3 9082 13714 8063

1/22/20

W9-CCW-941

BLOOD
of EMPIRE

By Brian McClellan

Gods of Blood and Powder

Sins of Empire
Wrath of Empire
Blood of Empire

Return to Honor (novella)

The Powder Mage Trilogy

Promise of Blood
The Crimson Campaign
The Autumn Republic
The Powder Mage Trilogy (omnibus edition)

Forsworn (novella)
Servant of the Crown (novella)
Murder at the Kinnen Hotel (novella)
Ghosts of the Tristan Basin (novella)
In the Field Marshal's Shadow (collection)

BLOOD
of EMPIRE

GODS OF BLOOD
AND POWDER

BRIAN
McCLELLAN

www.orbitbooks.net

Orbit
Hachette Book Group
1290 Avenue of the Americas
New York, NY 10104
orbitbooks.net

First Edition: December 2019
Simultaneously published in Great Britain by Orbit

Orbit is an imprint of Hachette Book Group.
The Orbit name and logo are trademarks of Little, Brown Book Group Limited.

The publisher is not responsible for websites (or their content) that are not owned by the publisher.

The Hachette Speakers Bureau provides a wide range of authors for speaking events. To find out more, go to www.hachettespeakersbureau.com or call (866) 376-6591.

Library of Congress Cataloging-in-Publication Data
Names: McClellan, Brian, 1986– author.
Title: Blood of empire / Brian McClellan.
Description: First edition. | New York, NY : Orbit, 2019. | Series: Gods of blood and powder ; 3
Identifiers: LCCN 2019013972 | ISBN 9780316407311 (hardcover) | ISBN 9780316407298 (ebook) | ISBN 9780316407328 (library ebook) | ISBN 9781478929369 (downloadable audio book)
Subjects: GSAFD: Fantasy fiction.
Classification: LCC PS3613.C35785 B58 2019 | DDC 813/.6—dc23
LC record available at https://lccn.loc.gov/2019013972

ISBNs: 978-0-316-40731-1 (hardcover), 978-0-316-40729-8 (ebook)

Printed in the United States of America

LSC-C

10 9 8 7 6 5 4 3 2 1

To Brandon Sanderson
For being the first pro to express serious confidence in my writing, and
for teaching me how to make a living at this weird job

THE CIRCLE HIGHWAY

THE HADSHAW R.

THE CIRCLE HIGHWAY

• MELN-DUN'S
QUARRY

UPPER
LANDFALL

GREENFIRE
DEPTHS

HADSHAW GORGE

MIDDLE
HEIGHTS

UPPER
LANDFALL

FALLEN
END

CLADEN
PARK

LOWER
LANDFALL

To the
Godstone
Fortress

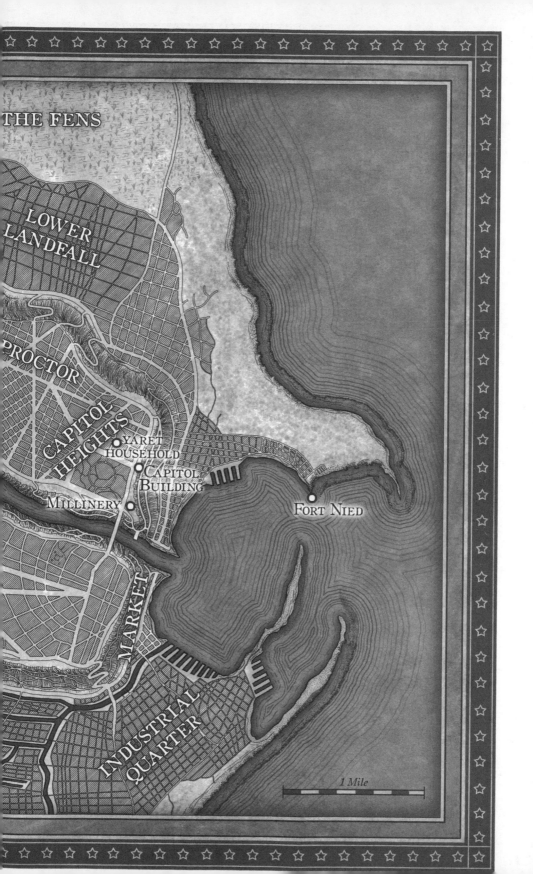

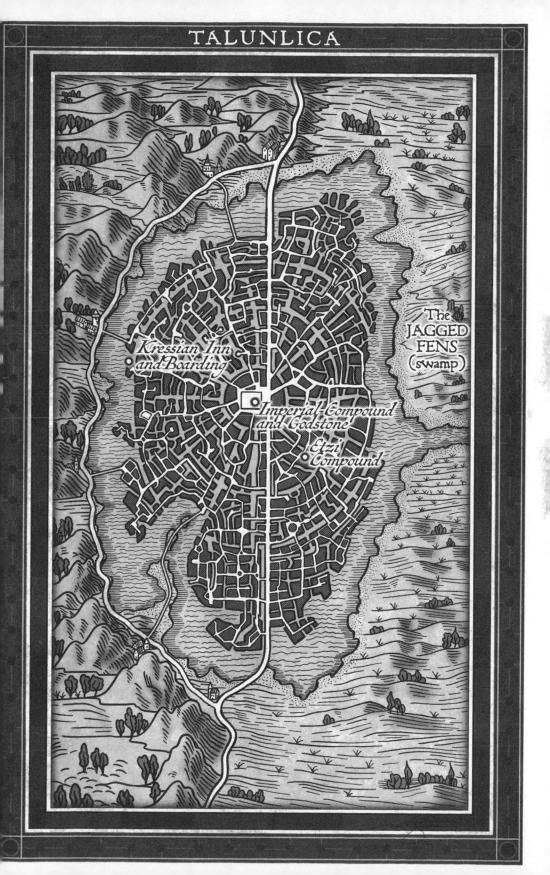

TALUNLICA

Kressian Inn
and Boarding

Imperial Compound
and Godstone

Etzi
Compound

The
JAGGED
FENS
(swamp)

BLOOD
of EMPIRE

PROLOGUE

K a-Sedial meditated in a pool of sunlight on the top floor of what had once been Lady Chancellor Lindet's town-home in Upper Landfall. It was a gorgeous room, filled with art, astronomical instruments, rare books, and engineering puzzles; the playground of someone who views education with a passionate eye. He'd left it largely untouched since taking control, and he had decided that he quite liked the previous owner. He and Lindet would have a very long, interesting discussion before he cut off her head.

He sat on a cushioned stool, facing east through a great stained-glass window, his eyes closed as he enjoyed this moment of quiet. Quiet was, after all, a rare luxury. He wondered if it would cease altogether in the days to come. Most people thought that *ruling* was a luxury. He scoffed to himself at the very thought. Ruling was a duty, a terrible responsibility that few approached with any measure of real success.

A rap on the door interrupted his ruminations, and Sedial rubbed at the pain persisting behind his left eye before placing his hands serenely on his knees. "Come."

The door opened to reveal the face of a middle-aged man with hard, angular features; a square jaw; and a military bearing. He was of middling height with a powerful frame wrapped in the black tattoos of a dragonman. Ji-Noren was, officially, Sedial's bodyguard. In reality he was Sedial's spy and military master, and one of about a dozen dragonmen that claimed loyalty to him rather than to the emperor.

"Yes?" Sedial asked.

"We found the girl."

"The girl?"

"The one you gave to Ichtracia."

Sedial snorted at the mention of his treacherous granddaughter. "Bring her in."

A few moments passed before Ji-Noren ushered in a petite Palo woman of about nineteen. She was very attractive, if Sedial had been young enough to still enjoy that sort of pastime. She trembled violently as Ji-Noren laid one hand on her shoulder. Plucked from among the poor natives in that immense slum, Greenfire Depths, the girl had been meant as a peace offering to Ichtracia, a slave to do with as she wished. Ichtracia had simply released the girl and ignored Sedial's orders.

Sedial looked the girl over for a few moments, reaching out with his sorcery in an attempt to find even the faintest trace of his granddaughter. If they had spent any amount of time together, there would be something there, even if just a whisper.

Nothing.

He produced a leather wallet from his sleeve and unrolled it to reveal a number of needles and glass vials. He drew one of the needles. "Give me your hand." The woman inhaled sharply. Her eyes rolled like a frightened horse, and Sedial almost commanded Noren to cuff some sense into her. Instead, he reached out and seized her by the wrist. He pricked a vein on the back of her hand, smearing the drop of blood with his thumb before releasing her.

He ignored the frightened sound she made and stared hard at the splash of crimson. He took a few shallow breaths, touching the blood with his sorcery, feeling it create a bridge between his body and hers, between his *mind* and hers. "When is the last time you saw Ichtracia?" he asked.

The girl's bottom lip trembled. Sedial squeezed ever so gently with his sorcery, and words suddenly spilled out of her. "Not since the day you left me with her. She sent me away within minutes of you leaving!"

"And you have had no contact with her since?"

"No!"

"Do you have even a guess at where she might be hiding?"

"I don't, Great Ka! I'm sorry!"

Sedial sighed and wiped the blood from his thumb using a clean scrap of cloth from the table beside him. He returned the needle to his wallet and rolled it up, then flipped his hand dismissively. "She knows nothing. Return her to the Depths."

Ji-Noren gripped her shoulder, but the woman refused to turn away. Her eyes locked on to his, her teeth chattering. "You..."

"I what, my dear?" he asked impatiently. "I'm not going to torture you?" He gave her his best grandfatherly smile. "Believe me, if I thought it would be of any help, you would be on the way to my bone-eyes at this very moment. But you are nothing more than a weak-willed bystander, and despite what you may have been told, I do not crush insects out of spite. Only necessity." He gestured again, and within a moment the girl was gone.

Ji-Noren returned a few minutes later. He stood by the door, waiting in silence while Sedial attempted to slip back into that blissful meditation he'd been holding on to earlier. It didn't work. The moment of peace had passed. His head hurt, the spot behind his eye throbbing intensely every time he used his sorcery. He gave a small sigh and struggled to his feet, crossing the room to a writing desk, where he lowered himself into the chair and began to sign a number of work orders redistributing Palo labor from the housing projects in the north down to a new fortress under construction in the south.

"We have no other way to find Ichtracia?" Ji-Noren asked quietly.

"No," Sedial replied as he skimmed a work order before adding his signature at the bottom. "We do not. Mundane means have failed—we've interrogated everyone with even a tenuous connection with her."

"And sorcerous means?"

"Dynize Privileged learned to hide themselves from bone-eyes long ago. Even our family blood is not strong enough to allow me to crack her defenses."

"What about the spy, Bravis?"

Sedial looked down at the bruising on his wrist. The bruising from one granddaughter—from Ichtracia's sorcery—the pain behind his eye from the other. "Ka-poel is protecting him," he said quietly, raising his gaze to a little box up on the shelf. The box contained the spy's finger, as well as several vials of his blood. They had proven useless, but he kept them all the same.

"I've widened the search to three hundred miles," Ji-Noren said. "We *will* catch them."

The reassurance just provoked a spike of fury in Sedial's chest. He pushed it down, signing his name on a work order and pressing it with his official seal. He shouldn't need soldiers combing cellars and ransacking attics to look for his granddaughter and that filthy spy. He was the most powerful bone-eye in the world. Finding them should be as easy as a thought.

The spot behind his eye throbbed. *Second* most powerful bone-eye, anyway. Despite his pained state, he felt a sliver of pride for Ka-poel. She would have made an amazing pupil—or a powerful sacrifice. She may still prove to be the latter.

"Ichtracia and the spy are either already on the other side of the continent, or they are hiding just beneath our noses. Continue to focus your efforts on the city." He rose to his feet again, knuckling his back and giving Ji-Noren a grin. "Ka-poel has spread herself thin. She protects dozens with her sorcery, instead of using it as a weapon. If she was not so distracted, she would have killed me."

Ji-Noren frowned, as if wondering how this could possibly be good news.

Sedial patted Ji-Noren on the shoulder. "She will continue to make the same mistake. Eventually, it will weaken her against my attacks, and I will break her."

"Ah. Do we know where she is?"

"To the west, still. I can't be entirely sure where, but I imagine she's looking for the last of the godstones."

"She doesn't know we already have it."

"No, I don't think she does." Sedial turned to the dragonman. "You're still frowning."

"We have many enemies in this place," Ji-Noren commented.

"As we expected."

"More than expected," Ji-Noren said. "And far more powerful. Have you read reports about what those two powder mages did to the army we sent after Lady Flint?"

Sedial ignored the question. One thing at a time. "Don't worry yourself, my friend," Sedial said as he crossed the room toward the door. It was nearly teatime, and he *might* just be able to enjoy it before another messenger arrived with some ridiculous problem that needed fixing. "We've won almost every battle we've fought on this accursed continent. We possess two of the godstones. Once we've broken Ka-poel's sorcery on the Landfall godstone, we will be in position to act."

"And Lady Flint, with that new Adran army up north?" Ji-Noren insisted. "They have the third godstone."

"But they have no idea how to use it." He paused, then added reassuringly, "They have, what, thirty thousand soldiers? We outnumber them four to one in that region alone."

"They have Privileged *and* powder mages now."

"We'll buy them off," Sedial said. "The Adran delegation will be far more pliant than Lady Flint's stubbornness. She may have gained an army, but she also gained the politics of the Nine. I suspect she'll find the latter much harder to wield than the former." He rested his hand on the door just as he heard footsteps pounding urgently up the stairs. He rolled his eyes and opened it just in time to see a messenger, covered in sweat and road dust, come to a huffing stop. "What is it?" Sedial demanded.

"We've done it, sir."

Sedial was taken aback. "Done what?"

"The godstone, sir. The Privileged and bone-eyes say that they've solved it."

It took a few moments for the thought to register. "They're certain? They've broken my granddaughter's seals?"

"Yes, Great Ka. Absolutely certain."

Sedial felt the grin spread on his face. He let out a relieved sigh and gave the messenger one curt nod before closing the door and hobbling back to the writing desk. "We've done it, Noren," he breathed.

"Congratulations, Great Ka," Ji-Noren said warmly.

Sedial reached beneath the writing desk and produced a small cigar box marked with his Household crest. It pulsed with sorcery as his fingertips touched it, and continued to grow warmer and warmer until he managed to prick his own finger and press the blood to a special knot on the bottom of the box. The box sprang open, revealing several dozen prepared envelopes layered in protective wards. He drew them out almost reverently and handed them to Ji-Noren. "Send these back to Dynize immediately."

"Are we sure we're ready for this?" Ji-Noren asked with some surprise.

"It is time to strike. Begin the purge."

"What of the emperor?"

"The emperor is just another puppet. He'll think that the purges are being conducted in his name."

Ji-Noren looked down at the orders. For a moment, Sedial thought he saw a flicker of hesitation. Understandable, of course. After such a long and bloody civil war, most Dynize were loath to spill the blood of their kin. Yet this was unavoidable. Enemies needed to be destroyed, both foreign and domestic.

"Can I trust you to stand beside me, my friend?" Sedial asked.

Ji-Noren's gaze hardened. "To the death."

"Good."

"This is how it begins."

"No," Sedial corrected gently. "It began decades ago. This is how it ends."

CHAPTER 1

Michel Bravis stood in the doorway of a small Kressian chapel, sipping cold morning coffee while he watched Palo fishermen pass him in the street, their early haul hanging from long poles balanced on their shoulders. He examined each man and woman carefully, ticking them off mentally as he watched for new faces or suspicious glances or any amount of curiosity tossed in his direction. They bragged to one another about their catch or tagged along in sullen, unsuccessful silence, but not one of them gave Michel a second glance.

He'd grown and shorn the blond dye out of his hair over the previous month, and he'd made sure to spend plenty of time in the sun each day to allow the natural strawberry red to come out in both his hair and his beard. A starvation diet had allowed him to lose nearly two stone, and every shop-window reflection reminded him that he had changed his look about as much as possible since leaving Landfall.

To the townspeople of this Palo fishing village about twenty miles up the coast from Landfall, Michel was nothing more than just another Palo vagrant displaced from his home with the Dynize invasion. He spent his mornings on the chapel stoop, his afternoons cleaning fish at the only processing factory, and his evenings tucked into one of the dozen local pubs listening to gossip and playing the occasional hand of cards with loose-lipped Dynize soldiers. He gathered information, he kept his head down, and most of all he waited for an opportunity to present itself that would allow him and Ichtracia to slip out of this place and head inland to find Ka-poel.

Michel finished his coffee, tossing the grounds into the gutter and stowing his tin cup before slipping inside. He listened to the clatter of the big chapel door swinging shut behind him and tried to resist fiddling with the still-painful stub of the finger Sedial had cut off, hidden beneath bandages and a false splint. He took a deep breath and walked up the center aisle of the chapel.

To all appearances, Ichtracia looked like a grieving widow. She wore a black shawl and veil and sat hunched as if in prayer on the second row of benches. Michel glanced around the empty chapel, then came to stand beside her, raising his eyes to Kresimir's Rope hanging above the altar. He noted that someone had written "Kresimir Is Dead" under one of the stained-glass windows of the nave.

The hard-drinking fisherwoman who acted as the town priest hadn't bothered to scrub it off.

"Are all Kressian churches like this?" Ichtracia asked, not raising her head.

"Like what?"

"Dull."

Michel considered the question. "The cathedrals are more impressive."

"I toured the one in Landfall. It certainly was big." She didn't sound impressed.

"Don't Dynize have churches?" It had never occurred to him to ask before.

"Not really, not in the same way. We're supposed to worship the emperor in the town square, but no one really does that, except on public holidays."

That sounded very similar to Michel's own relationship with religion. He'd never bothered with it as a boy, and as an adult he knew for a fact that Kresimir was indeed dead. He worked for the pair that had killed the Kressian god. "At least this keeps you from having to stay cooped up in our room all day," Michel suggested.

"This bench is going to be the death of me." Ichtracia stood suddenly, lifting her veil and stretching with a rather impious yawn. Ever since they had snuck out of Landfall, she'd been posing as his brother's widow. Or at least, that was their story. No one had actually bothered to ask them yet. The Dynize didn't have a strong presence here beyond the isolated, passing platoon, and the Palo simply didn't care.

But such was Michel's experience with aliases—they seemed unnecessary until suddenly one saved your life.

She continued, "Have you figured out how to get us out of here yet?"

Michel grimaced. Ichtracia had, to this point, taken their entire predicament rather well. She even seemed to enjoy playing the role of an anonymous widow, relishing every set of eyes that slid past her without a flicker of recognition. But the sight of the pulped corpse of her grandfather's bodyguard was still fresh in Michel's mind, along with her demand that she be taken to her sister. He was as cognizant as ever of the power imbalance between them and feared the moment her patience ran out.

"I have not," he answered her. Something passed behind her eyes that made the base of his spine itch. He gave her his most charming smile. "I'm trying."

"I'm sure you are." She didn't sound convinced. "Any news from the war?"

Michel came around and dropped onto the bench, waiting until she'd returned to her seat before he said, "A pitload of rumors. Lindet has retaken the Hammer and is pushing east across Fatrasta. Her army is immense but mostly conscripts, and the Dynize are rallying their field armies to put her down." He frowned. "There are a lot of conflicting reports coming out of the north—a whole Dynize field army disappeared. Another army has New Adopest under siege and is expected to take it and come south by the end of next week." To be honest, he was worried about that army. If they skirted the coast, they could march right past this little town, and Michel was not thrilled about the idea of thirty thousand Dynize or more, along with Privileged and bone-eyes, camped out nearby. Ichtracia claimed she could hide from any sorcery, but he didn't want to put that to the test up close.

"Anything out of Landfall?"

"Just troop consolidation. Sedial is building a fortress around the godstone and using Fatrastan labor to do it. Nobody knows how many Kressians and Palo he's hired, but rumor has it they're being paid and fed well, so there's not a lot of complaining."

Ichtracia sniffed. "You seem surprised that the Palo are being treated well."

"We've always been second-class citizens at best," Michel answered. "Slaves and subhumans at worst." He felt something else on the tip of his tongue—the guarded secret that the Blackhat je Tura had told him just before his death. For weeks he'd wanted to ask Ichtracia what she knew of her grandfather's attempts to activate the godstone, and for weeks he'd suppressed that urge. He wasn't sure whether he was worried she'd have no new information for him—or worried that she knew all about it.

"The Palo are Dynize cousins," Ichtracia said. "He won't treat them as well as our own people, of course, but they aren't exactly foreigners, either." She frowned. "A fortress around the godstone. I wonder if he's truly worried about Lindet and her conscript armies. Or if there's something else he's up to."

"No clue," Michel answered, studying the side of Ichtracia's face. *Did* she know? Was she lying to him this very moment? They'd been lovers and companions for some time now, but there were still a great many walls between them—and for good reason. He tried to shrug it off. It didn't matter. His only task now was to figure out a way to get them out of this town and across to the other side of the continent. Once he reunited her with Ka-poel, he could get back to Landfall and try to find out the truth.

The creak of the chapel door gave Michel a little jump, and he resisted the urge to look over his shoulder as Ichtracia leaned forward and assumed the role of praying widow. Michel touched her shoulder as if in comfort, then got to his feet. If he left now, he'd have a couple hours listening to rumors in the pub before his afternoon shift.

He froze at the sight of the man standing just inside the chapel door, blinking several times to make sure that his eyes hadn't tricked him. "Taniel?" he choked out.

Taniel Two-shot looked like he'd aged a decade in the few months since they'd last spoken. His riding clothes were filthy, his shoulders slumped, and his face was drawn out and haggard. A spot of silver had appeared at his temples and he gave Michel a tired smile. "Hello, Michel." He ran a hand through his hair. "You really are a damned chameleon. I would have walked right out of here without recognizing you if you hadn't said my name."

"What the pit happened to you?" Michel asked, slipping past Ichtracia and into the aisle.

"I fought a couple of Dynize brigades," Taniel said. It sounded like a joke, but he didn't smile when he said it. "I may have overdone it a bit." His eyes slid to Ichtracia, then back to Michel.

Ichtracia had gotten to her feet and now stared at Taniel in the same way Michel might have eyed an adder slithering through the door. Her fingers twitched as if for the Privileged gloves in her pockets. A look of uncertainty crossed her face. Michel cleared his throat. "Taniel, Ichtracia. Ichtracia, Taniel."

"Ichtracia," Taniel said, rolling the name across his tongue. "This is our mole?"

"I'm your sister-in-law, as I understand it," Ichtracia said flatly.

Taniel eyeballed her right back. "I thought your name was Mara."

"A nickname," Michel explained. "It was a pain in the ass to find her, but I did. Why didn't you tell me she was Ka-poel's sister?" He hadn't meant to ask—taking an accusatory tone with Taniel never ended well. But the question just kind of slipped out.

Taniel scowled for a moment before letting out a tired sigh. "I didn't think you needed to know."

"It might have narrowed things down." Michel heard his own tone rising. All the annoyance he'd felt over the secrecy, no matter whether it was important or not, began to slip through. "You also could have told me she was a Privileged."

"That's right." Taniel cocked his head as if listening to some distant sound. "You're hiding it very well. I didn't sense anything when I came through the door."

"I've practiced a lot," Ichtracia said. Her tone had gone from flat to annoyed. "So you're the god-slayer?"

Taniel's expression turned serious. "What have you been telling her?" he asked.

Michel threw up his hands, but Ichtracia answered before he could. "He hasn't told me anything. The Dynize have spies all over the world. You were supposed to have died ten years ago. When Michel told me who he worked for—who my sister is married to— I couldn't help but assume that you managed to finish the job you started on Kresimir."

Taniel snorted and walked to the last pew in the back of the chapel, sinking into it. "Lots of rumors," he said wearily. "I'm sorry about the misdirection, Michel. Pole and I decided together that it was best you figure out who and what Mar...Ichtracia was on your own. All we had to go on was the name Mara. A nickname, you say?"

"Something that our grandfather used to call us both as children," Ichtracia said. "It means we were his little sacrifices."

Taniel's apologetic smile switched from Michel to Ichtracia. "I see. Thank you for joining Michel. I can only imagine that we have a lot to catch up on about each other. And that you want to see your sister."

"Where is she?" A note of eagerness entered Ichtracia's voice.

Taniel hesitated. "West. I'm on my way to find her."

Michel watched Ichtracia. He wanted to tell her that she was in the presence of a great man. That she should show a little respect. But he was just annoyed enough at Taniel to keep his mouth shut. Besides, Ichtracia was no slouch herself. "Speaking of finding," he said. "How did you find us?"

"I went to Landfall first," Taniel replied. "I met with Emerald, and he told me that you'd accomplished your mission and pointed me in this direction. It's ... taken a couple of weeks."

Michel scowled. "We've been trying to figure out a way through the Dynize roadblocks ever since we left. How did you just ride right into Landfall?"

"One of Emerald's people was waiting for me north of the city with forged papers." Taniel patted his breast pocket. "No one's looking for a single Kressian rider, and the papers say I'm a spy for the Dynize. There were a few awkward questions, but I managed."

Michel made a frustrated sound in the back of his throat. If only it had been so easy for him and Ichtracia, they'd be on the other side of the continent by now rather than waiting in this little fishing village for an opportunity to slip away. "So you're here to take Ichtracia to Pole?"

Taniel gave Ichtracia a long glance. "I am."

"Wait," Ichtracia said, giving Michel a confused look. "You're coming with us, right?"

"You're more than welcome," Taniel added.

Michel gave them both a tight smile. "I should. But I need to head back to the city."

"You're mad!" Ichtracia exclaimed. She exchanged a glance with Taniel and then continued, "You know that Sedial is turning over the city looking for you, right? The moment someone recognizes you, you'll be captured, tortured, and killed."

Michel stared at his hands for a few moments, considering his words.

"Michel?" Taniel prodded.

"I've got unfinished business."

"What kind of business?" Taniel asked.

Michel avoided Ichtracia's gaze. Choosing his words with care, he said, "While I was there, I helped the Dynize hunt down the last of the Blackhats in the city."

"So Emerald told me," Taniel replied.

"I found and killed Val je Tura."

"The Gold Rose with the bastard sword?"

"The same. Before he died, he told me something." Michel hesitated again, looking sidelong at Ichtracia. "He told me that the Dynize were scooping up Palo and using them in a blood ritual to activate the godstone." The moment the last word left his mouth, he knew that he'd been wrong about Ichtracia—that he should have told her weeks ago. The blood drained from her face, her eyes widening. He expected an exclamation of surprise or denial or... something. Instead her jaw clamped shut.

"Pit," Taniel muttered.

"I need to go back to the city, find out if it's true, and try to do something about it."

"You'll get yourself killed," Ichtracia said, the words tumbling out over one another.

Michel gave her a tight smile. "Taniel, what is it I've been working toward all this time?"

"Palo independence," Taniel answered automatically.

Ichtracia seemed taken aback. "I thought that you planned on opposing my grandfather—to prevent the use of the godstones."

"That…that's Taniel and Ka-poel's fight," Michel said. "At the end of the day I have one purpose: to free the Palo of whoever is subjugating them, enslaving them, kicking them around. It doesn't matter if it's the Kressians or the Fatrastans or the Dynize. I have to pit myself against the enemies of my people. I'm of no use going along with you and Taniel. I need to head back into Landfall."

"I thought you said the Palo were being treated better under the Dynize?" There was a note to her tone that Michel couldn't quite place. It sounded like desperation.

"I don't know," Michel said with a shrug. "Maybe? Or it could be propaganda. Whatever it is, I need to go back to Landfall and find out the truth."

The silence between them all grew deafening. Ichtracia stared at the wall. Taniel stared at Michel. Michel examined both their faces, trying to read something in them. Finally, Taniel cleared his throat. "Ka-poel is on her way to Dynize."

"What?" The word tore itself from Ichtracia's throat as she whirled on him.

"She's going to find the third godstone. I'm on my way to join her."

"She's going to get herself killed, too! Why do all of you have a death wish?" Something in Taniel's expression must have confused her, because she stopped and took a sharp breath. "You don't know?"

"Know what?"

"We already have the third godstone. It's in Dynize, protected."

Taniel muttered something under his breath. "Good thing she has a bodyguard, I suppose. If that's true, I don't have a second to lose. I've got to cross the continent, catch a ship, and sneak into Dynize. It'll take me months to catch up with her."

Michel scoffed. Taniel's tone was optimistic, as if he were heading on a pleasure cruise. But anything could happen in months, especially if Ka-poel stumbled headlong into Dynize. He almost asked Taniel to forget that idea and come with him to Landfall. But there was no hope in that. Taniel would go wherever Ka-poel was.

"Are you coming?" Taniel asked Ichtracia briskly. Michel could see in his eyes that he'd already moved on from the conversation and was ready to bolt, like a racehorse waiting for the starting pistol.

"No."

Michel rounded on her. "What do you mean, no?"

"I'm going with you." Ichtracia's face had regained some of its color. Her jaw was now set stubbornly.

"You can't go back to Landfall," Michel protested. "You'll be in danger."

"No more than you," she retorted. Her left eye and cheek twitched, a cascade of emotions crossing her face in the space of a moment.

"Your sister . . ."

"I can meet her when this is over!" she said forcefully. Quieter, to herself, she echoed, "When this is all over. Do we have a way to get back in?" she asked Taniel.

"Emerald sent a couple of Dynize passports for the two of you," Taniel said. "They were meant for you to accompany me across the country, but I assume they'll get you back into Landfall without a problem."

Michel swallowed. He had been with Ichtracia long enough to see that she would not take no for an answer. His mentioning of the blood sacrifices had set something off in her. He felt like he should know what, but he was too taken up with his own plans to pinpoint the source of her distress. He immediately shifted his thinking, discarding all the ideas he'd had for a one-man operation and changing them to work for two.

"We'll take the passports," Ichtracia said.

"I think..." Michel began.

"Don't think," she snapped at him. "You should have told me about your intentions. You should have told me about the sacrifices. Mara!" She thumped her chest. "Mara! Sacrifice. That blood should have been mine! Instead, he's killing thousands of innocent people to get the job done. I'm going with you, and that's final."

CHAPTER 2

Ben Styke rested on the forecastle of a small transport ship called the *Seaward*, his big boz knife in one hand and a whetstone in the other, listening to the swell of the ocean and the calling of gulls undercut by the occasional slow rasp as he sharpened his blade. He wore a large, floppy hat to keep the sun from his face, despite the fact that Celine had told him on several different occasions that it made him look ridiculous.

He caught sight of one of the sailors staring in his direction and wondered if it was just the hat or *him*. Two weeks at sea, and the sailors still seemed uneasy to have twenty Mad Lancers and Ben Styke sleeping in their hold. The fear suited Styke just fine—if it meant that someone jumped when he said jump, it made his life easier. He wondered what they'd think if he told them about the genuine Dynize blood witch who had commandeered the first mate's cabin.

At the thought, Styke raised his head and swept his gaze across the deck for Ka-poel. He hadn't seen her much since they'd set sail.

In fact, ever since the battle at Starlight, she'd looked exhausted, and had slept no less than fourteen hours a day. He suspected that the sorcerous power struggle she'd had with her grandfather had done more damage to her than she'd care to admit. He wondered if he should ask her outright—he needed her in top shape for this mission—but immediately discarded the thought. She was still alive, still moving, and she had enough energy to snicker silently at his hat.

She'd be fine. She would have to be.

Styke lifted his eyes farther up, to the mainmast, where he spotted Celine just as she leapt from the rigging and walked—no, *ran*—out to the end of the spar. He swallowed a lump in his throat and the urge to yell, reminding himself that he was jumping between galloping horses at that age. Eyes narrowed, he watched as she deftly untied a knot, let some slack out into one of the sails, then retied it and returned to the rigging, where a trio of sailors gave her a proud cheer. He had to admit, in these last two weeks she'd become startlingly good at navigating the rigging, sails, and knots on the ship.

He had no intention of telling her of the chat he'd had with the first mate to ensure that the sailors did not ask her to do anything beyond her size or strength.

Styke returned his gaze to his knife, drawing it across the whetstone a few more times, and tried not to look to starboard, where the rocky, cypress-choked Dynize shore dominated the horizon. The sight of it would only frustrate him: so close he could practically touch it, and yet he was no closer to his destination.

Four days ago, just when they were nearing Dynize, an immense gale had scattered his fleet. Dozens of transports and their heavily armed escorts had been caught up in the storm. When it finally passed, the *Seaward* had found itself all alone and blown a couple hundred miles north of their rendezvous point on the Dynize shore. Styke had no way of knowing how many of the ships had been lost, or how badly they'd been dispersed. He didn't know if half of his Lancers had drowned, or been dashed against the shore, or if his entire army of twenty-five hundred cavalry had already landed and was waiting impatiently for him to arrive.

Regardless, the *Seaward* sailed south at speed, hoping to make up for lost time and avoid any Dynize warships along the way.

A shout brought his attention back up to the mainmast, where a boy in the crow's nest waved desperately toward the aftcastle. There was a sudden commotion, and the sailors sent Celine scampering down the rigging as their fun was replaced by an air of seriousness. The watchman gave another shout and pointed to the southern horizon, but the sound was lost on the wind.

Styke put away his knife and whetstone, climbed reluctantly to his feet, and headed across the forecastle, down the main deck, and up to the aftcastle where Captain Bonnie stood staring pensively through her looking glass to the southeast. Bonnie was an old seadog; a piece of shoe leather in tattered pants and a tricorn hat, her skin so dark from the sun she might have been Deliv for all Styke knew. He sidled up beside her and waited for her report. They were soon joined by Jackal and Celine. The Palo Lancer mussed Celine's hair and got a jab in the ribs for his effort, then gave Styke a very serious nod.

"You get anything new out of those spirits of yours?" Styke said just loudly enough to be heard over the wind.

"No," Jackal reported, glancing down toward the first mate's cabin below them, where Ka-poel was resting. "They still won't come near the ship, not with her hanging about. I almost coaxed one to me yesterday—there are the spirits of Dynize sailors this close to shore, and they seem less scared of her, but..." He trailed off with a shrug.

Styke opened his mouth to respond, but was interrupted by Bonnie. "Here," she said, thrusting the looking glass into his hands. "Directly southeast, ahead of us, you'll see a point on the horizon."

He put the glass to his eye. It didn't take long to find the point she'd referenced. Three points, actually; three sets of sails, all of them black with an arc of red stars across the center. "Dynize ships," he said.

"Very astute," Bonnie responded with a snort. "Any idea what they are?" He gave her a flat look until she cleared her throat and continued. "Two frigates escorting one of those big monstrosities the Dynize call a ship of the line. Trios like that have been sweeping the ocean ever since the Dynize invaded. We call them the three-headed serpent."

"Have they seen us?"

"They have much higher masts than the *Seaward*, so I'd be shocked if they haven't—and if not, they will any minute."

Styke felt his stomach lurch as he considered the possibilities. Their little transport was barely armed. He hadn't chosen it for his own vessel because of size or power, but rather because Bonnie was the most experienced captain in the commandeered fleet and knew the Dynize shore better than anyone else. "Shit," he said.

"Shit indeed." She raised the looking glass to her eye for another few moments. "They're already headed in this direction." She paused, furrowing her brow. "Ah. The frigates are beginning to split off. They've definitely seen us, and they're already preparing to widen the net. Probably hoping to get out far on our portside before we notice them." She half turned toward the first mate and barked loudly, "Bring her around to starboard!"

A flurry of commotion followed as sailors scampered to adjust the sails. Styke felt a growing alarm. "We're turning around?" he demanded.

"Yes, we're turning around," Bonnie replied acidly. "And don't try to wave that knife in my face, because that won't help shit. You may be Mad Ben Styke but I'm Perfectly Sane Bonnie. I can outrun those frigates without too much of a problem, but if I try to slip past them, they'll turn us into driftwood."

Styke wondered if she'd rehearsed that speech for just such an occasion. He glared toward the south, doing sums in his head. "And your plan is...?"

"My plan is to run away north until they can't see us anymore. Then we'll cut far, far east and come back around to reach the rendezvous. With any luck, they'll assume they chased us off and continue patrolling the coastline."

"And how long will that take?"

Bonnie shrugged. "Depends on the wind, the weather, and if we run into any more patrols. Fifteen days? Ten, if we're lucky. Twenty or thirty or more if we're not. We might even have to go resupply at Starlight."

Styke grit his teeth and shared a long look with Jackal. Twenty more days until they met back up with Ibana and the rest. Twenty days behind schedule. What a goddamned disaster. He briefly considered how badly it would go if he *did* wave his knife under Bonnie's nose. He might have a reputation, but her sailors outnumbered his Lancers three to one and he needed those sailors to get him to shore. The last thing he needed was to spark a mutiny against his commandeered authority.

The ship creaked as it came around, putting the Dynize vessels behind them and the shore on their portside. Sailors shouted and scrambled, accomplishing the maneuver in an impressively short period of time.

Styke's mind jumped to the old maps in Bonnie's cabin. They were the most up-to-date maps of Dynize available, which meant that the coastlines were all accurate, but inland hadn't been seen for over a hundred years. That *shouldn't* make a difference, not for his purposes. "Find us a place to put to shore," he said.

"Excuse me?" Bonnie's head jerked toward him, a look of disbelief on her face.

"You heard me. Get us as close as you can to the shore and weigh anchor. I want both your cranes put up and plopping my horses into the ocean. Give us three longboats and all our supplies, then you can run from those frigates to your heart's content and head straight back to Starlight."

"You're insane."

Styke tapped his knife. "Find us a beach where I can swim twenty-five horses ashore without getting them all killed."

"Don't you need us to get back to Fatrasta?"

"Not if I can meet up with the rest of the fleet."

"And you'll do that going overland?"

Styke grinned at her.

Hesitantly, Bonnie turned her eye to the shore and gave a weary sigh. "I think we might be near a place. I'll give the order. Tell your men to be ready to go in an hour. This will be the fastest landing you've ever experienced." Bonnie strode away, barking orders, and Styke turned back to Jackal.

"Are you sure this is a good idea?" Jackal asked.

"Not in the slightest," Styke responded. "But I'd rather cut through a hundred miles of swampy wilderness than sit on this goddamned ship for another three weeks while Ibana twiddles her thumbs."

"And if Ibana never made it to the rendezvous?"

"Then this will be the smallest invasion ever." Styke knelt down, putting his arm around Celine. "How well do you remember all that shit your dad taught you?"

Celine gave him a suspicious glance. "I thought you told me I'd never need to steal again."

"You don't want to?"

"I didn't say that."

"Good. Because I need you to pilfer all of Bonnie's maps of Dynize."

Celine scowled. "If she catches me, she'll throw me over the side."

"We're about to do something really stupid, and those maps are gonna be the only way to accomplish it. Besides, we're all going overboard anyway."

Celine considered this for a moment, then gave him a wicked little grin that he swore she learned from Ka-poel. "Okay, I'll do it. But not until we're about to jump into the longboats. That'll be the best way to make a clean getaway."

"Smart girl. Now, go wake up Ka-poel. Tell her she's home."

Styke stood on a rocky outcropping and watched as the *Seaward* disappeared around a nearby bend, heading north at full sail just out of gun range of the nearest of the two pursuing Dynize frigates. It would be close, but Captain Bonnie had been confident she could still make a clean getaway. The Dynize frigate fired off a single shot from a small bow gun, but Styke watched it splash into the ocean, well short of its target. Waiting until the *Seaward* was completely out of sight, he climbed down from his outcropping and headed down to the stream outlet, where his men were unloading the longboats.

"Report," he said to Jackal, splashing into the water and eyeballing a long-snouted swamp dragon half-submerged a little way upstream.

"Everyone made it safely ashore," Jackal responded. He sucked gently on his teeth. "One of the spare horses broke a leg coming around that reef. Had to put him down."

"Just the one?" Styke had heard the beast screaming, and the gunshot that put it out of its misery.

"Just the one," Jackal confirmed.

"That's better than I expected." He groaned inwardly. They had five extra horses, and more than a hundred miles of wilderness to cross with them. Facing difficult terrain, swamp dragons, big snakes, and whatever the pit else this blasted continent would throw at them, he expected to lose plenty more before they could meet up with Ibana. But having his feet on firm ground again felt good. At least he was in control of his own fate again. "Everyone has their armor?"

"They do. Markus has loaded up Amrec. Sunin is helping Celine get Margo saddled."

"Saddles stay dry?

A nod. "Sunin dropped her carbine. I had to give her one of the extras."

Styke rolled his eyes. "Why is she so old?"

"I think…"

"It was a rhetorical question." He looked around until he found Ka-poel and Celine sitting on the opposite bank of the inlet, then waded over to them. Even after two weeks of rest, Ka-poel looked thin and strung out, but her eyes were alert. She flashed a series of signs, most of which Styke followed. He let Celine translate anyway.

This looks like the Tristan Basin.

"It does, doesn't it?" Styke felt something fly into his mouth and quickly spat it out. "Same shitty trees and bugs and snakes and…" He trailed off, spotting the eyes of another swamp dragon watching them from forty feet upstream. "Swamp dragons look a little different, though. Keep your eyes out for them. Some of the bigger ones won't hesitate to snap at a man, and may even go for a horse."

Ka-poel rolled her eyes. *I know*, Celine translated the next gesture.

"Right. You grew up in that shithole, didn't you?" Styke glanced at the surrounding terrain. Despite the similarities, it was actually quite different from the Tristan Basin over in Fatrasta. While the Basin was very flat with thick, almost impassable flora, this swamp was littered with rocky outcroppings that ranged from boulders a few feet high to violent spines of rock that thrust above the mighty cypress trees. They hadn't even started their trip to the interior yet, but he could already tell that the rivers would be deeper, the lowlands unpredictable, and the terrain difficult for horses. "Just keep your eyes out for swamp dragons," he reiterated before turning back and wading to the longboats.

He cleared his throat loudly and gestured for the men to gather around, giving them a long, hard stare as they secured their horses, set aside inventory, and came to join him. He took a deep breath. Twenty men. Over a hundred miles of unpredictable swamp. This was going to be terrible.

"All right, here's the plan. Some of you might have already heard—we made landfall because our alternative was running with Captain Bonnie all the way back to Starlight and trying, from there, to rendezvous with Ibana." He gestured to Celine. "Bring me those maps," and then continued speaking to the Lancers, "Dropping us here means we have a chance to cut across the interior a damned lot faster than three weeks."

Someone coughed.

"Who was that?" Styke demanded. "Zac? Speak up."

Zac coughed again and looked around sheepishly. The scout tried to find some sort of backup from his brother, but Markus just shook his head. "Uh, Ben," Zac finally said. "Is this what the whole wilderness looks like?"

"As far as I know, yes."

"There isn't a damned way we're going to make it a hundred miles much faster than twenty days, not in this terrain."

Styke took the waxed leather map tube Celine stole from Captain Bonnie and popped the cap, then rummaged through the maps inside until he found the one he wanted. He spread it gently on the lip of the longboat, and everyone shifted to crowd around him. It was a map of a region in the northeast of Dynize called the Jagged Fens. "We're here," he said, pointing to a nondescript little inlet. "The rendezvous is here." He tapped on another spot. On the map, the distance seemed negligible, but Zac was right; it would be impossible in these conditions. "You see this?"

A few of the men leaned forward to squint at the paper. "Is that a road?" Markus asked.

"It's a coastal highway cutting through the Fens."

"This map is a century old," Jackal pointed out quietly. "Is the road even there anymore?"

It better be, Styke thought. This plan had sounded less crazy in his head back aboard the *Seaward*. Aloud, he said, "I don't see why it wouldn't be. We're just a couple miles to the east. I figure we can get there by morning. Once we're on packed dirt, we'll be able to ride hard to meet up with the rest of the Lancers. There are a handful of small towns between us and them. Worst case, we throw on our armor and ride through."

The small group began to murmur thoughtfully among themselves, and he saw the idea take root. He himself wasn't as convinced. In fact, he was beginning to think this might be one of his stupider ideas. But the important part was pointing the Lancers at a goal and getting them moving. He could deal with complications as they arose.

Styke rolled the map back up, then returned the map tube to Celine. "Keep this safe," he told her. "And the rest of you . . . finish inventory and get your horses saddled and ready to move. I want to be off the coast as soon as possible."

The group threw themselves into action, and Styke headed to give Amrec a once-over before making sure that Celine and Ka-poel's horses were hale and ready to ride. Less than a half hour passed before he could see the soldiers were ready to leave. He instructed them to haul the longboats farther upstream, and turned when he heard a voice call out his name. It was Celine, standing up on the vantage point he'd used to watch the *Seaward* slip away earlier.

Styke climbed up to join her and immediately saw the problem. Not far from shore, right around where the *Seaward* dropped them off, the big Dynize ship of the line had arrived and put down her anchor. The immense deck swarmed with sailors and soldiers, the latter of which were piling into longboats by the dozen. The first boat dropped into the water as Styke watched. Then the second, then the third.

He'd expected one of the frigates to send a small landing party to see what they were up to. But this big ship of the line was sending at least sixty naval infantry. Too many to deal with in a single, savage ambush, and probably better trained than normal sailors. The Mad Lancers needed to get off this coastline immediately.

"Is that bad?" Celine asked.

Styke pushed her gently down toward the waiting Lancers. "Yes," he said. "That's very bad."

CHAPTER 3

Vlora stood with her back to the entrance of her tent, thumbing absently through an old journal that she'd recovered from the bottom of her travel trunk just a few moments ago. At one point, it had been decorated with a rather ornate lock, but that had been dislodged by the jostling of tens of thousands of miles of travel. The black leather cover was well worn, the pages yellow from age and moisture, and the stitched teardrop of Adro barely visible in the center of the cover.

It was Tamas's journal, a seeming hodgepodge of dated notes and remembrances covering nearly two decades, the pages stuffed with old letters to and from his long-deceased wife. Vlora handled the pages with care, glancing at a few of the dates and letters, most of them written before she was born.

Someone cleared his throat behind her as she crossed her tent to set the journal on her cot, then turned to face the small group that had gathered at her request. Every movement brought pain, and she handled herself with nearly as much care as she did the journal, careful not to show just how badly her body had been mauled. She almost laughed at the efforts. Here she was, with her most trusted friends and companions, and she wouldn't allow herself to show them her pain. Well, no matter. They'd learn some of it soon enough.

Borbador sat on a stool in the corner of the tent, legs crossed, fingers drumming on his false leg while he puffed casually on an obscenely large pipe that he had to support with one hand just to keep it in his mouth. His face was expressionless, but his eyes had that thoughtful, amused look in them as if he'd just remembered something funny. He'd grown his ruddy beard out since Vlora last saw him, and she decided she preferred the look.

Privileged Nila stood behind Bo, leaning on his shoulder, playing with a strand of his hair, looking vaguely annoyed. Her hair was braided tightly over each shoulder, and she wore one of the crimson dresses that she liked so much. She looked up suddenly, meeting Vlora's eyes, and Vlora found her own gaze flinching away.

The rest of the party consisted of Vlora's three powder mages: the dark-haired Davd; the grizzled, highly experienced Norrine; and the quiet Kez ex-noble Buden je Parst. Vlora determined that it had been Bo who cleared his throat, and so let her gaze settle on him for a long moment before running it back across the others.

"Your recovery seems to be coming along nicely," Nila commented before Vlora could speak.

"You look...better," Davd offered.

Norrine looked up from cleaning her pistol. "We were worried about you."

Vlora waved away the encouragement and swallowed a grimace at the twinge that ran down her arm. She looked like a goddamned patchwork doll. Her entire body was covered with scars from the battle at the Crease over five weeks ago. Some of them, the smaller ones, were healing nicely. The rest...not so much. Neither Bo nor Nila specialized in healing sorcery, though they had both studied it in depth. It had taken them four days just to keep Vlora from dying and another five before she could be carried with the army as it traveled. Another whole week had passed before Vlora could walk on her own.

This was the first day she'd called her powder mages in for review; the first day she'd done anything beyond issue marching orders, ride along in a covered litter, or stew in the humid heat of her tent. She swallowed bile and clenched her fists behind her back. "Thank you for the kind words," she said softly. "But I have something important to discuss with the five of you. Bo already knows."

Nila looked up sharply, then down at Bo with a cocked eyebrow. "What is it?"

Vlora glanced across the group, swallowed again, cleared her throat, and found that she could not give voice to the thing that had haunted her since the second she regained consciousness. She coughed, tried to meet the eyes of her underlings, and failed. After a few moments, she forced herself to look Norrine in the eye—she was, after all, the most experienced of the mages. She would have to take up most of the slack.

"She can't use her sorcery," Bo announced. Vlora shot him a glare, but he continued. "The effort at the Crease has burned her out, made her powder blind."

All three of Vlora's mages stared at her. She could tell by their expressions that Norrine was not surprised—she'd probably expected it after seeing the carnage of the battle—but the other two were clearly taken off guard. Davd took a full step back, blinking in disbelief. Buden scowled. Before they could ask questions, she continued where Bo left off.

"This may or may not be permanent." Who was she kidding? It was possible to recover from powder blindness, but it took time. "You all know the stories, the notes Tamas kept about his students." She paused to blink away a few tears and take a deep breath. "The most important thing right now is that we continue as we have been. Absolutely no one beyond this room must know. Do you understand?"

There were a few dull nods.

"That goes for you two as well," Vlora said to Bo and Nila.

"Oh, come now," Bo objected.

"You are a bit of a gossip, dear," Nila said thoughtfully to Bo, studying Vlora with an intensity Vlora did not like. "Of course," she said. "We won't say a word."

"Yes, yes," Bo agreed. He glared at his pipe, then tapped it out against his false leg and stowed it in his jacket pocket. "You've been having us march south since you woke up. I assume that means you have a destination and a plan for what to do next?"

On to the next thing. Typical Bo, and Vlora was grateful for it. She had no doubt that she would dwell on the loss of her sorcery every spare moment from now until she died. Any distraction was welcome right now. "Of course. Thanks to you, I am in command of the greatest army on this continent. I intend on taking it to Landfall, where we will relieve the Dynize of their godstone and destroy it."

Norrine nodded along, as if this was what she'd expected. The other two powder mages still seemed too shell-shocked to respond. Bo lifted his hand like a schoolchild.

"Yes?" Vlora asked.

"I handed you a very nice army, but it's still the smallest fighting force by far. The Dynize and the Fatrastans both outnumber us by at least five to one. The Dynize want to kill you. The Fatrastans want to arrest you. Do you plan on fighting them both?"

"If necessary."

"What does that even mean?" Bo demanded.

Vlora wasn't entirely certain herself. The Dynize were enemy number one right now—they'd come dangerously close to killing her and her brigade of mercenaries. Fatrasta, though? Lindet's betrayal at Landfall still stung deeply. Vlora would not—could not—trust them. Which left her on a foreign continent swarming with enemy armies.

"It means destroying the godstone is our only purpose. We'll go through whoever we have to in order to accomplish that goal."

Bo exchanged a glance with Nila. After several seconds too long, he said, "Fair enough."

Vlora tried not to read too much into the hesitation. Taniel's initial reaction to the godstone had been to study it, and it had taken some insistence to bring him around. Bo was infinitely more curious than Taniel, so she would have to keep a close eye on him. He would never betray her outright, but he was a man rife with ulterior motives.

"You haven't actually told us how you plan on doing that," Nila pointed out.

Vlora gave her smile with humor she didn't feel. "The Adran way."

"Oh, well that explains everything."

Vlora ignored the sarcasm. "I just needed to tell the five of you about my . . . condition. Now that that's over with, back to business. Bo, I'd like you and Nila to check in with the artillery commander. We're going to end up in a full-fledged battle at some point in the next few weeks and I want you all coordinated. Mages, I'm going to want one of you on hand at all times. You'll have to be my sorcery—to tell me anything I should know and, if need be, to protect me. Eight-hour shifts, every day. I'll let you decide on the rotation. Dismissed."

The powder mages snapped their salutes and left the tent without another word. Nila followed them, pausing at the flap with a glance back, while Bo remained on the stool in the corner, watching Vlora the way an asylum doctor might watch one of his patients.

"That includes you," Vlora said to Bo, returning to her cot and picking up Tamas's journal.

Bo waited until Nila had gone, then said in a soft voice, "You're sure you're strong enough for this? We don't have Taniel anymore.

He's off to Adom knows where, and I'm not sure when he'll be back."

"Of course I'm sure." She was not. Not even close, and she knew it. Just lifting Tamas's journal brought a tremble to her hand that she could not afford to let her soldiers see. "I have to be."

"Right," Bo said flatly. He didn't believe her. "I'll be within shouting distance. If you need me..." He exited the tent, his false leg clicking as he went.

Vlora stood with her eyes closed in meditation for several minutes, *willing* her body to stop its shaking, pushing away the pain. It took all of her focus, and she instinctively reached for her sorcery every few moments, only to feel the pang of loss when it didn't come within her grasp.

Finally, she let out one trembling breath and fetched her sword from the corner. The blade was practically destroyed from her fight at the Crease; the steel notched, the tip bent, rust destroying what was left. There was still Dynize blood in several of the deepest gouges, and she hadn't had the energy to give it a proper cleaning. Still, the scabbard was in good shape, so she took the weapon as a cane and stepped out into the still morning air.

They'd set up her tent within spitting distance of the general-staff command center, on a knoll overlooking the Blackguard River Valley. Spread out before her was the army Bo had brought with him from Adro: thirty thousand infantry, eight thousand cavalry, and a full artillery contingent to accompany each brigade. It was, as she'd told her compatriots, the best fighting force on the continent—the best trained, the best outfitted, the best armed.

Across the valley, just on the other side of the small Blackguard River beside a picturesque copse of trees, was the town of Lower Blackguard. Her army had only arrived late last night, so this was the first time she'd set eyes on it herself. Still, she knew the area well by a study of local maps. The town's population was only around five hundred—it was the center of trade for the local tobacco and cotton plantations—but a city of tents now overflowed the town limits. The Fatrastan flag had been replaced by the black-and-red of the Dynize.

Vlora tore her eyes away from that flag and looked around. Soldiers had frozen in their tracks at the sight of her, staring openly. It was, she reminded herself, the first time they'd seen her out of a litter or her tent since the Crease. She gave the lot of them a cool, dismissive look before turning to Davd, who stood at attention beside the tent.

"Where's Olem?" she asked.

Davd started. "Uh, he's still gone, ma'am."

Vlora peered at Davd. There were bits and pieces missing from the last few weeks. Olem was one of them. She had no memory of being told that he'd ever left. "Where?"

"Escorting the godstone capstone to the Adran fleet, ma'am, as well as the Riflejack wounded."

"Ah, I remember now." She didn't. "Thank you. Let me know the moment he returns."

Davd looked nervous. "Yes, ma'am. Can I do anything else for you?"

"Tell me where our artillery unit is."

"This way, ma'am."

"Lead on." Vlora began the slow, methodical descent from the vantage of her knoll, leaning heavily on her sword. Davd kept pace with her, glaring at the passing camp followers and saluting soldiers with outward hostility as if their mere presence might upset her. His protectiveness was at once touching and irritating, but Vlora let it pass. If Davd's glares meant she was spared a few more hours until people started asking her stupid questions, so much the better.

They cut across the slope of the valley, ending up nearly half a mile away at a spot where the ground had been leveled for sixteen beautiful, polished four-pound guns and their crews. A woman in her midfifties with short, brown hair and a thin face strode among them, snapping orders and inspecting the guns. Her name was Colonel Silvia and she was the most experienced artillery officer in the Adran Army.

Vlora's approach was unnoticed until she was between two of the cannons. A crewman recognized her, snapping a salute and calling out attention. Within the minute, sixteen crews stood at attention beside their guns while their commander saluted, then warmly took Vlora's hand. "Good to see you up and moving, General."

"Good to be up and moving. What's the situation?"

Silvia looked toward the town of Lower Blackguard. "Roughly four thousand metalheads holed up in and around the town. They have a perimeter, but it's sloppy. We brought in a deserter less than an hour ago—I actually just came from a briefing."

Vlora lifted her eyebrows. "Oh?"

"Looks like this is the remnants of one of the brigades you and Two-shot gutted at the Crease. They don't have Privileged or bone-eyes, and only a handful of officers. About half of them are wounded."

Vlora barely heard anything after the word "Crease." This was what was left of a brigade sent to execute her, murder her men, and take the portion of godstone they'd brought from Yellow Creek. Flashes of the fight played across her memory, and the ache of her missing sorcery made her weak in the knees.

"Do we know what they have planned?"

"The deserter said they have orders to hold for reinforcements. I imagine if we give them a proper encirclement, they'll surrender by this time tomorrow."

Something ugly reared its head inside Vlora at that moment. Her lip curled involuntarily, and she couldn't help but think of the doggedness with which the Dynize had pursued her, of the betrayals of the Fatrastans, of the losses both personal and professional that she had suffered since the Dynize arrived at Landfall.

"Colonel, I want your battery to bombard the town into submission."

Silvia looked uncertain. "Shouldn't we demand their surrender first?"

"I think they'll get the message."

"And civilians from the town?"

Fatrastans. Betrayers. Enemies. "Try not to hit too many of them," Vlora said coldly. "Davd."

"Yes, ma'am?"

"Get Norrine and Buden. Kill every officer you see. I won't accept a surrender from any officer with an equivalent rank of master sergeant or above."

Davd swallowed hard. "Should we let them know that?"

"As I said, they'll get the message." Vlora turned away, gesturing for them to carry out their orders. That ugly thing was now rooted firmly in her breast, and she felt like she was watching someone else order the butchering of an enemy brigade. She tried to dig her way out of this fresh-found fury—and was unsuccessful.

"Where are you going, ma'am?" Silvia asked.

"To find a good place from which to watch."

CHAPTER 4

Vlora spent the day watching the heavy bombardment of Lower Blackguard. Throughout the morning and afternoon, more gun crews trickled in from the various brigades. They flattened sections of the hillside, brought in their guns and artillery, and joined Colonel Silvia in the relentless attack.

Word must have spread that Vlora had emerged from her tent, because a steady stream of messengers and well-wishing officers had cropped up by noon. She listened to their platitudes and reports, taking them all in with the same cool nod, and sat in her camp chair with her pitted sword across her lap. It felt good to let the sun play on her face after so long cooped up, and the report of the guns gave her a feeling of warmth that bordered on frightening.

The first white flag emerged from Lower Blackguard at about two in the afternoon. Vlora could tell by the lacquered breastplate that it was an officer, and the woman didn't make it halfway to Vlora's lines before she fell to a gunshot from one of Vlora's mages. The second white flag came out an hour later and met the same fate.

Just after that second one died, Vlora spotted Nila picking her way through the camp. The Privileged approached the artillery battery, where she spoke with Silvia and several of the gun crews, but did not add her sorcery to the bombardment. Vlora watched her cautiously, wondering how long it would take for Nila to approach and question her methods.

"You're shooting their messengers before they can surrender," a voice noted.

Vlora started and cursed under her breath. She'd been so focused on Nila that she hadn't heard Bo approach from behind. He had a collapsible camp chair over one shoulder and unfolded it, plopping down beside Vlora and letting out a pleased sigh as he unhooked his false leg and began to fiddle with the ankle mechanism.

"I swear that thing only makes noise when you want it to," Vlora accused.

Bo smiled but didn't look up from his leg. "You're punishing them," he said with a nod across the valley.

"If you want to call it that, sure," Vlora responded. She felt suddenly surly, uninterested in listening to any sort of reproach from anyone—even the adopted brother who'd helped save her life. She began preparing for an argument, cataloging Bo's past atrocities, ready to accuse the Privileged of doing anything and everything for his own ends.

She was surprised when he simply gave a small shrug. "Could be useful. But is it a great idea to shoot messengers under a white flag?"

She opened her mouth, closed it, and felt that ugly anger stir in her belly. "They would do the same to me without hesitation."

"You're certain of that?" Bo asked.

"Yes."

"Ah." Bo finally worked a bit of grit out of the ankle mechanism of his false leg and hooked it back to his knee. "Then, carry on!"

"I'm glad you approve."

Bo glanced across the valley, but he had that distant look in his eyes as if he had already moved on to other, more important thoughts. Vlora tried to read anything deeper from his expression but was unsuccessful. She sighed and looked over her shoulder to where Davd sat on the hillside some ten feet behind her—far enough to give her some room but close enough to come quickly if needed. Davd was smoking a cigarette, and Vlora wondered when he had started. She opened her mouth to ask Bo if he'd seen Olem, only to remember that Olem was still gone. His absence caused her to ache as badly as did the rest of her body. She wished he had not left.

"What's the state of Fatrasta between here and Landfall?" Bo asked.

Vlora pulled her eyes away from the bombardment. "You mean you've been here for over a month and you don't have your spy network in place? I assumed you'd know everything before I did."

"Don't be silly. I know *most* things before you do, not everything. But your soldiers are particularly loyal right now, what with their general sacrificing herself for their comrades and then rising from the ashes. It's hard to get much out of them."

Vlora snorted. "That's reassuring." She let her gaze linger on a group of Adran privates watching her from a distance of about twenty yards. She couldn't read their faces, not without a powder trance, but something about them left her unsettled. She tried to put them out of her mind and leaned forward in her chair, using her sword to scratch a bit of bare earth out of the grassland and then drawing in it. "Here's the coast," she said, making a line. "Here's us, and here's Landfall." They'd started out at the Crease, about three hundred miles north of Landfall. The army had managed to cover roughly half of that distance while Vlora recuperated.

She stabbed another dot into the ground. "The Adran fleet is shadowing our flank, dealing with any Dynize ships so that nothing lands behind us and making sure we're well supplied."

"And the enemy?" Bo asked.

"Field armies here, here, and here," Vlora answered. "All Dynize. The Fatrastans have been beaten badly, but they're not out of the fight. Rumor has it they've got at least four hundred thousand men fielded down here." She drew a circle around the area to the northwest of Landfall. "Mostly conscripts. They're better armed than the Dynize, but they don't have the discipline or sorcery. Lindet's a wily one, though, so I won't count her beat until I see her head on a spike."

"Is that what you intend to do with her?" Bo asked.

Vlora's stomach churned. "I'll deal with her when I have to. Regardless, we won't know about the true state of the Fatrastan military until we get around the south end of the Ironhook Mountains. The Dynize field armies are our immediate problem, particularly…" She jabbed at one of the spots she'd poked in the dirt. "That one there." She drew a small horn in the dirt, jutting out from the coast, on which was perched the city of New Adopest. Her last intelligence told her that the city was under siege by a Dynize army. "We'll lose valuable time if we go out of our way to confront them, but if we don't, we'll leave forty thousand infantry at our rear."

Bo gave the map a cursory glance and leaned back in his camp chair. "Hm."

It took Vlora a moment to register how little interest he actually had in what she'd just explained, and another to realize why. "You already knew all that, didn't you?"

"You sound just like him, you know."

"Who?" she demanded.

Bo rummaged in his pockets until he produced his comically oversized pipe and a match. He didn't answer until he'd puffed it to life. "Tamas."

A little tickle went up Vlora's spine. She snorted the thought away. "I sound like any competent general, you mean?" She gestured at the dirty map. "You already knew all this."

"Of course."

"Then why the pit did you make me explain it?"

Bo smirked.

"Well?"

"Just making sure you still have *it*."

Vlora was genuinely angry now. She climbed to her feet, lever-aging herself up with her sword. "Why the pit wouldn't I have it? Just because I'm practically an invalid doesn't mean I can't think anymore. I lost my sorcery, not my brain!" The last few words tum-bled out far louder than she'd meant them to, and she immediately looked around to see who could have heard them. Only Davd was close enough, and he was studiously looking elsewhere.

She knuckled her back, pulling at some half-healed muscle in her arm in the process. Being angry, she decided, hurt like the pit. "Damn you," she said to Bo.

He shrugged. "I handed an army to a woman who, for the last few weeks, couldn't even move without help. I needed to be sure I didn't make a mistake."

"Thanks for the confidence," she spat.

Bo's eyes narrowed, and she saw his mask of indifference split momentarily. "Don't confuse my brotherly love for you for stupid-ity. I wouldn't have handed you this army in the first place if I didn't think you would be able to lead it."

"Oh, stop it." Vlora felt her anger wane. "This army was meant for Taniel. Don't tell me you weren't surprised to hear that he didn't actually want to lead it."

Bo rolled his eyes and settled back in his chair, puffing steadily on his pipe. The tobacco was pleasant, with a distinct cherry scent—not nearly as harsh as Olem's cigarettes. Vlora pulled back into herself, nostrils full of smoke, ears filled with the report of artillery, eye on Lower Blackguard, and wondered when Olem would return.

A little after five o'clock, a lone soldier with a plain steel breastplate left the Dynize camp, walking slowly with hands held in the air, shouting something that was lost beneath the din of the bombardment. He collapsed when he reached the Adran lines.

A few minutes later, a messenger approached Vlora. The young woman snapped a salute. "General Flint, ma'am, there's a Dynize soldier here offering unconditional surrender."

"A common soldier?" Vlora asked.

"Yes, ma'am. I was told your orders were to accept surrender only from a sergeant or infantryman."

That ugly thing writhing in her belly almost put words in her mouth, and Vlora had to bite her tongue hard to resist the urge to order the bombardment to go on all night. "Right. I did. Tell Colonel Silvia to cease fire. Order the Third to march down and take possession of Lower Blackguard. I want a full report of the town and the Dynize prisoners by nightfall. Dismissed."

The messenger had been gone for a few minutes before Bo cleared his throat. "You almost continued the bombardment, didn't you? I could see it in your eyes."

"Shut up," Vlora snapped, getting to her feet. She could feel Bo's gaze on her back as she slowly made her way back to her tent, retrieving Tamas's journal before heading to the general-staff headquarters. The pain of making herself walk such a distance was dragging at her by the time she reached the command tent, and she had to straighten her shoulders and adjust her collar before she nodded to Davd to throw the tent flap open.

As she stepped inside, the chatter of discussion died within moments. All eyes turned toward her. The big tent was full of officers and their aides—brigadier generals, colonels, majors. Most of them had already swung by earlier in the day to offer their platitudes, but they still seemed shocked to see her here.

"Good afternoon," she said softly. She looked around to see if the commander of the Third was present, and was glad when he wasn't. She wanted him to oversee the surrender of the Dynize camp personally. "I know many of you are waiting for orders," she continued, "and that you're all curious what we're doing on foreign soil in the middle of a war that isn't ours.

"Rumors may have reached you about the artifact of great power that the Dynize possess and that the Fatrastans wish to steal back. The rumors are true. I have seen the artifact myself, and we are in possession of the capstone of its counterpart. A third artifact is still unaccounted for. According to our intelligence, if the Dynize leader is able to possess all three of these so-called godstones, he will have the sorcerous ability to make himself or his emperor into a new god.

"I will tell you right now: We are not here to win a war for either the Dynize or the Fatrastans. We are here to take the Landfall god-stone from our enemies and destroy it, after which we will with-draw and these sons of bitches can kill each other to their hearts' content. Understood?"

There was a round of nods. One of the colonels in the back raised a hand. Vlora ignored it.

"Thank you all for coming so far on the word—and krana—of Magus Borbador." She allowed herself a smirk, and gave a moment for the few chuckles to die down. "Thank you for giving me the opportunity to lead you all in battle once again. The Dynize in Lower Blackguard have surrendered. We're finished here, and I'm simply waiting on my scouts before I plot our next move. I'd like to review the troops in an hour, if you please. That is all."

Vlora ignored a storm of questions as she cut through the middle of the room and searched for a seat in the far corner, where she sank down in relief and opened Tamas's journal, reading with ears deaf to the rest of the world. Only when a messenger approached, informing her that the troops were assembled, did she close the journal and return to her feet, limping along with the book tucked under her arm.

She stepped outside and her breath immediately caught in her throat.

The valley below the command tent was filled with soldiers standing at attention in perfect, still silence. Nearly forty thousand sets of eyes stared directly at her, unblinking, unwavering. She couldn't help but wonder what Bo had promised these men and women to get them to come all the way across the ocean and leap into a war, and whether her reputation had swayed any of them to come.

She dismissed the thought immediately. Bo must have promised them a fortune. He certainly had the money.

Distantly, a voice called out, "Field Army, salute!"

There was booming answer of "Hut!" and the snap of forty thousand arms. Vlora watched in awe, trying to remember if she'd ever been in command of so many troops at once.

"Looks pretty good, doesn't it?" Bo asked, emerging from behind the command tent.

Vlora managed a nod.

"You know, technically you should be addressed as Field Marshal."

Vlora considered it. She fought momentarily with her terrible subconscious, which rather liked the sound of Field Marshal Flint. " 'General' will do for now," she told Bo. She stepped past him, walking the few dozen paces to where the general staff stood assembled nearby. She was barely able to tear her eyes off the army before her as she approached, and a line from Tamas's journal struck her.

With an Adran Field Army, he'd written during the Gurlish Wars, *if it was stripped of buffoons and properly supplied, I could conquer the world.*

She thought, for that moment, that she felt the thrill that must have compelled him to such a conjecture. "My friends," she finally said to the general staff, "my voice is not up to a speech, but please pass on to your soldiers that this is the finest army I've ever seen." She lifted her head just as a rider crested the top of the hill. The rider paused, clearly taken by what he saw, but Vlora lifted an arm and waved him closer.

It was one of her scouts. The man swung from his horse by the command tent and approached with a sort of reverence, saluting Vlora and then the general staff. "What news?" Vlora asked. "Speak up so the generals can hear you."

"I come from the southeast," the scout reported. "With word from New Adopest."

"And how does it look?"

"They're still under siege by the Dynize. They beg for aid from Lindet, but none of the Fatrastan armies have been able to break north. The messengers I met claim that the city won't last out the week."

Vlora glanced at the general staff, knowing what must be going through their heads. She'd already told them that they weren't here to take sides, but Fatrastans were almost entirely Kressian, with an enormous population of emigrated Adrans. Some of the general staff probably had friends or relatives in New Adopest. It had, after all, been settled by their ancestors.

Vlora needed to teach a lesson—a lesson to her officers, to the Fatrastans, and to the Dynize. She raised her voice. "Send orders to the fleet. They're to brush aside the Dynize sea blockade, but I don't want them to make contact with the city."

"And us?" one of the brigadier generals asked.

"Most of these men haven't seen blood since the Kez Civil War. I don't want to reach Landfall with rusty troops. Let's go give them some practice."

CHAPTER 5

Styke knelt in the thick, clinging underbrush, trying to ignore whatever creature was crawling across the back of his neck, and watched as two squads of Dynize naval infantry splashed through a streambed almost close enough for him to touch. The soldiers seemed alert, watchful, each of them looking in a different direction to cover all approaches while the two leads tracked Styke's Lancers across mud, water, and rock.

He pressed his back against one of the mighty stone outcroppings that rose sharply from the swamp. Not a sound—not a breath. He was too close. One of the soldiers looked right past him, stabbing a short bayonet into the foliage and missing Styke's knee by inches. Satisfied, the woman moved on. A few moments later the last soldier paused right beside Styke. He said something in Dynize that Styke couldn't quite catch, then turned directly toward him and began to undo his trousers.

Styke was willing to put up with all sorts of creeping things for the sake of an ambush. He would not, however, allow a man to piss on him. He grunted, knife flashing up, and slashed the man's throat before he could say a word. Styke lunged from the underbrush before his first victim had hit the ground. He thrust into the next soldier, cut the throat of a third, and took two steps back before the rest of the squad could turn to face him.

"Now!" he yelled, flinging himself back into the underbrush.

Farther up the stream, twenty carbines fired at once, cutting through the two squads of infantry. Styke listened to the bullets whiz by and crack against the stone mere feet from his head, then counted to ten before he returned to the open.

Only six members of the original two squads remained standing. The Lancers fell upon them, swinging carbines and knives, but to their credit the Dynize infantry did not go down without a fight. Wounded to a man, they closed ranks and returned fire, then brandished their bayonets. Styke waited for them to route and retreat toward him, but not a one of them did.

Within the minute they were overwhelmed, but at least four of Styke's Lancers had taken wounds, and two of those were on the ground. He joined the group, taking a moment to wipe his blade on the jacket of a fallen Dynize before barking out, "No time to slow down. We've got at least six more squads on our heels. Jackal, get the horses. Sunin, see to the wounded. We've got to stay ahead of these bastards or this swamp will be the last thing we see."

As they jumped to follow his orders, Styke let out a piercing whistle. A few moments later both Ka-poel and Celine emerged from the trees farther up the streambed. Celine looked around at the bodies like a child unimpressed by a bunch of broken dolls, while Ka-poel's study was far cooler, almost academic.

"If one of these is still breathing," Styke said, "I need him to talk. Can you do that?"

Ka-poel's hands flashed. Celine translated. *I thought you don't like my methods.*

"I don't. But I'd like to stay alive right now."

Ka-poel rolled her eyes and headed around the sixteen-or-so fallen Dynize. She checked three of them before finally squatting beside one, a man with the haggard old face of a seasoned veteran. The man's mouth was full of blood, his teeth clenched tightly, but he grinned defiantly at them as he clutched a length of intestine falling from a gaping stomach wound. Ka-poel dipped her fingers in his blood, then dabbed them on his forehead and cheeks. The soldier's eyes narrowed, then widened in realization, and he began to shiver violently, clawing at his own stomach as if to hurry his own demise.

"Seems like they know what a bone-eye is capable of," Styke commented. He looked over his shoulder to make sure that his orders were being carried out. The men had already begun to bring their horses back to the streambed and out of the rocky recess where they'd been hidden.

Ka-poel pressed two fingers against the dying soldier's throat. The man's struggles weakened, his eyes glazing over. She nodded.

Styke knelt beside him, looking over the soldier, the coppery scent of Ka-poel's sorcery in his nostrils. "Can you understand me?" He spoke in Palo, throwing in the few Dynize words he knew.

"Yes," the soldier responded.

"Good. How many of you are on our tail?"

"Nine squads."

"How many in a Dynize squad?"

"Eight to ten." The answers were mechanical, spoken in that Dynize that sounded so much like heavily accented Palo.

"Your orders?"

"Kill you. Capture a few. Find out why you're dropping such a small group on the homeland."

"Is your ship continuing in pursuit of ours?"

"Just the escorts. Our ship of the line will return to port to let them know about a possible invasion."

"Of just twenty men?"

The soldier blinked blankly. "We are very cautious. The homeland is not well defended right now."

Styke tried to think of any other questions that a common soldier might be able to answer. That last bit was good news, but he knew better than to take the man at his word. It was very unlikely that he actually knew how many soldiers the Dynize had left to garrison their own cities. "Not well defended"—could be relative, considering the size of the Dynize invasion force.

Still, this meant that *someone* would be told that Styke had put to shore. Whether the Dynize cared enough to come looking was another matter. But they needed to hurry.

"How far behind us are the rest of your comrades?"

Sweat poured down the soldier's forehead. He was dying, and quickly. Styke wondered how long Ka-poel could keep him alive. "I don't know. We spread out to entrap you. The others may already be on your flank."

"Piss and shit." Styke stood up, raising his head to the sky. "We need to find that road well before nightfall," he shouted. "Form a line and get ready to move out. I want to—"

He was cut off by the distant caw of a raven, followed by another, then a long-drawn-out croak. He paused and looked around for Jackal. "Did you hear that?"

Jackal nodded in confusion. "That was Markus's signal."

"That the enemy on our left flank has been taken care of," Styke replied, not bothering to hide his bafflement.

"Yes."

"By himself?"

"I'm not sure," Jackal said. "Should I go find him?"

Styke felt his gut twist. Something was wrong here and he couldn't quite place it. "We need to keep moving. If we're fine on our left flank, it won't hurt to get to the road. Markus can catch up with us. Get on your horses," he told Ka-poel and Celine. Once

Celine's back was turned, he knelt down next to the soldier he'd been interrogating and quickly dispatched him.

"Ben," Jackal said.

"What is it?" Styke's eyes fell on Jackal, only to see that the Palo had frozen in place, alert as a dog with its hackles up. Gripping his knife, Styke turned to follow his gaze.

A pair of figures had appeared on a knoll to their right. One of them was Zak, Markus's brother. The other was familiar, and it made the hair on the back of Styke's neck stand on end.

It was the dragonman who had walked out at the Battle of Starlight. Ji-Orz. He wore the same naval infantry uniform as the soldiers Styke had just ambushed, and he regarded the entire group of Lancers with an air of appraisal. He and Zak descended the knoll, and though Zak was stiff, he didn't appear to be under any duress. He swallowed hard when they reached the stream and cleared his throat. "Boss," he said, "this man says he's a buddy of yours."

Styke met Ji-Orz's gaze and slowly wicked the blood off his knife with two fingers. "Dragonman."

"Hello, Ben Styke," Orz said in Adran. "I have come to make a deal."

"Hold on," Styke cut him off. "First, how the pit did you get here?" He looked sharply around at the gathered Lancers. He had no doubt that they could deal with the dragonman—but it would be at great cost.

Orz raised one eyebrow, his gaze sweeping casually—*too* casually—across the Lancers, lingering for half a moment on Ka-poel. "How do you think?"

"You stowed away on the *Seaward*?" Zak blurted.

The dragonman glanced at Zak, his face expressionless. "Yes."

"Where?" Zak again. Styke thought to silence him, but he was curious, too. The *Seaward* was not a big ship.

"Just under the prow. There was enough space to hang in the

rigging out of sight. If the captain had ordered any work done on the keel on a slow day, I would have been discovered."

"You just hung there for two weeks?" Styke asked flatly. Styke had spent the better part of the journey carving and watched the gulls up on the forecastle. Orz had probably been less than a handful of paces away the entire time. The idea was disconcerting.

"I snuck on board for food and water on two nights. But otherwise, yes." Orz answered as if it was no great deed.

"Through the storm?"

"It was…unpleasant," Orz answered. "Most of my clothes were torn away. I had to abandon my dragon leathers. That's why I'm wearing these." He plucked at the ill-fitting Dynize uniform. "Does that satisfy your curiosity? Or would you prefer to believe that I swam here?"

Styke considered the question for a few moments. It had been over a month since Ji-Orz left the battle at Starlight. In theory, that was plenty of time for him to slip down the coast, hop a Dynize vessel, and then put to land with the soldiers currently on their tail. But it would have to be a damn big coincidence that Orz wound up on the same ship that would eventually give chase to the *Seaward*. He shook his head. Either way gave him a strange story. Either way he didn't trust the dragonman. "All right. Assuming you hitched a ride with us…why?"

A serious smile flickered across Orz's face. "Because I needed to get home."

"And you couldn't just find a Dynize vessel?"

"I left in the middle of a battle, disobeying direct orders from Ka-Sedial himself. I am not…how do you say, a person 'welcome' among the Dynize."

"Yet you're going back."

A nod. "By now, my betrayal will be well known among the Dynize in Fatrasta. Dragonmen will have been sent to look for me. Coming back here is the last thing Ka-Sedial will expect."

Styke studied Orz closely, trying to foresee where all of this was going. "But they'll find out eventually."

"Yes, they will." Somehow, Orz's serious face grew even more tense. "Sedial knows he cannot punish me, so he will punish those close to me. He will have dispatched agents to seek my family. I've returned to do what I can to protect them from the coming reckoning."

Styke glanced to his side. Ka-poel stared hard at the dragonman, flicking her gaze once toward Styke but betraying nothing of her thoughts. "Is he telling the truth?" Styke asked.

Ka-poel drew a pen knife from one pocket, then presented an open palm toward Orz. Orz's eyes immediately narrowed. "No," he said firmly. "I assume that you're the one who broke Sedial's hold on me. If that is true, I thank you. However, I will not allow a bone-eye to take my blood again, not willingly."

Ka-poel snorted. She gave a few short gestures and stepped back next to her horse. *I think he's telling the truth*, Celine translated.

"All right," Styke said, breaking a sudden stillness. He realized his shoulders were tense, his fist clutching the hilt of his knife so hard that it hurt. He forced himself to relax and put his knife away. "We know why you're in Dynize. Now tell me why you're *here*. What's this proposition? And make it quick, because fifty or more of your countrymen are swarming that swamp behind us, and I need to either get ahead of them or set up a trap."

"Sixty-four," Orz said softly.

"Sixty-four what?" Styke found himself losing patience, and had to consciously restrain himself from reaching for his knife.

"Sixty-four of my countrymen. They won't be a bother."

A shiver went up Styke's spine. He jerked his head at Zak, who immediately took off into the swamp to check on Orz's claim. Orz continued, "My proposition is this: If you help me get home and get my relatives to safety, I will help you make the rendezvous with the rest of your cavalry."

"Why do you think we need your help?"

"Because you won't make it twenty miles without me." Orz paused for a just a moment, as if to let the information sink in, then continued, "I've been listening to your Lancers gossip for weeks. I listened at Starlight and I listened on the ship. I know that you're here to destroy the godstone, and I know that you plan on meeting up with your Lancers and finding the stone in the middle of the swamp. As for the godstone: good. Dynize is better without Sedial getting his hands on such a weapon. As for your plan . . . it is inherently flawed."

The surrounding Lancers began to murmur among themselves, exchanging glances and reaching for weapons. Styke could sense the swell of uncertainty within them, and it was not a feeling that would make this journey any easier. He half considered lashing out with his knife, silencing the dragonman before he could sow any more doubt. But that, he decided, would not end well. "How is our plan flawed?" Styke asked between clenched teeth. He looked once more at Ka-poel. Her head was cocked to one side, as if she was listening very carefully to what the dragonman had to say.

Orz didn't seem to notice the stir his words caused. "Because you don't have updated maps of Dynize. No outsider has set foot on our shore and been allowed to depart again for over a hundred years, and that means you have no idea how the Jagged Fens have changed since your map was made. The Fens are no longer a wilderness. They may seem it from the outside, yes; we've been very careful to keep our shoreline looking static to foreign sailors. But the Fens have been tamed. The godstone you seek is not sunk into some swamp. It was rediscovered forty years ago and excavated. The scholars and sorcerers did not think it wise to move it, so instead we built a city around it. We moved the entire capital. The godstone is now the centerpiece of the emperor's palace, less than sixty miles from where we stand. The road you wish to use is a heavily trafficked highway rather than a backwater dirt track, and there are at least eight population centers between here and the capital."

Styke took a step back, feeling like he'd been punched. To pit with riding through the damned wilderness. If Orz was telling the truth, he was now separated from both his army and their target by several cities and whatever garrisons they might hold.

Orz spread his hands. "May I see your map?"

Numb, Styke gave a nod. Celine handed over the map case, and Styke passed it to the dragonman. Orz carefully drew out the regional map and unrolled it, giving it an appraising glance. "From what I overheard, you planned on landing here, correct?" He pointed to the rendezvous.

"Yes." Styke briefly considered that he was giving vital intelligence to the enemy. What if Orz snatched the maps and made a run for it, taking knowledge of the invasion back to his people? But Styke was still trying to process Orz's claims, and he felt suddenly sapped of all energy to consider intrigue.

"It's a good place to land. Inhospitable, dense swampland. You're lucky, because they'll have some time to make preparations and scout before they are discovered." Orz tapped another spot, roughly two-thirds of the way down the coast between their current location and the rendezvous, and about twenty miles inland. "This is the Dynize capital, home of the godstone. It's named Talunlica. To reach your rendezvous, you will have to pass through or very close to Talunlica, and you will not be able to do so undetected.

"As I said," Orz continued, "I will exchange my help for yours. My parents live in the capital. They are the former heads of a Household and have since stepped down. 'Retired' is your word, yes? If you help me get them safely out of the city and into hiding, I will make sure you reach the rest of your army."

Styke had no idea how reaching Ibana and the rest of the Mad Lancers was going to help. He'd brought twenty-five hundred cavalry over—enough to seize and secure an artifact in the middle of the swamp while they figured out how to destroy it. But the Dynize had built an entire damn city around the thing. How was he going to meet up with Ibana, storm a city, crush a garrison, and give Ka-poel time to unravel the damn thing's secrets?

He took a deep breath, letting the emotions roll over him, turning his uncertainty into focus. One thing at a time. "How do you propose getting twenty foreign cavalry through the center of government in a place where foreigners aren't allowed?"

That serious smile crossed Orz's expression again. "Foreigners are not completely unknown in Dynize."

Ka-poel gestured emphatically. *Explain.*

"Shipwrecked sailors, foolish explorers, and the descendants of a handful of merchant families that were allowed to remain in Dynize when the borders closed. There is an entire"—he paused, searching for the word—"'subculture,' I think you'd say, surrounding foreigners. It would take far too long to explain, but the vast majority of them are slaves—the only legal slaves remaining in the empire."

"You want us to pose as slaves?" Styke demanded. He immediately envisioned his time in the labor camps, chained together with convicts, forced to dig ditches for his evening gruel. He had to stifle a surge of fury in his breast.

"Yes, slaves," Orz said, speaking quickly as several of the Lancers gave voice to the same fears that had risen in Styke. "But I do not think 'slave' has the same meaning to you and me. In Dynize, a slave is a member of a Household. They do not get to choose their Household, but they do have jobs, families, security. Many of them act as Household guards. Still slaves, yes, but treated well."

Styke relaxed somewhat, rolling his shoulders, and nodded for Orz to continue.

"I am a dragonman. Very few people who see these tattoos dare to question my word. I can pass myself off as escorting twenty slaves and"—he gestured to the armor strapped to Amrec's saddle—"an acquisition of Kressian armor from up north. We will pose as members of a Household that has little to no presence in the capital. As long as we keep moving without hesitation or delay, there shouldn't be any problems." Orz spread his arms, looking around at the assembled Lancers and once again allowing his gaze to linger for a few seconds on Ka-poel.

A niggle of urgency touched the back of Styke's mind, and he glanced toward the swamp, hoping to catch sight of either of his scouts. Those damned Dynize soldiers might be on them at any moment, and he needed to set up an ambush or get moving. "We're getting more out of this than you are," he said. "Why?"

"Because," Orz said simply, "your plan will disrupt the local politics and mask the disappearance of my parents. And I don't think you have any real chance of success. It is a fool's errand, and I find myself drawn to it in the same way I was drawn to spitting at the feet of an emperor I didn't love even though I knew I would suffer the consequences."

"He thinks he's giving charity to a bunch of simpletons," someone said angrily from the back of the group.

Orz held up one finger, a genuine smile cracking the corner of his mouth. "On the contrary. I have seen Ben Styke kill several dragonmen in single combat. I have seen the carnage wrought by the Mad Lancers against the very best Dynize cavalry. And I have seen her"—he pointed at Ka-poel—"break the strongest bone-eye in the world. You are the only group I can possibly imagine succeeding at this mission, and even if you all die in the attempt, you will cause Ka-Sedial many sleepless nights. That is enough for me."

Styke weighed his options. Was this a ruse? Or was everything Orz had said true? If so, did Styke have any other option beyond trusting him? He glanced at Ka-poel and considered demanding Orz give her his blood. But what if Orz *was* telling the truth, and the very request drove him away? That would leave Styke and his men stranded in enemy territory with no way of reaching the rest of the Lancers.

His attention was drawn back to the swamp as a pair of figures sprinted out of the undergrowth and across a wide, shallow stream. It was Zak and Markus. The pair were coated in swamp slime, faces dirty, eyes wide. They pushed their way through the assembled Lancers, and Markus took a deep breath, glancing fearfully at Orz, before nodding excitedly at Styke. "Uh, sir..."

"Spit it out," Styke ordered.

"Ben, the landing party is dead."

"What do you mean, dead?"

"Sixty-four of them. All dead. Looked like most of them were picked off in small groups, most of them without a chance of drawing their weapons." He glanced at Orz's clothing. "One of them was naked."

Styke slowly turned to Orz. "You killed your own people."

Orz shrugged. "It wasn't the first time. It won't be the last. They were of a Household that was my enemy during the war, so I feel no guilt. Besides, I thought it the only way to convince you of my intentions."

Sixty-four men, slaughtered in what must have been less than an hour as they were strung out through the swamp. Styke hadn't heard a single gunshot in that time. He twirled his ring thoughtfully, pressing his thumb against the tip of the silver lance until it hurt. "What do you need to get us past Talunca?"

"Talunlica," Orz corrected. "Dynize colors, for a start. Passports. Weapons. Whatever we can't get off the dead, we will acquire at the next large town. And I'll need your men to stay completely silent for the next week—we cannot risk anyone finding out they don't speak Dynize."

"Right." Styke glanced once more at Ka-poel. She gave him a small nod. He wished that Ibana were here to hash this out with him. She was more level-headed about this sort of thing.

"Backtrack, boys. Let's strip the dead and get ourselves cleaned up. Orz here is going to teach you all how to write 'I've taken a vow of silence' in Dynize. Once we're on the main road, the first of you to talk to anyone but me gets my ring through the front of your skull. Got it?" There was a round of reluctant nods, and the Lancers began heading back the way they came, most of them giving Orz a reluctant glance as they passed.

Orz snorted. "That might work in an emergency."

"Good. Because I damn well don't trust you, but I know you're telling the truth about at least one thing."

"Oh?"

"That this is a fool's errand," Styke said quietly, "and we're probably all going to die."

CHAPTER 6

Y ou're sure about this?"

The question was, Michel knew, about three days too late. He stood in front of Ichtracia in a hired room on the outskirts of Lower Landfall, where their Dynize passports had gotten them past the last of the major roadblocks that governed all highways in and out of the city. The room was tiny and cramped, most of it taken up by a big, flea-ridden bed that usually slept six strangers so that the boarding house could accommodate more bodies when the dockside inns were full.

What little space remained was occupied by a short wooden stool. On the bed was a razor, a bowl containing a small amount of lime-and-ash mixture, and an actor's face-painting kit. Ichtracia's clothes—the black mourning vestments that she'd worn for almost a month—lay on the floor to be burned. Ichtracia sat straight-backed on the stool, like a princess sitting for a portrait.

Her gaze flickered up to him briefly. "I said I was, didn't I?"

"You did."

"You question me a lot." There was a note of warning in her voice.

Michel clenched his jaw and tried to ignore it. "I do, because most people only *think* they can become a spy. Actually doing it is a different matter altogether." Her forehead wrinkled, her mouth opened, and Michel held up his hand to forestall an argument. "Yes, I know that you'd rather just smash your way back into Landfall and demand answers. But by your own admission you are loath to kill your own people—and even if you weren't, Sedial is surrounded by dragonmen, bone-eyes, and Privileged. We're not going to smash anything. We're doing this my way. Agreed?"

"Agreed," Ichtracia said after a long hesitation.

"Good."

"I have a question first."

Michel paused, frowning at Ichtracia. "What's that?"

"Why didn't you tell me about the sacrifices?"

"Because..." Michel hesitated. Telling her that he hadn't been sure if he could trust her was not going to help their relationship. A half-truth, then. "Because I couldn't confirm it, and I didn't think you could, either. It was just something told to me by a dying Blackhat."

Ichtracia stared at him for a few moments—long enough that he feared she would question him further—before giving him a curt nod. "Go ahead."

"All right," Michel said, trying not to sound relieved to move on. "Training. We're going to move as quickly as we can, which to an outsider might seem positively sluggish."

"How so?"

"Spies don't run. They saunter. Everything we do needs to be calculated but *look* casual. We need to blend in, operate with thoughtful consideration. Our second job will be to make contact with Emerald and find out exactly what's going on in the city—if he has any evidence of the blood sacrifices. Once we've confirmed

how, exactly, the Dynize are exploiting the Palo...Well, that's
when the fighting begins. We rally the Palo. We fire them up."

Ichtracia cocked her head. "You skipped the first job."

"Our first job is to make you into a spy. It's not going to be
pretty." Michel picked up the razor, took her long auburn hair in
one hand, and began to cut. He talked as he worked.

"We'll start by changing your appearance. Your mannerisms
will be next. I don't have time to teach you to act like a Palo, so I'll
have to correct you as we go. Your Adran accent is excellent, which
is a major boon to us. Your Palo...well, we're going to have to work
on that. We can pass you off as from a northern family with Adran
connections and an Adran education. It's not too far-fetched."

He worked the razor carefully around her ear. Locks of hair
fell to the floor, forming a skirt around the feet of the stool. He
was careful to leave about an inch on the top, half an inch on the
sides—a common northern look for city Palo women. The shade
of her hair was fine, but he wanted to convince both the Palo *and*
Dynize that she was a native—that meant making her unrecogniz-
able. The fact that most of the Dynize upper crust knew her face
made this particularly difficult, so he'd need to lighten her hair
with the lime and ash mixture.

"We'll need a name for you."

"I don't know Palo names."

"I was thinking 'Avenya'?"

Ichtracia repeated the name several times. "I like it."

"I had a great-aunt named Avenya," Michel told her. "She helped
raise me for a few years before she died. It's not a common Palo
name, but it's known."

"Avenya," Ichtracia said out loud again. "Yes, that will do."

"Good." Michel continued his instructions. "When you're
infiltrating a group, confidence is easily half the job. Talk, walk,
and act like you belong. Be useful, engaging, charming. Avoid
confrontation."

"Be like you," Ichtracia said.

Their eyes met for a moment. She had made it very clear that despite their continued codependence and cohabitation, she had not forgiven him for lying about who and what he was. "Yes. Like me."

She nodded for him to continue.

"Because we don't know who to trust, we're going to approach the Palo under our pseudonyms. We're not their enemies, but if they discover our real identities, they will *think* that we're their enemies. So we, in our own minds, must consider them the target of deception. The Dynize probably have hundreds, maybe thousands, of spies and informants in Greenfire Depths, and that makes it doubly difficult to decide who we can trust."

"Is there anyone?" Most people would have had a tinge of despair in their voices when asking such a question, but Ichtracia seemed to take it as a matter of course.

"To trust?" Michel asked. "There will be. Starting with Emerald." He finished with the razor and tossed it on the bed. "It's a hack job, but I couldn't find scissors on short notice. I can tidy it up when we get to the Depths."

"You couldn't find scissors, but you *could* find a face-painting kit?"

"You'd be surprised at how many people have one on hand at all times, even in a Palo fishing village. Doesn't matter where you are—people want to look nice for a day at the fair or to impress a loved one." He picked up the kit and rummaged through it until he found a bit of charcoal. He stepped back, looking closely at Ichtracia's face. "Your features are distinctly Dynize. Anyone with half a brain can tell by looking at you."

"You're going to fix that with face paint?"

"I'm not giving you rosy cheeks and a blue forehead," he assured her. "I've met face painters—professionals who would never stoop to working a children's street festival. The very best of them could make you look exactly like me."

"You're joking."

"It wouldn't last through a rainy day or a particularly sweaty afternoon, but yes," Michel said. "They're damned artists, and I'm not going to do anything so severe. What I *can* do is apply a bit of shading to your nose and cheekbones. A little back here"—he brushed his fingertips across the nape of her neck, then over her brow—"and a little here. Very subtle alterations to the angles."

"And this isn't immediately obvious to anyone who looks at me?"

"I sure hope not," Michel said, only half joking. "It should stand up to most scrutiny, and it shouldn't be so heavy that if you *do* get caught in the rain, anyone will really notice that much of a difference. They'll just think something is a bit off, but pass it off as nothing. A person's brain will trick them in all sorts of ways if they *think* they already know who you are."

He put one hand under her chin and tilted it up, examining her for several minutes before he finally lifted the bit of charcoal. Their eyes met briefly, and he found her expression oddly determined. He'd already taken note of the thrill she seemed to get when no one recognized her, and he wondered if this next step was just an extension of that. The problem was, they were going into Palo life in the Depths. No more private rooms. No servants or free access to booze and mala. No comforts to which a high-ranking Privileged might be accustomed. He'd tried to impress this upon her for days without any emotional response from her.

He considered something he'd been thinking about since they left Landfall with Sedial's goons on their heels. He opened his mouth, reconsidered, then licked his lips several times before rushing ahead. "I have a question for you."

"Yes?" One of her eyebrows flickered upward.

"Why do you trust me?"

"I don't," she said firmly.

"Clearly you do," he replied, somewhat more forcefully than he'd intended. "You followed me out of Landfall on my word, hid in a fishing town for weeks with barely a complaint, and now you're letting me change your entire face and take you into one of the most dangerous places in Fatrasta…"

"Greenfire Depths is that bad?"

"Yes, it is. And don't change the subject." Michel had momentum now, and he didn't want to lose it. "Aside from wanting to see your sister, what could possibly convince you to come with me?"

"Are you trying to get me to say I'm in love with you?"

The question brought him up short. He froze like a panicked deer, mouth suddenly dry. The idea hadn't even occurred to him. He fumbled for an answer.

"Because I'm not," she said calmly. "I'm not even sure I *like* you after all of this. But I suppose I *do* trust you. Back in the fishing village, when you told me and Taniel that you planned on going back into Landfall to save your people? That was the first time I've truly felt like I saw the real you. I think I've found your true intentions, and that intrigues me." She took a deep breath. "And there's the blood sacrifices."

They hadn't spoken about it since her outburst at the fishing village. "You think there's truth in what je Tura told me?" Michel asked carefully.

"*You* do."

"Yes, but I'm just a spy. I only have my suspicions. You're a Dynize Privileged." She was evading the question. Michel fixed her with a look that, he hoped, told her that he wasn't going to let her get around it.

Several moments passed. Finally, she said, "I do think there's truth in it. Since I was a child, my grandfather has made it very clear that I am a tool. His little *Mara*. Blood holds the key to unlocking the stones, and as a Privileged *and* his granddaughter, my blood is stronger than most. But I'm not there, so…"

"Why didn't you mention it before?"

"Because it never occurred to me that he would turn to other options. Stupid, I know. Sedial would never let my absence damage his plans."

"So you think he's using the blood of others to unlock the stone?"

"A *lot* of others," Ichtracia said flatly.

"How many?"

"Thousands."

Michel shivered. "Pit."

"Exactly." Ichtracia raised her chin imperiously. "I don't much care about the Palo. I'm not here to fight for their freedom. But I can't help but feel as if the murder of all those people could have been avoided if I'd just volunteered. I can't let that pass."

"It's not your fault, you know."

"I know," she snapped. There were tears in the corners of her eyes, but she wiped them away before they could fall. The gesture smudged the face paint Michel had just applied, and he made a mental note to fix it. "I'm not a fool. But something has been twisting my guts around ever since you mentioned the sacrifices. I *have* to do something about it. You know, I want to meet my sister more than anything. To find out I have kin, and to find out that she is *fighting* for something, rather than sitting in a mala haze. It shames me into action. I can meet her when this is all over."

Michel decided it would be prudent not to push her any further. He gave her a curt nod.

She wiped her eyes once more and suddenly smiled. "I do not like you, Michel, but I do enjoy you. Watching you work. I can't help but be impressed. You convinced an entire Dynize Household that you were a spy, and *then* convinced them that you'd changed your ways for good. And *then* I find that you hadn't actually been a spy for the people we thought you were a spy for in the first place. If I hadn't been personally involved, I would have found that very funny. I think it will be a pleasure to see what you do next."

"Weirdly, that puts a lot of pressure on my shoulders," Michel answered.

"Good. You deserve it. Are you done already?" She gestured at her hair and face.

He shook away his thoughts and stepped back up to her. "We still need to dye your hair."

"Fine. Go on. Have I answered your question?"

She *did* trust him, but she didn't like him. And they were still sharing a bed. An emotionally confusing answer. "Yes. Thank you."

"Then answer one for me: What do you plan on doing to hide your hand?"

Michel swallowed hard. He'd been avoiding this subject for days, and it made his stomach churn. "The same thing I do with the rest of my body: hide it in plain sight."

She gave him a quizzical look.

"That sorcerous surgery technique you used on me..."

"If you want me to reattach your finger, we would need the finger in the first place."

Michel chuckled nervously. "That's not quite what I had in mind."

CHAPTER 7

Michel stood on the southern rim of Greenfire Depths, try-ing to ignore the terrible pain in his left hand. The stubs of his now two missing fingers felt like they were on fire, and it had taken several shots of the worst kind of rotgut Palo whiskey to get to the point where he could even think through the agony. Despite the very fresh feeling of losing his ring finger and having had the wound over the pinkie stub reopened, what remained of both fingers was expertly handled by precise applications of sorcery and bits from his face-painting kit.

The wound looked healed-over naturally, at least a year old, with no sign of bruising around the knuckle of either finger. It was, he decided, the worst thing he'd ever done to sink into a character. He hoped it was worth it. The Dynize were looking for a man with the month-old scar of a single missing finger—not the healed-over stubs of two.

He breathed in deeply, attempting to put the pain from his mind, and took in the familiar smell of garbage, shit, piss, and sweat that rose from the Depths on the afternoon heat. The mixture of smells was joined by the stale odor of burned wood and garbage, residual from the fires set by rioters during the siege of Landfall. He hadn't returned to the Depths proper since well before the invasion. Black-hats never went down there alone, and only seldom in force. Even for someone like him, who had friends scattered throughout the cavernous slum, it would have meant taking his own life in his hands.

Now, masquerading as a full-blooded Palo, he should be fine to walk the winding web of enclosed corridors that passed as streets—at least during the day.

Should be.

The idea of heading down there sent a flutter through his stomach. Beside him, Ichtracia stared into the Depths with a look of mild disgust. Her presence was a gamble. If they ran into real danger, she would resort to her sorcery without hesitation, and the moment that happened they would paint a large red flag over their heads for the Privileged and bone-eyes in Landfall.

She'd taken well to her disguise. He'd thought that cutting her hair and giving her softer features would lessen her imposing presence. If anything, it had increased it. Wearing loose workman's trousers and a sharp vest over a cotton button-down, her pale skin and confident demeanor told the story of a northern Palo businesswoman, someone who was more used to the confines of factories or political buildings but with a history of giving orders.

At least, he hoped that's what other people saw when they looked at her. Creating a disguise to match an amateur could be extremely difficult.

"People *live* down there?" Ichtracia asked, craning her neck to get a better view of the immense quarry as it wrapped around the nest of patchwork buildings below.

"You've seen it before, haven't you?" Michel asked in surprise.

"Driven past it in a carriage," she replied. "I never stopped to get a good look."

"You don't sound thrilled."

"I'm certain we have slums in Dynize. I have never seen them."

Michel opened his mouth, but Ichtracia cut him off. "If you ask me if I'm sure about this one more time, I'm going to toss you off the edge of this cliff. You just had me cut off your bloody finger for the sake of a disguise. I think I can handle a slum and some dangerous Palo."

He snapped his jaw shut. "Understood. We have an appointment to keep. Shall we?"

They descended by a narrow series of switchbacks carved into the wall of the quarry known as the Southern Ladder, steep enough that Michel's shins hurt like the pit by the time they reached the bottom. The towering hive of buildings blocked out the sun and a good part of the midday heat, leaving the bottom of the Ladder cool, dark, and very damp. The smell of soot was so strong down here that it gave him a headache, and he wondered how the Palo continued existing in such a place.

The air felt closer, more oppressive, and Michel had to force himself to breathe so as not to get overcome by claustrophobia. Ichtracia's eyes narrowed, her jaw tightened, but she did not comment on the stifling atmosphere.

Michel had worried that the slums would be abandoned from the fires, that the bulk of the Palo population would have been conscripted for Dynize labor or had fled the riots or had left of their own accord. But the bottom of the Ladder was as crowded as ever, people shouldering past them. No one seemed to give either him or Ichtracia a second glance, though within ten steps he had to wave off three different street vendors trying to sell them unidentifiable meat, half-rotten vegetables, and used boots that had probably come off the corpse of an Adran mercenary.

Michel headed into the interior at a measured pace, slipping into the rhythm of this place with almost startling ease, a hard, *Don't talk to me* look on his face, and with one shoulder forward to cut through the jostling crowd like a knife. He paused every few moments to make sure Ichtracia was behind him. It became instantly clear that she was not used to navigating crowds; after all, she was used to people moving *for* her. Not the other way around. She was shoved and buffeted so badly that she was almost thrown to the grime-encrusted street.

He finally moved back to stand beside her when he spotted her reaching for a pocket in anger. He took her by the hand. "Your gloves," he whispered, pulling her along, "they're in your pockets?"

"Yes."

He swore silently to himself. "That's a good way to get them stolen."

"I couldn't leave them back in the room."

Michel pulled her into a recess where two disjointed buildings met and took the bag off his shoulder. "Put them in here. My bag is less likely to get stolen off my shoulder than your pockets are to get picked."

"I want them at hand," Ichtracia protested. Her tone was almost pleading rather than commanding. He could tell that she was feeling this place already—learning why it was still a fetid slum even after a decade of effort by Lindet.

"You have an extra pair tucked beneath the soles of your shoes, right?"

"Yes, but..."

"We can't risk anyone snatching a glove off you and selling it to Sedial," he said in a low, urgent tone. "Would Sedial hesitate even a moment in marching a whole field army down here to find you, no matter the cost?" A vein on Ichtracia's left temple throbbed visibly. She finally reached into her pockets, pulling the gloves out in a wad, and stuffed them to the bottom of Michel's pack. He said, "Next time we get some privacy, I'll show you a little trick Taniel showed me that a friend of his uses to hide his gloves and keep them at hand."

Ichtracia nodded. She looked visibly ill, and Michel tried not to feel a little bit vindicated. *This*, he wanted to tell her, *is what it feels like to be powerless like the rest of us.* He wisely kept his mouth shut.

As they proceeded deeper into the interior, he noticed that more than just the fires had changed Greenfire Depths. There was a glut of Dynize propaganda. Posters and handbills had been plastered to every wayward intersection of roads and hallways, proclaiming a better life for the Palo under Dynize rule. A common motif was a printed drawing of two freckled hands clasped in friendship, and "Dynize and Palo: Cousins United" written in big block letters in Palo, Adran, and Dynize.

Michel stopped to examine one of the posters and found a tiny checkmark hidden inside one of the freckles of the left hand of the drawing. He pointed it out to Ichtracia. "I know the artist. He used to work as a Blackhat propagandist. The Dynize must have turned him."

"It's easier to make friends than enemies," Ichtracia said.

"If only Lindet had learned that." Michel bit off a further reply. He still only half believed that the Dynize were sacrificing Palo. It was impossible to buy into it completely. All the newspapers and propaganda spoke of unification. The Palo seemed to be treated well enough. He struggled with the thought of the changes he'd already noticed compared to what he had expected. What *had* he expected? As much as the fires and propaganda had left a mark, this *was* still Greenfire Depths.

They continued on until they reached a narrow strip of road where there was stone beneath their feet and sky above their heads—a sliver of blue between two tall, dilapidated buildings. A view of the clear sky was a rarity in the Depths, and the road was flanked by shops crammed in as tightly as humanly possible as well as dozens of dark entrances that led to mala dens, whorehouses, gambling houses, and a thousand hidden crannies. The road was packed to the point of barely being able to move, and Michel had to take Ichtracia firmly by the arm and shove a path through.

He caught sight of a narrow doorway and cut across the crowd in that direction. They reached the side of the road and gained purchase on a doorstep, where Michel double-checked the sign above the door. It was a picture of a man in a baker's hat sitting on a bench, pants down, above the words THE SQUATTING MILLER. Ichtracia in tow, he stepped inside.

They descended a trio of steps into a cool, dank room lit dimly by gas lanterns. Despite the press of bodies outside, the room contained just a handful of people. Michel stopped on the bottom step to allow his eyes to adjust to the low light, and quickly picked out a familiar figure in one corner.

Emerald sat with his back to the wall, one knee pulled up in front of him on the bench, sipping from a pewter cup. His green-tinted glasses were pushed up on his head, his stark-white skin and hair distinguishing him from the handful of Palo in the room. Michel zigzagged through the benches and tables and dropped down across from him. "I'm surprised you wanted to meet in public. And in the Depths, no less."

Emerald tipped his head forward, his glasses falling onto the bridge of his nose. "Kresimir," he swore, squinting back and forth between them. "You two look nothing like yourselves."

"That's the idea," Michel replied as Ichtracia took up a position just behind him, leaning against the wall.

"It's the Dynize," Emerald said, a note of unease in his voice. "They've started sending their own people to work in the morgues. I'm still technically in charge, but I don't trust the eyes and ears in my own territory now. That's why we're meeting here."

"They like to have a grasp on all public services," Ichtracia said, leaning over Michel's shoulder. "I'm surprised it took them this long."

Emerald eyeballed Ichtracia. He'd made it very clear, when Michel had limped to him just after the confrontation with Ka-Sedial, that he did not trust her. He had obviously not changed his mind. "Yes, well, it's going to make my hobby a little harder. I'm known in the Depths. I help out at one of the Palo clinics from time to time. I've done enough favors for people that I'm left alone—so yes, any meetings we have from now on will have to be here."

"That's a lot of favors," Michel commented. "Being a spymaster is a hobby, now?"

"Yes," Emerald snapped. "And you should do well to remember it. If you rely on me too much, you may arrive one day looking for help and find that I've packed up and left for Brudania."

Michel ground his teeth. Emerald was right, of course. He'd been very forthright about the fact that he could only be so useful before putting himself at risk. "Then let's make this short. I need every update you can give me."

Emerald looked skeptical. "What, you want troop movements? The arrival of Dynize politicians?"

"No, no," Michel said, rubbing the bridge of his nose. "Sorry, I should narrow that down."

"You should."

"We need to know about the Palo," Ichtracia said.

"What about them?" Emerald asked.

"Rumors," Michel said. "Public leanings. Events. Whatever has happened since I left."

Emerald grimaced. "Not much, to be honest. The riots died down while you were still here. Aside from the fires during the initial Dynize attack, the Palo seem to be the least affected by the invasion. Some of them have left, of course. Others have moved into abandoned houses in Upper Landfall. Everyone else..." He gestured around them. "They're just going about their business."

Michel exchanged a worried glance with Ichtracia. "That's it?"

"You're going to have to be more specific if you want more," Emerald said with a hint of exasperation.

"Disappearances," Ichtracia suggested.

Michel nodded. "Right. People going missing. Children, the elderly. People who won't be missed."

Emerald considered the question for a moment. "Those kinds of people always go missing during a war. You're looking for something specific?"

"We are, but I don't think you should know. Not yet."

"Understood." Emerald seemed to accept that bit of compartmentalization without further comment. "Nothing in particular has come to my attention, but I *can* look into it. Check morgue records. Ask around quietly. As I said, people disappear during times of conflict. But if there's something out of the ordinary, a pattern should emerge." He frowned. "The Dynize are recruiting Palo by the thousands, which is going to make the job harder."

"For what?"

"Construction. Public works all over the city. A great big fortress down south, surrounding the godstone. They've even started a conscription program. If there are two hundred thousand Palo left in Landfall, roughly a fourth of those are being shuffled around by Dynize programs."

Michel had heard these rumors already, but he wanted to get Emerald's opinion on them. "And you don't find this suspicious?" Michel asked.

"Not really. The Palo are being treated quite well. Very few complaints come out of either the labor camps or the army reserves, though I suppose the Dynize have control of what gets in and out." Emerald nodded to himself. "I can do some digging, but beyond that..." He spread his hands helplessly.

Michel swore to himself. He'd hoped that Emerald would be able to give him some sort of evidence for or against these sacrifices. Instead he'd painted a picture of accepted enlistment and bureaucratic shuffling. If the Dynize wanted to make a few thousand people disappear, they could do so easily in all that hubbub. "Do what you can, but be as circumspect as possible."

"That's what I do best."

Michel looked over his shoulder at Ichtracia, who gave him a small shake of her head. No ideas there. He'd have to work on his own angle and hope that Emerald could come up with something. Frustrated, he mentally moved on to the next thing on his checklist. "What is the mood of the Palo right now? Do they support the occupation?"

"You might as well ask if every Kressian worships Kresimir," Emerald replied blandly. "Everyone has their own thoughts on the Dynize. Like I said, the Palo are being treated pretty well. Fair pay, chance at rank in the military, equal housing. Compared to Lindet's regime, they're living the dream."

That was not what Michel wanted to hear. If the Palo were truly better off beneath the Dynize, it would force him to change his entire plan of attack. In fact, it might *remove* his plan of attack. How could he justify helping Taniel against the invaders when the invaders were so much better than the alternative? Then again, if the Dynize were plucking the young and infirm and using them for blood sacrifices, he couldn't think of a Palo he knew who'd find that an acceptable option for their future.

"That's not everyone, though?" he asked.

"Of course not. I couldn't even give you an estimate at what percentage of the populace supports the Dynize. It's high, though."

"Do they have some sort of leader? Someone local who has the Dynize blessing?"

"They do. Meln-Dun."

Michel snorted. That snake who manipulated Vlora Flint into capturing the last Mama Palo? It made sense, though. He'd obviously sold out to the Dynize a while ago, *and* he was in a position of leadership as the biggest employer in the Depths. "Did Ka-poel appoint a new Mama Palo before she left?"

"She did," Emerald replied. "Mama Palo is the other big political leader. She hasn't done a lot since the invasion—when Meln-Dun found out that he'd missed his target, he was furious. He's had a private little task force chasing her around for the last couple of months. She has to keep her head down and stay on the move, and it's losing her a lot of support."

"The Dynize aren't hunting her?"

"The Dynize don't care. They've identified Meln-Dun as the leader of the Landfall Palo and left all internal matters to him."

"As long as they think he's bought and paid for," Ichtracia spoke up, "they won't worry about him or the Palo until after the end of the war. External threats first, then internal."

Michel leaned back, considering. "So we're isolated here?"

"Pretty much," Emerald replied. "Besides their propagandists and some spies, the Dynize want nothing to do with the Depths while they're still fighting a war on two fronts."

The gears in Michel's head began to turn, and he set aside the blood sacrifices for the moment to focus on the more immediate enemy: Meln-Dun. The Dynize puppet would have to go. But Michel knew the Depths and he knew the Palo. Meln-Dun's authority depended on his status as a community leader and employer.

"We could kill him," Ichtracia suggested.

"We're spies, not assassins."

"You're a spy," she countered.

"How do you plan on killing him without alerting your grandfather to our presence?"

Ichtracia's lip curled, but she didn't retort.

Michel said, "These are my people. I'm going to avoid killing—or having them killed—as much as possible. I believe you understand that?"

Ichtracia gave a sullen nod.

"Besides, killing Meln-Dun would only cause chaos. We don't want chaos. We want to organize against a common enemy." Michel thought furiously, a plan beginning to form in the back of his head. He chuckled quietly to himself.

"Is something funny?" Emerald asked.

"Yes," Michel said. "Yes, it is."

"What's that?"

Michel ignored the question. "That task force that Meln-Dun has chasing Mama Palo. Can you get me on it?"

"Are you joking?"

"Not at all."

Emerald scratched his chin. "I can make introductions through one of my contacts. Do you have a good cover story?"

"Leave that to me." Michel tapped the table between them. "If I can join his task force, I can steer their investigation and have a reason to creep around the quarry."

"What for?" Ichtracia asked.

"So I can set up Meln-Dun."

"You want to discredit him?" she asked.

"To the Dynize, yes."

"And to the Palo?" Emerald asked.

Michel grinned. "We're going to make that snake a Palo martyr."

CHAPTER 8

By the next morning, Styke and his small group had reached the Jagged Fens highway. As they emerged from the wilderness, wearing looted, quickly mended uniforms and carrying the passports of Dynize naval infantry, it quickly became obvious that Orz was, indeed, telling the truth.

The highway was a full-fledged cobble road packed with traffic. It wound through the swamp, lined with frequent farms, homesteads, inns, mail-relay stations, and campgrounds. They passed through a town big enough to have its own garrison within four miles, and stood aside and watched as a platoon of fresh-faced recruits marched by, wearing shiny breastplates that had never seen a scratch.

Styke did not mind admitting that he was both shocked and impressed. The Dynize had hidden behind their closed borders for a century now, but aside from the odd story from a sailor or the curious newspaper column, everyone in Fatrasta had ignored their presence entirely. Not a soul suspected that they'd built an entirely new capital just a short voyage from Fatrastan shores.

During that first day, Styke waited with clenched teeth for something to go wrong or for Orz to betray them in some way. Everyone they passed on their journey certainly gave them long, curious looks, but the moment their eyes fell upon Orz—riding bare-chested on one of Styke's extra horses, his black spiraling tattoos and proudly displayed bone knives signaling his station to all—passersby would turn their attention to seemingly anything else.

It didn't take a perceptive man to realize that dragonmen had a reputation among their own people.

Orz's demeanor seemed to belie this casual fear that travelers exhibited toward him. He rode up and down the small column, lecturing Styke's Lancers on Dynize custom, home life, Households, politics, ways of thinking, and language. He switched at ease between Adran, Palo, and Dynize, though he only used the latter when a stranger was within earshot. He talked all day and into the night, his tone measured but friendly, his energy up like a man who was glad to be back in human company.

They camped alongside the road without incident, and the next morning Orz began the day riding beside Styke at the head of the column. Styke hadn't found a dead naval infantryman big enough to provide him with a uniform, so he had elected to wear his normal traveling clothes with a hastily made Household crest sewn to the left breast. Sunin had made the crest at Orz's instruction, and Orz assured Styke that the lopsided peregrine would mark him as a Tetle Household guard to anyone who knew enough to ask.

They rode in companionable silence for the first half hour of the journey, and Styke noted that Orz looked over his shoulder more than occasionally at Ka-poel. Styke could not sense any real fear, but there was no doubt that the way Orz felt about bone-eyes was similar to the way normal folks seemed to feel about him.

"You don't like her riding behind you," Styke commented after the fifth such glance.

Orz started, as if he hadn't even realized he was looking back at Ka-poel, and then gave a slight shake of his head. "Bone-eyes can't be trusted," he said.

"You'll find no argument from me," Styke replied. "I haven't met your Ka-Sedial in person, but he seems like a real piece of shit."

Orz did a quick scan of their surroundings. "Never say such words aloud in this country," he rebuked, "no matter what language you speak them in. Sedial has informants in every Household, including those belonging to his enemies. Even with him across the sea, his influence is such that you could be executed just for insulting him."

Styke bit back a reply. People had tried to kill him for less, certainly, but that was in Fatrasta, where he had friends and a reputation. If an entire city garrison turned on him in an instant, he wouldn't wager his luck in getting off this continent alive. "Right," he finally answered, "I'll keep that in mind."

"Besides," Orz said in a low voice, "I'm speaking of *every* bone-eye."

"Her?" Styke turned and looked back at Ka-poel, who seemed engrossed in making one of her little wax dolls. "I'll admit, I'm becoming fond of the little blood witch."

"Does she have your blood? Or any part of your body? A fingernail, or a bit of hair?"

"Probably."

"Do you have any idea what she's capable of?"

Orz spoke in a measured tone, but Styke thought he sensed a hint of urgency in the question. "Do *you*?" he countered.

"She broke Sedial's hold on me, which means she's incredibly strong."

Styke thought back to the battle at Starlight, then even further to the thick of the Hock and those Dynize dragoons that harried them halfway across Fatrasta. "You mentioned that you saw the aftermath of the Mad Lancers' fight with those dragoons. Did you happen to come across their camp?"

Orz stared at him.

"There should have been two slaughters. The first was on the road, when we ambushed them. The second was at their camp, where—"

"I saw both," Orz interrupted.

Styke gave him a sidelong glance. "The second was all her. She took control of most of the camp with her sorcery and interrogated the commander. Once it was done, she turned them against each other until there was no one left alive. She told me later that it took quite a lot of preparation to pull off, but... well, I've never seen anything like it. Privileged could only dream of having that kind of direct power over people."

"Pray that you do not see such a thing again." Orz's head began to turn, but he seemed to catch himself at the last moment. His eyes narrowed. "Most of the camp, you say?" He let out a long, shaky breath. "Most bone-eyes can only keep track of a single puppet at once. Some, a handful. I've heard rumors that Ka-Sedial has as many as a few dozen, though he can only directly control one or two at a time. Hundreds, though?"

Styke was surprised at the awe that leaked through in Orz's tone. Was Ka-poel really such an aberration? Was she really so wildly powerful that she warranted a strong man's fear? He checked himself on that last mental question and barked a laugh. Of course she was. Orz might have seen the aftermath of that camp in the Hock. Styke had *been* there.

"Is there something funny about the bone-eyes?" Orz asked.

"No, I was thinking of something else." Styke twirled his Lancer ring and watched a Dynize family pass by in a horse-drawn cart full of a type of unfamiliar fruit. "This civil war of yours... when did it end?"

"Nine years ago."

"And before that, there were two emperors?"

A nod.

"What gave you such loyalty to yours?"

Orz opened his mouth, paused, seemed to consider his words. "He was kind."

"Kind?" Styke couldn't help the small laugh that escaped with the word.

Orz didn't seem to take offense. He simply nodded. "Not just in a personal way. He was crowned when I was a child, when the civil war was at its bloodiest. My Household loyalties were on his side from the beginning, of course, but he made it his life's work to end the war. Not to win it—just to end it. He negotiated fiercely, without pride, simply working for a way to end the bloodshed. He finally offered to give up his own power, and instead of putting him gently into retirement, Ka-Sedial engineered his assassination."

"Do you blame him?" Styke asked. "A retired emperor seems like a flashpoint for rebellion."

Orz snorted. "I understand the reasoning. But I had met him. I even guarded him for thirteen months, just after my training ended. He was a man of his word. He would have pulled out his own heart before allowing the civil war to ignite again. I don't care if Sedial's reasoning was good or not. I care that he and his false emperor slaughtered mine and then expected us to fall into line."

"Were you there when..." Styke let the question drop off.

"He died? No. If I was present then, he'd either still be alive or I would have died defending him."

Styke wondered about the man who could command such loyalty. "Where do the bone-eyes come into this?" he asked, resisting the urge to look at Ka-poel. She had ridden a little closer as they spoke, and he had no doubt she was listening in on the conversation.

"Bone-eyes are supposed to be like Privileged or dragonmen—we are tools of the state. Wards of the emperor. At the beginning of the civil war, the bone-eyes split nearly down the middle onto either side. As time went by, especially after Ka-Sedial came into power, more and more of them were swayed under his leadership. They became a cabal unto themselves. The few bone-eyes that remained on our side at the end were murdered with their emperor."

"So Ka-Sedial owns the bone-eyes?"

Orz nodded.

"And based on what I've seen her do"—Styke jerked a thumb over his shoulder—"that means that Sedial effectively runs the country."

Another nod.

"And most everyone is happy with this arrangement?" Styke tapped his ring against his saddle horn, watching a platoon of young Dynize recruits march by on the highway.

"Not at all," Orz answered. "But they fear the bone-eyes. And they fear a return to the bloodshed of the civil war. You have to understand, the war lasted *decades*. When Sedial assassinated our emperor, no one had the energy to fight anymore. Peace was more important. Politicians on both sides were just eager to secure their positions in the new order of things. Sedial offered complete amnesty to his enemies, and they took it."

"And then they let Sedial goad you into another war."

Orz swayed unhappily in his saddle. "It was a . . . what's the word? 'Unifying.' It was a unifying tactic. People were tired of the fighting, but it's also what they knew best. Turning all that expertise and energy against an outside entity was the smartest thing Sedial's ever done." Orz passed a hand across his face. "Sedial is a man of limitless ambition. I fear what he will do with all three godstones."

"That's what I'm hoping to stop," Styke offered.

Orz gave him a cool look. "I fear what *anyone* would do with all three godstones."

"Point taken." Styke watched the side of Orz's face for a moment, wondering if he would still have to fight him at some point in the future. Everything about the man, from his knives and tattoos to his posture, indicated violence. All except the way he spoke. Orz was as tired of the bloodshed as the rest of them. The idea seemed anathema to Styke. Violence had been his life's work. He had never gotten sick of it. Even in the labor camps, he'd just been taking a rest.

What would it be like to leave it behind for good? *Could* he?

"Were you planning on letting me live, back at Starlight?" he asked.

Orz didn't look at him. "No."

Styke remembered the fight well. He'd been badly wounded. Completely tapped out, running on strength reserves that he wasn't entirely sure were his own. Orz could have easily killed both him and Lindet. "You didn't have to answer that honestly."

"I would have killed you, because I wouldn't have had a choice," Orz replied. "If I had shown an ounce of hesitation, Sedial would have taken control of me. He would have raped my mind and used my body as one of his puppets. I would have done anything to prevent that. But..." This time he did look back at Ka-poel, speaking loudly enough to include her in the conversation. "I felt his hold upon me snap in those last few moments. I assume she did it when she got close enough to his other puppet—your old companion that he had in thrall. It was like a yoke lifting from my shoulders and with that"—Orz smiled—"I couldn't help but spit at his feet like I'd spit at the feet of his emperor." He nodded respectfully to Ka-poel and then turned forward. "That's why I didn't kill you."

"And that night at my mother's grave?"

"He wasn't watching. Acting as the eyes of a bone-eye is like having someone standing over your shoulder. With practice, you can get a sense when they're paying attention and when they're not." He cleared his throat, then urged his horse a little faster. "Come, let me show you something."

Styke rode to follow, and when he'd caught up, he saw Orz pointing into the bushes. "What is it?"

"Nothing," Orz replied. "I just didn't want her to overhear us. I'm not sure if I could have killed you, Ben Styke. That bone-eye back there has her mark on you, and it is a damned powerful one."

Styke opened his mouth to reply that he'd asked Ka-poel that very question and she'd denied that she helped with anything more than a nudge. He realized that she had no reason to tell the truth. "In what way?"

"She is not controlling you. You'd know. But she is protecting you."

"A little protection can be handy."

"But when does it end? When *does* she take control at a vital moment? A friendly warning: Be wary." Orz turned around and rejoined the small column as it reached them, nodding once again to Ka-poel.

Styke let them pass, watching his soldiers and eyeballing passing Dynize. Slowly, he lifted one arm to his nose and gave a deep, powerful sniff. His Knack was not perfect, but he'd always been able to smell sorcery. There was, perhaps, the slightest hint of copper about himself. He smelled it on Ka-poel and he smelled it on Orz.

How strong *was* Ka-poel's hold on him? He thought back to all the battles he'd fought since they first met—to the wounds that should have incapacitated him, to the exhaustion that should have left him on the ground. He'd fought through all of it because that's what he was used to—he was, after all, Mad Ben Styke. But the legendary Mad Ben Styke had been a young man, unbroken by the labor camps. He was something else now, and maybe there was wisdom in Orz's warning. Maybe he wasn't as strong as he thought he was.

The thought gave him a moment of disquiet deep in his belly. Ally or not, he did not like the idea of being enhanced by Ka-poel's blood sorcery.

CHAPTER 9

Michel sat cross-legged on the floor of a rented tenement room deep in the guts of Greenfire Depths, working by the dim light of a gas lantern. The lantern was fed by a shoddy-looking tube that jackknifed out of the ceiling, touched the back of the lantern, and punched into the next room via a gap large enough for a cat to squeeze through. He could clearly hear talking and laughing through the paper-thin walls, so when he himself talked, he made sure to keep his voice down.

He finished removing the stitches on one side of Ichtracia's vest pocket, then flipped the vest inside out. "Hand me your left glove," he told her. She sat on the floor beside him, watching him work, and occasionally reading aloud from a Palo book with an affected northern accent. Or at least what she seemed to think was a northern accent.

She handed him the glove. "The Palo have been oppressed for hundreds of years," she read. "Since the arrival of the Kressians, who have sought to steal our land, break our spirits, and enslave our people."

"No, no," Michel cut her off. "Longer 'o' sounds. Your accent is all over the place. You've got to be consistent."

Ichtracia's eyes narrowed, but she repeated both sentences and continued reading until the end of the paragraph. "Better?"

"A little. You'll have to keep practicing if you want to hold an actual conversation with anyone from up north."

"Is that a risk?"

"Enough of one that you should be ready." Michel finished putting a handful of stitches into the hem of her Privileged glove, attaching it to the inside of the vest with enough strength that it wouldn't fall out but not so firmly that it couldn't be loosened with a quick tug. "Try this."

Ichtracia stood up, putting on her vest. She put one hand slowly into her pocket. It took several tries, then with a quick yank she pulled her hand back out, loose threads hanging from the glove that was now on her hand. She smirked. "That works better than I expected." She lifted her hand and inspected the symbols on the back of the glove. "No damage that will prevent me from using my sorcery."

"Good. I'll put it back in and do the other glove," Michel said. "You'll want to practice this a few dozen times every night."

"Are you serious? It worked like a charm."

"The first time, yes," Michel answered. "But maybe not the second or third or tenth time. We want to make sure you're comfortable enough with the process that you can do it while someone is shooting or stabbing you. You've seen a card trick before? Or watched someone twirl a knife?"

"Yes."

"They had to practice that thousands of times before they got it right. This is a trick, too. Not as complicated, but it could save our lives. I'll redo the stitches. You practice."

Ichtracia snorted and handed the glove back to him, then the vest. "This sounds stupid, but now that I've seen such a simple trick, I'm shocked that every Privileged doesn't have spare gloves stitched into their clothes."

"Maybe they do?" Michel asked.

"Perhaps. But most Privileged I've met wouldn't stoop to such a *trick*."

Michel began restitching the glove into the vest. "Taniel's friend—Borbador—is full of tricks. Or so Taniel tells me. Borbador was a street rat who never quite took to the Privileged cabal. He wasn't the strongest, or the smartest, but he was by far the cleverest. From what I've been told, you'd either like him or hate his guts."

Ichtracia sat back down beside him. "I'll keep that in mind if I ever meet the man."

"You might," Michel said. "If that rumor of an Adran army up north is true, then there's a chance Borbador is with them." He checked his voice and glanced at the wall of their room, where the sound of laughter had waned. He heard a grunt and a giggle, then chuckled himself. The occupants had gotten on to something else. He finished restitching the glove and had just turned his attention to the other pocket when he heard footsteps stop outside their door. The pause was brief, and a piece of paper was slid under before the steps continued down the hall.

It was a note written in cypher. He read it aloud, quietly. "Meln-Dun is looking for foot soldiers without links to the city to help him find Mama Palo. You have a meeting at three o'clock at the quarry. Contact name is Dahre. Expendable." He read it to himself several more times, then held it up to the flame of the gas lamp above his head. Within moments it was ash and a wisp of smoke. "Sounds like Emerald has gotten us a job," he said.

"Shouldn't we make contact with this Mama Palo before we go work for the enemy?"

"If I knew where to find her, I would," Michel replied. "But she's to the wind."

"So you're going to use Meln-Dun to find her?"

"If the tool is there, I might as well use it. Are you ready?"

Ichtracia swallowed hard, then nodded.

"Good. Practice your accent while I finish with the gloves. Then we're heading to meet Emerald's contact."

Michel and Ichtracia navigated the web of streets, paths, rickety bridges, and shortcuts that connected the tenements of Greenfire Depths. They headed down to the river, then followed it upstream to the only corner of the mighty old quarry still producing rock for construction.

The working quarry was walled off from the rest of Greenfire Depths by a high palisade fence, and Michel found the gate thrown open to the streets and a large crowd gathered. What looked like a foreman was speaking from atop a large limestone column, flanked by thugs with truncheons. Michel shoved his way along the edges of the crowd, careful to keep one hand on Ichtracia's arm. They proceeded through the gate and worked their way to one of the large wooden warehouses that were crowded into this corner of the quarry floor.

The sun was directly overhead, peeking through the wide spot of open sky between the end of the Palo tenements and the walls of Greenfire Depths. Michel shaded his eyes as he reached the doors of the office building, where he tipped his hat to a truncheon-wielding guard. He cleared his throat, rolled his shoulders, and sank into his character.

"We're here about work," he said, adopting a northern Palo accent. He assumed the body language of a confident man-about-town, with his shoulders relaxed, eyes half-lidded but watchful, and a polite but forceful note in his voice.

The guard was a young woman with a smashed-up face pitted

with old scars. She gestured with her truncheon. "So is everyone else. They're only hiring thirty new workers to fill the Dynize orders, so best of luck with that."

"No," Michel said, "not that kind of work. I've got a meeting with Dahre."

The guard cocked an eyebrow. "Right. Head inside. Upstairs, first door on the left."

Michel jerked his head for Ichtracia to follow. The inside opened out into a wide, long room filled with the clank and scrape of stonemasons carving blocks of a thousand different sizes while foremen organized sledge teams to haul the finished products down to the river. An iron staircase took them up the closest wall to where a series of large offices overlooked the workspace, dangling precipitously from wooden girders. Michel strolled up to the first door and pounded on it, then slumped casually against the wall while he let his eyes travel across the big workroom.

Nothing seemed out of the ordinary. Stonemasons went about their work under the watchful eye of the foremen, and there were a couple of truncheon-wielding thugs, but the latter seemed more intent on watching the doors than enforcing any sort of labor code. He did spot a single Dynize soldier, dressed in morion helmet and breastplate, standing at attention on the catwalk that stretched off from the offices.

"Who is it?" a voice responded to his knocking.

"Name's Tellurin," Michel responded. "Got a meeting with Dahre."

There was a shuffle, the sound of a chair being pushed back. "I thought there were supposed to be two of ya." A bald head stuck out of the doorway. "Ah. There *are* two of ya."

"Tellurin and Avenya," Michel introduced himself. "Got a recommendation to come down and see ya about some work."

"You're the thief-takers from Brannon Bay?" Dahre eyed them

both up and down and seemed more impressed by Ichtracia than he did by Michel. Disguise or not, she had the unmistakable confidence of someone who commanded respect.

Michel stifled a smile at Dahre's appreciative nod. "That's us."

"Good, good." Dahre stepped out of his office, closing the door behind him, and shook both of their hands. He was tall, well over six feet, and paunchy around the middle from too much time behind a desk. He seemed the jovial sort, not the kind of man Michel would want to stab in the back. More was the pity. "Follow me, let's go find the boss."

As soon as his back was turned, Michel shared a glance with Ichtracia. He hadn't actually planned on meeting with Meln-Dun. A lieutenant, certainly, but not the man himself. He must be more itchy to get rid of Mama Palo than Michel had even expected. Dahre spoke over his shoulder as they zigzagged through a handful of offices and then took a catwalk that extended the length of the building and headed up toward a single office at the far end. "What brings you down from Brannon Bay? Most people are leaving Landfall, not coming to it."

"No work," Michel responded. "City is flooded with refugees, speculation has hit every industry."

"I'd think that would be ripe for thief-takers."

"You'd think." Michel injected a note of irritation into his voice. "But everyone wants someone found. Nobody wants to pay the price."

"Aye, aye." Dahre laughed. "That's the way of things. Believe it or not, the Dynize have been pretty good to us." Michel couldn't tell whether Dahre meant the Palo or Meln-Dun's organization. Probably both. "We've had to triple the size of the quarry since they arrived. Stone for that big fortress they're building south of the city. They've got work camps and factories and they're paying with anything you can imagine—ration cards, jade, gold, and even Adran krana."

They reached the end of the catwalk and Dahre stepped to one side, indicating that they should head up to the office. He continued, "Surprised you came to us looking for work. Dynize are convinced the city is full of spies. Paying good money for anyone willing to help round up Kressians connected to Lindet."

Michel made a noncommittal sound in the back of his throat. "Figured we'd come to the city and work for someone we can trust before we put ourselves in the employ of foreigners."

"Smart man." Dahre rapped once on the office door. A sharp bark answered, and he stepped past them and went inside, gesturing for them to follow.

Michel barely kept himself from blanching the moment the door opened. The office was spacious, decorated in an old-world style of the Nine, with musty carpets, low light, and dark wood-and-leather furnishings. But the first thing his eyes fell on was a woman sitting in one corner, arms crossed, the black tattoos of a dragonman spiraling up her neck. She wore swamp dragon leathers and pared her nails casually with the end of a bone knife, her leg thrown over one arm of the chair.

The dragonman studied Michel's face, then Ichtracia's, and then her gaze fell back to her knife. Michel's heart hammered in his chest and he prayed that Ichtracia hadn't reacted to the sight of the woman. He raised one eyebrow at the dragonman, as one might toward a curiosity, then turned to the man sitting behind a low ironwood desk.

Meln-Dun was a Palo in his fifties, wearing a tailored Kressian suit with big, ivory buttons and a turned-up collar. He sat straight-backed, a paper held to his face like a man who was nearsighted but refused to wear spectacles. Dahre rounded the desk and whispered in Meln-Dun's ear. The quarry boss gave Michel and Ichtracia the same weighing glance as Dahre, then turned his head toward the dragonman. "Could you give us a moment? Local business."

The dragonman didn't move. "Local business is Dynize business," she answered, her eyes remaining on the knife.

Meln-Dun's lips pursed. "Not that kind of local business. If you please."

Michel paid careful attention to the ticks of the short exchange, curious about Meln-Dun's relationship with the Dynize. He certainly seemed to think he was in charge, but the dragonman didn't jump at his bidding. Interesting. Slowly, almost carelessly, the dragonman got to her feet and strode out the door, leaving it open behind her. Michel turned to watch her cross the catwalk, using the opportunity to lock eyes with Ichtracia. She gave the smallest shake of her head.

No recognition from either of them, it seemed.

"You're the thief-takers I was told about?" Meln-Dun said. He pulled a cigarette out of one drawer of his desk, lit it, but didn't offer any to Michel and Ichtracia. "I'm glad to hear we found you before the Dynize did." His eyes dropped to the missing fingers on Michel's hand, briefly, before returning to his face. "Dahre here has been chasing a problem all around the Depths for a couple months now without any real progress. I'm hoping you can change that."

"I hope so, too." Michel took his hat off, nodding to Meln-Dun before dropping into the dragonman's still-warm seat. It was an affected mix of politeness and confidence that had always gotten him far in infiltrations. "If you need people found, we're the ones to do it." Ichtracia leaned against the door, and Michel caught Dahre eyeballing her body for a moment before he went to the one tiny window and squinted outside.

Meln-Dun took several drags on his cigarette. His fingers trembled ever so slightly, and Michel wondered just how much of his soul he'd had to sell to the Dynize to become the de facto king of Greenfire Depths. "I'm curious how you propose to find anything in Greenfire Depths if you're from Brannon Bay. This place is, as you may have already noticed, unique."

"I'm from here," Michel said with a derisive snort. "Parents died when I was a boy. Ran the streets for a few years until an uncle up in Brannon Bay came and found me and gave me a trade. I agree that coming in blind would be foolish, but me? Well, I know the place. And Avenya here learns quick."

"Do you still have local ties?" Meln-Dun asked, almost too quickly.

"Like I said, street kid," Michel answered. "If I have any local ties, I haven't talked to them since before the Revolution."

"Excellent. We need trackers, but we're more in need of eyes and ears without the preestablished...loyalties of the Depths. We need a woman found—a local folk hero of sorts. Goes by the name of Mama Palo."

"Heard the name," Michel said, digging in one ear with his remaining pinkie as if he wasn't at all concerned by the person in question. "Freedom fighter, right?"

"That's right."

Michel spat on the wood floor. "I've dealt with their type before. Idealist pricks, the lot of 'em."

A small smile grew behind Meln-Dun's cigarette. "I think I like you, Mr...."

"Tellurin."

"I like you, Mr. Tellurin. You and your friend are hired. Discuss the terms with Dahre. He's heading up the search and already has some boys working their way through this godforsaken rat's nest."

"I can have you join up with them tomorrow," Dahre added, nodding along with his boss.

Michel got up, cocking his head and straightening his shirt. "Thank ya, right, sir. You won't regret it. By the by, how do you want this lady brought in? Truncheon and ankles dragged in the dirt?"

"Dead," Meln-Dun said mirthlessly, face hardening. "I want her and all her followers slaughtered. Will that be a problem?"

"The knife, then," Michel said, pulling a face. "Price will be a little higher, especially if she's as popular as you say and we have to disappear quick after the job."

"Price isn't an issue."

"Then we have a deal." Michel returned his hat to his head and touched the brim. "Right you are. Sir?" he said to Dahre.

Dahre led them out of the office and back along the catwalk. Michel lagged behind a little bit, glancing over his shoulder at Ichtracia as they passed the waiting dragonman. Once they had left her far behind and were back among the rest of the offices, he waited for Dahre to get far ahead of them and quietly asked, "That dragonman. Anyone you know?"

"Don't think so. There are a lot of dragonmen. Don't think she recognized me, either."

"Didn't look like it. But keep your eyes open."

"Meln-Dun doesn't want the Dynize to know that he's having problems with Mama Palo," Ichtracia said.

Michel resisted the urge to scratch at the painful stubs of his two fingers. "I got the same impression. We'll have to figure out how to use that."

"They seem awfully trusting," she said cautiously as they approached Dahre's office. She wasn't outwardly nervous, but her eyes moved just a little too quickly, like someone trying to watch every angle at once.

"This isn't high politics," Michel answered quickly. They would have time to talk later, but anything he could do to calm Ichtracia's nerves would help her stay in disguise better. "Down here, among the Palo, you get jobs on a handshake, a nod, and knowing a guy who knows a guy. People pass through all the time. If they screened them all they'd never do anything else."

"That sounds ... distractingly easy."

"That's not the hard part," Michel responded. "The hard part will be shaking these assholes off our trail once we're ready to move on."

CHAPTER 10

The Adran Army marched down the coast for four days and
swung around onto the Cape of New Adopest, where they
descended from the hilly northland and onto a vast river delta that
had long been stripped of its old forests. Cotton and tobacco plantations stretched to the horizon, broken only by the intertwining
branches of the New Ad River.

Vlora sat on her horse, watching from a knoll beside an abandoned plantation house as her army marched over the first of
a dozen bridges that stood between her and New Adopest. The
distance wasn't far—another twelve miles or so—but she fully
expected it to be a hard-fought twelve miles, with burned bridges
and a dug-in enemy waiting for them at the end.

Soldiers saluted her position as they passed, and Vlora returned
the gesture a handful of times before it became too tiring to lift her
arm and she fell to answering with a nod.

"Are you all right, ma'am?"

The question brought her out of her foggy thoughts, and she

turned to find that Norrine had ridden up beside her. She blinked sweat out of her eyes. "When did you get here? Where's Davd?"

"Just relieved him, ma'am," Norrine responded, pointing to where Davd was riding down to join the army on the road. "Do you want me to get him?"

"No," Vlora answered, hearing the response come too quickly from her lips. "No, that's okay. I just..." She hesitated for a few moments, before continuing in a quiet voice, "There are gaps in my memory from the Crease."

"Perfectly normal, ma'am. You almost died."

Vlora opened her mouth, frustrated at not being able to voice her frustration. "I know, I know. I'm just worried that the gaps are widening. That they're happening to me still. Do you understand? I keep looking around for Olem, even though you and Davd and Bo have told me a dozen times that he's on an errand."

Norrine looked down at her rifle, which was slung across her saddle horn, then looked on toward the horizon without answering. Perhaps there *was* no answer. Vlora gestured dismissively. "Sorry, it's not your problem."

"It is my problem, ma'am," Norrine responded slowly. "You're my commanding officer. But I'm not great on advice. Better at shooting and fighting."

"Me too, Norrine."

"They say time heals all wounds. You probably just need time."

"I don't have any."

They fell into an uncomfortable silence, and Vlora was relieved when she spotted Bo and Nila making their way from the column up toward her position. They approached, turning their horses to fall in on her opposite side from Norrine. Bo scratched his head, jerking his chin toward the horizon in the direction of New Adopest. "Does something feel off about this?"

It took a moment for Vlora to retool her thoughts and focus on the strategies she'd need to employ for the next few days. She'd felt a vague unease since this morning, but she'd just chalked it up to the fear she felt over gaps in her memory. She swept her gaze across the horizon, finding nothing worrisome, and turned to Bo. "I'm not sure what you mean."

"I'm not, either," Bo said. "You're the trained strategist. I just feel like..." He chewed on the inside of his cheek.

It was Nila who spoke up. "Why is that bridge still there?"

The question set off a spark in Vlora's mind, and that feeling of unease grew stronger. Bo was right. Something *was* wrong. She met Nila's eyes. "They *have* to know we're coming."

"Absolutely," Nila answered. "We have an entire field army. They should have known we were coming weeks ago and made preparations. And even if somehow they missed us, our fleet will have already engaged theirs. They know we're here. They know about our approach."

"I don't follow," Bo said.

Vlora snorted. For as brilliant as Bo was, he could be daft as pit at times. "There's a Dynize field army between us and New Adopest, correct?"

"Yes."

"If you knew that an enemy was on the way to relieve the city, wouldn't you have burned all the bridges between you and them?"

Bo opened his mouth in a silent "ah-ha."

"We're not far," Vlora continued. "We'll be approaching their rear by the end of the day. So why aren't they trying to slow us down? Where is their delaying action?"

"Maybe their general is an idiot?" Bo suggested.

"Maybe." Vlora looked to the south, where the main trunk of the New Ad River slashed the Cape in two horizontally on the map. It was a wide, deep river and their destination was on the north bank—so she'd kept her army on the same side. But now something about its positioning bothered her. "Could this be a trap?"

"In what way?" Nila asked.

Vlora shook her head. "Perhaps they're trying to lead us out onto the Cape and then bottle us out here with a bigger army?"

"That's a terrible trap," Bo pointed out. "We have an enormous fleet right off the coast. All we'd have to do is embark and land somewhere north or south of the Cape."

"It would slow us down by a week or two," Vlora reasoned. "Enough time for them to get reinforcements."

"Are we reading too much into this?" Nila asked. "It could very well just be enemy complacence, or stupidity, or..." She trailed off with a shrug. "Put it to your generals. Or leave a brigade or two back here."

The temptation to divide her forces was strong, but Vlora fought against it. Splitting the army now, with several field armies still south of them on the mainland, could just play into the enemy's hands. This excursion to New Adopest was supposed to be a brief one, meant to isolate and break a portion of the enemy's strength. "We stay as one." She raised her hand, signaling for one of the half-dozen messengers awaiting her word down by the road. A boy in a loose-fitting uniform, probably no more than fifteen, rode up the hill and snapped a salute.

"Orders for General Sabastenien," Vlora said. "I want him to send his cavalry across the New Ad, where they'll shadow our movement, scout the south side of the river, and report back at regular intervals. Dismissed." The messenger was off before she'd finished the last word, and she watched the boy go with a frown. "I do feel like I'm missing something," she said.

"You have scouts ahead of the vanguard?" Nila asked.

"Of course." Vlora stewed in her uncertainty. "If they haven't burned any of the bridges, we'll be within scouting range of the enemy siege by nightfall. We'll find out what's waiting for us then."

The enemy, as it turned out, had only burned one bridge. It was the bridge between one of the smaller tributaries of the New Ad and the Dynize camp. The river was shallow enough to ford but deep enough to slow their crossing if the enemy decided to make a contest of it. And based on their defenses, they *would* make it a contest.

The Dynize army had formed a half-moon series of fortifications around the distant city of New Adopest with ditches, gun emplacements, and watchtowers. But they'd also done the same thing on the other side, facing outward, effectively turning their besieging army into a town capable of withstanding siege itself. The closest of the earthworks was placed just fifty yards beyond the river. Vlora could see, through her looking glass, the morion-helmed soldiers manning those earthworks and gun crews checking over the artillery that would face her were she to attempt a direct assault.

"They definitely knew we were coming," Vlora said to no one in particular. She was surrounded by most of her general staff, all on horseback, and all examining the enemy and the city beyond them through their looking glasses.

"We can brush those aside with sorcery," someone suggested. Vlora didn't bother lowering her looking glass to see who.

"No, we can't," Nila shot back. "They have at least eight Privileged over there. I'm strong, but with just me and Bo we'll have our hands full handling that many at once."

"Davd?" Vlora asked.

Her powder mage hesitated for a moment before answering. "Those Privileged are hanging really damn far back. Almost to the front they have with New Adopest. If I didn't know any better, I'd think that they've learned not to get cocky around powder mages."

"So they have strong positioning, and they're being smart," Vlora said. "That's unfortunate." She fought a spike of frustration. All of this would be so much easier with her own sorcery—she wouldn't have to ask for reports on the enemy Privileged or use a looking glass to see the earthworks.

"It's nothing we can't take," General Frylo said. He was an older man, a veteran of the army that Tamas built before the Adran-Kez War, and newly arrived with Bo and Nila. "But we'll lose a lot of men doing it unless we can come up with something clever."

Vlora swept her looking glass across the enemy fortifications, through the middle of their camp, and then to the buildings of New Adopest barely visible through the afternoon haze. There wasn't a lot of high ground out here, so visibility was no more than a few miles, and even that was sketchy. The enemy could be doing practically anything behind those fortifications and she'd be none the wiser. She swung her looking glass to the river, where a few hundred Dynize cavalry were fording the river toward a token force holding south of the city.

"General Sabastenien, do we have word back from those scouts we sent across the river?"

Sabastenien shook his head. He was not much older than Vlora, in his mid-to-late thirties. He'd been a brigadier with the Wings of Adom mercenary company during the Adran-Kez War and then recruited to the regular army by Tamas. "They ran into resistance the moment they crossed. Dynize cavalry are screening us, keeping us from getting a foothold over there."

"How many did you send?"

"Two hundred dragoons, with orders not to engage."

"Send four hundred. I want to know what's going on to our south, and I want to know by tomorrow afternoon."

"Yes, ma'am."

Vlora considered the order, wondering if she should send more. The enemy might be contesting their scouts for some vital reason, or just to foul Vlora's intelligence. She needed to know either way. But at what cost? "Make it five hundred," she corrected. "And give their commanding officer discretion on whether to engage."

"Of course, ma'am. Right away."

Vlora turned her looking glass back on the enemy camp and listened for the distant report of cannon fire. If the Dynize had been shelling New Adopest before she arrived, they had stopped now. Perhaps they thought their guns would be better turned in her direction? They wouldn't be wrong, of course.

"Do you see that?" someone asked.

"What?" Vlora asked, lowering her looking glass for a moment and sweeping the horizon.

"There." It was Sabastenien speaking. "One o'clock. From their camp."

Vlora followed his instructions and used her looking glass to find a pair of Dynize riders coming over the earthworks. They forded the tributary and began the long trek toward the Adran lines, waving a white flag. Neither soldier wore a breastplate nor any decoration.

"Deserters or messengers?" Bo asked.

"Messengers, by the white flags," Nila responded.

Vlora could hear a very pregnant question in the air. The entire general staff had an air of expectation, and she could practically feel Bo wanting to ask if she was going to give the orders to shoot them. The terrible urge in her stomach certainly wanted her to. But these weren't the soldiers that had almost killed her. She had to remain in control of herself. She lowered her looking glass and took her reins in one hand, then headed at a slow pace out to meet them. "Bo, Davd," she called over her shoulder. "With me."

She drew up a few hundred yards in front of her own lines and waited for the messengers to reach her. One was a middle-aged man with short-cut hair, thoughtful eyes, and a clean-shaven face. The other was an older woman—very old, looking just on the edge of frail. Her hair was dyed as black as Vlora's and she had deep smile lines on her cheeks. It was the man who spoke, in broken Adran. "We're looking for General Flint."

"You've found General Flint," Vlora replied. "What do you want?"

"We're here on behalf of General Etepali of the Spider Brigades of the Emperor's Immortal Army."

"On what errand?"

"To seek an audience with General Flint."

Vlora examined the two, unable to keep her lip from curling. They were too sharp-eyed, too clean and well-mannered to be common soldiers and yet they weren't wearing anything that marked them as officers. She wondered if word from Lower Blackguard had spread ahead of her. She remembered meeting with the Dynize general just before the Battle of Windy River. Her head had been nothing but a trophy to him. Arrogant prick.

"Why should I agree to meet with your general?"

"Mutual respect," the old woman said, spreading her hands wide.

"I've yet to meet any of your officers who looked at me as any more than a rabid dog waiting to be put down."

The pair of messengers exchanged a glance, something passing between them. The man replied, "Mistakes were made."

"I've splattered your mistakes across the hills of Fatrasta."

"A good reason to talk to you rather than fight you, no?" the old woman asked. Her Adran was much better than the man's. More refined and practiced. An interpreter, maybe? Or someone more important?

"A good reason for *you* to talk to *me*," Vlora shot back. "Not the other way around." Beside her, Bo cleared his throat. "What is your advice, Magus Borbador?" Vlora asked sharply, with far more acid in her tone than she'd intended.

"Never hurts to talk," Bo said quietly.

"Doesn't it? It hurts right now, and I have Dynize blades and bullets to thank for that."

The messengers exchanged another glance. The woman nudged her horse forward a few steps. "A gift," she said, tossing a bundle to Vlora.

Vlora fumbled the small package but managed to avoid the embarrassment of dropping it. It was a bit of cloth wrapped in twine. She managed to unbind it, and a small piece of metal dropped into her hand. It was a silver powder keg. No, not any silver powder keg. *Hers*, with initials carved into the back. It still had her blood in the grooves. "How did you get this?" she demanded.

"A dragoon," the woman explained. "He cut it off your uniform just before your friends arrived from Adro. He played dead to avoid the slaughter, and then fled. He stumbled into our camp two days ago."

"And why give it back?"

"It's our custom," the woman said, using two fingers to frame the small stud in her ear that looked an awful lot like a human tooth, "to take trophies from the dead. We do not take them from the living. General Etepali believed you should have it back."

"Did he?"

"She," the man corrected.

Vlora felt the urge to send the silver powder keg back, along with the heads of the two messengers. The thought had barely entered her mind when she shook it off. What kind of response was that? To what end? Was that really the woman she was becoming? "I'll meet your general," she snapped. "In my camp. Eight o'clock."

"Do you give your word as an Adran officer that she will be unharmed?" the old woman asked.

Davd urged his horse up in a few quick bounds, bringing it abreast of the messenger's mounts. "Don't question my Lady Flint," he growled.

The old woman seemed unperturbed. "Your Lady Flint has murdered numerous Dynize officers. My general hopes to keep her own life intact, at least until the actual fighting begins."

"Stand down, Davd," Vlora ordered. The last thing she wanted to do was speak with a Dynize officer. It would come to nothing, of course. The Dynize would not give up their prize of the godstones and Vlora would not give up trying to take them. But a small bit of honor managed to wriggle past the ugliness that had made a home inside her. Tamas himself had pinned this powder keg to her breast. Having it again, even without the sorcery that it represented, was no small thing. "I give my word. I'll talk to her. But once the fighting starts..." She shrugged.

"Understood." The messengers bowed and turned around, trotting back toward the Dynize earthworks.

Vlora returned to the general staff. Deep in thought, she barely heard someone asking her what had happened, and waved off any other questions. "Set up camp," she ordered. "I want our own earthworks dug by morning in case of a counterattack. Make sure we secure the coast and have a line of communication with our fleet. Someone find out why Olem hasn't returned yet. Oh, and set up the general-staff tent. I'm having a guest tonight."

CHAPTER 11

We have to talk," Styke said.

He fell to the back of the column, where Ka-poel lagged a dozen paces behind the last of the Mad Lancers, sitting back in her saddle, riding with a tuneless whistle on her lips and a casual eye on passing Dynize. She stopped whistling as he approached and made an open-handed gesture at her left side, her sign for Celine.

"No," Styke answered. "Just the two of us. I think I've got enough of a grasp of your sign language for a conversation."

She pursed her lips, giving him the impression that she already knew what this was about. Over the last couple of days they had made decent headway—according to Orz, they were less than twenty miles from the capital. The men were well rested, their couple of wounded were recovering well, and so far no one had bothered to ask why a group of foreign soldiers was traveling in the company of a dragonman and a bone-eye. Styke was impressed that the ruse had lasted as long as it had, though the logic behind it was sound.

No one goes out of their way to question authority figures. In Dynize, it seemed that was doubly the case.

With the current calm, it seemed a good time to get Ka-poel alone and hash out whatever was going on between them, sorcery-wise. Styke let Amrec fall in beside Ka-poel's horse, matching paces.

"You're using your sorcery to protect me." It wasn't a question. Ka-poel did not answer, so he went on. "You told me before that you're not."

The flurry of gestures that shot back at him was almost too much for him to follow.

"Slow down, slow down," he said.

She repeated herself slowly. *Which do you believe?*

"I believe that you're protecting me."

You say that like it's a bad thing.

"I say that like you lied to me."

Ka-poel snorted. *Lies among friends.*

"Lies among friends is me telling Markus that the cut of his jacket doesn't make him look like a fat sack of shit. Lies among friends is *not* you digging your blood-witch hooks deep into my flesh."

To protect you. The strength of the gesture emphasized the word "protect." She continued, *I protect my friends. You. Taniel. People who may be in danger from other bone-eyes.*

"How many of those people do you prop up with your sorcery? How many of them can shrug off wounds, fight through crippling pain, react with astonishing strength?"

Ka-poel narrowed her eyes at him. *Only you and Taniel.*

"Right. And that stuff between you and Taniel? I don't give a shit. You've got your own deals. I get that. But me and you . . ."

Is this because I'm not sleeping with you like I am Taniel? There was an unmistakable mocking tilt to the gestures.

"Don't be a child. I'm mad because Taniel gave you his permission. I did not."

And why don't you want my protection?

Styke considered his words for a moment. "Because I'm Mad Ben Styke. I may be a bit in love with my own legend, and maybe that's a fault of mine. But my strength? My resolve? I want those things to be *mine*. Not a loan from some blood sorcerer. Do you understand what I mean at all?"

For a moment, Ka-poel looked almost pouty. She turned away, scowling, and took nearly a full minute before finally looking back at him. She gave a small nod. She continued to gesture. *Maybe. But you're a fool for turning down such a gift. I don't give it lightly, you know.*

"Yeah, but like I said: I didn't ask for it. You can't guilt someone into accepting a gift they don't want."

I only give you enough to keep you alive. It doesn't take much. You're very strong on your own.

Styke felt like she was finally listening. Bargaining. Stroking his ego. A small weight left his shoulders, and he realized that he'd been afraid of what would happen if she simply told him that he belonged to her now. But this was not a dialogue between master and slave. He took a deep breath. "All right. Let's start this over. How does it work?"

It's a sort of link between us. I can allow you to feed off the strength of my sorcery, giving you more or cutting you off when you do or do not need it. Once the bond is established, it doesn't take much effort on my part to keep it going. Giving you too much strength does *exhaust me, however.* The explanation was so long that Styke had to make her repeat the series of gestures twice before he got it all.

"So is that why you were so tired after Starlight? Because you gave me so much strength? It seems like you're only now recovering from it."

Ka-poel smirked. *No. You drew some energy from me during that fight, but most of it was going to Taniel.*

"I'm guessing he needed it?"

Our communication isn't perfect, but I understand he faced down a couple of Dynize brigades.

Styke was in the middle of drinking from his canteen and spat half of it down the front of him. "By *himself*?"

I'm not sure. But he drew enough power from me to do so.

"He's really that strong?"

We're *really that strong,* Ka-poel corrected. She seemed to recognize her own arrogance and made a small gesture of humility. *It nearly killed us both. Neither of us can repeat that performance. I've called him to join me here, actually, though it will take him some time to reach us.*

Taniel's presence would certainly be helpful, Styke conceded to himself. Even if he had only a fraction of the strength required to fight a couple of Dynize brigades. He dismissed the thought and focused on the present. "Look, I know you think this is necessary. But my strength . . . it must be my own."

Are you sure?

"I'm sure."

A small war played out over Ka-poel's face. He could practically feel her weighing the options, wondering if she should make the decision for him—or simply lie to him again. Her mouth finally settled into a firm line and her hands flashed. *I'll withdraw my power. But I also don't want another bone-eye getting a hold of you.*

"So you want to keep a close eye on me?"

But I won't do it without your permission.

There was the bargain. Styke grunted, feeling as if he was still being played somehow. But she had a point. Ka-Sedial was a world away, with no method of leverage, but there might be other bone-eyes in the capital just as capable of taking control of him. Given the choice, he'd rather risk Ka-poel's sorcery than a stranger's. "All right. But just a watchful eye. I'm not Taniel. I'm not your champion. I'm just a temporary bodyguard."

Ka-poel leaned across the gap and patted him on the cheek. The gesture had all the gentleness of an elderly grandmother, but the moment her fingers touched his skin, he felt an electric shock that traveled from his face to the tips of his fingers and toes. He flinched back, but the feeling was so brief that he thought he had imagined it. A few moments passed, and he squinted his eyes against a sudden headache. He looked down at his hands, flexing his fingers, feeling them react just a tiny bit more slowly to his commands. Little aches that he hadn't realized were there came into focus; from the old, healed-over bullet wounds to the sorcerously stitched stabs and slashes from Starlight.

The cascade of painful echoes hitting him from every part of his body were at once hateful and welcome. He found himself gasping for breath, eyes burning, while a sense of freedom lifted his heart. He nodded to Ka-poel and realized that he was grinning stupidly.

You like that? she signed with a cocked eyebrow.

"It's not a matter of liking it," Styke replied. "I *know* it. I recognize it. This body is mine again."

I never . . . , she began, but let her hands drop. She gestured dismissively, rolling her eyes.

Their conversation was interrupted as the group ahead of them turned off the road into a large inn complex. The stop was not unexpected, and the place was fairly deserted, so the Lancers dismounted and began to water their horses at a large fountain. Styke pulled away from Ka-poel and attended to Amrec, then made sure that Celine had properly taken care of Margo.

Watching while Celine brushed down her horse, and giving the occasional pointer, Styke was soon joined by Markus and Zak. "Where's our local guide?" Styke asked.

"Requisitioning supplies from the owner of this place," Zak answered.

Styke lifted his eyes to the road and watched as some fifteen soldiers marched into the large courtyard of the inn. Most were barely old enough to wear the uniforms, and their morion helmets and breastplates fit poorly. Several had bad sunburns, telling of inexperience when it came to marching all day.

Keeping one eye on the soldiers, he asked Markus, "Is something wrong?"

"Just curious if we're going to be able to scout at some point," Zak answered for his brother in a low whisper. "I know how little you like going blind into things, and we've been riding on the word of that foreigner for the last couple days. We're sitting ducks all gathered up into one group, with no eyes out front or back."

"You're right, I don't like it," Styke answered. Speaking in Palo wasn't the same as Dynize, but it was close enough that if they were overheard, it might be mistaken for bad Dynize. "But our friend hasn't lied to us yet. And having either of you ahead or trailing us only makes it all the more likely that you're stopped and questioned. No, we stay with the dragonman. All of us."

The brothers nodded unhappily. "Could Jackal speak to his spirits? Get a lay of the land?" Markus asked with a mix of hesitancy and hope.

"I haven't asked him lately. He hasn't had much luck with the blood witch around. Speaking of which…" Styke looked around for Jackal. His eyes landed on the big round fountain in the center of the courtyard, where the newly arrived soldiers had begun to water their horses and themselves. The soldiers didn't give Styke and the rest of the Kressians more than a few curious glances— they seemed to write off the naval infantry uniforms without a second thought.

But Jackal was kneeling beside the fountain, dunking his head in the water, then slicking it off his head and face before repeating the action. Anyone with eyes could see that Jackal wasn't quite Dynize and it seemed to make the soldiers more than a little curious.

Three of the Dynize soldiers gathered around him in a loose knot that quickly tightened. Zak and Markus both took a step in their direction, but Styke grabbed them by their shoulders. "Go find Orz," he told them, then began to walk slowly toward the fountain, acting casual, his hands behind his back instead of in a fist and on his knife like he wanted them. He hoped the situation resolved itself before he even reached the fountain.

"Where are you from?" he heard one of the guards ask in Dynize.

Jackal had been learning Dynize along with the rest of the soldiers. But, like the rest, he was in no state to speak openly with a native. He ignored the soldiers and dunked his head again. When he came back up, one of them—a tall woman with head shaved around a single topknot—grabbed him by the shoulder.

"Where are you from?" she asked again, somewhat more aggressively.

Jackal smiled at her and tapped his ears, then his throat, and shook his head.

"What are you, mute?" The woman's tone took on a mocking edge. The two men with her both laughed at the question, though Styke wondered what could possibly be funny about it. One suddenly snatched Jackal beneath an arm, jerking him to his feet. Jackal spun with the pull, letting himself stumble into the two men and using the motion to disguise that he'd pulled his knife.

Styke was on them in a few quick strides. He quickly shouldered between Jackal and the three soldiers, looking down on them with a measured calm while he struggled internally not to draw his own weapon.

The woman took an involuntary step back. Styke put a hand on the chest of one of the men, pushing him gently. Orz had taught him the equivalent expression for "Let me buy you a drink," so he used it. "You've had a long day in the sun," he suggested in broken Dynize.

"Is there something wrong?" The sergeant in charge of this crew sidled over to Styke, looking him up and down with one long glance and then turning his attention to the three soldiers. "Well?"

Topknot's lip curled. "This slave was disrespectful," she said, gesturing to Jackal. "And this one." She gestured at Styke. "I want them whipped."

Styke felt himself a hairsbreadth from violence. He and Jackal could cut the four of them down without drawing a sweat. The other eleven might be a problem, though. "I apologize," he said, bowing very slightly at the waist. Orz had said that bows were important here. "This slave cannot speak."

"But he can still answer a question!" Topknot's blood was up.

"How?" Styke asked, hoping that his inflection said just how obvious the question was. He couldn't help but wonder at her background. She had to be a noble of some kind, or at least what passed for nobility in Dynize. A bastard of a prominent Household maybe, sent to the infantry to get wise. She couldn't be more than seventeen, but she had the arrogance of a Kez officer.

She glared at him, ignoring the question.

"I'm sorry," Styke repeated.

The sergeant didn't seem all that interested in the spat. He turned to Styke and gave a regretful sigh. "It is within her right. You are slaves." His face and tone expressed sympathy.

"I have apologized." Styke realized that he was gripping the handle of his knife and forced himself to let go. "I think we should take this no further."

"I—!"

Topknot was cut off by the timely arrival of Orz. The dragonman swept into the confrontation smoothly, putting himself between Styke and the sergeant in much the same way as Styke had between Jackal and the soldiers.

The sergeant's nostrils flared and the three soldiers immediately retreated several steps. "This property does not belong to you," Orz said to Topknot in a dangerously low voice.

The sergeant was white-faced. He backed away, bowing low with every step. "No, there is no problem, Servant of God. My apologies."

Orz glared the group back to the other side of the courtyard and then walked, unhurriedly, around the Mad Lancers. "It's time to go," he told them quietly, a note of urgency in his tone. They were soon on the road and, once they'd gone around a bend and were safely out of the sight of the inn, were riding double-time at Orz's suggestion.

"What happened back there?" Orz demanded, pulling Styke up to the front of the column.

Styke found himself gripping his knife again. He let go. "They took an interest in Jackal."

"They don't see a lot of Palo here. Kressians are rare, but everyone has seen a slave and knows better than to fool with them. Palo, though?" Orz let out a litany of words that Styke had not learned. "Those recruits are nothing more than goddamn children," he finally finished. "We've sent so many soldiers overseas that they've lowered the recruiting age to sixteen. It's become a point of pride among the Households to put their less useful members into the infantry to fill out the ranks, no matter how unqualified or privileged."

Styke hadn't been that far off with his guess, then. "How do you know all this?"

"Because I've been questioning every innkeeper we pass for the last couple of days. I haven't been a free man in Dynize for years. I need information. That's why I was taking so long to get supplies."

"Will this be a problem?"

"Only if they follow us," Orz said, glancing over his shoulder.

"They backed off in a hurry when they saw you."

"And a good thing, too. A blind man could have seen the violence in you."

"I was restraining myself," Styke protested.

"Like a dog at the end of a chain." Orz spat angrily. "Slaves don't have such violence in them, Styke. Even the Household guards know their place. They don't stand up to Dynize."

"What good is a guard who isn't allowed to fight?"

Orz swore again. "It's complicated! If I had been standing there and ordered you to kill them, it would have been acceptable. But not on your own."

"That's stupid."

"That's the way things are done!"

Styke bit down on his tongue, trying hard not to argue. This wasn't his land. He couldn't be himself if he wanted them to get through this alive. "I won't allow them to attack one of my men."

"Even to save the rest?"

"No."

Orz inhaled sharply, studying Styke's face. His calm seemed to return to him in the span of a few short breaths and he shook his head. "You are a wonder, Ben Styke."

"I'm an officer. A shitty one, most of the time. But I've always protected my men from the injustice of tyrants. It's one of my few good qualities, and I've reached the age that I'm just not going to let that go." The words flowed without Styke even thinking about them, and he was a little surprised at himself. It was something he'd always *known* he felt strongly about, but the logical part of his brain told him that he should have been more flexible. He should have let Jackal take a beating for the rest of them.

But he'd never let it go when lives and wars were at stake in Fatrasta. Why here?

"All right," Orz finally said. "Let's just keep well ahead of those soldiers. We reach the city ahead of them, then we disappear. They might gossip at some point, but as long as we move quickly, it shouldn't be a problem." He did not sound like he believed it.

"Is it so rare for slaves to stand up for themselves?"

"Yes," Orz answered without hesitation.

"Why?"

"Because they are conditioned. Before they reach any level of station within a Household, they are broken and remolded. If they cannot be broken, they are killed." Styke bit his tongue to hold back a retort. The anger was still there, festering. He twirled his ring to keep himself from checking his carbine.

"What do you think happens to dragonmen?" Orz asked, shooting him a look. "Dragonmen, bone-eyes, and Privileged are all tools of the state. But the truth is, everyone in Dynize belongs to someone else. Even the heads of the Households belong to the emperor. Foreign slaves are lower than Household grunts. It makes them a target."

"You could have mentioned that before."

"You're with a dragonman and a bone-eye. The chances of you actually being a target were not very high."

Styke ground his teeth. He suddenly felt very tired, and he wondered if Ka-poel's sorcery had been giving him energy that he did not have. It seemed likely. He was tired and hurting, and he definitely did not want to ride another ten hours before they next slept. "All right. We ride late tonight. I don't want to meet those soldiers again. We'll stay ahead of any questions."

CHAPTER 12

To their credit, Meln-Dun's men had set up a fairly thorough command center for their search of Greenfire Depths. It was located in one of the offices above the warehouse. Two walls were covered in police sketches of known associates of Mama Palo, as well as long descriptions of anyone whose sketches they hadn't managed to acquire. A third wall allowed light in through big, leaded windows with broken panes. The final had a massive map of Greenfire Depths scrawled with notes and marked with large red X's.

Michel was mostly interested in that map, but the moment he entered, he took a few seconds to examine the motley group of searchers. They included two women and six men, in addition to himself, Ichtracia, and Dahre. All were Palo, of course, though he could tell from the variety of dress that they came from—or attempted to mark themselves from—all walks of life. Only two wore the traditional brown cotton laborers' suits found most commonly among city Palo. Both women wore buckskins. Another dressed like a Brudanian merchant with a tricorn hat and a finely made blue cotton jacket.

Dahre himself sat in a chair pushed back on two legs, his feet up on the corner of a ratty old sofa, a pewter mug of coffee in one hand. He looked like a tired old police captain about to give the morning briefing to his sergeants, and the very sight of him made Michel wistful for Captain Blasdell. He wondered what had happened to her, and hoped she'd gotten out of the city ahead of the Dynize purges.

Dahre touched his forehead in greeting. "Everyone, this is Tellurin and Avenya. They're thief-takers from up in Brannon Bay, and they'll be helping us with the search." He went around and introduced the searchers. Michel cast the names to memory but only took particular note of two of them: an older man with a harelip, who glared at them at the mention of "thief-takers," and one of the pair in buckskins—a young woman who smirked at Ichtracia, then rolled her eyes openly at Michel.

The rest of the group seemed pleased to get additional help. Those two, however, could be trouble.

"This is a decent setup you have here," Michel said, heading immediately to the map of Greenfire Depths. "I'm guessing one of you has police experience?"

The glare on the old man's face softened slightly. "Aye, that was me. Twenty-five years with the Palo Irregular Division here in the Depths."

"Couhila, is it?" Michel asked.

"That's me."

"Very well done."

The glare softened a little more and the old man gave Michel an appreciative nod. Police generally didn't like thief-takers, seeing them as little more than localized bounty hunters, but few people would argue that an experienced thief-taker was often the best option for tracking down someone in hiding. Michel's take-charge tone was calculated to take advantage of that reputation.

Dahre pointed to the young woman who'd rolled her eyes at Michel. "Devin-Mezi here helped the Dynize back when they did a big search of the catacombs for that Blackhat bomber. She was with the Household in control of the search, and offered a lot of good suggestions."

Michel tried not to bristle. Devin-Mezi would *definitely* have to be watched. If she had been helping out in the Yaret Household, there was a good chance she had seen his face on more than one occasion. "Good." He nodded. "All this is very good." He pointed at the X's. "Are these the spots you've already checked?"

A round of nods answered him. It was, he could tell at a glance, the one big flaw in their organization of the search. They were hitting random spots—probably by virtue of tip-offs and false leads. There was no method to the madness, and Michel said as much. "Just hitting the spots where we have intelligence isn't going to find us a Palo freedom fighter. No, this Mama Palo...she's probably mobile, able to double back and change hiding spots at will. If she's at all smart, she has a portable map that looks just like this and that tells her wherever you've been raiding."

"How will she know where we're going to hit next?" Devin-Mezi asked, her lip curled.

Michel looked between Devin-Mezi and Couhila. Those were the two he was worried about, and he needed to make an enemy of one and a friend of the other. His compliments already seemed to have worked on Couhila. "Because she's clearly not an idiot," he snapped back. "Freedom fighters don't last long if they can't keep ahead of the local magistrates. She's probably got as many eyes and ears as you spread throughout the Depths." He knew for a fact that she did, and that she *was* smart. Ka-poel would have left her most capable agent in charge.

"So what do we do about it?" Couhila asked.

Michel nodded respectfully. "These are great tools," he said, gesturing around the room. "But we need to use them smarter. Brannon Bay doesn't have a rat's nest like Greenfire Depths, but it does have slums. The only way to flush someone out is by working methodically." To emphasize his point, he punched a finger at a landmark in the southeastern corner of the Depths and then punched another spot, then another, working inward from the Rim. "We crack down on anyone who knows them. We spread around money and threats, leaving a network of informants behind us everywhere we go."

Dahre lifted his pewter mug, sipped from it, then spoke for the first time since making introductions. "That is, uh, very ambitious."

Michel shrugged it off. "I worked for some old-hand thief-takers and their very rich clients up in Brannon Bay. You said money was no object, so—"

"Within reason," Dahre cut in.

"Within reason," Michel agreed. "We can't do this on a budget, of course, but based on what you already have set up here, I think we can do it without going crazy. A couple more thugs, plus fifty thousand krana for bribes—"

He was interrupted again, this time by Devin-Mezi. She burst out laughing. "Fifty thousand a person? What, are you planning on taking a cut of each bribe?"

"Total," Michel snapped at her. "Spread fifty thousand around the Depths with a little bit of thought and we'll find this freedom fighter right quick." He glanced at Ichtracia, who still stood near the door with her hands in her pockets, eyeballing the group. She had already begun to get more comfortable around the Palo, but he could still see a bit of wariness in her eyes, her body tensed as if ready to run or fight. "Look," he said to Devin-Mezi, "if you want to jump around chasing ghosts, fine by me. I've got a weekly retainer. But my finding bonus is bigger the quicker I get things done and this is the way to do it. Or I'll walk."

Dahre got to his feet quickly, clearing his throat. "No, no!" he said. "No need to walk away. I like where this is going. Method might be the very thing we need to find this bitch and get back to settling the Depths."

Devin-Mezi sneered at Michel. Couhila looked pleased with himself. Michel noted that the old police sergeant wasn't a fan of the young upstart. He could use that information to his advantage. "Right. You mentioned the catacombs. Are they on the map?" Michel asked.

"As many as we could piece together. That big Blackhat purge shuffled through a thousand miles of catacombs, so we know them a little better than we did before, but there's still a lot of space." Dahre approached the map, squinting at it. "To be honest, most of the more traditional Palo are scared of them. Superstition and all that. She might be hiding out there, but there are still cave-ins, booby traps, bad air, and the real threat of getting lost. I'd wager next week's wages that she's here in the Depths."

Michel began shaking his head before Dahre was finished talking. He agreed with the foreman, but he also didn't want them to actually catch Mama Palo. He needed them to get close—just close enough that he could find her on his own. No harm in muddying the water a little. "I respectfully disagree. Danger might keep some of us away from the catacombs, but not a freedom fighter. Their whole life is danger. The prospect of getting lost won't scare them. We need to look under every rock, search every tunnel. If you have extra people, put them on regular sweeps."

Dahre scowled, but gave a reluctant nod.

Michel examined the map for a few moments. "We start here," he said, pointing to a spot not all that far from the quarry. "The first thing we do is canvas. Minor bribes, promises of jobs and riches. Then we act quickly on any information we get in this area. Smash-and-grab sort of raids that might let us get our hands on a lieutenant or anyone else who knows more about Mama Palo's whereabouts."

"This technique. It's just like the Blackhats," Couhila said. By his tone he was just trying to be helpful, but a round of scowls followed the suggestion.

Michel spat on the floor and made a disgusted face. "Unfortunately, yes. Those shitbags are good at this sort of thing."

"I don't like using their tactics," the Palo dressed like a Brudanian merchant spoke up.

"You think the Blackhats invented this kind of thing?" Michel said, turning aggressively on the man. "No. This kind of thing has been happening for a thousand years. If you want to make a political statement about it, be my guest, but do it after we've done our jobs." He let his glare pass around the room, noting Dahre's smirk. The foreman knew exactly what Michel was doing and he seemed to approve.

Of course he did. This was just another job to finish.

"All right, let's get going," Michel said, pointing around the group. "The Depths has as many as twenty levels, right? You two, take the top levels. You three try to drop down just below them. You three get the bottom level. Me and Avenya will fill in everything else. Remember, we're not trying to grab anyone, not immediately. Right now we're just asking questions, spreading around a little bit of money. Maybe some of these Dynize rations cards. You find anything, you report it to me and Dahre."

The group began to split up. Michel waited until most were gone and went over to Dahre. "Sorry for taking over there," he said quietly. "Didn't mean to step on your toes." Polite and likable. The best way to infiltrate an enemy.

Dahre waved it off. "You know what you're doing. I'm just a quarry foreman who the boss trusts." He grimaced. "You get this damn thing over with quick and I'll buy you a drink. Pit, I'll recommend we keep you on retainer."

"I'll do what I can," Michel promised, then headed for the door. He waited until they were some distance from the quarry and had lost their new coworkers before he rubbed both hands through his short hair and bent over, staring at the slime-covered ground and taking long, unsteady breaths. He let his disguise slowly drop, losing the quietly confident smile and the thoughtful look in his eye. His body was suddenly seized with the tension of being someone else the whole day, and he saw a bit of a tremble in his fingertips.

"I don't think I ever realized how terrifying you are."

Michel looked up at Ichtracia. Her body language was still very tense, but now she was watching him with a strange look in her eye. "Me?"

"Yes, you. Watching you slide into a different person like it was a suit of clothes. Glad-handing. Warm and friendly. When I found out that you weren't who you said you were, I thought both myself and Yaret were fools for taking you in. But now that I've seen you work..." She let out a small laugh and shook her head. "I knew you were good at what you do, but that is absolutely frightening."

Michel smiled at the compliment, but he didn't feel it. There was a sour note in his stomach that he couldn't ignore—one that he'd felt on several occasions. Dahre, Couhila, even Devin-Mezi. All these Palo working for Meln-Dun weren't bad people. "I like Dahre," he said quietly.

"He seems like a competent sort. But he was taken in by you in an instant."

"More's the pity."

"You don't want to do your job?" Ichtracia seemed surprised by this.

"It's not about 'want.' I need to, so I will. But deceiving all these people day in, day out. It..." Michel trailed off. He'd been about to say "it takes its toll," but considering that Ichtracia was one of those people he'd deceived, he didn't expect much empathy. Slowly, he pulled his mask back on. "Let's do a little groundwork for Dahre's group. See if we can get a whiff of Mama Palo."

Ichtracia watched him carefully for a moment, clearly thrown off by his shift back into character. "Think we'll find her?"

"We better. My whole plan hinges on making contact. But we've got other work to do as well."

"Setting up Meln-Dun?"

Michel grinned. "That's the fun part, yeah."

CHAPTER 13

The Dynize general arrived ten minutes early, riding up to the Adran perimeter with an honor guard of thirty soldiers and two Privileged. Vlora greeted them on foot, flanked by Davd, Nila, and Bo while Norrine and Buden kept watch for any trickery that might be afoot.

Vlora raised a hand in greeting, standing straight with her sword at her side and wearing the returned powder-keg pin on her dress uniform. It was all she could do to remain standing after a long day of reviewing the freshly laid camp, and she half hoped that this enemy general proved to be as prickly as her colleagues and would give her an excuse to cut this worthless summit short.

She made an effort to still her negative thoughts. Just behind her, soldiers had finished setting up the general-staff tent with chairs and refreshment near the earthworks and had begun lighting torches to fend off the coming dusk.

The Dynize general was a stout woman in her midfifties, with a scar that traveled down the side of her face and one eye cloudy from what seemed likely to be the same wound. She wore a turquoise dress uniform and earrings of colorful feathers, as well as a cavalry saber at her side, the hilt festooned with ribbons.

"Lady Flint," the general said, swinging down from her horse.

Vlora extended her hand. The general gripped it, hard enough that it hurt, though Vlora couldn't tell whether the act was intentional or if she was simply that fragile. She smiled shallowly through the pain. "General Etepali?"

"Correct."

Vlora felt her exhaustion weighing on her, chipping at what little restraint she still held. "General, I can't help but wonder why you requested this meeting. It seems rather pointless, considering that we both know we'll be fighting a battle tomorrow."

Several of the general's retinue gasped audibly.

"I'm not trying to be rude," Vlora added, "just trying to save us both some time." The words sounded forced in her own ears, and she realized how dismissive and angry she sounded—well past rude and on to insulting.

Etepali took in a sharp breath and muttered something before finally saying, "You'd treat a fellow general with such disdain?" Her expression spoke of the same haughtiness as the other Dynize generals she'd met, and Vlora found herself letting out an irritated sigh.

"I don't have time for this," she said, fully ready to turn her back on the group.

"Wait, wait." The voice came from somewhere at the back of the retinue. A horse muscled its way through the small crowd ridden by the old woman who'd come as a messenger earlier. She rode up beside her general's horse and swung down with the restrained enthusiasm of an experienced rider. She said something quickly in Dynize, and General Etepali gave a short bow and backed away.

Vlora found herself frozen, one foot off the ground for her to turn back to her camp. "What's this?" she asked cautiously.

"She's not General Etepali," the old woman said. "I am." She strode forward, taking Vlora by the arm like a grandmother. "Shall we leave the Privileged and the officers outside and go have us a conversation?"

"I…" Vlora found herself dragged gently past her own guards and toward the general-staff tent. She waved off Davd with a subtle gesture and shot Bo a look before being pulled inside.

The tent had been set up for twenty people. A table at the far end was laid out with Adran spirits and an assortment of breads, sweets, and salted meats that Bo had somehow magicked up from the camp followers. The old woman dropped Vlora's arm just inside the tent and looked around with a critical eye. "This is very nice, thank you." She made a beeline for the refreshment table, leaning down to peer at the labels on the bottles before pouring two drinks. She brought one to Vlora, then found a chair and pulled it around and took a seat.

Vlora looked dumbly at the drink in her hand. "I'm sorry, but I'm not entirely certain what's going on here."

"My officers," Etepali explained, "were very insistent that I not meet you in person. I told them that I'd come as an observer and let someone else pretend to be me."

"You thought that I'd kill you under a flag of truce?"

The old woman sipped her drink, examining Vlora with bright, intense eyes over the rim of the glass. Her silence answered Vlora's question.

Vlora rubbed her jaw to relax the muscles and crossed the tent, sitting down facing Etepali. "I didn't mean to be rude out there. But I repeat my earlier question."

"Why waste time by meeting?" Etepali asked. "Because who wouldn't want to? You're Vlora Flint. Hero of the Adran-Kez War. Hero of the Kez Civil War. Mercenary commander extraordinaire!" There was an air of gentle mockery about the last title, as if it didn't belong with the first two.

"There's no way that my reputation goes all the way to Dynize," Vlora said flatly.

Etepali gave Vlora a coy smile. For the second time, Vlora found herself trying to guess Etepali's age. She couldn't be any younger than sixty. Perhaps closer to seventy. "You'd be surprised." She looked at her glass, smirked, and continued, "But no, it doesn't. I have a biography of Field Marshal Tamas that a spy brought me a few years ago. It mentions you briefly, but otherwise I knew nothing about you before arriving in Landfall. I've been reading, though, and there is quite a lot of literature on the famous Vlora Flint."

"So what about me?"

"You're interesting. Fiery. Loyal. Principled. Conflicted. You remind me of me."

At another time, Vlora would have liked this woman. She knew that right away. But she was tired and irritable, and that terrible urge for violence was still planted firmly inside of her. All she could think about was a few hours of restless sleep and the inevitable battle that would come tomorrow. "I suppose I should take that as a compliment."

The old woman puffed out her cheeks, letting a breath blow through her lips slowly before answering. "I don't mean to be self-aggrandizing, but you don't know who I am. You couldn't. So I'm going to tell you." She drained the last of her drink— single-malt Adran whiskey, now that Vlora had taken a chance to sip her own—and continued. "I, too, was a young general. Decorated to the rank at thirty-five, during the height of the violence of the Dynize civil war. I've fought in over sixty battles. I've commanded half of them, and I've only lost two." She held up a pair of fingers to emphasize the point.

"Are you trying to intimidate me?" Vlora asked, slightly taken aback.

"Of course not. I'm just giving you context. When I read that biography of Field Marshal Tamas, it was like seeing a ghostly reflection of myself in a mirror. Not his life experiences and campaigns, of course. But the way he thought. His passions. His strengths and weaknesses. It was startling. And then I found out that he had three children: a warrior, a mage, and a general. Now, I would be as interested as anyone else to meet the warrior and the mage." She cast a glance toward the flap as if to indicate she knew exactly who Borbador was. "But the general..." She shook her head with a small smile. "I never had children of my own. Men aren't my interest, if you catch my meaning. If I had a daughter, however, I like to think she'd be a lot like you." She leaned back, took another sip of whiskey. "That, my dear, is why I wanted to meet you."

Vlora blinked at the old woman in surprise. "That's it?"

"Of course that's it. I'm old, Vlora. Can I call you Vlora? Yes, well I'm old, Vlora, and I've fought so many battles that I'm far less interested in the results than in who fought them."

"You're not like the other Dynize generals I've met."

"Sedial's lapdogs? Of course not. Assholes, the lot of them—just like their master."

Vlora snorted.

"You're surprised I'd call the Great Ka an asshole?" Etepali shrugged. "He is. I've told him to his face, and I'm not the only one who wishes that someone else had gotten credit for ending the civil war. My cousin Yaret, well, he..." She laughed. "Sorry, I'm going too far off topic."

"No, no...this is quite interesting."

Etepali gave her a knowing smile. "Looking for Dynize gossip? Somewhere to twist the knife? I'm not going to defect, Vlora. We will have a battle tomorrow. It's possible that one of us will die during the fighting, and I wanted to meet you before that happens."

Vlora frowned down at her glass. She thought about the silver powder keg at her lapel, and she set down her glass and carefully unbuttoned the powder keg, holding it up to the lamp light. "What happened to the man who took this from me?" she asked.

"I had him shot."

"Why?"

"Because by his own admission he led a cavalry charge against a single, half-dead woman and then played dead when it didn't work out for him. I don't have room for that kind of cowardice in my army."

"He was following orders, I assume."

"Then he should have followed them all the way. He should have died trying to finish you off instead of pulling a corpse over himself and hoping your Privileged friends didn't notice him. By the way," she said, swirling the amber liquid in her glass, "this is very good. May I have the rest of the bottle?"

Vlora made a fist around the powder-keg pin. "It's yours."

Etepali beamed. "Wonderful. I appreciate your generosity." She fetched the bottle and stood behind her chair as if to signal that the meeting was over, and shook the bottle at Vlora. "If I win tomorrow, I hope that you'll share the rest of this bottle with me in the evening."

"Before you take my head for Ka-Sedial?"

Etepali snorted. "As much as he thinks he is, Ka-Sedial is not the emperor. And I'm not a barbarian. You won't be mistreated in my care."

"That's something, I suppose."

The old woman wagged her finger at Vlora. "It's more than something. It's my promise. A word is worth a lot, Vlora. Don't forget it in your grief and anger."

Vlora looked up sharply, but Etepali had already turned her back. She disappeared out through the tent flap in a few strides, leaving Vlora alone in the large tent, a half-finished glass of whiskey in her hand. A few moments of loneliness passed before the flap stirred again and Vlora was joined by Bo.

"That was awfully short," he said.

"It was, wasn't it?" Vlora asked distantly.

"Did she make demands?"

"None."

"She left here with a two-thousand-krana bottle of whiskey."

"I gave it to her. For this." Vlora held the powder-keg pin up to the light.

"So what did she want? Don't tell me she came all the way over here to pilfer some Adran booze."

"She wanted to meet me."

Bo scrunched up his nose. "The whiskey was more worth her time, I'd say. Is something wrong?"

Vlora swirled the glass under her nose absently and then finished it in three large gulps. The burning sensation in the back of her throat felt good. "I have the oddest feeling that I'm missing something."

"About Etepali?"

"About this entire meeting. A subtext I didn't read." She set her glass on Etepali's chair and struggled to her feet. "Tell them to clean this up. I'm going to bed. We have a battle to win in the morning."

CHAPTER 14

"D o you know who she really is?"

The question came unexpectedly as the Mad Lancers set up camp, fumbling in the dark around the only empty site they'd spotted for several miles. Styke looked up from lighting the tiny lantern he kept in his saddlebags to find Orz's shadowy face staring at him hard through the darkness. It was very clear which "she" he was talking about.

Styke finished lighting his lantern. He'd found a spot on the edge of the campground for himself, and the only person within earshot was Celine. He rounded his horse, ignoring the question while he used his lantern to light Celine's and then helped her get her saddlebags down from Margo. Once he'd finished, he returned to Amrec and hung his lantern from a tree branch overhead.

"I'm not sure if *she* knows who she really is," he finally replied.

"Don't be cryptic with me, Ben Styke," Orz said. "I need to know."

At first, Styke hadn't been sure if Orz was asking because he wanted to discuss Ka-poel's lineage or whether the dragonman wasn't actually certain. This made it clear it was the latter. Styke opened his mouth, a reply on his tongue, and thought back to his own relation to Lindet. He'd kept that secret his entire life. "It's not my place to say," he finally said.

"*Do you know?*" There was an urgency to Orz's tone.

"I do."

Orz's jaw tightened in the shadows cast by the lamp. Styke imagined that if he were anyone else, Orz would resort to casual violence to get his answers. Styke wondered if he still might, and let his hand rest lightly in his saddlebag, fist tightening around one of the extra knives in his pack. A long silence stretched between them.

"It's something I didn't consider important at first. A foolish oversight on my part," Orz finally said. "I assumed that Palo had their own bone-eyes and that she was one of them."

"They do," Styke replied. From what he'd been told, there were a few blood sorcerers in the deep swamp, but most Palo were bone-eyes in name only—elders of the tribe, wise men and women.

"Perhaps they do. But I've been studying her face since we encountered those soldiers. She is not Palo. She is Dynize. I don't know how I missed something so obvious."

"Don't be too hard on yourself," Styke said. He pulled his hand from his saddlebag and worked to relieve Amrec of his burdens, setting up his bedroll and laying the saddlebags beside it.

Either Orz didn't notice the flippant remark or he chose to ignore it. He continued, "Knowing that she is Dynize brings up so many questions. Why was she in Fatrasta? How did I not know that such a powerful bone-eye existed? Is she a member of Sedial's cabal, broken from her master and changed sides? Is she a hidden weapon of the Fatrastans? Is she a member of another Household?"

Styke disregarded the barrage of questions and continued to work in silence, getting the saddle off Amrec and then taking some time to brush the beast down and check his hooves. Orz watched, a frustrated look in his eye, squatting at the edge of the lamplight like a creature who'd crawled out of the swamp and wasn't certain he liked what he saw.

"If she has connections with the Dynize," Orz voiced his thoughts again, "then she would have known about the capital. She would have known about the Jagged Fens. Did she warn you?"

"She didn't know," Styke answered quietly.

"She is not *of* Dynize, but she has a Dynize name and a Dynize face." He scowled. "I've heard rumors of Dynize fleeing the mainland from the very beginning of the civil war until the very end. Is she a lost Household? Are those common in Fatrasta?"

"Not that I'm aware."

Styke finished his work and turned to face Orz. He'd noticed that the dragonman was guarded with his expressions, choosing when to let his inner thoughts play out upon his face. At the moment he appeared deep in thought, looking inward, the wheels of his brain in motion. Nearly a minute passed and no spark of understanding appeared in the dragonman's eyes. He straightened suddenly and snatched Styke's lantern. "Come with me, girl. I need you to translate," Orz said to Celine before striding across the camp.

Celine looked at Styke, startled. Styke felt his heart flutter. There was going to be a confrontation, and he needed to be there. "Come on," he said, taking her hand. "But if he starts to get angry, I want you to get behind me." They followed in the dragonman's footsteps.

Ka-poel was down by the stream, no more than thirty yards from the edge of the camp. She was alone, sitting in the dark, her legs pulled up with arms wrapped around her knees. It was the position of a fearful child, and even with the dragonman standing above her, lantern swinging, she stared into the middle distance as if her mind was in another place.

"Ka-poel," Orz said.

Her eyes flickered to him briefly. A finger twitched—such a small gesture, but it held the venom of a person who preferred to be left alone. *What do you want?* the movement demanded.

He seemed to get the gist, though if he read the subtext, he didn't care. "I need to know who you are and what you plan to do with the godstones."

Styke approached slowly with Celine, and urged her with one hand to move around to where she could face Ka-poel and see her hands easily. Ka-poel looked at all of them without moving her head, her expression darkening before being overtaken by something akin to resignation. Her hands flashed. *It's a long story*, Celine translated for her.

Orz hunkered down next to Celine. "I have time."

I don't wish to discuss it right now.

"I don't care."

Ka-poel looked up sharply to meet Orz's eyes, but the dragon-man did not flinch away at her glare. They froze into a sort of battle of wills, and Styke found himself holding his breath, wondering which of the two would break first. If Orz made a move toward violence, Styke would need to step in. But he was also aware just how much they needed Orz's help. He wanted to take the two of them by their collars and shake them, but he imagined that such an attempt would just earn him a pair of knives in the gut.

Neither of them broke the staring match, but slowly Ka-poel's hands began to move.

I don't know it all.

"Explain."

Ka-poel hesitated. She was not nearly as good as Orz at concealing her thoughts, and her face was writ with irritation. Styke wondered if she would refuse just out of stubbornness, and found himself letting out a breath he did not know he had held once she continued.

I'm an orphan. I grew up in a Palo tribe in the Tristan Basin in western Fatrasta. I've always known I was different. I've always known that I was Dynize, and that my sorcery was strong. The rest I have only begun to piece together. She made a downward sweeping gesture of uncertainty that Celine either did not know how or did not bother to translate. *Most of what I know about who I am has come in just the last few months.*

"If you're Dynize," Orz asked, "how did you come to be in Fatrasta?"

That is one thing I'm still trying to discover.

"But you know who you are?"

Mostly. I know who, but not why. I know that my nurse brought me out of Dynize. She told me stories of wars and palaces whose names are lost to my memory. She told me to fear other bone-eyes—to fear the men of the dragon and to fear the turquoise soldiers.

Celine broke her translation for a moment and looked at Ka-poel curiously. "Dragonmen and Dynize soldiers?"

Ka-poel nodded, giving Celine a sad smile before continuing on. *I know that my name is Ka-poel. I know that I have a sister named Mara. I also know that my grandfather is the bone-eye you call Ka-Sedial.*

Styke looked sharply to Orz. The dragonman sank farther back on his haunches, his chin lifting slightly to regard Ka-poel down the length of his nose. If anything, he seemed more wary than alarmed by this new information. "Ka-Sedial only has one granddaughter. Her name is Ichtracia."

Say that name again. There was an urgency to the gesture.

"Ichtracia."

A small smile cracked Ka-poel's weariness, and she went through a series of gestures that Celine did not translate. It took Styke a moment to realize that she was spelling out her sister's name.

"Her name isn't Mara," Orz said again.

A nickname, Ka-poel explained. *It's all that I could recall. I'm not even certain whether I heard it myself or my nurse told it to me. It's been too long.* She spelled "Ichtracia" one more time with her fingers. Slowly. Fondly. She wiped something away from the corner of her eye. *I have gathered rumors from the Dynize that I've met. Some willingly. Others... not. I have tried to piece together my own life. From what I know, Ka-Sedial had his son and daughter-in-law murdered, along with two of their three children. Ichtracia is the third child.*

Orz settled back even farther until he was sitting, and he no longer looked like a man performing an interrogation but a child listening to a story. "There are rumors," he said. "But no facts are known. Ka-Sedial's son and his family disappeared long ago—all except Ichtracia. Supposedly they were strangled and burned for some untold treachery. Ichtracia was the only one spared."

I am one of those two other children that were said to have died.

Orz pulled a very distinct impression of disbelief across his face. "That is quite a story."

Do you know anything else about it? About my past? Ka-poel leaned forward eagerly.

"I don't." Orz made a noise in the back of his throat. "Like I said, rumors. What you've already heard is the unofficial story, and Ka-Sedial never gave an official one."

Do you know who my parents were?

Orz frowned. "Distantly. I know your mother fought on my side of the civil war." He snorted angrily. "*Your mother.*" He shook his head in disbelief. "I take you at your word, yet this is too fantastic to believe."

Fantastic or not, this is my life. I've never known what it meant. I still don't.

"So what are you using these soldiers for?" Orz gestured around at the Mad Lancer camp. "What hidden goals do you have? Which of them have you seeped your influence into without their knowledge?" His voice began to rise, the cadence of his speech increasing.

Styke took a long step forward, laying a hand on Celine's shoulder. "That's enough," he said.

Orz shot to his feet so quickly that Styke fell back into a defensive stance. The dragonman whirled on his heel and stalked into the night without another word, leaving Styke with a mixture of anger and relief. He looked down at Ka-poel, who herself was staring in the direction that Orz had gone.

"Is this going to be a problem?" he asked.

I don't know, she gestured. *I thought he already knew who I was.*

"I thought the same thing. But he didn't, and telling him now hasn't made him trust us any more." Styke ground his teeth. "Why is he so angry about it?"

He doesn't know whether to believe me. Even if he does, how can he trust me? I am Ka-Sedial's kin. Ka-poel frowned. *I think this is a very confusing time for him.*

Styke tapped the side of his lantern, staring off into the dark after Orz. "I really hope he's still here when we wake up in the morning."

CHAPTER 15

Vlora sat astride her horse, nodding gently into the morning sun, desperately trying not to fall asleep as the distant beat of drums marked out three full brigades of Adran soldiers falling into rank. Her head hurt from a night without rest, her body ached from her wounds from the Crease, and her mind still wondered at the conversation with General Etepali the night before. She knew instinctively that she had missed something in the encounter and it clawed at the back of her brain.

"Sleep well last night?" Bo asked cheerily, riding up beside her.

"Not a wink. You?"

"Like a baby. Nila brought a young captain back to the tent last night, and I'll tell you..." Bo made the shape of a woman with his hands.

"Please don't," Vlora cut him off. "And what the pit do you think you're doing, sleeping with my officers?"

"It's very boring here," Bo said defensively. "Besides, it was Nila's idea. She figures we can, uh, spend time with someone from every regiment in the entire army by the time this stupid thing is over."

"I hate you so much right now." Vlora poured a bit of water from her canteen onto a handkerchief and pressed it to her forehead. She knew about Nila and Bo's proclivity for play, of course—they were Privileged, after all, and had the libidos that went with their sorcerous power—but it served as a reminder that Olem had still not returned. She only now realized that the ache of his absence had become almost physical, joining all of her wounds to a pulsing nest of pain in the back of her head. "Are you and Nila ready to deal with anything they throw at us?"

Bo pursed his lips. "Odd, that."

"What is?"

"We can't find them."

"The enemy Privileged?"

"Right. They've either left, or they're very, very good at hiding."

"You're out of practice. Talk to Norrine and Davd."

"Already did. They can't find any Privileged, either." He spread his hands. "There's a lot of sorcerous noise over there—color left over from the Dynize bombardment of New Adopest—but not enough to hide a bunch of Privileged. There were eight yesterday, and now..."

"Shit," Vlora said under her breath. She searched the horizon, reaching for her sorcery instinctively and clutching at nothing. The one time she *wanted* to do everything herself, and she literally couldn't. She beckoned over a messenger. "Send people to the First, Second, and Fifth. Tell them that we don't know when to expect a sorcerous barrage, and I'm holding our own power back to counter any surprises. They are to proceed with the battle plan."

The messenger bolted, and Vlora gestured to Bo to join his wife at the front before settling back to watch the proceedings. Her left flank marched over the horizon to the north, swinging around the enemy earthworks with heavy cavalry support. Her right clung to the river in a tight column while their cannons rained down a withering cover fire on the Dynize artillery platforms. The center, directly in front of her, ground forward in a line four-deep, bayonets fixed, prepared to ford the river tributary as soon as pressure had been applied to the flanks.

Vlora swept up and down the length of the river tributary with her looking glass, that feeling of uncertainty still wedged in her gut. The Dynize returned fire with their heavy guns, but by the time her men reached the tributary, she had the odd feeling that the return fire was too sporadic, that there wasn't enough movement on those earthworks.

It was with some surprise that she saw her own cavalry sweeping down the length of those earthworks before her center had even reached the other side of the river. The cavalry galloped over a handful of Dynize, swept through multiple artillery platforms, and then rode out of sight beyond the earthworks. Her soldiers crossed the river and followed them without a single scrap of resistance from the enemy line.

Messengers soon came flooding back to her, all of them with the same story: only a token resistance. A few hundred Dynize soldiers threw down their weapons the moment the Adran infantry arrived. There was no sign of General Etepali, her officer corps, her Privileged sorcerers, or the main body of her army.

The Dynize were gone.

Vlora walked through the Dynize camp, the seeds of their deception unfolding before her eyes.

It was clear that most of them had already been gone by the time she met with General Etepali last night. Every third tent had been left standing, and all the campfires stoked just enough to smolder.

It was shockingly clean—the Dynize had taken everything with them but the tents—evidence of an ordered withdrawal rather than a frantic retreat. The withdrawal had forded the river within sight of New Adopest, but around the bend from Vlora and her troops.

Exhaustion tugged at her shoulders, slowed her feet, but Vlora was galvanized by her anger. She strode around the camp in wider and wider circles, ignoring the soldiers who stared at her as she passed, swearing under her breath.

On her third circle, she ran directly into General Sabastenien and his bodyguard. Sabastenien was dismounted, examining the ground at his feet. He shook his head as Vlora approached, said something to one of his bodyguards, and came to meet her. "Ma'am."

"It's the same damn thing."

"Excuse me, ma'am?"

"The same damn thing I did to the Fatrastans and Dynize when they cornered me at Windy River. This was why I couldn't sleep last night. I had an inkling of what was happening, but I just couldn't put the pieces together." Vlora was angry at everything—her officers, her scouts, the enemy, and especially at herself. "Your cavalry. Were they ever able to gain ground south of the river last night?"

Sabastenien pulled a wry face. "They just reported in. They met stern resistance until dark, then pulled back and conducted a night crossing after midnight. When morning came, it was like the enemy had never been there. Except…"

"Except what?"

"Evidence of a mass exodus. Easily thirty thousand men. They must have crossed the river over the last few days and headed west while we were heading east."

"Yeah," Vlora said crossly, "I figured as much." Everything came into focus. The tributary bridges had been left standing to give Vlora an easy ride *on purpose*. Had they been burned, she would have taken a longer time getting to New Adopest—she would have spread out her forces to look for a better route and been more insistent about scouting south of the river and caught wind of their retreat. Those cavalry she saw crossing yesterday afternoon must have been the tail end of their forces. "Why?" she demanded, half to herself. "Why would Etepali slip away when she had such a good defensive position?"

Sabastenien clasped his hands behind his back. "If she only had thirty thousand, and she knew the size of our force and our off-shore fleet, then she was wise not to allow a confrontation here. Slip around us, head back to the mainland. She loses New Adopest, but she puts herself in position to be reinforced by the rest of the Dynize Army."

A messenger approached, starting when he saw the look on Vlora's face.

"What is it?" she snapped.

"Sorry, ma'am. One of the Dynize soldiers. He had a note for you."

Vlora snatched the note from the messenger and broke the seal. It was written in Adran in a gorgeous, flowing hand in crimson ink.

My dear Vlora. It was a pleasure to meet you last night. I'm sorry for the deception, but I felt I was not prepared to face you in open battle at such a disadvantage. I'll save the rest of the whiskey. I do hope we have an opportunity to share it one day, regardless of the outcome of our next meeting. Best, Etepali

Vlora crumpled the letter and dropped it, pinching the bridge of her nose. "Used my own tactic against me and I didn't even see it coming."

She heard horses and looked up to find Bo and Nila approaching at a trot. The two Privileged dismounted, and it was Nila who came to Vlora's side and picked up the letter she'd dropped. She read it silently and handed it to Bo.

"If you laugh, Privileged Borbador, I will shoot you in the face," Vlora said.

Bo turned a chuckle into a cough, then began to hack and spit. "I would never," he said when he recovered.

"This isn't funny."

"It's *kind* of funny."

"No, it's not. I now have the most decorated general in Dynize at my back. She's put herself in a position to block my progress off the Cape and bring in reinforcements. What's more, I missed what should have been an obvious deception."

"We all have bad days," Bo suggested.

"My bad days get people killed."

Sabastenien cleared his throat. "Ma'am, I understand we've received messengers from the city. They're hailing us as liberators and have asked that you come meet with the mayor."

"I don't have time," Vlora said. "Get everyone turned around. I want you to take command of our combined cavalry and head upriver. See if you can get in front of Etepali's army. Harry them. Slow them down."

"We're going after her?"

"Yes. I'm not going to let her get reinforcements, not if I can help it."

"What about the prisoners?"

The words "execute them" floated on the tip of Vlora's tongue. The terrible urge rooted in her belly almost pushed them out, but she managed to choke them off. "Hand them over to the city garrison of New Adopest."

"And the city?"

"Strip their granaries and munitions. Take everything we might need to fight our way to Landfall."

Sabastenien's eyes widened. "We're sacking the city?"

"Not a sack," Vlora replied. "Keep the men in line, but requisition everything. If they disagree, signal the fleet to fire a few salvos at their harbor." This was it—the second lesson she needed to teach both her allies and her enemies: that Fatrastans were not their friends. The Adran Army was not here to liberate. They were here to accomplish a task. "Get to it, General. I want you at the head of our cavalry and after the Dynize within the hour."

CHAPTER 16

Michel didn't like the idea of leaving Greenfire Depths. Through some cruel corruption of the laws of nature and in defiance of common sense, it had become the safest spot for him in Landfall. He climbed out of its stinking, twisted embrace with reluctance and joined the morning traffic heading east across the plateau, wearing thick cotton laborer's trousers, a vest, and a wide-brimmed straw farmer's hat to shade—and hide—his face.

He let the crowd pull him along, nudging his own trajectory every couple of blocks until he'd navigated to Proctor, not far from where his mother had lived before she'd been whisked inland by Taniel's agents. He wondered, not for the first time, where she was and how she was doing. He wondered if she'd forgiven him for all those years of making her think he was a Blackhat stooge.

Michel slipped down the basement stairs of a large tenement near the edge of the plateau, trudging the length of a musty hall until he reached the last door on the left. The lock had, by some miracle, not been smashed, and the door showed no signs of tampering. He let himself in with a key hidden behind a loose brick. The single-room apartment was lit by one rectangular window not much bigger than his head, and the air was thick and full of cobwebs.

It took him just a couple of minutes to move the mattress out of the corner, lift the dusty old rug beneath it, then find the knots in the floorboards that allowed him to pull them up, revealing a hidden cubby that could, in an emergency, fit a person. It currently contained a handful of Taniel's old fake passports, a few thousand krana in cash, and a long map case that he'd stolen from the Yaret Household after the successful search of the Landfall catacombs.

He took some of the cash, ignored the passports, and then spent the next hour examining those old maps of the catacombs. Once he was satisfied, he copied down a bit of one of the maps and then stowed them back in their original spot, leaving the place exactly as he had found it.

He returned to Greenfire Depths and picked up Ichtracia from their shared apartment before heading to Meln-Dun's quarry to meet his fellow hunters.

The crew was in good spirits and, at Michel's orders, headed out into the Depths to spread around bribe money and listen for rumors. Michel pocketed a thick wad of petty cash and Dynize rations cards from Dahre. He led Ichtracia out into the street, down along the river, and then into one of the tenements that the two of them were meant to be searching. He waited inside for several minutes, watching the street behind them through a crack in the tenement wall.

"What are we doing?" Ichtracia asked.

"We're making sure no one is following us."

"You think they would?"

"I don't," Michel said reassuringly, "but better safe than sorry. Okay, I think we're fine. Follow me." They went up two levels and then left the tenement for the spiderweb of the Depths. Even with a working—if dated—map of the quarry in his head, Michel got them lost three times before he found their destination: a tall building, almost entirely still in one piece, near the very center of the Depths.

"We're here," Michel announced.

"What is *here*?" Ichtracia asked skeptically.

Michel rapped on the door. A peephole opened and a pair of eyes stared out at them. "Do you have an appointment?"

"I don't," Michel said, "but I do have this." He counted off exactly eighty-three krana in Adran bills and held it up to the peephole. It was snatched quickly and the hole closed. "This," he told Ichtracia quietly, "is the home of the most successful Palo arms dealer in Fatrasta. Don't say anything. Just look menacing." He held up one finger to qualify that statement. "But not too menacing."

The door opened suddenly, and they were greeted by the smiling face of a Gurlish hunchback. The man bobbed his head twice. "Up the stairs," he instructed, pointing them toward a narrow staircase. "All the way to the top."

Michel frowned at the narrow lift beside the stairs. A sign on the lift door said, OUT OF ORDER. He shrugged and nodded to Ichtracia. They began their climb.

They were on the sixth floor when he heard the very distinctive hum of a steam-powered engine somewhere in the bowels of the building. They reached the eighth floor at almost the exact same moment as the lift. The hunchback doorman stepped out, gave them a cheeky smile and a bow, and opened the door for them. Michel paused to catch his breath, nodded, and stepped out into the sun.

The roof was a narrow bit of gently sloped shingling that rose higher than almost all the other buildings in the Depths—almost to the rim of Upper Landfall. A man lay out nude on a blanket, his face covered with a washcloth and the rest of him bared to the sun. His freckles were thick and dark, his skin as wrinkly as a prune. He might have been a hard-living forty-year-old or an exceptionally fit octogenarian. Michel did not know, nor did anyone else who worked with him. Their host raised the washcloth as they stepped onto his roof, then lowered it back over his eyes.

"Afternoon," Michel said. "You're Halifin?" He'd met Halifin on three different occasions, of course. But Halifin didn't need to know that.

"Have we met before?" the supine figure asked.

"We haven't," Michel said. He didn't bother introducing Ichtracia to the arms dealer or the arms dealer to Ichtracia. This was a business where names didn't matter. "I need to put in an order."

"If we've never met, how did you know where to find me?" Halifin muttered from beneath his washcloth.

Michel tensed involuntarily, stealing a glance over his shoulder at the hunchback. The fool still had that big grin on his face, but a pistol had appeared in his hand. He didn't point it at anything; rather, just let it hang loosely there. Ichtracia's eyes tightened, and Michel gave her a slight shake of his head. "I was recommended," he offered.

"Of course you were," Halifin said. "All my new friends are recommended." The hunchback's pistol disappeared as quickly as if it were a magic trick. "What can I do for you?" Halifin asked. Never once did he touch the washcloth over his face, or attempt to cover his nudity.

Michel produced the map he'd copied of a little corner of the Landfall catacombs from his pocket, then wrapped it in a wad of Adran krana. He handed it to the hunchback. "I need twelve crates of Hrusch rifles delivered to this spot by tomorrow night."

"You're sure I don't know you?" The voice was almost playful.

"I'm sure," Michel replied flatly. "Do I have an order?"

Halifin sniffed. "Hrusch rifles are in steep demand. The Dynize are buying them up like kids in a candy store. Trying to update their arms."

Michel reached into his pocket and produced another thousand krana in a tight, folded clip. He handed it to the hunchback. "Does that cover it?"

No apparent signal passed between the hunchback and Halifin, but the latter yawned loudly. "Yes, I do believe so." He waved his hand, and the hunchback gave him both the money and the map. Halifin lifted the corner of his washcloth with one hand, unfolded the map with the other. "Behind Meln-Dun's quarry? Are you working for that old hawk?"

Michel gave him a shallow smile. "Is the delivery location a problem?"

"No, it shouldn't be. Nobody likes going into the catacombs since the Dynize cleaned them out last month. It'll be a good spot to stash the guns."

"Wonderful." Michel tipped his hat and wished Halifin a good afternoon. He refused a ride on the lift from the hunchback and waited until they were back down in the street—or what passed for a street in this neighborhood—before letting out a relieved sigh. He loosened his collar a little and wiped a bit of sweat from his brow.

"Did we just buy guns from a naked man?" Ichtracia asked, staring back toward the door.

"We did," Michel confirmed, taking a mental inventory of how much money he still had left in his pocket.

"Why are we buying guns for Meln-Dun?" Ichtracia asked.

"Think about it," Michel answered, his own thoughts already moving on to the next several steps of his plan.

"This is how you're going to make him a martyr?"

"One part of it, yes."

"Are you going to explain that?"

"No." He saw her annoyed expression and spread his hands. "Compartmentalization. If you're captured, I don't need to worry about other parts of my plan coming apart."

"If I'm captured, you'd be smart not to stick around for more than a few seconds," Ichtracia pointed out.

"You're probably right. But I haven't survived this long without a little caution." He shook his head. "Look, this may sound silly, but I do best not thinking too hard about my own plans."

"You're worried about someone overhearing your thoughts?"

"I keep myself"—he tapped his chest—"the real me, buried deep. When I worked for the Blackhats, I refused to even think Taniel's name. It's not about hiding my thoughts. It's about being as much of the person others expect me to be as possible. There's less room for screwups. We're already working a hundred times faster than I would have preferred, with you learning to govern your accent on the fly." He shook his head. "We better get back to our posts. Pretend we've gotten some work done."

They returned to their canvassing area. Michel put Ichtracia just behind him so she could watch how he worked, and fixed a gentle smile on his face. Starting at one end of the street, he began to move down it at a leisurely pace. He slapped men on the shoulders as if they were old friends, gently touched women on the elbow, meeting everyone's eyes with a pleasant smile and a quiet word. "Hey there, I'm looking for someone," he'd say, slipping a two-krana note into a hand. "Someone who goes by 'Mama Palo.' Any idea where I can find her?"

"No," came the answer. "I heard she was dead," or "Not gonna find her anymore, she went up north." Occasionally someone would turn away, or leave quickly after Michel passed. He'd note their face but keep moving.

Hours went by and Ichtracia had just begun to work the other side of the street on her own when Michel spotted a familiar face jumping through the crowd, waving at him. It was Couhila. The old man's face was alight with a grin. "We found her!" he babbled before he'd even reached Michel. "Dahre has called a meeting. We have to head back!"

Michel forced a surprised smile onto his face and subtly waved off Ichtracia's alarmed expression. "Shit, shit, shit, shit," he muttered under his breath. Already? What kind of horribly rotten luck was this? His heart started thumping as worries shuffled through his head. What if they'd captured her already? Pit, what if they'd *killed* her? He widened his grin as Couhila got close. "That's fantastic," he forced himself to say, gesturing for Ichtracia to join them. "Let's get back quickly!"

They followed Couhila back to Meln-Dun's quarry and up to Dahre's office, where the rest of the group had already gathered. There was a nervous energy in the room, and Dahre had the sort of well-earned smirk that Michel himself might have been wearing in the same situation. For a few moments he forgot where he was— for a few moments these were the good guys, his allies, celebrating an imminent victory. Michel held on to the feeling, accepting the comradeship, holding his gnawing fear at bay.

"All right, all right," Dahre said, motioning for them to quiet down. "We haven't *caught* her yet."

Michel suppressed a sigh of relief.

Dahre continued, "But the canvassing has turned up the best lead we've had so far." He crossed the room to pluck one of the sketches off the wall of Mama Palo's known associates and waved it in the air. "This man, Kelinar, is a minor lieutenant of Mama Palo's. Devin-Mezi found him today during her search. She was able to talk him down, feed him some cash, and offer him a fat reward for information. He took the bait."

Devin-Mezi looked smug enough that you'd think she'd captured Mama Palo already. Michel did his best not to roll his eyes, and focused on the sketch. The name Kelinar was vaguely familiar in a distant way, as was the face. Perhaps they'd crossed paths briefly at some point, or maybe he'd spotted the face on a list of criminals wanted by the Blackhats. As far as Michel knew, he wasn't someone very high up in Mama Palo's organization—but that might have changed, or he might just be in the right position to offer up his employer.

"What does he know?" Michel asked.

"He knows where Mama Palo is, how many guards she has, and even the room she's sleeping in." Dahre grinned. "He says she's about to change safe houses and that he can deliver us the location of the next one. If he does...we've as good as got her."

"Good, good," Michel said out loud. Inwardly he continued to swear. Beside him, Ichtracia wasn't nearly as good at hiding her true feelings. She was forcing a smile but looked vaguely alarmed. He hoped no one noticed. He was working through options with that desperation that he'd only recently warned Ichtracia was a bad way to operate as a spy. He might have to find this turncoat and silence him, or dig out Mama Palo himself to warn her.

None of this was how things were supposed to go down.

"Do we have him in custody?" Michel asked.

Dahre shook his head. "We had to cut him loose or his friends would get suspicious. He's going to report back tonight. At least, if he wants his money, he will."

"Did he say where they are?"

"Not until he gets paid."

Michel forced himself to breathe evenly. The turncoat might get cold feet and never come back. Or pit, he might be conning Dahre. He hoped it was one of these options. He wasn't ready to move against Meln-Dun yet, and he certainly couldn't afford to lose Mama Palo and her resources before he'd even made contact with her.

"How long until we move against her?"

"Our new friend said she's going to move tonight and settle into her new safe house tomorrow. We give her a little bit of time to get complacent. Three days, I think."

Michel tried to think of a good argument to delay their actions further, but came up with nothing. He nodded lamely. "When he comes back, we'll want to give him a good interrogation. Nothing violent, mind, but put the screws to him. Make sure we're getting exactly what we paid for."

"Good call," Dahre agreed. "Couhila, can you deal with that?"

"Of course," the old man said.

Michel almost swore out loud. He'd meant for *him* to do the interrogation. *Alone.* Pit and damnation. Nothing to do now but go along with things—and move his own time line forward. He let the others talk, half listening as everyone suggested interrogation tactics, questions for the turncoat, and how best to surround and isolate Mama Palo's position. At the first chance he got, he took Ichtracia off to one side.

"What the pit are we going to do?" she hissed. "If they kill her…"

"We'll deal with that if we have to. In the meantime, I've got work to do. Don't expect me back tonight."

"Where are you going?"

"To Upper Landfall." He didn't offer any more information—if he told her the details she would *definitely* not let him go.

CHAPTER 17

The day after General Etepali's deception, Vlora had turned her entire army around, crossed to the south side of the New Ad, and was marching double-time in pursuit of the slippery Dynize Army. She could feel an energy about her soldiers—a feeling of being cheated out of a battle, an eagerness to match bayonets with the Dynize that she herself shared. Rumors swirled that the Dynize were afraid of Vlora, and that seemed to put the soldiers in good spirits. From the gossip she heard through Bo's informants in her own army, they considered Landfall—and the godstone— already won.

She knew that the morale of a marching army was a fickle thing, but she also knew better than to squander it while it lasted.

Her own mind dragged, and her body was full of aches and pains that she couldn't get rid of. She'd learned very quickly that despite her powder blindness, liquor still had very little effect on her senses—it took several bottles of wine to feel even slightly woozy. A small part of her held out hope that this was a sign that the condition was not permanent. A much larger part of her spat with fury that there was nothing to take the edge off her anguish.

She hid all of it behind a carefully constructed mask that allowed her to face her soldiers without tears in her eyes. She turned that mask on Borbador when he approached her late in the afternoon while she watched her men. After two hard days of quick marching they were beginning to flag.

"How are you holding up?" he asked, letting his horse fall in beside hers.

"Alive," she responded.

"Well, that's a relief." He didn't press the question. "Odd thing to ask, but are you getting proper reports from your officers?"

Vlora shook off her ennui and gave him a sharp glance. "Why?"

He shrugged. "Just curious. Everyone seems to be stepping pretty softly around you."

"I don't know," she said with frustration. "Olem usually acts as a liaison between me and . . . well, most everyone else."

"He's not here."

"Yes, I know." She didn't hold back the anger she felt at the statement. Olem *should* be here. He was her second-in-command. Her friend and lover. She *needed* him. "Any other bits of wisdom you care to share with me?"

The venom in her voice washed off Bo like water over a turtle's shell. "Not wisdom," he replied. "Just information. You heard the New Adopest mayor has been dogging us since last night?"

"We're thirty miles from New Adopest."

"Exactly. He's been chasing us, trying to get an audience with you."

"Nobody told me."

"Would it matter?"

"How?"

"Would you see him?"

Vlora waved off the question. "No."

"Sure. But you probably should know that sort of thing anyway."

Bo chewed on his lip. "Look, I'm not going to fill in as a liaison for you and everyone else like Olem, but I am going to make sure you get a full report of important things."

"How is the New Adopest mayor important?"

"He's the mayor of a major city that your fleet is in the process of sacking."

"I'm not sacking it. I'm requisitioning from it."

"Against their will."

"That's how requisitioning often works."

Bo rolled his eyes. "It's near enough the same thing in their eyes, and don't pretend like you don't know it. They were on the edge of capitulating when we arrived. Few stores, ammunition and medical supplies low. We're taking what little they have left."

Vlora wrestled with the idea, trying to summon that persistent fury to quash all sympathy. Was she doing the right thing? Winters in Fatrasta were practically balmy compared to Adro, but they were on the cusp of it, which meant a long time until another harvest. Was she leaving those people to starve if the war didn't break? She hardened her heart, staving off the questions swirling in her mind. She was trying to save the world from another god. Sacrifices must be made.

"Since when did your heart start bleeding?" she shot at Bo.

"This isn't bleeding-heart shit," Bo retorted. "This is commanding-officer shit. You need to know these things and consider them with every decision. I'm pretty sure we both learned that from the same person."

Vlora's hand went protectively to her saddlebags, where Tamas's journal was close at hand. "Don't do that," she said quietly.

Bo glared hard for a few moments before relenting. "Sorry."

They rode in silence for some time before Vlora ran a hand through her sweaty hair and called to a messenger. "Word for the fleet," she told the boy. "Tell them to go light on the requisitioning. Leave the city grain—but take all the munitions we can get our hands on."

The boy snapped a salute and was off.

She glanced at Bo, who was studying his saddle horn. He'd said his piece. She'd relented a little. Life would go on. "Davd," she called over her shoulder.

The powder mage left his casual guardsman's position a few dozen paces behind them and rode up to join them. "Yes, ma'am?"

"Have we heard from Olem?"

Davd went pale. "No, ma'am."

Vlora scowled at the reaction. "What do you mean, 'no'?"

Davd looked to Bo, but Bo himself seemed surprised by the answer. "I mean we haven't heard from Colonel Olem, ma'am."

"We've been in steady contact with the fleet ever since we got onto the Cape. He accompanied the godstone capstone and our wounded weeks ago. But we haven't heard from him?"

Davd was visibly sweating now. It made no sense. Had something happened to Olem? Were they *hiding* it from her? The whole thought was inconceivable. "Davd," she said sharply. "What's going on?"

"Nothing, ma'am. We just haven't heard from him."

Bo nudged his horse back, then around to the other side of Davd. "Probably best if you just come out and say whatever it is you have to say," he said gently.

Davd looked over his shoulder, swallowed, and finally met Vlora's eyes. He was no coward—she knew that from all the fighting they'd gone through together—but he was still young and he'd always gotten nervous before her moods. He cleared his throat. "Olem dropped the capstone off to our fleet several weeks ago," he said.

"And?"

"And the wounded."

Vlora was getting impatient. "And where is he?" she hissed.

"No one knows." Davd looked away again. "He left his uniforms with his travel chest on one of the ships, took a horse, and disappeared. The last time anyone saw him, he was riding west. They thought he was coming back to join us. We scoured the countryside for him—no sign of him or his horse."

Vlora couldn't comprehend what Davd was saying. "He left?" she asked dully.

"Yes, ma'am."

"Did he say anything? Tell anyone where he was going?"

"No, ma'am."

Vlora could see on both Bo's and Davd's faces that there was more to the story—Davd because he knew it, and Bo because he'd figured it out. She wanted to lean across and shake answers out of them both, but there was a sudden fear in the pit of her stomach. Did she *want* those answers? This sounded like Olem had abandoned his commission. He would never. She refused to believe it.

"What happened to Olem?" she asked Davd, trying—and failing—to keep her voice steady.

Davd looked like he wanted to be swallowed up by the earth.

"Does everyone else know?" Vlora demanded. "Is this some joke among the army? Some secret to keep from the general?"

"No, ma'am."

"Then, what is it?"

"I can't know for sure, ma'am."

"Guess."

Davd looked around one more time before he took a deep breath and swallowed hard. "The colonel was furious after the Crease, ma'am. I've never seen him so angry. He broke an infantryman's arm, knocked the teeth out of another. It took eight men to restrain him when he found out that you were back there holding the Crease on your own."

The sensation in Vlora's stomach grew more defined. Her heart hammered in her chest.

"The only thing that brought him back to his senses was the arrival of the Adran Army. Bo and Nila swore to him that they'd do everything in their power to save you, but I think the damage had been done by then. He wouldn't even go with them to help. He just fell into a silent fury. It was scarier than when he was breaking arms. He stuck around just long enough to find out that you'd pull through. Then he took the wounded and the capstone to the fleet."

Vlora ran through a thousand rationales in her head, trying to stave off the rising panic. "Damage?" she echoed, her own voice sounding ghostly. "What damage was done?"

"You betrayed him, ma'am." Davd met her eyes this time. He was dead serious.

The only thing Vlora had to curb her panic was fury. She let it loose, let it catch her under the arms and lift her into the air. "Leave," she whispered.

"You had him attacked and trundled off like a sack of potatoes," Davd went on, his voice getting stronger. "You're the woman he loves and you wouldn't even let him die by your side. It was too much for him. He snapped."

"You should go now," Vlora said louder.

"I don't think he's coming back," Davd said.

"Get out of my sight!" The words tore themselves from Vlora's throat, and she found herself standing in her stirrups, sword half-drawn. Davd kneed his horse and leapt forward, tearing off to join the column. She barely noticed him going, staring at the pommel of her sword. She jerked unnecessarily hard on the reins, brought her horse to a stop, and turned away from Bo and the column and anyone else who might be able to see her face.

Olem was gone. How could any of this be worth it anymore?

CHAPTER 18

Michel returned to the forlorn safe house in the basement of the tenement in Proctor. It was a brief visit—just long enough to find the passport given to him by the Yaret Household during his time in their service. While it did identify him as a member of the Yaret Household, it didn't give his name. It *should* be just enough to get him out of a tight situation if necessary.

He returned to his apartment in Greenfire Depths and fell asleep early beside Ichtracia, where he dreamed of betrayal, prisons, and torture. When he awoke in a cold sweat, his pocket watch told him that it was almost two in the morning. He dressed silently, careful not to wake Ichtracia, and headed out into the Depths on his own.

The Depths at night hadn't changed one bit—it was still a dangerous place, even for Palo, and he kept his ears tuned for following footsteps and his eyes darting for movement in dark alleyways. The important thing was that he was more worried about thieves than he was about Dynize agents. It wasn't until he reached Upper Landfall that his nerves began to fray. The streets here were all but empty, trafficked by Dynize patrols and couriers on official business. The curfew had grown more severe since his last night. He was stopped three times on his trip across the plateau, and with each one he was able to present the passport and move on without question.

The capital building was dark, guarded by a small number of bored-looking sentries in their colorful uniforms and steel breastplates. He waited and watched, making sure that someone—anyone—still used the big building this late at night so that his presence wouldn't be out of place. Once he'd seen a handful of tired clerks and slumping messengers come and go, he allowed himself to approach.

The Yaret Household passport worked without a second glance from the sentries. Michel was soon inside, walking quickly down the marble halls, his footsteps echoing softly. A few gas lamps splashed long streaks of flickering light, deepening the shadows and giving the Dynize flags, Household regalia, and military colors a sinister feel.

He passed only the occasional person as he navigated the long halls—the same late-night sorts he'd seen outside, in addition to a handful of maids, janitors, and guards carrying out their nightly routines. None of them gave him a second glance, and he was soon heading down the stairs into the bowels of the building.

These stairs did not hold good memories for him—the last time he'd descended this way, he was following a woman who he *thought* was a member of Yaret's Household. She'd beaten him severely before Yaret had managed to find him. Michel had taken his revenge, but he could still feel the strike of her blackjack against the base of his neck.

He descended three flights of stairs. There were no windows to show the moonlight down here, and the few lit lamps were tokens to guide lost clerks rather than any real effort to conquer the darkness. He was glad for the echoing loneliness of it, and took extra care to muffle his steps. The last thing he needed was some helpful guard discovering him this far beneath the more trafficked areas of the building.

He found a series of rooms by virtue of his memories of their description—another benefit of his time with the Yaret Household. Under the Lindet regime, these had been filing rooms, a place to put intelligence and information until the professionals could sort out their importance. The Dynize had seen no need to change their original function. Yaret's people had brought thousands of cases of files down here, all of them recovered from various corners of Landfall, most from Blackhat archives and safe houses. The files had been considered important enough to keep, but not important enough to work through with any urgency.

Each door was marked with big block numbering and a small placard that listed the location from which the contents had been scrounged. Some of the rooms held files from several dozen locations, while others contained information from just one or two places. He tapped each placard gently as he found it, whispering the names to himself until he reached one that simply said, MIL-LINERY. FIRST FLOOR.

The old Blackhat headquarters at the millinery had been an important source of information for the Dynize, but most of the good stuff had come from the third floor. The first floor had contained little more than public and lightly classified records.

He opened the door, slipping inside and locating the gas lamps by the tiny glow of their pilot lights. He turned them up, one by one, until the entire room was well lit, revealing hundreds of filing cabinets. A quick search showed that half of them had been marked by some efficient Dynize clerk. The other half were a jumbled, unsorted mess. He prayed that what he needed was in that first half.

Michel bent to his work, muttering to himself as he went. Despite Lindet's hasty exit and the Dynize reorganization, he was fairly confident that the files he needed were here. All he had to do was figure out which cabinet they'd been stuffed in.

He worked methodically, starting with the labeled boxes and perusing papers for names, dates, and anything that might help him narrow down his search. There was method to the madness of both the original Blackhat clerks and the Dynize. It took him over an hour to confidently surmise how those two systems had been shuffled. It was another hour and a half before he'd found the right corner of the room, and then one more after that when he finally put his hands on a file labeled *Lady Flint Landfall Operation*.

He checked it thoroughly, making sure he had the right thing, then pulled out his pocket watch. Almost six in the morning. Well past time to leave if he wanted to be gone before the morning rush. He rounded the room, careful to remove any evidence that anyone had been here during the night.

He was just about to head to the door when he heard whistling, accompanied by the low, unsteady sound of someone walking with a limp. Michel swore under his breath, rushing around the room, turning off the lamps. He'd just dimmed the last one and ducked behind a row of boxes when the whistling stopped outside the door. Several moments passed. Michel held his breath, waiting, until the door finally opened to cast a light across the now-dark room.

Someone entered and crossed to the opposite side of the room in the darkness. Michel took the opportunity to slip out of his hiding spot and pad toward the door. He was almost there when a lamp flared to life behind him and a firm voice called out in Dynize, "You there! Stop!"

Michel froze, considering his options. His back was still to the stranger. He could make a run for it and risk that the guards wouldn't hear any yelling this deep in the building. Or he could try to talk his way out of things. He wondered if his passport would be enough to silence any questions. It depended entirely on the person behind him—whether they were a low-level clerk or someone more important.

At this hour? They were likely a low-level clerk here for a mundane job. Michel fixed his best *Why are you bothering me?* expression and turned to face the stranger.

His expression disappeared in an instant, and Michel had to struggle to hide the shock that replaced it. The man behind him was bald, lean, and short. He wore a cotton suit in the Fatrastan style, but he was most definitely a Dynize. He frowned at Michel for a moment, clearly confused. It took several seconds for a flicker of recognition to pass behind his eyes and his mouth to fall open.

"Michel?"

Michel swallowed hard. "Tenik." The two stared at each other from across the room. Michel considered making a run for it. Tenik clearly couldn't keep up—his left leg was dragging badly and his left arm was in a sling. But how close were the capital-building guards? Would they be able to hear his shouts before Michel had slipped safely into the streets? "Not exactly a place I expected to find you."

"Nor I, you." Tenik's expression hardened. "What are you doing here?"

Michel didn't answer. Tenik probably didn't expect one. He let his eyes travel across Tenik's left side. The last time he saw Yaret's cupbearer was right before an explosion had separated them in the catacombs almost two months ago. "Your arm...," he said lamely.

"The explosion," Tenik explained. "I'm unable to move like I once could, so Yaret has made me an archivist. My job is to oversee all of this." His eyes wandered briefly across the lines of cabinets. "We're sorting through it. Trying to find anything of use."

Michel gripped the files in his hand. "Best of luck with that. There's a lot to go through."

"I see *you've* been making use of it." Tenik's eyes flashed to those files. "Yaret figured you might come back at some point."

"Here?" Michel asked in surprise.

"Not necessarily. But to the city. He said that you're too attached to Landfall. That your expertise is here, and you'll want to use it."

Michel frowned.

"We found your file," Tenik said

"Ah." Michel's Blackhat file. He'd never actually seen it himself, but he could guess what was in it—highly classified information about his undercover operations. A handful of commendations that no one but him and two or three Blackhat Gold Roses had ever actually known about. He wondered if his file had information about those last few weeks before the Dynize invasion, or if his tasks for Fidelis Jes had been lost in the chaos. He hoped the latter. The less anyone knew about him and his actions, the better.

"We knew you were a spy," Tenik said, "but it was interesting to see what you'd done for the Blackhats. Your transition from spy to bureaucrat. But you never stopped being a spy, did you?"

Again, Michel didn't answer.

The surprise left Tenik's voice, replaced with a firm note of disappointment. "The last time any of us saw you was at the catacombs. Yaret sent you home for a job well done, and then..." Tenik gestured mysteriously. "The next thing we knew, Ka-Sedial's people were crawling all over us. Sedial himself was screaming about how he had proof that you were still working for the enemy, and Yaret could not protect you."

"Sedial ambushed me at Ichtracia's. Tortured me."

"Sounds like he was right to do so," Tenik snorted. "How the pit did you escape?"

Michel scowled. If Tenik didn't know about Ichtracia's involvement, Michel wasn't about to tell him.

"So, did you leave Landfall?" Tenik asked after a moment of silence. "My bet was that you never left—that you'd slipped off to hide someplace that we wouldn't think to look."

"I did leave. For a while."

"But you're back."

The tension grew thicker. Michel resisted the urge to look toward the door so as not to betray his next move. He needed to run, but his feet felt glued in place. "Yes."

There was more to the injuries in Tenik's body language. He seemed tired, his face haggard and his shoulders slumped in defeat. He looked at Michel, then at the door, then limped over to a chair in the corner and sank down into it with a grateful sigh. "Ka-Sedial has made you an enemy of the state. Claims that you're still working for the Blackhats."

"He knows I'm not," Michel replied before he could stop himself.

"So do we," Tenik said. "Problem is, none of us at the Household have been able to figure out who you *are* working for. You're not a Blackhat. You helped us hunt down and kill and turn too many of them." He leaned forward. "Who the pit *are* you working for? There's no one else."

Michel gave Tenik a tight smile. He was acutely aware that every word he spoke here could be used against him. But he was also tired—tired of the masquerades and the lying. Yaret had taken him in. Tenik had been Michel's partner. He woke up in the middle of the night sometimes thinking of ways to help Yaret against his enemies in Landfall, only to remember that he now *was* one of those enemies. "I *was* working for you."

Tenik's tired face twisted. "No, you weren't." There was venom in his voice. "You were *using* us. We still don't know to what end—something to do with Sedial, or so we've gathered. His granddaughter has disappeared, but we haven't been able to discover anything else. What was it, Michel? Yaret adopted you. I considered you a friend. What are your true colors?"

The real hurt in Tenik's voice twisted something in Michel's gut. He had to use every bit of self-control not to spill out every secret, not to attempt to explain himself at any cost. "What am I?" he asked.

"A spy. A traitor."

"No. What *am* I?" Michel was angry now. Tenik's dismissive words about there not being anyone else to work for had touched something inside of him. "Who are the people that everyone uses but no one thinks about? Who are the rightful heirs to Fatrasta? Who has been kicked and beaten and enslaved since the Kressians first set foot on our shores?" He heard his own voice echoing and had to rein in his anger.

Tenik gave a sudden, quiet gasp. "The Palo?"

Michel clenched his teeth. He'd said too much. Betrayed himself. He kicked himself that he hadn't turned to run yet.

"By our dead god," Tenik breathed. "You're a Palo freedom fighter. That explains so much." Tenik's expression softened. He suddenly laughed.

The sound made Michel bristle. "What's so funny?"

"We're on the same side!" Tenik said excitedly. "Don't you see? We're *freeing* the Palo. We're bringing them back into the fold. Treating them better than they've ever been treated. You're our cousins. Our kin."

"The Palo don't belong to you," Michel said flatly.

That flare of excitement disappeared from Tenik's face, replaced by confusion. "You don't think fealty to the emperor is a price worth paying for a better life?"

"Not under threat of the sword," Michel said. He held up one hand. "I'll give you this—you do seem to be treating the Palo better. The whole idea gives me an ounce of peace and hope for the future. But there's something rotten in the guts of your empire. Why do you think I continue to fight? Sedial is at the heart of it. He knows that I know, that's why he hates me." It wasn't strictly true. But it was close enough.

Tenik regarded Michel warily. "You are not what we thought."

"I've worked hard to make that the case." Michel paused. Despite all of this, it still hurt him to see Tenik in such a condition. "Will they allow you a Privileged healer?"

"I'm on a waiting list," Tenik said, looking away. A thousand little ticks crossed his face, too quickly for Michel to read with any depth. When he finally looked back at Michel, he was a mask of fury. "Leave."

Michel flinched at the word. It was so angry. So final. He gave Tenik a curious glance.

Tenik went on. "For better or for worse, you were my brother for the space of a summer. I will not call for the guards and drag you before the Great Ka. I'm going to tell Yaret that I saw you, and he's going to decide whether or not to report that to Ka-Sedial." Tenik leaned forward. "I'm going to let you take whatever you have in your hand and leave. You used us, but you used us well, and Yaret was able to further the Household due to your actions. For that, I'll let you go."

Michel opened his mouth, but Tenik lifted a finger. "Once!" he continued. "Just this once. The Yaret Household has disavowed you. Struck you from our records. You are an enemy of the state. If I see you again, I will not hesitate to call for a guard if I cannot kill or capture you myself. I suggest you leave the city. Don't make me follow through on this threat."

Tenik's gaze fell to the floor.

"I *am* sorry," Michel said.

There was no response. Michel slowly backed out, waiting for that fateful shout. He reached the hall and let himself take a few quick breaths, then hurried out of the archives and up toward the first floor. He kept his eyes on the ground, walking quickly, hoping not to be recognized by any of the early-morning staff that had just begun to arrive.

He was able to reach Greenfire Depths without incident. He wanted nothing more than to head back to the safe house and crawl into bed next to Ichtracia, to try and catch up on some of the sleep that he'd missed. But the meeting with Tenik had rattled him and he doubted that sleep would come. He navigated the early-morning traffic and headed to the one post office in Greenfire Depths.

The Dynize had kept the postal system open, oddly enough. Letters and packages wouldn't leave Landfall, of course, but they would be moved around within the city without being molested. He'd heard that the Dynize themselves had begun to use the post for official, but unimportant, communication—just another way they had co-opted the previously created systems within Fatrasta.

Michel flipped through the file once more, sitting on a stoop outside the post office. He read it carefully, blacking out the three times his name was mentioned and making sure there was nothing else that could lead back to him. Once he'd finished, he wrapped the file in paper and slid it into an envelope.

He smiled politely at the woman at the counter and handed the package to her. "Hello. I'd like this delivered to the Yaret Household tomorrow morning. Eight o'clock. No earlier. No later." He slid her a hundred-krana note. "This is very important."

CHAPTER 19

Styke rode alongside Ka-poel while he kept a wary eye on the dragonman at the head of the small column. Orz had not spoken to any of them for two days. It was a sharp contrast to his talkative self after the landing, and it left a worried knot in Styke's stomach. He tried to ignore it. There wasn't much else he could do.

"You didn't know your sister's name?" he asked Ka-poel.

Ka-poel started out of her own thoughts. She gestured for him to repeat the question, then leaned across the gap between her and Celine to tap the girl on the knee. Celine dutifully translated what she said next.

No. I had a vague memory of a girl and a name I associated with her. Mara. Ka-poel paused for a moment, some unreadable emotion flickering across her face. *I've actually spoken to her. No. "Spoken" is the wrong word.* She tapped the side of her head. *I've communed with her.*

"Is that another thing a bone-eye can do? Like when Ka-Sedial spoke through that poor bastard at Starlight?"

It's different from that. More direct. I discovered the ability a year or two ago when Ka-Sedial first tried to reach into my mind. I used it to find Mara, and to gain knowledge of the upcoming invasion.

"You *knew* about the invasion?" Styke asked. "Did you bother telling anyone?"

Who would have believed me? Lindet? No. Taniel and I began making our own preparations. But this communication. It is not perfect. It requires a blood link and a strong willingness, and even with those things it is less like speaking and more like—she made several gestures that Celine just shook her head at, then continued—*It's more like two mute children drawing pictures to each other.* She smiled briefly at something. *Taniel and I sent a man to find Mara. From what Taniel has told me through our own link, our man found her and brought her out of Landfall. I can only imagine what frustration he felt when he found out her name wasn't actually Mara. But he succeeded. I hope my sister is safe. I hope I live through the coming months so that I may meet her.*

It was the first time Ka-poel had acknowledged that their mission had a chance of failing, and it caught Styke off guard. "You're awfully introspective today."

Ka-poel frowned at him. *I am learning who I am. Where I came from. I saw into the heart of my grandfather and saw his lust for power. It was an ugly thing, but worse—because I saw the same in my own heart when I took control of that group of dragoons in the Hock. Do you know what it is like to learn who you are? What you are?*

"Yes," Styke said, sucking in a deep breath. He thought of the men he'd killed in his search for vengeance, and the men he'd spared. "Yeah, I think I might know what that's like."

Then, you know how awful it can be.

Ka-poel's hands ceased flashing and she fell into a brooding stillness. Styke watched her for a few moments, then lifted his head to look along the column. The men had taken to their roles well and without complaint, though they still cast suspicious glances at Orz whenever the dragonman wasn't looking. They remained silent when there was company on the road, didn't sing or laugh into the night, and listened to the dragonman's lectures. They were all old Lancers, though, and he would have expected nothing less. They'd endured harder times during the Revolution, though perhaps the stakes were higher now.

They emerged from the swamp about midday, leaving the main highway and cutting west into some hilly terrain that took them up and around the back of a small mountain. The road was lined with houses here, creating an almost suburban feel. After a couple hours of climbing, Styke finally urged his horse up next to Orz, giving the dragonman a sidelong glance before speaking.

"Have we turned to go around the city?"

Orz shook his head. "Going around would take too long."

"Then, where are we headed?"

"A western district. But I've taken a short detour."

Styke felt himself tense. "Why?"

"To show you something."

"Which is?"

"Soon," Orz responded cryptically, pointing up the trail. Styke fell back to the rear of the column again and kept his hand on the butt of his carbine, watching the road carefully. If Orz was going to spring a trap, he would have done it already. Wouldn't he? He tried to shake off the distrust, but signaled silently to Jackal to keep eyes open. The signal was passed up the column behind Orz's back.

They soon rounded a bend and climbed a crest in the road. Styke was so busy watching their flanks that he only heard the first gasps. His head jerked forward and he urged Amrec on quickly, only to come over the crest himself and pull hard on the reins.

An immense valley spread out before them, cradled in low mountains on the western side and spilling out into the Jagged Fens on the east. It was at least five miles wide and ten miles long, at a guess, and it was filled by a lake that stretched for most of the length and breadth of it, though the geography was clearly not what had elicited gasps from the Mad Lancers.

A city had been built upon the very waters of the lake—an immense metropolis constructed along causeways of raised dirt and stone, crisscrossed by canals as thin as alleys and as wide as thoroughfares. Both roads and canals were lined with stone villas, cornered by marketplaces, pierced by the sharp angles of archaic city walls and huge temples that rose half a dozen stories above all the other buildings.

"Talunlica," Orz announced, gesturing expansively with one hand at the entirety of the valley.

Styke rode several paces out ahead of the other Lancers, until Amrec's hooves were at the edge of a cliff, and leaned forward to stare at the city. It was infinitely complex at a glance, divided into sectors that themselves were divided. He'd seen planned cities before—some of the more purposefully founded towns on the Fatrastan frontier—but none of them gave even the slightest inkling of what lay before him now. Even to his untrained eye, the entirety of the place had been laid out with purpose, every stone planned, every road with a destination.

It was a city that had been created not just to live in but to be *seen*.

"It's beautiful, isn't it?" Orz spoke with a smugness that seemed unfitting to his character.

"It is." Styke was genuinely impressed, and he immediately saw why Orz had chosen to make this detour. If they had ridden directly into the city, it would have been a hard thing to explain, a hard thing to grasp. Even now, staring at it from above, he felt like there were patterns to the design that his eye couldn't see, like the finest of Gurlish rugs in a rich man's house.

His eyes traveled to the center of the city, to the one large island from which the rest of the man-made avenues and canals seemed to radiate. The island was walled off with immense stone facades, each sharp angle punctuated by squat turrets that looked big enough to hold entire gun batteries. He felt his vision pulled beyond those walls, to a great black monolith that sprouted from the center of the island. At this distance it looked small, but based entirely on perspective the thing had to be at least as tall as the Landfall Plateau.

"Is that it?" he asked. His voice came out as a harsh whisper.

"That's it," Orz answered.

For the first time Styke became conscious of Ka-poel at his side, sitting forward in the saddle in the same pose as himself. Her eyes jumped around the city as if to take in every detail. If she had noticed the monolith in the center, the goal of their expedition staring them in the face, she gave no indication of it.

"Come," Orz finally said. "We'll head to one of the western districts. I know of an inn that caters to slav—to foreigners. It'll be the best place to bunk down for a night or two while we take care of business in the city."

"Shouldn't we go around the city? Maybe just you and I can go in to retrieve your parents?"

"We could," Orz agreed, "but it would take far too long. If we want to reach the rest of your army with any amount of speed, we'll have to cut through Talunlica."

Styke nodded absently, his eyes still glued to the godstone. Even at this distance he thought he could smell the coppery tinge of blood sorcery on the wind, but dismissed it as his imagination.

Orz rode off, followed slowly by the rest of the Mad Lancers, until Styke was left alone.

No, not alone.

Ka-poel nudged her horse closer to his and reached out, giving his hand a quick squeeze. She signed briefly—a simple set of gestures that needed no translation.

Thank you for bringing me home.

They descended from their mountaintop vantage and skirted the base of the lake for several miles before turning into one of the long, straight avenues that connected the city of Talunlica with the shoreline. The crowds grew thick, the stares less interested, as the Mad Lancers entered a place where foreigners were a more common sight than in the rest of Dynize.

Despite the grids, canals, and walls, Styke was surprised to note that the city itself did not seem to be built with self-defense in mind. The aesthetics were for beauty and civilian function. There were as many barges and canoes traveling the waterways as there were carts and carriages traversing the avenues. Aqueducts lined each street, bringing fresh water from the mountains and, according to Orz, taking black water down to where the lake fed a river into the Jagged Fens. There was lush greenery everywhere, from small squares filled with towering cypress tress to floating islands of loamy soil that acted as community gardens.

The inn Orz had promised was a sprawling compound in one of the western districts. Orz explained that it was one of the older buildings in the city, built on one of the many islands and originally a headquarters for a Household that had grown rich off trading foreign slaves during the war. Now it was used as a stopping point for slaves traveling to and from the city. An old brass placard outside the gate was easy enough to translate: THE KRESSIAN INN AND BOARDING.

The owner was a middle-aged man with a bored expression

whose eyes widened briefly at the sight of Orz before taking on a businesslike calm. He sat behind a low stone desk in the corner of the compound courtyard, wearing a thin cotton shirt and a single feather hanging from the one braid in his long hair. A handful of stable boys played dice nearby.

Orz swung down from his horse, gesturing Styke to follow, and the two approached the owner. Orz produced a coin—stamped copper by the look of it—and set it on the innkeep's desk. It was the first time Styke had seen such a coin, but the innkeep simply nodded as if it were proper currency.

"These are my wards," Orz told him. "Give them somewhere they can drink and not be bothered." *Or bother anyone else* seemed to be the implication.

"Of course, Servant."

"This man here is named Ben," Orz jerked a thumb at Styke. "He speaks with my authority. Understood?"

The innkeep gave another brisk nod and barked a series of quick orders to the stable boys. Within minutes the horses had been taken, clean water provided to the soldiers, and they were all led to a building in a far corner of the compound. It was two stories with a flat, shaded roof, a large great-room, and several dozen cells that each provided a small sleeping compartment. A couple of slaves— Gurlish women in their late fifties—were whisked away to another part of the inn.

"Can we relax here?" Styke asked Orz quietly as the innkeep flitted around the room, making sure that everything was made right and all the soldiers comfortable.

"For now," Orz answered. "We shouldn't stay more than a day or two, or we will attract attention. But that's all the time we need."

Styke gestured Jackal over. "They've been good. Let them kick their feet up tonight. Gamble, drink. But keep away from the locals." He caught the eye of the innkeep and said one of the first words Orz had taught them in Dynize: "Beer!"

A small smile played out across Orz's face. "Dynize spirits aren't great," he told Styke, "but our beer is some of the best."

"I need some myself," Styke replied. He could already taste it.

"You'll have to wait."

"Oh?"

"Yes. Bring Ka-poel and Celine. We're going out."

CHAPTER 20

Vlora's quick march off the Cape of New Adopest was arrested by the arrival of a messenger from General Sabastenien. The messenger was a young man coated in sweat and dust, looking tired and vaguely shell-shocked. His salute was halfhearted and his horse was limping.

"Message from our cavalry, ma'am," he said before he'd even come to a stop near Vlora and a small group of officers with whom she'd been conferring.

Vlora blinked at the messenger through a haze and wondered if she looked as tired and strung out as he did. She hadn't slept in almost thirty-four hours. Olem's abandonment was still forefront in her mind, despite all she'd done to bury it beneath loads of work. It took all of her energy just to keep her face neutral, her eyes dry, and her mind focused on the duties of commanding a field army. She wondered how she managed to stay upright in her saddle. "Report," she barked.

"Yes, ma'am. We managed to catch up with the Dynize earlier today. Got in a few good hours of dogging their rearguard and harassing their train. Unfortunately they reached their reinforce-ments just a couple hours ago and we were forced to pull back when they about-faced on us."

"Reinforcements?" Vlora echoed.

"Yes, ma'am. Another Dynize field army has joined them. They've arrayed themselves to give battle at a bit of hilly ground just as we're coming off the Cape and onto the mainland. General Sabastenien says they're trying to use the terrain to neutralize our superior cavalry."

"It sounds that way." This was one of the things Vlora had feared about heading onto the Cape in the first place—that the Dynize would try to bottle them up here. Now it had come true, and they were outnumbered two to one. She would have cursed herself for a fool if she didn't know that the alternative would have been leaving Etepali to run rampant behind her. "Anything else?"

"General Sabastenien has found a defensible position for us to camp tonight and is waiting there—it's about two miles from the head of the column. That's all."

"Good. Get some rest, Private. I'll send one of my own messen-gers with a reply."

"Thank you, ma'am."

Vlora turned her attention back to her officers. They whispered among themselves, brows wrinkled, already talking strategy of fighting two field armies at once. She wondered if they blamed her for letting Etepali slip away. *She* certainly blamed herself.

"My friends," she said, "you heard the report."

"Yes, ma'am," came the echoed reply.

"Any suggestions?"

A colonel whose name had slipped her mind said from the back, "We can just go around them. Call in the fleet to ferry us down the coast."

"Maybe," Vlora said, "but that's risky. It'll force us to break up our strength."

"We can swing around to the north and try to hit them one army at a time," someone else suggested.

"We'd have to be damned fast," Vlora replied, shaking her head. She'd already decided to acknowledge Etepali as a clever commander, and that meant assuming she was smart enough to counter any of the simpler strategies that Vlora might attempt. The way she saw it, she had two choices: to punch them hard and fast, giving them little time to prepare; or to pull up into a defensible position and draw the enemy to her. The former was risky and would throw them right into the maw of an enemy that outnumbered them. The latter could waste precious weeks and depended on the general of this new field army to be aggressive and daft.

Vlora fell into her own thoughts, half listening while her senior officers discussed possible strategies. The only bright side to all of this was that none of them seemed particularly bothered by the idea of fighting a superior Dynize force. Several minutes passed while she listened and slowly grew alarmed by their cavalier attitude. She finally roused herself.

"Gentlemen and women," she said loudly, quieting the group. "I'd like to remind you that while we have the edge on the Dynize technologically, they have more Privileged *and* they have bone-eyes. If any of you doubt the effectiveness of the bone-eyes, I invite you to speak with the officers from my mercenary company. They'll tell you how the Dynize refused to break at Landfall."

The group fell into a rocky silence.

"We'll still beat them," Vlora added, injecting as much confidence as she could bring to bear. "I would just prefer to do it with fewer casualties. So I remind you to not plan anything stupid in the assumption that we're going to walk all over a bunch of backward savages. The Dynize are neither of those things."

"Yes, ma'am," came the chorus of answers.

She nodded for them to continue their planning, and turned forward in the saddle, ready to sink back into her own malaise. Every strategy she reached for, every plan she began to grasp, seemed to fall apart before she could fully get her head around it. Her mind kept turning to how much easier this would be with Olem at her side—a thought that made her feel angry and guilty all at once. She brought her head up and scanned the horizon for a distraction—any distraction—from her own brain.

Her eyes fell on a row occurring about a hundred yards away on the other side of the marching column. It was too far for her to make out the details of what was going on, but it seemed that at least a dozen of her cavalry were attempting to corner someone on horseback. One of her cavalry finally broke away, riding across the column and coming to join her.

"What's going on, soldier?" she asked, nodding in the direction of the row.

"Sorry, ma'am. Wouldn't normally bring this to you, but there's some kind of incident with a local."

"What kind of incident?"

"It's a Palo, ma'am. Claims he knows you. Claims he has important intelligence for you."

Vlora scowled. "And why didn't you send him to me?"

"Well, he's a Palo, ma'am."

"And what difference does that make?"

The cavalryman opened his mouth, closed it again, and looked deeply uncomfortable. "I thought we didn't have any allies among the natives, ma'am."

Vlora grit her teeth and reminded herself that these soldiers were freshly arrived from the Nine, where Palo were still considered a backward curiosity. "Bring him here," she ordered. "Wait, did this Palo give you a name?"

"Calls himself Burt, I think."

"Brown Bear Burt?" Vlora asked, feeling her mind shed some of her exhaustion. "Never mind, take me to him. Now!"

She followed the cavalryman across the column to find Brown

Bear Burt in the center of a knot of cavalry. He had a pistol in one hand, his boz knife in the other, and was gripping the reins with his teeth while he brandished both at the cavalry. He was sweaty, dusty, and worn, with a bloodstain on the left sleeve of his riding jacket. His horse looked worse than he did, favoring one leg and swaying badly.

"Lady Flint!" Vlora's accompanying cavalryman announced loudly.

Vlora rode into the group. "What the damned pit is the meaning of this?" she demanded. "This man is my friend and a guest, and you will treat him as such! You, summon a medic. You, get him a fresh horse. Jump, god damn it!" The knot of cavalry scattered to the wind, leaving Vlora alone with Burt.

Burt spat his reins out of his mouth and let out a litany of curses in several different languages as he holstered his pistol and knife. "Your boys are seriously protective of you," he finally said.

"I'm sorry, they—"

Burt waved away the apology. "Disheveled-looking foreigner armed to the teeth and demanding to see your commanding officer? Probably for the best." He squinted and blinked at her. "You look like you got run over by a herd of cattle. What the pit happened to you?"

"Long story. Why are you here, Burt? I thought you were taking the trunk of the godstone up to the Palo Nation."

Burt took a deep breath and stripped off his jacket, taking a good look at his arm. "Grazed," he muttered. "Hurts like the pit." The wound was recent.

"That's not from my men, is it?" Vlora asked.

"No, no. Damned Dynize. They get itchy when you refuse to stop for their questions. I *was* escorting the godstone up north. But a whole lot happened after you left Yellow Creek."

Vlora felt like a stiff wind might knock her off her horse at this point, and she could see the storm clouds in Burt's eyes that heralded a whole lot of bad news. She gripped her saddle horn. "There wasn't much left of Yellow Creek last I saw it."

"And there's nothing left now." Burt spat into the dirt. "A few days after you left, a whole Dynize brigade rolled in. I'd left a few of my boys behind to keep an eye on things and they came and got me when the Dynize arrived."

"Looking for the godstone?"

"That's what we thought at first. They put the whole town to the sword. Butchered everyone. Men, women, children. Anyone they couldn't catch they chased into the mountains. Then they brought in a handful of Privileged and began work on that scree slope below where Little Flerring busted up the godstone."

Vlora stared at Burt, horrified. "Why?"

"They pulled something else out of the mountainside." Burt sniffed. "Something hidden way down below the godstone."

"Hidden?" Vlora echoed.

"Buried," Burt corrected. "Probably not on purpose."

"What was it?"

"Big old block of stone. Flat, like a mighty table. It looks just like the godstone, and I suspect that it's a pedestal of some kind."

Vlora ran her hands through her hair. The capstone was now with her fleet, and everyone who knew anything about it—Prime Lektor and Julene, specifically—were there protecting the damned thing. The root of the godstone had gone with Burt. So what was this new piece that the Dynize had found? If it was truly a pedestal, it might be integral to the godstone as a whole. She looked around for a messenger. "I need to talk to Prime," she muttered.

"That Privileged from Yellow Creek?"

"Yeah."

"I have a damned mind to hold his feet to the fire to find out if there's something we—all of us—missed." Burt seemed to push away his exhaustion, his face hardening. "Whatever it was, the Dynize killed a lot of my friends to hide it."

Vlora searched her saddlebags and produced a canteen of rum, handing it to Burt. He took a swig, sputtered, and spat. "Kresimir on a cracker, I thought that was water." Once he'd recovered, he took a more measured sip and handed the canteen back, wiping his face with his jacket. "Thanks, I needed that."

"So what happened to the stone they pulled out of the mountainside?" Vlora asked.

"They headed south," Burt replied. "I was halfway across the Ironhooks when I got the message. Sent the rest of the godstone on to my people and grabbed what men I could and headed back. They were gone by the time we reached Yellow Creek—they dragged their prize to the Hadshaw and loaded it onto a keelboat. Made it about a hundred and fifty miles before we caught up to them."

"You chased a Dynize brigade with a handful of irregulars?"

Burt eyeballed her. "You think I'm gonna let them get away with killing my friends? Of course we did. Managed to butcher a handful of them at a joint in the river, killed three of their Privileged, but lost a lot of my own boys."

"Three Privileged," Vlora said flatly.

"Yeah, three of the bastards. I subscribe to the Ben Styke theory of killing sorcerers: Hit them hard and hit them fast. Kill them before they can put their gloves on. Palo Nation irregulars are the best guerrilla fighters in the world, Flint." He made a few motions as if drawing a map in the air. "We managed to get ahead of them and sink the keelboat hauling that pedestal, but like I said, we took a bad hit. What irregulars I have left are back there right now, harassing the shit out of the Dynize to keep them from recovering their prize. I've sent for backup, but when I found out you had an entire army over here, I thought you might be closer."

"Shit," Vlora said quietly, her mind racing. She pictured a map of the region in her head. "If you sank their keelboat about a hundred and fifty miles south of Yellow Creek, that means they're... almost dead west of us right now."

"That's right."

"I've got two Dynize field armies between me and them."

Burt grimaced, touching his arm. "I did notice that."

One of Vlora's soldiers returned with a medic. Vlora and Burt both dismounted, letting the medic clean and stitch Burt's wound while another soldier brought him a new horse and went about switching saddles and bags between the two animals. "Don't let that limp fool ya," Burt told the soldier, "she's still good to go. I want her back, so don't go shooting her for the afternoon stew. Ow." The medic pulled on the stitches and tied off a knot. Vlora dismissed her, leaving the two of them alone again.

"I'm not sure what I can do," Vlora said hesitantly.

"I'm not, either," Burt replied. "If I didn't need the help, I wouldn't ask for it. Whatever it is the Dynize got their hands on, they wanted it pretty bad, and that means I want to take it away."

"I don't disagree." Vlora felt the beginning of a plan forming in the back of her head. "When did you sink that keelboat?"

"About eight days ago."

"And how much longer do you think you can keep them occupied?"

"Maybe another week or two, if we're lucky. They're damned persistent and they've got readier access to their friends. I won't be surprised if they already have a couple more brigades heading up river to help them."

"No," Vlora said thoughtfully. "Me neither." Her mind was working overtime now, spinning through a hundred different possibilities. This was an opportunity to get ahead of the Dynize, to take away another vital piece of their sorcerous puzzle. She waved down one of her messengers. "Send word to the general staff," she ordered. "Tell them that we're going to bring the column up right against the Dynize camp."

The messenger blinked in surprise. "Tonight, ma'am?"

"Yes, tonight. I want us camped on their front door, so close we can throw rocks at each other. Have my powder mages find the enemy Privileged immediately, and tell Bo and Nila I'll have separate orders for them." She paused, chewing over her half-formed plan. "Oh, and send someone to fetch Colonel Silvia. I want to know how many flares our artillery have."

CHAPTER 21

Y ou're really not worried about being recognized?" Styke
asked as they left the Kressian Inn. As if to answer him, Orz
stopped just outside the gate and threw a light scarf over his shoulders, flipping it up to shade his face from the sun—and hide his
tattoos. He gazed thoughtfully back at Styke for a few moments,
his mind clearly elsewhere, before answering.

"Not worried, no," Orz said, tapping the shawl. "This is a precaution. I suspect everyone who might recognize me is fighting in
Fatrasta."

"And if not?" Styke asked.

"If not, I still have this." Orz produced a card from his pocket
and handed it to Styke. It had a broken seal of black wax stamped
with three stars, and inside was a very official-looking letter. Both
the envelope and the paper inside were made of heavy, waxed paper,
which explained how it survived Orz's stowaway. "This is my letter
of pardon from Ka-Sedial," Orz explained. "If something happens
to me, I want you to recover it from my corpse. It's not as good as

having me with you in person, but it might get you past check-points and awkward questions."

Styke glanced over the card thoughtfully and handed it back. This felt like some kind of a trap—an opportunity for him to turn on Orz, steal the letter, and use it to get him to his destination. "You trust me to know about this?"

Orz shrugged. "I have no reason not to. I've been watching you for weeks, remember? Trailing you for much longer. You're a killer, but you're not an assassin."

Styke snorted. "I suppose that's a compliment."

"It is," Orz replied. His gaze swiveled to Ka-poel and Celine. "You, bone-eye, walk with me in front. Girl, stay with Styke and walk a few paces behind us." He headed down the street without further explanation. Ka-poel scurried to keep up with him. Styke took Celine by the hand, frowning at the dragonman's back, and followed.

The first thing that struck Styke as they headed into the middle of the city was the stares. No one seemed to do it openly, but out of the corners of his eyes he caught passersby glancing curiously in his direction, lifting eyebrows or even outright ogling. As soon as he turned his head, everyone seemed to continue on with their day as if he weren't there.

He tried to ignore them, focusing his attention instead on Orz and Ka-poel. They walked side-by-side like old friends, and he could hear Orz speaking to her in a low voice. Ka-poel's hands moved in response, but as they were in front of her, Styke couldn't see her replies. It seemed curious to him that Orz had requested Celine to come along but didn't bother to have her translate. Had he picked up on Ka-poel's sign language so quickly?

A deeply unsettling thought struck him—if Ka-poel had broken Sedial's hold over Orz, she might have had some sort of connection with the dragonman ever since. In which case, how the pit did she *not* know that he was a stowaway on the *Seaward*? Or *did* she know? And if so, why hadn't she said anything?

The thought swam around inside his head, and he argued with himself over possibilities and motivations. He grew increasingly frustrated with the train of thought, doubly so because he knew that if he asked her outright, he couldn't expect a straight answer.

"Ben, why are you squeezing me so hard?"

Styke looked down at Celine, who was actively attempting to extricate her hand from his. He let go and she almost fell, shooting him a glare. "Sorry," he told her. "I was thinking about something."

"You're thinking too hard," Celine said pointedly. "You're scaring people."

Styke glanced around and noted that an approaching Dynize woman took a sharp turn at an intersection the moment their eyes met. She hurried away, leaving Styke to attempt to peel the scowl off his own face.

"You wouldn't be a very good actor," Celine told him.

"Eh?"

She pursed her lips and began to skip along at his side, seemingly no worse the wear from his squeezing her hand. "You can't hide your thoughts. 'An open face,' my da used to say. Read you like a book."

"I would have turned your dad inside out if we met on the street," Styke shot back, somewhat more aggressively than he'd meant to.

Celine giggled. "Nah, he would have avoided you bad. He would have read you and taken a different street."

"Smarter than I've given him credit for."

"Maybe," Celine said with a tiny shrug, "or maybe not. Thing is, we're far from home and you need to act more like you belong if we're gonna get back." The words were heavy and thoughtful, but her tone was as light as any child's, as if she didn't really understand the weight of them.

"Where the pit are you getting that kind of talk?" Styke asked. "You're too young for it."

"Sunin. Ka-poel. The Lancers." Celine continued to skip. "They know you're doing your best, but they're a little bit worried."

"Worried about what?"

Celine stopped suddenly, for just a couple of beats, then ran to catch up. She wore an expression as if she'd just figured out that relaying this kind of gossip to their officer made her a snitch. "Nothing," she said evasively.

"Spill it," Styke told her.

She pulled another, more comical face, then continued. "It's like I just said."

"And you're going to elaborate."

"That you can get us out of this," she said in a quick rush. "It's not the fighting that worries them—they know you're the biggest and meanest and that you'll always carve a path through the enemy to get them home. But we're not in a spot that you can fight us out of. You've got to be meek, and they don't think you can do it."

Styke chewed on the inside of his cheek. His first response was anger, tinged with indignation. His soldiers had lost faith in him? But he quickly moved past that and forced himself to listen—to *really* listen—to those words. Celine sounded as if she were parroting them straight from one of the older Lancers. Probably Sunin. That old shithead. "What do you mean, 'meek'?"

"Like this," Celine said, gesturing around them. "We're walking behind Orz, but you still look like you're in charge. But you're supposed to be pretending to be a slave." Styke gestured for her to talk more quietly, and she went on in a softer voice. "You're supposed to be a slave, but you don't act like it."

"And how am I supposed to do that? It's not like I can help my size."

"No, but you can help your posture. Your expression."

"I don't follow."

"Hunch your shoulders," Celine suggested. "Don't scowl at everyone. Don't make eye contact. You remember what it was like to be at the labor camp?"

Styke let out a little involuntary growl. "Yes."

"Act like that."

"I'm not going to be a slave again."

"But you can pretend to be one to save all our lives."

"I can't believe I'm having this conversation with a little squirt like you."

Celine fixed him with a serious look. "I remember the camps," she said solemnly. "And I remember when my da went on benders and I had to fend for myself in the streets. I remember what it's like to have to stay unnoticed."

There was something in that youthful solemnity that finally broke through to Styke. He looked away, lifting his eyes to the skyline of Talunlica—an unfamiliar skyline, in an unfamiliar city, in an unfamiliar country.

He knew the Lancers talked among themselves. That's what soldiers did. But for the last week they'd followed orders to the letter, without showing an ounce of hesitation, and not once had they let their own doubt spill over to where he could see it. He'd given them a plan to see through and they'd follow it. He rubbed the back of his head. He missed Ibana. He needed someone on hand who would tell him when he was being an idiot, tell him when his orders went beyond foolhardy to suicidal. Because maybe that's all this jaunt was.

"You're a good kid," he finally said.

Celine grinned up at him. "I thought you said I was a pre... preco—"

"Precocious little shit. Yeah, you're that, too." Styke took her hand again. "Okay, how's this?" He forced the scowl from his face and turned his eyes downward. As they walked, he tried to hunch his shoulders, making himself remember—truly remember—those afternoons at the labor camp. Avoiding the beatings of the guards. Dodging fights with the other inmates. Just trying to get by. He remembered shrinking into himself, ticking off the hours until the next parole hearing.

He couldn't even remember what had broken inside himself to become such a mouse. Whatever it was, it had healed. He would die before he let himself become that again. But...Celine was right. He needed to at least act like a mouse again to get his people through this damned city.

"That's better," Celine said, examining him with a critical eye. "Don't make eye contact with people."

"You really pay attention to this sort of thing?"

"Didn't you?"

He grimaced. "Right. I'll practice this. And when I'm finished being a 'slave,' I'm going to burn this city to the ground."

Celine giggled as if he'd said something funny, and the two of them fell into a silence. Styke did his best to keep his head down but his eyes open, and he gradually felt like it was working. People stared less when he was hunched over. Some didn't even seem to notice him. His own perception felt as if it had widened and he began to grasp things he hadn't before—to see the occasional foreign slave, to notice the different castes among the Dynize, including their varied clothing, the way they walked, and even their postures.

Beside it all, he kept adding to the map of the city in his head. Talunlica was wide and open, with few enormous buildings to block out the horizon and many definite landmarks because of the surrounding mountains. But the nature of its construction presented a whole different set of challenges. The avenues jumped from island to island, with smaller bridges and causeways creating shortcuts between them. He had to keep track not just of the physical roads but also of the waterways and their widths and depths, which he noticed were marked to aid the boat traffic—of which there was a considerable amount.

He was so focused on taking all of this in that he didn't really notice where they were going until they arrived. Celine tugging on his hand prevented him from running into Orz. Styke looked up in surprise, rubbed at his nose, and suddenly realized that his nostrils were full of a dusty, angry scent.

They were in a wide city square at the convergence of several avenues. Orz had led them out of the main traffic to a parklike area off to one side. Despite the crowds, the park was quiet and contemplative. People picnicked, lounged, and even prayed, and it took Styke a moment to realize why.

The godstone rose above them. They were not at its base—that was behind a large stone wall that separated the imperial compound with the rest of Talunlica—but this park had been very clearly set aside as a place for some sort of worship of the stone. A short fence cordoned it off from the road, tall trees provided shade, and decorative facsimiles of the godstone about Styke's height dotted the perimeter.

Styke couldn't take his eyes off the godstone. It wasn't even the smell of sorcery that transfixed him, nor the strange knotting in his gut at the sight of it. No, it was simply the size—a single cut piece of stone that rose at least two hundred feet into the air. The effort to put it there must have been incredible. He'd seen the one in Landfall, of course, lying on its side. But this was both bigger and the center of a city that had been designed around it. There was a grandeur here that fused ancient and modern and made an impression even on him.

He allowed Orz to lead their small group to an isolated spot at the water's edge in one corner of the park. He leaned against a stone wall and craned his head to gaze at the stone, slack-jawed.

"It's something, isn't it?" Orz asked.

"I had my doubts," Styke replied.

"Worth fighting a war over?"

"Let's not get carried away."

Orz laughed. "What about you, Sister Pole?"

Ka-poel's examination of the stone seemed far more clinical than Styke's. She looked it up and down, one finger tapping against her jaw. She gestured, and Celine translated dutifully: *I need to get closer.*

"This is the closest we can get," Orz said. "This park is technically within the imperial compound, but the walls were moved when they realized that people were blocking traffic to worship the stone."

"I heard a rumor," Styke said, "that the stone in Landfall was driving people mad."

"Not a rumor," Orz replied. "The power of *this* stone is dampened by the bone-eyes, but it still drives someone mad every week or so."

"That doesn't make me want to stand near it."

Orz seemed amused by the note of reluctance in Styke's voice. "Doesn't it? There is a whole town dedicated to those who've been driven mad by the stone. It's got a very nice view from that mountain over there." He pointed to their northwest. "They're considered holy men. Many of the worshipers here come every day in the hope that they're claimed next."

Styke snorted. He'd never taken much to religion himself. "Aside from the idea of messing with things clearly beyond the scope of normal humans," he said, "I'm shocked that a people advanced enough to create this city are stupid enough to worship a stone that drives them mad." He watched Orz through the corner of his eye, curious if his words would offend.

The dragonman just shrugged. "Everyone needs to believe in something to feel truly whole. Sometimes that's an emperor or a god or a politician. Sometimes it's themselves. Other times it's the promise of an ancient stone driving them mad. It mitigates the pain of real life, I believe."

"Is this what you wanted to show us?" Styke asked. Ka-poel was still engrossed in the stone, her fingers twitching in no understandable language and her lips pursed. She looked like she was itching for that closer look.

"Among other things," Orz said.

"And what are those other things?"

"Just this." Orz gestured expansively. "I wanted to show you the city, to let you feel its heartbeat. You still intend on attacking it, unless I'm mistaken."

Styke looked around, but they were well out of earshot of anyone else. "That's the idea."

"I wanted to show you that it *is* just a city. These are normal people living normal lives."

"Most cities are full of them," Styke replied, unsure as to what Orz was getting at.

"Yes, and that's my point." Orz sighed. "These aren't evil people. They've been goaded into a foreign war by an evil man, yes. But most of them will never see Fatrasta. They don't know or even care about the machinations of Ka-Sedial. They're just living their lives and they look to the godstone as a representative of something better."

"A new god?" Styke asked skeptically.

"A uniting god. Past glories of an entire hemisphere under one banner, living in peace."

Styke harrumphed.

"Is it a sin to hope for better?"

"At the cost of my own people? Yes."

"Your own people are usurpers. They came across the ocean mere generations ago. They slaughtered, subjugated, and enslaved the Palo and took the land for their own."

"I mean Fatrastans," Styke replied, feeling a little heated. He pulled his anger down.

"Fatrastans? The concept of a Fatrastan people is less than a generation old."

"Does it matter whether a people is a decade old or twenty centuries?"

"I'd imagine it does," Orz replied.

"I feel like you're arguing that the Dynize are right in attacking my people," Styke said. "But right had nothing to do with it. They're still my people, and they're still being attacked."

"That's not what he's arguing." Celine sniffed, climbing up on the stone fence beside Styke.

"Eh?" Both he and Orz looked at her.

"He's just trying to say that people are the same everywhere. They're just trying to live their lives." Celine produced a pebble from one pocket and tossed it over her shoulder into the water behind them, smiling at the distinctive *plop* that it made when it landed. "He's trying to ask you not to slaughter everyone when you attack the city."

Orz blinked at Celine for a few moments, then a grin spread across his face. "This child never ceases to astound me. Yes, Ben Styke. That's what I'm asking."

Styke chewed on the inside of his cheek. It was both a simple request and a difficult one. Attacking a city was never pretty and often included a great deal of bloodshed on both sides. The attackers, no matter how modern-minded and disciplined, always had their blood up by the time they got inside—and that often led to sacking and looting. His gut instinct was to tell Orz that the Mad Lancers were above all that, but he remembered what Valyaine had told him back in Bellport. The Mad Lancers had done everything and anything they'd wanted during the Revolution, always with a word of justification. They'd do the same here.

Celine suddenly slipped from her seat and headed across the park. Styke was about to call after her when he saw her destination—a gathering of children not far from them, all seated in a semicircle around a large wooden box with black curtains. Exchanging a glance with Orz, he followed her over.

It was a puppet show, and he found himself smiling as he joined Celine at the back of the semicircle. The puppets were in the middle of some sort of conflict. On one side were morion-helmed puppets with freckled faces. On the other were comically oversized giants in sunflower yellow. This was the Fatrastan War, he realized immediately. For a brief moment he thought that the giants were supposed to be him, but then he realized that they were just ordinary Fatrastan soldiers, made larger to show their menace.

It did not take long to follow the gist of the show. On one side, the Dynize. Conquering heroes, overwhelming the larger, angrier Fatrastans. More freckled puppets joined from the Fatrastan side, these ones bent and downtrodden until the Fatrastan soldiers had been slain. Palo. Freed from servitude.

One of the Fatrastan giants fell with a sword through the belly and was tossed out onto the ground by the puppeteer. Styke found his eyes drawn to that one puppet, lying broken on the stone, and he found himself considering Orz's words. It was easy to dismiss this all as propaganda, but it was harder to dismiss the fact that Lindet would spread the exact same kind of propaganda throughout her own people.

Everyone wanted to feel like they were the good guys, just as Styke had always denied the unjust ferocity of the Mad Lancers within his own head.

He took Celine by the hand and led her back to Orz and Ka-poel. "Does everyone here think that we're monsters?" he asked Orz.

"Many of them, yes," Orz admitted. "We have a very deep cultural feeling of superiority that goes back thousands of years. It's not difficult to build upon that. They're wrong, of course. I've seen your people and I believe they are no different from my own. That's why I began this discussion."

"I don't think I agree."

"Oh?"

"At least, not personally." He thought of those big, fallen puppets. "*I* am a monster. I've had to be to protect my country. Just like you dragonmen."

Orz didn't reply.

Styke went on slowly. "I don't intend on sticking around," he said slowly. "Once I've found Ibana, we're going to get in and out. Fight our way to the compound and take over the godstone, then defend it just long enough for Ka-poel to do her thing." He didn't mention his contingency plans—kidnapping the emperor, setting fires, fomenting chaos. He hoped that it didn't come to any of that. The faster they were able to destroy the godstone, the better. But this little walk had also told him how the people of Dynize felt about their godstone, and he wondered if the Mad Lancers would flee the city at the head of a mob once they'd destroyed the thing.

They'd have to deal with that when it came up.

"Let's go," Orz said, leading them away from the imperial compound and back the way they'd come. They turned off a main avenue and proceeded down a narrow causeway until they were practically alone in the middle of the lake, between two of the islands of city. Orz pointed. "Do you see that small street jutting into the water over there?"

Styke picked it out. "Yes."

"That's where my mother and father live. And that there"—he swept his finger across the water, up the shoreline, and centered it on a walled compound about a mile from the godstone—"that is my old Household. My brother runs it now."

"He has an entire compound?"

"Pay attention, and you'll see them dotted all over the city. Hundreds. My brother's is one of the smaller ones, to be honest. His name is Etzi, and he is the Minister of Drainage."

Styke snorted.

"Don't laugh! It's a small Household but an important job. Etzi's task is to keep the city from flooding during the wet months or the lake from draining during the dry. He oversees sewage and the hunting of swamp dragons that make their way into the lake."

"How are we going to convince your brother to abandon his Household and go into hiding?"

"We won't. I don't even want him to know we're here."

"Then, why show me?"

"I want you to avoid that compound when you invade."

"Ah."

"I don't want my brother involved. He is not like my parents— he loved our emperor, and he took some convincing to reconcile with Sedial when our emperor was assassinated. But he has a good life now. I'm not even going to speak to him before we leave."

"He's not in danger from Sedial?"

"I don't believe so. He's too important..." Orz trailed off, his eyes fixing on the horizon just above the city, staring at nothing. "This is the cost of being a 'monster,'" he said quietly. "It is losing all you love. I recommend that you regain your humanity as much as you can, Ben Styke." Before Styke could answer, he cleared his throat. "Come, let us return to the inn. We'll need some rest before we go to fetch my parents tonight."

CHAPTER 22

Michel spent the better part of the next day with Dahre's crew, canvassing the Depths for alternative leads and discussing the best plan of attack for cornering Mama Palo. He made plausible excuses to slip out of the quarry to make his own arrangements—studying maps, walking out an escape route, and even buying a pistol. He kept Ichtracia close in case the whole thing went badly.

Against his own instincts he began to fill her in on his plans. Things were moving too quickly now to keep her entirely in the dark. She took the explanations in stride, weathering them as she had everything else, with a steely-eyed acceptance and, maybe hidden beneath it all, a touch of nerves.

They returned to their apartment at dark. Michel went over everything in his head again and again as he lay in bed, listening to Ichtracia's gentle snores. His own nerves, he decided, were too thinly strung by the uncertainty of all this.

Michel was just beginning to drift off when the sound of

footsteps in the hall brought him back to wakefulness. It took him a moment of confusion to figure out what his subconscious was telling him—dozens of people walked back and forth down this hall every day, after all. The steps, he decided, had very definitely stopped outside of their door.

He'd only just made this connection when he heard another noise—the click of a latch. In an instant Michel's adrenaline was pumping, his heart hammering. A thousand explanations passed through his head as to why someone might be coming into their room unannounced: an innocent mistake, an assassin, a message from Emerald. It was the second that he feared, though he wasn't entirely sure who would try to kill him. If it was the Dynize, they'd have just swarmed the building with soldiers and kicked the door in.

All of this flashed through his mind in the few moments it took for the door to open. It happened quickly enough that he didn't have the chance to so much as poke Ichtracia. Her steady, deep breathing continued beside him, and he tensed himself, eyes open to slits, and watched the silhouette of a figure appear in the doorway. His brand-new pistol was beneath the bed, out of reach, and unloaded anyway. His knuckledusters, however, were just beneath his pillow.

He kept his own breathing steady so as not to betray his wakefulness as a second figure appeared in the doorway. Michel caught sight of the very distinct glint of a knife. The first figure paused by the foot of their mattress, turned back to the second. Something was whispered between them.

Michel lashed out with one foot, felt it connect with a knee. The figure cried out and tumbled to the floor. Michel was on his feet in a flash. He snatched up his knuckledusters, trying to seat them onto the fingers of both hands while getting his bearings in the dark room. The first figure let out a string of curses in Palo, while the second one attempted to leap at Michel but was blocked by the flailing heap his companion had made on the floor.

Michel saw another glint on the floor and stepped on the blade of a knife before it could be retrieved by its owner. He'd only just managed to do so when she surged to her feet, catching him in the stomach with her shoulder and throwing him hard against the wall. His breath was snatched from him in a wheezy grunt, and he pounded his fists on her back.

They wrestled for several moments, Michel's attention fully on the woman with her arms around his waist, when he felt fingers take a handful of his hair and jerk his head to one side. Something sharp touched his neck and he felt a bead of something wet on his skin—for the sparest of moments he was convinced that his throat had been slashed. He froze, hand going to his throat, but was shaken hard by the second attacker's fingers in his hair.

"Move," a voice hissed, "and you're a dead man."

Michel felt his eyes bugging out, his whole body trembling. He was far from a true fighter, and all their movements had been a frenetic scramble up to this point. That knife at his throat, however, had taken all the fight out of him, and he found his body frozen in self-preservation. A small voice in the back of his head told him that he knew how this would go—a few questions and then a bloody smile. Fighting back was all he could do. But his limbs wouldn't answer his commands.

He raised both hands and sagged against the wall. The figure at his waist pulled away and stood up, and in a moment of shock, Michel caught sight of her face in the light of the hall. Devin-Mezi. He let out a disbelieving scoff. "What the pit?"

"Wake your friend up," Devin-Mezi ordered. "We're going for a walk. Get the door," she told her companion. "And the light." She took control of the knife at Michel's throat, then tugged his knuckledusters off his splayed fingers. The man closed the door behind him and reached over their heads to turn up the lantern. Two things struck Michel the moment there was enough light to see by:

The first was that her companion was none other than Kelinar—the very same turncoat who'd offered to sell Mama Palo's whereabouts to Meln-Dun's searchers. Michel barely had time to register this when he noted that Ichtracia was not only awake but sitting up.

And she was wearing her gloves.

Kelinar's left arm snapped backward, the bone splitting through the flesh and splattering blood across the wall. He tried to reach for his arm but froze in place, his mouth opened in a soundless scream. The knife flew out of Devin-Mezi's hand and clattered against the wall. She, too, froze in place, though both of her hands still appeared to be able to move. She clawed at her throat, unable to make a sound.

The two assailants remained suspended that way for several moments before Michel was able to get the thundering of his heart under control. He pushed Devin-Mezi away from himself and took control of both of their knives. There was a thumping on the wall.

"You there, quiet down! Some of us have to sleep!"

"Sorry," Michel called back. "Right away!"

A few choice curses came back through the wall, and then silence. "Let them breathe," Michel said quietly to Ichtracia. She still sat in bed, her fingers twitching gently, her face screwed up into the kind of mild annoyance one might feel upon losing a small amount of money at the horse races. She gave him a curt nod, and Devin-Mezi and Kelinar both took in a sudden gasp of air. Kelinar collapsed to the ground, curling up around his ruined arm, while Devin-Mezi sank against the wall.

"Scream," Ichtracia said, "and I will pop your heads like boils. Understand?"

Devin-Mezi nodded urgently. Kelinar trembled and dry-heaved, clutching at his shattered arm.

Michel tried not to look at the blood pooling beneath Kelinar. His own hands trembled from the rush of the fight and he had to take several deep breaths to steady himself. He could break down later. Now he had to ask questions. He shifted his gaze to Devin-Mezi. "Who the pit are you, and why did you just try to knife us?"

The would-be assassin stared at Ichtracia, wide-eyed, her fingers trembling. Michel had to remind himself what it was like for a civilian to come across a Privileged—terrifying at best.

"Didn't go how you expected it, did it?"

Devin-Mezi shook her head. "We weren't going to knife you," she whispered. "Just ask some questions."

"And what were you going to do after asking questions?" Michel shot back. He knew how this worked. *Go for a walk*, she'd said. That was Blackhat shorthand for *Make them walk to their own grave.*

Devin-Mezi shook her head again.

"Why were you trying to knife us?" Michel asked again, this time firming up his tone. He let the silence hang for two beats before adding, "If you don't start answering questions, I'm going to have my friend do the same thing to each of your fingers as she did to *his* arm."

"Too competent," Devin-Mezi muttered. "Too quick."

"You want to explain that?"

She spoke under her breath, eyeballing Ichtracia a few moments before her jaw tightened and her eyes narrowed. "I'll die first."

Michel worked through his own emotions for a few moments before he waved Ichtracia off with a subtle gesture. She didn't look too eager to start torturing people, and despite having sat through plenty of Blackhat "questionings," he had no stomach for it himself. It would be, he decided, a last resort. Ichtracia swung out of bed and he watched her dress absently, his thoughts churning through cause and effect.

There was a chance that Devin-Mezi was a Blackhat. She might have recognized him and decided to kill him. Any Blackhats left in the city would certainly have reason to do so. That phrase, "Go for a walk," was definitely Blackhat shorthand, but that didn't necessarily mean anything. It was commonly known around Land-fall and might have easily been picked up by anyone who spent any time on the wrong side of the law.

Maybe she was simply who she said she was. Perhaps one of Meln-Dun's people had recognized Michel as a Blackhat and they'd decided to bump him off. But again, this was the Depths. Meln-Dun, of all people, wouldn't need to act in secret.

So if she wasn't a Blackhat and she wasn't working for Meln-Dun, who was she?

Michel glanced at Kelinar—a low-level lieutenant of Mama Palo's who'd agreed to sell out his comrades. Or was he? A few things clicked into place, and Michel snorted a laugh. "You're set-ting up Meln-Dun, aren't you?" Michel asked. Devin-Mezi looked at him sharply. It was all he needed to see to confirm his suspicion. "You're a mole. A plant. And this poor bastard is your accomplice."

"I don't follow," Ichtracia said. She was dressed now, and turned back toward the other two with a sneer fixed on her lip.

"My guess," Michel said to her, keeping his eyes on Devin-Mezi, "is that they both work for Mama Palo. She's infiltrated Meln-Dun's group and has been guiding them toward a trap. Her friend here is the bait. What's the plan, Devin-Mezi? To get Dahre and his crew into one spot and kill them all? Look, you're going to have to say something eventually." He glanced significantly at Ichtracia.

Devin-Mezi followed his eyes. "More or less," she finally said.

"Pit." Michel rubbed his eyes and touched his neck, where he found blood still dripping from a scratch there. It was beginning to sting. But nothing like poor Kelinar's arm. "Where is Mama Palo?"

"Do what you want," Devin-Mezi snapped back. "I'm not going to tell you."

"Haven't you wondered why I've got a secret Privileged with me?" Michel demanded. "Has it occurred to you that maybe I'm not what I claim to be, either?"

"We should kill them," Ichtracia cut in. "They know what I am."

Michel couldn't tell if she was being serious or helping him feed Devin-Mezi's fear. Either way . . . "Look, I'm trying to find Mama Palo for my own purposes. I'm only working for Meln-Dun to piggyback onto his search. Understand?"

Devin-Mezi stared hard at him. "What are you, then? A Dynize agent?"

"Hardly."

"I don't believe you."

"Believe anything you want." Michel shrugged. "But I don't have a lot of time. This trap of yours, they plan on springing it tomorrow night?"

She didn't answer, but he could see confirmation in her eyes. She glanced toward her knife still dangling from his hand. "You'll have to kill us both," she insisted. "I'm not giving you any answers."

Michel took a deep breath and glanced at Ichtracia. They were in a world of hurt now. She'd used her sorcery, which would quite likely alert Sedial—if not to *their* presence, then at least to the presence of a Privileged. Devin-Mezi also knew of their presence, even if she didn't know who they were. He knew he should cut his losses and leave her and her companion rotting in a ditch. But if he didn't have the stomach for torture, he *definitely* didn't have the stomach for cold-blooded murder.

"Let them go," he told Ichtracia.

"What?" Both Ichtracia and Devin-Mezi said the word at the same time, with equal amounts of surprise.

"I'm not going to torture you, and I'm not going to kill you," Michel said. "You don't believe me, but we're on the same side. So instead of drawing this out any longer, I'm going to let you go. Take your friend there to get his arm seen to, then go inform Mama Palo that I'm trying to find her."

"She doesn't know you," Devin-Mezi replied, suspicion dripping from the words.

"She should," Michel replied. He didn't know who the new Mama Palo was. He could only hope it was someone high enough up the organization to know his name, or the names of one of his aliases. His own, he decided, was too risky to give out. Instead he gave one of the latter. "Tell her that Puffer is trying to come in. He wants to talk, and he wants to talk soon."

"Puffer?" Devin-Mezi asked. "Like the fish?"

"Exactly like the fish. It's an old code name of mine. If Mama Palo has been around long enough, she'll know it." Michel jerked his head toward Kelinar. "Go on, before I change my mind. I'll be here for three hours. Come back and find me once you get an answer. Come alone." He ignored Ichtracia's doubtful expression and watched while Devin-Mezi collected her companion off the floor. Kelinar was still sobbing quietly when she led him out the door. Michel stepped into the hallway and watched until they were gone, then darted back into the room.

"What the pit was that?" Ichtracia asked, removing her gloves.

"That was me trying to make contact," Michel answered. "I appreciate your intervention, but we need to move." He immediately began to throw their things into his shoulder bag. Ichtracia followed suit, collecting her meager possessions into her pockets and handing him her one extra set of clothes.

"Where are we going? I thought you told her we'd be here."

"This building has two exits. There's a decent spot up three levels where we can see both of them. We're going to go spend the rest of the night there."

"And if she comes back with more assassins?"

"Then we disappear," Michel replied. "And all our plans will be ruined."

CHAPTER 23

Vlora patrolled the hastily assembled Adran camp. Per her orders, they were set up in the hills just off the Cape, so close to the Dynize that she could see the light from their campfires flickering against the low cloud cover to her west. *Recklessly* close. If the terrain had been flat and visibility good, the Dynize would have been able to open fire with their field guns and abuse Vlora's camp all through the night—but their choice of rough terrain had limited their own options, which Vlora used against them.

The reason for camping so close was clear—it meant that Vlora could force a battle at first light, keeping the sunrise at her back to blind her enemies. Her men would barely have to roll out of bed to start the battle, meaning they'd be as fresh as possible and ready for a day of bloody line fighting and bayonet charges. The lack of space left the Dynize with little room to practice subterfuge or maneuver.

At least, Vlora *hoped* those were the fears going through her enemy's minds. The reality, if they had somehow managed to grasp it, was far more ridiculous.

Vlora managed to keep herself upright due to a combination of coffee, catnaps in the saddle, and no small amount of bloodthirsty energy. By all rights she should be on her back in her tent, looking for ten hours of sleep before she dared a major battle. But she didn't have that kind of luxury, so she turned all of her anger, grief, and hatred into single-minded eagerness. It was time to meet the Dynize in battle—for real this time—and to show them what it meant to fight an Adran army.

Vlora's camp was laid out in a half-moon shape. To the west were the newcomers—the Dynize reinforcements of some thirty thousand infantry. To her northwest was General Etepali's field army. Vlora had made a great show of digging in—fortifications on all sides of her camp—but had set the bulk of her engineers on that northwest side. It was the side that she was most worried about.

Her inspection of the Adran camp was swift, beginning just after nightfall and ending at the general-staff tent. She strolled inside, doing everything in her power to look well rested and eager, despite all the pains wracking her body. The tent was packed with officers from colonel to brigadier general, as well as her three powder mages, Nila and Bo, and Brown Bear Burt.

Conversation ceased when she entered. She returned the offered salutes and let her gaze wander around the space for a few moments. Expressions ranged from eager to steely, and it was in the eyes of the latter she could see that some of her senior officers had begun to get an inkling of how furious she really was.

General Sabastenien was closest at hand. "How is everyone holding up?" she asked him.

"Troops? Or officers?"

"Both," she answered in a voice loud enough to include everyone in the tent in the conversation.

"Troops are good. The Third, Fifth, Sixth, and Eighth have all spent the last few hours resting per your orders. There's some trepidation over a night attack. No one likes the risk of accidentally bayoneting their friend because they can't see a damned thing."

"Of course. And the officers?"

A brief moment of hesitation. "About the same."

Vlora met the answer with a small smile and took in the room again with her gaze. "I understand that the order of battle tonight is...unorthodox. There *will* be confusion. There *will* be friendly fire. If you have questions or reservations, now is the time to voice them."

A cacophony erupted from the officers. Vlora quieted them with a raised hand and began addressing the questions one at a time— working through preparations, the plan of attack, and all the way through a dozen different contingencies. The questions seemed to be gently geared toward finding out whether Vlora had gone completely insane or not. By the end of it most of the officers seemed satisfied, though not necessarily pleased with the idea of sending four brigades of infantry on a night attack.

Once the questions were over, she dismissed the officers to see to their brigades, leaving her with the Privileged and powder mages. She addressed the mages. "Have the three of you found your vantage points?"

They nodded. Davd avoided her gaze. He hadn't said a word to her since she shouted him away yesterday. A part of her knew that she should apologize—he was just the bearer of bad news. But her stubborn streak remained firm, her voice clipped and impersonal.

"You're sure about leaving you without a mage?" Norrine asked doubtfully.

"Yes, I'm sure," Vlora responded. "I'm staying on the edge of our camp with a bodyguard. I'll be fine."

"But you can't see in the dark without your sorcery," Norrine pointed out. "You'll be blind."

"No more blind than they are," Vlora countered. "Besides, once things have started, I won't be issuing commands. This is one bat-tle I need to just point in the right direction and then cut loose."

"That's awfully cavalier," Bo said, looking at his fingernails.

"Can you think of any alternatives?" she asked. She'd briefed them all earlier on Burt's message and the mysterious artifact the Dynize had recovered from Yellow Creek. They'd all agreed it was imperative to find it and steal it. "If we sit on our thumbs, we risk letting the Dynize get away with that thing."

"Why can't we attack in the morning?" Bo drawled.

"Because they're expecting just that," Vlora responded. "Did you not hear the entire question-and-answer session I just had with my officers? Or were you dozing off?"

"He was dozing off," Nila interjected.

Vlora turned her attention on Nila but held her temper in check. She had the type of relationship with Bo that would allow her to be cross with him but stay friends in the morning. Nila, on the other hand, would take it more personally. "I don't want the two of you participating in the attack."

Bo arched an eyebrow.

"It'll be too chaotic," Vlora explained. "It's already going to be bad enough without slinging sorcery around. No, when the signal goes off, I want you to help Colonel Silvia with the lights."

"You're going to use us as a couple of giant lanterns?" Nila asked flatly.

"No. I'm also going to put you in the northwest corner of the camp. You're going to be there when General Etepali counterattacks."

"When?"

"When," Vlora confirmed. "I'm not just expecting her to slam into us from the flank, I'm counting on it. You're going to make sure she gets a face full of shit when she does it."

"And the other Privileged?" Bo asked.

Vlora jerked her thumb at her powder mages. "They'll be dead before they can bring their real strength to bear on us."

The group reluctantly agreed to Vlora's orders, and she sent them scattering out after her officers. Vlora found herself alone for the first time in days and sank down into one of the chairs in the general-staff tent, rubbing her eyes. Every fiber of her being throbbed with pain and exhaustion. Each time she moved a limb, she could practically hear it screaming in protest. She'd pushed herself plenty harder before, but never without the benefit of her sorcery.

She steeled her resolve. She had no choice. She could not allow anything as petty as human weakness to slow her down.

She closed her eyes briefly, thinking of Olem. She wondered where he'd gone. What he was thinking. Had it been so easy for him to cut loose from her? Had she hurt him so badly? She wished he was here so that she could apologize to him. She wondered if he'd accept the apology—or if there was nothing she could say or do to make things better.

She remained in black contemplations until a messenger arrived to tell her it was time.

The night was tinged with just a sliver of moonlight peeking through the clouds. It wasn't ideal—a full moon on a cloudless night would have made it easier for her soldiers to keep from shooting one another in the attack—but she intended to use that confusion against the enemy. She allowed a messenger to guide her to the edge of camp while her eyes adjusted to the dark, where she found thousands of her soldiers kneeling quietly. The only sounds were the whispered orders of officers and the creak of leather gear and rattle of the occasional rifle.

If there were any nearby Dynize scouts, they would be mighty suspicious. But her powder mages had already swept the region between her camp and the enemy, putting spies and picketmen to the knife.

Some time passed, and Vlora's eyes grew more accustomed to

the night. A messenger moved cautiously up a broken trail to her position. "General Flint?" a voice asked.

"Here."

"Everyone has reported in, ma'am."

"Officers have hooded lanterns and pocket watches?"

"Yes, ma'am." The messenger thrust one of each into Vlora's hands. The lantern was covered, betraying only the smallest bit of light in the cracks of its construction. She held the pocket watch up to it. Almost one in the morning. She kept her eyes glued to the hands of the watch, counting down the minutes, then the seconds.

The watch had barely struck one-ten when hushed orders rippled off to either side of her, spreading across the front. A whisper of cloth and jangle of gear followed as the group set off. Vlora stood in the darkness, watching the glint of steel in the moonlight and the occasional glow of an officer's lantern descend slowly over the ridgeline and then down into the first of two steep, narrow valleys that separated her camp from the Dynize.

Her blood hammered in her ears with the anticipation of it all, and the bleakness of her earlier thoughts felt like an itch that covered her body. She needed action to scratch that itch. But she'd done her part—made the plans, given the orders—and now had nothing to do but wait.

"Pit be damned," she whispered to her small bodyguard of ten infantry. "I'm not sitting back here for this. Let's go kill some tinheads." She was moving before she'd finished talking, scrambling up and over the ridge while her bodyguard struggled to keep up. She joined the infantry moving down into the first ravine. She moved mechanically, not allowing herself to acknowledge the aches and pains. She was halfway to the top of that third ridge when she realized how bad of an idea this was.

But she had gone too far. She *was* going in with her soldiers.

They reached the top of that ridge. Vlora almost tripped over a body, throat slit from ear to ear looking like a great black grin in the sallow moonlight. It was a Dynize sentry. She left the corpse behind and lifted her eyes to the Dynize camp.

It was still, but not silent. Soldiers and camp followers moved about in the shadows of their campfires, taking a piss or mending uniforms by firelight or just restless on the day before the battle. She was close enough to hear snores. Someone sang softly nearby. All around her, Adran soldiers crouched at the ready, breath held as they waited practically on top of the enemy.

She felt a momentary pang. This wasn't going to be a battle. There was no honor or justice in this.

That pang was cut off by a heavy thumping sound. Another followed it, and then another, too close together to count. The air was filled with a distant squeal that grew steadily louder until suddenly a blossom of red light erupted above their heads. It was joined by another, and another, until the sky was full of flares.

A nearby sergeant, a woman's voice, bellowed in Adran, "Like pigs in a pen, boys. Charge!"

Vlora drew her sword and allowed herself to be swept forward by the sudden rush of the infantry.

CHAPTER 24

Styke waited until his small group of Lancers had drunk themselves past the ability to do much damage. Then he slipped out the side door of the inn's bunkhouse, rounded behind the latrines, and met Orz on the side of the road. The dragonman wore long sleeves and a cape and hood to cover his tattoos. He seemed to blend with the shadows effortlessly. Styke hoped that their outing didn't require *too* much stealth, as he had neither the training nor the size for sneaking.

Orz handed him a hood. "Over your head," he said quietly. "Just to keep your face hidden. The fewer questions asked, the better."

"Are we going to run into any problems?" Styke asked, following instructions.

"We shouldn't. The curfew for slaves is at dusk. If we're *actually* stopped, it should be enough that you're with me. But I'd prefer not to be bothered."

"Right." The dragonman had managed to acquire for Styke some local clothing big enough to fit him—cream-colored pants and jacket accented with turquoise and sapphire. The clothes were much looser than anything he'd ever worn and he'd spent the last couple of hours wearing them in the hope that some practice would keep him from tripping on all the hanging cloth. He pulled the sleeves down to his wrists and shoved his hands into his pockets. "I'll do what I can not to be noticed."

Orz gave him a wry glance. "Will they be fine without us?" he asked, jerking his head to the inn behind them.

"Should be," Styke replied. "Jackal is in charge. He doesn't drink much these days. Ka-poel is sober, and if I can count on anything these days, it's that those assholes jump at Celine's word faster than they jump at mine."

"A daughter they never had?"

"Lots of them have kids. Half of those died during the Revolution, mostly at Kez hands. They spoil her, but she's too clever to let that go to her head." Styke adjusted the fall of his loose pants, took a couple of experimental steps. "Are we going far?"

"It's a couple of miles." Orz pointed to the south. "My parents, if they're still there, live just on the other side of the palace. When my brother took over the Household, they had a falling out. My mother picked a spot to live close enough that she could scrutinize anything he did but far enough away that she wasn't technically under his influence or protection. Shall we?"

Styke gestured for Orz to lead, and fell into step just a half pace behind the dragonman, remembering what Celine had told him earlier. He kept his head bent, shoulders hunched, with the hood pulled far enough forward to shadow his face without obscuring his vision. He watched Orz's shoulders for a few moments, noticing a hurriedness to his stride that hadn't been there before—a trace of nerves, perhaps—and then turned his attention to memorizing landmarks and street names.

"Do you get along with your parents?" he asked.

Orz shot a glance over his shoulder.

"I'd like to know what we're walking into," Styke explained.

Orz snorted. "I do not. Not with my parents, nor with my brother."

"Any good reason?" Styke chewed on his words, thinking them over. He'd never been one for talking about this sort of thing. But it seemed necessary. "Or just old family wounds? I'm familiar with both."

"I don't even remember the old family wounds. Small things that made us hate each other, I'm sure. But the schism between us—my brother and me—and my parents is deeper than that. When my emperor..." He paused, clearing his throat as they were passed by a handful of men and women giggling among themselves on a night out. "When our emperor was murdered, my parents switched sides. Not just pragmatically as adherence to the treaty, but with enthusiasm. They gave their minds, hearts, and souls over to Ka-Sedial within hours of the news. Not even a grain of remorse. They bullied my brother into doing the same. I couldn't forgive them for that."

This new bit of knowledge set off warning bells in the back of Styke's head. "You're sure this is a good idea, then? How do we know they won't turn you over to Ka-Sedial's people the moment we show our heads?"

"We don't."

Styke reached out and seized Orz by the arm without even thinking about it, jerking the dragonman to a stop. Orz whirled on him. "I'm helping you do this because you brought us out of the jungle. But if they turn on us—if this comes back to my men..."

Orz looked down at Styke's arm, nostrils flaring. "I will not allow it to come back to your men. I'm not going in blind. I know that they may betray us and I will be watchful. If they do not agree to come immediately, we will leave them behind."

"You're sure?"

"I'm sure."

"And your brother? Are you going to warn him?"

"There is no need. Ka-Sedial won't send assassins against a

Household head. My brother is well liked and supports Ka-Sedial publicly." He raised his gaze to meet Styke's eyes. "I don't do this because I am a fool. I have friends—people I knew in my youth who I haven't seen for ten years—who will likely disappear because of my actions in Fatrasta. They'll be tortured and killed. They may not even know why. But these are my parents. I have to at least *try* to spare them a similar fate."

Styke let his arm fall and they continued walking. He felt a tightness in his chest now, a new wariness that went beyond being in a strange place. This was a risk they didn't need. But they wouldn't have gotten this far without Orz. Styke owed him several times over now. No choice but to take a deep breath and help him with the errand.

And hope it all didn't go tits up.

They passed around the outer walls of the palace and cut east, leaving the wide avenues and entering an area that seemed to have more in common with the suburbs of Landfall. The houses were smaller, closer together, each of them fronted by a road and backed by a canal, built on foundations of stone surrounded by packed dirt. The houses here were mostly light-colored brick with reed-and-thatch roofs. The occasional group of children still played in the floating gardens despite the late hour. About half of the houses had already gone to bed, while the others were lit by lanterns.

They turned onto a short road that wasn't even a street anymore, just a dirt and gravel path that dead-ended at the water and was lined by more of the closely packed brick houses. Orz stopped abruptly.

"Do you see anything?" Styke searched the windows, roofs, and gardens of the dead end but saw nothing out of the ordinary.

Orz shook his head. "If Ka-Sedial warned one of his puppets, then my parents are already dead. If not, then we have beaten Sedial's men by at least a week. Come. It is the second-to-last house on the left."

The house was one of the few with a lantern still burning. As they approached, Styke caught sight of a single elderly woman sitting in a small room furnished with a table, two chairs, and a small, clay stove. The woman must have been in her late sixties, the freckles on her arms and face so thick that her skin looked entirely ashen. The resemblance was immediately apparent; she had the same cheekbones as Orz, the same thoughtful eyes. Her head was bowed over a length of knitting that extended between her knees and under the table.

Orz examined the old woman without a trace of emotion crossing his face. He lifted one hand. "I will be no longer than ten minutes." Without further explanation, he crossed to the door and stepped inside. Styke positioned himself by the open window, where he had a good view of the interior, including the look on the old woman's face as Orz closed the door behind him and threw back his hood.

The old woman's mouth opened, her jaw slack. Several seconds passed before the corners of her eyes tightened and she looked back down at her knitting. "You are dead to me," she said.

"Mother," Orz replied as if she hadn't just verbally cast him out.

The old woman began to knit furiously. "Did you escape?"

"No." She looked up sharply. Orz rounded the table to stand beside her, putting one hand on her shoulder. "Where is Father?"

"He's dead. Five years now."

The only response from Orz was a hard swallow. "They didn't tell me."

"Because you are dead, too. If you didn't escape, how are you here? Why are you here?"

"I was released. By Ka-Sedial."

"That's a lie," the old woman said, brushing his hand off her shoulder. Styke could see a flash of pain in Orz's eyes and was tempted to look away. This wasn't a drama that should be witnessed by other parties. But he remained glued to the window, unable to stop watching.

"It's not," Orz said stiffly. "Ka-Sedial released me. And then he betrayed me. I've come to warn you before he punishes you for my sins."

"I've already been punished for your sins," the old woman snapped, finally looking up at her son's face. "We were ostracized. Humiliated. Your father's heart gave out from shame. That you would spit on our emperor. Our *god*!"

Styke could see Orz drawing into himself throughout the lecture, his eyes growing more distant, his jaw tightening. "He is not my emperor, and he is far from a god. He is nothing but a puppet for Ka-Sedial, that..." He visibly wrestled for control of himself. Farther up the path, Styke heard a door shut and a figure walk off toward the main street. He attempted to sink deeper into the shadows.

The old woman suddenly shot to her feet, crossing the room as if it were difficult to be so close to her son. "The war ended, Orz. Were you so in love with it that you couldn't stop fighting?"

"Fighting?" Orz demanded, gesturing broadly to the east. "Do you think any of us stopped fighting? What do you think is going on at this very moment? I came from Fatrasta, where our mighty armies are stripping a land that is not our own."

"Ours by right," the old woman sniffed. She glared at her son, crossing to the table and unhooking the lantern. She took it with her and hung it in the opposite window above the stove. She opened the stove and added a few twigs, blowing life into some leftover coals. "I suppose you're here," she said angrily. "I'll make you tea."

"I'm not staying long enough for tea," Orz replied coldly. "I came here to warn you. To take you away before you could be hurt."

"Take me away to where?" she replied bitterly.

"Somewhere you can hide until this is over."

"Until what's over?" She turned to peer at his face.

"The war."

"To what end? You speak as if you expect us to lose. The treason—"

"Realism is not treason, no matter what the bone-eye propagandists want you to think," Orz talked over her. "We may win. We may lose. Ka-Sedial has attracted more attention than he cares to admit—I doubt you're getting any truth of the war in our newspapers."

"We're winning. What else do we need to know?"

Styke marveled at the willful ignorance of the old woman. She clearly wasn't stupid, but there was a set to her jaw that spoke of someone who had decided how the world was and refused to let it change.

"Kressian attention," Orz said. "Fatrastan resistance. Military technology that we can't match. I saw a lot in Fatrasta." Styke thought he detected a hint of something in Orz's voice. As if he was trying to convince *himself* that Ka-Sedial might lose.

"It doesn't matter," the old woman said, snatching a pot down from above the stove. "Here, fill this with water from the fountain, I—" Her words were cut off by a cough, and several things happened at once. Styke saw a flutter beyond the opposite window, then the deceivingly quiet shatter of the glass lantern. A familiar soft strumming sound was the next thing that registered, causing the hair on Styke's arms to stand on end.

In the same heartbeat, a hail of bolts slammed through the old woman, shredding her frail body. Styke flinched back, and when he raised his head back to the window, she was on the floor and Orz had stumbled back against the wall, clutching at his stomach. He had at least one bolt in his stomach, one in a shoulder, and another in his chest. Somehow, he stayed on his feet.

Styke had barely begun to move when the house next door suddenly discharged six shadowy figures. They were dressed much like he was but in darker clothes and carrying strange crossbows. Two took up stations on the path while a third kicked in the door.

Styke froze. The group was so focused on Orz that none of them seemed to notice him kneeling in the dark.

Through the window, he watched in amazement as Orz's bone knives appeared in his hands. The dragonman managed to cut down the first two assassins to enter the house. The third assassin casually braced himself and fired a pair of bolts point-blank into Orz from the pathway. Orz stumbled back, tripped, and fell over the table onto his mother's corpse.

The third assassin stepped into the light, and Styke immediately spotted the black tattoos on the man's neck. This new dragon-man grinned grimly down at Orz. "You shouldn't have come back, old friend." Orz wheezed something in response. The dragonman bent over, picking up one of Orz's knives from where it had been dropped. He gestured at Orz's mother. "She was all too willing to help set the trap. A good woman. A loyal woman. She'll be remembered for that loyalty."

Styke ground his teeth at the sudden change of fortunes. None of the remaining assassins had noticed him yet—the dragonman was inside and two were crowded around the door, crossbows held at the ready. The fourth was checking on her fallen comrades. The way Styke saw it, he could cut and run and hope none of them noticed his departure. He'd have to get back to the inn, sober everyone up, and get them moving. Then hope that Ka-poel could take Orz's place as their Dynize figurehead and get them safely to the Mad Lancer rendezvous.

It was the smart thing. Orz had done a lot for them, but he hadn't done enough to warrant a fight with another dragonman. Besides, with so many crossbow bolts in him he looked like a hedgehog. He was dead already.

Styke's heart fluttered. He remembered Orz's refusal to fight him over his mother's grave. He felt the injustice of Orz having to watch his *own* mother die. His fingers twitched, teeth clenched.

"Shit," he whispered, discarding his hood and drawing his knife.

The two assassins at the door didn't even have the chance to turn. He punched his knife through the neck of the one on the left, withdrew it in one quick motion, and slammed it hard into the other's kidneys. He put his shoulder to the man's back and lifted him, charging forward with the body as a shield.

The dragonman danced aside—or attempted to. Styke arrested his charge just a few steps into the room and, with one palm outstretched, shoved the dying assassin off the end of his knife and into the dragonman, who had nowhere to dodge in such a tight space.

The fourth assassin was on her feet by the time Styke turned. She raised her crossbow, catching the blade of his knife across the stock. He reached past both weapons with his left hand and snatched her by the throat, whipping her around and tossing her at the dragonman. The dragonman, extricating himself from the first body Styke threw at him, simply ducked and darted at Styke fast as a bullet.

Styke managed to catch the dragonman by the wrist, blocking a knife headed for his ribs, while the dragonman did the same to his own knife hand. The two remained locked that way for several seconds, struggling in a contest of strength. Styke felt his arms begin to tremble and had a brief vision of Ka-poel's smug face looking down at his corpse.

He slammed his forehead against the dragonman's nose. The dragonman's head snapped back, blood exploding across both their faces. Styke managed to bury an inch of his Boz knife into the dragonman's thigh, while the tip of the bone knife zigzagged a bloody line down his own arm. They spun, grappling, tripping and slipping on the corpses. Styke jerked his knife downward and sideways to open the wound, using the momentum to shove the dragonman backward against the now-hot stove.

Neither the sudden smell of cooking flesh nor the knife tearing through his thigh brought more than a grunt from the dragonman. Styke tried to lean harder, working his blade for an artery, but the dragonman suddenly slipped to one side and rolled backward across the stove and out the very window the crossbow bolts had come through less than a minute before.

Shouts came from the street, and Styke could picture the dragon-man going for one of those strange crossbows. Kicking the dying assassins out of his path, he snatched Orz by the back of his shirt and lifted him onto one shoulder as he ran through the front door. He caught sight of people standing on the path, gawking at him, as well as a single shadowy figure in the space between the houses. Styke didn't waste time trying to get a closer look. Jamming his knife into its sheath, he sprinted for the end of the road.

"I hope whatever bone-eye sorcery they carve into you guys keeps the swamp dragons away," he huffed as he ran. He threw Orz ahead of him just as his feet left firm ground and he turned the leap into a sloppy dive, hitting the dark, murky water hard enough to take the breath out of him.

CHAPTER 25

Vlora stumbled through the chaotic haze of the Dynize camp, choking on smoke and bewildered by the harsh glow of flares combined with the flickering flames from burning tents. It was all too much to process, shapes and shadows leaping through the night as Dynize staggered from their tents only to be bayoneted by a wave of Adran soldiers.

This was the first time Vlora had fought in a battle without her sorcery—ever—and it was the absolute worst circumstances she could have chosen. She had no conditioning for this sort of thing, no experience with the heightened cacophony of bloodshed, for the confusing nature of the sounds and sights of a fight in the dark. Her sorcery would have slowed it all down, given her time to think and adjust. Without it she felt as helpless as a fresh recruit, and it terrified her.

"Ma'am! One of our Knacked has located a bone-eye!" someone shouted in her ear.

Vlora tried to rein in her senses, to grasp enough of what was going on around her to give orders. Her bodyguard consisted of ten grenadiers—eight men and two women, the biggest and meanest of her infantry corps. Joining the fray had essentially cut them loose, and they expected her to sweep along with them as they joined in the bloody slaughter. She could see the confused looks in their eyes when she didn't move readily, react quickly, and bark orders. She wasn't behaving like a powder mage, and they knew it.

"Where?" she demanded, focusing on one of the grenadiers. "Lead on!"

She struggled to keep up as they began to jog through the smoke. A coughing Dynize infantryman crawled from his tent only to take a bayonet between the shoulder blades. An officer emerged from the haze, half-dressed and waving a sword. Her grenadiers swarmed him before he even had the chance to call out.

"Here, ma'am," one of the grenadiers barked, running toward a tent. She could see a shape inside, the silhouette struggling to buckle on a breastplate.

"Take care of it."

The order was carried out quickly and savagely, bayonets pincushioning the hapless bone-eye in his own tent, then dragging him out into the light, where someone slit his throat to make sure the job was finished. Vlora found herself horrified at the process.

She couldn't help but wonder if her sorcery had given her some sort of cushion against these horrors. Had it calcified her? Kept her from seeing the blood of battle for what it truly was? Or was this something different—nothing that could be called a battle. These Dynize weren't even vaguely ready to defend themselves. Her soldiers poured over them with ease. She turned her attention on her surroundings, looking at the faces in the flickering light. Some of them attacked the helpless infantry in their tents with childish joy. Most seemed steely-eyed, acting with methodical, mechanical effort. They knew that every soldier they didn't kill was one that would have the opportunity to shoot back at them in the morning.

Vlora grasped onto that thought. This was the right thing to do, wasn't it? Minimizing danger to her own people was all that mattered. The Dynize infantry were just so many sacks of meat to churn through.

"Ma'am! Ma'am!"

Vlora focused on the face of one of her female grenadiers. She realized that she didn't even know any of their names. These people were here to protect her life. How could she not have bothered to learn who they were?

"Are you all right, ma'am?"

"Yes, yes. What is it?"

The grenadier pointed to the horizon. It took a few moments for Vlora to tell the difference between the various lights in the sky—sorcerous conflagrations had now joined the flares. An experienced eye was good enough to see that this wasn't just Nila and Bo adding to the fireworks; they'd gotten into it with someone, likely General Etepali's Privileged. "Bo and Nila are on it," she told the grenadier. "Focus on this camp."

"Yes, ma'am!"

As the night wore on, the mood of the conflict shifted. Pockets of Dynize appeared, usually organized by a sole officer, offering token resistance to the rampaging Adrans. Vlora pushed herself through her own muddled mind, urging her bodyguard toward these pockets, making sure they put them down as quickly as possible to keep the Dynize from forming a coherent backbone.

Sorcery continued to rage on the northern horizon, and it helped Vlora orient herself in the confusion. Messengers passed through the haze on horseback, sometimes looking for her and other times just informing captains and sergeants of developments. She learned through these that Etepali had indeed counterattacked. Her Privileged had engaged Bo and Nila and her infantry was pushing hard at Vlora's flank. So far, the men she'd left to protect those heavy fortifications had managed to hold the line.

She lost all track of time and space. One of her grenadiers fell to a Dynize officer. Soldiers in one of those pockets of resistance had managed to leave her limping with two new cuts on her left thigh. Her own inability to do more than raise her sword left her with an inner terror and the continuing knowledge that she shouldn't be here in the thick of things. She risked not just her life but also her reputation.

She shoved herself onward, forcing herself to be an avatar that she didn't feel she was any longer, pushing harder toward those pockets of resistance. She even began to run, shouting at her men. It felt surreal, like she was floating above herself and watching someone else control her body.

Vlora was so caught up in the chaos around her that she barely noticed the orange-lacquered breastplate on a Dynize officer less than twenty feet from her. She had to backpedal mentally, turning her head toward that breastplate, words of caution on her lips.

The enemy general was a small man with a long, braided mustache. He wore the morion helm and lacquered breastplate, and he shook a cavalryman's sword over his head. His eyes fell on Vlora at almost the same moment that she looked back to examine him, and the two froze in the heat of the moment. Unfortunately for Vlora, the general's bodyguard was quicker.

Two forms erupted from the night, hitting her grenadiers like a pair of cannonballs. She saw flashes of bone knives, of ashen-freckled bare chests covered with snaking black tattoos. The dragonmen cut through three of her grenadiers before the group even had the chance to react.

"Form up!" Vlora yelled, far too late. "Dragonmen on the left flank; keep them at the tips of your bayonets!" She threw herself backward, dropping her sword and snatching up the bayoneted rifle of a fallen grenadier. For the first time all night, her vague feelings of stupidity burned into something sharper—the terror of knowing she could die within moments.

A bayonet skewered one of the dragonmen through the belly, but the dragonman barely flinched, using the opportunity to jerk the grenadier closer and slice her throat with one of his knives. He soon fell to the bayonets of the others, but the gap gave his companion the opening he needed to slide around to the side of the mass of grenadiers, hitting them in the flank. All but two went down, and those last threw themselves between the dragonman and Vlora with a pair of angry roars. Blades flashed, bayonets jerked.

The entire confrontation lasted for mere moments, passing so quickly that Vlora could barely follow it. She stood stupidly with the recovered rifle hanging loose from numb fingers as the last of her grenadiers fell to a dragonman's knife. The enemy general stood just behind his champion, shouting something in Dynize, waving that saber at Vlora. The dragonman had not come out of the fight unscathed—he was covered in cuts, stabbed through at least twice. He would have been an easy target if Vlora had had her sorcery, and perhaps an even fight even if she was in better health.

The dragonman brushed off his wounds and began to stalk toward Vlora. It took all of her courage to stand firm, renewing her grip on the rifle in her hands. They circled each other for a few moments before the dragonman ducked and lunged, coming in under the point of her bayonet, knife flashing forward. She backpedaled hard, feeling the blade nick through her jacket and flesh. She tripped, slid, and fell so hard that the dragonman stumbled over and past her.

Flashes of the battle of the Crease passed through Vlora's mind, those moments when she knew her fate was sealed hitting her between the eyes. Her hands trembled. She clutched the rifle to her chest, trying to get a good enough grip on it to stab upward at the dragonman who now loomed over her, knife poised for the killing blow.

There was a sudden thunder in her ears, and her eyes filled with the flash of hooves. She shook and shivered in the onslaught, not daring to move. As quickly as they arrived, the hooves were gone, and she craned her neck to watch the rear of a platoon of Adran cuirassiers as they thundered back into the fire-licked darkness.

The dragonman and his general were both gone. Vlora slowly staggered to her feet, casting about until she found her opponents—both of them reduced to a pulp beneath Adran hooves. She widened her gaze, taking in the horror of her slaughtered bodyguard, and then further to look around at the bodies of Dynize infantrymen that coated the grounds of their camp for as far as she could see.

She bent and was sick all over her own boots. Clawing at her throat, trying to breathe, she began to stagger back to camp.

History, she realized in a moment of clarity, would call this a victory.

CHAPTER 26

Michel and Ichtracia moved to a damp overhanging roof that viewed the exits of their former safe house. It was recessed beneath another walk, a good place to watch without being seen, but wildly uncomfortable. Ichtracia settled down next to him and scowled into the darkness, placing one hand on his knee. He reached down and squeezed it.

"You all right?" he asked.

"Of course." Her tone was confident. Her face—what little of it he could see in the shadows—was not.

He cleared his throat. "You, uh, sure?" he asked slowly.

There was a long silence. He finally felt her gaze turn on him and heard the soft tremble of a sigh. "Just remembering," she said with a shake of her head. "It's been a few years since I've had to deal with an assassination attempt. You never really get used to them."

"That's right. You've dealt with this sort of thing before?"

"You haven't?"

"Been woken up by an assailant? Once. It wasn't pleasant, and I've slept lightly ever since."

Ichtracia remained quiet for several more minutes. He could sense her reluctance to speak, and was surprised when she finally did. "I barely slept between the ages of eight and thirteen. I was so scared of them coming back to kill me. Then I started taking mala."

Michel had always assumed that she took the mala to deal with her contentious relationship with her grandfather. It had never occurred to him that it was for a far more practical—and personal—reason. He let out a soft *ah* and put an arm around her shoulder. She leaned into him, her head resting on his shoulder.

"How do you switch sides so easily?" she asked.

"Well, it's not actually easy."

"It *looks* easy for you." She paused. "Dahre and his people. They all seem so...decent. Average. Just normal people living their lives. I've been with them for just a couple of days and I've stayed aloof, but I find myself wondering more about them—their home lives, their loves and hates, their inner thoughts. I wonder where they'll be next year or in a decade."

"That's called empathy," Michel said, trying not to sound condescending. "It's an important tool for a spy."

"So you've told me. But the deeper I get into these people, the more I *care* about them."

Michel didn't reply. It was something he struggled with for every person he had to deceive. He'd felt it so strongly just the other night when he saw Tenik again. "It's hard," he whispered.

"I never imagined." Ichtracia's voice trembled. "I think...I think I'm beginning to see why you do it."

"Oh?"

"We're deceiving them, but we're also down here among them. The Palo, that is. I'm beginning to feel the bottled-up anger. The way that you eat and breathe the oppression by stronger people. I can see it in everyone's eyes. Even the well-to-do have it—like Dahre. There's a little pain that's in the eyes of all the Palo that isn't there for the Kressians or Dynize. It's…" She trailed off for a moment, then continued thoughtfully, "It's like I've found an entire people who know what it's like to live beneath my grandfather. It's terrifying but…wonderful at the same time. Does that make sense?"

"Misery loves company?"

She laughed softly. "Yes, I suppose it does."

Michel was surprised when she suddenly leaned in and kissed him, then settled back against his shoulder to wait. He fell into his own thoughts, considering her words, turning over what it meant to be *of* a people but also of none. He eventually had to push those thoughts away before they took a dark path.

Over the next few hours, his anxiety began to lessen as no one returned. No assassins. No Dynize. Just no one. Frustrating, but not deadly. He was just beginning to think it might be time to abandon their hiding spot and move on to a new safe house when he caught sight of Devin-Mezi approaching one of the tenement exits. She paused just outside, beneath a gas lantern, looking around furtively. Michel nudged Ichtracia. "Our friend is back."

"I still think you should have let me kill her." Ichtracia yawned.

"We'll find out if you were right soon enough."

Devin-Mezi headed inside. Michel remained rooted to his spot, watching for any sign of hidden companions, until he was satisfied that Devin-Mezi had come alone. He slid back from the ledge. "With me," he told Ichtracia, heading down a narrow staircase and then dropping onto the next level down. A steep ramp led them to the exit, and they arrived at almost the same moment that Devin-Mezi reappeared, her face screwed up in a look of frustration.

"You're late," Michel said.

Devin-Mezi jumped and whirled, drawing a knife. She eyeballed him for a moment, then Ichtracia, before putting her knife back. "You said three hours."

"It's been three and fifteen."

"I had to get Kelinar to a doctor."

"Will he be all right?"

"I have no idea." Devin-Mezi glared at Ichtracia.

Ichtracia smiled back at her softly. "Careful who you try to knife, next time."

"There won't be a next time," Michel intervened. "Well. You're back. I take it you're here to fetch us to Mama Palo?"

"I am. I was told to take the Privileged's gloves, first."

"Over my dead body," Ichtracia snapped.

"Either I get your gloves, or I don't take either of you anywhere." Devin-Mezi folded her arms. Michel had to give it to her—she had guts. To come back and say that to a Privileged took both courage and stupidity. Just as it would be stupid for Ichtracia to give up her only pair of gloves just before heading out to meet with strangers. Luckily, Ichtracia had several pairs hidden about her person. He pretended to hesitate before turning to Ichtracia. "I'm going to give her your gloves," he said, swinging the pack off his shoulder. He dug inside for a moment before handing them to Devin-Mezi.

Ichtracia's lip curled, but she didn't respond.

"Good enough?" Michel asked.

Devin-Mezi held the gloves up to the light suspiciously.

"Like I said," he continued, "we're on the same side. If that doesn't prove it, I don't know what will."

"All right," Devin-Mezi replied hesitantly. "Follow me."

They were led through the twists and turns of the Depths at an alarming rate, heading up, down, across, and under a dozen different levels. Michel stopped trying to keep track of their path and instead watched for landmarks. By the time they reached their destination, he had only a vague idea that they were deep in the center of the Depths—very deep, with real ground beneath their feet.

They went through a nondescript white door and were suddenly stopped by a pair of heavily armed Palo. Both men wore two pistols and a sword, and both took a pistol in hand as the door opened. They relaxed at the sight of Devin-Mezi but kept their eyes on Michel and Ichtracia.

"The visitors that Mama requested," Devin-Mezi introduced.

Whether the two had been told what Ichtracia was, or were just naturally wary, they fell in behind Michel and Ichtracia without a word. Michel reached into his bag and handed them his unloaded pistol. "I'll want this back," he told them before being herded through another door.

They might as well have stepped into a nobleman's townhouse, so different was this next room from the rest of the Depths. It was a wide, open room with immaculate plastering, well-lit by gas lanterns, and genuine art on the walls. Mattresses covered the floor, each taken over by a sleeping form, and Michel was more than a little surprised by the sight of it. This had the feel of one of Taniel's safe houses, and the extra bodies told him that it might well be Mama Palo's headquarters.

They picked their way through the impromptu bunkhouse and went down a hallway. There was more art on the walls; the plaster and trim were all the familiar materials used by the upper crust of Landfall. Michel's curiosity about the new Mama Palo grew tenfold. Whoever she was, she had good taste.

Devin-Mezi knocked on a door at the end of the hall. A muffled voice answered, and she opened the door. Michel took a deep breath, shared a glance with Ichtracia, and followed Devin-Mezi inside.

The room was spacious enough to have once been a drawing room. It had been commandeered as a bedroom and office with a large, four-poster bed shoved into one corner and a desk and several tables taking up the rest of it. Michel's impression of a headquarters immediately solidified at the sight of all the maps and papers spread across every surface. There were even rifle crates piled in one corner, stamped with the Hrusch family logo.

The last thing in the room to fall under Michel's eye was the woman sitting behind the desk. Like many Palo, she could be considered petite, just a shade over five feet tall with waist-length hair combed out over one shoulder. She was young, a couple years younger than Michel at best, but she had an aura of command about her, even sitting there in her nightgown with hair down. Her chin was resting on one fist, the other hand holding a book up to the lamplight, and it was only her eyes that moved when the small group paraded into the room. Her name was Jiniel, and the moment Michel saw her, he had to stifle a grin and a spike of fear all at the same time.

A normal reaction, he decided, for someone seeing an old lover for the first time in years.

"Cousin," Devin-Mezi said, "this is the guy calling himself Puffer. Careful with the woman. I've taken her gloves, but she still might be dangerous, she—"

"Out," Jiniel said.

"Cousin?"

"Not you. The other two. No need for guards."

"Cousin, are—"

Jiniel snorted loudly, and the sound sent the two guards scurrying. Once the door had shut behind them, Jiniel set down her book and stretched, letting out a severe yawn. "The woman's name is Ichtracia. She's a Dynize bone-eye." Devin-Mezi swore, and had begun to go for her knife before Jiniel held up one hand to forestall a fight. "If she's here with Michel, that's enough for me."

"Michel?" Devin-Mezi muttered, turning toward Michel with a look of confusion. Her jaw suddenly dropped. "*You're* Michel Bravis?"

Michel had never heard his name spoken with a tinge of awe

before. He wasn't sure where it came from, but he knew within moments that he liked it. "That's me."

"I had no idea, I—"

Michel cut her off gently with a question he'd been wondering since their first introduction at Meln-Dun's quarry. "Did you really work for the Yaret Household?"

"I did. I was there the same time as you. I only ever saw you once, but you look nothing—"

"Michel," Jiniel interjected, "is our best spy. I'd be shocked if he still looked anything like he did a month ago. He certainly looks nothing like he did three *years* ago. How are you, Michel? It's been too long." There was a note of exhaustion to Jiniel's voice that elicited a bit of worry in the back of Michel's mind. He was not, truth be told, all that surprised to find her here as Mama Palo. Despite her age, she was one of the cleverest people he'd ever met. Add in a great deal of intelligence and charisma, and she was a natural successor for Ka-poel's authority in Landfall. But in the time he'd known her, she'd always had the most boundless energy. To hear such weariness seeping into her voice was not good.

"It has," he agreed, waving his three-fingered hand at her to answer her question. "Sorry for coming in like this. Your cousin here tried to knife me earlier tonight."

"So I heard." Jiniel leaned forward, resting her elbows on her desk and nestling her chin behind her hands. She looked hard at Michel, then at Ichtracia. "I'm sorry about that. We had no idea it was you—just some asshole mercenary here to ruin our plans."

"That's fine. I didn't know you had a cousin. Or that you were the new Mama Palo. I forgot to ask Taniel the last time I saw him."

"I'm sure he had other things on his mind."

"He definitely did," Michel agreed. He noted that Jiniel's gaze was still on Ichtracia and glanced over his shoulder to find her hanging back near the door, hands thrust in her pockets. She hadn't said a word in the brief time since they entered, and the look of appraisal on her face said that she was sizing up Jiniel the same as Jiniel was doing to her. She shot Michel a quick glance full of a thousand questions. They'd have to be answered later, he decided. For now, he needed to explain her presence. There was an awful lot to go through, and he wasn't sure whom to trust and how much to trust them.

"Why *do* you have a Privileged with you?" Jiniel finally asked.

A moment's consideration passed before he decided to tell Jiniel. He didn't have much choice. But that didn't mean he had to spread it around. He gave Devin-Mezi a significant look, and Jiniel spoke up immediately. "Give us some privacy, Cousin."

Devin-Mezi hesitated only a moment before showing herself out. Once she was gone, Michel let out a breath he didn't even know he'd been holding in. "You don't trust her?"

"I do," Jiniel answered. "But the less she knows, the better."

"Compartmentalization," Ichtracia said.

"Exactly. I see that Michel has started training you how to think like him."

"It's an...education," Ichtracia replied.

"It is. He trained me, too. Michel, are you going to tell me why the granddaughter of the Great Ka is running with you?"

Michel sucked on his teeth. "She's Ka-poel's sister."

He couldn't think of a time in the past that he'd seen Jiniel genuinely surprised, so the look on her face now was one that he cast to memory to enjoy for the rest of his life. He let the statement sit for a moment, then leapt into a very brief explanation of their adventures over the last few months. Jiniel remained silent throughout the whole thing, her fingers steepled in front of her face. Once Michel had finished, with a few interjections from Ichtracia, Jiniel opened a desk drawer, removed three glasses, and poured a finger of Palo whiskey into each. Michel took two glasses, handing one to Ichtracia. They all downed the unspoken toast in silence.

Jiniel chuckled and ran a hand over her face. "I thought I had had a pit of a year. But you . . . by Kresimir, that is some story."

Michel rubbed the stubs of his missing fingers gingerly. "When I say it all at once, it certainly is." He looked back at Ichtracia again. This was not the first time he'd been in the room with an ex-lover and a current lover at the same time, but that didn't make it any less uncomfortable. He was willing to bet that both women had already sussed out that much about the other—Jiniel spoke to him too warmly; Ichtracia hovered too close. Nothing was said, of course, but the very energy in the air put him on edge.

"These sacrifices," Jiniel said, pouring them each another round. "You're certain about them?"

It was the one part of Michel's story that had gotten a deep frown from Jiniel, and he was not surprised to hear her come back to it so quickly. "That's the problem. I have the word of a Blackhat, and Ichtracia's own certainty."

"But no evidence."

"No evidence."

Jiniel sighed heavily. "I haven't heard anything. Disappearances, yes. But those happen in times of war and chaos. People die, drift away, or are nabbed by enemy agents."

"These would be . . . a few thousand disappearances in total since the invasion."

"That's not very many people in a city this big," Jiniel said. "I'm sorry. Nothing has snagged our notice."

"I need to find out," Michel said, "and if it *is* true, the word needs to be spread."

"Of course! But I barely have enough resources to keep our organization going. We've been running from Meln-Dun's men, attempting to sift through Dynize propaganda to find out how they really intend to treat us, and dogging what few Blackhats were left after that purge you conducted through the Dynize." Jiniel paused, her face scrunched up in a scowl. "What you're saying is such an outlandish story that we need some kind of evidence to move forward on it."

"And what can you do if we *can* find evidence?" Ichtracia spoke up. She moved to sit on the corner of Jiniel's desk, crossing her arms and looking down at Jiniel as if daring her to comment on it.

"Fight back." There was a note of helplessness in her voice. "Do what we can."

"I have a plan for that," Michel said, "but I'll need your resources."

"Then give me something to work with."

Proof of Sedial sacrificing citizens in a blood rite of some kind. When Michel crammed the thought into so few words, it sounded simple. But if *no one* had noticed anything wrong yet? Maybe he was chasing a breeze, and the ghost of je Tura was laughing at him from the afterlife. He tapped his chin. Not no one. No one *important*. He needed to find the unimportant people who might have noticed. "I'll come up with proof. For now, I need you to call off this trap you're preparing for Meln-Dun's men."

"Call it off?" Jiniel scoffed. "It's happening tonight—and it's not just a little trap. We're going to ambush his goons at the same time we send a strike team into the quarry."

Michel inhaled sharply. "You're planning on assassinating him?" Jiniel nodded.

"Don't."

"The plan is in place."

"You have to scrap it." Michel paused, considering. "Wait. No, don't scrap it. But I think I can make it unnecessary."

"What are you planning?" Jiniel asked cautiously.

"Something that will eliminate Meln-Dun's threat to us without having to kill fellow Palo *and* without bringing the Dynize down on our heads."

"I'm listening."

Michel gave her a tight smile. "Compartmentalization."

"I forgot how much I hate it when you use that word," Jiniel said.

"Right?" Ichtracia added.

"Okay, Michel," Jiniel continued after a moment of thought. "If you can make my attack unnecessary, well...I'll be damned impressed."

"I'll do it," Michel promised. "Give me twelve hours."

CHAPTER 27

Styke swam until he could feel his strength beginning to wane, and then pulled Orz down one of the countless tiny canals of Talunlica. It was a waxing crescent moon that shone a pale light across the city, giving him just enough light to navigate by and— he hoped—just enough darkness to hide within. He found a tiny inlet, shallow enough for him to touch his toes to the bottom, and broke a bit of reed weaving off one of the floating gardens to hook underneath Orz's arm. He put his own shoulder beneath Orz's other arm and lowered himself into the water so that everything below his nose was covered.

Occasionally he could hear distant shouting. There were a few splashes early on, and torchlight in the distance, but the Dynize did not seem readily equipped to organize a search. Styke mulled over his options. The dragonman had survived their conflict, which meant that he had seen Styke's face. He would know to look for an immense foreigner. Once he had a little bit of time to gather more searchers and widen the net, he might find Styke hiding in the water—or even discover Styke's men at the inn.

Styke vacillated between abandoning Orz in an attempt to reach his men and get them out of the city, and remaining with the dragonman. His thinking drifted slowly toward the former option. Orz was as good as dead, bone-eye sorcery or not, and even if he *could* survive, he was just deadweight.

He paused midthought as he felt Orz's body shift. Lifting them both a little out of the water, Styke pressed his ear up against Orz's mouth. "You still breathing, you tattooed asshole?" Styke whispered. For a few moments he thought that Orz had finally given up the ghost, but to his surprise the dragonman took a sudden deep breath.

"Bolts...have to get...out."

"Those bolts are the only thing keeping you from bleeding out right now," Styke told him. "I can't speak for the infection this damned lake water is gonna give you, but I doubt that's our first worry right now."

"Mo...moth...mother."

"Sorry," Styke replied. He closed his eyes and saw, once again, the old woman's body being torn apart by crossbow bolts. He remembered the lantern she had hung in the window—a signal, probably. He also remembered, very distinctly, that she'd sent Orz out for water right before the ambush. Styke wondered if she'd had a change of heart at that last moment. They'd never know. Not that it mattered.

Orz's breath began to come a little stronger, ragged and loud. Styke craned his head to try to get a good look at the nearby street. They were just off one of the countless little dead-end streets much like the one they'd escaped. Farther down the canal someone was smoking in the evening air, facing the opposite direction, but otherwise the area was abandoned and the occupants asleep.

"Should I be worried about swamp dragons, or do they stay out of the lake?" he whispered to Orz.

There was no answer.

"Shit." Styke craned his head again, this time trying to pierce the darkness and get a good look at the silhouette of the surrounding mountains. It wasn't an accurate way to get his bearings, but it would be a start. He lifted Orz's arm and hooked the dragonman's limp fingers around the reeds of the floating garden, then swam out a couple of feet to get a better look. It took a few minutes, but he was eventually able to spot the black shadow of the godstone stabbing into the sky—probably a quarter of a mile to his northwest.

He had just one option: Get Orz to Ka-poel. She might be able to strengthen the blood sorcery that had kept him alive this long. But to do so, he'd need to risk the avenues, where frequent city guard patrols would spot him within minutes. He considered swimming, or a boat. Both avenues were more than likely to get him lost and confused.

He swam back to Orz. "You have any suggestions on how to get out of this?"

Orz took a ragged breath but did not answer.

Styke eyeballed a canoe tied up behind one of the nearby houses. Perhaps there *was* another option. He disentangled Orz from the reeds and set off across the canal with the dragonman in tow. Reaching the opposite bank, he found a couple of brick steps just above the waterline and leveraged himself, then Orz, onto dry land—careful to move slowly to make the least amount of noise.

"Sorry," he whispered to Orz, then dumped him off the land and into the bottom of the canoe. There was a loud *thunk*, and he grimaced into the darkness, waiting for a face to appear in a window, or a door to open.

Minutes passed. No one came to investigate the noise.

Styke found a paddle and untied the canoe before lowering

himself in. Using deep, slow strokes, he pushed off and began to head down the middle of the canal.

He was working on a map of the city that he'd built in his head. There wasn't a lot to go on—his earlier view from above the city, then their walk to the palace complex, and finally the trip to Orz's mother's house. But it would have to be enough, he decided. He certainly wasn't going far.

Once he was moving, he rooted around in the bottom of the canoe, finding an old wool blanket tucked under the stern. It reeked of fish, but he tossed it over his head as a hood and continued to paddle.

Pulling out into open water gave him a better chance to orient himself. He'd managed to make quite some distance in his panicked swim. There was a wide channel, at least half of a mile between his current location and where he believed was the site of the ambush. The houses over there were lit, the streets filled with moving lanterns. There were a couple of boats in the water, but they hugged the shore as if the searchers had not expected him to get far with a body in tow.

After getting his bearings he decided to cling to the bank, keeping a wary eye on the distant searchers. His progress was slow but fairly quiet, and the occasional soul that he passed in the night gave him little more than a friendly wave. He returned those waves and continued on.

As he'd decided earlier, heading back to the inn would be too risky by water. He didn't know the canal routes at all, and getting lost would put him at great risk.

He did, however, have a pretty good idea where to find the Minister of Drainage.

He rounded several small islands and suburban promontories, leaving the lamps of the searchers behind him, before spotting a watchtower ahead in the darkness. It was—he hoped—the same watchtower that marked the Etzi Household. Eventually the complex defined itself in the gloom: a large, walled villa at the end of a man-made cape. It looked to be about the size of a small village, with dozens of buildings rising above the short walls. Easily big enough to house a small army or, as Orz had put it, a minor Household.

By the time Styke reached the villa complex, he was exhausted. His arms and shoulders ached, his eyes hurt from trying to peer into the gloom. He pulled up alongside the single cobbled road that led to the villa and rolled onto the land. After a few moments of rest, he reached back into the canoe to fetch Orz.

Miraculously, the dragonman was still alive, letting out a loud groan when Styke lifted him.

Styke had thought to drop Orz on his brother's doorstep and make his escape. But the noise brought an answering sound from within the walls, and within a few moments there were a handful of clacks and a low squeal as one of the big, iron-strapped doors of the complex opened. An old man with a gray mustache held a lantern high on the end of a pole, thrusting it toward Styke.

"What's this here?" he demanded in a low voice.

Styke swore under his breath. He considered making for the canoe, but the idea of trying to flee yet another scene did not sit well with him. He'd made his decision. It was time to throw himself on the mercy of others. And if that failed, he'd go for his knife.

The man took another step closer. "I asked you a question! Is that a body?"

Styke answered in broken Dynize, filling in any words he wasn't certain of with their Palo counterparts. "I'm looking for Meln-Etzi. Is this his home?"

The old man took a half step back, calling something over his shoulder into the door behind him. "Yes, this is the Etzi Household." Then he scurried forward, lowering the lantern to play on Orz's face. He let out a gasp. "Go fetch the master," he barked to a young girl who had appeared in the doorway. He lifted his lantern, peering at Styke. This time he actually fled back to the door, standing with one hand on the wood as if to slam it shut in Styke's face if he made a move.

"I'm his slave," Styke attempted.

The old watchman didn't answer. A few minutes passed and some small commotion took him inside, only for him to reappear a moment later.

Styke had expected to find Orz's brother to be older, but he was surprised at the appearance of a bespectacled man in his midthirties who wore a hastily thrown-on robe over silk pajamas. Like Orz's mother, the resemblance was uncanny. But while Orz had hard, unbending features, this man seemed soft and thoughtful. He paused in the doorway, his watchman peering over his shoulder as if his master would protect him from this hulking foreigner.

"Who are you?" Etzi demanded.

Styke bit his tongue, remembering Celine's lecture, and bowed his head respectfully. "I am Orz's slave."

A grunt answered. "Do you know who I am?"

"His brother."

Etzi took the lantern from his watchman and thrust it in Styke's face for a handful of moments, then gave another grunt and knelt beside Orz. He took a deep breath, looking him up and down, then pointed at Styke. "You, carry him inside. You." His finger twitched to his watchman. "Fetch Maetle. Be quick about it and don't wake anyone else up."

Styke obeyed, lifting Orz with both arms—in a manner somewhat gentler than he'd been treating him so far—and followed Etzi through the door. They didn't have far to go, ducking through a darkened servant's entrance just inside the compound walls and emerging into a long kitchen with high ceilings, the likes of which would have been recognizable in any lordling or merchant's manner hall. Etzi gestured for Styke to set Orz on one of the long preparation tables and then walked briskly around the kitchen, shuttering windows, before turning up the lamps.

Etzi returned to the kitchen table and stared at the body of his brother, forehead creased, as if Styke wasn't even present. Styke was glad for the silence—questions would start soon, and he'd never been a very good liar. The longer he had to think of some story, the better.

The watchman soon returned, followed by a woman in her midtwenties. To Styke's surprise, she was not Dynize—or at least, not a full-blood Dynize. She had dark brown hair and only a hint of freckles on her cheeks and arms. She carried a satchel over one shoulder and wore a nightgown, still rubbing the sleep out of her eyes as she entered the room.

She froze at the sight of Orz, letting out a tiny gasp before rushing to his side and, in the process, shouldering Styke aside. He relinquished his spot to stand in the corner of the kitchen, where he could watch all three entrances as well as the figures swarming around Orz's body. He casually rested his hand on the hilt of his knife.

Etzi had called for Maetle, and Styke could only assume this was she. He couldn't smell any sorcery on her, but he'd seen a lot of surgeons in his day and she had the air. As if to confirm his suspicions, she disgorged her satchel onto the table beside Orz's head, revealing bottles, bandages, tiny sacks, and a full complement of small blades, tweezers, saws, and tools that Styke didn't even recognize. Her equipment was tidily organized, everything labeled, and she quickly arranged a handful of items close at hand and pushed the rest away.

"Well?" Etzi asked.

Maetle paused with her hands hovering over Orz's chest. Styke could still see a slight rise and fall. Maetle responded to her master in Dynize, speaking so quickly that it was hard for Styke to follow. "He's still alive."

"I know that!"

"And he may yet live. I can't be certain." She hesitated. "I've read about this sort of thing, but I've never dealt with it myself."

"A pincushioned fool?" Etzi asked.

"No," Maetle shot back. "Dragonmen and the bone-eye sorcery that makes them . . ." She cleared her throat and continued in a gentler tone. "Sorry, master. The bone-eye sorcery that makes them strong. Supposedly it can help them survive wounds beyond anything a normal person could weather. This . . . he should have bled out . . . you, how long has he been like this?"

Styke's head jerked up. He realized he'd been starting to nod off even while listening. "A couple of hours."

Maetle gave him a peculiar look. "What did you say?"

"I said . . ." He realized he'd answered in Adran. He swore inwardly and switched to his poor Dynize, repeating himself.

Maetle's gaze remained on Styke for a moment before she returned her attention to her patient and master. "He should be dead already. Bled out. But dragonmen can go into a sorcery-induced trance that slows their heart and the bleeding."

"But you don't know if he'll survive?" Etzi asked.

"I don't. But I need to remove the bolts, clean the wounds, and find out if they punctured anything vital. Shall I begin?"

Etzi rubbed his chin, staring down at his brother's body. The silence dragged on. A minute. Then two. Styke felt as if he could see Orz's breaths growing slower. Finally, none of Celine's lecture about remaining meek could keep him from losing his patience. "Well, are you going to save him?" he demanded.

All three of them looked up sharply. The watchman raced across the room and smacked Styke hard across the face. The sharpness of the blow seemed to shake off some of his exhaustion, and he set his teeth. The watchman drew back his hand. "You do not speak to the master of the house in such a manner! You are a slave, you . . ." He swung again, and Styke caught him by the wrist before the blow could fall. The old man seemed confused, then immediately began to struggle against Styke's grip.

"Let him go," Etzi ordered.

Styke ground his teeth. "Are you going to save your brother or not?"

"Let him go," Etzi repeated. Styke knew the tone well, no matter the language it was spoken in. He'd heard it as a young man in the military, and he'd heard it every day for ten years in the labor camps. It took a supreme act of willpower not to snap the watchman's wrist. Finally, he released the man.

The watchman stumbled back, wringing his hands. "What kind of a slave—"

"That," Etzi cut him off, "is not a slave. What is your name, foreigner?"

Styke bit down hard on his tongue. He'd only ever been good at ending confrontations with violence. It would not work this time—at least, it wouldn't work in his favor. "Ben," he answered.

"This man," Etzi gestured at Orz, "is already dead. He died when he spit at the emperor's feet. He was imprisoned and declared an un-person. Now he is here, as if having clawed his way out of a grave." He used a word next that sounded fairly close to an old Palo legend of the undead. "My duty would be that of any man confronted with a zombie: to call the authorities to destroy it. Tell me, Ben, what would you do in my place?"

Styke sniffed. "Metaphor means nothing in the face of the truth," he said in Adran, trying to think of the right words in Dynize.

"Metaphor is all I have," Etzi replied, also in Adran.

It was not the first time Styke had been surprised to hear a Dynize speak passable Adran. He continued in his own language. "Ever buried anyone by accident?"

Etzi's eyebrow raised.

Styke continued, wishing he had more time, trying to balance delicacy with urgency. "Happens occasionally. Someone slips into a coma, or comes down with a disease of the heart that makes them sleep as if dead. I've heard one story of a woman digging herself out of her own grave. Other stories tell of strange sounds at night in the graveyard and when the body is dug up, there are claw marks on the inside of the coffin."

"What is your point?"

"My point is that sometimes you think someone is dead. But they're not. All that matters now is what's in front of you."

The watchman had retreated to the door that led back out into the courtyard, as if waiting for permission to run for the city guard. Maetle remained by Orz, one hand resting gently on his chest, eyes glued to Styke. Etzi stared into the middle distance between Orz and Styke, forehead still furrowed, spectacles perched on the tip of his nose.

"You called for a surgeon," Styke said. "You wouldn't have done that if you didn't care."

The tension was suddenly broken by a hammering on the front gate of the complex, followed by a call for the watchman. Everyone in the room looked to Etzi, who himself glanced toward the source of the sound in annoyance.

The hammering continued.

"It's the city guard, master," the watchman said in a low voice, casting meaningful glances at Orz's body. "They can deal with this."

Styke found his hand gripping the hilt of his knife, his stomach wrapped in knots. This was it. How he'd die. In a stranger's home in a strange land, failing the men he'd left back at the inn to get drunk. The authorities would clean this up in a few days. No one back home would ever know what had happened. No glory. No memories. Just the disappearance of Mad Ben Styke and the Mad Lancers.

"Answer them," Etzi said sharply. "Say nothing of this. Leave them outside and then go to my rooms to fetch me."

"Master?"

"Go! Maetle, turn off those lanterns. Ben, lift my brother." The orders were barked in a low tone, decisive and quick. Etzi ducked under one of the preparation tables and came back up with a handful of flour. Styke had no sooner lurched forward and lifted Orz than the flour was tossed across the table. Etzi snatched up a flat blade and scraped the mess—including water and blood from Orz—onto the floor, then threw down more flour. At a casual glance it looked like little more than a common kitchen mess.

"With me," Etzi said, striding to the corner of the room. He opened a door to a spacious pantry and quickly shuffled several crates, then reached down and slid his finger into a ring. Lifting it revealed a dark, narrow hole. "Old smuggling cache," he explained quickly. "You'll have to drop him in there and follow him down before he swallows too much water."

"You are joking," Styke said in Adran.

"I am not."

A primal fear stuck in Styke's throat—fear of the dark, fear of the sound of water gently lapping just a few feet below them. There was no adrenaline to fuel him into the water now, and he blanched. He could feel the silliness of it even as the fear swept through him. "I won't even fit."

"You either go down there or you start by killing me and then however many city guard you can manage until they put you down. It's your choice. The knife or the hatch."

Styke was taken aback. Etzi had no fear in his eyes, just business-like expectation. It was a strange thing to loom over such a bookish person without eliciting the tiniest bit of worry. He gave a growl and shifted Orz from two arms to one, slipping his hands under his shoulders and lowering him, feetfirst, down the hatch. He got down as far as he could before dropping Orz, his body slipping into the water. Styke followed, forcing his shoulders diagonally through the narrow space. As soon as his head was below the floor, the hatch was closed and he could hear things being moved back on top of it.

He was in complete darkness, his feet touching slick stone about five feet below the waterline. He lifted Orz with one arm and reached cautiously with the other, getting a feel for the area. It appeared to be an open rectangle—just enough room for a rowboat to come and go, probably pushed in by someone in the water until it was directly below the hatch and then unloaded. There was a thick layer of slime on everything, including the iron rungs of the ladder, indicating it hadn't been used in quite some time.

Styke tilted his head, listening carefully to the muffled voices out in the courtyard.

"Foreigner...dragonman...betrayal...searching..." He only picked up bits and pieces, but it became quickly apparent that they were searching for him. Protestations from Etzi. Questions. Demands. Voices raised. Then the sound of feet on the kitchen floor. At least a half-dozen pairs. Styke gently pushed himself away from the ladder in case the hatch was opened.

Doors were slammed. "Search here," he heard someone say from the kitchen. There was the shuffling of pots and pans, the sliding of drawers and the creaking of cupboard hinges.

"If you're going to empty that, you should put it back," Etzi said in a perturbed tone. "Oh, for the love of the emperor. Do you think I've hidden a giant and a dead man in the silverware drawer? You, hang that back where you found it!"

The door to the pantry opened. A sliver of light cut down through the floorboards into Styke's hiding spot. He drew his knife slowly, so as not to make a sound in the water. Someone kicked over a crate. The door shut again. Styke let out a cautious breath, and the pounding of footsteps followed several men out of the kitchen. Styke put his knife back and pushed himself up against the slimy stone wall of the smuggler's nook, listening to the distant sounds of rooms being ransacked.

Time crept by and Styke summoned his last reserves of strength just to hold Orz's head above the water. He had no idea how long he'd been there, or how long it had been since he'd heard the noise of searchers. He was just beginning to think it was over when the kitchen door opened again and he heard two distinct sets of footsteps crossing the floor, accompanied by two voices.

One was Etzi, speaking in a tired, conversational tone: "...happy to serve the emperor in any way possible, but if you could avoid waking up my entire Household next time, I'd be most grateful."

"I'll do what needs to be done," the second voice answered in a harsh, clipped tone. Styke recognized it. It belonged to the dragonman who had ambushed them at Orz's mother's house. He realized that one of the sets of footsteps had a distinct limp, and it brought a smile to his face. The smile quickly disappeared when he realized that the dragonman must not have admitted his role in the murder of Etzi's mother.

"And I'll lodge a complaint to the emperor if this happens again," Etzi responded. "You know, I have a very talented surgeon on staff if you'd like someone to look at that leg." The door from the kitchen to the courtyard opened and the voices grew too muffled to understand.

Over an hour must have passed before there was a flurry of footsteps, the scraping of crates, and then the hatch above Styke opened. He was momentarily blinded by a lantern being lowered down, then looked up to see the faces of Etzi, Maetle, and the watchman. Etzi seemed irritated. Maetle concerned. The watchman resigned. "Come on," Etzi said in Adran. "Hand him up to us. I hope he's still breathing."

Styke squeezed himself out of the hatch after Orz had been hauled up, then stood dripping water on the floor while the three Dynize conferred among themselves. The watchman was sent away, then Etzi turned to Styke. His face was thoughtful, and he looked at Styke with a considering eye. "The dragonman. You gave him the limp?"

Styke shrugged. He didn't have energy for anything else.

"He claimed Orz had given him the limp and killed his men. But they wouldn't have been able to stick Orz with so many bolts without an ambush, and he clearly wouldn't be fighting after that. So it must have been you. Well, I'm glad my brother has been keeping good company. Come, carry him to Maetle's room. You can rest there."

"And Orz?" Styke asked.

"You need to keep quiet and hidden. I don't trust the emperor enough to not have spies in my Household. Maetle will do what she can. It'll be a miracle if he's still alive in the morning."

CHAPTER 28

Styke rolled off his uncomfortable reed mat and sat up, hitting his head hard on a piece of furniture. He rubbed furiously at his forehead, taking a few moments to orient himself in the darkness before remembering that he was in Maetle's office, sleeping underneath her desk. He craned his neck and crawled out from underneath it, climbing slowly to his feet. He guessed it was around five o'clock in the morning.

The Etzi Household surgeon had her own quarters in the western corner of the compound. It wasn't large—a bedroom, office, and infirmary—but it was sequestered away from the rest of the sleeping areas. The last thing Styke remembered was laying Orz on the infirmary bed and collapsing onto the reed mat while Maetle began work on the dragonman. He stepped across the room, poking his head into the bedroom and listening to a woman's soft snores, before stepping into the infirmary.

Orz was still there. His clothes had been cut away and his chest wrapped in bandages. Styke had to lower his cheek to Orz's mouth to feel the slightest of shallow breaths. He wondered if Ka-poel's sorcery would allow *him* to survive such a mauling and if perhaps he'd been too hasty in rejecting it.

Too late now. He needed to move—to get out of here before sunrise and get back to the inn. The city guard would be searching for unfamiliar foreigners. Styke needed to get his men out of the city as quickly as possible. Their best chance would be to ride south as hard as they could, posing Ka-poel as their local master and not stopping to answer questions. They should be within twenty or thirty miles of the rendezvous. They could make that in two days if they were quick about it.

He wondered if the landing had ever happened, if he was riding his twenty Lancers toward an empty jungle with Dynize soldiers on their tail. It was too late to hesitate at this point. The only way out was forward. Even if it got him, and everyone who depended on him, killed. He swore several times under his breath and gathered his clothes from the back of Maetle's office chair. They were still damp, but they'd have to do. He began to dress.

"Ben?"

He jerked around to find Maetle sitting up in bed. He quickly began to pull his boots on. Maetle was up in a flash, lighting a lamp beside her bed and hurrying out to him. "What are you doing?" she demanded.

Styke was too tired to answer immediately, fumbling for the words in Dynize. "I have to leave."

"You can't."

"I have to." He finished tying his boots and took a step toward the door. Maetle darted around him and threw herself against the door, arms spread.

"You can't leave," she said firmly.

Styke sucked in an angry breath. He didn't have time for a girl a third his size to tell him what to do. He reached for her shoulder, intent on moving her as gently as he could manage.

"You touch me and I'll scream."

"What is wrong with you?" he growled. "I have to go. People are depending on me."

"People are depending on you not to leave!"

Styke scowled at her. "I don't know what that means."

"It means that Master Etzi has put this entire Household at risk for you. If you're spotted outside the compound, you will be taken, and they'll question you, and they'll find out that he is hiding a fugitive."

"Then I won't be spotted," Styke said, reaching for her again. Her determined glare made him drop his hand.

"You're hard to miss."

"And if you scream, everyone in the compound will know I'm here."

"Better to keep it within the compound than for the city guard to find you."

"Shit," he growled. He was feeling desperate, now. The damned Dynize could be coming for his men anytime. He needed to be there for them. He tapped one finger against his ring and stared at the door. "I have to go," he said quietly. "You don't want to stand in my way."

Maetle thrust one finger up between them. "Wait. Hold on." Styke rolled his eyes. He'd humor her for exactly ten more seconds, and then he had to move. She rushed to the corner of her infirmary, rooting around in a cabinet before returning to the door. "Here," she said, lifting something to his face. "Smell this."

Styke couldn't help but take a deep whiff. He jerked back involuntarily from the slightly sweet, chemical smell. It filled his nostrils, his mouth, and his lungs in the course of a few moments. He took a step back, then another, his feet feeling heavy. "God damn it," he slurred. "I can't believe I fell for that." His vision grew dim and he began to fall.

*   *   *

When Styke awoke, he was lying on his back on the floor with daylight streaming in through the high windows of the infirmary. His vision swam for the first few minutes of consciousness, and it took him some time after that before remembering how he had ended up in this position. The thought made his aching head pound even harder, and he had to force his temper down to acquire any clarity of thought.

"The effects shouldn't last long. A couple hours at most."

Styke's body still felt as heavy as a rock, so he tilted his head toward the source of the voice. It was Maetle, sitting on the end of her bed, gazing at him with trepidation.

"Why does my mouth taste like shit?" Styke asked.

"I had to dose you directly," Maetle said. "A couple of drops between your lips to make sure you'd stay down. I gave you enough to knock out a horse, so don't expect to be able to move for at least thirty minutes."

Out of curiosity—and no small amount of spite—Styke flexed his fingers. He felt one arm twitch, then the other, and soon his body seemed to be obeying his commands—albeit with the speed of molasses. He let out a groan and rolled over and up into a sitting position.

"By the emperor," Maetle swore.

It was a small thing, but it made Styke grin. He didn't need Ka-poel and her sorcery. He was still Ben Styke. The grin faltered at the brass band that began playing in the back of his head. A spike of worry shot through him as he considered Celine, Ka-poel, and his Lancers. They might still be waiting for him—they may have even been captured. "Pit, this hurts. What time is it?"

"About two in the afternoon."

Styke tried to root around for some anger toward this diminutive woman. It was there, certainly, but he couldn't quite grasp it. He remembered their argument clearly. She'd done what she felt was necessary to protect her home. It just might have gotten all of Styke's men killed at the same time. He looked across at her, trying to put himself in her place and realizing that she knew absolutely nothing about him—why he was here, who he was—she just knew that he was a foreign giant who'd brought her a dying man.

He wondered what Etzi knew or suspected, and how much he should be ready to share. As far as he knew, he was trapped in this room until at least sundown. "Where's your master?" he asked.

"He went to the games."

"The games?" Styke echoed.

"It is a forum. An area where the powerful gather to gossip and craft deals."

"Ah. I can barely..." He had to substitute Palo words and hope they were close. "I can barely think in Adran right now. Do you speak any Kressian languages?"

Maetle's face lit up. "I do," she said in Kez. "It's a family language going back several generations. Do you understand me?"

"Your accent is very strange," Styke answered in kind, "but yes, I can understand you. So you're Kez?"

"Half Kez, half Dynize," she responded, lifting her legs to fold them beneath her on her bed. "My family were traders who remained in Dynize when the borders closed."

"So you're slaves?"

Her eyebrows went up. "My family? No, no. Free foreigners, they call us. Established. Looked down upon, but tolerated." She frowned. "If you're not a slave, how did you come to be in Dynize?"

"Do you know what's going on in Fatrasta?" Styke asked.

"We're fighting for our land. For the godstone."

"You're fighting for *my* land," he countered. "I met Orz there. We came here." He shrugged, unwilling to tell her more than that.

Maetle didn't seem all that bothered by talk of the war. He could see it in her face and manner—the war was a distant thing, not a concern of the here and now. He'd seen the same distant, casual disdain in the eyes of anyone he'd ever discussed a foreign war with. There were no stakes for them, and therefore no passion. At worst, it was barely an event. At best, a passing interest. He'd probably been in the same situation himself before.

But this war was his and he had to fight back indignity at her dismissal.

"In Fatrasta," she asked, "are you a warrior?"

Styke nodded, one hand twitching for his knife and realizing for the first time it wasn't there. "Where is my knife?" he asked quietly.

"I had to take it," she responded. "You seem prone to violence."

Styke crawled to his knees, then gained his feet. "Knife. Now."

Maetle set her jaw. A few moments passed before she gestured to her office. "Behind the desk."

Styke found his knife and returned it to his side, then lowered himself onto Maetle's office stool. It creaked angrily beneath his weight but did not give way. He was still trying to gain full control of his thoughts and body. The attempt was slow-going, but it seemed to help to talk. "No one has discovered us?"

"I put a note outside my door that I am ill," Maetle said.

"And no one demands your presence for their own hurts and sicknesses? This compound must have hundreds of people." He could hear them, when he strained—the sound of children playing, people passing within a few yards of this small house. He decided to lower his voice, just to be sure they weren't overheard.

"Dynize don't ask questions," Maetle responded.

"Ah. Orz mentioned that. Very obedient people."

"You don't approve?"

"Obedience has its uses."

"To society?"

"To powerful people."

Maetle scowled at him. "You don't believe in obedience to the land? To laws?"

"I'm a soldier," Styke said. "Laws only apply to me in times of peace."

"You don't sound happy about that."

"I wish society were more consistent. Do you know Fatrastan history?"

"A little. What they taught us in preparation for the invasion."

"I fought in the Fatrastan Revolution. I was a monster for my people, and when the war was over, they did this to me." He pointed to the still-visible scar along his cheekbone that had now been restitched by sorcery twice. He then held up his hand. "And this. I refused to die, so they made me a prisoner."

Maetle looked horrified. "And yet you still fight for them?"

"Life is complicated," Styke said. It was an irony that he considered from time to time. But he was, he'd decided, fighting for Fatrasta—for the people—and not for the assholes who put him in chains. He shook his head. "When will Etzi return? I need to get out of this place. To find... others."

"Other foreign soldiers?"

Styke didn't respond. Perhaps he'd already said too much.

"He should be back soon. He never stays at the games longer than he needs to." She looked away when she spoke of him, and Styke thought he caught a hint of something.

"You like your master?"

"Of course I do! He's a good man."

"You're sleeping with him."

Maetle's cheeks reddened. "How dare you."

Styke held up his hands at her anger. "Forget I said anything. Tell me about him."

Maetle's mouth formed a hard line and she held her glare for several seconds before finally looking away with an irritated sigh. "He's the head of a Household. He's a good master. Thoughtful, fair. He does everything for the sake of the Household. Taking in his brother is the first time I've ever seen him make a selfish decision."

"Selfish?" Styke echoed.

"Against the Household, I mean. Very dangerous."

And she was protective of her master. He rubbed his head. She was also the reason he was held up in here for the rest of daylight instead of riding hard through the suburbs at the head of his men. "I think I got that." He looked up sharply and saw that a curtain had been drawn between the infirmary and Maetle's bedroom and office. "Orz, is he..."

"Yes," Maetle answered just a little too quickly. "Dragonmen are very hardy. Hardier than I expected, certainly. One of the bolts punctured his left lung, but it doesn't appear to be filling with blood." She hesitated, and he could see the discomfort in her face. "I know that bone-eye sorcery is different from Privileged sorcery. Beyond that..."

"It might just be enough," Styke said. He felt like he should be ambivalent over Orz's survival—bringing him here was nothing more than a debt paid. But he still remembered that night at his mother's grave, and he found himself hoping that the dragonman would pull through. It took him a few moments to realize that his own survival could depend on it—if Orz died, the whole Household might just as well turn on him.

Styke's head began to clear, and with little else to do he spent the next few hours questioning Maetle about her country, the language, traditions, and everything else he could think of. She seemed more than willing to talk—even enthusiastic—and it occurred to him that she'd probably never met a Kressian who wasn't a slave or somehow naturalized to Dynize. His curiosity seemed to surprise her, and though she never said as much, he got the impression that the Dynize considered the rest of the world to be barbarians who needed to be saved from themselves.

Which, he was almost certain, was how the Kressian countries would view the Dynize if the situation were reversed.

Talking helped stave off the anxiety he had over his men back at the inn—but didn't contain it entirely. He glanced at the window often, counting down the hours until dusk. He was just beginning to lose his patience in the late afternoon when there was a quiet knock on the door. Maetle gestured for him to hide, then answered the door. It was Etzi.

The Household head looked pensive—Styke had the distinct impression that he looked that way a lot—and he glanced down at Styke's knife before speaking.

"You didn't tell me that my mother was dead."

Styke's mouth went dry. He glanced at Maetle, whose face had gone white. "I didn't think it was the time."

"Nor that the dragonman who visited here last night killed her." Etzi held up one hand to forestall a response. "It is good that you did not. I'm not a violent man, but I would have refused his entry into the Household if I had known it, which would have been suspicious. It might have undone us." He took a couple of deep breaths. "She died doing what she felt was right."

Styke bit his tongue. Hard.

"My brother?" Etzi asked Maetle, the question hanging in the air.

"He's alive," Maetle answered. "For now." She hurried behind the curtain and returned a few moments later with a glass of something dark. It smelled like bourbon. Etzi took one sip and handed it back with a gesture of thanks.

"I need to get out of here," Styke said gently. "I have other responsibilities."

Etzi looked him up and down. "I'm sure you do. The men at the inn, they are yours?"

Styke stiffened.

"They were taken by the city guard early this morning."

"How bad was it?" Styke braced himself.

"Bad? They didn't put up a fight. Half of them were too drunk to stand. The other half took their arrest in stride."

"And the little girl that was with them?"

Etzi shook his head. "There was no girl."

"Or a Dynize woman?"

Another head shake.

Styke chewed on the inside of his cheek, unsure whether this was good news or bad news. The fact that they hadn't put up a fight must have been Jackal's doing. He'd have realized that it was better to keep them all alive and together than get them all killed. And where had Ka-poel and Celine slipped off to? Unlike the rest of them, Ka-poel could walk the city at will, and Celine had enough Palo in her mongrel blood that she probably wouldn't get a second glance from most people.

"What are they doing with them?" he asked.

"Questioning them." Etzi's eyes narrowed. "And getting nothing in return. There's a Palo with them, and he's claiming the whole group are slaves that have taken a vow of silence. It's obvious that they're not slaves. What they really are has everyone's curiosity piqued."

Styke returned Etzi's gaze coolly and wondered if the Dynize would summon a bone-eye. All he could do was hope that Ka-poel had taken some precautions.

"You're going to make me ask?" Etzi said.

Styke remained silent.

"Who are they? Who are *you*? What are twenty foreign soldiers doing in Dynize with a disgraced dragonman?"

Styke crossed his arms. "Would you believe me if I said we were invading?"

"No," Etzi answered immediately. "No, I would not."

"Good." Styke rubbed his eyes. His men imprisoned. Ka-poel and Celine in the wind. And himself unable to leave this place for fear of getting caught. Somewhere to their south, the Mad Lancers were biding their time in the deep jungle, waiting for Styke to catch up with them. What the pit could he do now?

There was another knock on the door, and Styke hid himself around the corner while Etzi answered it. He heard a confused voice speaking in Dynize. It sounded like the watchman from last night. "Master, there is someone here demanding to speak with a giant."

Styke reached for his knife.

"Who?" Etzi asked. He sounded as confused at the watchman.

"A mute woman and her foreign slave girl. They are dressed for travel and have three warhorses with them."

"Hold on." Etzi closed the door and turned to Styke, one eyebrow arched.

Styke let his hand fall away from his knife, a wave of relief sweeping through him. That damned blood sorcerer had brought Celine and, from the sound of it, had even thought to escape with all their horses. "I suggest making her comfortable," Styke told Etzi.

"Who is she?"

"The bone-eye who broke Ka-Sedial's hold on your brother."

CHAPTER 29

Just before dawn, Michel slipped into the catacombs through an old basement entrance in an abandoned townhouse in Upper Landfall. He descended steep hallways and staircases, guiding himself with an oil lantern and maps cast to memory. He wasn't completely certain he was heading the right way until the descent flattened out and he came across an alcove carved into the side of the tunnel.

In that alcove were stacked twelve crates of Adran rifles. Michel swept back the canvas covering the crates and pried one open. Everything there. Just as ordered. He couldn't help but smile to himself. Good old Halifin. Neat, punctual, and reliable.

Just to be sure, Michel checked each of the crates. They needed to be full to be convincing and he had no interest in risking this whole setup just because of a little laziness on his part. He finished his task and covered them back up, then pulled the pistol out of his shoulder bag and loaded it. Time to put things in motion.

He emerged from the catacombs less than fifty paces from the location of the hidden guns. A narrow tunnel let out behind an outcropping in the far corner of Meln-Dun's quarry, and Michel emerged in the dim morning light and listened for several minutes for any sounds of patrolling guards or wandering quarry workers before poking his head out from cover. He was just above where the quarry fence met the rock wall of the Depths. This part of the quarry was long disused, far from most of the blasting and digging and as distant as one could get from the sounds and smells of Greenfire Depths without actually leaving it.

Michel barely had to glance to his right to look down upon a small but tidy-looking foreman's house: Meln-Dun's residence when he didn't have time to head to his country manor. Michel watched for several more minutes, looking for guards, signs of movement, or anything else suspicious. Nothing. He threw his bag over his shoulder and scrambled down from his hiding spot, crossing to the back of the house in just a few steps.

His heart was raging but his head was cool, and Michel carefully checked each step off in the back of his head. No room for mistakes here.

Picking the lock on the front door took just a handful of seconds. He slipped inside, paused to get his bearings. The house was a one-room residence with a wood-burning stove in one corner, a one-person dining table in another, and a card table in the center of the room. Like the outside, everything here was tidy. Meln-Dun had a maid come twice a day, his three meals delivered from his favorite restaurant, and few visitors outside of his foremen, who came to play cards two nights a week.

Meln-Dun valued his privacy, and only took his Dynize visitors at his office a few hundred yards from the little house. No whores. No friends. Michel had been certain he'd be alone.

After a thorough examination of the house, Michel cracked the door to the one bedroom. One body in the bed. Gentle but deep snoring. No weapons within sight. He pulled his bag off his shoulder and produced his pistol, taking several deep breaths as he left behind Michel Bravis and became Tellurin the thief-taker. With a sharp inhale, he burst through the bedroom door shouting.

"Meln-Dun! Meln-Dun!"

The quarry master leapt from his bed, hands flailing, night-clothes asunder and pure confusion covering his face.

Michel brandished his pistol but did not point it at Meln-Dun. "Quickly, master, is there anyone here?"

"What? No, no, of course not!"

"The Dynize," Michel said desperately. "Are they near?"

"No, I..." Meln-Dun's eyes began to focus and they fell on Michel's pistol. "What are you doing?" he asked in horror.

Michel looked at the pistol as if confused himself, then pointed it at the ceiling. "Sorry, master, I had to be sure."

"Sure about what?" Suspicion crept into Meln-Dun's tone. "Who are you?" he demanded. "Wait, I know you! You're—"

"Tellurin," Michel stated. "I've been working for Dahre. Look, there's little time to explain, but Dahre has ordered me to get you out of here."

"What are you talking about?"

"We've uncovered a plot." Michel grabbed Meln-Dun by one shoulder to steady him. "Mama Palo, that insidious bitch, has set you up! She's convinced the Dynize that you're running weapons and spying for the Lady Chancellor Lindet."

"That's mad!" Meln-Dun continued to flail around, clearly try-ing to fight off the dregs of sleep still clinging to his mind. "Where's Dahre?"

"Of course it's mad, but she's managed to do it. We uncovered the plot just an hour ago. Dahre is trying to clean everything up, but the Dynize might be here at any moment. If they get their hands on you, they'll execute you without hesitation." Michel swore several times, working himself into a desperate fury.

"I'm their friend! They've been good to me!"

"They don't trust anyone," Michel hissed. "Why do you think they've had that dragonman hanging around the quarry?"

Meln-Dun's eyes grew wide in understanding. "That dragonman. Pit. Oh, pit," he wailed. "What do we do?" Meln-Dun began to clutch at Michel's arm. Michel smiled inwardly. He had him.

"It's all right. We'll take care of it. I have to get you out of here. We put you in hiding for a couple of weeks and smooth things over with the Dynize. It'll take us some time to unwind the evidence that Mama Palo has planted, but I'm convinced we can do it." Michel gestured. "Quickly, get dressed. Grab anything of value. We have to move fast!"

Meln-Dun threw himself into action, and it quickly became apparent that he'd already put some consideration into what items he'd take with him were he forced to flee, but he'd never actually practiced packing them. He attacked his bureau with vigor, dressing as he did a whirlwind job of his own bedroom. The wardrobe was flung open, a loose board removed from the floor, and a small strongbox retrieved. Meln-Dun fetched a checkbook, two thick bundles of Adran krana, and a couple of small leather satchels, tossing them all into a shoulder bag not unlike Michel's.

Within five minutes he was standing in the center of the room, looking around, breathing heavily. "I think I have everything," he told Michel with a fearful nod. "We go?"

"Not that way," Michel said, taking Meln-Dun by the arm. "Out the back. Through the window. Let's go."

Meln-Dun crawled out first. Michel hesitated, giving the room a once-over as well. While Meln-Dun had been trying to think of other valuables to take with him, Michel gave it a critical eye. The place looked, even to an amateur, like Meln-Dun had fled in a panic.

Perfect.

He crawled out after the quarry boss and left the window open behind them. He took Meln-Dun by the arm. "This way," he ordered. They scrambled up the rock face, Michel being sure to scuff and mark the rock as much as possible, leaving a clear trail behind him. They went up and over, and Michel showed Meln-Dun the narrow entrance.

"Pit," Meln-Dun exclaimed in wonder as he crawled inside. "Just feet from where I was sleeping. I had no idea this was here!"

Michel didn't answer him. They gained the main tunnel and were able to stand, and Michel felt around for his lamp. He was able to get it lit within a few moments, illuminating the tunnel and Meln-Dun's frightened face. That expression almost—*almost*—made Michel feel bad for what he was doing. But it didn't quite crack it. Meln-Dun had executed an old woman to cement his own position and then sold out the Palo to the Dynize invasion. There was no sympathy for a man like that.

"Where do we go now?" Meln-Dun asked.

"This way." Michel led Meln-Dun down the tunnel, past the covered crates of Adran rifles. Meln-Dun was so busy fretting he didn't even glance at them. They took a right turn and continued down a long hallway that zigzagged for some length roughly parallel to the wall of Greenfire Depths. Michel could hear Meln-Dun muttering to himself and half listened, noting the fear and desperation turn to indignation, then turn to anger.

"How dare they?" Meln-Dun asked himself. "How could they turn on me like this, after everything I've done? Greenfire Depths is mine! *Mine!* They need me if they want to keep the Palo contained."

The muttering erased any trace of guilt that Michel still felt. Once the anger began to grow, he put Meln-Dun in front of him. The quarry boss didn't even seem to notice the change, or the pistol that Michel now had pointed at his back.

"Take a left," Michel told him. "Down there. Good, now to the right. Okay, we're almost there."

"Where is *there*?" Meln-Dun asked.

"To a safe place," Michel answered. They took a short set of worn stairs up and past a handful of marked tombs, emerging into the basement of an old Kressian church. Michel ordered Meln-Dun to climb up into the chapel, and they soon emerged into a worn-out room with a handful of pews, lit only by Michel's lamp and a sliver of morning light coming in through the one stained-glass window high up in the roof of the building.

"Is this it?" Meln-Dun asked, looking around.

Michel let out a long, relieved sigh and dropped into one of the pews. "This is it."

They remained in silence for nearly a minute before Meln-Dun began to get antsy. "What are we waiting for?"

"Friends," Michel said loudly. The code word echoed off the high chapel ceiling. He'd barely said it when a pair of figures emerged from behind the altar. Another came up from behind one of the pews. The chapel doors were thrown open, and four more entered.

Meln-Dun whirled, peering at faces in the dim light. "Dahre? Is that you?" He took a step back. "I don't recognize any of you. Tellurin, who are these people?"

Jiniel was the first figure Michel recognized. Ichtracia stepped into the light of his lamp a few seconds later. Michel lifted his pistol and pointed it at Meln-Dun. "Meln-Dun, meet Mama Palo."

The quarry head tried to run. He caught a fist in his belly and doubled over, collapsing to the feet of one of Jiniel's foot soldiers. She looked down at him dispassionately until another foot soldier got a good look at his face. "It's him, ma'am."

"What's going on?" Meln-Dun moaned from the ground. He was silenced by a swift kick from one of the foot soldiers.

"Son of a bitch," Jiniel breathed. "I can't believe you actually pulled that off."

Michel put up his pistol. "He's yours," he reported.

"And what did you leave behind?"

"The Yaret Household will receive anonymous evidence of Meln-Dun's collusion with the enemy general Lady Flint within the hour," Michel said. "They'll rush to confront him and find that he's fled ahead of any accusations that might be leveled. They'll further find a stash of Adran rifles just behind his house. The evidence will all be there. They'll shut down his quarry and put a price on his head."

"How can you be sure?" Jiniel asked.

"I'm not completely. But that's how they'll operate. The best part of all of this is they'll tear apart his organization. Imprison a few for questioning. Scatter the rest. If they try to cover up his alleged involvement with Lady Flint, we'll leak it to the newspapers."

"You *tricked* me," Meln-Dun hissed in horror.

Ichtracia laughed. Pure mirth, tinged with a small, terrifying splash of cruelty. Michel stood up. "Good-bye, Meln-Dun." He took Jiniel by the arm and led her out through the front doors of the chapel, then turned to her. "Remember, you're not to kill him."

"He deserves it," Jiniel sniffed.

"I have my reasons."

"You're going soft?"

"Softness has nothing to do with it," Michel replied. "What I have in mind for Meln-Dun is far better than a quick death."

CHAPTER 30

Vlora examined both the Adran and Dynize camps in the morning gloom. Smoke from the charred remains of the southern Dynize camp obscured her view and made her eyes water. The place looked like the floor of a butcher shop that had recently burned down, the ground carpeted with the bodies of the dead, dying, and wounded in between the smoldering remains of tents and supply wagons.

The northern Dynize camp—General Etepali's—looked practically cheery in comparison. It had been hastily abandoned in the wee hours of the morning, leaving behind tents, unnecessary gear, and random spots of tidy occupation where the camp followers hadn't been fast enough to follow their retreating army. Vlora's own soldiers were currently picking through the scattered remains to look for anything of value that General Etepali might have left behind.

Vlora stared at it all through bleary eyes, functioning on a few hours of deep sleep, smarting from fresh stitches from one of her medics. Last night felt like a nightmare to her, a series of half-remembered events that barely formed a cohesive narrative. Yet here she was, looking at what remained.

Someone had thrown a blanket over her shoulders at some point, and she clung to it like a drowning man to a plank of wood. Beside her, General Sabastenien read out reports. She half listened, nodding when she was expected to nod and saying a word or two when she was expected to respond.

"Final word has come in from our scouts," he was in the middle of saying. "It seems that once General Etepali realized what was happening last night, she woke her soldiers and organized an attack. They pushed our flank hard—that was a stroke of brilliance, having us build those barricades, by the way—but once they realized they couldn't take advantage of the attack, they pulled up stakes and retreated. They're about five miles directly to our southwest now."

"About what I expected," Vlora said dully.

"I wonder why she attacked our flank in *our* camp," he mused out loud, "rather than attacking our troops that were undertaking the slaughter of her allies."

Vlora roused herself enough to look at Sabastenien. "Because she didn't expect us to leave anyone to defend our rear. She expected us to be completely absorbed in the slaughter, which would have allowed her to crush our camp and then sweep in behind us. That would have been more effective than going to the aid of her allies."

Sabastenien blinked at her. "She allowed her allies to be slaughtered as a distraction?"

"It might have worked, too. It's why I left Nila and Bo back in the camp."

"I suppose you're right." Sabastenien cleared his throat. "She managed to do some damage, I'll give her credit for that. Most of our casualties last night came from her. About two thousand men killed or wounded." He let out a half sigh, half laugh. "Initial estimates on the Dynize are twenty thousand casualties. I'd say that's a resounding victory. Congratulations, Lady Flint."

Vlora tried to smile. "Thank you," she whispered.

"General, could you excuse us for a moment?" It was Bo, sidling up to Vlora's left and nodding at Sabastenien. Bo looked a little worse for the wear, with bags under his eyes and a tiny bit of his hair singed off the top. Vlora wondered just how close Etepali's Privileged had gotten to overwhelming him and Nila.

"Of course," Sabastenien replied, tipping his hat to Vlora. "Lady Flint. Magus Borbador." He retreated down the hillside.

Vlora felt Bo take her by the elbow and allowed herself to be steered back into her tent. They were barely inside before Bo released her and began to pace violently, then finally rounded on her. "What the pit is wrong with you?" he demanded.

She tried to find her voice, failed.

"Are you trying to get yourself killed? Are you that bloody-minded right now that you accompanied our troops on a night attack *in your condition*?"

Under normal circumstances she would have snapped right back. His tone was accusatory and venomous. Nobody talked to her like that. But all she could see was the faces of her dead grenadiers.

Bo continued, "I just talked to Davd. He saw that fight with the dragonmen. Said that you would have died before he had the chance to load his rifle if not for a handful of cuirassiers that rode down that dragonman. Blind luck. The cuirassiers didn't even notice you." He leaned forward, taking her gently by the sides of the face. She could see the anger in his eyes warring with concern. "You are not a powder mage anymore, Vlora. You can't do that!"

"Just because I'm no longer a killing machine doesn't mean that I shouldn't lead from the front," Vlora managed.

"Yes, it does," Bo responded, letting go of her and resuming his pacing. "And we're not just talking about the lack of your sorcery. You almost died less than two months ago. You shouldn't even be out of bed for more than an hour or two, let alone charging into an enemy camp in the middle of the night. You..." He stumbled on his words, turning to peer at her face. A sudden realization seemed to dawn in his eyes. "You *were* trying to get yourself killed," he whispered.

"Don't be absurd." The very idea cut through Vlora, stunning her.

"This is about Olem, isn't it?" he asked. "Did you engineer this whole battle, planning on getting yourself killed over *some soldier*?"

"Olem isn't *some soldier*," Vlora finally snapped. "He is the love of my life *and* he's your friend. He abandoned us. Me. He walked away from this thing, and..." Vlora sputtered, her words stumbling into a cough that threatened to knock her off her feet. "I didn't engineer anything," she finally managed. "I made a tactical decision."

"A tactical decision to get yourself killed," Bo said, his voice rising. "You know that this isn't just about you, right? This is about an entire army that crossed an ocean to help you stop something horrible. Never mind that you have more important things to worry about than Olem—people here are ready to *die* for you, Vlora. They *have* died for you. Or have you already forgotten the grenadiers who were torn apart by those dragonmen?"

Faces flashed across Vlora's vision. Bloody, startled faces. She didn't even know the names of those grenadiers.

Bo's outburst was interrupted by the tent flap being thrown open. Nila strode into the room and grabbed Bo by the shoulder. "Out," she ordered, shoving him back out the flap before he could respond.

Vlora stared into the middle distance, unable to move, unable to respond. *Had* she tried to kill herself? Death by enemy wasn't unheard of. Officers whose lives had taken a dark turn and volunteered for dangerous missions. Soldiers who charged without orders. Was it possible that she'd tried to off herself, without her even knowing?

Bo's words suddenly hit her—she'd heard them when he spoke, but now that he'd been shoved outside, they seemed to slam into her gut like a kick from a horse. He was right, of course. She'd gotten her bodyguard killed. All of them would still be here if not for her insistence on charging in with the infantry. She lifted her eyes, looking at Nila without seeing her. "They'll call it a victory," she muttered.

Nila sighed. "Yes, they will. And so will you."

"I can't. Have you seen that?" She pointed a finger toward the Dynize camp.

"I've spent the better part of the morning helping the wounded," Nila answered gently. She came to Vlora's side, and Vlora allowed herself to be guided to her cot. They both sat down, and Nila pulled Vlora's head against her shoulder.

Within moments Vlora was weeping. She didn't even feel it start, but suddenly the tears were flowing and her shoulders heaving. She felt a hand on the back of her head, gently stroking her hair, and Nila spoke in a soft, soothing voice.

"The victory is in how few of those dead and wounded are your countrymen," she said. "So very few. These soldiers are your responsibility, and if you have to resort to a dirty trick to keep them alive, then so be it. You've done it, and you can move on. The Dynize are *not* your responsibility. They belong to whoever sent them to die by your hand.

"I know that you miss Olem. We all do. He's a fantastic commanding officer and a friend to us all. I don't know where he's gone. I don't even know if he's truly abandoned us. What Davd told you the other day was true—you betrayed him at the Crease. You did it as a lover rather than as a commanding officer, and that's what hurt him. You have to let that go. Adom willing, when this is all over, you'll be able to find him and make this right.

"At this moment, however, you have a decision to make: You can back out of this. Cede command. There are a half-dozen generals in your army who are all the equal of anything the Dynize can throw at us, and not a one of them would think less of you for stepping down after all that has happened. They know you're in pain. They worry for you. You can let them take care of you for a change.

"Or," Nila continued, "you can take responsibility. Claim this carnage as a victory and move on. Galvanize yourself and your troops. Come back stronger than before. Sweep your enemies aside. Forget Olem's absence. Focus on your goals and leave the self-recriminations for when this is all finished."

Nila fell silent, and Vlora wept out her anger, grief, pain, and frustrations. They remained in that embrace for some time, long after Vlora had dried her tears and her mind and heart felt empty, a shell devoid of the torrent that had so recently been raging within her. The ability for rational thought finally returned, and Vlora used it to probe within herself, looking for that ugly, furious thing that had dominated her thoughts for so long. It was still there, lurking in the corners of her mind, but it felt smaller and diminished.

She finally sat up, looking Nila in the eyes. "Thank you."

"Of course. Bo's good at a lot of things. Dealing with complex emotion isn't one of them."

Vlora barked a laugh. "That would require him to let his guard down."

"You say that like it's not a family trait."

"Unfair."

"But true." Nila lifted the hem of her dress and used it to dry Vlora's cheeks. In all the time they'd known each other, it was probably the most intimate gesture that Nila had made toward her.

They sat in companionable silence for some time. Vlora stared at her hands, deep in thought, considering everything that Nila had said. She was right, of course. She *could* step down. Any of her generals could conduct this campaign and do Adro proud in the course of doing so. But none of them had seen the godstone, felt its dark power. None of them knew, firsthand, all the things she knew. They hadn't met Lindet and Ka-Sedial. They hadn't defended Landfall.

The moment she had accepted command of the army, she had taken responsibility. And she had to accept that. She might be physically and emotionally fragile. But she was still sound of mind and great of will. Any excuse that she gave in ceding command might be accepted by everyone else. But she'd never forgive herself.

Vlora stood and walked to the tent, poking her head outside. Norrine was standing guard just a few feet away, and Vlora wondered if she'd heard the exchange. If she had, none of it showed on her face. "Pass on orders for the general staff," she told Norrine. "I'm allowing one day for our men to rest. Our medics are to treat our wounded first, then the enemy. Let General Etepali know that we won't interfere with her retrieving her dead. We won't be taking any prisoners—anyone we scooped up will be left in her care."

Norrine nodded. "Yes, ma'am. Anything beyond that?"

"Let the general staff know that we're marching due west tomorrow afternoon. We're going to relieve Burt's Palo Nation irregulars and find out what the Dynize wanted so badly in Yellow Creek." Vlora stepped back inside and smiled at Nila. "Again, thank you," she said quietly. "I have a lot to cast off. But cast it off I will. This is a war I must win myself."

CHAPTER 31

The Etzi Household infirmary was crowded with people, all of them standing in a circle around the unconscious form of Orz. Ka-poel stood at his head, with Celine beside her, and Styke at his feet. Maetle and Etzi remained on the other side. The latter two stared at Ka-poel as if she were some kind of adder slithering around their feet, while she didn't seem to notice their attention.

I can speed up his healing, Ka-poel said, translated by Celine into Adran, *but not by much. The sorcery that surrounds dragonmen is similar to the link I have with Taniel—but rather than a constant exchange of sorcerous energy, it is a onetime thing: a blessing of sorts. I think I can strengthen it a bit. Like repairing a ship with material stronger than it was originally made from.*

"Do what you can," Styke replied. "We need him."

Ka-poel looked at Etzi. *You're his brother. If you're willing, I'll use some of your strength.*

"Neither Orz nor I have ever been on good terms with bone-eyes,"

Etzi responded. "Orz can't speak for himself, but I certainly don't want you cutting into me."

Ka-poel made a gesture that was somewhere halfway between accepting and rude. *I'll use my own, then.* She immediately set to work pricking her thumb with a needle from her satchel and touching the blood to Orz's lips. She worked slowly and deliberately, all focus on the body before her. The group watched silently for several minutes until Etzi finally spoke up.

"So the Fatrastans have bone-eyes. None of our spies told us that."

Styke bit his tongue. He preferred to be straightforward, but even he knew when to let an assumption lie. If anyone, including Etzi, found out exactly who Ka-poel was, they might lose their only chance of surviving in this damned city. He gently tapped on the small of Celine's back—a signal for her to stay quiet—and just grunted in response. "Your Ka-Sedial is finding out a lot about Fatrasta that he didn't know."

"And may it give him the worst kind of headache," Etzi said, as if invoking a curse. He rubbed at his temples.

Styke eyeballed Etzi. "I thought you were loyal to Ka-Sedial."

"I am loyal to the empire," Etzi replied, ducking his head slightly as if realizing he'd let something slip. "I am loyal to my family and my Household. Ka-Sedial is none of those. Now, what do I do with you?"

Styke had no response. He had no plan. Everything had been predicated on getting through the city unnoticed and meeting up with Ibana farther down the coast. So far he'd had no indication that Ibana's army had even landed—which could mean that they hadn't, or it could mean they'd avoided detection. And now twenty of his men had been arrested by the Dynize. He'd considered a thousand different courses of action over the last couple of hours and had been unable to land on any that weren't completely suicidal. He just didn't know enough about the layout of the city, the garrison, or the people to come up with anything proper.

"You're going to help us, right?" Celine asked. So much for keeping quiet.

Etzi blinked at her. "You're a bold little one."

"You have no idea," Styke muttered.

"Your brother is going to live," Celine said. "We've saved him, so you're going to save us. Right?"

"It is more complicated than my brother's life," Etzi told Celine. "It is the lives of my entire Household." He turned his attention back to Styke. "I will speak bluntly. Fraternal love is only some of the reason I hid you and Orz from the dragonman last night."

Styke straightened, listening carefully.

"Orz probably does not know this himself. If he was only released a couple of months ago, he will not be up on local politics."

"Which are?"

Etzi gave a hard sigh and said something to Maetle in Dynize that was too quick for Styke to follow.

"It's your decision, master," she responded.

Etzi rubbed his temples again. "Dynize has been on the brink of a new civil war for almost two years. Sedial's consolidation of power has divided the nation, and his invasion of Fatrasta has both taxed everyone's loyalty and kept us from tearing one another apart. He's probably aware through his puppet-spies that the capital is politically volatile right now, but if he knew the true extent of it, he would be back here at the head of his biggest army."

This sounded very much like information Styke could use. If he had the brains to figure out how. He was a soldier, not a politician. "It's that bad?"

"It is. The death of my mother, the search for you and Orz, even the arrest of your soldiers—these things happened practically hours ago and they've already sparked a wave of debates on everything from slave policy, to the use of sorcery by the government, to questioning Sedial's authority all over again. I went to the games earlier today to hear the gossip. Assassinations happen from time to time, of course, but they don't usually happen in the...I suppose you'd call them the 'middle-class suburbs.' She was a retired Household head. She should not have been collateral damage."

"So you hid us because you might be able to use us?"

Etzi gave him a sallow smile. "As I said, times are uncertain. Despite my brother's disgrace, he is still a dragonman. And you are the man who saved him, so..."

"I'll try to stay useful."

"I'm not entirely certain how," Etzi said. A troubled look crossed his face, and after several moments of silence he produced a piece of paper from his pocket and tapped it against his brother's leg. "Tell me something, Ben."

Styke shrugged at him to go on.

"When someone in Fatrasta goes to university for an education, do they usually go on to work in their field of study?"

"Usually...," Styke said. "But not all the time."

"My own education was in the legal system."

"Oh?" The word must have sounded more sarcastic than Styke had meant, because Etzi chuckled dryly.

"We don't operate entirely on traditions and imperial word," Etzi said. "In fact, the emperor rarely involves himself in day-to-day politics. He lets Sedial and the Household Quorum—our governing body—take care of all that. Sedial is far away right now."

Styke could see the thoughts turning behind Etzi's eyes. "And universities?"

"Sorry," Etzi said, passing a hand over his eyes. "I was a legal student. I was very good at it, and I'd intended on making my career as a lawyer. I wouldn't—I thought at the time—inherit the Household until I was quite old. But then Orz was disgraced, my parents stepped down as heads, and I found myself here." He gestured at the compound surrounding them. He tapped the paper against his brother's leg once more and unfolded it. "Laws are often put into place by the powerful to control the weak. But they can also be used against the powerful—especially when those powerful people aren't present. Do you know what this is?"

Styke shook his head.

"Maetle took it out of Orz's pocket last night. It was sealed in wax, well-protected from the elements. It's stamped with Sedial's seal and signed by his own hand, and says that Orz is working on a conditional pardon on a task from the Great Ka himself."

Styke finally began to follow. "What do you mean to do with it? Claim publicly that Orz was unjustly attacked by assassins?"

"Exactly." Etzi had a strange look in his eye now. Styke had seen that look before—on Ibana, when she thought that one of his insane ideas might actually work.

"But the assassin could only have been waiting for him at Sedial's command," he protested.

"Give me a timeline of events. When did he betray Ka-Sedial's orders?"

Styke ran through a very basic outline of the past six weeks, leaving out the fact that he'd been separated from an army intent on capturing the very city in which they stood. It wasn't an entire lie—but it did make it out to seem like Styke and his men had come from Starlight to help Orz in return for his sparing Styke's life. Both Celine and Ka-poel looked at him a couple times during the story but neither tried to correct him.

Etzi nodded along. When Styke had finished, he said, "Based on your own version of events, a messenger from Sedial could not have beaten him back to Dynize."

"Sedial must have given the order through a puppet."

Etzi snapped his fingers. "Exactly! Puppets are not acknowledged by the legal system. Everyone knows they exist. Everyone knows they are wrong. But the bone-eyes have always had power and they avoid being held accountable by pretending—through laws—that puppets don't exist."

"So you're saying that any order given through a puppet is illegal?"

"Not technically illegal. It just doesn't hold any legal weight." Etzi bounced the paper up and down in his hand. "*This* carries legal weight."

"So you're not going to hide him?" Styke asked.

"It would be foolish to try. The longer I keep him hidden, the more they can claim that I know I've done something wrong. But if I take his presence public, with this conditional pardon..."

"You're taking the fight to Sedial's representatives in the city."

Etzi grinned in a way that reminded Styke of Orz. "And that bastard who murdered my mother."

Styke knew right away that he was out of his depth. He didn't know the legal system in his own country, let alone in this strange place. He could do nothing but trust that Etzi knew what he was doing. But this all dealt with the Orz problem and Etzi's Household. "And me and my men?" he asked.

Etzi's mind was clearly elsewhere. "You saved my brother from assassins. Legally, I'm honor-bound to protect you."

Styke bit his tongue, considering what to tell Etzi. On one hand, the army down south might never even have landed—they might have sunk, or headed back to New Starlight, or landed somewhere far from here. On the other hand, if word suddenly arrived about Styke's army, all of them carrying the same skull-and-lance banner that he had in his saddlebags, it might get both him and Etzi's Household executed as spies.

It didn't feel right to treat a host in such a way. But Styke's primary concern had to be staying alive—at least until he knew whether Ibana had actually landed and decided to wait out his arrival. "So what do I do?"

"You remain here, as my guest. Sedial's representatives in the city will ask for clarification from him directly, which will take at least six weeks. I muddy the water legally, Orz heals—he just needs to be able to ride—and we get you all moving again."

"And my men?"

"As I said, I'll muddy the waters. I'll put effort into seeing them released as accessories to whatever task it is that Orz is up to." He paused, frowned. "Dynize is a tinderbox right now. I suspect that either Sedial's allies will try to keep this quiet, letting me have my way in order to keep from stoking more discontent…"

"Or?" Styke asked.

"Or they will make an issue out of it."

Styke examined Etzi's face. There was a resolve there that he hadn't seen last night. It made him like the man, for all his bookish nature. "You're sure that you're up to protecting us?"

"At the end of the day, I can claim ignorance. I protected my brother, who I thought had been pardoned." Etzi paused thoughtfully. His nostrils flared and he leaned across Orz. "No. That's not just it. That dragonman murdered my mother. All politics aside— all relations and intrigue and everything else be damned. I will not let that go. Do you understand?"

"I think I do."

"Good. I'll ask you to hide in here for another day while I prepare."

CHAPTER 32

My love is dead.

It was the last entry into Field Marshal Tamas's journal for almost thirteen months, and Vlora found herself staring at that page for hours on end. She examined the paper, stained with thirty-year-old teardrops. She studied the letters, written in a trembling hand. She sat in contemplation, staring at nothing with the journal open to that page on her lap.

Two days had passed since what the men had taken to calling the Midnight Massacre. It wasn't a name that would reflect well on Vlora in the history books, but she did not contest it. How could she? In those two days she had searched Tamas's journal for his mistakes—for any campaigns that had gone poorly, atrocities attached to his name, Pyrrhic victories. She'd found records of every one of those things, but he'd never written in terms of absolute regrets. The closest he'd ever come to self-recrimination was ending three of his entries with the words "I will learn from this."

She *knew* that he had regrets. She'd spent her teens in his household, listening to stories about the Gurlish campaigns over the dinner table. It made her wonder if perhaps he knew that others might study this journal for posterity and he was presenting a confident face for history.

Which made this one, raw entry all the more emphatic. *My love is dead.* Nothing more. Just a date—the date that he would have been informed that his wife had been executed by the Kez. Everything about that page spoke of grief, as one might expect. Had Tamas been a normal person, this page would be nothing more than a record of the death of a loved one. But Tamas wasn't normal, and the following entry—those thirteen months later—would no doubt give goose bumps to anyone with even the faintest knowledge of recent history.

> *Vengeance. Retribution. Justice. There is no word strong enough for what I am about to put in motion. Whether I succeed or fail, history will remember me as a man with ambitions. I spit on the very word. This is not about ambition. There is nothing I could gain that will fill my heart. I only seek to expunge those who took her from me. I will erase their legacies from history or die in the attempt.*
>
> *They have no idea what they've done.*

It would be well over a decade from the time this entry was written to the day that Tamas overthrew the last king of Adro and provoked a war that would see the king of Kez murdered by his own kin. Vlora shuddered upon the reading.

In the context of history, this was a declaration of war against the noble institutions of two countries. A war that the son of a poor apothecary would one day win. Weighty words. Significant. But after the Midnight Massacre, Vlora couldn't help but see the cost of them. Hundreds of thousands had died. Millions had suffered. All for the grief of one man. She couldn't condone that, just as she couldn't condone her own poor decisions in the wake of her loss.

I will learn from this. She took a deep breath and closed the journal, setting it on her pillow and falling into a long, thoughtful contemplation. Outside her tent, she could hear the sounds of an army breaking camp, the joking of two porters while they waited for her to vacate her own quarters so they could pack her tent and baggage into a cart.

She put on her jacket and bicorn, using her sword as a cane as she limped out of the tent and squinted into the morning light. There was a light mist on the broken terrain of eastern Fatrasta, burning away quickly beneath the intensity of the rising sun. The army was spread across several rolling, abandoned cotton farms and she felt as if she was looking at that sea of tents with new eyes. She had to change. To learn. To become better.

Davd was on watch outside her tent. He stiffened when she emerged, snapping a salute. The two young porters dashed a last joke between them and then came to attention. She waved one hand at them. "Five minutes," she said. "Make yourselves scarce, then come back and break everything down."

"Yes, ma'am!" they replied, chasing each other off into the camp.

Their absence left a loud silence between Vlora and Davd. He stared straight ahead, rifle shouldered, his posture painfully stiff.

"At ease," she told him.

He didn't move.

She clenched her teeth. *Learn.* Letting out a long breath, she said, "Davd, I want to apologize for the other day. You were only telling me what I asked to hear, and my outburst was entirely inappropriate."

It didn't seem possible for Davd to stiffen further. His shoulders tightened and his hands clenched his rifle until his knuckles were white. "It was my fault, ma'am."

"Look at me," Vlora said.

Davd flinched.

"*Look at me*," Vlora commanded.

Davd's head gradually turned until they looked each other in the eye. "Ma'am," he said, swallowing hard.

"It's not your fault. It's mine. For the last two years, you powder mages have been among my most valued companions. You aren't just subordinate officers; you are friends. I shouldn't have done anything to compromise that. Please forgive me."

A few moments passed before, like a deflating watchman's balloon, Davd sagged. "Of course, ma'am."

Vlora reached out and touched Davd on the elbow. "Thank you. I'm going to try to be a better officer. I'm going to try to learn from my mistakes."

"You aren't—"

Vlora cut him off gently. "No platitudes. I get enough of those from my general staff. The rest of this war will be painful. I need all the friends I can get, and I hope you're one that I can count on the most."

"Without question." The formality had left his voice, but his posture was still overly rigid. It would take time for their relationship to mend. Vlora hoped that it might one day return to what it once was. She gave him a grateful nod.

"I'm going to find Bo. Accompany me?"

They found Borbador wearing a gaudy silk dressing gown, puffing on his pipe while a dozen porters broke down the small canvas palace that he and Nila called a traveling tent. Nila was nowhere to be seen, but a half-dozen officers were gathered around Bo, wearing nothing more than what Vlora could only assume were Bo's extra dressing gowns. They stared bleary-eyed at the porters as if they'd badly overslept and had been kicked out of the tent. Only Bo was fully awake, as if this were a normal ritual for him.

One of the officers spotted Vlora, whispered something to his companions, and the whole group scattered. Vlora tried not to memorize their faces—she didn't want to know—and came up to stand beside Bo. Davd gave them a respectful distance.

"You weren't kidding about working your way through my officer corps, were you?"

"Not at all," Bo replied happily.

"I would insist on being invited to one of your parties, but that would probably be gross, wouldn't it?"

Bo cocked an eyebrow at her. "Gross has nothing to do with it. You'd bring the mood down like nothing else."

"I can be fun."

Bo barked a laugh so hard that it threw him into a coughing fit. He doubled over, slapping his knees, until Vlora thumped him on the back. He wiped a tear out of the corner of his eye and recovered, one last chuckle escaping his lips. "Right. You're just a barrel of laughs. Especially these days."

"That hurts," Vlora replied. It did a little, but the arm that Bo draped companionably over her shoulders helped take the sting out.

"My dear sister, you wouldn't know what to do at an orgy. And I mean that as a compliment. You're a very organized, ordered person. A dozen limbs going every which way would just put you into a fury."

"Thanks. I think."

"No problem. How soon are we marching?"

"The head of the column has already hit the road."

"Ah. I should probably put pants on. Oi! You there, don't pack that trunk. It's got my pants in it!"

Vlora examined the side of Bo's face. It was easy to write off his excessive debauchery as the habits of a Privileged, but he also used it to bury his own deep trauma. She decided, in light of her recent realizations, that she should judge him less for it.

"I need a favor," she said.

"Oh?"

"I need a real, honest answer. Do you have any idea where Olem went?"

Bo froze. "No?" he said.

"Are you lying to me?"

"No," he said somewhat more confidently.

She stared at him, looking him in the eye until he began to squirm. "I have an idea," he finally said. "But I can't be certain. He didn't say anything when he left, but everyone I've asked seems to think he didn't want to be followed or found."

"Can you spare a couple of plainclothes scouts?" she asked.

"You mean spies?"

"Yes, I mean spies."

Bo's nose wrinkled. "You want me to chase him down?"

"I just want you to find him. I'll write four copies of a letter for your spies to carry. Once they find him, I just want them to hand over the letter. No need for anything else."

"What's in the letter?"

"An apology."

"Probably a good idea."

Vlora narrowed her eyes. "Well?"

"Well what?"

"Will you help me?"

Bo clicked his tongue thoughtfully. "Of course I'll help you. You think I would dare stand in the way of true love?"

"Don't," she warned.

"Sorry," he said immediately. "I don't mean to make light. I know you're hurting. I'll do what I can, but I can't promise results."

"I just need a letter delivered. No other expectations."

He considered for a moment. "Yes, all right. I can do that."

"Thank you," Vlora said quietly. "As you said, I'm an organized person. I'm trying to put my personal life in order so that I can finish this campaign."

"Good idea."

She let the remark pass. "How do things look between here and the Upper Hadshaw?"

"I talked to one of your scouts about twenty minutes ago. Looks like General Etepali's army is still at the site of the Midnight Massacre, cleaning things up and helping the wounded. Seems she's going to be a bit more cautious about getting between you and your goals."

"You know," Vlora said wryly, "I should have that scout shot for reporting to you before reporting to me."

"Oh, come off it. They reported to your general staff before me. Besides, you and I are on the same side." Bo grinned at her, but the smile faltered. "Are you sure about leaving Etepali behind us?"

"Not at all. But speed is of the essence right now. If I take the time to deal with her, we might lose whatever the Dynize recovered from Yellow Creek."

Bo pursed his lips, nodding. "Fair enough. As far as we know, the road between here and the Upper Hadshaw is clear. We still have one Dynize army about twenty miles due south and holding their position. A second Dynize army is about forty miles to our southwest and marching to join the first. They probably found out about the Midnight Massacre yesterday, and I imagine that, like Etepali, it will make them more cautious."

"Good. Then we'll march double-time to the Upper Hadshaw. If we put our backs against the river, we won't have anyone behind us anymore."

"And as many as three field armies in front of us."

"We'll deal with that when it happens."

"Oh goodie," Bo said flatly. "I do have some bad news."

Vlora ran a hand over her face. "Is this news that I want to hear?"

"No. But you need to."

"Shit. Go ahead."

Instead of answering, Bo walked away. He didn't go far, stopping at the trunk he'd yelled for the porters to set aside. He opened the top and threw off his robe without ceremony or an ounce of propriety. He rummaged around, producing a pair of pants with an "Ah-ha!" and began to dress. Once he'd found a shirt, he finally looked up with a grave expression.

"The politicians have arrived," he said.

"Excuse me?"

"I had to do *a lot* of wrangling to take an entire field army out of Adro. Even if most of these soldiers weren't on active duty, they're still Adran citizens, and this isn't just one crack brigade off playing mercenary. Their departure threw the entire Adran legislature into a tizzy. I had hoped it would take them months to get their act together and send someone after us."

Vlora felt a creeping despair. "They've sent someone to stop me?"

"You're getting forty thousand Adrans involved in a foreign war," Bo said. "Of course they've sent someone to stop you. That doesn't mean they're going to succeed, but they can probably be a huge pain in the ass."

"Do you know who it is?"

"Word arrived late last night. A squadron from Adro has arrived carrying their special envoy with orders to find out what the pit we're up to."

Vlora's heart fell further. "And who is it?" she asked again, her tone firmer.

"Delia Snowbound."

"Oh." Lady Snowbound was not just a political enemy. She was one of the few old nobles who'd survived Tamas's purge. The rest of her family had died before the end of the Adran-Kez War, and she was able to return to the country under a general amnesty. She'd dedicated her career to dismantling Tamas's legacy—overseeing general disarmament, the forced retirement of hundreds of officers, and even gaining leverage over the head of the government, Ricard Tumblar.

It was no stretch to assume that she'd *asked* to be assigned as a special envoy. She'd do anything to stick a needle in Vlora's eye.

This wasn't just a complication. It was a disaster.

"She's on her way here?" Vlora asked, feeling suddenly faint.

"She'll be here in a couple of days."

"Do we know her specific orders?"

"No. Just that she has the full authority of the Adran government behind her."

"Pit."

Bo closed his trunk and sat on it to put his boots on, swearing quietly at his prosthetic. "I'd have chosen a stronger word. You want something to happen to her?"

"Are you suggesting I order the assassination of an agent of my government?" Vlora's head snapped around to make sure there was no one within earshot. Even for Bo, that went over the line.

Bo shrugged. "Just asking."

"No. We're not going to have her killed, as much as I'd like to." *Learn. Become better.* "Do you have any suggestions?"

"Unfortunately I don't think there's enough money in the world to buy her off. She hates you more than you hate her."

"Any *helpful* suggestions?"

She and Bo fell into a long silence, staring anxiously at each other. This could derail her entire campaign. She'd expected to face an inquisition from the Adran government at *some* point. She had, after all, gotten deeply involved in a foreign war that her mercenary company had never been hired to fight. She just didn't expect a reckoning until she got back to the country. She'd already accepted the possibility of being forced into an early retirement or even exile over all this. But if those things happened right *now*?

She briefly entertained Bo's suggestion before rejecting it again. She was not about to resort to the assassination of her own countrymen.

"You look like you have an idea," Bo said.

Vlora churned through her options once more, grasping for anything that might prepare her for the arrival of the special envoy. "Not a very good one. But something."

"What is it?"

"Did you bring any military attorneys with you?"

"A few." Bo shrugged. "Most armies have them. Don't you?"

"I do, but I want to consult with as many as possible before Lady Snowbound's arrival. Send them to meet with me after lunch."

CHAPTER 33

Two days after kidnapping Meln-Dun, Michel received his first report from Emerald. The file was left behind a false wall in a tenement block near the edge of Greenfire Depths. Michel picked up the blind drop and took it back to the room he and Ichtracia had been given in Jiniel's headquarters. He went inside and closed the door, turning up the lamp to give the report a good read.

He was on his second read-through when Ichtracia slipped inside and sat down next to him.

"No one will talk to me," she said.

"Hmm?" Michel reread a sentence, then pulled his attention away from the report and looked at Ichtracia.

"They're scared," she added.

"Do you blame them? You snapped the forearm of one of their enforcers with the flick of your fingers."

"It was barely a twitch, to be honest."

"Huh?"

"A twitch of my fingers." Ichtracia held up her bare hand and demonstrated. Her ring and pointer fingers moved in a slight, but dangerous, gesture.

Michel gave her a wry look. "That doesn't help. Why are you trying to make friends, anyway?"

"Isn't that what I'm supposed to do? Be friendly and helpful?"

"As a spy, yes."

"As an outsider," Ichtracia said. "Whether or not I'm spying on these people, I need to make them realize that I'm on their side. Remember what I said the other day? About finding a people who shared my . . . particular servitude?"

"I do."

"I meant it. I want to be closer to them. I *want* to be on their side."

Michel was surprised to hear a note of earnestness in Ichtracia's voice. He set aside the file and looked her in the eye. She was lonely, he realized. He'd found his people, but at the same time it had isolated her. They no longer had the shared experience of being two fugitives on the run. He was fighting while she waited around to enact plans he did not share with people she did not know.

"You're on *my* side," he told her gently. "These people don't know you. They don't trust you. Jiniel will take you in on my word, but to be honest, none of these people know me, either." He let his own unhappiness leak out. "I've been listening the last couple of days. Overhearing. Turns out I'm a bit of a legend with these people. They watched me infiltrate the Yaret Household and think I'm some kind of wizard for engineering the downfall of the Blackhats. But the only one who *does* know me is Jiniel, and we haven't spoken for years."

He continued, "These are my people, but I'm an outsider, too. You and I need to stick together. Do what we can to earn their trust. But they've got a hundred different projects and missions going on. We'll go about our own business, using what resources they can spare. Which will be less than we need, I'm sure."

"You don't have faith in them?" Ichtracia asked curiously.

"It's not that I don't have faith in them. It's like...like I just said. They've got their own missions that they think are more important. They don't mind working against the Dynize, but they think our claims about blood sacrifices are fairy tales."

Ichtracia snorted angrily. "If *they* won't help, then what do we do?"

"We give them a reason to help. We find evidence." Michel hesitated a moment, thinking of compartmentalization. Against his better judgment, he needed Ichtracia to trust him more than he needed to keep her in the dark. He handed her the report from Emerald and waited while she read through it.

She handed it back a few minutes later. "Nothing," she said in disgust. "No trail on missing people. No evidence of blood sacrifice. This doesn't help!"

"Right," Michel agreed. "But the rest of it."

She sighed. "Your setup of Meln-Dun worked."

"It didn't just work. It worked amazingly well. These are actual memos from within the Dynize government." Michel waved the report at her. "The Yaret Household found three separate instances of Meln-Dun working with Adran agents over the last decade that I didn't even know about. On their own, they're just a bit of bribery and light racketeering—nothing that the Blackhats would have used to move against him. But taken with Dynize paranoia, these paint Meln-Dun as an enemy of the state."

"Meln-Dun is down. Mama Palo can begin to operate in the open again. How does this help us?" Ichtracia was clearly frustrated.

Michel smiled, trying to keep any sense of condescension out of his tone. "Because with this," he said, "we can break Meln-Dun in the way I need him broken."

The now-former quarry boss was being kept in a dank little cell *underneath* Greenfire Depths. The stone down there was cold, oozing water that drained down through a crack in the floor. When Michel put his hand on the slimy wall, he could feel the vibration of the steam pumps that kept the lower levels of the Depths from flooding. They were well below the Hadshaw River here—below even the nearby ocean.

Michel let himself into the cell, hanging his lantern on a hook in the low ceiling and turning to face the man huddling in the corner. It had been two days since his kidnapping, and Meln-Dun did not look well. He was pallid and shivering. His bed was a mess of damp straw barely held together by something vaguely resembling a mattress cover. All he had for his waste was a bucket in one corner. By the smell of it, it hadn't been changed since he arrived.

Ichtracia had wanted to come along, but this kind of questioning was most effective if Michel could work one-on-one with the prisoner. He gave Meln-Dun a sad smile. "I'm sorry about the lodgings."

"No you're not." Meln-Dun's words were angry, but they had no bite. He looked more pathetic than anything else—a man who didn't take much to feel as if he'd been broken. Michel had to remind himself that most people ended up that way. No matter how much courage a man thought he had, it amounted to nothing when he'd lost everything dear to him. "What are *you* here for? To torture me?"

Michel peered at Meln-Dun. Per his instructions, it appeared he hadn't been touched. "You think that's what I do?"

"I don't know. I can hear them talking, you know. They're planning on killing me. They hate me. They want to make sure my death lasts a long time."

The "they" clearly referred to the guards posted outside the cell. Michel wondered whether he should put a stop to that kind of talk. If they actually planned to go through with their threats, it could ruin all his hard work. If, on the other hand, it was a bit of wishful chatter...well, that could be useful. "Of course they hate you," he said with a sigh. "You sold out their leader's predecessor to Lindet, then sold yourself to the Dynize."

"I did what I had to."

"For yourself. Yes, I understand that. I'm here to talk to you about what else you can do for yourself."

Meln-Dun studied him through distrustful eyes for several moments. "What do you want from me?"

"Information."

"I don't have anything of use to you."

"That's for me to decide."

Meln-Dun's lip curled. "I'm not going to tell you anything."

Michel put on a strong air of world-weariness. It wasn't a hard act. He found a dryish spot on the wall to lean against and let out a heavy sigh, careful that he look as unconcerned as possible. "That's your choice," he replied.

"It . . . it is?"

"Sure. I'm not interested in bloodying my knuckles with your face. I'm just here to ask a few questions."

"And if I don't answer them?"

Michel shrugged. "Not my problem."

"What does that mean?"

"It means I turn around and walk out of here. Nothing changes. You stay down here, shivering in the darkness, listening to the brutal fantasies of the guards and eating whatever slop they feed you until you catch pneumonia and die alone."

Meln-Dun's teeth began to chatter audibly.

"Or," Michel continued, "you answer my questions. I leave you a light, get you an extra blanket and a dry mattress. Small kindnesses, you know?"

Meln-Dun stared at him as if he were a demon crawled from the very pit. "What's going to happen to me?" he whispered.

"I just painted a pretty vivid picture," Michel replied. "I mean, they could lose their patience and execute you, of course. Nice and fast. That would probably be better." Michel was careful to phrase the actions in terms of "them" versus "me." Two different entities. Give the prisoner something hopeful to grab on to.

"I mean if I help you."

Michel took a deep breath. "You're never going to be a free, powerful man again, Meln-Dun. But if you help me, it gives me leverage to help *you*. Best-case scenario is that, once the war is over, you are retired to the countryside with a permanent guard but some amount of comfort and autonomy."

This best-case scenario didn't seem to sound all that best-case to Meln-Dun. He visibly withdrew into himself, his face twisting in horror, hands clutching at his knees. "You're not going to win, you know," he said, his voice stronger. "The Dynize. They're going to beat you."

"If I were you, I wouldn't root for them."

"They'll free me." Meln-Dun raised his chin. "They'll free me when they flush you out. All of this will be explained to them, and—"

Michel lost his patience, tossing a careful selection of Emerald's report onto Meln-Dun's lap. "I'm guessing you can read enough Dynize to see what those say?"

Meln-Dun slowly lifted the reports, flipping through them as he peered at the words.

"Those," Michel explained, "are internal memos regarding the traitor Meln-Dun."

"These aren't real."

Michel shrugged again, as if it didn't really matter. "I could mock those up, probably. Getting the grammar right might be hard unless I found a native speaker willing to do some forgeries for me. I didn't need to, though. We stole those right from the capital building."

Meln-Dun read through the report again and then looked up sharply at Michel. "You set me up. Everything you told me when you woke me up the other day—"

"Was all true," Michel said with a gentle smile. "Except for the part about me working for Dahre. You *were* set up, and the Dynize *did* come and try to arrest you about an hour after we left. Whatever suspicions they had—and I gave them quite a lot to work with—were cemented when they arrived only to find that you'd fled with all your valuables." Michel scratched the back of his head. "You're dead to them now, Meln-Dun. Doesn't matter what the truth is. They think they know, and if they ever find you, they will execute you without a second thought."

Meln-Dun stared at Michel in horror. This was, he admitted to himself, a form of torture. Michel produced a newspaper from his pocket and handed it over. "Third page. The Dynize have already taken over your quarry. Several of your foremen have been apprehended for questioning. They're not leaking any more information, of course. They want to keep the betrayal quiet. But they've quietly put a price on your head."

"What are your questions?" The sentence seemed to tear itself from Meln-Dun's throat. Michel had finally gotten through to him.

"Are the Dynize kidnapping Palo for their own purposes?"

There was a flicker in Meln-Dun's eyes, so quick that Michel might not have noticed it if he weren't watching carefully. Recognition. Then fear. Meln-Dun turned away, looking at his feet. "I don't know anything about that."

"You're sure?" Michel prodded gently.

"I'm sure." The protestation had a firm, desperate finality to it, as if Meln-Dun was hoping that if he exclaimed hard enough, it would put the matter to rest. "What else do you want to know?"

"I want to know about the disappearances," Michel pushed.

Meln-Dun suddenly surged to his feet. "I know nothing about them!" He stared at Michel, his whole body trembling, until he melted back onto his bed. He turned his face to the wall.

Michel watched him for the next couple of minutes. They remained there in silence, the only sound that of trickling water and Meln-Dun's unsteady breathing. Michel knew beyond a doubt that he'd touched something. But whatever it was—if Meln-Dun knew the truth that Michel feared was behind the abductions—it was too sinister for the greedy old snake to address head-on. Michel needed to give him time that he didn't have.

"Do you know *why* you haven't been tortured and killed?"

Meln-Dun shook his head fearfully.

"Because I'm holding the wolves at bay, Meln-Dun. Because I think you're more useful to the Palo cause alive than dead. I can convince them of that, but only if you point me in the right direction." No response. Michel swore inwardly. "I'll give you twenty-four hours. Give me an answer, or I'll let Mama Palo decide what to do with you." Michel opened the door. "I'll leave you the light, and the papers. Give you something to read. To think about." He closed the door behind him, nodded to the guards, and headed up to street level.

Ichtracia was waiting for him, sitting against the wall in an empty room above the holding cells. "Anything?" she asked, getting to her feet. There was an anxiety in her tone and mannerisms. She wanted to know—to be vindicated in her hatred of her grandfather. For some reason, that thought gave Michel a moment of sadness.

"Something," Michel replied. "Definitely something."

"You don't sound like it was something."

Michel considered the conversation. "I think we're on the right track. I think Meln-Dun was privy to the disappearances, maybe even had a hand in them."

"No evidence, though? He didn't give us a trail to follow?"

"Not yet." Michel glanced back down toward the cells. Twenty-four hours. "Not yet, but he will."

CHAPTER 34

Styke lay on the floor, staring at the ceiling of Maetle's infirmary, considering the thousands of hours he'd spent doing the same in the labor camps outside of Landfall. He'd come up with games to pass the time—sorting pebbles, thought experiments, even new war hymns to sing while fighting. He couldn't recall any of it now; all flushed away in the flurry of excitement that followed his release. He wished he remembered. It might make being confined in one corner of Etzi's Household compound a little easier to bear.

This was by far the most helpless he'd felt since leaving the labor camps. Well, second-most helpless, after his duel with Fidelis Jes. But this was worse than sitting in his cabin on the *Seaward*. At least there he could go up on deck and watch the waves. Here, however, he had to wait for days hiding in a tiny room in a foreign city at the mercy of a single man.

A tiny part of his brain wished for something to go wrong; that soldiers would suddenly fill the doorway, bayonets fixed, here to arrest or kill him. At least then he could draw his knife and do *something.*

A noise caught his ear and he twisted to look toward the door. There were a lot of noises around the compound—children playing, Household maintenance, men and women going about their trades inside the walls of the Household or heading out into the city for their work. It was a busy, thriving place that reminded him of his earliest memories of childhood on the plantation. Before the madness took his father.

This particular sound came from several voices, and it was getting closer. He rolled to his knees and stood up, facing the door when it opened to reveal five figures: Etzi, Maetle, the night watchman, and Ka-poel and Celine. The latter two had been living out in the open in the Household for the last few days. No one was looking for them, nor seemed to question their presence.

Etzi nodded seriously at Styke. "I'm sorry to keep you cooped up like this longer than expected." He ran a hand through his hair. He looked tired, but pleased. "But we've finally made some progress. Follow me."

Styke pulled on his boots, checked his knife, and followed Etzi out of the infirmary. It was midafternoon and he had to shade his eyes from the sun, squinting to try and see any of his surroundings. Three days being stuck inside and his legs felt cramped, his shoulders tight. Etzi led him down an immaculately kept series of gravel walks that connected and ran between the buildings of the compound until a narrow alley opened into a grass courtyard. The ground here was slightly depressed so as to create a sort of amphitheater, and it was filled with several hundred people.

Styke fought a moment of panic at all the Dynize faces looking at him. He felt foolish, like an ape in a zoo, and had to remind himself to stand tall, hands clasped behind his back, his face impassive.

There was surprise written on most of the faces, and they stared at him with open curiosity as murmurs laced back and forth through the small crowd.

"I've assembled the Household," Etzi told him, leading him to a spot at the head of the tiny amphitheater.

"You could have warned me."

"Ah. I thought Maetle told you. My apologies." Etzi scowled, giving Styke no time to consider the gathering. "You'll have to excuse them. Kressians are rare enough, but I doubt any of them have ever seen anyone of your size. Now then…" He lifted one hand, and the amphitheater fell silent as quickly as Styke's Lancers would responding to his orders.

"My friends," Etzi addressed the Household, "for the last three days, we have been harboring a pair of fugitives. These fugitives were unjustly and illegally attacked in the same violence that ended my mother's life." Whispers of sympathy and anger tittered through the assembly. Etzi stilled them with a gesture. "One of those fugitives is my brother, Ji-Orz." Gasps followed the announcement, and the ripple of excitement was harder to quiet. Styke gathered from the outburst that Orz was well known. Etzi continued over it. "Orz was released and pardoned by the Great Ka in Fatrasta. Why he was attacked, we do not know. But we will get to the bottom of it, even as he struggles for his life in our own infirmary."

Many of the crowd glanced toward Maetle, nodding and whispering as they put together her mysterious sequestering with Orz's presence. "Master!" someone called. "Who is the giant?"

A flicker of a smile caught the corner of Etzi's mouth. Instead of rebuking the questioner, he gestured to Styke. "This man is named Ben. He is a warrior from Fatrasta, and he is an ally of my brother. In fact, he saved Orz's life. He will be our guest while my brother recovers from his wounds, and I want you all to treat him as you would a member of this Household. Understood?"

Styke cleared his throat and eyed the group. The faces staring back at him looked as normal as any group he might find in a city or town—men, women, children; tradesmen, laborers, students; even a handful of soldiers. It reminded him again of the plantation when he was growing up, except that on the plantation there had been a very clear divide between his family and all of the "help." Here, it seemed as if everyone *was* family. It felt odd, but not bad.

He spotted Celine and Ka-poel in the back corner and gave them a small nod. Celine waved back at him. No one seemed to notice.

Etzi said a few more words and then dismissed the Household. He turned to Styke and gave him a tight smile. "The Household is open to you now."

"And it's wise that they know I'm here?"

"Everyone knows you're here," Etzi said. "I've spent the last two days laying the groundwork for a suit against Ka-Sedial's agents who attacked you and Orz. I took it to the Quorum Hall this morning."

"And you're sure they're not going to come here asking questions?"

"It will take them weeks to get that far," Etzi replied confidently. "A lone dragonman and a handful of foreign soldiers is a curiosity, to be sure. But they care far more about the murder of my mother—a retired Household head—and they care about the overreach of the Ka. I told you, things here are boiling over. No one is happy, and Sedial isn't here in person to silence the debates."

Styke opened his mouth, but he was interrupted by the approach of a child. It was a small boy, perhaps Celine's age, with a mop of dark red hair, a broad face, and a stout, almost chubby body. He cleared his throat loudly, and both Styke and Etzi looked down.

"Sir," the boy said, the slightest tremor in his voice. "Celine says that you are the head of her Household."

Styke blinked back at the child, looked up toward the corner to find Celine watching him, and then over at Etzi, who shrugged. "I suppose that's true."

"May Celine and I play, sir?"

Etzi clearly and unsuccessfully tried to hide a smile. He took a step behind Styke's shoulder and said in a low voice, "One of the boys tried to kiss her yesterday."

"And I didn't hear about this?"

"She knocked his front teeth out. Baby teeth—he'll grow more—but the children are scared of her now."

Styke cocked an eyebrow at Celine, then looked down at the boy in front of him. "And this one?"

"He doesn't scare easily. His name is Jerio. A distant cousin of mine. Much more polite than the other boy. And much smarter."

Styke cleared his throat. "That's up to her," he answered in his broken Dynize, kneeling down next to the boy and holding up one finger. "But I'd suggest not making her mad."

"Thank you, sir!" Jerio said, turning and running toward Celine before the last word had left his mouth. He reached Celine, and the two had a quick exchange before they both ran down one of the corridors that left the amphitheater. Styke felt like he had just witnessed some sort of strange, childlike ritual. Celine had made it clear that she could not only fend for herself but that her guardian was bigger than anyone else in the city. She was now forging alliances. Celine, he realized, was going to be a terrifying teenager.

"Sir!" someone called. This time the word was directed toward Etzi. A young man approached in a hurried walk, his face pale, and whispered something in Etzi's ear. Etzi looked up sharply at Styke.

"What is it?"

"*That* dragonman. He's outside."

"I thought you said it would be a couple of weeks before he came calling."

Etzi swore under his breath and hurried after the young man. Styke followed, checking his knife as he went. They navigated the corridors of the compound and were soon at the front gate. This was the first time Styke had actually seen it since carrying Orz in here three nights ago. It looked smaller in the daytime, an open-air vestibule that led off in a half-dozen directions. The big doors were closed and a concerned-looking soldier stood on a raised platform that let him look over the wall. Etzi climbed up to join him.

Styke elected to remain on the ground, putting his back to the wall and keeping his eye on the gate, listening.

"Good morning, Servant of God," Etzi said in a formal tone.

Styke couldn't see the dragonman, but he could imagine the condescending sneer on his face. He seemed the type.

"Open the gate," the dragonman called. "There are traitors I must arrest."

"You must be mistaken."

"I am not. And I am not in the mood for games. Open the gate."

Etzi, to his credit, did not seem as cowed as everyone else. Probably because his own brother was a dragonman. He shook his head. "You know the law, Servant. Take your henchmen and be gone. The men inside this compound are under the protection of myself and the Household Quorum."

"This doesn't have to go badly for you."

"It won't," Etzi replied with a hard note in his voice. "I am doing my duty. Or do you forget what it's like to have a mother and a brother?"

"You're making a mistake."

"If you force your way into this compound and lay a finger upon my brother or his friend, the Household Quorum will turn on your master with a fury he is not prepared to fight. Go ask him. Go speak to one of Sedial's puppets and find out just how much he's ready to risk for a single dragonman."

"It's not just about Orz." The dragonman had the tone of someone trying to be reasonable with an unruly child. "It's about that giant."

"He's also under my protection."

"You have no idea what kind of snake you're dealing with."

"He strikes me as more of an ox," Etzi said. "Now, go on back to one of your master's puppets. Tell him he has to wait for the law to run its course just like everyone else."

Styke heard the distinct sound of someone spitting at the base of the gate, then the tramp of a dozen pairs of feet receding down the causeway that led away from the compound. Etzi remained on the guard post, watching them go, before descending. His face was troubled. "That one is going to be trouble."

"You knew that," Styke pointed out.

"Yes, I did. What did he mean about you being a snake?"

Styke shrugged. He wasn't about to tell him about the army that might be south of the city. "He still have that limp?"

"Ah, yes. I forgot that it may be personal for him. However, I had the sense that it was more than that. Something from Sedial."

"I killed a few of Sedial's dragonmen."

"You don't strike me as a boastful man, Ben," Etzi said in a manner that very clearly told Styke that he didn't believe him.

Styke shrugged again and deflected. "Orz said that the emperor is under Sedial's influence."

"It is a...rumor." Etzi shifted uncomfortably from one foot to the other as if Styke had just committed some blasphemy.

"What happens if the emperor himself orders you to open that gate and hand Orz and me over to the dragonman?"

"The emperor doesn't get involved," Etzi said. He cleared his throat, avoiding Styke's eye, and turned toward the watchman at the gate. "Keep this door closed at all times. No strangers in or out." He took a deep breath and nodded at Styke. "Again, thank you for your patience. I have a lot to do to prepare for the days ahead. Feel free to get to know the compound. If you want to leave, I'll send you with an escort. Good day." He strode away before Styke could respond.

The whole exchange had been hurried, a very obvious cover-up of the fact he hadn't answered Styke's question. Styke grit his teeth, unable to do much more than that. He tried to remember Celine's advice: Don't attract attention. That's all he needed to do until Orz recovered.

But he also needed to be realistic. Etzi was using him for his own ends. The winds could shift at any moment and this safe haven would be upended. Styke needed to make sure he had his own plans in motion.

He hurried to catch up to Etzi, who'd already rounded a corner and was giving orders to a couple of his Household members. He looked up in expectation when Styke approached. "I'm sorry, Ben. I have a lot to do."

"Just one request: I want to visit my soldiers in prison."

Etzi considered this for a moment and gave a hesitant nod. "I'll try to arrange it."

CHAPTER 35

Michel spent his free time integrating both himself and Ichtracia into Mama Palo's command structure. Ichtracia's eagerness to *belong* to something came in handy, and although she kept her aloof demeanor, she remained omnipresent—hanging around Jiniel or her lieutenants at every moment, giving insight into Dynize operations, and never hesitating to offer a helping hand whenever it was needed.

Her gloves remained out of sight, and her true nature was only revealed to a handful of Mama Palo's inner circle, with those sworn to secrecy. Michel kept his ear to the ground, listening for any rumbling that the Dynize Privileged and bone-eyes had become alerted to her flash of sorcery the other day. As time went by and soldiers did *not* march into the Depths by the thousands, Michel began to relax.

They'd gotten lucky.

Michel himself did much the same as Ichtracia. He was immediately slotted into Jiniel's command structure just below Mama Palo herself. But while her lieutenants seemed to accept this new state of things, he could tell that it was uncomfortable for them. His reputation as a maverick spy won him admiration, not loyalty. As he'd told Ichtracia, he was still an outsider. He'd have to work to change that.

In the meantime, the fact that he *had* a reputation gave him anxiety. A known spy was a bad spy. All it took was a single informant, or even one pair of careless lips mentioning his name at the wrong time, to bring the might of Ka-Sedial down upon them. He wondered if he should change his identity again and work from the shadows, or leave the city altogether. Jiniel was about as good a leader as the Sons of the Red Hand could get: competent, intelligent, fervent. But she was short-handed, her attention divided among a thousand different directions. She needed Michel almost as much as he needed her.

He was pondering this conundrum, sitting on the floor in the corner of Jiniel's office, when Ichtracia burst in through the door, a victorious grin on her face.

"What's gotten into you?" Michel asked.

"Meln-Dun has called for you. He's agreed to talk."

Ichtracia accompanied Michel into Meln-Dun's cell. The quarry boss huddled on his mattress, the spent lamp hanging from the ceiling, and the newspapers and reports Michel had left for him sitting on his lap. He had the thousand-yard stare that Michel had seen on more than one broken convict. Michel replaced the spent lamp with his own and leaned casually against the one dry spot on the wall. "You wanted to talk."

"You have to guarantee that they won't torture me," Meln-Dun croaked.

"I'm not guaranteeing anything," Michel replied coolly. "As I said, I'll do what I can to make your life more comfortable. But my ability to do this depends completely upon how useful you can be."

Meln-Dun stared at him for several moments, a flurry of emotions crossing his face. He barely even glanced at Ichtracia. Once again, a sliver of pity nearly broke into Michel's thoughts. He steeled himself, remembering who Meln-Dun was and everything he'd done.

"You want to know about the disappearances," Meln-Dun finally said, looking down at his hands.

"I do."

"It was Ka-Sedial."

Michel glanced at Ichtracia. She was watching Meln-Dun just as intently as he was looking away in shame. "Go on."

"He came to me just after the invasion. Told me that he needed people that wouldn't be missed. Said that if I could provide him with two hundred a week, he would make sure that my quarry remained independent, that my people would be taken care of."

Michel had expected this. He knew the sinister implications. But hearing it out of Meln-Dun's mouth made his gut twist. "So what did you do?"

"I provided them," Meln-Dun whispered. "Kresimir help me, I provided them. Old men. Children. Drifters and dispossessed. I put a couple of my foremen in charge of the gathering. I didn't want to know the details."

"You're a monster." The absolute lack of emotion in Ichtracia's voice caught Michel's attention more than any amount of anger. Her face was a stone wall, but her eyes smoldered. He prepared to throw himself between them if it came to that.

Meln-Dun looked up, his lip curled. "I did this to survive."

"You did this to enrich yourself."

"And save my people! Thousands depend on me for work! Tens of thousands depend on my quarry and work projects for survival! Without me, the entire Depths is doomed!"

"Don't flatter yourself," Michel said, trying to hold in his own anger. He needed to remain uninterested, detached. "So you gathered up the unwanted. What happened to them?"

"Like I said, I didn't want any details."

Michel almost swore out loud. The testimony of a condemned man might be enough evidence to convince Mama Palo and her lieutenants, but it wasn't enough to galvanize the population. He needed more. "You don't know *anything*?"

Meln-Dun flinched. "I know they were taken to a keelboat every night at about one. A handful at a time."

This was something. Michel leaned forward. "And?"

"They shoved off downriver."

"Toward the bay?"

A nod. "I don't know what happened to them after that. I didn't ask; I didn't want to know."

"Are you still making deliveries?" Ichtracia demanded.

"No. No! I ... the requests stopped. Ka-Sedial said that he had enough."

Michel didn't like the look of alarm that crossed Ichtracia's face, and he didn't stop her when she crossed the room to snatch Meln-Dun by the front of the shirt. Despite her size, she jerked him around to face her and shook him hard. "How long ago did the deliveries end?"

"Weeks ago! He said he didn't need any more. I think ... I think we gave him a couple of thousand people in total."

Ichtracia released Meln-Dun, dropping him and staggering away. Her whole body trembled, and she fled from the room without another word. Michel watched her go, then turned his attention back to Meln-Dun. "Is that all you've got?"

"It is," he whispered. "I don't know anything else about it. I'll give you the names of the foremen I had doing the work. I'll give you the keelboat launch. That's all I have, I swear."

Michel swallowed his disgust. Meln-Dun didn't need to know exactly what those "unwanted" Palo would be used for to know that it wouldn't be pleasant. He'd sold the lives of his own countrymen and worse, those that couldn't defend themselves. There was a strong temptation to go back on his word and let Mama Palo's foot soldiers tear the bastard apart. He wrestled with the thought for several moments before leaving the room in disgust.

"Give him a better mattress," Michel told the guards outside. "And a permanent light." He stormed off to find Ichtracia.

She'd retreated to the street outside. He found her on the stoop, her whole body still shaking. Michel took one of her hands gently, sitting down beside her.

"I should have seen it happening," Ichtracia whispered. "I should have put a stop to it."

"You couldn't have known."

"I *should* have. I was willfully ignorant." She rubbed her face hard enough to turn her cheeks red. "I knew that Ka-poel—I didn't know her name then, just that my grandfather had an adversary—I knew that Ka-poel had somehow locked the godstone. I knew that Sedial and his Privileged and bone-eyes were trying to remove that lock. I just thought they were…"—she gestured mysteriously— "doing magic things to solve the problem. I never went near it myself. I *should* have known that those magic things would require blood, and lots of it." She cradled her head in her hands. "And that blood should have been mine."

Michel frowned, trying to catch up. A slow realization entered the back of his head. "So if the blood of those people was being used to undo Ka-poel's sorcery, and the deliveries stopped weeks ago, that means…"

"That Sedial already managed to unlock the godstone," Ichtracia finished.

"Shit."

"Yeah. Shit."

"If he's had it unlocked this long, then what is he waiting for?" Michel asked.

Ichtracia shook her head. "He doesn't know everything. Perhaps he's been studying it, trying to figure out how to activate it. Or maybe he's waiting until they can get their hands on the third god-stone. Or waiting until he's finished off his enemies. I don't know, but he must have a good reason for not having used it yet."

Michel let out a shaky breath. "This is bad." He wished he could tell Taniel and Ka-poel. They *needed* to know. He would get the information to Emerald as quickly as possible, but even if the albino knew how to find them, it would take weeks to reach them. "Okay, one thing at a time. This makes it even more vital that we rouse the Palo. But to do that, we need evidence."

"You think anyone will care?" Ichtracia said, a note of defeat in her voice.

"About the abduction and blood sacrifice of thousands of their kin?" Michel finally let his anger out. He was mad, but he was not helpless. He *could* do something to avenge these people. "Of course they'll care. Ka-Sedial has made a mistake." He got to his feet.

"Where are you going?" she asked.

"To follow the path Meln-Dun just gave us. To find evidence. Are you coming?"

Michel got the name of the keelboat landing from Meln-Dun. He and Ichtracia found it without a problem, near the southeastern exit of Greenfire Depths. There was nothing particularly unique about the landing—it was one of dozens within the Depths. Michel examined it thoroughly, asked a few of the workers about smuggling opportunities, spread around a little bit of money. No one reported anything out of the ordinary. Michel wasn't surprised. With many weeks since its last insidious use, these might not even be the same people.

Michel hired a small, two-man canoe. Ichtracia sat in the front while Michel took the back, giving her a brief boating tutorial as they pushed into the middle of the river.

There was plenty of traffic on the river, both from the Depths itself and from farther upriver, shipping supplies and soldiers back and forth from the bay. Michel allowed the gentle current to take them and kept his eyes on the rock walls of the plateau. They were soon out of the Depths and entirely buried within the canyon. He watched for smugglers' coves, outcroppings, low entrances to the catacombs—any place that the Dynize might take a keelboat full of old people and children.

"They're taking them down to the godstone south of the city, correct?" he asked Ichtracia.

She nodded unhappily. "From what I understand, the longer the blood is separated from a person, the less useful it is. The most potent use will be direct from them."

"That's how je Tura described it," Michel said, shuddering at the memory. "Men, women, and children, their blood being spilled directly onto the godstone."

"That sounds right."

"So if they kidnapped them from the Depths, loaded them into the keelboat, then..."

"They would take them south."

"Right." Michel kept his eyes on the walls of the plateau, but began to suspect that he'd find nothing here. Already loaded onto the keelboat, it would be easiest to take the prisoners out through the bay and down the coast a couple of miles. "There's a barge landing on the coastal plain near the godstone. I'd be willing to bet that's where they're unloaded."

They continued down the river in silence, dodging keelboats and river barges, letting the current take them out into the bay, where they canoed past the big Dynize ships laying in anchor. It was a calm day, the ocean like a sheet of glass, so they proceeded out past the breakers and turned south to hug the coast. They were not alone, either—plenty of traffic moved up and down the coast, making them just one of hundreds of boats, ships, barges, and canoes.

Once they were out of the harbor, the stink of dead fish and city sewage dissipated, and Michel found himself breathing the ocean air in deeply. He wondered why he didn't do this more often, then remembered that he'd been an active informant for most of his adult life, which left very little room for innocent pleasures.

"You act like you've done this before," Ichtracia said.

They were the first words spoken in almost an hour, and Michel reluctantly brought his mind back from its pleasant trance. "When I was a kid," he said, "I used to steal a canoe after the really bad storms and paddle up and down the shoreline looking for anything washed up from shipwrecks."

"Isn't that...dangerous?"

"Wildly. But you can see more when you're out on the water. Trick is to stay close enough to land that you don't get swept away, but far enough that you don't get bashed against the rocks. A day like today? An absolute breeze." Michel continued to paddle with long, even strokes, propelling them through the calm water. His arms were beginning to hurt, but he didn't mind.

The shoreline was his main concern. Much of it was marshy scrubland, providing a barrier between the ocean and the plains beyond—the same kind of horrid swamp that Lindet's forced labor camps had spent the last ten years trying to irrigate around the plateau. This was broken by the occasional rocky outcropping and, even less often, a gentle sandbar big enough to constitute an actual beach.

"Should I be looking for anything in particular?" Ichtracia asked.

Michel shook his head slowly. "I'm not even sure myself. Things out of the ordinary, maybe?"

"I don't know what constitutes ordinary on a coast like this."

Michel didn't answer. He was beginning to suspect that he'd taken this expedition as a way to get out of the city more than anything else. What *did* he hope to find out here? A trail, like he'd said, but the most likely trail led right to the barge landing that he could now see about a mile to their south. Not too much longer and they'd have to turn back. That landing was likely heavily guarded. He didn't want to risk talking his way past those guards, not with Ichtracia in tow.

They proceeded another half mile before he dug in his paddle and turned them around, heading back north. The pleasant feeling was gone now, replaced by frustration. Had he just wasted an entire afternoon paddling up and down the coast? His mood began to sink further, and he was just beginning to lose his concentration when Ichtracia spoke up.

"You see something in those rocks there?"

He followed her outstretched finger toward one of the rocky outcroppings. There was nothing out of the ordinary about this one—it had a small gravel beach at its base, upon which the trunk of one of those giant trees from up north had washed. As a child he used to love those giant trunks. He would climb all over them, inspect their roots for caught treasures, and pretend they were his mighty ship run ashore.

"Nothing," Michel answered her.

"There's a kid hiding behind the roots."

Michel watched carefully for several minutes. Finally, he saw a little flash of color and a movement. "Okay, I see it. Two kids, looks like." He pulled in his paddle, letting them drift, and considered their options. They'd seen relatively few people along the shore between here and Landfall. It would be smart to walk all the way back, question everyone as they went, but those long stretches of marsh made such an endeavor difficult.

"They're awfully far from the nearest fishing village," Michel said, looking up and down the coast. They were, it seemed, trapped on that outcropping by the marsh. "They might be local, though. We can go ask if they've seen anything out of the ordinary."

He turned the canoe toward shore. By the time they reached it, both of the children had disappeared. Michel looked around the empty little beach and up toward the rocks, hesitant to go looking through that tangle. He pushed the canoe farther onto the beach. "Stay here," he told Ichtracia. "I don't want a couple of damned kids getting the drop on us and stealing our canoe."

"They'd do that?"

"It's what I would have done for fun at that age," he said over his shoulder. He headed up the beach, around the ocean-worn tree trunk, and began to climb the rocks. He got to the top and looked around. They were, indeed, trapped on the outcropping, surrounded by marsh. He couldn't see any kids, and he couldn't see any likely path that they would have taken to get here.

He could see the godstone from here. It was a couple of miles away, rising from the plain like a twig thrust into a sandbar. Around it swarmed a small city, constructed entirely by the Dynize since they arrived. There were laborers, soldiers, scientists, Privileged, and bone-eyes. The walls of a mighty fortress, as of yet unfinished and covered in scaffolding, surrounded the monolith itself.

The very idea that that thing was active and usable, bathed in the blood of thousands, made him want to look away—to spill the content of his stomach into the rocks. He wasn't sure whether it was the sorcery of the stone or just his own horrible knowledge, but the whole horizon seemed to pulse with dark purpose. He shuddered and turned back toward the beach.

Only to come face-to-face with an old Palo man, bent and gray.

Michel almost tumbled from his perch in surprise. The old man held a driftwood branch over his head, as if preparing to swing. His clothes were torn and weather-beaten, his beard and hair unkempt and unwashed. He seemed as surprised that Michel had turned around as Michel was that he was there, making a *oop* noise.

"Were you just about to hit me with that?" Michel demanded.

The old man brandished the stick. "Give us your canoe," he said.

Michel eyeballed the makeshift weapon. The old man's arms

trembled so hard that it almost fell from his hands just hanging there, and he doubted it could be swung with any strength. Michel raised one hand toward the old man and another toward the beach, where Ichtracia could no doubt see that something was happening. He didn't want her to do anything rash, not out in the open like this.

"Whoa there," Michel said gently. "Hey old-timer, can I help you with something?"

"You can give us your canoe." Despite his trembling limbs, the man's voice was strong.

"So you can go where?" Michel asked. "It doesn't look like you're fit for rowing anything."

The old man tried to brandish the stick again, but finally let out a defeated sigh and let the weapon slip from his fingers. Michel gave him another quick appraisal. He was whip-thin, the gauntness of his face speaking of malnutrition. Michel wondered how long he'd been out here. Was he a hermit? A shipwrecked sailor? Did he have something to do with the godstone? It was the final thought that sharpened Michel's curiosity.

"Who is 'we'?" Michel asked.

The old man wilted to the ground. "No one," he said, waving Michel off. "Just me. Go on, get out of here."

Something about this was very strange. Michel took a cautious look around, remembering the small figures he'd seen from the water. Two children. Alone, he had just written them off as local kids playing on the shore, much as he would have when he was a child. But with this old man... "Do you need help?"

The old man didn't look up.

Michel continued, "If you need help getting back to Landfall, I don't mind rowing you to the city. But I'm not gonna let you strand me and my friend here." He tried to read the old man, to get a feel for who and what he was. Mad? He didn't *seem* mad. Just half-starved. "Look, I'll make you a deal. I'm trying to find out if there's anything strange about that new citadel over there. You help me..." He trailed off, because when he gestured toward the god-stone, the old man flinched. Not a small flinch, either. He might as well have cowered. Michel's breath caught in his throat.

An elderly Palo man and a couple of children. The unwanted, the uncared-for.

Michel crouched down, staring intently at the old man. "Do you know something about that place?"

"No," the old man growled. "Nothing. Now, go."

It was an obvious lie. Michel continued on in a gentle, firm voice. "How long have you been here?"

No answer.

"Are you from Greenfire Depths?"

Still no answer.

Michel looked around for any sign of the kids. He thought he saw a bit of red hair poking up behind a nearby rock. It moved. He didn't give any indication that he'd seen it, keeping one eye on the man and one on the rocks. "I'm from the Depths. I'm trying to find out about people who went missing there. I think some of them were taken to the new Dynize citadel."

"I have no idea what you're talking about." The old man was a terrible liar. He was also clearly terrified. Michel caught sight of a tattoo on his wrinkled skin: the roots of a cypress tree on his upper arm. Michel knew the mark—it belonged to a large contingent of Palo soldiers who'd fought for Fatrastan independence.

Michel pursed his lips and spoke in a strong, confident tone. "I am a Son of the Red Hand, and you have no need to fear me, brother."

The old man looked up sharply. His whole body convulsed and shuddered, and he suddenly sprang forward. Michel caught him in surprise, and soon found himself holding an old man who wept against his shoulder. "A friend!" the old man cried. "By my life, a friend!"

It took some time to calm the old man. The children were coaxed from their hiding spot—three of them, all looking as ragged as the old man, but none nearly as starved. They gathered around Michel, touching his clothes and his hair. He recognized the parlance of the street urchins of Greenfire Depths and replied to them with their own vernacular. They clapped and laughed, and asked when they could go home.

Michel struggled to maintain his professionalism. He would get them back to the Depths, of course. But he had to know their story. He prodded the old man twice before it all came pouring out in short, staccato bursts.

"Soldiers gathered us up. At least, I think they were soldiers. Armed Palo, carrying Dynize muskets. I was pulled from my tenement late at night, threatened into silence. They took us to the docks. Old people, like me. Kids. So many kids." The old man spoke between deep breaths, every moment threatening to burst into tears again. "Keelboats. Down the river. Down the coast. Marched us to the citadel. To that...thing. The Dynize, once they had us, kept us placid with talk of food. Spoke of service to a higher cause. Religion. Gods. I didn't understand any of it. I've heard promises before, you see." He tapped the tattoo on his arm. "I snuck off when I could. Got lost. Then I saw them...the bodies. It was the smell that got me first, and then the sight. Within the citadel. A mass grave. Bloodless corpses."

The man began to shake and shudder. Michel put a hand on his shoulder to calm him. Several more minutes passed before he could speak again.

"I saw them bloodlet a child. A child, damn it! Slit her little throat like she was an animal to put in the stew, then dashed her brains against the base of the monolith. I fled. Managed to gather these three. I don't think anyone even noticed. There were so many of us, and the night was dark and the soldiers sleepy. We left through a drainage ditch in the citadel wall. But...but I got lost in the dark. Led them across the marsh. It wasn't until morning that I realized I'd trapped us on this forsaken rock."

"Why didn't you head back to the city?" Michel asked.

"Fear," the old man replied unashamedly. "Fear of the snakes and the bottomless marsh. Fear of the Dynize. Fear that we'd be rounded up the moment we returned."

"How long have you been here?"

The old man looked at the oldest of the children, who held up one hand, fingers splayed.

"Five weeks. We survived off fish we caught with our hands. There's a little cave down under these rocks. Big enough to keep us out of the rain and sun."

Michel looked around the group. He didn't let himself react to this story. He couldn't afford to. He had to harden himself. This was a horror, but he had a job to do. He looked toward the beach, wondering how long he'd been gone, only to find Ichtracia standing less than ten paces from them. The fury on her face told him that she'd heard enough. He took a long, calming breath and turned back to the old man.

"Do you still have any fight in you?"

The old man looked down at his own trembling hands. This time, there was shame in his eyes.

"Not that kind of fighting," Michel said reassuringly. "A different kind. I want you to come back to the Depths with me. Meet Mama Palo. Tell your story."

"To who?"

"To everyone."

CHAPTER 36

Vlora watched an approaching column with no small amount of trepidation, knowing that if she'd still had her sorcery, she could spend this time closely studying the faces of the men and women, gaining an early edge on her political enemies. Instead, she was left to stew in her impatience, while her mood grew darker with every passing moment.

Her army had stopped for the night, and she could smell the smoke from fires as company cooks began to turn rations into something vaguely resembling dinner. She'd been told she would enjoy venison herself—a bit of meat shot by one of the camp followers and sold to the general-staff chef. She doubted she would *actually* enjoy it. Everything seemed to taste of ash these days, even after her recent realizations.

One of her first duties as a commanding officer receiving politicians was to invite them to dinner. Vlora had no intention of doing so, and decided she would have to get her pleasure from the petty snub.

"That's almost two thousand soldiers," Bo said. Nila was off aiding the wounded, but Bo had elected to join Vlora. General Sabastenien was here as well. No one else had bothered. Delia Snowbound was not popular among any of the soldiery, and less so among the senior officers. Even under the best of circumstances Vlora herself had trouble dealing with Delia without losing her temper. It was not even close to the best of circumstances.

"The High Provosts," Vlora spat. Even at this distance she recognized the flags flying above the infantry column. One of them was the classic crimson with the mountains and teardrop. The one below it was small but no less bold—a contrasting military blue with the same exact emblem, but an added chevron below the teardrop. The High Provosts were a wing of the military police created after the Adran-Kez War as a sort of royal guard for the new ministerial government. Delia Snowbound and her allies had managed to gain control of the High Provosts and turn them into a check on the military leadership of the country. It had been the High Provosts who oversaw the disbanding of much of the Adran Army.

Delia herself was insult enough. But the presence of two thousand High Provosts was a slap to Vlora's face and a clear statement of Delia's intentions—she wasn't just here to make sure that Vlora played nice in a foreign war. She was here to remove Vlora from power.

Vlora couldn't let Delia get the better of her. Not now. She had to remain calm.

Bo glanced in her direction and did a double take. "Are you okay?"

"I'm practicing a pleasant smile," Vlora told him.

"You look like you're about to chew your own leg off."

"That's why I'm practicing."

"Maybe just not smile at all. Try total neutrality."

Vlora rubbed at her jaw, trying to work some of the tension out of it. "How about now?"

"You look constipated."

"Sabastenien?" She turned to her general.

Sabastenien cleared his throat, seemed about to say something, then think better of it.

"He agrees with me," Bo said confidently. "Just relax. This won't be that bad."

"Two thousand High Provosts and Delia Snowbound. How could it possibly be worse?"

"Four thousand High Provosts?" Sabastenien suggested.

"You're not helping." Vlora leaned back in her saddle, attempting to loosen the knot between her shoulders. The column continued their approach, and she noticed that hundreds of her soldiers had turned out to the edge of camp to watch. She had a pang of fear. High Provosts were paid better than the regular army, and their numbers had been heavily recruited from the surviving scions of the old noble families who'd been exterminated by Tamas and their sympathizers. She worried that she wouldn't have to do or say a damned thing for her soldiers to turn on the provosts.

Anything they did on their own initiative would reflect poorly on her.

The column finally reached the edge of camp and came to a stop. A small group detached itself from the main body and rode up the hill toward Vlora. She recognized both Delia and the man at her side. Delia was a tall, slim woman with hawkish features and an overbearing air, her nose turned up and her lips fixed in something close to a permanent sneer. Her long blond hair trailed all the way down across her horse's back. She wore a riding jacket and pants as if she'd turned out for a fox hunt rather than to join a military expedition.

The man's name was Valeer, and what he lacked in height—being only an inch or two taller than Vlora herself—he made up for in arrogance. He'd inherited the High Provosts from their original commander and done his very best to turn them into Delia's private little army. He wore the blue-and-crimson uniform of a High Provost, with an epaulet on his left shoulder.

The pair looked every bit the part of the old aristocracy, and the presentation was, Vlora understood, absolutely deliberate.

"Provost Marshal Valeer," Vlora called as the two approached. "To what do we owe the honor?"

Neither of them answered until they'd ridden up close to Vlora and her companions. Valeer eyeballed both Bo and Sabastenien before turning to Vlora. "A military crisis," he said.

"Lady Flint," Delia greeted with a nod.

Vlora ignored the clear implication from Valeer and returned Delia's nod. "Lady Snowbound. What an auspicious visit."

Delia looked around. "You had warning of our arrival?"

"We did."

"Then where is the rest of the general staff?"

"Having dinner, I believe."

"We should join them."

"Should we?" Vlora asked. Her voice cracked. Beside her, Bo cleared his throat. "Pardon me," Vlora continued, pressing a hand to her chest and coughing. "I mean to say, I'd rather not interrupt anyone's dinner. They are dining with their troops tonight."

"I see." Delia cast a long look at Bo. He smiled back at her.

"Lady Snowbound, is there something I can do for you?" Vlora asked in her most neutral tone. Even to her it sounded defensive. "We only found out about your impending arrival yesterday morning and—"

"Lady Flint," Delia cut her off. "Marshal Valeer and I have come to relieve you of your command. I would rather have told you the news formally, in front of the general staff, but there you have it."

"In front of witnesses, you mean?" Vlora asked lightly.

Delia ignored her. "We've been instructed to send you, Magus Borbador, and Privileged Nila back to Adro to answer to the governing council. They turned a blind eye to your brigade of mercenaries, but you are still a sitting member of the Adran Republic Cabal and an Adran general, and the fact that you're now leading a field army across a foreign continent puts our entire web of international relationships in peril. Once you are gone, Valeer and I will remain behind and attempt to sort out this war that you and Borbador seem to have thrown us into."

Vlora leaned forward onto her saddle horn and frowned at Delia. The silence stretched into nearly a minute, and Valeer was the first one to break it, shifting uncomfortably in his saddle. "Did you hear her?" he asked. "You've been relieved of your post, effective immediately. You should gather your general staff to pass on the news and formalize the changing of command."

"That's not happening," Vlora said.

"Pardon?" Delia looked taken aback.

Vlora made a show of checking her pockets, then removed a small book from one of them. She'd borrowed it from the Riflejack military attorney. She licked one finger and flipped through the book, then ran the tip of that finger along the page to a sentence that had already been underlined for her. She quoted, "Under extraordinary circumstances, and in possession of individual knowledge that affects the well-being of the motherland, a ranking general may operate his or her army in foreign territory independent of orders from Adopest."

Delia sneered. "You believe that you can invoke Tamas's Clause. At me?"

It took Valeer a moment to catch up, but eventually his eyes widened. "That clause was written during the Gurlish Wars to give Field Marshal Tamas leave to operate without waiting for orders that might take months to arrive."

"The clause is still very much on the books," Vlora assured him.

"And you think it applies to this circumstance?"

"Absolutely," Vlora replied confidently. "These are extraordinary circumstances, and I possess individual knowledge that affects the well-being of the motherland." She shrugged. "I'm afraid that since you must have left Adopest between six and eight weeks ago, you couldn't possibly know about those extraordinary circumstances. Therefore, I can override your request to hand over command of this army."

"It was not a request," Valeer barked. "It was an order from your government!"

"Speak that way to Lady Flint again and I'll slap that mustache off your face," Sabastenien said coolly.

Both Vlora and Delia held up a hand in a mirror gesture to silence their subordinates. It almost made Vlora laugh. "An ill-informed government," she assured them.

"Tamas's Clause does not allow you to act with impunity," Delia warned.

"No, of course not," Vlora replied. "I would never dream of it. Accordingly, I will order a briefing drawn up for you and Valeer. It should be ready tomorrow. Once you know everything that I know, I'm sure you'll agree that these circumstances are extraordinary and you will take your provosts and return to Adro."

That last bit was, Vlora knew, wishful thinking. But she couldn't help but try to steer them that way. Delia's nostrils flared and her horse pranced to one side, as if sensing its rider's anger. She spoke through clenched teeth. "We have the authority to take your command."

"And I have the authority to tell you to buzz off," Vlora replied. "Don't think I mistook your intentions, showing up with two thousand provosts. You may hate me because of who my father was, but you can't possibly think me a fool. I have no intention of risking my legacy on an unsanctioned foreign invasion—I will be vindicated in my actions."

Delia snorted and turned her horse away. "Prepare your briefing," she snapped over her shoulder as she began to ride back to her provosts. "We shall be the judge of this."

*   *   *

Vlora felt herself once again missing Olem as she looked over a hastily-drawn-up briefing titled "The Dynize-Fatrasta Conflict." Normally, Olem would handle this sort of thing and she trusted him so implicitly that she wouldn't even have felt the need to read the draft. That sense of loneliness cut deep every time, refusing to go away until she consciously pushed it aside. She had no more time for self-pity. There was too much riding on her ability to think clearly.

She read through the briefing for a fourth and fifth time, adjusting the language here and there in light pencil. She finally called for a secretary to take it to be read over by a handful of her Riflejack officers. Instead of a secretary, it was Bo who popped inside.

He took the draft out of her hand without a word and dropped onto her cot, reading through it quickly. "This looks good," he finally said, handing it back. "I would change 'threat to Adran interests in the region' to 'Adran interests worldwide.' A new god would, after all, be a worldwide threat."

Vlora made the change without comment. "Hand this to the secretary outside."

Bo did as she asked and returned, taking a seat back on her cot and frowning at the wall.

"Well?" she asked him.

"Well what?"

"I assume you've spent the last couple of hours making contact with any spies or old allies you have among the High Provosts."

"Ah. Yes, that I have. Not a very good lot unfortunately. Delia specifically made sure that most of the High Provosts she brought with her have good reason to hate me."

"She has always been annoyingly thorough."

"Indeed. I was able to bribe a lieutenant."

"Get anything good out of him?"

"Her," Bo corrected. "But yes, a few interesting tidbits. It turns out that when Delia began to put together her expedition, she was absolutely convinced that I had just left to invade Fatrasta."

"What *did* you tell everyone?"

" 'Cabal business.' " Bo shrugged.

"You got forty thousand soldiers into a fleet on 'Cabal business'?"

"It's easier than it sounds when you do it in little chunks. Only the generals actually knew what we were doing. The rest of the soldiers all thought they were going on small, isolated missions. They didn't find out until they reached a rendezvous well off the coast."

"You say that like it isn't a terrifying feat of subterfuge."

"It took some planning," Bo admitted. "I'm honestly surprised we left without a major inquest by the First Minister."

"Well, they've caught up with you."

"Right! About that—so, they thought I was leaving to invade Fatrasta. However, they found out about the Dynize invasion just before they left and didn't really get any new information until they reached our fleet a few days ago. They thought they were coming to arrest a rogue group of generals and a couple of Privileged—those provosts include half a dozen mage breakers among their number. Instead, they find out that I've handed command to you and that no one is planning any sort of foreign invasion. Everyone in the fleet, and indeed our own general staff, considers this a peacekeeping mission."

Vlora frowned, feeling a tiny thread of optimism. "Are you saying we might be able to convince Delia that we're in the right?"

"I'm saying that Delia is going to spend the next few days rethinking her position. She didn't actually know you'd be here until she met with our fleet commanders. Seems to have thrown her off a bit. Quoting Tamas's Clause at her has her in an absolute fury. I have no doubt she's going to figure out how best to make your life miserable—but I'm fairly confident you can keep your command without going into open rebellion against the Adran government."

"And if that happens?" Vlora asked.

Bo crossed his legs and tapped absently on his prosthetic. "Let's not get ahead of ourselves. I break a lot of rules because I can get away with it, but I'd really rather not get involved with actual treason. I imagine most of the general staff feels the same way."

"So, no treason," Vlora mused. "I'll keep that in mind." She took a few deep breaths. Delia had arrived and Vlora still had her command. One step at a time. But she had to remain vigilant. Delia hated her, Bo, and every other officer and soldier who'd helped with Tamas's coup ten years ago. She wasn't going to give up simply because of a clause named after the very man who had executed her family.

CHAPTER 37

Styke sat in the corner of the courtyard of Etzi's Household compound, tucked in the shade while he whittled horses out of Cypress wood and watched Celine play in the shallow bowl of the amphitheater. It was early afternoon, and the heat had already made him sweat through his shirt. All around him the Household carried on its duties; washerwomen, cleaners, and gardeners passed through the courtyard regularly. It had been two days since Styke had been introduced, and they still glanced at him furtively every time they came near.

The children seemed less bothered by his presence. Jerio, Celine's quiet, serious, chubby little friend, had taken to stealing pastries from the kitchens every morning and bringing them to Styke. It was not a subtle gesture—very clearly meant to win Styke's favor—and it was working well. Any boy clever enough to keep Celine's attention was a good kid in Styke's mind.

The pastries didn't hurt.

He finished whittling a horse and blew the dust off his fingers, then set it down with a half-dozen others. He'd already distributed one to each of the children in the compound, but this group was being saved for something special.

He adjusted each of the horses so that they stood in a perfect line on the flagstone, then raised his eyes to check on Ka-poel. Unlike Celine, she hadn't taken to the Household. The language barrier saw to that. She spent her time shadowing Styke, watching people come and go, and fiddling with little bobs and bits that she kept concealed in her lap. Knowing a little how her sorcery worked, he wondered if she was gathering leverage over the Household or simply taking stock of what she'd already gathered. She didn't bother to tell him.

Etzi had very pointedly *not* told his Household that she was a bone-eye. He'd told them nothing about her, as far as Styke could discover, beyond the fact that she was a guest and was to be treated as such. Even her connection with Styke was not explicit, though the Household must have picked up on it at some point.

He left her to her devices and turned his head at the steady sound of approaching footsteps. A few moments later, Etzi emerged from a corridor, walking unhurriedly but businesslike toward Styke. It was the first time since Styke's introduction to the Household that he'd even seen the Household head. Whether Etzi was avoiding him or just busy, Styke couldn't say.

They exchanged a cool nod, and Styke climbed to his feet and dusted off his trousers. "Afternoon."

"Good afternoon, Ben," Etzi said with a friendly but tired smile. "I apologize for my scarcity—this suit has taken up every second of my time the last few days."

"Of course," Styke said, resisting the urge to demand an update. He was still trying to follow Celine's rules for going unnoticed, and one of them was simply not acting like himself. He needed to be polite. Gracious.

"I do have news, both good and bad," Etzi said. "The bad news is that I haven't been able to get your men released into my care."

Styke wasn't surprised. "And the good?"

"You have permission to speak with them. I have an hour of spare time right now, and a carriage waiting. It'll go easier if I accompany you."

"Excellent." Styke forced himself to smile. He needed an opportunity to put his own plans in motion, and although Etzi might be a better chaperone than an escort of prison guards, he also spoke flawless Adran—which meant he could overhear whatever Styke said to his men. "I would appreciate it. Celine!" he called, then gestured at the horses he'd been carving. Celine paused in her play to nod. He then exchanged a glance with Ka-poel. "Let's go," he told Etzi.

The carriage was not ideal. It was small and narrow, with two seats facing each other in a covered box and a driver out front directing a single horse. The wheels squealed loudly beneath Styke's weight, and he could tell by the nonplussed expression on Etzi's face that such a sound was not common. They rode in silence for a couple of minutes before Etzi gave him an embarrassed smile.

"I'll get a larger carriage next time," he promised. "It's easy to forget just how big you really are."

Styke hunched his shoulders to keep them from splitting through the thin wooden walls, and resisted the urge to get out and walk. "Don't mention it."

"It's better this way," Etzi went on. "You're the buzz of town right now, and even on foot you're likely to draw crowds."

Styke leaned forward to look out the narrow window, watching the people pass. Occasionally someone spotted his face and exclaimed to a companion, pointing, but by the time they'd made a ruckus, the carriage had long passed.

"You'll be pleased to know that I was able to retrieve your men's horses from the foreigner's inn where they'd been lodged," Etzi said.

Styke perked up. "Yes, I am. Thank you for that. And..."

"And that strange armor, yes, I've retrieved that, too." Etzi got a peculiar look on his face. He reached beneath his seat and drew out a bundle. "You're lucky the innkeep didn't take too close a look at those saddlebags, else that armor would have disappeared by the end of the first day. Magical armor." The last two words were more of a mutter than anything else, and he pinched the bundle by one corner and held it up in the small space between them, letting it unfurl. It was the skull-and-lance of the Mad Lancers. Probably came right from Jackal's saddlebags.

"Company standard," Styke explained. That peculiar look was beginning to bother him.

"Yes, so I gathered. Very striking. Striking enough that it caught my memory." Etzi reached beneath the seat again and drew out a book—very nice, leatherbound, if rather worn. Styke recognized the stitched title down the side: *A History of the Fatrastan Revolution*. They'd only gotten books occasionally in the labor camps, but this one was hard to miss. It was written four years after the end of the Revolution and had become a best seller overnight.

Styke clenched his teeth while Etzi flipped to an earmarked page.

"Our spies have smuggled us many books over the last few years," Etzi explained. "The heads of larger Households get the pick of them, of course, but a few trickled down to me. It says here that this is the standard of the Mad Lancers. There's even a sketch, which is what caught my memory." Etzi turned the book to show Styke a rendering of the flag that was lying across Etzi's lap.

Etzi closed the book, set it on the seat beside him, then carefully folded the flag back up. Styke remained silent throughout the process. When he was done, Etzi said, "The odd thing to me was that Colonel Ben Styke, an apparently infamous hero of that war, was executed for treason. The Mad Lancers were disbanded. Odder still, a cavalry unit under this banner was seen at the Dynize capture of Landfall. Fighting for the Fatrastans."

Styke stared at the banner for a few moments, considering. His position was fraught, and he'd never been a good liar. What was it that Markus had once told him? The easiest way to lie is to tell a half-truth? To steer the conversation? "Ben Styke wasn't executed," he finally said. "He was put up against a wall and shot."

"That sounds an awful lot like an execution."

Styke tapped the still-visible scar on the side of his jaw, then the one on the back of his hand. "Not if you're more stubborn than a dozen bullets."

"I see." Etzi opened the book again, flipping through it seemingly at random. "This Ben Styke was a giant of a man, a monster and a hero. A god among men, if the author is to be believed."

"There are a few exaggerations."

"The one about killing a Kez Warden with your bare hands?"

Styke did not fail to notice that Etzi had switched from "he" to "you." He grimaced. "I was a lot younger then."

"You know, when you said that you've killed dragonmen, I assumed it a boast. Perhaps, I thought, you finished one on the battlefield. But the man described in this little chapter here—this tall tale—would be more than capable of fighting one of our emperor's holy warriors."

Styke cleared his throat and looked out the window. If Etzi knew who he was, and knew that Styke fought for the Fatrastans, it made both their positions weaker. It made Styke's position downright dangerous.

"I don't want to know," Etzi said.

"Eh?" Styke looked up at his host sharply.

"I don't want to know," Etzi repeated. "I don't want to know why you're here. I don't want to know whose side you're on, or what you intend to do in my country. I don't believe you're a spy, and if you're part of an invasion force, your presence here on your own is testament that it has failed spectacularly."

He continued, "Ignorance, as they say, is bliss. I've begun a legal battle that I cannot—that I will not—stop, and you and Orz are the linchpins. All this"—he gestured at the book and the folded battle standard—"will remain hidden. No need to let it out, as long as both you and your men remain silent. All *you* need is a few weeks for Orz to recover enough to walk. Then you'll be out of my hands, and whatever comes out, I can claim ignorance."

Styke decided not to tell him just how close his guess was. "You're taking a great risk."

"Revenge isn't sweet without risk," Etzi said with a cold smile that reminded Styke of Orz. "My greatest hope is to have Ji-Patten executed for the murder of my mother. But at the very least, I will have given Ka-Sedial a handful of sleepless nights."

"That doesn't seem worth it," Styke observed.

"It takes a lot of work to make the Great Ka lose sleep."

Their conversation was cut short by the carriage lurching to a stop. Etzi leaned forward and looked out the window. "We're here," he announced. A moment later the driver opened the door for them, and Styke followed Etzi out into the sunlight.

Styke found himself in a walled courtyard of rough-cut red stone. The courtyard was large enough to accommodate a dozen carriages like theirs, and was about half full. The traffic continued around them, citizens coming and going, and more than a few stopping to stare at Styke. Etzi ignored them, so Styke followed suit, continuing after his host across the dusty drive and up a wide set of stairs. They proceeded down a high-arched corridor and then a side hall toward a suite of offices.

Despite the archaic look of the building—it was more ancient castle than the rest of the construction in the city—it had a very modern feel to it that reminded him of the prisons in Fatrasta. The hallways bustled with activity, city guardsmen marching here and there, long-coated investigators speaking with administrators and lawyers in low voices, slouching criminals in irons being ferried about.

Etzi strode past them all without stopping, until they reached a large, official-looking door. Etzi announced himself to the guardsman outside, who nodded briskly and disappeared, only to reappear a moment later with a handful of keys. "Good afternoon, Meln-Etzi," the guard said, nodding to the Household head but not taking his eyes off Styke. "Arrangements have been made. If you'll follow me?"

Styke tried to ignore the work stoppages as he passed, his shoulder blades itching from the feel of eyes following his every move. They wound back through the halls, then took a short causeway out through the open air and entered a second building. It looked more like a prison and less like an administration hall—the windows were barred, the doors double-hinged. Cells marched down either side of the dank hall and around a corner.

"Ben?" His name was echoed a dozen times, and suddenly faces appeared at the bars of those cells. Three or four to a cell, his Lancers began a clamor that the guard unsuccessfully attempted to silence.

Styke searched the faces for a few moments. No one seemed hurt or otherwise mistreated. They seemed surprised to see him, with a mixture of giddiness and caution. "All right, quiet down," he said. Silence fell.

The guards glared at Ben. "They won't say a word for three days, and now he arrives and they won't shut up," one of them muttered in Dynize.

Styke looked up and down the row of cells again, then glanced to Etzi. "Can I get any privacy with them?"

"I'm afraid not," Etzi replied. He coughed into his hand. "I thought they had taken a vow of silence?"

"They're not great at it. Everyone all right?"

A round of nods. "The food here sucks, Ben," someone grumbled loudly.

"I prefer our road rations."

"They seem to be in good spirits," Etzi commented.

"They're hard to get down. All right, you idiots. Etzi here is Orz's brother. He's working on a lawsuit to get you released. He's our friend."

One of the guards stepped forward. "Speak in Dynize," he snapped.

Styke grinned at him. "You don't understand me?" he asked in Adran.

"I'm watching you," the guard warned.

"How about now?" Styke switched to Kez. He received a blank look, so he continued in that language. "Etzi is trying to get you out," he repeated, "but you're not to trust anyone here. Don't tell anyone anything. Got it?"

Another round of nods. "How's Celine and Pole?" someone asked.

"They're with me, safe. We're staying at Etzi's compound. Orz and I were ambushed by enemy agents. Etzi has taken us in. That's all you need to know for now. Hopefully you won't be here long." More nods, and Styke ran a hand over his face. No grumbling. No remonstration. He deserved both, for leading them into this shitty mess. He wished again that Ibana were here, just so someone would tell him he was an idiot.

"What language is that?" Etzi asked.

"Kez," Styke answered, searching the faces for Jackal. He found the Palo leaning against the wall toward the end of the hall, and headed down that way. The guards followed him, scowling, and he grinned over his shoulder at them.

Jackal nodded to him as he approached and said in a low voice, "The woman guard there speaks a few words of Kez, so don't let them fool you. One of the men speaks passable Adran. They're listening."

Styke leaned against the cell, one hand on the cold stone. "Sorry about the other night. We were ambushed."

"I gathered as much. They told us you were captured, but once Pole and Celine disappeared, I figured everything would work out."

"Have they questioned you?"

"Quite a lot. We've given up nothing."

"They didn't bother to collect your things from the inn," Styke said. "Etzi grabbed them. He knows who we are but is keeping silent." He spoke quickly, in Kez, hoping that the words would be too fast for a half-schooled Dynize guard to keep up. By the frown of concentration on her face, he was right.

"Are we safe?"

"Speak up!" one of the guards said angrily. "No whispering! Speak in Dynize!"

"For now," Styke answered, ignoring the guard. "But I still have no intelligence on Ibana."

Jackal gave a small nod. "Do you remember that marshal in New Adopest?"

Styke had to search his memory. Jackal had been picked up as a "public nuisance" by a marshal in New Adopest while on leave during one of the few short lulls during the Revolution. Styke hadn't even had to get involved—Jackal simply escaped the city prison and rejoined the Lancers before news of his arrest had even reached Styke.

"Similar situation?" Styke asked, resisting the urge to case the locks, bars, and walls.

"Yes."

"Good. If you need anything—*anything*—just look for Etzi's Household."

Another small nod. "Yes, sir."

Their conversation was finally broken up by the irritated guards, who made a stink about a time limit. They hurried Styke and Etzi out of the prison and back to the main administration building. Etzi argued with them the entire way—complaining about the time limit—but didn't physically resist. The guards grumbled about foreign languages and secret deals. Styke didn't object. He'd gotten what he came for.

They were soon alone in the courtyard, waiting for their carriage to return. "You should have spoken in Dynize if you wanted longer," Etzi told Styke.

"My men barely understand it," Styke replied, staring up into the sky in thought. He wondered how long it would be until Jackal attempted to escape. The last thing he needed was Jackal getting caught and killed—or worse, taken alive—but the risk was necessary. He needed to find out about Ibana.

Etzi shrugged. "I can ask for you to meet with them again soon, but you'd probably have to agree to speak a language the guards can understand."

"It's all right," Styke assured him. "I just wanted to make sure that they were being treated well."

"Are you satisfied?"

"I am. For now. I'm guessing they don't like us having visits like that."

"You guess correctly."

"Would it be easier if you had one of your Household check in on them every day?"

"Significantly."

"Do that, then." Styke remembered to add a "please" and "thank you" at the end, hoping it didn't sound insincere. It wasn't as if he was ungrateful—he just wasn't used to being all that polite.

"Of course." Etzi waved it off. He scowled as their carriage rolled into the courtyard. There was a boy riding on the running board, and the moment the boy saw Etzi, he leapt off and ran on ahead. "Master, master!"

"Yes?" Etzi asked, greeting the boy with a touch on the shoulder.

The boy looked both directions, wide-eyed, and then leaned forward to whisper loudly. "Master, Orz is awake!"

CHAPTER 38

Michel gave the old man a day to recover—a good meal, sleep in a real bed, a bath and shave, and gentle conversation. Still, he refused to give his name. Whether he did not want to be associated with a checkered past or simply feared the telling of his tale to come back and haunt him, Michel could not decipher. He dubbed the old man Survivor, and he took him and the three children to Jiniel and her lieutenants and listened carefully while he told his tale.

The reactions varied. Devin-Mezi looked on in horror. Another lieutenant was aghast with disbelief. Two more wept openly. Jiniel herself listened in stoic silence, her jaw tightening, veins bulging from her forehead as more details came out. Once Survivor had finished his story, she gestured for the children to give their own testimonies. Everyone was finally sent away, leaving Michel and Ichtracia with Jiniel and her four lieutenants.

No one spoke. Michel could read the shock on their faces. He gave them several minutes to process the information before he cleared his throat.

"You wanted evidence," he said.

Devin-Mezi swore.

"I did not imagine..." Jiniel trailed off.

"I didn't, either," Michel replied. "I suspected the details, but I didn't consider the real implications of this."

Jiniel looked around at her lieutenants, then focused her eyes on Michel. "What do we do?" There was a note of helplessness in her voice. "We are outnumbered. Outgunned. The Dynize hold everything. We have been doing what we can to safeguard the Palo from our position here, but we've been operating on the assumption that the Dynize are our friends. Now we know they aren't. They are using us, just as everyone else has used us."

"You're wrong about that," Michel said. He'd been thinking about this for weeks. Planning. Considering.

"About what?"

"That we're outnumbered and outgunned. The Dynize have recruited Palo into every facet of their lives. We clean their houses, run their new labor camps, build their citadel around the godstone. They're even training us to fight for them. They may have the armies, but this is our land. We outnumber them ten to one. We *exist* here. They made a tactical choice to include us in their new empire—a good choice, from their perspective. But they then thought they could steal away our lowliest citizens and use them in their blood magic. If they'd stopped at the first, you and I might be reaching out to help them take their fight to Lindet. But they didn't."

"So we have the people," Devin-Mezi replied bitterly. "But we *are* outgunned. We have what, a few thousand fighters?"

"Right now? Yes. But an angry population can mobilize to arms in a frighteningly short amount of time."

"You're suggesting we rise up?" Jiniel asked.

"I am."

"We'll be slaughtered."

"There will be casualties," Michel admitted. The idea stuck a knife in his gut, but he *had* to ignore it. "There might be a *lot* of casualties. But if we don't stop the Dynize now, we will forever be a people in bondage."

Jiniel examined him over steepled fingers. "Michel and Ichtracia, can you give us a moment?"

Michel nodded. He and Ichtracia retreated to the hall, where they stood in silence while a murmur of voices came to them through the door to Jiniel's office. Ichtracia still looked shell-shocked with anger. Of all the people here, Survivor's story seemed to have struck her the deepest. Michel thought about what she'd said weeks ago—of her claim that all that blood could have been avoided if she'd just offered her own. He wondered if she still felt the same way. He wondered if she had doubts. He knew he did.

"I might be goading my people into walking into a slaughter," he said quietly.

"You're hesitating?"

"Of course I'm hesitating. Like I said, I might be—"

"Don't." The word was whispered forcefully. "Just...don't. These people—*your* people—need to fight. You're giving them the best chance."

Michel did not reply. He sank into his own thoughts and plans, turning them over and over again in his mind while they waited. Finally, after what felt like hours, they were summoned back inside.

Mama Palo and her council looked shaken but determined. "You've clearly considered this," Jiniel said. "And we've agreed that you should be in command. How do we do this? How do we rouse the Palo? How do we fight back?"

Michel sat down. "Word travels fast in the Depths," he began. "We are going to fight the Dynize the same way that Lindet has kept us down and divided—the same way the Dynize have tried to keep us down. Putting all this in motion won't take long, but the results could come in a week, or in months. So we begin our propaganda campaign immediately."

"You have a plan for this?" Jiniel asked.

"I do. But also know this: Once we unleash this thing, there is no going back. There is no controlling it. Landfall will suffer. We will suffer."

Jiniel looked around at her lieutenants once more. "We are agreed."

"Good. It's time to start the fire that will burn everything down."

Styke stood outside the Etzi Household infirmary, trying not to listen to the rising voices within. On the other side of the doorway stood Maetle, her eyes on the ground, twiddling her thumbs.

A particularly loud shout issued from within, mostly consisting of a string of obscenities. Everyone else had already cleared out of this wing of the compound, leaving Styke and Maetle alone. He wished he had his whittling, or something to read, or anything to pass the time while the two brothers fought inside.

"Should I go?" he asked Maetle.

The nurse finally looked up, met his eyes momentarily, then resumed staring at the opposite wall. "He said to wait here." She shrugged. "So we wait here."

"Is this sort of thing normal?"

"The shouting? Oh, no." Maetle scowled, as if the question itself were impertinent. "You overhear arguments and lesser dramas living with the Household, but Etzi is a gentle man. His relationship with his family, though . . . " She trailed off.

Styke didn't push her further. "Understood."

It was at least fifteen minutes before the arguing died down to something more civil, the words less pronounced and more difficult to make out. Another ten minutes after that passed before the door opened and Etzi emerged, red-faced and hair mussed. "Stubborn bastard," he muttered, running a hand across his face. He seemed to realize he was not alone, looking first to Maetle and then to Styke.

"Did he hurt himself?" Maetle asked in a gentle tone.

Etzi had the wherewithal to look embarrassed. "He might have strained himself a little."

"I need to check on him."

"Wait." Etzi held up one hand. "First, he wants to talk to Ben. I'll be in my office if anyone needs me." Etzi strode off, muttering under his breath, gesturing angrily to himself.

Styke watched him go, then turned to Maetle. She shook her head. "Best see what he wants. Try not to get him too worked up. I know dragonmen are tough, but the more he exerts himself, the longer it will take him to recover."

"Right." Styke stepped inside and closed the door behind him. Orz lay on his back, his head craned forward. He was as pale as a ghost, with rivulets of sweat pouring down his brow and cheeks. His eyes opened when Styke reached his side, and they took a few moments to focus on Styke's face.

"You stupid piece of shit," Orz said weakly in Adran.

Styke rolled his eyes and sat down beside the bed, drawing his knife and using the tip to clean dirt from beneath his fingernails. He'd been accosted by more than one angry, injured soldier in his time. Nothing to do but weather it. "You're welcome."

"Don't 'you're welcome' me. I told you I didn't want to involve my brother."

"Yeah, well, I didn't have much choice after you walked into an ambush."

"You should have left me to die."

"Maybe." Styke shrugged. "But I didn't. I still have use for you."

There was a long moment of silence. Orz closed his eyes, his breath coming out in shallow, ragged gasps. Just when Styke thought that he might have passed out, his eyes flashed open once more. "He thinks I got our mother killed."

"You kind of did."

Orz's brow wrinkled. Another tense silence, and he let out a wheezing laugh. "You would have made a terrible doctor."

"There's a reason I do what I do."

"Yes. And despite what Etzi may think, my conscience is clean. I did not kill her. I was trying to save her." He made a fist, then let his fingers relax, then repeated the effort as if to judge his own strength. "I thought I knew Sedial's mind. I won't make that mistake again."

"Probably for the best," Styke commented.

"Etzi knows nothing of our designs here?"

"I haven't told him and he's made it clear that he doesn't want to know."

"Etzi is no fool."

"He told you about the suit?"

"Yes. It's our best chance at vengeance, but it may still get him and his entire Household killed. He's being careful not to attack Sedial openly, but the Ka will still see it as a slap in the face. When he returns—"

"If he returns."

Orz took a few long breaths. "You think your sister can best him? When we left, she had all but lost the continent."

"She was on the back foot," Styke admitted. "But she's not a fool, either, and she won't pull punches."

Orz eyeballed Styke. "No, I imagine she won't. You know, I was spying on a group of officers camped outside of Starlight when the rumor came around that you were her brother. One of them actually spit his drink on the other two." He let out a weak chuckle.

"There's a reason we kept it hidden for most of our lives."

"Family provides a weakness that can be exploited by your enemies," Orz said, touching his bandaged chest with two fingers.

"Among other things, yes." Styke used the tip of the knife to root a blackberry seed out from between his teeth. "This sorcery you've got keeping you together—is it strong enough to put you back in a saddle?"

"Not immediately. But not nearly as long as a normal person, either."

"How long?"

"A few weeks, I'd say. It'll hurt, but I'll be able to ride."

Styke didn't think they had that long. "We need to get out of here as soon as possible. Preferably before someone finds my army down south."

"Have you confirmed that they made landfall?"

"No. But I've dispatched a man to do so."

"And if they haven't?"

"Then I'll have to change my plans right quick." Styke twirled his big Lancer ring with one finger. "We'll get you out of the city, head down the coast, and try to find a port where we can bribe, threaten, or beg our way back to Fatrasta."

"An ignominious end to your venture."

"Quite."

"Will you give up on the godstone?"

"I never said that. But I will need to regroup."

"Good to have contingency plans."

"I'll need a lot of those. I'm not completely confident that Etzi can get me out of the city, or save my men from Sedial's goons, or even keep himself alive through the next few weeks. I'm going to keep my knife handy."

Orz did not respond, but he gave the smallest of nods as if he agreed with Styke's assessment. "You saved my life," he said suddenly.

"It sounded like you'd rather I hadn't."

"It doesn't matter what I want. The fact is you did save it, and for that I thank you."

"Help me get out of the city and we'll call it even."

"Done. But I have another request, one I am loath to put upon you."

Styke hesitated. Orz was no longer a stranger, but it was difficult to call him a friend. They shared an odd kinship, that was for sure, but he didn't know how much more involved he wanted to become in the dragonman's life. "What is it?"

"If I die," Orz said, "and if it is within your power to do so, I want you to kill the dragonman who murdered my mother."

Styke considered the request. He had enough experience now that he felt he *could* kill a dragonman. But he also knew he was taking his life in his hands every time he crossed paths with one of them. It was not something to take lightly. "I'll consider it."

"A smart man would say no without hesitation."

"Have I ever struck you as a smart man?"

"Smarter than you'll admit, Ben Styke." Orz let his eyes fall closed and let his head fall back. His sweating had intensified again, his hands trembling. "How is Ka-poel?"

"Keeping her head down."

"Etzi was not happy about you bringing a bone-eye into his Household."

"He hasn't said anything to me."

"Because he's considering."

"Considering what?"

Orz did not answer. Several moments went by, and Styke leaned forward. "Orz?"

Nothing. The dragonman's ragged breaths became slow and shallow, but steady. He was out. Styke stood up, tapping his ring against his thumb, and left the room quietly. "He's asleep," he told Maetle, who nodded in appreciation and headed inside.

Styke thrust his hands into his pockets and looked up to the cloudless sky, admiring the vibrant blue of it. He could hear Celine laughing somewhere nearby, and the happy shouts of her playmates. The sound boosted his mood, but he knew that this moment of comfort was an illusion. Everything he'd seen and done here had complicated his feelings about Dynize—complications he could not afford. Sedial's agents would soon strike back, and he still had a job to do on this continent.

There was a storm on the horizon. The only question was who would unleash it first: him, or his enemies?

CHAPTER 39

Vlora listened as an aide finished giving a long, comprehensive briefing of the Dynize-Fatrastan situation to a tent jam-packed with senior officers and newly arrived dignitaries, but primarily, to Delia Snowbound and Provost Marshal Valeer, both sitting in the front row. The briefing had begun the moment the army stopped to make camp over an hour and a half ago, and everyone had been listening in complete silence for the entire duration.

Bo and Nila had chosen the presenter strategically—a young, clean-cut officer with a penchant for public speaking. He'd been with Vlora for these last two years in Fatrasta, so he could talk with personal passion and experience, but he had no personal ties to the Adran coup of a decade ago and would not, in theory, offend Delia and Valeer by his mere presence.

Vlora had half listened. She'd written the majority of the briefing, after all. Her real concern was watching the faces of the special envoys, hoping against hope that she might be able to get through their thick skulls and impress upon them the importance of every-thing that was going on across the continent.

Their expressionless absorption of the information did not give her a lot of optimism.

The young aide finished the briefing with an overview of the Midnight Massacre. Vlora had decided not to sugar-coat it, hop-ing that if she gave Delia the ammunition to humiliate her before the government back in Adro, the special envoy might not ruin everything now. It was a minor gamble as these things went—Delia would find out about the Midnight Massacre eventually, if she hadn't already. But if there's one thing Bo had taught her about politics, it was to play to the plans and prejudices of her enemies.

The aide cleared his throat, thanked the audience, and took a seat. Vlora waited a few beats and then climbed to her feet, leverag-ing herself with her sword, and limped to the center of the room. She swept her gaze across the stern visages of her general staff. They knew most of this already, of course, but she had wanted them here to solidify their loyalty. Delia would try to get to them over the next few weeks. She needed them all on board with her concerns—and her plans in dealing with those concerns.

"Taniel Two-shot is alive," Delia said, breaking the silence.

It was not the first thing Vlora had expected to hear, and it threw her off guard. "That is correct," she answered, swearing quietly to herself. She *should* have expected it. He would no doubt immedi-ately rise to the top of Delia's shitlist, making Vlora grateful that he'd left after the Crease.

"It sounds very much as if he's gone native." Delia paused, as if expecting an answer. When Vlora did not respond, she went on. "I will need to gather more information, but in the meantime I want him brought in for questioning. Take a note, Provost Mar-shal. Taniel Two-shot should be considered an enemy of the state of Adro. Nothing he says or does should be trusted until we are able to debrief him."

Vlora's stomach turned. An arrest warrant for Taniel. She wasn't worried about him, of course. As far as she knew, he was on the other side of the continent by now. She exchanged a glance with Bo. "Lady Snowbound, I would recommend against taking an antagonistic stance with Taniel."

"Would you?" Delia asked lightly.

Vlora could sense a trap, but she went on anyway. "Taniel helped save the lives of my mercenary company, and he's a war hero back from the dead. If the men find out that he's wanted for questioning, it might not go well for morale."

"That's not my problem, Lady Flint," Delia said in a clipped, professional tone. "As long as you remain in command, I expect you to keep the discipline among your troops. My order stands." She removed a pair of reading glasses from her breast pocket and put them on, gazing down at a stack of notes that she'd been adding to throughout the briefing. "Now, may I continue?"

"Go ahead," Vlora said through clenched teeth.

"My first point of order is this: The moment at which you ceased being a common mercenary thug and began operating as an agent of the Adran government is the moment that you accepted command of this army. What was the date and time of that?"

Vlora glanced at Bo again, who just shrugged. "I'm not entirely certain. I'd have to check."

"Do so. Now, as I mentioned before, we shall regard Taniel Two-shot as a foreign national. Any interaction with him or his agents is highly suspect. Fortunately for you, it appears that he left this camp before you became cognizant enough to take command of the army." She swept her gaze across to Bo. "That is not the case, however, for Magus Borbador. Magus, you may have cowed many members of the governing council with threats and bribes, but you won't find me nearly as lax with your blatant disregard of Adran law. Raising an army at the behest of a foreign national?" She scoffed. "You've broken dozens of laws."

"I left my legal counsel in Adro," Bo said lightly. "I'm afraid you'll have to wait and take it up when you get back home."

"Dozens of laws, I say! You've consorted with an enemy agent, smuggled an entire field army out of Adro, and engaged the forces of a sovereign nation, all without proper authorization from your betters. As you yourself have reminded me in the past, this is no longer pre-coup Adro. Privileged cannot get away with doing whatever they want."

Bo adopted a dismissive air, removing his pipe from his pocket and slowly, meticulously cleaning it before packing in new tobacco and lighting it with the flick of gloved fingers. Despite his presentation, Vlora could see in his eyes that he was fuming. He *had* to have known that Delia would throw all of this in his face. Had he been so confident in his own position that he hadn't bothered preparing a rebuttal?

Delia continued, "We may be in a backwater, but I'm sure we can convene a perfectly legal tribunal to try the case. I have no interest in waiting to deal with your cabal lawyers back in Adro."

A cloud of smoke rose from Bo's puffing. He regarded her coldly. "Try it."

"Are you threatening me, Magus Borbador?" Most people would sweat bullets dealing with a Privileged, even these days. But Delia didn't blink.

"I wouldn't dream of it," Bo replied. "As Lady Flint tried to do a few minutes ago, I just want to remind you where you are."

"Surrounded by war hawks," Delia spat, looking around the room. "Don't think I don't know. And don't think that if I disappear on this expedition, every single one of your careers won't end the moment you return to Adro. There's not a single one of you who won't face charges for your complacency in this farce. How extensive those charges are will depend entirely on your cooperation."

There was a general, uncomfortable shift in the audience.

Several of the general staff clearly took the threat to heart—faces went pale, uneasy mutters were exchanged in the back row. Others hardened, as if this were some kind of challenge. Delia was known as a woman not to be trifled with, but those angry stares made Vlora wonder if she'd have to post an extra guard outside Delia's tent just to make sure none of her officers took this into their own hands.

"'Farce'?" Vlora's voice cracked as she repeated the word.

Valeer leaned over and whispered in Delia's ear. She inhaled sharply, her gaze returning to Vlora. "A poor choice of words," she said, sorting through her notes for a few moments as if to gather her thoughts. She finally continued. "Despite our mutual antagonism, we are all Adrans, and this is, for better or worse, an Adran expedition. Your briefing was most thorough, and I'm not an idiot—we are clearly dealing with something that warrants the attention of not just the Adran government but likely the governments of the entire world." She paused to whisper back to Valeer. They had a quick conversation, and she went on.

"In my authority as special envoy, I declare thusly: The organization and launch of this expedition is in question. However, I believe that question should be dealt with once we return to Adro. Furthermore..." She paused, sighed. "Furthermore, the expedition *is* here, regardless of legality. I agree that the situation warrants Lady Flint's invocation of the Tamas Clause."

A collective breath was released in the room, and Vlora's added to it. She felt a knot between her shoulders loosen just a tiny amount. But she didn't allow herself to grow too complacent. Delia clearly wasn't done. "And?" Vlora asked.

The special envoy fixed Vlora with a long, thoughtful gaze. "The Tamas Clause requires that the head of the army in question engage in constant, good-faith negotiations with whatever force he or she has engaged. Have you done that?"

"I met with the Dynize general outside of New Adopest," Vlora said, slightly confused. That part of the clause was wide open to interpretation. Not much Delia could do to pin her with treason.

"And before the Midnight Massacre?"

"Strategy necessitated that we not meet with the enemy directly before the battle."

"I see." Delia wrote something down. No doubt a note to make sure Vlora suffered for that mistake. But she still wasn't done here, and Vlora found herself on edge. "Good." Delia looked up. "Well, now that I'm here, I invoke my powers as special envoy to take over any and all negotiations on behalf of Adro with the Dynize and Fatrastan governments."

Vlora felt as if she'd been punched in the gut. There it was. Delia had just established herself as the Adran authority in the region. Vlora was still, essentially, field marshal of this army. But Delia's political authority—using Vlora's own declaration of the Tamas Clause—now put her in position to second-guess all of Vlora's decisions, all the while engaging in talks with the Dynize that could at any minute put a stop to all of Vlora's plans.

She felt herself suddenly so weak and tired. All of her work, all of her anguish, now put in the balance. This could have happened with any special envoy, of course, and she knew deep down that Delia was right—the Adran government couldn't afford to allow an entire field army to operate in a foreign war without any oversight. But the fact that it was Delia made it a thousand times worse. Vlora had every confidence that Delia would go to great lengths to undermine her at every turn.

"All right," Vlora said weakly. "Is there more?"

"Much more, but it can wait until I've better mapped the lay of the political landscape." Delia tapped her pencil against her chin. "The army needs to stop marching so that I can make contact with the Dynize and Fatrastans."

"That's not happening." Vlora was done. She couldn't even muster indignation. Just flat annoyance.

"Excuse me? Were you not paying attention to—"

Vlora cut her off. "You're in charge of the politics. I'm still in charge of the army and I'm waging a goddamn war."

"A war that I am charged with ending!"

"Independent of my actions," Vlora replied. "Begin your negotiations. Make contact with Sedial—I imagine that the two of you will get on very well with your mutual loathing of me. But I will not give up strategic advantage so that you can make overtures to a blood-hungry warlord. If you have any other questions, feel free to put them to General Sabastenien or Magus Borbador. I'm going to get some rest."

The last thing she heard when she left the tent was Delia's indignant huffing, but the sound didn't give Vlora any pleasure. She stood outside for a moment, trying to gather her thoughts, when she was joined by Bo. She held up a hand to forestall whatever it was he was about to say. "I'm too tired, Bo."

"I know, but I have something you want to see."

"Can it wait until the morning?"

Bo cleared his throat, glancing around to make sure no one would overhear him, and then said in a low voice, "If you'd like. I received a coded message from Taniel."

The words sent a spark through Vlora, giving her just enough energy to react. "Give it to me."

Bo produced a folded paper and slipped it to her. "Came by messenger a few hours ago. I spent the meeting translating it."

Vlora opened the paper. It was a long letter, containing a great deal of mundane gibberish that a distant spouse might write to keep their other half informed. At the bottom was one short paragraph, written in Bo's handwriting: the real message.

Third godstone is in Dynize. Styke has gone after it with Ka-poel. Problems with the crossing. Their position is fraught. Possible Dynize allies. On my way to join them as quickly as possible.

When you reach Landfall, make contact with Michel Bravis. Fully trusted spy. This will be my last update before setting sail.

—T

"In Dynize." She sighed. "Which means they probably already have it in their possession." The idea made her stomach twist.

"Seems likely."

Vlora read it again and looked at Bo. "His last update? Were there others?"

"No idea. It's possible he sent us a couple of messages that we never got. Or he's just warning us that we won't hear from him again."

The tension of sitting through that briefing after a hard day's march had left Vlora dizzy. She gave the letter back to Bo. "We can't expect any help from Taniel, except for the man he left in Landfall."

"Could be useful. Interesting that Styke is in Dynize now."

"Yeah, with several hundred of the cavalry I loaned him. That madman." She rubbed her face. There was nothing she could do for Styke or Taniel but go ahead with her own plans. And to do that...well, she needed sleep. She bid good night to Bo and headed to her tent, forced to lean on Davd's arm for the last few dozen paces to her own quarters. She went inside and collapsed onto her cot without removing her uniform.

A few hours of sleep, then she'd review the daily reports by candlelight. Not enough time to rest. Even more than before, speed was of the essence.

CHAPTER 40

Vlora sat on horseback in the center of an abandoned town just off the highway in east-central Fatrasta. The air was choked with the dust of her army marching past just over the next hill, and the oppressive afternoon sun made her want nothing more than to find a nearby tree and take a nap. But they'd ridden into the foothills and then back down onto the plains, which were chock-full with cotton and tobacco. Trees here were few and far between.

General Sabastenien sat beside her, examining the silent town with a frown. "We've come across a dozen towns like this in just the last twenty-four hours," he said. "Completely abandoned. Stripped of all resources, signs of violence, no one to tell us what has happened."

"Violence?" Vlora echoed. The town, she didn't mind admitting, spooked her. Doors hung off their hinges; wind whistled through open windows. Livestock pens were empty. There wasn't a soul in sight. She couldn't even spot any dogs or cats anywhere. Out of sight, a lone crow called.

"Mass graves," Sabastenien said solemnly.

"By Adom," Vlora swore.

"We haven't had the time to exhume any of them, but from what we've gathered, it seems that whole populations were marched to the edge of town and shot, then buried."

"Who would do this?"

"There are really only two options: the Dynize or the Fatrastans. Lindet may be a dictator, but I never pinned her as the type to slaughter her own people."

"Maybe her armies are stripping the countryside and killing the witnesses?" Vlora didn't believe it herself.

"Maybe?" Sabastenien allowed.

"Why would the Dynize do this?"

He shook his head. "Your bet is as good as mine."

"Why haven't I been told about this?"

"As I said, it's just been the last twenty-four hours. We had to come some distance from the Cape of New Adopest before we ran into these abandoned towns."

Vlora's scowl deepened. There was a mystery here, something she couldn't quite get her hands around. It had to relate to the current war, but she couldn't come up with a good excuse to slow down and investigate. She just had far more urgent matters on her hands. "Could it be something else? A local warlord using the war to establish their own power base?"

Sabastenien spread his hands. "I wish I knew."

"Right." Vlora sighed. "We can't afford to stop, but I want you to put together a fire team and a couple of surgeons. Next time we come across one of these towns, give them an hour to try and figure out what happened. Oh, and tell Nila and Bo. They'll want to check for any signs of sorcery."

"Yes, ma'am."

A chill went up Vlora's spine as she realized her mistake.

Sabastenien was not one of the few people privy to her condition. He simply nodded and turned his horse back toward the column. If he'd caught her slipup, he didn't mention it. She stilled her thumping heart and rode after him.

She found Bo about a half mile up the column. She let her horse nudge his way in between Bo and Nila's horses. The two exchanged a glance, both of them giggled, and then Bo broke into an open laugh as Vlora began to ride between them. "What's so funny?" she asked, casting a look at each of them.

"Nothing, nothing," Bo said.

"Nothing at all," Nila echoed.

"Privileged shouldn't giggle," Vlora growled. "It completely destroys your image."

Nila cleared her throat, regaining her composure before her husband. "She's right, you know."

Bo nodded gravely.

As much as these two could get on Vlora's nerves, she had to admit that it was good to hear genuine laughter. Her general staff tended to be an older, more serious lot, while her soldiers were always so formal around her. The fact that Bo and Nila seemed to actually find joy in just about every situation helped mend her heart.

She rolled her eyes. "Have you heard about these abandoned towns?" she asked.

Both of them shook their heads.

"Talk to Sabastenien. Something strange is going on and I want to make sure there isn't a sorcerous component."

Bo shrugged. "We can do that."

"Have you been keeping an eye on Delia?"

"Do you really have to ask?" Nila replied indignantly.

"What do you have?"

Bo snorted. "Nothing we didn't expect. She wasted no time in sending out emissaries. Riders went out from her High Provosts last night after the briefing. Looks like she's sent people to all three of the armies closing in on us, as well as down to Landfall *and* down around the Ironhooks to try and meet up with Lindet."

"She's moving quickly," Vlora commented.

"Very quickly," Nila confirmed. "Last night after you retired, she met personally with every one of your general staff."

Vlora resisted the urge to growl like a dog. Delia was going to do everything in her power to turn the generals against her. "And?"

"The meetings were private, so we didn't have any spies to listen in," Bo said, "but I've talked to a few of them, and she's just doing the same thing with each: veiled threats, half promises, and demands for intelligence. Half of your general staff is terrified of her and the other half wants to add her to the unmarked grave where Tamas buried all of her noble cousins ten years ago."

"'Terrified,'" Vlora spat. She tried to rein in her disgust. If she wanted to, she could retire tomorrow and travel the world comfortably for the rest of her life without many regrets. Unlike her, most of the generals had a lot to lose—*they* had families, hard-won careers, reputations, and more that Delia could threaten. They weren't stupid, and only the most stubborn of them would openly defy her. "Any impressions?"

"Too early to tell," Bo said. "I will note that Delia is no fool, and she's never indicated that she would sell out the country just to spite her enemies."

Vlora hesitated. She and Delia had butted heads on several occasions throughout the Kez Civil War. While she had to admit that Delia had never sold her out directly, she'd made several decisions for the sole purpose of spiting Vlora—and this was part of what made her so unpredictable. When would she do what was best for Adro, and when would she do what was worst for Tamas's old allies and kin?

She let her meditations turn toward Sedial. The Dynize warlord was himself an enigma. He'd shown both ruthless cunning and petty vindictiveness. Would he hold his grudge toward Vlora and keep up the fight? Or would he lose his nerve at the sight of an Adran field army and grab on to whatever terms Delia offered to end the conflict? Dynize itself was also a mystery. Their armies had proved to be both numerous and strong, and it was impossible to tell just how many more they had ready to send over from their mainland.

She scowled at the sky, wishing it was late enough that she could call a halt. Many more miles to go today, though. "Is Prime Lektor with us?"

"He is," Nila said. "Hiding with the baggage train, I understand." She sniffed in irritation.

Vlora cocked an eyebrow at her. "You met him?"

"Nila is under the impression that Prime is a bit of a worm," Bo explained.

"Oh?" Vlora asked. "You know what he is, right?"

"I know exactly what he is," Nila grumbled. "A man with that much power has responsibilities. Instead, he's a coward. He prefers to put his head under a rock and study his books rather than take an active role in the world."

"I think the term you're looking for is 'pacifist,'" Bo suggested.

"I know what a pacifist is," Nila objected, "and I've met pacifists who wouldn't raise a fist to hurt a fly but would still work for the betterment of mankind."

"Prime," Bo said as if in an aside to Vlora, "is terrified of Nila."

"I can't imagine why." Vlora rolled her eyes. "Keep him close. This pedestal we're going to retrieve from the Palo Nation irregulars is part of the godstone he studied in Yellow Creek. We'll need his expertise."

Nila snorted but offered no other comment.

"Lady Flint!" A voice cut off Vlora's next thoughts, and she turned to find General Sabastenien riding toward her. She waited until he was close before raising a hand in greeting. He returned the gesture. "Ma'am, I have news about these abandoned towns."

"So soon?"

"One of our scouts just brought in a survivor. Would you like to meet him?"

Vlora cast a glance back over at Bo and Nila, then gave a nod. "Lead on."

They left the two Privileged behind and headed to the baggage train, where Sabastenien directed her toward the back of one of the wagons. It had been pulled off the road, a bit of canvas thrown over the back to shade it. The driver was off to one side, watering the mule, while an officer and a surgeon tended to a figure sitting on the open tailgate. It took Vlora a moment to realize that the figure was a young man—rather than a child—hunched over and clutching at a blanket tossed over his bare shoulders.

Vlora dismounted and approached to a respectful distance. The officer watched thoughtfully while the surgeon asked questions in a gentle tone.

"How long has it been?"

The young man shivered violently. "Three weeks, I think. What's today?"

He was given the date.

"No—four weeks. I remember because it was Nan's birthday."

"And you've been hiding in the hills all this time?"

The young man looked up, squinting at Vlora before turning his gaze back to the ground between his knees. "It was about a week before I got up the courage to come down to the town... but they'd stripped us of everything. Cattle, flour, fruit and veg. They even found the bottle of spirits that Dad kept under the floorboards for a rainy day."

"Who?" Vlora cut in.

The officer gave Vlora a nod and then asked softly, "Donovel, this is General Flint, the leader of our expedition. Do you think you could tell her what you told me a few minutes ago?"

Donovel looked up again, this time with a sharp sort of recognition. "Flint? Flint?" he echoed. "You crushed the Dynize at Landfall?"

"Aye," Vlora answered gravely.

He suddenly lurched forward, leaving the wagon tailgate and nearly falling face-first in the dirt as he caught Vlora by the hand. "It was the Dynize," he said desperately. "They swept through like locusts. Took everything we had, bundled up all the Palo, then dragged all of us Kressians to the edge of town and shot us. My dad, my Nan. Everyone I know and love."

Vlora's jaw clenched. "Do you know why?"

"I wasn't there," Donovel said. Tears began to form. "I was out tending the goats. Heard the first shots, so I went and hid. They got my goats a couple hours later, but they didn't get me. I managed to hide near the old windmill—good view of the town. I saw what they did to everyone, and I saw them leave again." The words came out in a jumbled panic, barely understandable.

Vlora resisted the urge to shake off his grip, instead giving his hand a little squeeze. So it was the Dynize. But why? What purpose could they possibly have to gain in killing Kressians and kidnapping Palo? Hard labor? If so, why didn't they take the Kressians, too? A sudden thought struck her. "This was a month ago?"

A nod.

"Describe the banners this army had."

Donovel sketched out the normal black with red stars, but also a number of secondary banners of varying shapes, designs, and colors. Vlora gave a sidelong look at the officer and surgeon. "Any of that sound familiar?"

The officer spoke up. "It wasn't that field army that slipped us outside New Adopest."

"General Etepali."

"Not them, no."

The surgeon nodded to herself. "No, ma'am. It was the army that you and Taniel Two-shot..." She trailed off.

Vlora held back a snarl, turning back to Donovel. "Your kin have been avenged."

His eyes grew wide. "You're certain?"

Vlora unbuttoned the front of her jacket and pulled it aside to show him a puckered scar that ran from her collarbone down and across her left arm. Even after all this time it was a nasty-looking wound. "I got this from their dragoons. I'm alive. They're not."

Donovel threw himself against her, nearly knocking them both to the ground. He wept openly now, his whole body shaking and trembling. Vlora stiffened, then let her arm fall around his shoulders while he cried against her chest. She allowed him to remain there for several minutes while the surgeon and officer looked away respectfully. Even Sabastenien, still mounted and some distance off, bowed his head.

Vlora finally gestured to the surgeon, and with her help managed to get Donovel back into the wagon. She stepped away, bringing the officer with her. "Anything else to report?" she asked, jerking her head at Donovel.

The officer frowned, glancing at Sabastenien. "Well, ma'am, I was just put in charge of this thing minutes ago—right before this poor fellow stumbled into our baggage train."

"Right, of course. I'll leave you to it."

"Thank you, ma'am. I'll try to find out what I can."

"The why of it is our most pressing matter," Vlora told him, then headed back to her horse. She allowed Sabastenien to dismount and help her into her own saddle. Once they were both riding, the brigadier general cleared his throat. She looked at him sidelong. "Something wrong?"

"No, ma'am. It's just..." He scowled. "You know that Major Gustar is a friend of mine, right?"

"I didn't," Vlora answered.

"I took the liberty of checking all the communiqués received from him after you sent the cavalry off with Colonel Styke."

"And?"

"And I just went and looked—and he definitely mentioned finding a couple of towns just like this while they crossed the center of Fatrasta. I didn't think anything of it before, but now..."

"This seems very out of character for the Dynize. All the major cities they've captured are still fully intact, correct?"

"As far as our spies have been able to get back to us."

"Then why the towns?" She shook her head. "Very strange. That poor bastard back there—make sure he gets good care. And keep an eye out for more like him. If the Dynize missed one, they may have missed more. Wait!" She pulled back on her reins.

"Ma'am?"

"Did you come across any Palo when you relieved me and Two-shot at the Crease?"

"No, ma'am. Not a one."

She turned and rode back to Donovel. "You there, quickly," she called. "Do you have any idea what happened to the Palo that were carted off? Did they go with the army?"

Donovel blinked back at Vlora through teary eyes. He seemed not to understand the question, and then a light went on. "No, ma'am. They didn't. They were sent west, back the way the Dynize had come. Just marched off with a handful of guards."

"In chains?"

"No. Just walking. Seemed to me they were allowed to take their valuables with them, too."

Vlora scowled. "Right. Thank you." She turned back to Sabastenien as he caught up with her. "Next time we take prisoners, I want you to personally see to it that we get some answers."

"Of course, ma'am."

Vlora left him with a nod, riding back to the column and falling in with Norrine. The powder mage greeted her with a raised hand, but said nothing. Vlora was grateful for the quiet. These empty towns set her on edge, and she needed the time alone to meditate on their meaning.

CHAPTER 41

Michel watched from the darkened corner of a pub in Greenfire Depths as Survivor and his young wards told their stories of Dynize horror to a packed room. This was only their fourth appearance in public and yet word had spread like wildfire. Palo packed the entrance of the little pub, spilling out into the street, straining to hear every word. Drinks flowed, fury stewed, and gossip bubbled. Michel could *hear* the growing indignation in the whispers around him, *see* it in the body language.

Michel was jostled aside as Jiniel joined him and Ichtracia in the corner. She bent an ear toward the story being told for a few moments, then turned to him and Ichtracia. She looked serious, but pleased.

"We're getting requests from every corner of the Depths," she said in a low voice. "Everyone wants Survivor to come tell his story."

"Congratulations," Michel replied, "you're now the booking agent for the greatest act in the city."

"It's not an act," Ichtracia said. She was listening intently, though she'd heard the story half a dozen times already. She wore the same look of horror as she had the first time and seemed no less affected. If anything, her emotional response seemed to grow with each telling. Michel remembered once that she'd called herself a monster in service of the state. He could no longer believe that. She seemed to care just as much as he did.

"Maybe it should have been," Jiniel said cynically. "We could have gotten this up and running earlier if we'd just hired a couple of actors."

Michel could see Ichtracia begin to react to the cynicism. He cut in quickly. "No. First off, we didn't know the details. Second... well, no actor is this good. No actor can be this convincing." Survivor was, he had to admit, a natural storyteller. Not in a dramatic way, but with the gravitas of a grandfather who's lived through a dozen wars. He spoke in a clear, measured tone, tired emotion leaking through into his words with each retelling. He never smiled or tried to play to his audience. There was a raw honesty to his words that no actor could possibly capture.

Jiniel nodded in agreement, and Ichtracia settled back into her seat.

"Other than pub owners looking for something to bring in an audience, do we have any rumblings?" Michel asked.

"'Rumblings' is a good word," Jiniel answered. "It's all over the Depths. Just on the way over here, I saw a couple of teenagers pulling down those Dynize propaganda posters. I've got word from friends on the Rim that gossip has already reached Upper Landfall and the Palo who moved up there after the evacuation."

Michel trusted Jiniel not to overembellish, but he tried to remain cautious. Survivor had only started his public stories early this morning. It was now almost midnight. Eighteen hours, give or take, was not much time for word to spread. But if it was already reaching Upper Landfall, this was, as a friend of his in theater used to say, a performance that "had legs."

It needed to be more than a performance. It needed to be the galvanizing cry for an entire people.

"What other intelligence do we have?" Michel asked. "I've been following Survivor around all day. Tomorrow I'm passing him off to Devin-Mezi, but for now I need to catch up."

Jiniel reached into her pocket and drew out a sealed envelope, sliding it across the table to him. "A message from your mysterious friend," she said.

Emerald. Michel had seen no reason to reveal his identity, even to Mama Palo. He took the envelope and opened it, reading it quickly. He tapped Ichtracia on the wrist.

"Hmm?"

"Confirmation," Michel said unhappily. "Our friend has heard rumors out of the citadel to the south. They've unlocked the godstone and are actively studying it. No word on whether they already know how it works and are just being cautious, or if they're waiting for something."

"Probably both," Ichtracia replied. "Sedial has collected every known scrap of information on the damned thing. If anyone knows how it works, it's him. He spent years studying the Talunlica godstone."

"Talunlica?" Jiniel asked.

"The Dynize capital," Michel explained. "It's where they have the second godstone."

Jiniel scowled at them both. "Did they kill orphans for that one, too?"

"I . . . I don't think so." Even Ichtracia seemed uncertain. "They found it in the swamp and constructed a city around it. But there was no protective sorcery to break. They didn't need blood to make it work."

"I'm not sure if that's better or worse," Michel said.

"Neither am I." Ichtracia's uncertainty deepened. She seemed about to say something, but to think better of it. She glanced purposefully at Jiniel, and Michel made a note to ask her what she'd wanted to say the next time they were in private.

Michel waved the envelope from Emerald. "This just confirms something we already suspected. But it does mean that we need to move faster. We need leverage on Ka-Sedial."

"What, to blackmail him?" Jiniel asked.

"Even if we had anything, blackmail doesn't work on Sedial," Ichtracia said flatly. "I've seen it tried. He kills everyone suspected of involvement, and sorts out the corpses later."

"That's not what I meant." Michel tapped the envelope on the table thoughtfully. "I just mean anything we can use against him or the Dynize. You have your agents sweeping up any information they can get their hands on?"

Jiniel nodded. "I've impressed upon all of them how important it is."

"And how important it is not to get caught?"

"That, too."

"Good. It's a fine balance to walk. The last thing we need is someone getting caught, dragged in, and tortured, and revealing our entire organization."

"Come now," Jiniel said, smirking. "You taught me better than that. None of them know who they're working for. There's at least three layers between me and them."

"Good."

"Ah," Jiniel said, raising her chin toward the door. Michel soon saw Devin-Mezi struggling through the press. The lieutenant finally reached their table and leaned over them.

"I've got something to show you," she said, indicating all three of them.

"Here?"

"No. The barkeep has a little room in the back. I had it emptied."

Michel and his companions pushed their way through the common room and into the back, where the barkeep did indeed have a

private room. It was barely big enough for the four of them, dominated by a small dice table. Once they were all seated, Devin-Mezi
produced a thick binder and tossed it down on the table.

"What's this?" Michel asked.

"Intelligence," Devin-Mezi said. "One of our people got hired as
a maid for a townhouse near the capital building last week. Turns
out the owner is a dragonman—too dangerous for us to keep her
there for any length of time. This morning, we had her snatch up
every important-looking document she could get her hands on and
then made her disappear."

Michel raised both eyebrows at the binder. "Why didn't I know
about this?"

"You've been busy," Devin-Mezi said, jerking her head toward
the commotion going on in the common room.

"I authorized this," Jiniel cut in. "Like she said, it was safer to
do a smash-and-grab than to try and keep someone that close to a
dragonman."

Michel glanced at Ichtracia, who shrugged. "They're probably
right. Dragonmen can be arrogant, but they pay more attention to
their immediate surroundings. Far more likely to notice someone
acting suspicious."

"Fair enough." Michel undid the cord on the binder and let the
contents spill out onto the table. He was immediately taken aback.
This didn't look like the contents of a warrior's desk—this looked
more like it had been pilfered from a general or politician. There
were sealed envelopes, work orders, army missives, quartermaster
reports. And that was just at a casual glance. "Wow," he managed.
"This is quite the coup."

Devin-Mezi gave them all a self-satisfied grin. "I thought so."

"You're sure this came from a dragonman?" Ichtracia asked,
leaning over the pile while Michel sorted through it.

"I am."

"Do you know his name?"

"Ji-Noren."

The name tickled the back of Michel's memory, but Ichtracia's reaction was far more telling. Her eyes grew wide and she drew in a sharp breath. "You're kidding."

"I think that was his name?" Devin-Mezi said.

"No, no. I believe you." Ichtracia swore under her breath. "You just robbed Ka-Sedial's right-hand man."

There was a moment of silence as that sank into the group. "Oh," Devin-Mezi replied.

"You don't rob Ji-Noren," Ichtracia continued. "He's one of the most dangerous men in the empire, easily in the top five besides Ka-Sedial himself." She looked at Devin-Mezi. "Whatever you think you've done to hide the woman who did this, do better. Get her out of the city. *Far* out of the city. No doubt he's already discovered that these are missing and begun a search." She ran a hand through her hair. "Pit, you've kicked a hornet's nest."

Michel watched everyone for their reactions. Devin-Mezi immediately took on a defensive expression, while Jiniel scowled at the pile of papers. He stepped in before anyone could say anything else. "Okay, so we've robbed the wrong person. Devin-Mezi, I want you to clean this up. Do as Ichtracia just said and get anyone else who might have been seen around his townhouse out of the city." He reached beneath the table and squeezed Ichtracia's leg. She seemed to relax slightly. "We're going to see what we can gain by this. We might have done something stupid by accident, but that doesn't mean we can't benefit."

Devin-Mezi waited for Jiniel to give a nod before leaving the room.

"He's that terrifying?" Michel asked Ichtracia.

"I'm a Privileged, and I'm scared of him. That man you told me about, the enforcer for Chancellor Lindet?"

"Fidelis Jes?"

"Yes, him. Ji-Noren is like Sedial's version of him. Not as blood-thirsty or egotistical, but equally effective."

"Okay. Well, we'll deal with this. In this meantime..." Michel resumed going through the stack of intelligence. No use in worrying about mistakes already made.

Ichtracia suddenly perked up, leaning forward again and searching through the stack with one hand. She fished a little bundle out from the middle: a number of envelopes, all bound together with a black ribbon. They were stamped with the three-star seal of the Dynize emperor. "I know these," she said.

Something about the way she said it struck Michel. "Those in particular?"

"Yes." She got a distant look on her face. "In Sedial's study. I saw them by accident."

"Well, let's see what the old man has to say," Jiniel said, reaching for the bundle.

Ichtracia snatched it away. "No. These are warded. Very subtle. I almost couldn't sense it, but now that I've touched them, they could have any sort of nastiness stitched into them. Open one, and it could burn the envelope, or cripple you, or even alert the owner that they've been touched."

"Shit," Michel said. "Can you do anything about that?"

Ichtracia stared at the envelopes for a few moments. "The wards are very tightly wound. But given a day or two, I should be able to pick them apart."

"Any idea what's in them?"

She shook her head.

"All right." Michel returned his gaze to the rest of the intelligence. "Let's sort this out. Ichtracia will unwind what she has there." He pointed to Jiniel. "You and I will figure out what we can use. The rest leaves the city."

"To go where?"

Michel sucked on his teeth. "We can send it to either Lindet or Lady Flint."

"Lady Flint? The woman who killed the *last* Mama Palo?" Jiniel asked in disbelief.

"Or Lindet."

"Those are terrible options."

"Maybe. But Lady Flint is a friend of Taniel and Ka-poel's, and she's actively fighting to get the godstones away from Sedial. And Lindet...well, Lindet has fought the Dynize to a standstill out west. She's probably going to lose, but anything we can do to distract Sedial is a good thing right now."

"Why don't we make a copy and send one to each of them?" Jiniel asked.

"Fantastic idea."

"I was being sarcastic."

"I wasn't. Get it done." Michel glanced at the envelopes in Ichtracia's hands. Something about them seemed off—so different from all the other missives and reports in the stack. Despite the official seal, they looked more like love letters than orders—thicker envelopes made out of heavy, expensive paper. He tilted his head, turning his ear toward the common room where one of Survivor's young wards was talking about the horror of the Dynize citadel.

"Whatever you have on your schedule for Survivor, double it," he told Jiniel. "And get our printers going on the propaganda we've sketched out. I want everyone in Greenfire Depths to see a poster or handbill describing the evils of the Dynize by the end of the week. We have no idea when Sedial will use the godstone. We have to work as quickly as possible."

CHAPTER 42

Styke was awakened by a commotion in the Etzi Household compound. He was soon sitting on the edge of the bed, his boz knife lying across his lap as he tried to get his head around the sounds of a hushed, but angry confrontation. He couldn't make out any words, but there were multiple voices involved.

He, Ka-poel, and Celine had been given a small room not far from the kitchens. It wasn't a large space, and it suffered from being close to both the noise of the kitchens and the front gate, but it was private. He looked to the other bed, which lay perpendicular to his own against another wall, and listened for Celine's quiet snores. She and Ka-poel were cuddled up together, but when he sought Ka-poel's face, he saw the twin dots of the early-morning light reflecting off her eyes. She'd heard the ruckus, too.

He guessed by that light that it was around five or five thirty. He rubbed his eyes, then found his ring and slipped it on, followed by his pants and jacket. The voices outside continued. It might have nothing to do with him, but...

The thought ended with a gentle knock on the door. He got up to answer it, only to find Maetle waiting outside. She shifted from one foot to another. "You're dressed?"

"Heard a commotion."

"You'd better come," she told him.

Styke stuck his knife in his belt and followed her out into the compound. It was just two short turns before they reached the front gate. Two groups had already gathered—one consisted of Etzi, the night watchman, and four of his Household guards. The sight of the other group almost made Styke miss a step, and he swore quietly. It was Ji-Patten, along with six of the city guard.

"You!" Ji-Patten snapped, taking two steps toward Styke.

Styke entered the courtyard, but only just, leaning against the kitchen wall and cocking his head at Ji-Patten. He didn't have to pretend a yawn. It came naturally, and he made no gesture to stifle it. "How's your leg?"

The dragonman's nostrils flared, but he didn't rise to the bait. "What did you say to your men the other day?" he demanded.

Styke raised both eyebrows. "I asked them how they'd been treated."

"What else?"

"That's it."

"Liar."

Styke sniffed and turned to Etzi. "What is this?"

Etzi frowned at the dragonman, then turned that frown on Styke. "They're making serious accusations, Ben. I suggest you handle them respectfully."

"From him?" Styke jerked his chin at Ji-Patten.

"From him," Etzi confirmed, clearly reluctant to do so. "He is an agent of the emperor."

Styke yawned again and stood up straight, dropping a half bow toward Ji-Patten. "O mighty dragonman, what are you so angry about this morning?"

"Ben!" Etzi hissed.

"I will not allow you to goad me, foreigner," Ji-Patten growled. "If the laws didn't prevent it, I would teach you respect."

"You think you can do that with six men?" Styke asked, jerking his head toward the guardsmen behind Ji-Patten. He was beginning to get annoyed himself. "You want a bigger limp? Is that what you want?" He caught himself, remembering Celine's words—remembering that he was a guest here. Gritting his teeth, he snapped his head back and forced down his own rising ire. Etzi's scowl deepened, and Styke held up one hand to forestall whatever he was about to say.

"I apologize," Styke growled. "Not enough sleep, you see? What can I do for the Servant of the Emperor?"

Etzi took a deep breath, nodding at Styke's apology and then turning expectantly to the dragonman. Ji-Patten's eyes remained narrowed, but he bit back his tone when he next spoke. "One of your men has escaped."

"Oh?" Styke asked, trying to sound surprised.

"The Palo. During the changing of the guard at midnight. No one noticed until just an hour ago."

"Have you bothered to look for him?"

"Of course. We're scouring the city and widening our net. He *will* be found. What I want to know is what you said to him the other day."

"I already told you," Styke insisted. "I inquired whether they were being treated well. Nothing more. I didn't have time to before your guards hustled me out."

"If you had nothing to do with this, then you must help us find him," Ji-Patten said. "He must be returned to his cell until this… suit of yours has been resolved." His eyes darted briefly to Etzi.

"What do you expect me to do?" Styke demanded. "Ride through the city calling his name? Neither of us knows anything about this place. I don't know why he escaped—certainly not on my orders—but he should be easy enough to find." Styke narrowed his eyes. "How do I know that you haven't snatched him yourself?"

Ji-Patten looked taken aback.

Styke pushed on. "You've already shown that you have no problem murdering an old woman in a nighttime ambush. What's to say you didn't snatch one of my men to take him off for questioning?" Styke feared that perhaps he was right. What if Sedial's men had snatched Jackal before he was able to escape, and had taken him away to be questioned by bone-eyes? He'd have to check with Ka-poel to see if she was protecting Jackal.

"That's preposterous," Ji-Patten objected. It was clear he wasn't used to being confronted in such a manner. As a dragonman, he probably expected everyone to bow and scrape—even the Household heads.

"It better be," Styke said. "I protect my men. You find him—for his own safety—or you'll have me to answer to." Despite his fears, he grinned inwardly. Too bad Celine couldn't see him now. Terrible actor—bah.

Ji-Patten looked from Styke to Etzi and then back at Styke. "Damn you both. There will be consequences for this." He pointed a finger at Styke. "The first is this: As an agent of the emperor, I bar you from seeing the foreign prisoners until this suit is over." He whirled suddenly and strode out through the open gate, heading toward the horses waiting at the other end of the long causeway. Styke noticed that his limp was less pronounced, as if it was healing quickly, and he thought of the sorcery that had kept Orz from dying due to a punctured lung. If they did end up fighting, that wound would not give Styke as much of an advantage as he wanted.

The compound gate was soon closed, and Etzi ran a hand across his face. He was clearly exhausted, his cheeks flushed, bags beneath his eyes, and hair mussed. He took several long breaths before turning to Styke. "What...," he began, then held up a hand. "Never mind. I don't want to know." He stepped forward and said in a voice low enough not to be overheard by his guardsmen. "One of your horses went missing. Two hours ago. The boy watching the stables said that it just disappeared. Do you know anything about that?"

"No," Styke answered. How Jackal had managed to slip into the stables and out again on a warhorse without waking anyone up was beyond him.

"Good." Etzi let out a shaky breath. "I hope whatever you're doing is worth not speaking to your men again. This will make my task more difficult."

"I'm not doing anything," Styke said. The words came out dull and heavy. Not very convincing.

"Of course not," Etzi said, waving the subject off. "I'm going back to bed. I suggest you do the same."

Styke followed Etzi's suggestion, returning to the guest room, where he found both Ka-poel and Celine sitting up in bed. He removed his shirt and sat down on his own, yawning. "Do you have anything on that Ji-Patten?" he asked Ka-poel.

She shook her head and gestured. *Dragonmen are more cautious about not leaving behind detritus for bone-eyes.* Styke didn't need Celine to translate.

"Makes sense. Well, if you get the opportunity don't hesitate. That bastard is starting to annoy me."

Ka-poel pressed her lips into a hard line. *I am spread thin.*

"So you can't help?"

I'll do what I can. But a dragonman is harder because of the sorcery that gives him his strength.

"How about my Lancers?" Styke asked. "If they are questioned by a bone-eye, can you keep them from being compelled to answer?"

That tight-lipped expression turned up into a wicked little smile. *They've already tried.*

"And you didn't tell me?" Styke took in a sharp breath and swore.

They were ... unsuccessful. And quite baffled as to why.

Styke frowned. "Good. Wait. Could this tip your hand to Ka-Sedial? He doesn't know you're here, but if he finds out..."

I understand. I'm being very cautious.

"I hope so." Styke looked at Celine. "You should go back to sleep, little one."

"I will," she yawned. "Are you going to fight Ji-Patten?"

"Maybe."

"Don't let him kill you."

"I don't intend to."

Celine got up and joined Styke, sitting on the edge of his bed and putting her head in the crook of his arm. Her expression was very serious. "I mean it. You're not allowed to let him kill you."

"How do you like the kids here?" Styke asked, changing the subject.

"They're fun," Celine said dismissively. "A lot nicer than the kids in Landfall. Jerio is my favorite, though." Her tone became suddenly excited at the mention of his name. "He's very clever. And very funny, too. He doesn't let the bigger kids bully him. They're almost as afraid of him as they are of me."

"Why is that?"

"Because he doesn't back down." She scowled. "That's not allowed here."

"Here?"

Ka-poel's hands flashed from across the room. Styke nodded to her to repeat herself. *She means in this society.*

"Ah. People here aren't allowed to stand up for themselves?" he asked Celine.

She waggled her head from one side to the other. "Kind of? It's not that they can't, it's just that they're expected to do what they're told by people stronger or more powerful than them. I heard one of the adults call Jerio a troublemaker because he thinks for himself."

"He was polite to me."

"Like I said, he's clever."

"Clever to be polite to the biggest man in the compound?" Styke asked, amused.

Celine nodded matter-of-factly.

"So this Jerio doesn't bow and scrape to the kids bigger than him—only to the people he considers to be worth the subservience?"

"What does 'subse . . .' 'subse . . .'"

"'Subservience'?" Styke explained the meaning of the word.

"Exactly," Celine said. "He won't subserve to people who can't actually hurt him."

Styke tapped his ring, thinking about the confrontation with Ji-Patten and the impression that he didn't know how to deal with a soldier who stood up to him. There were levels to the politics here that he could only sense on the edges of his awareness. Etzi was more confident with those levels, and Celine seemed to have already sussed them out. He wondered, if all of them survived this war, whether he should let Celine spend time with Lindet. They would either love or loathe each other. Celine certainly was already showing she had a mind closer to Lindet's than his own.

He took a deep breath, thinking of Orz's words the other day— the promise he'd requested of Styke to fight and kill Ji-Patten. "If something happens to me, I want you to keep your head down. Survive."

Celine squeezed his hand and said in a sleepy voice, "Don't worry, I will. But nothing is going to happen to you, Ben. You're too strong."

Styke looked across at Ka-poel. She wore a small smile, gazing at Celine. The moment she noticed Styke's glance, the smile disappeared and she lay down, rolling over to put her back to him. He wondered, not for the first time, what she was up to every day. Biding her time. Making plans. Preparing for that storm he sensed on the horizon.

Probably making better use of her time than carving a wooden army for the Household kids. Styke leaned back in bed, letting

Celine settle against his shoulder. She soon dozed off, filling the room with her soft snores.

Styke was awakened again by a knock on the door. He gently slid Celine off his shoulder and padded over to answer it, only to find Etzi standing outside. One of his guards was shadowing him, something that Styke hadn't seen before.

Etzi wore a worried frown. He looked up at Styke, hesitating a moment, then said, "There is nothing you can do, but I wanted to let you know that Sedial's counterattack has begun."

"In what form?" Styke asked.

"Mobs," Etzi said. "They began this morning. They're roaming the city, posing as discontented laborers angry about the foreigners in the city. Several slaves were caught and lynched."

"You're sure this has to do with us?"

"I have no proof," Etzi said, "but I am certain. Only seven Dynize were murdered by the mobs. All of them belonged to my Household."

"Shit," Styke breathed.

"Yes. Yes indeed. It has begun, Ben Styke. I would like to say that you are safe within the compound, but...sleep with your knife at your side."

CHAPTER 43

Michel finished his morning's work and retired to a small, dark pub not far from Mama Palo's headquarters, where he ordered a drink and kicked his feet up onto the chair opposite. He'd worked nonstop for almost thirty hours, but for the first time in weeks he felt like he was getting somewhere; Survivor and his young wards were now the talk of the Palo slums, telling their stories of horror to anyone who would listen.

And, it seemed, everyone *wanted* to listen. Grumbling spread as fast as word of mouth. Thousands of Palo had already begun to abandon the military training camps outside the city. Hundreds of laborers had quit their jobs in protest. Community leaders were demanding answers about this citadel-under-construction and the godstone within it.

Michel and Mama Palo's people worked tirelessly behind the scenes to stoke the fire. They produced propaganda, took meetings with community leaders, and whispered in all the right ears.

The Dynize, for their part, barely seemed to have noticed anything was wrong. The stories had been circulating for less than two days. Michel wondered how long the Dynize would remain in ignorance—and then how long after that until they responded. The response, he knew, could come in many different forms: violence, denials, cover-ups, or combinations thereof. He and Jiniel were working on contingency plans for whatever the Dynize decided to do. He hoped it was enough.

He had to believe it would be enough.

"Have you seen this?"

He jumped as a newspaper was thrown down on the table in front of him and realized that he'd been half asleep in his chair. Ichtracia sat down across from him, taking the beer that he hadn't even noticed had been delivered, and draining half of it. He rubbed his eyes and yawned, turning the newspaper so that it faced him. Before he'd had a chance to read more than the main headline, Ichtracia snatched it back and began to read. Her eyes moved furiously across the lines for several moments.

"Are you going to let me see it?" Michel finally asked.

She handed the newspaper back and turned away. Michel watched the side of her face for a few moments. Her jaw was clenched and a vein stood out above her cheek. Something had clearly set her on edge. Was it the newspaper article?

"Your fomentation is working," she said. "The Palo are going nuts."

"You don't sound happy about that."

"It's working too well, I think." Ichtracia tapped the newspaper. "A Palo woman was caught defacing the capital building. She wrote *We will never be slaves again* in horse blood in very large letters."

Michel skimmed over the details of the article. He wondered if it was one of Jiniel's operatives or just someone inflamed by all these rumors. Either way, the culprit had been thrown into prison. The newspaper claimed that she was a madwoman and would be dealt with leniently, but that the Dynize city guard would be more active the next couple of weeks. He pushed the newspaper away and looked up at Ichtracia again. She fidgeted, not meeting his eyes.

"Are you all right?" he asked.

"It's barely been any time at all. I've been reading the reports going across Jiniel's desk. These stories have been circulating for, what, a day and a half at best? And people are already defacing buildings and throwing rocks. I heard there's supposed to be a march across Upper Landfall in just a couple hours."

Michel ran his tongue along his teeth. That was new, and not one of his plans. Jiniel might have organized it. "The stories *are* true. In the right political atmosphere, truth has wings."

"It doesn't matter if they're true or not. What shocks me is that people are eating it up so quickly. I know you're good at what you do, Michel, but you're not *that* good."

Michel stifled a smile. "Your point?"

"Then, what is it? The Palo were singing Dynize praises just a few days ago, and now they're on the edge of rioting."

Michel considered the question for a few moments. "You have to understand our people. We've been put down and kicked around for so long that we were desperate for relief—any relief. Lindet and her Blackhats had us terrified into inaction, and for good reason. She was brutal. So when the Dynize came along and treated us so well, we took it without asking too many questions. What's that old saying? Don't look a gift horse in the mouth?"

"It's 'Don't look at a gift goat's hooves' in Dynize," Ichtracia replied. "I get your meaning. But you haven't answered my question."

Michel tapped the side of his head. "We didn't turn our noses up at a gift. But we've also been burned before—dozens of times in living memory. Everyone you see around us here in the Depths, we all loved the Dynize treatment. But we were all thinking the same thing: Everyone else has betrayed us. When will the Dynize? We Palo were all just waiting for the Dynize to show their true colors. And now that they have, we're pissed about it."

"As simple as that?"

"As simple as that," Michel confirmed. "That anger is exactly what we're trying to stoke."

"Like I said. I think it's working too well."

Michel pursed his lips. "Why?"

Ichtracia shifted uncertainly. "It's changing so fast. I'm worried what Sedial will do when he finally grasps the situation. He can be a subtle man, but not when he's taken by surprise."

"Honestly, I'm worried about that myself." Michel drank the rest of his beer and pushed it to the edge of the table. "Is that what's bothering you?"

There was a long, worrying pause. "No."

"Then...?"

Ichtracia took a deep breath and retrieved something from the inner pocket of her vest, laying it on the table in front of Michel. It was the stack of envelopes she'd claimed from those reports stolen from the dragonman's home.

"You broke the wards already?" Michel asked in surprise.

"Sedial thinks his favorite Privileged are the best at everything. They're not great at wards."

"You're better?"

"Enough to only need a day to pick through them. Once I unwrapped one, the rest were easy." Ichtracia smiled, but it came across as pained. "You going to look at them?"

Michel kept his eyes on her as he picked up the top envelope and flipped it open, finally looking down. The lettering was neat, and he knew enough about Dynize to recognize the tone as formal. He read through it slowly, translating the words as he went, his hackles rising with each new line. It said:

By Order of the Great Ka, Written with the Full Authority of the Emperor of Dynize

*At the appointed hour, the bearer of this order is given author-
ity to execute a complete and utter purge against the Household of
Yaret. All men, women, and children in the immediate Household are to be put to death. All ancillary Household members will
be branded as slaves and scattered to the wind. All possessions
will be seized and all dwellings razed. The name of Yaret will be
struck from Imperial record.*

*The execution of this sentence is the will of the Emperor, for
the good of His domain. Any who question it will be scattered
with the offending Household.*

Michel inhaled sharply and read it again. "Did I translate this
right?"

"It's a purge order targeting Yaret and his Household."

"I did, then." He set the envelope down. "Why Yaret?" was the
first thing he managed to say. "Was it because of me?"

"You?" It seemed to take Ichtracia a moment to realize that
Michel was blaming the purge order on his infiltration of the Yaret
Household. "Oh, no. Not at all. Sedial and Yaret have always hated
each other. Look at the date on the top right-hand corner. This was
written before the invasion fleet left Dynize, and it's signed by the
emperor. Besides, look at the rest of the envelopes."

Michel began to pick them up, one at a time, reading through
them quickly. Each one was a copy of the former—only the names
were changed to target a different Household. When he realized
that they were all identical, he stopped bothering to read and
instead just counted the pile. There were twenty-three in total.
Everything clicked. "These are all of Sedial's Dynize enemies,
aren't they?"

Ichtracia gave him a small nod. "The ones in Landfall, yes. It's
thorough, too. Anyone who has stood up to him in any major
capacity over the last decade has been targeted. There are a few

names missing, but I'm not sure if that means he's decided to spare those Households or if he's just handed the purge orders to a different lieutenant. My guess is the latter."

Michel swore and checked the execution date again. Just nine days away. He took several deep breaths, forcing aside his sudden worry, trying to detach himself from the situation. He needed to think about this rationally. He could use this—the Palo cause could use this. If there was to be a purge, it would throw the Dynize into chaos and the Palo could rise up and . . .

He felt his thoughts circling, unable to focus. He rubbed the bridge of his nose.

Shit.

"You should probably head back to headquarters," he told Ichtracia, leaving money for his beer and gathering all the purge orders into his bag.

She didn't move. "What are you going to do?"

"You sound worried," Michel said, giving her a soft smile.

"And you look resigned. I don't like it."

Michel suddenly felt so tired. It wasn't his usual exhaustion, either, but something deeper. It was the same thing he'd felt that night when he was confronted by Tenik, and confessed that he worked for the Palo. It was the pain of being so many people at once. He realized why Ichtracia had been so on edge: She knew what he'd do when he saw the orders. He closed his eyes for a moment, leaning on the table until he could gather his resolve.

"You can't go to Yaret," Ichtracia told him gently. "You'll risk everything."

"I'm not stupid," Michel replied, pushing himself away from the table and heading toward the door. He could hear Ichtracia swear under her breath and run to catch up to him. She fell in beside him outside, and the two of them trudged through the haphazard dripping caused by rain trickling down through the myriad roofs and gutters in Greenfire Depths. Michel headed up to the rim of the Depths, deep in thought, fighting the powerful urge of self-preservation that told him to turn around and head right back down there and figure out a different way to use the purge orders.

He crossed Upper Landfall, entered the capital district, and found one of the Palo street kids that had become de facto spies and runners for several of the large Households up here. With Ichtracia hiding in an alley nearby, he beckoned the kid over and held up a two-krana coin.

"Do you know where the Yaret Household is?"

The child nodded seriously. Through the layer of grime on his face, Michel could barely tell he was Palo—or whether *he* was actually a *she*. He dropped the coin in the kid's hand, then gave him a hastily scrawled note. "I want you to deliver this to Tenik in the Yaret Household. Tell him that you're to be paid twenty krana for your troubles."

The kid's eyes widened. He snatched the note from Michel and took off running without asking any more questions. Michel shadowed him around the corner and then three streets over to be sure that he did, in fact, run to the Yaret Household. Once he was satisfied the kid wouldn't take the note somewhere else, Michel retreated back to Ichtracia.

"What next?" she asked him.

"I've asked Tenik to meet me tomorrow afternoon. Either he'll show up alone and we'll give him the purge orders..."

"Or?"

"Or," Michel said grimly, "he'll show up with a small army bent on capturing me."

CHAPTER 44

Vlora was inspecting the evening camp, preparing to retire early and get some rest, when Bo approached her at a brisk walk, his pipe hanging out of the corner of his mouth and his prosthetic squeaking loudly. She lifted an eyebrow at him as he fell in beside her. "Evening."

"Evening," he replied, taking her by the arm. "The first of Delia's emissaries has returned—with company."

"Shit. This soon? It's only been two days."

"Three days."

"Who is it?"

"General Etepali."

"Herself?"

"Yup."

Vlora let out a string of curses. "I thought Etepali was still burying bodies back at the Cape of New Adopest."

"Turns out she's been following us about ten miles back."

"Of course she has. She's *here* already?"

"The first of Delia's little summits," Bo confirmed. "Started five minutes ago in Delia's tent."

Vlora changed directions, nearly losing her grip on her sword and falling flat on her face. She recovered thanks to Bo's arm and began heading toward the corner of the camp where Delia's High Provosts had pitched their tents. Bo went along with her in silence, with Norrine trailing along behind them.

As they approached the edge of camp, Bo asked, "Do you expect to be present at every one of Delia's meetings?"

"Haven't decided yet."

"She's not going to like that."

"I don't care. Besides, I want her on her toes. I don't trust her worth shit, and..." Vlora fell silent as she maneuvered around a couple of campfires and approached a large tent marked with the emblem of the High Provosts. A handful of Dynize officers and their bodyguards milled outside the tent with an equal number of provosts. The provosts shuffled into Vlora's path as she approached.

"Sorry, ma'am, this summit is for the special envoy and her guests only," one of them said.

"Move."

"Sorry, ma'am, I—"

Vlora cut him off in a quiet voice. "Lay a hand on me and I'll make sure that your bodies are never found. *Move.*"

The lead provost cleared his throat, looked at his companions, then stepped aside.

"Thank you," she said to him sweetly. "Borbador, why don't you keep these gentlemen entertained?" Loosening herself from Bo's arm, she swept inside the tent.

There were only four people inside: Delia, Valeer, Etepali, and one of Etepali's senior officers. The group seemed like they had only recently seated themselves, and they looked up in surprise as Vlora entered. Delia's eyes narrowed slightly and Valeer looked openly indignant. "Lady Flint—" he began.

"I'm sorry I'm late," Vlora cut him off. She looked around for a fifth chair, found one in the corner of the tent, and dragged it over to the group before falling gratefully into it. "Evening inspections take a long time, you know?"

The glares from her two political "allies" were unmistakable, and Vlora saw the cool look that Etepali gave all three of them. She wondered, briefly, if this had been a mistake. Even a fool could feel the tension between the Adrans, and Etepali was no fool. She was probably already trying to figure out how to exploit this internal rift. None of this showed on her face, of course, and she raised a glass to Vlora. "My dear Lady Flint. It's so good to see you. Has your health been improving?"

"Yes, thank you."

"Excellent. I'm very pleased to hear that."

"I must confess, I didn't expect you to catch up with us so quickly," Vlora said.

Etepali's companion scowled, but Etepali herself just smiled pleasantly. "There were a lot of bodies to bury, of course, but there *is* still a war on. I left some of my auxiliaries to take care of the cleanup."

"Still hoping to drink that bottle of spirits?"

"I'll carry it with me until we have the chance to share it." Whatever effect the Midnight Massacre had had on the morale of the Dynize, it didn't seem to have touched Etepali. Vlora felt her own smile slipping, so she turned back to Delia.

"Sorry, Delia. Don't let me interrupt. I'm just here to observe the peace talks."

A pregnant pause hung in the room before Delia reached across the table beside her and shuffled a pile of papers and notes. She cleared her throat, gaze lingering on Vlora, before turning to Etepali. "As I was saying before Lady Flint arrived, I want to thank you so much for answering my request for a meeting."

"Of course," Etepali responded, swirling the liquid in her glass.

"I've only just become acquainted with Adran liquor, but I find myself enamored. I wouldn't miss it for anything."

Delia blinked back at the old woman for a moment. "Yes, well. I'd like to lay out the initial plan to bring the Adran theater of this war to a close."

"So soon?" Etepali seemed surprised. "You've only just arrived."

"Indeed we have, but our purpose here is not to wage war. It is, rather, to make sure that Adran interests in this part of the world are upheld."

Etepali leaned forward. "I'm sorry. What, exactly, *are* Adran interests in this part of the world? I understood that you don't actually own any of Fatrasta anymore."

"We don't," Delia replied with a tight smile. "But we do have a trade alliance with Fatrasta—one that has been disrupted badly by your capture of so many Fatrastan cities."

"I wasn't aware that a trade alliance with Adro warranted such a heavy response. A whole field army, just over some trade routes! My heavens, I'm certain that the Great Ka would have rethought the entire invasion if he had an inkling that a Kressian nation would intercede on behalf of the Fatrastans."

Vlora couldn't quite tell whether Etepali was being sarcastic or not. She spoke in that tone that so many old women are able to master—part condescending, part sincere, part baffled. Vlora watched Delia carefully to see how she'd respond.

Delia shuffled her papers again. "We're not, strictly, intervening on behalf of the Fatrastans."

"Oh?" Etepali exclaimed. Definitely sarcasm.

"This is about the so-called godstones," Delia said.

"I see. Well, I wouldn't know anything about those."

"You wouldn't?" Delia asked in surprise.

"I know *about* them," Etepali admitted. "But I don't have any orders to deal with them in any capacity. In fact, I don't actually have any orders to deal with you, either. My last order from the

Great Ka was to capture the city of New Adopest. By all rights, I should have headed right back there the moment Lady Flint left us behind her to clean up the Midnight Massacre."

"So why aren't you?" Vlora spoke up.

"I'm a general," Etepali replied. "I may follow orders, but I can also take *some* initiative. I've deemed an Adran field army to be of greater importance than a small coastal city."

Delia frowned at Etepali. "When you say that you don't have orders..."

"To deal with you? I should have said, rather, that I don't have any *authority* to deal with you." Etepali shrugged. "I have absolutely no political autonomy. None of us generals do, unless we're accompanied by one of the Great Ka's adjuncts."

Delia became visibly deflated, while Valeer scowled at both Etepali and Vlora. "Do you mean," Delia asked, "that this is a waste of time?"

"I'm afraid so," Etepali said, draining the last drop from her cup and leaning forward to pat Delia on the knee. "It's nothing personal, of course. You and your friend here seem very lovely. And General Flint, of course, though I should probably be bitter about her maneuver back there on the Cape." She got up and walked over to a small table in the corner, where she poured herself another glass.

"I have a question that I believe you *can* answer," Vlora said, taking advantage of Delia's befuddlement to interject. "My soldiers have been coming across empty towns. According to the survivors, a Dynize army has been murdering Kressians and kidnapping Palo. What do you know of that?"

Etepali's composure was broken, if only for a moment. She covered for herself by taking a sip from her glass. "Nothing."

"You're certain?" Vlora asked.

"Certain. As I said, every army has different orders." Etepali shrugged.

Silence blanketed the room. Etepali's officer and Provost Marshal Valeer stared at each other. Delia glared at the papers in her lap. Etepali drank her second, then third glass. Vlora tried to watch everyone at once.

Finally, Etepali gave a tiny, happy burp and set her glass down. "Well now. I'm afraid I'm not much use to you. You'll have to wait for your emissaries to return from Landfall. Thank you so much for the drink, though. Have a good evening!" With a wave, Etepali was joined by her officer and left the room. Within a few minutes, her group had departed, judging from the sounds outside, leaving Delia's tent silent.

Vlora cleaned her nails on her jacket. "Don't take it too badly," she said to Delia. "She did the same thing to me out on the Cape. I'm pretty sure she initiates these meetings just to find out the character of her enemies."

Delia remained quiet for a few moments before her head jerked up. "You are not authorized to be here," she snapped.

Vlora pretended to be surprised by the outburst. "I'm the commanding officer of this army. I am authorized to be anywhere I want."

"And I'm the head of the Adran special envoy! I—"

"Don't," Vlora warned. "You won't win this argument. It's been fifty years since a commanding officer has been subordinate to a special envoy, and there's nothing in Adran law that changes that. You're welcome to make overtures, and you're welcome to try and stop this war. But my word here is still final. Strategic necessity trumps political maneuvering."

"You're saying that as if you can do whatever you want," Delia accused.

"No, I'm not," Vlora said flatly. "You're here now, there's nothing I can do about that. I'll let you do your job. But I *have* to be allowed to do all of mine—and one of those is making sure that you don't endanger the lives of my soldiers in the course of your negotiations."

"Do you expect to stand over my shoulder throughout all of this?"

"I certainly hope not. I don't have the energy." Vlora wished she could take more pleasure in Delia's anger. And she did take a little, to be sure. But she also knew that this was but a momentary set-back for Delia. Within the next few weeks, she'd make proper contact with Ka-Sedial, and when that happened, Vlora couldn't be certain how the wind would blow. She stood up, giving a small bow to Valeer and Delia. "I want to suggest something."

"What?" The word came from Delia in a half snarl.

"I want to suggest we put aside our differences and work through this conflict. This expedition could be used to greatly enhance Adran wealth and prestige."

Delia became very still, regarding Vlora suspiciously.

Vlora took this as an opportunity to continue. "We've landed a field army in the middle of a conflict. We're greatly outnumbered, but we have the best-armed and best-trained troops on the continent. We can use our position to leverage concessions out of both Fatrasta and Dynize. Money, trade, even land. The Fatrastans are on the back foot. The Dynize are overextended. A skilled politician should be able to exploit that. Barter a peace, and break off a chunk for Adro in the process. Pit, if we can do that before any of the rest of the Nine is forced to get involved to protect their interests in this hemisphere, we might even be lauded as heroes."

Vlora could see the gears turning in Delia's head. Her suspicion slowly faded, replaced with a haughty coldness. She regarded Vlora with pursed lips. "I'll take it under advisement."

Haughty coldness was about the best Vlora could hope to expect out of Delia. "Of course. Thank you. And in the future, if you'll give me some warning, then either I or my representative will be on time for these meetings. And I might be able to share information with you that keeps you from wasting your time."

Delia gave her a tight nod. Vlora took it as a sign that it was time to leave. She made her good-byes and slipped out, where she found Bo surrounded by provosts. The whole group burst into laughter as she headed toward them. She pried him from their midst and, still shadowed by Norrine, they headed back toward her tent. "What was that all about?" she asked.

"I was telling jokes," Bo said.

"By Adom." Vlora sighed.

"Oh, come on. Even you find the one about the Kressian priest and the Warden a *little* funny."

She rolled her eyes. "The summit was a no-go. Etepali drank Delia's liquor and then told her that she had no authority to negotiate."

"I can't help but wonder what her angle is," Bo said.

"Etepali? I think she's crafty and bored. Regardless, Delia was furious, but I did manage to plant a seed in her head."

"Oh?"

"Suggesting we can work together to use this expedition to enrich Adro."

"Think she'll go for it?"

"Maybe. I'm just trying to keep her distracted. Whatever happens, I'm not leaving this continent without the second godstone and, hopefully, Sedial's head."

"Oh, good," Bo said cheerily, producing his enormous pipe from within his jacket. He tapped it out on his wrist, added new tobacco, then slipped on one of his gloves and twitched a finger. The pipe began to smoke immediately and he gave her a grin. "This will be fun."

CHAPTER 45

E tzi wrung his hands in the first show of genuine nerves since
Styke had arrived at the compound. Both men were in the
compound stables, just across the courtyard from the kitchens. Etzi
paced in the straw, while Styke rummaged through his saddlebags
that hung from a crossbeam outside Amrec's stall. He paused in his
rummaging to reach over the door and let Amrec nuzzle his hand,
patting the warhorse on the nose before returning to his search.

As Etzi paced, his face drawn up into a focused frown, he grumbled, "I don't know why they're summoning you to the Quorum
Hall."

"So you've said," Styke replied, finally finding the wax-paper
package that contained his carefully folded dress uniform. He set
it on the floor, unwrapped it, and checked the cloth for stains or
damage. "Can someone iron these?" he asked.

"Gorlia!" Etzi barked. A stable girl detached herself from a pile of
hay at the end of the stables and ran to attention. "Are your hands
clean? Good. Take these to the steward. They must be ready in

thirty minutes." The stable girl took off, and Etzi resumed his pacing. "There *should* be no need for your presence. Ji-Patten is going to try something. I can sense it."

Styke laced both arms over the stall door and scratched Amrec's cheeks. Etzi's disquiet filled the building, but his own was no less present. He'd never been good with politicians, officers, or any sort of authority figures. Not one-on-one, and much less so in groups. Yet they'd summoned him to stand before the Household Quorum. According to Etzi, everyone who was anyone would be there: five hundred or so Household heads or ranking representatives, all present to gawk at the foreign giant being protected by one of their own.

The whole idea made him want to break something.

"Anything I need to know before I go up there?"

Etzi flinched. "You cannot—I emphasize, *cannot* speak to the Household Quorum the same way you spoke to Ji-Patten. We are a people steeped in tradition and decorum. For a foreigner to even enter into the Quorum Hall is uncalled for, but if you so much as raise your voice..."

"Then what? They'll have me whipped?"

Etzi sniffed. "We're not barbarians. Half the people in that room have already formed an opinion about you. Of those, they can be divided between Sedial's allies, who have been told what to think, and Sedial's enemies, who hope to use you."

"And the rest?"

"The rest are those I hope to influence. In my lawsuit I've framed you as Orz's traveling companion and friend. They'll be curious what the friend of a dragonman looks like."

Styke turned around, leaning against the stall door. Amrec nibbled at his ear. "Would this be easier if I just called Ji-Patten out?"

"Eh?"

"A duel. Can I just have some sort of trial by combat?"

Etzi's eyes widened. "No! No," he repeated again, shaking his head. "That's not how we do things here. Remember that dragon-men are the property of the emperor. Attempting to duel one would be like calling out god himself. Do that, and they'll think you a savage." He held up a finger. "Pretend that you're speaking with your own governing body."

Styke bit his tongue and nodded.

Etzi went on. "Speak when spoken to. Ji-Patten knows you are a man of violence. He may even try to provoke you into attacking him."

"I can't rise to his provocations?"

"No. This is important." A flurry of emotions crossed Etzi's face. "It is more important than you can imagine. Any violence in the Quorum Hall will be taken as an affront to the members. I know that I don't tell you much, and that you are confined to this place, but you have to understand: There is a war of ideals taking place within the Household Quorum right now. My lawsuit has unleashed something larger than I imagined, and may very well shake the foundations of Sedial's power."

Styke intertwined his fingers to hide his own nerves. He'd rather charge five hundred soldiers alone than stand in front of them, expected to be a compliant little child. "You think this will be that important?"

Etzi didn't hesitate before he nodded, and his face was so earnest that Styke felt as if he had no choice but to believe him.

"All right," Styke said. "I'll be on my best behavior. Have one of the boys saddle my horse. Where do I find the steward to get my uniform?"

Styke rode in the center of Etzi's Household guard—three dozen soldiers in breastplates, morion helmets, and white-and-turquoise uniforms in a slightly different style than those of the city guard or regular soldiery. Etzi rode at his side with his head high and his gaze cool, all trace of nerves left back in the stable. Styke followed his example. He wore his dress uniform, an outfit he'd brought with a mind bent toward accepting the surrender of an enemy army, not attending a trial.

He gripped his reins with his white gloves, half wishing he'd brought the skull-and-lance banner and flown it from his lance. But he was not here to intimidate. He was here to grin at Ji-Patten, answer a few questions, and go on his way. Respectful. A tad arrogant—but not too much so. Upright. Friend of the pardoned dragonman, Orz.

He'd dismissed Etzi's earlier claims that Styke had become some kind of celebrity, but reassessed them in light of the crowds. The route from Etzi's Household to the Quorum Hall was packed. People gawked from the streets, windows, and rooftops. They waved handkerchiefs at him. They called him names. A thrown piece of fruit barely missed his head, and at another point three pretty young women appeared in a window wearing next to nothing, calling to him in broken Adran.

A city divided indeed.

They rode up the main thoroughfare toward the palace complex, but took a sharp left before coming within the shadow of the godstone. Their path crossed a wide square of tiled marble, approaching a building of immense, dusty red stones whose face stretched across the entire side of the square and more beyond. A mighty archway led inside. Styke followed Etzi's lead, dismounting and giving Amrec's reins to one of the Household stable boys.

"Are you ready?" Etzi asked.

The question only caused Styke's nerves to jump. He forced himself to grin. "Of course."

Etzi gave a curt nod and led Styke through the archway and down a long hall. Styke removed his hat, holding it under one arm, feeling the reassuring cadence of his cavalry sword slapping against his thigh. Their footsteps echoed in a silence, disturbed only by a distant roar. The roar grew in intensity with every step. They turned at the end of the hall, walked through another archway, and the roar resolved itself into the sound of hundreds of people speaking over one another in a huge concert hall.

The hall was shaped like an amphitheater, with seats rising up in three directions from a platform of white marble. They had entered directly onto that platform, and Styke suspected that the distinct feeling of smallness imposed by the high-domed ceiling, the rising seats, and the crowd that hushed upon his entry was all thoroughly engineered.

The sudden silence left him with an imagined echo in his ears. He stood stiffly at attention, back straight, trying to remember the last time he'd bothered to show the respect of parade posture to an audience. During training, maybe?

"Meln-Etzi," Etzi presented himself in a soft voice. The voice carried clearly throughout the room, not requiring him to speak any louder. "I present to the Household Quorum my guest, Colonel Ben of Fatrasta, companion of my brother, Ji-Orz."

Continued silence.

Etzi gave a small frown. "I was instructed to present him here?"

"You were," a voice boomed.

Styke glanced to his right to find Ji-Patten stepping up onto the speaker's platform, about ten paces from Styke. The dragon-man seemed in his element, an easy smile on his face, something strangely triumphant in his eyes. Styke was momentarily confused, and then his eyes fell upon a group sitting at the front of the audience just over Ji-Patten's shoulder.

It was his men, all twenty—or nineteen rather, without Jackal—of his Lancers. Styke's fists clenched involuntarily and he resisted the urge to reach for his knife. The Lancers returned his gaze with curious ones of their own. Even without exchanging a word, Styke could feel their nervousness and confusion. They didn't know why they were here any more than he did.

Etzi bowed his head respectfully to Ji-Patten. "Servant," he said formally. "May I ask what a representative of the emperor wants with my guest?"

Styke ran his eyes across the audience. It was as varied as any street crowd—old and young, men and women. No children, of course. All of them wore formal, loose-fitting clothing embroidered with Household crests. There were a lot more than five hundred people in this chamber, and he realized that many of them were assistants or those who were second in command. *Everyone* had turned out to see this.

See what? He realized something else, and that was that no one looked like they were ready to participate. They wore the curious expressions of people who'd turned out for a boxing match. This was a spectator sport, and *he* was one of the participants.

But in what way?

"You may," Ji-Patten answered after a moment of theatrical pause. Another such pause followed the statement.

Etzi coughed into his hand, clearly unimpressed. "Servant, I was told that my guest would not be disturbed by the Quorum. He is the companion of Ji-Orz, who is on a task from the Great Ka, and he is beyond reproach."

"This matter does not concern your guest."

"Then why is he here?"

"It concerns one of his soldiers."

A murmur went through the crowd. It was quickly hushed by the crowd itself. People leaned forward in their seats.

Etzi blinked back at Ji-Patten. Styke took a deep breath, reminding himself that this was important—he needed to remain silent. Let Etzi handle things. Any word he spoke would be used against him in the minds of the Quorum. Etzi finally cleared his throat and cast an expansive look across the Quorum. "I'm not sure I understand."

"Your guest—Colonel *Ben*." He emphasized "Ben" as if he knew it wasn't his full name. "I have not called into question his place alongside Ji-Orz. But he is a commanding officer, is he not?"

"He is."

"To these soldiers?" Ji-Patten thrust a finger toward the Lancers sitting behind him.

Styke noted that several of his soldiers were already looking at one of their own. They knew as much Dynize as Styke, and even those who weren't quick with languages had already gotten the gist of what was going on. Zak squirmed in his seat, sweating heavily, while his brother whispered urgently in his ear. Styke wanted to walk over to them and demand to know what was going on.

"He is their commanding officer, yes," Etzi said to the last question, the words much slower and more hesitant. Whatever was about to happen, it had blindsided him.

"Good." Ji-Patten strode to the Lancers and snatched Zak by the front of his shirt, dragging him off his seat and onto the speaking platform. The rest of the Lancers surged to their feet, but Dynize soldiers sprang to attention around them, forcing them back down at bayonet point.

"What's going on?" Styke whispered angrily.

"Quiet!" Etzi snapped at him. "Ji-Patten, explain yourself!"

Ji-Patten dragged a struggling Zak into the center of the platform until they were mere feet from Styke and Etzi. Zak wiggled and squirmed, but to no avail against the iron hold of the dragonman. Ji-Patten locked gazes with Styke, ignoring his prisoner as if he were a panicking rabbit. "Yesterday morning, your man murdered another prisoner."

"It was self-defense!" Zak shouted.

"Silence!" Ji-Patten cuffed Zak on the side of the head, hard enough that Zak's struggles ceased entirely and his face took on a look of confused stupidity. "He murdered another prisoner," he repeated.

"Then he should have a trial." Styke forced the words out, trying not to look at Zak and certainly not to look at the worried faces of his men.

"Exactly! I am glad you agree, Colonel Ben, because the trial has already been conducted. This soldier has been found guilty of murder. A tribunal has sentenced him to death."

"What tribunal?" Etzi demanded. "What trial? This is preposterous!"

It took every ounce of willpower for Styke to keep himself from falling forward, knife drawn. A cold fist seemed to curl around his stomach, leaving him ill and weak. This was it, then? This was Sedial's first real blow—a way of getting at Styke without laying a finger on him and, presumably, to show Styke that he could do anything he wanted to the soldiers in that prison.

Ji-Patten's glare drove Etzi back to Styke's side. "Meln-Etzi, remember yourself! The trial has occurred and there will be no dispute."

"What do you want?" Styke demanded.

"Ben!" Etzi whispered in warning.

"Want?" Ji-Patten asked. "I want justice. Nothing more." A bone knife suddenly appeared in his hand, as if drawn from thin air. The audience gasped. Ji-Patten spun it in his fingers, offering it hilt-first to Styke. "As a show of respect, I will allow you, his superior officer, to carry out the execution."

Styke stared at the hilt of the knife. His fingers twitched. He felt Etzi touch his arm, and heard his urgent whisper. "He's trying to provoke you, into either violence or rebuttal. If you claim not to recognize the judgment, he'll hold you in contempt of our courts and bring you into the suit. If you..." Styke stopped listening. All he could hear was the murmur of the audience. All he could feel was fury. All he could see was red.

"I won't have his blood on my hands," he finally answered stiffly.

"I see." Ji-Patten took a sudden step back. He jerked on Zak's collar, rag-dolling the Lancer to one side. His knife hand suddenly dipped, almost too fast to follow. Zak stiffened, letting out a terrible gasp, and then slid from Ji-Patten's fingers to splay on the floor. Blood poured from the side of his neck, spreading across the platform. Etzi retreated back almost to the entry hall. Styke let the blood pool around his boots, unmoving.

The Quorum was silent enough to hear a pin drop. Through it, suddenly, burst a sob. Markus tried to crawl over the soldiers holding him back. At a gesture from Ji-Patten, he was suddenly allowed to run forward. He slipped in his brother's blood, sliding and stumbling, until he cradled Zak's head in his lap. The weeping filled the hall.

Ji-Patten returned his knife to his shirt and strode over to Styke. Styke towered a full head above him, but Ji-Patten approached until their chests almost touched. Styke ignored him, looking down at the sight of Markus holding his brother.

"Not strong enough to do the deed yourself, are you?" Ji-Patten demanded.

A little part of his brain told Styke that he had won. Somehow, in a twisted way, he had bested Ji-Patten. This spectacle had been a battle of wills. If he raised a fist now, he would ruin it all. His hands trembled.

"You should have done it yourself," Ji-Patten growled. "Are you not man enough?" He raised a hand slowly. His palm opened. The gesture was so clearly conveyed as to be impossible to miss. Ji-Patten drew back and slapped Styke across the face.

Styke shifted his gaze to look at Ji-Patten.

"Do I have your attention now, Ben Styke?" Ji-Patten whispered.

"Servant!" Etzi shouted angrily. "Stop this at once!"

"Will you not fight back?" Ji-Patten asked. His hand raised again. Another slap, this one significantly harder, like the sharp crack of a belt across Styke's jaw.

Styke sniffed. "Is that all you've got?" he asked just loudly enough that his voice carried.

Ji-Patten took a step back and raised his arm once more. Closed-fist this time. "If I kill you with this blow, I will barely be punished." A whisper. Styke didn't respond. He kept his eyes locked with Ji-Patten's.

The fist struck him just below the heart and felt like a kick from a warhorse. Styke leaned into it, letting his weight absorb the impact, refusing to be driven back even half a step. It took a few moments to regain his breath, but he let nothing show on his face. Slowly, deliberately, he let the corner of his lip twitch upward in a sneer. He put every bit of his fury into it.

Ji-Patten's cheeks twitched; his eyes widened. His expression very clearly said that he'd killed men with such a blow—and Styke did not doubt it. That punch would have made Valyaine proud.

"Your god needs a new servant, Ji-Patten," Styke said loudly. "Because I've been struck harder by a child." His voice echoed throughout the audience hall. The Quorum watched, every one of them slack-jawed.

Ji-Patten drew back his fist again.

"Servant!" Etzi barked. "Enough."

The words finally seemed to get through to the dragonman. He blinked, shaking his head slightly, and only now seemed to see that he was standing in Zak's blood. He cast about him in disgust, then turned and strode off the platform and down to the side exit, leaving bloody footprints behind. "Return them to their cells, and burn the murderer's body," he barked at his soldiers.

Styke remained where he was while his soldiers were filed out. He watched them drag Markus through his brother's blood, then take away Zak's body. Porters appeared to clean up the blood, while the Quorum erupted into a shouting match that drowned out any thoughts that may have been creeping through Styke's head. It wasn't until he felt a gentle hand on his arm that he allowed himself to be led into the same large hallway through which he'd entered. Once they were out of sight of the Quorum, he sagged against the wall, resting a hand on his chest and staring at the blood all over his boots.

"I'm sorry." Styke looked up at the soft words. Etzi stood across from him, looking ashen and defeated. Etzi continued, "I didn't know they would stoop so low."

"Evil men will stoop to anything they see fit," Styke responded without feeling. "I've done so myself." He wanted to shout and flail, to pick up Etzi and throw him against the wall. The vision of Markus cradling his brother's body was now burned into his memory.

"Thank you for not responding." Etzi gazed at Styke's cheek. It still burned, and he imagined that it was very red.

"Once in a very great while, I do as I'm told," Styke said. His fury was still there, burning in his belly, but it seemed muted and distant. He pressed his thumb against the lance tip of his big ring until he felt it draw blood. "But your arrogant prick of a Great Ka still hasn't learned his lesson."

"What lesson is that?"

"That I'm Ben Styke."

CHAPTER 46

Michel stood on the southern edge of the Landfall Plateau, eyes intent on the park down below where he'd asked Tenik to meet him at four. It was only noon, and he intended on being there early enough that no one would get the drop on him. He worked through his nerves, testing contingency plans in his head, knowing that he was being a fool.

"You're actually flustered," Ichtracia said. She stood next to him on the edge of the plateau, enjoying the sun on her face, looking out across the floodplains toward the distant tower of the godstone.

The statement took Michel off guard. "I'm what?"

"Flustered." Ichtracia bit off a laugh. "I've never seen you flustered."

"This isn't funny."

"Not even when my grandfather had you tied up and was cutting your finger off," Ichtracia continued. She seemed almost pleased, and it was getting on Michel's nerves. "You were angry and in pain and desperate, but you weren't flustered. This is..." She rubbed her face, physically wiping the smile away. "I shouldn't laugh. You're right, this isn't funny. But seeing you so conflicted is kind of..."

"Vindicating?" Michel asked. The word came out as an angry snarl.

"A little," Ichtracia said as if she didn't notice his anger. "But I was thinking *humanizing*. Just another piece of the real Michel Bravis." She suddenly stepped forward and, to Michel's surprise, took his face in her hands. Before he could react, she kissed him gently on the lips. "It's all right. We're going to warn Yaret, aren't we?"

Michel swallowed. He *was* flustered. Flustered and conflicted. He was going against all of his instincts and training. He was operating off a half-cocked plan that might get him killed—or worse, dragged through the streets and delivered straight to Ka-Sedial. "Yes. I can't just drop these off." He patted his bag, where he was carrying the purge orders. "I need them to know they come from me, I need them to—"

"You need them to know that you wouldn't abandon them," Ichtracia said.

Michel swallowed a lump in his throat and nodded. He should have felt better from Ichtracia's show of understanding. But for some reason he just felt defeated. "I told Tenik to meet me at the garden where we spotted Forgula. I'm hoping it's specific enough that he gets the message but vague enough that if it's intercepted by Sedial, I can't be traced."

"And where's that?"

Michel pointed off the plateau to a spot down in Lower Landfall. They could see the park from here.

"You know this is risky?" Ichtracia asked. He could hear the concern in her voice.

"I'm aware. This is why I don't think you should—"

Ichtracia cut him off. "I came with you to Landfall to watch your back. I'm not going to stop because you're doing the right thing."

That *did* make him feel better, but not in the way that he expected. The words were even more intimate than the kiss she'd just given him. "*Is* it the right thing?" he asked. "The Palo…"

"You've given them everything. You don't have to give them your friends, too." Michel noticed that the corners of Ichtracia's eyes were red. She continued, "I've never been allowed to have friends. Allies and enemies. I…envy you the opportunity to save someone you care about."

Michel took a shaky breath. "Thank you."

They headed down the side of the plateau and toward Claden Park. Michel gave the park a wide berth and found an old factory overlooking a row of townhouses with a clear view of the area. They did a circuit of the factory before finding a rusted iron ladder that led to the roof. He slapped the side of the building. "All right. Up you go."

"You're not coming?"

"No. You're taking this spot. Like you said—watch my back. I told him to meet me here in four hours, so we might have to wait a while. If I wave twice, I want you to join me. If I wave three times, stay put. If I wave once…well, get the pit out of here."

Ichtracia hesitated for a moment before giving him a nod. The intimacy and concern she'd shown on the plateau were gone, replaced by a cold, businesslike demeanor. She began to climb.

Michel didn't wait for her to get into position before heading to the row of houses just in front of the factory. He could make his way up to one of those roofs. He'd be in sight of Ichtracia, and he in turn could watch for Tenik—and find out whether Tenik, as requested, had come alone. If everything went smoothly, he and Ichtracia would be heading back to Greenfire Depths by nightfall.

He found the roof access near the end of the row of townhouses— a narrow iron staircase for chimney sweeps. It was about ten feet off the ground, so he began looking for something to use as a ladder, when he heard footsteps coming up behind him. He pulled his gaze off the staircase and adopted a purposeful limp, so that anyone coming across him might think he was just a cripple looking for a shortcut through the alley.

"That's not going to work, Michel."

The words felt like a cold knife through the gut. Michel stiffened and broke into a run, only to make it a half-dozen steps before several figures cut off the end of the alley. They wore morion helmets and carried muskets, with the Household symbol of Yaret draped over their cuirasses. Michel skidded to a stop and spun to look back the way he'd come.

Tenik stood about fifty paces back, leaning heavily on a cane. The cupbearer looked unimpressed and tired. He was flanked by four more soldiers. Michel searched desperately for an escape. This wasn't how this was supposed to go. Not at all. Ichtracia couldn't see him from here, and even if she could, he didn't want her to attack Tenik. He bit his lip, looking for a way out and finding nothing.

Tenik limped across the space separating them. His face was red, his brow covered in sweat.

"I thought I said to meet me in the park," Michel said, unable to think of anything else.

"Which is exactly why we're waiting for you here," Tenik replied, giving Michel a shallow smile. "You did train me in some of this stuff, remember? I figured all I needed to do was beat you here and figure out where you'd be watching from."

"Well." Michel swallowed hard. "I'm impressed."

Tenik snorted. "Why are you still here, Michel? I warned you, didn't I?"

"You did."

"I keep my promises."

"Yeah." Michel eyeballed the soldiers again, then glanced over his shoulder at those behind him. Definitely no way out. It wouldn't be long before Ichtracia began to wonder what was taking him so long, but it might still be ten or twenty minutes before she came down to check. He considered running, but even if he *could* get past the soldiers, the look in Tenik's eye told him that he would definitely get shot in the back.

"I'm either killing you or taking you in," Tenik said regretfully. "Pick one."

"You're not going to ask why I wanted to meet?"

"If you come in, you'll be telling us a lot of things."

"It doesn't look like I have much of a choice."

"There's always a choice," Tenik replied. "You have two right now." He lifted his hand, and Michel turned to see a carriage pull up to the end of the alleyway behind him. The windows were shaded with drapes matching the decoration on the soldiers' cuirasses. Michel even recognized the driver as one of the Yaret Household, though he couldn't remember the woman's name.

He realized that Tenik *was* giving him a choice—an out. Michel could run. He could be gunned down in the street. It wasn't a pleasant choice, but it was still a way to save himself and all the information stored in his head. It was a way to avoid the endless tortures that Sedial had no doubt planned for him.

"Does Sedial know that you've found me?" Michel asked.

Tenik gestured once more to the carriage.

If Michel got into that carriage, he was a dead man, and everyone he knew would die along with him—Jiniel, Emerald, Mama Palo's entire organization. He would spill it all to the bone-eyes. He tensed, spreading his feet to prepare to run.

"Tenik," a voice suddenly called. "Please stop the theatrics. Bring him over here."

Michel turned in surprise to find the carriage door open and Yaret himself peering out from within. The Household head motioned impatiently. "If you want to talk to me, Michel, you'll have to do it quickly before Sedial's spies know that I've left the house. Now, come!"

Michel considered one more dash to freedom—or death—before turning toward the carriage. He joined Yaret within. The carriage was rolling before he'd even sat down, and he could hear Tenik giving instructions to the bodyguard from the running board. He laid his bag across his lap and met Yaret's eye.

Yaret looked much the same as he had when they'd last met, if a little worn around the edges. He gave Michel a fatherly smile and shook his head. "Tenik told me that you'd changed your appearance drastically, but I didn't believe that it was this much. No wonder you're still avoiding detection." He glanced down at Michel's two missing fingers and clicked his tongue, but did not comment on them. "I like you, Michel, but your immediate fate depends very much on whatever it is you wanted to tell us."

Michel let himself relax into the carriage bench, taking on an air of confidence that he did not feel. The winds had just shifted, and he could sense that this was now a negotiation rather than an execution. "Tenik told you who I really am?"

"He told me that you're claiming to be a Palo freedom fighter. Though whether that's your real identity or not, then"—Yaret gave a small shrug—"I find it strange that you're now fighting the Dynize, when it seems from my perspective that we have given you Palo a hundred times more freedom than you ever had beneath the Kressians."

"That's . . . a discussion we can have later," Michel said.

"If there is a later."

"I think there will be." Michel reached into his bag and fetched the purge order that he'd set aside from the main bundle. He handed it to Yaret. "I stole this from Ji-Noren's apartment yesterday morning."

"You robbed Ka-Sedial's best dragonman?" Yaret said in disbelief. He reached into his breast pocket for a pair of reading glasses, clicking his tongue again. "You're one bold . . ." He trailed off as he got the glasses onto the bridge of his nose and opened the envelope.

Michel watched his eyes flick across the page and the blood drain from his face. Yaret rapped on the ceiling. "Tenik!"

"Master?" the response came.

"Stop the carriage and join us."

The instructions were followed, and Yaret's cupbearer was soon sitting next to Michel. Yaret gave him the letter.

"Where did you get this?" Tenik demanded breathlessly as soon as he'd finished reading.

"Ji-Noren's apartment," Michel answered.

"Could it be a forgery?" Yaret asked.

Tenik glanced sharply at Michel, studying him for a moment, before cautiously shaking his head. "This is the imperial seal. This is Sedial's scrawl. This is his signature. This is the *emperor's* signature." Tenik sniffed the paper. "It's even the powder Sedial uses to dry the ink. If it's a forgery, I've never seen the like."

Michel reached back into his bag and produced the bundle of purge orders. He gave them to Tenik, who immediately began to open each, listing off the Household names aloud and setting them aside. "Master," he said to Yaret, "these are all our allies. Our relatives. Everyone we—"

Yaret cut him off with a raised hand and turned back to Michel. "You know what this means, don't you?"

"Sedial is about to consolidate his power," Michel replied. "And he has the emperor's backing to do it. He'll wipe out anyone who might oppose him in the future."

"Not just here. He'll have sent five times this many orders back to Dynize. The rest of my Household will be in danger." Yaret inhaled sharply and seemed to struggle to gain control over his emotions. He narrowed his eyes at Michel. "You risked everything to bring this to us?"

Michel didn't answer.

"You knew that Tenik would follow through on his promise to kill you. Even now, we could take you directly to Sedial and hand you over in an attempt to get this sentence commuted." Yaret shook the envelope under Michel's nose.

"I figured that was a possibility," Michel admitted.

"But you did it anyway."

Michel glanced sidelong at Tenik. "I'm pretty good at reading people, and neither you nor Tenik struck me as the type to betray someone trying to help you. And as Tenik said to me—for the space of a summer, you were my friends. My family. I may be a spy, but I'm not a monster. I'm not going to stand aside and allow your Household to be slaughtered simply to save my own skin."

Yaret tapped the envelope against his chin, looking down at the pile of purge orders in Tenik's lap. There was a sudden knock on the door. It opened a crack, and one of the soldiers stuck his nose in. His eyes were wide, his tone frightened. "Master."

"What is it?" Tenik asked sharply. "Speak up, man. Is it the Great Ka?"

"No, it's...I can't entirely be certain, but I think that there's a Privileged watching us from the rooftop."

"A Privileged?" Tenik asked. "Who could possibly...?"

"She looks different, but I think it's Ichtracia."

Both Yaret and Tenik looked at Michel. He swallowed his unhappiness at the discovery and shrugged. "She's with me. You probably shouldn't make any sudden moves until I leave the carriage."

To his surprise, Yaret began to chuckle, waving his hand to dismiss the guard. "Remain where we are," he ordered. "Let me know if she approaches or puts on gloves." As soon as the door had closed again, he glanced at Michel. "You turned Sedial's granddaughter."

"I'm not sure if I turned her," Michel replied, "or just gave her more choices."

Yaret sighed, staring at the purge order in his hand. "This," he said, tapping the order, "is not unexpected."

"Master?" Tenik asked, a note of warning in his voice.

"It's all right. Michel may not be on our side, but he's not our enemy, either. At least, not to the Yaret Household." He studied his fingertips for a moment, clearly coming to some decision, before continuing. "Michel, for almost two years we have been planning on removing Sedial from power."

Michel scoffed. "You *what*?"

"It's been a long time in the planning, with the utmost secrecy, known only to the Household heads involved in the plot and their closest cupbearers. Most of the names on this purge are in on it." He gave Michel a sad smile. "Together with our allies back in Dynize, we've been planning a bloodless coup that would force Sedial into retirement, destroy his hold over the emperor, and keep us from extending this damned war to the whole of the Nine."

"When," Michel asked flatly, "did you plan on doing this?"

"That's the trouble with conspiracies among many," Yaret admitted. "We haven't actually agreed yet. Before he uses the godstone, that's for sure."

"You'd better be ready to act quickly then, because it's active."

"It can't be," Tenik protested. "He's supposed to tell us."

Michel shook his head. "I'm almost certain he's managed to activate it and is only waiting until he has the third stone in his possession. Ichtracia agrees with me."

Yaret waved the purge order at Tenik. "I think we should set aside any trust that we have left for the Great Ka. We shouldn't be surprised that he's moved forward in secret. And this…this changes everything." He pressed his fingers against his chin, staring at the paper, deep in thought.

"Will you act?" Michel asked.

"I'm not sure if we can. Our conspiracy to remove the Great Ka from power has been so carefully planned. We seek to avoid another civil war at all costs. We planned to weaken his public support, distance him from his allies, and then force him to resign." Yaret flipped the envelope back open and read through the purge order once more. "Eight days. I don't know what we can do." He gestured. "Michel, you should return to Ichtracia before she gets nervous. I don't want an incident."

Michel looked at Tenik, half expecting the cupbearer to object to his being released. But Tenik seemed to have already forgotten he was there.

"I'm sorry," Michel said.

Yaret looked up. "Don't be," he said with a smile. "I'm not sure if I or any of my Household will be alive by the end of next week. But at the very least, you've given us a chance to fight for our lives. Thank you. Now, go, before the People-Eater gets twitchy."

Michel stepped out of the carriage and glanced up to see Ichtracia's relieved face looking down at him from above. Not only had she spotted the carriage and followed it, but she'd managed to flank their position from high ground. He felt a stab of pride, and headed down a nearby alley away from the carriage. None of the soldiers stopped him as he left.

He was able to fetch Ichtracia, and the two of them were halfway across the city before they spoke again. "I almost had a heart attack when you didn't show up on that rooftop," Ichtracia finally said.

"But you found me. Thanks for that."

"I take it that Tenik was grateful for the news?"

Michel walked to a café and sat down, ordering two iced coffees. He didn't want to stay out in public for too long, but he also needed a shot of energy. The encounter with Yaret had left him feeling emotionally exhausted. "It was Yaret. He came out to see me in person."

"Oh?" Ichtracia snorted. "Sedial did say the old fool liked you more than he should have."

Michel turned to Ichtracia. "Does Sedial have any idea that there's a coup planned against him?"

"No one would dare."

"Yaret just told me. Dozens of Household heads are in on it."

"You're joking." Ichtracia sat back in her café chair, watching his face carefully. "You're not joking. Damn. No. As far as I know, he has no idea. I never thought the Households would have the guts to oppose him."

Michel took his coffee when it arrived and drained it, then stared into the cup. He felt troubled, cursed by the feeling that he would never see Tenik or Yaret again. "I got the impression that they're not going to get the chance. They've been planning for years, yet Sedial is going to strike too quickly." He waited until Ichtracia finished her coffee, then stood up, trying to cast the Yaret Household from his mind. He couldn't spare them anything else. He couldn't afford to. "Let's go. We have work to do."

CHAPTER 47

Despite everything that had happened—the Midnight Massacre, the arrival of the special envoy, the loss of her sorcery, and her own deeply disruptive emotional swings—Vlora felt herself nervous with excitement. She stood in the stirrups against the protests of her aching body to watch the horizon, and every time the army stopped, she would consult her maps.

They were nearing the Hadshaw River. She recognized this territory now, the flat plains replaced by gentle, rolling hills, with the shadowy specter of the Ironhook Mountains to their west and the true foothills to their north. She and Taniel had swept through here a few months ago on their mad dash to Yellow Creek. All of that felt like a dream now, and it saddened her to remember the sorcery in her veins like lightning, pushing both of them on long after their horses dropped from exhaustion and they were forced to trade with the locals for new ones.

Burt's arrival at her side in the middle of the afternoon was sudden, if not unexpected. He rode up to her as she examined the horizon, a cigar clamped between his teeth, and studiously examined the same horizon until she lowered her looking glass.

"You know," he said in greeting, "I recognized you pretty early back at Yellow Creek. I've been to Adro and I've heard the stories and read the newspapers. But damn me if I'm not a little impressed."

Vlora turned to him in confusion. "Oh?"

He gestured to the column marching past them. "A real-life Adran field army. As a kid who grew up reading everything he could about Field Marshal Tamas, this tickles the pit out of me."

"I've always thought it much like any other field army," Vlora said offhandedly, though even as she spoke, she knew she was lying.

"Nah." Burt waved her off. "I've seen field armies. Fatrastans, Kez, Deliv. I've even seen the Dynize now. But there's something different about Adran soldiers. A higher step, a more efficient march and camp. Did you know that on average an Adran army marches roughly three miles farther in a day than the next fastest army in the world?"

Vlora pursed her lips. She was sure she'd heard that somewhere. "Tamas's reforms during the Gurlish Wars," she told him. "We were already very good before he came along—we had to be, being the smallest nation in the Nine. But once he was field marshal, everything changed. He gutted the officer corps and began promoting by merit. He started using the Privileged cabal less in his campaigns. Speed and organization replaced the old system bent on gaining glory for noble officers."

"It shows." Burt nodded, ashing his cigar. "Anyway, I wanted to let you know that we've made contact with my irregulars."

Vlora's head came up. "We're that close?"

"Just a few miles from the river," he confirmed. "My boys are hurting, I've got to admit. They've kept the Dynize pinned down at the river, but the Dynize outnumber them significantly, and it's beginning to show. I'm headed to their camp now to get the lay of the land."

"I'm going with you," Vlora said, the words leaving her mouth before she'd even considered them. She swore inwardly. She *couldn't* make such rash decisions anymore. She needed to be thoughtful, cautious. What if this was a trap? What if the Dynize counterattacked while she was with Burt? "If that's all right," she added. "I'll need to give a few orders and gather a bodyguard."

"Of course," Burt said, raising both eyebrows. "We'd be honored to have you."

"Give me thirty minutes," she said, turning and riding down the column.

She found General Sabastenien and Bo together on the side of the road, smoking their pipes while they stared off to the south. "Does every damn person in this army smoke something?" she asked as she approached.

"Ma'am." Sabastenien greeted her with a nod. Bo raised one hand and furiously puffed up a cloud.

"You're just the two I'm looking for. Anything to report on this business with the Dynize and Palo?"

"Nothing much new," Sabastenien said unhappily. "There doesn't seem to be a sorcerous aspect to the kidnapping—simply racial. The Dynize are grabbing all the Palo and sending them to the river. From there we can only assume they're sending them downriver on keelboats."

"They'd have to be going by the hundreds."

"Thousands, more like," Bo interjected.

"Forced labor?"

"I'm not so sure anymore," Bo said, holding something out to Vlora. It was a yellowed handbill, decorated with a pair of freckled hands and the words DYNIZE AND PALO: COUSINS UNITED.

Vlora snorted in disbelief. "They're kidnapping them to turn them into allies?"

"It certainly seems that way," Sabastenien said. "Of course, we have no idea if all of these promises of equality actually mean anything. But if they do, the Dynize are clearly consolidating what they think of as *their* people. It could be for labor, for conscription, for census taking…pretty much anything."

"But why kill the Kressians?"

"Purifying?" Bo suggested. "There was more than one shah during the Gurlish Wars who killed every Kressian that crossed her path. She believed that she had to cleanse the continent before her chosen gods could return again."

Vlora shivered. "That is terrifying."

"And it could have far-reaching implications. We haven't heard of anything similar in the big cities yet, but if the Dynize decide to wipe out every Kressian on the continent, they have enough soldiers to begin at any time."

"Shit," Vlora swore. "All right, Sabastenien, I want you to take this theory to Delia. Use it as leverage. Not even *she's* bitter enough to let Adran expatriates die by the tens of thousands to spite me."

"Yes, ma'am."

"And while you're there, I want you to sit in on her little summits. She has more representatives coming in today to talk, right?"

"She does," Bo confirmed. "From the other two armies on our tail."

"Sit in on those," she repeated to Sabastenien. "Keep notes. Don't say anything unless Delia seems like she's about to promise the world."

Sabastenien nodded sharply.

"Bo, come with me."

"Where are we going?"

"To meet with Burt's irregulars."

Sometime in the last week, Burt and Bo had become the closest of friends. It shouldn't have surprised Vlora at all, but this was the first time she'd seen them together, and she was pleased that the two of them were laughing, joking, and going on at length as they left the main army and headed toward Burt's irregulars camp. They were even sharing Burt's cigars.

Vlora was playing this little visit safe. She'd brought Norrine, Davd, Bo, and three hundred of her cavalry with her. If the Dynize managed to get the drop on them, the tin-heads would be in for a pit of a fight.

The trip was not as long as she'd expected, and they were only about three-quarters of a mile off the main highway when Burt's messenger led them behind an abandoned plantation building and down into a steep, wooded ravine that separated the property between two of the plantations. The ravine looked innocuous from afar, but once they'd descended a narrow mule track, it seemed to open up and revealed a well-worn camp.

They were challenged by a sentry who, once Burt and his guide had been identified, emerged to join them on the mule track. The young woman saluted Burt and regarded Vlora, Bo, and their escort with wide eyes. "You weren't kidding when you said you were going for help, boss," she said.

"I've always told you the importance of making friends," Burt replied, gesturing to Vlora with his cigar.

Vlora scowled at the camp. "Where is everyone?"

"They're keeping the Dynize pinned down," the sentry reported. "Those buggers have gotten awfully restless the last couple of days."

Burt swore. "Did they manage to get that damned pedestal out of the river?"

"They did. Last I heard, they've got it into a keelboat and are preparing a flotilla to get them going again. Tomm and the lads are trying to sink it."

As if to emphasize the point, a distant boom reverberated through the ravine. "That would be them," the sentry said.

"Grenades," Burt explained. "Some of my irregulars apprenticed with Little Flerring when we were in Yellow Creek. Made some improvements on the standard Adran army explosives. But they still have to get real damn close to use them." He swore several more times. "There's only so much we can do as skirmishers. If we're close enough to use grenades, the Dynize might be able to wipe us out." He turned his gaze on Vlora, asking an unspoken question.

Vlora froze. She'd sworn to herself not to make any stupid decisions that put her and her men at unnecessary risk. With a whole field army less than a mile or two behind her, she was about to bring overwhelming force down on the Dynize. No need to endanger anyone. But the Palo Nation irregulars were putting their lives on the line to stop the Dynize. She couldn't just let them all die.

She nodded at Burt, then the sentry. "Lead on. Let's go give them a bit of relief."

The sentry led their group down the ravine for several hundred yards before bringing them up the other side and out into the open again. They crossed yet another plantation, rounded a hill, and were suddenly in clear view of the Hadshaw River Valley.

The river was perhaps three hundred yards down the hillside from them, flowing gently through the plantation fields that ran all the way down to its banks. The banks themselves were held by a Dynize brigade, which was camped on either side of the river and held a wide stone bridge that, unless she was mistaken, marked the crossing of the very highway Vlora's soldiers were marching down at this moment. The river was packed with keelboats, lashed to the bank and to the bridge.

It took her only a moment to spot their target—the largest of the keelboats, loaded with a rectangular stone roughly the size of one of the covered wagons frontiersmen favored for transportation. There was, at this distance, nothing special about the stone. It lacked ornamentation, and though it was the same color as the godstone they'd cracked back up in Yellow Creek, it didn't give her the same sense of dread. Perhaps, though, that was simply because she had no sorcery.

The keelboat was directly under the stone bridge, which was the epicenter of a sizable engineering project—cranes, counterweights, stabilizing equipment—that had clearly been used to bring the stone out of the water and plop it onto the keelboat.

Even as Vlora took all of this in, she saw Burt's irregulars engaged in a fierce firefight on the edge of the river. There were only a few hundred of them compared to the thousands of Dynize, but they had managed to push hard and bottle up a decent number of the enemy on the bridge itself. The irregulars fired and reloaded at an astonishing speed, powder smoke rising from their little group as they locked down the reeling Dynize. Occasionally a grenade would burst among the Dynize line, adding to the confusion.

Even with their momentum, the irregulars couldn't hope to reach the bridge. The Dynize were on the back foot, but they had the strength in numbers. Vlora reined in, took a deep breath of the powder smoke on the wind, and snapped off orders.

"Captain," she barked to the commander of her bodyguard, "take your dragoons and relieve the irregulars. Burt, pull your men out of there. My soldiers will provide covering fire."

"That keelboat is starting to move under the bridge," Burt warned. "If it gets moving, there's no stopping it."

"It's not going anywhere. Go!" Vlora's dragoons responded immediately, galloping down the hill at full speed while drawing their carbines. Burt urged his own horse after them. "Do we need to get you closer to sink that keelboat?" Vlora asked Bo.

Bo wiggled his fingers like a father about to show his child a trick, then slipped on both of his gloves, tugging at the hems theatrically. "Not even a little. And I'll do better than sink it."

For the faintest breath of a moment, Vlora thought that she felt something. It might have been a cold breeze, or it might have been muscle memory from watching so much sorcery, but when Bo's fingers began to twitch, she could have sworn that a tickle went up between her shoulder blades. She drew out her looking glass and turned it on the keelboat.

"Do you have orders for us?" Norrine asked. Both she and Davd had dismounted and prepared their rifles.

"Wait," Vlora said, watching carefully. Almost a minute passed, and she ignored the shouting of her dragoons and the sudden pop of carbine fire as they reached the irregulars. The keelboat emerged from beneath the bridge, but instead of gaining momentum, it began to slow again. Within seconds it had stopped entirely, and the Dynize soldiers on board frantically pushed and shoved with their poles to try to get it moving again. It took her another moment to see the band of ice forming around the base of the keelboat. The ice began to spread, locking the keelboat in place. "All right," she told Norrine, "ignore their officers. Clear that keelboat of life. I want the three of you to keep it locked up."

It was almost fifteen minutes before Burt returned with his irregulars and Vlora's dragoons. The former were badly mauled, hauling as many wounded and dead along with them as they had still walking. The latter had suffered light casualties, but their blood was obviously up as their captain requested permission to continue his skirmish with the Dynize.

"Denied," Vlora replied, listening to Davd's rifle bark. A Dynize soldier attempting to board the big keelboat tumbled into the water. The Dynize brigade had crossed over to this side of the river and finally drawn up into lines. They waffled on the bank, as if undecided on whether they should charge Vlora's small group or remain to defend their ward. Vlora rummaged in her saddlebags until she found a white handkerchief, and handed it over to the captain. "Put this on the end of your sword. I want you to let the enemy general know that I will give him generous terms to surrender if he orders his men to throw down their muskets immediately."

Vlora sat back and waited while the captain headed back down the hill with a few companions. A group emerged from the Dynize lines, and the two envoys began their meeting.

While she waited, the head of Vlora's army crested the road directly behind her. She was soon joined by General Sabastenien and Nila. Sabastenien snapped a sharp salute. "We heard fighting and brought the cavalry, ma'am."

"Well done." She gestured to the meeting below them. "Hopefully they won't be necessary, but..."

She trailed off as the meeting adjourned, far quicker than she would have expected. The captain returned with his report.

"They won't surrender."

"They saw that we have more cavalry alone than they have soldiers?"

"They did. The general..."

"Doesn't trust me?" Vlora guessed.

"Not exactly," the captain replied. "I got the impression that he's more scared of whoever is giving him orders back in Landfall than he is of you."

"Damned fools," Vlora muttered. "All right. We do this the hard way. Nila, burn out the front lines. Don't let your fire hit the keelboats, I want those intact. Sabastenien, I want you to ride down whatever hasn't burned. Send a thousand dragoons downriver to find a ford. I want them to flank the Dynize and kill or capture everyone who tries to run."

"Yes, ma'am."

Nila tugged at the cuff of her sleeves, frowning down toward the enemy. "You don't want me to give them a warning shot?"

"They've had their warning. The Dynize general is more scared of Ka-Sedial than he is of dying by our hand. Besides, I want that stone secured by nightfall. We've got three enemy field armies coming up behind us and I don't want anything left of this rabble by the time we put our back to the river. Nothing left to do but get to it. Oh, and Sabastenien?"

"Yes?"

"If they throw down their weapons, I want them spared."

"Better for our own morale," he agreed, switching the reins from one hand to the other and drawing his sword and calling out to his officers. The column of cavalry began to split up, forming into groups and spreading out across the valley. Vlora forced herself to turn and watch the coming battle.

CHAPTER 48

It took the Adran Army longer than Vlora expected to crush the Dynize. Despite Nila's flames raining down on them from above, they held their line against Vlora's cuirassiers for the better part of the afternoon and well into the evening. It was dark by the time her dragoons managed to flank them and the Dynize finally fell apart beneath the two-sided onslaught. Weapons were thrown down, and Vlora's infantry finally came over the hill to make camp, organize the prisoners, dispose of the dead, and secure the keelboats and the stone pedestal that had been the focus of all this effort.

Vlora slept fitfully that night and was up early, heading down to the river's edge with Davd in tow. The ground still smoldered from Nila's sorcery, but at least the corpses were cleaned up—one of her brigades had spent most of the night transporting the bodies downriver a mile and burning them all so that they wouldn't spread disease as her own soldiers dug into the position.

"What's this bridge called?" she asked Davd, leaving the river-bank and gaining the stone bridge, where early-rising infantry were in the midst of moving aside all of the engineering equipment so that they could use the whole span.

"Ferrymore, I believe," Davd told her. "Sight of an old ferry. The bridge is relatively new."

"And well made." Vlora kicked a stone. No wonder Burt's irregulars hadn't destroyed it. They probably had no way of doing so. She walked across the bridge, returning salutes from her soldiers, and descended to the opposite bank, where she found that the keelboat containing their prize had been lashed to the opposite bank. She spotted Nila's colorful dress moving around the side of the pedestal and Bo standing on the bank with a number of Dynize prisoners. Vlora joined him.

"Who are these?" she asked.

Bo took a step away from the prisoners. "Officers," he reported. "Their general died in the melee, but we have a colonel and three majors. I'm trying to find out what the bloody pit this stone is for."

"Burt thought it was a pedestal."

"Yes, and he might be right. But... might also be wrong."

"What else could it be used for?"

He shrugged. "Not a goddamned clue. Nila was up all night trying to get something out of it by lamplight."

"Are these any help?" Vlora jerked her chin at the prisoners. Three men and a woman, all of them staring at their feet in dejection. They'd been disarmed but were not bound, though a rifleman with fixed bayonet had been assigned to watch each of them.

"Remember how Etepali told you that every army has their own orders?"

"Yes?"

"Seems that Sedial takes the old 'Don't let one hand know what the other is doing' approach very seriously. Not only are the officers in the dark, but it turns out they didn't even know where they were going until they got to Yellow Creek. Once there, they dug this thing out of the mountainside and were told to get it back to Landfall. No other information."

"Who was giving the orders?"

"The Privileged that Burt's irregulars killed in their ambush."

"Ah." Vlora made a sour face.

"Turns out that they did have a bone-eye with them, too, yesterday."

Vlora stiffened. "Neither you nor the powder mages noticed?"

"Nope. He wasn't very powerful, and apparently he killed himself rather than be taken prisoner."

Vlora threw her arms up. "Have we just stumbled across Sedial's most devoted blind followers?"

"We might have at that," Bo said seriously.

"Pit on a stick. Where is Burt?"

"Probably still sleeping."

"Have you been up all night, too?"

Bo nodded. "Baggage train is just arriving. We don't even have our tent yet."

"Well, see if you can get anything else out of them. Oh, and do me a favor."

"Yes?"

"Make sure no one tells Delia a damned thing about this stone."

"Done."

"Thanks." Vlora turned and, with a deep breath, boarded the keelboat with the pedestal. As she'd expected, she felt nothing from the stone. No dread, no sorcerous aura, not even a sense of preternatural foreboding. It was just a cut rock. She had been wrong about one thing—up this close, she could clearly see that the stone was covered in script and symbols that, unless her memory was playing tricks on her, matched quite well with those on the godstone.

She rounded the end of the stone and crossed to the other side, where she found Nila squatting beside some writing, her lips pressed into a firm line, eyes narrowed. "Shouldn't Prime Lektor be here?" Vlora asked.

"He was with the baggage train last night," Nila answered without looking up. "I've sent someone to fetch him, and if he's not here in an hour, I'll go myself."

Vlora snorted. Nila was wildly powerful, but the fact that she was so dismissive of one of the ancient Predeii pushed past amusing and bordered on madness. Was Nila stronger than even *she* let on? Or did Prime's inactivity just bother her that much? "Anything yet?" Vlora asked.

"Not a bit." Nila pressed her palm against the stone and shook her head. "I haven't actually seen a complete godstone yet, but this piece here is entirely unlike the capstone we have with the fleet. They're made of the same material and they're covered with the same writing, but unlike the capstone, this is entirely inert. Not even an inkling of sorcery coming off it."

"Burt claimed it was writhing with dark sorcery."

"Perhaps. It might have gone dormant somehow. Or whoever had given him that report was overreacting. I won't know for sure until I've had more time to study it."

Vlora frowned, wondering if she'd made an enormous mistake. This quick march from the coast had cost them lives, time, positioning, and easy contact with her fleet. She had three field armies bearing down on her. Had she done all of this for a piece of rock that held, at the end of the day, no importance? She couldn't believe it. No, Sedial had sent his soldiers to retrieve it for a reason. Now it was her task to find out why.

She watched Nila's examination and was just about to head back across the river to check in with her general staff when she caught sight of Prime Lektor walking slowly over the bridge toward her. "Speak of him and he shall appear," she muttered.

Nila snorted and still didn't look up.

Prime paused on the bank just off the bridge, examining the pedestal with a sour look. He avoided Vlora's gaze and seemed to be avoiding even *looking* at Nila. He was rooted in place, and even when Vlora gestured for him to join them, he didn't respond. Irritated, Vlora left the keelboat and went to him.

"What is your problem?" she demanded.

The Predeii started. "What do you mean?"

"Why are you standing here with a constipated look on your face? Nila and Bo have been at this thing all night."

"I'm sure they're doing a fine job," he said.

"And I'm sure the only reason we brought you with us is to figure out what the pit this is and why the Dynize want it."

Prime turned his face toward Vlora, but his gaze remained locked on the stone slab. He didn't answer.

"Why are you avoiding it?" she demanded.

His attention finally shifted to her, and his tone took on an imperious note that she associated more with that of an ancient sorcerer. "I would like to remind you who I am and that your friend Taniel is no longer here. I will not be bullied and disrespected."

Vlora resisted the urge to back down. Prime was immensely powerful, it was true, but she just couldn't bring herself to care. She couldn't afford to. Either he was a threat that could destroy them all, or he wasn't. And she suspected that despite his willingness to kill her back at Yellow Creek, he didn't have the nerve to make a move against four powder mages, two Privileged, and a whole field army. "Why are you afraid of Nila?" she asked.

Prime's expression visibly tightened.

"Is she stronger than you?" Vlora pushed.

"No," Prime said confidently. "She is not."

"Then why are you afraid?"

"I'm not..." He trailed off, then gave a frustrated huff. "She doesn't need gloves."

"Is that scary?"

"No gloves to touch the Else. That is unheard of outside of the gods themselves. Combine that with her considerable strength, and yes, she is terrifying. But not personally. Not for the reasons you think."

"Then for what reasons?"

Prime fixed her with a serious consideration. "Because it means that sorcery is continuing to evolve. It means that things are changing again. She might be an aberration, or she might be the beginning of a new pattern."

"You mean that Privileged won't need gloves in the future?" That was, Vlora admitted silently, a little terrifying. Their need for gloves was one of their biggest weaknesses.

"It won't be immediate. I suspect that if this is an evolution, it will take hundreds of years." Prime fell into a contemplative silence, then drew his own gloves out of his pockets and tugged them on. "Yes, I've been avoiding this. I don't know what it is, and that also scares me. I sense nothing from it, but it very clearly matches the godstone. My lack of knowledge—as in the case of your friend Nila—terrifies me. But I'm here now, so I might as well get to it." Once his gloves were on, he made a shooing gesture. "Let us work, Vlora. We'll tell you what we can, when we can. In the meantime, I expect you have a very large battle to prepare for."

CHAPTER 49

Styke stood in the hallway just outside the Quorum Hall in his dress uniform, trying not to look as annoyed as he felt. His feet and back hurt from standing for hours, and his head ached from trying to listen to the proceedings as voices echoed out of the hall and arguments often stumbled over one another, becoming difficult to keep up with for a nonnative speaker.

Etzi had assured him that his presence wasn't necessary, but Styke had felt it his duty to attend these last three days since Zak's execution. He had many reasons: the hope that he could keep any more of his men from being dragged in to be used as pawns; to get out of the compound; even as a sort of penance for being unable to prevent Zak's death.

For these three days, Styke had barely slept. His mind raced. His knife hand twitched. The world felt on the edge of disaster, and he wasn't even allowed to speak to the rest of his Lancers. He wondered where Jackal had gotten to—if he'd managed to locate

Ibana—and when or if he'd return. Styke stared at his big skull ring, twirling it absently.

In the Quorum Hall, Etzi thundered on. Etzi was in a fury—he spoke passionately about the need for oversight of the emperor's tools, for the reduction of Ka-Sedial's local power, and for the legal loopholes that allowed the bone-eyes to operate with impunity. Occasionally one of his allies would join in, adding that they needed better representation of the provinces or pointing out that the emperor hadn't done his customary tour of the empire for two whole years.

It was these latter arguments that really began to impress Styke with how big Dynize really was. He'd seen it on a map of the world, of course, but his entire experience had been limited to the eastern coast—and just a tiny sliver of that. Dynize was as big as the Nine, and though the people shared a common racial identity, it became clear that they were much divided. Of thirty total provinces, four in the west were already in open revolt after having their resources stripped by Ka-Sedial to fund the Fatrastan War. Another seven had sent envoys to the capital to request that Ka-Sedial be forced into retirement.

This was, as Etzi had put it, a powder keg. He hoped to control it. Styke was beginning to think that getting out of the capital and waiting for it to blow up might be his best option—but he had no idea how to do so.

One thing at a time, he reminded himself as he listened to one of Etzi's enemies rail against the "weak-willed mice" that would see the empire crumble. He recognized that rhetoric well. It was used by politicians and their financiers when they stood to gain from the continuation of conflict. It was the same rhetoric Lindet had used to silence her enemies just after the revolution—though she had used it to justify the formation of the secret police rather than continue a foreign war.

Ka-Sedial and his allies, Styke realized, needed this war to tighten their power. The emperor was either their puppet or he was impotent. Styke couldn't help but wonder how long until, like Lindet and her Blackhats, Ka-Sedial turned the knives against his internal enemies.

As soon as the war was won, he imagined.

His thoughts were cut off when the impassioned speeches gave way to the quiet roar of hundreds of people breaking out in small discussions. Styke turned to see Etzi emerge from the Quorum Hall. Etzi walked with purpose, his head up and face flushed, looking like a man who could see some sort of victory on the horizon, but when he got closer, Styke noted the small signs of exhaustion—the crow's feet, the drooping shoulders, the deep, slow breaths.

Etzi scowled as he approached. "I've asked them to bring you a chair every day for three days." He glanced over his shoulder. "They refuse to do it. What kind of petty..."

Styke waved it off. "How are the debates going?"

"Well, I think," Etzi said, running a hand through his hair and then straightening his formal tunic. "The debates themselves are." He shrugged, as if to say *only slightly more than unimportant.* "It's these moments of discussion that are important. We have a ten-minute recess for toilet and refreshment, but most everyone will remain in the Hall discussing the debates, forging deals, strengthening alliances—or preparing to break them."

"I'm not experienced in politics, but doesn't all of that happen in private?" Styke had been to plenty of Lindet's parties during the war, and he'd been keen enough to realize that's where all the important dealing happened.

"Yes," Etzi confirmed, "but the groundwork for them will be laid here. A glance, a gesture, a few token words—they're all just preparations for later meetings. This evening will be a busy one. The Quorum has spent the last few days trying to decide how they feel about your man's execution."

Styke forced himself to contain his anger at the fresh wound. "I haven't even heard my name spoken, let alone the event discussed."

"Formally?" Etzi asked, shaking his head. "Of course not. No one wants to be on the record directly addressing the emperor's justice. But we'll talk about overreach and Sedial's position of power."

"So it's all between the lines?"

"And in private, yes."

"So..." Styke ground his teeth. "What does everyone think?"

Etzi cleared his throat, avoiding Styke's gaze. "Everyone thinks that Ji-Patten was within his rights to execute a foreigner convicted of murder."

"I—" Styke began angrily.

Etzi cut him off. "However, they're not stupid. Everyone, even Sedial's allies, acknowledge that the judgment was less than legitimate and the execution of the sentence rushed. Ji-Patten made that obvious when he tried to provoke you after the fact."

Styke rubbed his chin. He could still feel the sting of the slap, and the spot on his chest that Ji-Patten had full-on punched had developed into a bruise that looked like he'd been kicked by a mule. "Are they going to do anything about it?"

"Actively? They can't. But it has convinced several of the unaligned Households that Sedial is out of control."

"That's not good enough." Styke could hear the anger in his voice, tried to rein it in, and did not succeed.

To his surprise, Etzi smirked.

"What?" Styke demanded.

"It's..." Etzi tilted his head, as if considering his words. "Ji-Patten struck you. Three times."

"So?"

"And you laughed at him. Belittled him. Any other time they might have taken that as an insult against the emperor, but considering the current climate, the fact that you spat in the face of a dragonman has garnered you quite the following."

"In the Hall?" Styke asked in confusion. He had done his best to hold on to his anger but had still expected the political fallout to go poorly for him.

"In the Hall. In the public. Word leaked. Those roving mobs that have been killing foreigners and some of my men? One of them was attacked by another band this morning. They tore each other to shreds. I don't have any interest in mobs of any kind wandering the capital, but it gives me a distinct amount of pleasure to hear that the common people won't just lie down for Sedial's paid thugs."

"You're certain those mobs are paid thugs and not just angry citizens?"

Etzi gave a small but confident nod. "It was leaked from Sedial's Household. One of his cupbearers has been arming and paying unemployed citizens to attack foreign slaves. An ally of mine is going to gather witnesses and prepare a suit against the cupbearer for inciting insurrection."

Styke bit his tongue, cutting off an outburst about lawsuits, lawyers, and politicians. Etzi had made it very clear that he and his allies didn't want to reignite the civil war—that their intention was to use the law to destroy Sedial's power base. But Styke had followed this kind of naivety in the newspapers during his own sister's rise to power. She had won because she had kept her enemies engaged with lawyers of her own, and all while conducting an operation of blackmail, spying, and violence on the sly.

If Sedial was anything like Lindet, he wouldn't allow Etzi's long game to continue for enough time to actually do real damage. Though, to be fair, Sedial was on a whole different continent and distracted by a war. Maybe, Styke allowed himself to hope, just maybe Etzi's people could play this game through to the end.

Etzi reached up and patted Styke on the shoulder. "Don't worry, my friend. Sedial is losing the unaligned Households. The winds are shifting. My mother and your man will be avenged."

"Will they?" Styke asked quietly.

"I promise." With that, Etzi gave a nod to himself and then turned to head back inside the Quorum Hall.

Styke sagged against the wall, watching him go. He had no doubt that Etzi was on his side—though he still wasn't sure he wouldn't be thrown under the turnip cart if push came to shove. His fear was that Etzi would lose.

Styke considered what Valyaine had told him back in Bellport. About how the Mad Lancers had been monsters, using the war to sate their base desires. The words rang truer the more Styke thought about them, but he also knew that without her own monsters, Fatrasta would never have won the war against a bigger, meaner nation. He was a necessary evil.

Etzi didn't have that necessary evil. He didn't want it, didn't think he needed it. But Styke had his own agenda, his own vengeance to be had.

A small group emerged from the Quorum Hall, and Styke looked up at them coolly. It was Ji-Patten, escorted by four of his black-clad soldiers. Styke resisted the urge to reach for his knife. They marched down the center of the hallway, and it became clear that they weren't going to acknowledge Styke's presence.

"You ever heard of a dragonman by the name of Ji-Kushel?" Styke asked in Dynize.

Ji-Patten took several more steps before slowing. He gestured to his men, who came to a stop around him.

"Ask one of your boss's puppets what I did to Ji-Kushel. Then ask him what I did to the dragonmen who he sent to avenge Ji-Kushel. Ask him why he hates me so much."

"Wait for me outside." The order came in a clipped, emotionless tone. Ji-Patten's escort responded without hesitation, marching on to leave him and Styke alone in the hallway. Once they'd gone, Ji-Patten turned toward Styke. "What did you do to Ji-Kushel?"

"We dueled."

Ji-Patten's nostrils flared.

Styke continued, "It took me all day to clean his brains out of my ring. Sedial dug up Orz and five other disgraced dragonmen and sent them after me. I killed two of them. The rest died fighting my people." He leaned forward. "You're not special."

"We have the blessings of the bone-eyes."

"Little good it did any of you. Sedial doesn't just hate me. He fears me. He fears anything stronger than one of his precious dragonmen."

Ji-Patten stiffened. "You're not stronger than a dragonman."

"I've got three notches on my knife that say otherwise," Styke told him. "Ask Sedial. Or one of his puppets, or however the pit you communicate with him."

"You're trying to provoke me."

"What? Like that weak slap you gave me the other day?" Styke gave him a toothy grin, trying to make sure it looked insolent rather than leaking out the pure rage inside him. He didn't want to give Ji-Patten the satisfaction of knowing how close he'd come to succeeding. "No. I've been told that you don't duel here in Dynize, so there's no point in provoking you. Didn't bother Ji-Kushel, but I guess he was on another continent." Styke shrugged. "I'm just letting you know that Sedial is trying to cover for your brotherhood. He tried to avenge their honor and only made things worse."

He saw a flicker in Ji-Patten's eyes, but the dragonman didn't betray anything else. They stared at each other for several moments, until the quiet roar of discussion in the Quorum Hall subsided and Etzi began another long, passionate speech.

"Your men are waiting for you," Styke said, jerking his head toward the exit. "Be a good dog and go terrorize whoever else Sedial doesn't like."

Ji-Patten snorted, then pivoted on one foot and headed for the exit without a word. Styke didn't bother watching him leave. He let his head fall back against the wall, feeling the tension in his own shoulders and letting out a deep breath. He would have to wait a few more hours until Etzi finished with the Quorum for the day. But he wouldn't need to come back tomorrow.

His message had been delivered.

CHAPTER 50

Michel worked his way along the back of a crowd in Upper Landfall. He was surprised at the size of it—thousands of people, mostly Palo, waving signs and shouting slogans. They took up the entire center of the square, with even more marching in a continuous circle around them. Everyone was angry, and he couldn't help but feel a confused mix of pride, guilt, and terror.

Pride because he'd organized the anger behind this protest. Guilt because he knew that eventually people were going to get hurt.

And terrified because the Sons of the Red Hand had nothing to do with this gathering. The anger that he'd stirred up by having Survivor tell his story around the Depths had taken on a mind of its own. He'd nudged community leaders, conducted an enormous propaganda campaign, and paid hundreds of gossips to spread the word, but this...this wasn't him. He could feel the vibrato of the furious crowd deep in his chest. He could sense the impending violence.

The protest was, if he wasn't mistaken, occurring in the very same public square where the Blackhats executed the decoy Mama Palo earlier in the year. He wondered if that had been planned, or if this was some kind of coincidence. He wondered if anyone even remembered the poor old woman.

He continued to stay near the edges of the mob, but made his way toward the bandstands set up to one side of the square. A few dozen Palo were already on them, speaking among themselves or shouting back and forth to whip up the crowd. Michel recognized many of them as prominent speakers, activists, and leaders of the Palo community. None of them were as rich or powerful as Meln-Dun had been before his fall, but they were still a force to be reckoned with.

Once Michel had found himself a good spot to listen to the speeches, he craned his head toward the nearby streets. Stone-faced Dynize soldiers were already gathered in tight knots on the roads or positioned on the rooftops. Their muskets were still shouldered, but Michel knew how quickly that would change. He hoped that nothing here turned violent and rethought his own positioning in the crowd.

Better to not be able to hear very well but have a clean exit than to get caught up in a stampede if this got nasty.

He repositioned himself near a wide alley just as a shush went through the crowd. One of the men on the bandstand approached the podium. He clutched a speech in one hand and waved with the other, looking out over the assembled masses with a stern visage.

He introduced himself as Horiallen, and Michel remembered that he owned a mill that provided most of the grain to Greenfire Depths. Jiniel had met with him two days ago.

"My friends!" he began. "Thank you for joining me here today, for a show of solidarity." There was a cheer that quickly died out. "We've gathered as a people to ask questions of the new rulers of Landfall—to demand answers." He pointed at a particularly prominent group of mounted Dynize soldiers watching from nearby.

"Vicious rumors are being spread about our new overlords. These whispers are almost too horrible for me to mention, but I know for a fact that we've all heard them by now. Rumors about Dynize sorcery. Rumors about blood sacrifice!" His voice rose to a fever pitch. The crowd grumbled, people shifting about angrily.

"We want to know if these rumors are true! We want to know who will pay for the blood of our children and our grandparents!"

The grumbling grew louder. Shouts of agreement rose from the crowd. Michel looked around nervously and took a few steps back. The tension was thick enough to chew on, and it wouldn't be long before some damned fools tried to vent their anger on the watching Dynize soldiers. He swore under his breath, but the word caught in his throat as someone suddenly clutched him by the wrist.

He spun, his other hand digging into his pocket for his knuckle-dusters, only to find himself face-to-face with Tenik. His eyes darted around, looking for some sign of an ambush, but it quickly became apparent that Tenik was alone. It was also apparent, for anyone who looked under the hat that Tenik had pulled down over his face, that he was a Dynize in a sea of angry Palo.

"What are you doing here?" Michel asked, taking a step back to stand beside Tenik.

"Looking for you." Tenik replied in Adran but spoke in a low voice, clearly conscious of his accent. He let go of Michel's wrist and leaned heavily on his cane.

"This is not a good place for you," Michel warned.

"I'm just figuring that out. I feel like we're on the edge of a damned riot. Is this your doing?"

"In part. But I don't have any control of it anymore." Someone nearby scowled at Tenik. Michel took him by the shoulder and steered him through the crowd. "Keep moving. We don't want anyone to notice what you are. Pit, if you need to talk, we probably should get out of here."

"We *definitely* should get out of here."

"Palo making you nervous?" Michel asked lightly.

"Yes. *And* Sedial has sent four hundred cudgel-armed thugs to disperse the crowd. It's going to get really bad really fast. If I hadn't found you just now, I would have left myself."

"Shit." Michel turned, steering them back toward the alley he'd picked out as his escape route earlier. The crowd cheered at the speaker, drowning out whatever it was that Tenik said next. It took them a couple of minutes, but they soon broke through the marchers and headed into the alley. They were just turning the corner when Michel caught sight of a greater number of Dynize soldiers arriving on horseback at the other end of the square. "Just in time," he muttered.

Michel and Tenik emerged onto the next street. It was still crowded here, with people trying to hear what was going on in the square, but they were able to walk without shoving their way through the press. He heard a loud voice echoing behind him, as if amplified by sorcery, telling the crowd to disperse. An angry roar answered it.

"Faster," Michel said, offering Tenik his arm. Tenik took it and limped along quickly as they made their escape. The angry shouts of the crowd were soon interspersed with screams. A ripple of fear went down the street. A few people began running toward the sounds. More began running away.

They managed to find a safe place out of the way in a burned-out building on the rim of Greenfire Depths. Tenik sank down to the ground, breathing heavily, one hand on his damaged leg and a grimace on his face. Michel listened to the distant sounds of the chaos. No gunshots so far. That was good, at least. "The damned fools."

"Who? The people protesting or the ones who showed up to deal with it?"

Michel looked down at Tenik and said, "Both. The protesters should have held their march down in the Depths, where they'd be less likely to be interfered with. And the Dynize…" Michel spat. "They're just going to make things worse."

"What do you expect them to do?" Tenik asked. The question came across as petulant. The protest had clearly shaken him, even if he hadn't already been inclined to side with his countrymen.

Michel didn't answer the question. He offered Tenik a hand, pulling him back to his feet. "This rumor going around about the street children and blood sacrifices. Is it true?" Tenik asked.

"What do you think?" Michel glanced at his friend sidelong.

Tenik shifted uncomfortably from his good leg to his bad one and back again. "I can't say I'd be surprised."

"It's true."

"You're sure?"

Michel nodded.

Tenik rambled off a number of curses in Dynize. "How does Sedial hope to contain this? The arrogant piece of shit, he…" His voice began to rise, but he seemed to catch himself. He turned to Michel. "Once again, the Yaret Household is in your debt."

Michel frowned. "In what way?"

"The very night that you warned us about the purge orders, they came for Yaret."

"An assassination attempt?"

"A squad of six of them. We had already tripled our guard, and yet they still killed nine of us and wounded that number again. Yaret barely escaped with his life." Tenik bit his lip so hard that it drew blood. "Sedial tried to kill my master, Michel! If you hadn't warned us, he would have succeeded. If he had sent a couple of dragonmen, my entire Household would already be dead."

Michel felt the thrill of Tenik's anger and tried not to let himself get swept up in it. "You're sure they were Sedial's men?"

"We identified two of them. More than enough to be certain."

"I thought the whole point of the purge order was so he could legally sic his soldiers on you."

Tenik winced. "It is. But those purge orders were specifically prepared by the emperor. Your theft of them meant that Sedial couldn't just march the army into the city. So he resorted to assassins, and he moved up his timeline. No doubt fearful that the orders might end up in someone else's hands." Tenik took an unsteady breath. "If not for your interference, we would all be dead."

"You can thank a light-fingered maid," Michel replied. He ran his hands through his hair and began to pace. The roar of an angry crowd had died down now, replaced by more screaming. Even many blocks away, he could see people rushing back and forth out in the street.

"Sedial's trying not to kill anyone," Tenik explained, gesturing back toward the square. "He's not a fool. He's hoping that a few hundred beatings might send the message for the Palo not to ask too many questions."

Michel wondered if it would work. Perhaps. The Palo had been cowed before by Kressians, and then by Lindet. They could be cowed again. But they'd had a taste of real freedom under the Dynize. He wondered if they'd let that go.

"They're going to try again."

Michel turned his attention back to Tenik. "The assassins?"

"Doubtlessly. Sedial does not give up, and he's already moving forward. Three major Household heads have been found dead in the last three days. One of the killings was definitely an assassination. The other two were made up to look like a mugging and an accident, respectively."

"Do your people believe it?"

"Some of them," Tenik admitted. "Some of Sedial's allies will no doubt be in on it. There are plenty of good people on his side— people who'd never back him if they knew for certain what he was up to—but they also believe anything he says. A lot of bodies would have to pile up before they believed that this was really a purge."

"So they're as bad as any one of his other allies."

"For now, yes. Yaret is reaching out quietly, trying to rally some opposition and inject doubt into the more honorable members of Sedial's inner circle. I don't know if it will help." Tenik leaned over to rub his leg and wound up bent over, limp, his eyes shut. Michel could see the hopelessness in Tenik's body language: He probably believed he was already dead.

"Is there really nothing Yaret can do to defend himself?"

"If Sedial wants us dead, he will have us dead," Tenik answered. "That doesn't mean we won't fight back, but..." He trailed off for a moment. "Yaret's cousin is one of our most celebrated generals. She's in charge of a field army up north, chasing after Lady Flint. We've sent word to her about the assassination attempt. She's our closest ally, but I'm not sure if there's anything she can do to help us short of marching her entire army down here to demand that Sedial stop the purge. And I don't think she's going to do that."

"What if I can buy you more time?" Michel asked, a thought beginning to form in his head.

Tenik looked up sharply. "How?"

"I'm not completely sure. But I might be able to hide you—to give you time to negotiate, or rally Sedial's enemies, or just wait out the purge until you can escape to Yaret's cousin."

Tenik snorted. "That's impossible. You'd have to hide several hundred immediate Household members. Maybe more, if we pull some of our military officers out of the infantry. The rest are too low-ranking to require protection—Sedial won't bother assassinating them—but hundreds of people. Where could you possibly put us?"

Michel stifled a smile. Tenik was in such deep despair that he couldn't see the answer hiding literally right under his nose. "Are the Yaret Household still the only ones who have all the maps of the catacombs?"

"What maps you didn't steal when you—" A wave of shock

swept across Tenik's face, followed by a gasp of relief. "Damn you, Michel. How the pit did I not see that?" He stood up straight, like he'd been animated by some new strength. "Those catacombs are endless. We could disappear without Sedial even noticing, and even if he did, we could hold out in there for weeks. He'd have to send Privileged in to find us, and he doesn't have any to spare." He began to pace, leaning heavily on his cane, talking quickly. "We'd need to pack up our valuables. Take food, bedding, lanterns, rope. Spread everyone out to avoid the bad air. It'll take planning and logistics, but we could do it. There's an entrance not far from the Household. We could all disappear within days."

"I can lend a little help for the logistics," Michel offered, though he knew that Jiniel would slap him if she heard him say so. The Sons of the Red Hand already had way too much work for their existing plans. They couldn't afford to take in hundreds of strays. But he was already working through the argument he'd give to her lieutenants: allies among the Dynize. A bona fide source of intelligence, straight from the Minister of Scrolls. Adding kindling to a budding Dynize civil war.

And, it would let him save some friends that he desperately wanted to help.

He pulled out a scrap of paper and a nub of pencil. "Send two of your most trusted people to this address," he said, scribbling. "We can coordinate getting your people off the streets and well hidden. We might even put some of them in the Depths. I'll see what we can spare in supplies."

Tenik took the paper, but a sudden reservation crossed his face.

"What is it?" Michel asked.

"You . . . you don't have to do this."

"I know."

"But you're doing it anyway. I didn't ask for help. Yaret sent me to do so, and I was getting around to it, but I hadn't actually asked."

"I don't need to make you ask," Michel said reassuringly. He reached out, patting Tenik on the shoulder. "Like I told you before. I'm a spy, not a monster."

"But..."

"You were—you are—my friend, Tenik. Yaret was, for a small moment, my master, and a good one. I don't need to abandon that."

Tenik stared at the scrap of paper, then finally met Michel's gaze. "Thank you."

"It's not often I have things I can offer other people," Michel said. "It's kind of nice to be able to help."

Tenik suddenly pulled him into an embrace, squeezing him hard before hurrying back toward the street and falling into the flow of the crowd. Michel stood still for a few minutes, listening to the sounds of the city. The screaming had all but died down now. He could still hear the occasional rough shout of a soldier. Somewhere nearby, a window shattered. "How long have you been standing there?" he asked.

Ichtracia emerged from the shadows of a brick building just around the corner from where Tenik had been standing. She pursed her lips and looked toward the street. "I followed the two of you from the protest."

"And you didn't want to announce yourself?" Michel should have been mad, but he was mostly bemused. He was actually a little proud of her—staying silent, listening in on a conversation, sneaking about; she was becoming a better spy every day.

"I was curious what you'd talk about. Also I wanted to make sure that Tenik wasn't trying to lead you into some kind of trap. Do you trust him?"

"I do," Michel replied. "But I'm also going to check with Emerald and try to verify his claims. The last thing I need is to be suckered into helping them only to find out that Yaret or Tenik have been turned into puppets by Sedial."

"Be careful."

"I will," Michel promised. "Thank you for watching out for me again."

She smirked at him. "How did you know I was around the corner?"

"I could see your shadow."

She looked back to her hiding spot and rolled her eyes. "Damn it. I thought I'd done so well, too. How did you know it was me and not someone else?"

"You have a, uh, particular shape. Even your shadow."

Ichtracia snorted. "Right. I'll have to remember that. You think that protest has died down?"

"Sounds like Sedial's thugs are still chasing people off. But I'm guessing we're far enough away that we'll be fine."

"Good." She fiddled with her vest pockets where she kept her hidden Privileged gloves. "Let's go find something to eat. Spycraft makes me hungry."

CHAPTER 51

Vlora was more than a little surprised to get a visit from Delia Snowbound in the middle of the afternoon. It was the third day since they had arrived at the Hadshaw River and crushed the Dynize there, and Vlora was hiding from the worst of the afternoon heat in her tent by the river. Tamas's journal lay open beside her, forgotten in a flurry of reports and her own strategic planning. Norrine announced Delia, and Vlora, startled by the suddenness of it, forgot to pretend that she wasn't around.

Delia swept the tent flap aside and stepped in, turning her head quickly to take in Vlora's residence as if inspecting the lair of some great beast. She gave Vlora a brisk nod and clasped her hands behind her back, standing formally just inside the flap.

Vlora blinked at her, pulling her own thoughts out of her plans and then clearing away several of her maps and notes from her spare chair. "Lady Snowbound. This is unexpected. Please have a seat."

Delia glanced at the chair as if it were a scorpion. She gave Vlora a grimace that was probably supposed to be a smile, then crossed the tent in a few overly brisk steps and sank into the offered seat. She put her hands on her knees, raised her chin, and looked around at everything except at Vlora herself.

Vlora took a deep breath. "What can I do for you?"

"Lady Flint. I wanted to let you know how the negotiations are going."

"Oh?" Vlora had last gotten an update from Sabastenien yesterday morning. Unless she was mistaken, Delia had more meetings this morning and she expected to hear Sabastenien's opinion of them later tonight. She didn't bother to cut Delia off, though. It would be interesting to hear her version of events.

"You've put me in quite the pickle."

Vlora pursed her lips and braced herself for a lecture.

Delia continued. "We have three armies bearing down on us, and they have finally received orders from Landfall on how to deal with us. While they *do* have room to negotiate, it seems the three generals are in agreement that they don't actually *need* to negotiate. They feel their armies are more than enough to deal with our one. They'd rather try their luck at a battle than give up anything."

"That does sound like the Dynize I've gotten used to dealing with."

"That's why I'm here." Delia took a deep breath, looking around nervously again before finally seeming to relax into her seat with a frustrated sigh. "We need to talk strategy. Whatever hate exists between us needs to be set aside so we can discuss our situation frankly."

"I'm not the one with all the hate." The words slipped out before Vlora could rethink them.

"Because it wasn't your family who was slaughtered," Delia snapped. She visibly wrestled control of herself and her tone returned to normal. "Yes, I hate you. I hate your family. I hate everyone who helped Tamas in his bloody coup. But I'm not a fool. We are in a dire situation and I need your help resolving it."

Vlora didn't let herself rise to the bait. *Tamas is dead*, she wanted to say. *Besides, your parents were a part of the old system that had to die.* Instead, she plastered a neutral expression on her face. "Go on."

"As I said, the Dynize do not believe they need to negotiate. I have given them generous terms and reminded them that furthering this conflict increases the chances of the Nine getting involved. They don't seem to be all that worried about the latter—it would take the better part of a year for anyone to raise an army and then sail it here, after all, and the Dynize seem to think all of this will be wrapped up by then."

"What do *you* think?" Vlora asked.

"I think they're mad. Whatever crimes were committed by the general staff and Magus Borbador to get us involved... well, those will be dealt with later. And whatever I think about the Adran Army's role in the coup, you are still the best in the world. They should be treading lightly around us. Instead they are preparing to attack."

Vlora stiffened. Her last report put all three of the Dynize armies holding about five miles away from the river, arrayed in a semicircle. She had a few companies down to their south to keep the Dynize from fording the river for a flanking action, but otherwise there'd been no conflict. "You're sure?"

"I'm dealing with generals right now instead of politicians, and they are not good at concealing their intentions. If they wanted a deal, they'd be negotiating more aggressively. But they aren't."

"What, exactly, are they asking for?"

Delia pursed her lips. "They want your head, for starters."

"I see." Vlora sighed. This again. Sedial's petty idiocy.

"As much as I'd enjoy handing it over, I have neither the authority to do such a thing nor, in the end, would I. You are an Adran citizen."

"Thank you."

"Don't thank me. I'm just doing my job." Delia tapped one finger against her knee. "They're also asking for complete disarmament. They want us to hand over everything more dangerous than a bread knife, march straight back to our fleet, and depart for Adro without looking back. Personally, I think we're in a better position than that. The fleet still commands the waters on this side of Fatrasta and despite our numerical inferiority, we are the Adran Army."

It amused Vlora to hear Delia express so much confidence in her soldiers, and Vlora found a tiny part of her warming to the woman. She quashed that warmth. *Always be on the lookout for a trap from a person like this.* "Your assessment goes along the same lines as mine," Vlora said slowly.

"I thought as much. But even so, I need to ask you directly: If we are beset upon by these three armies, do we have any hope of winning?"

Direct and to the point. Vlora leaned back in her chair, puffing out her cheeks and letting out a long, thoughtful breath. She looked around at her mess of a tent. Notes and maps everywhere, a dozen different plans of battle sketched out as well as a dozen contingencies for each of them. So much preparation time was a luxury she hadn't had for months, but the Dynize were treating her carefully now and taking the time to make their own plans. She grimaced.

"This is not a fight I want," Vlora said.

"You can't win?"

"I didn't say that. I just said that I don't want to fight it," Vlora said. "We *can* win. We've beaten worse odds before."

"Against the Kez, who didn't have blood sorcerers."

"Blood sorcerers die just as easily as Privileged, and I still have my powder mages," Vlora said. "The bone-eyes don't concern me. The numbers do, but we have our backs to the river and several hundred keelboats that allow us to ferry men quickly. We control the only bridge for tens of miles. Our guns are now on the hillside behind us, putting them out of enemy reach but in position to blast their own artillery to pit should they attempt to bring it forward. And at the end of the day, both our infantry and our cavalry are better than theirs."

Delia sat in silence, absorbing the information. After a few moments, she said, "You didn't mention Nila and Bo."

"They'll have their hands full of the enemy Privileged for the beginning of the battle. But once my powder mages have neutralized them..."

"Nila's fire."

"Nila's fire," Vlora confirmed. "The Dynize still haven't figured out just how big of a gap there is between their combat abilities and our own. Powder mages are too powerful a trump card, and they don't want to accept that." She paused, considering General Etepali. The old woman had shown more freethinking and wiliness than her allies, but she had yet to live up to the reputation she'd claimed upon their first meeting. Either she had exaggerated her own abilities or she still had tricks up her sleeve. Vlora wasn't looking forward to finding out.

"But you said you don't want to fight," Delia said.

"I did. Because whatever happens, I will lose a great many soldiers. I care about my soldiers."

"You think the losses will be worth the victory?"

Vlora clenched her teeth. This conversation had revealed something, and she suddenly put her finger on it. Delia was still negotiating as if this were a regular war. She didn't understand the severity of what they were fighting for. "Any losses are worth it, Lady Snowbound. If the Dynize are able to create a new god, they won't just win this war. They will reign supreme over the entire hemisphere. They will cause upheaval that reaches the Nine and beyond."

Delia gazed back at Vlora, and it was in this gaze that Vlora began to suspect that Delia wasn't ignorant of this—she simply didn't believe it. Vlora opened her mouth to continue, but shut it again. Delia hadn't met Kresimir. She hadn't experienced the beginning of this current war. She had no context to put this in except for simple politics. Vlora found herself suddenly terrified.

She didn't want a dogmatic believer. Those tended to be dangerous in their own right. But she *did* want someone who would take her at her word, and Delia's silence told her that she thought Vlora was a fool. A healthy dose of helplessness joined her terror. She resisted the urge to argue. She didn't have the time or the energy. All she could do was attempt to steer Delia using her own methods.

"Are you going to attack them?" Delia asked suddenly.

Vlora hesitated. It wasn't that she didn't trust Delia, but Vlora didn't want her to know all of her plans. "I'm going to play this defensively. If I do, we can win. I agree with you that the Dynize terms are unacceptable."

"Good." The word was clipped, final. Delia stood up and gave Vlora that same grimace-like smile. "That is what I needed to know. I will suspend negotiations until after the battle. If we can defeat them when outnumbered three against one, I suspect they will be on the verge of giving us anything we want."

Vlora waited until Delia was gone to let out a scoff of disbelief. This was pure, sharklike politics. Nothing more, nothing less. A tiny part of Vlora could respect that. Envy it, even. But there wasn't room here for playing politics. If she won this coming fight, she'd give Delia the ammunition to end the war on whatever terms she wanted. And if she didn't win...well, they'd all be dead anyway.

Vlora waited about ten minutes before she left her tent and headed across the river to the pedestal. She found Prime, Nila, and Bo with their heads close together, huddled on the far side of the keelboat, examining a bit of writing. "Anything?" she asked.

Bo waved her off without looking up. "We're working on it," he said with a strong note of irritation. "We'll let you know as soon as we find out."

Vlora left the keelboat and paced on shore, feeling a sudden desperate need to *do* something. Her first instinct was to plan an attack—to launch something bold against one of the three armies hemming them in, in an effort to even the playing field. She resisted that urge—it was a trick she dare not attempt again with Etepali present—and instead headed back to her tent, to where her plans and contingencies were. She needed to prepare for anything.

She paused just outside her tent, one of those contingencies floating at the corner of her mind. "Davd," she asked her shadowing mage, "any news on those keelboats?"

"We've got around three hundred of them," Davd said.

The keelboats were packed into the river behind them, hidden by a sorcerous fog, courtesy of Bo. The enemy knew she had them, of course, but she didn't want the enemy to know how many were there. They factored into several different contingencies and might prove to be the crux of a coming battle. "Still two hundred short," she muttered. "Tell me if we find any more," she said, heading into her tent.

That talk with Delia should have calmed her nerves. Instead she found herself trembling with excitement and trepidation.

CHAPTER 52

Styke woke to a gentle knock on his door and opened it to find Jerio standing in the moonlight outside, holding something up to him. Styke looked around. It was probably two in the morning and no one else was around. The night watchman's torch flickered off the walls of the compound, and a single gas lamp in the corridor illuminated the side of the boy's face.

"What is it?" Styke whispered.

Jerio bobbed his hand up and down until Styke reached out and took the card. "This was delivered for you at the front gate. I'm assisting the watchman tonight, so . . ." He trailed off, watching while Styke turned the card in his hands and then opened it.

"Who delivered it?" Styke had to step out of the doorway, closing the door behind him quietly, and walk over to the gas lamp to read the writing. It simply said, *Unity Square.* There was nothing else on the paper.

Jerio looked over his shoulder. His eyes widened slightly, and he replied in a whisper, "Their face was covered, but... I think it was a dragonman."

"Why do you think that?" Styke asked, looking sharply at the boy.

Jerio hesitated a moment before touching both his wrists. "Tattoos."

Styke clutched the card in his fingertips. Most people might consider this a strange cypher, but he'd been a fighter long enough to know exactly what it was: a challenge. It was not only unsurprising; it was expected. His discussion with Ji-Patten had been a thrown gauntlet. The dragonman had just answered.

Styke's heart immediately began to hammer, his fingers twitching and his rage building. He could practically *taste* the fight—the blood on his lips, the knife in his hand, tearing at Ji-Patten like a wild animal. The satisfaction of vengeance in a gruesome kill was at his fingertips. He had to consciously keep himself from grinning like a lunatic. "Did you read this?" he asked.

Jerio shook his head.

"Did the night watchman?"

Another shake of the head.

"Good kid. Where can I find Unity Square?"

Jerio had to repeat the directions twice for Styke to really understand them in Dynize. The square wasn't far—a handful of city blocks—but from the mental map he'd created of the city he was fairly certain that it was an isolated public space surrounded on three sides by water. A good spot for a duel. He dismissed Jerio and returned to his room, where he began to quietly dress. His mind churned with strategies and worries. Was this an ambush? Would Ji-Patten come alone? Would Styke be able to win this fight? What happened if he lost?

The last thought buzzed around in the back of his head like a persistent fly. It wasn't a familiar worry—he never really considered it as an option. He was, after all, Ben Styke. Even without Ka-poel's sorcery, he had smashed a dragonman's head in with his ring.

Was that luck? a little voice asked. *What if luck turned the other way? What if the dragonman proved just a little too strong or fast?* He sought to mentally bury the voice. Risk be damned. There was vengeance to be had.

Styke's eyes fell on Celine's sleeping form. She was snuggled up against Ka-poel in the spare bed, both of them snoring softly. He thought of the set of horses he was still carving for her and her friends, and scowled down at the boz knife lying on the floor between his bare feet. He thought of the idea that Celine *had* friends—it was the first time since he'd taken her under his wing at the labor camp that he'd seen her thrive with children her own age.

He never made a conscious decision. One moment he was picking up his knife, ready to head to the next fight. The next, he was kneeling beside the bed, his brow furrowed in a scowl, reaching out gently to touch a shoulder.

"Ka-poel," he said softly.

Her eyes opened, reflecting the moonlight coming in through the window. He gave her a moment to extract herself from Celine and climb out of the bed. They both went into the compound corridor outside, where he could see her hands. *What is it?* she asked.

"The dragonman, Ji-Patten. Have you made plans for him?"

She pursed her lips, head tilting to one side. *You gave me orders to keep my head down.*

"I also asked you to make plans for him. Did you?" Styke insisted.

Yes.

"I need to deal with him," Styke said, his eyes flicking toward the door of their shared room where Celine was still sleeping. "But the risks…"

Ka-poel blinked at him, clearly taken aback. *Risks?* The gesture didn't convey sarcasm, but the crooked smile certainly did.

"Yes, risks," Styke said through clenched teeth. "I'm not invincible. Nor do I want to be. I've already gotten one of my men killed, and for once in my damned life I'm going to consider the consequences before I act."

The smile disappeared, replaced by a thoughtful frown. *I'm try-ing to save my strength for the godstone.*

"Does it take a lot for you to control a dragonman?"

The bone-eye sorcery that makes them strong also protects them from other bone-eyes, much like the protection that I have been giving you and your men. You want him to slit his own throat in the middle of the night? Willing him to take such a definitive action will be difficult, but not impossible. It was a long series of gestures, and Styke had her repeat herself twice before he'd gotten it all.

"But will it also alert every bone-eye in the capital that one of their own is acting against them?" he asked.

It will likely alert Ka-Sedial himself.

Styke considered the note with the words "Unity Square." "What if I don't need anything quite so grandiose?"

Ka-poel tilted her head to one side and gestured. *What did you have in mind?*

Styke's memory had been spot-on: Unity Square was a public gar-den not far from the Etzi Household. It had flower beds, mani-cured lawns, stone pathways, and even a fountain. All of it thrust out into the lake, connected to the rest of the city along one side by an avenue that was almost entirely devoid of traffic at three o'clock in the morning.

It was not a good ambush spot—no high buildings, walls, or towers within crossbow range, and the only privacy was a copse of trees around the fountain. Bad for an ambush, good for a duel. No doubt the reason that Ji-Patten had chosen the place. It put to rest Styke's worries that he was walking into a trap. Ji-Patten, for all his underhanded dealing, was still a warrior. Warriors had pride, espe-cially in their fraternity. This wasn't about killing Styke for a mas-ter. This was about killing Styke for honor. Like a goddamn fool.

Styke glimpsed a figure near the fountain as he approached.

There were no lights in the garden, but the moon was bright and Ji-Patten was unmistakable. His tall, muscled figure lounged casually against the fountain, flipping an object—one of his bone knives—up into the air and catching it. Styke kept his hands out of his pockets as he approached, letting his eyes search the darkest corners of the park, breathing deeply to maintain his calm.

He reached the edge of the small grove and stopped, drawing his knife.

"I'm surprised you came, foreigner," Ji-Patten said, taking his own knife in hand and holding it casually at his side.

"I'm surprised you're going around your master for a fight."

"Who says I am?" Ji-Patten replied. Both their tones were casual, almost friendly, but Styke could hear an eager tension in Ji-Patten's voice. He imagined that Ji-Patten was just as ready to end this as he was—to rid himself of a troublesome foreigner stirring up contention among the political elite in the city.

"I do," Styke said. "If your master wanted me dead, I would have woken up with a knife between my ribs anytime in the last ten days."

Ji-Patten shifted slightly. A bit of nerves, maybe? "And leave Etzi with more ammunition in his crusade?" he spat back. "With this, well"—he gestured at the empty park—"no witnesses. They won't even find your body. You'll just . . . disappear."

"And Etzi will have a note, written in your hand and delivered by you, drawing me out for a duel in the dead of the night," Styke said. "You're not dumb, dragonman. You're just single-minded. I sympathize. I'm usually the same way."

"The note can be dealt with," Ji-Patten said, lifting his knife. His irritated tone told Styke exactly what he needed to know: This duel was, if not against orders, then certainly without sanction. "Come, foreigner. We've talked long enough."

Styke finally stepped into the grove, adjusting the grip on his boz knife. Ji-Patten didn't waste another breath. He leapt from his spot against the fountain, over the tangled roots of one of the trees, sprinting at full speed. The movement would have been hard to follow in the daytime, and was hardly more than a dark blur in the moonlight. Styke didn't bother trying to intercept him. He took two long steps to one side, putting a tree between himself and the dragonman.

Ji-Patten's knife hand lashed out, reaching toward Styke, just as his shoulder slammed into the trunk of that tree. There was a heavy grunt, the branches shook, and Ji-Patten bounced away, spinning so hard that his knife flew out of his hand and off across the cobble path outside the grove. He stumbled to his feet, looking like a man who'd had four too many drinks and couldn't be convinced to sleep off the booze on a pub bench.

Styke kept his distance, watching. Ji-Patten threw both arms outward to either side as if maintaining a balancing act. He stared hard at Styke, and even in the darkness he was clearly confused. He took one step forward, then a second, and fell directly on his face.

"He's dealt with," Styke said loudly.

It took a few moments for a small figure to emerge from the shadows across the avenue and reach the park. Ka-poel entered the grove at a stroll and paused beside Styke, looking down her nose at the dragonman. Styke felt a pang of sympathy for Ji-Patten. He could think of nothing more terrifying for a seasoned warrior than to be helplessly manhandled by forces he could not control. He remembered Markus crying over the body of his brother, and stifled the sympathy.

He took a step to Ji-Patten, tucking one toe beneath the dragonman and flipping him over onto his back. He did a quick search and found the dragonman's spare knife, pocketing it. He then knelt on one of Ji-Patten's arms and gripped him by the chin.

"Will Ka-Sedial hear us?" he asked Ka-poel in Kez.

She shook her head.

"Normally," Styke said, switching back to Dynize and addressing Ji-Patten, "I would have taken you up on your offer. I love a good fight, and I've killed three of you shitheads already. But your murdering my man the other day reminded me about my responsibilities—and it made me realize that you don't deserve the dignity of a fair fight."

"What have you done to me?" Ji-Patten demanded in a harsh whisper.

Styke jerked Ji-Patten's head toward Ka-poel. "Wasn't me."

Ji-Patten's eyes narrowed at Ka-poel for a brief moment before widening. "No. The bone-eyes belong to us."

"Not all of them," Styke answered. He twirled his Lancer ring, feeling along the lance-and-skull with his thumb. He didn't feel sympathy, but this whole thing *did* feel dirty. Underhanded. He discarded the thought. "The mobs breaking out in the city. They're your doing, correct?"

Ji-Patten's eyes grew wild, and he began to thrash and convulse. Styke leaned harder on his arm and pinned the other arm to the ground with the tip of his knife. The dragonman gave a pained grunt.

"I asked you a question."

"Yes," Ji-Patten hissed.

"What else do you have planned for me and Etzi?"

More convulsing. Styke glanced at Ka-poel to find her staring at Ji-Patten with hands balled into fists, shoulders squared in determination. Finally, words squeezed themselves out of Ji-Patten's lips. "I don't know. I only follow orders."

"And what are your orders?"

"Stoke the mobs. Bribe and threaten Quorum members. Wait for a ship from Fatrasta."

"A ship?" Styke said sharply. "Carrying Orz's condemnation?"

"No. The Great Ka hasn't even bothered to send it."

"Then what is on the ship?"

Ji-Patten had stopped struggling. He glared hard at Styke, reminding him of the cavalry commander that Ka-poel had taken control of in the Hock back in Fatrasta. "Orders."

"What kind of orders?"

"I don't know."

"But you suspect."

The glare intensified. Styke glanced at Ka-poel again, only to find her drooping. "Hey!"

She gestured something he could not see. He swore under his breath. She was still weaker than he'd expected, and she'd put too much energy into this. He leaned forward until his face was next to Ji-Patten's ear. "For Zak, you deserve far worse than this. But I'll satisfy myself with ruining everything you and your piece-of-shit masters have built. I swear it." He reversed the grip on his knife, jerked his arm up, and brought it down hard.

It took a few moments for the body to stop moving. When it finally had, he got to his feet and crossed to Ka-poel, offering her a hand. She waved him off and stumbled over to the fountain, sitting down on the stone rim. He squinted to see her hands moving in the moonlight.

The protections around him were stronger than I thought. As was his will.

"Will you be all right?"

I need to sleep.

"Go. Back to the compound. I'll take care of this."

Ka-poel gave Styke a nod and headed back to the avenue. He waited until she was out of sight, watching for any potential witnesses to their conflict, before returning to Ji-Patten's body. Despite the death of his enemy, he was left with a very particular disquiet. It took him a few moments of consideration to pinpoint the cause of this feeling, and then a few more to realize that it was twofold. The first came from the realization that Ka-poel still wasn't as strong as she should be. The second was the secret that Ji-Patten had refused to divulge.

What orders was he waiting for? And when would the messenger arrive from Fatrasta? Styke could only wonder, and hope that Jackal returned soon with news of Ibana.

Styke swore under his breath again, cursing the dragonman, Sedial, and all the rest of the Dynize. Sedial's faction was about to make some kind of a move. Something bigger than him or Etzi. But what? He walked around the grove to find the knife that had gone skidding off along the garden path. He placed it with the other and returned to the body.

Kneeling down, he tapped Ji-Patten on the forehead with the tip of his boz knife. "You got off easy," he said. Then he began to prepare for a long night's work.

CHAPTER 53

Vlora was roused from a restless sleep by the light of a lamp and the gentle shaking of her shoulder. She rolled over and squinted into Buden's face. He took many of the night shifts as her bodyguard because it kept him from having to relay orders and cross paths with every aid and messenger in the army. Even after a decade, she couldn't tell if he preferred solitude on account of his half-missing tongue or because of shame over his noble Kez parentage.

"Buden?" She tried blinking the sleep from her head. "What is it?"

"Visor," he muttered, the word barely understandable.

"Who?"

"E...E..." Buden scowled at her. "'Yni eneral."

"Etepali?"

A nod.

"Pit and damnation." Vlora rolled to her other side and fished her pocket watch out of her discarded jacket, then held it up to

Buden's lamp. It was a little past two in the morning. "What the pit is going on?"

He shook his head.

"Light the lamps and give me a few minutes to dress, then send her in."

Buden did as instructed, leaving Vlora alone to try and summon some sort of clarity of thought from her sleep-addled brain. She sat on the edge of her cot, staring at her bare legs, wondering what the pit Etepali could possibly want to meet with her about at two o'clock in the morning. Was this another trick from the old general? A test of Vlora's character? The beginning of a ruse? The latter concerned her the most and was what finally got her moving. She made a mental checklist of everything she'd need to do the moment Etepali left—recheck the pickets, send scouts to scour their flanks, wake the general staff.

She was still running through that mental checklist as she buttoned up her jacket when there was a knock on the main post of her tent and the tent flap was thrown open. The wiry old Dynize general ducked inside, followed by Buden's scowl. Vlora gave Buden a small nod and he withdrew.

Vlora limped across the tent and cleaned off a chair—the same that Delia had sat in yesterday afternoon—and offered it to Etepali. She, in turn, remained standing by the tent flap with her hat in hand. She wasn't dressed in her uniform, but rather a loose-fitting shirt and trousers, the style of which Vlora had seen on a few of the Dynize prisoners they'd taken unaware. Civilian clothing.

"General," she said cautiously.

Etepali gave her a tight smile, her eyes never leaving Vlora's face. "Lady Flint. Thank you for receiving me at such an hour."

Vlora found her own chair and sat. Something was wrong here, but she still wasn't awake enough to figure out what. "Are you alone?" She looked around urgently to make sure her battle plans were covered, only to remember she'd transferred most of them to the general-staff tent just before bed.

"I am."

"I see. What can I do for you, General? Drink?"

"No, thank you." Etepali pursed her lips and stared at her hands for a few moments before finally returning her gaze to Vlora's. "I wanted to tell you something that I did not the other day."

Vlora remained silent, gesturing for her to continue.

"You asked about the missing Palo and the dead Kressians."

"I did."

"Yes, well. I was not honest before. I do know exactly what you're talking about."

Vlora was fully awake now. She leaned forward with bated breath, wondering if she should send for Bo and Sabastenien.

Etepali continued, "The order came not long after landing. My own army, we landed off the coast about twenty miles north of Landfall, about three days after what I understand your soldiers call the Battle of Windy River. Our orders were to secure our landing position and work our way up the coast, controlling every port—a task that we have been about ever since. But we also received a secondary order, one directly from Ka-Sedial. Anytime we came across a small, isolated town, we were to strip the town of resources, slaughter the Kressian inhabitants, and gather the Palo to be sent to Landfall."

"Only the towns?"

"Only the towns," Etepali confirmed. "The orders were very specific about making sure that they were isolated. I was given the understanding that Sedial didn't want any witnesses left behind."

Vlora regarded the old woman warily. "Do you have any idea why?"

"Why for the action, or why for the witnesses?"

"Both. Either."

Etepali gave a tired sigh. "Sedial does not like to tell us his why for anything. As you Adrans like to say, he keeps his cards close to his chest. I have a few guesses. One of our propaganda points for the invasion was that we were freeing the Palo—gathering our cousins back into the bosom of the empire. While we have vast resources, there is only so much we can ship over here, so Sedial is gathering labor and conscripts."

As Bo had suspected. Vlora nodded.

"As for the murder of the Kressians—I think that Sedial is making room for our own immigrants. He promised land to tens of thousands of families that fought for him during our civil war. Clearing Kressians from the isolated farmsteads and villages makes room for our own people, and eliminates any witnesses that might report such an action to the Nine."

"To keep us from getting involved?"

"I suspect, yes."

"We'd find out eventually."

"Perhaps. But years from now, after we've fully cemented our place on the continent. No one cares about atrocities decades after the fact, when trade is good and the rich are getting richer." Etepali passed a hand over her eyes. "But this is speculation on my part. I don't know Sedial's mind. No one does but his closest lieutenants." She paused. "Regardless of the reasons, I ignored this order. I don't slaughter civilians. I didn't during our civil war and I won't now. I think the whole idea is bloodthirsty madness. Sedial has many faults, the foremost of which is that he believes he can control everything, that he can shape the world in his image."

"Hence the godstones."

Etepali made a sour face as if Vlora had cut to the quick of it. "Perhaps," she said evasively.

"Why are you telling me this?"

"Also," Etepali said, holding up a finger, "I noticed that you're collecting keelboats. Well, if you haven't found them already, there should be well over a hundred stored up a tributary to the Hadshaw just seven miles to our north."

Seven miles. Just outside of Vlora's current scouting range. This felt like a trick to her, and she instinctively pulled back from the conversation, trying to see where Etepali was leading her with all of this. A hundred keelboats would give her a great deal more options than she had before—allowing her to move almost her entire army up and down and across the river at will. It made the river a highway for her and an obstacle for the Dynize. Another edge in the upcoming battle.

"Why are you telling me this?" she asked again, putting steel into her voice. If something was going on here, she needed to get to the bottom of it. "You're not turning on your allies because of some murdered civilians."

"I never said I was turning on my allies," Etepali replied harshly. She seemed to check herself, pulling back her temper with a scowl. Vlora realized this was the first time she'd seen her lose her composure. Etepali shook her head. "Do you remember me mentioning my cousin?"

"Vaguely."

"I have a cousin named Yaret. He is a Household head—a minister with the government in Fatrasta. Much younger than me, almost like a son in a lot of ways. Clever, thoughtful man. One of my favorite people in the world." Etepali's face had taken on a hard, distant look. "A few hours ago, I received word of an attempted assassination."

"Against this Yaret?"

She nodded. "Many of Yaret's Household were killed defending him."

"Who ordered the assassination?" Vlora asked. "Lindet? Why would she want to kill a random—?"

"The assassins were Dynize," Etepali cut her off.

Vlora sank back into her own chair, a thousand implications scrambling through her head at once. The veneer of distrust she held for Etepali was marred and she found herself genuinely curious.

"Like myself," Etepali continued before Vlora could ask any

questions, "Yaret fought on the other side of the civil war. We were Sedial's enemies, and though we put aside our differences, we've still opposed him in smaller ways politically."

"You think Sedial ordered the murder?"

"I *know* Sedial ordered the murder. The message I received included a special note, written in invisible ink in Yaret's own hand, that he has evidence that Sedial is about to begin a purge of his domestic allies." Etepali was angry now, though she was hiding it well. Her nostrils flared, a sweat breaking out on her forehead. If this was an act, it was a very good one. "I have believed for years that there would come a day when Sedial no longer found us—his former enemies—useful. That one day he would turn on us."

"And this is the day?"

"It is. I always thought that he would rid himself of his enemies *after* using the godstone. Not before."

"Have you prepared for this in any way?"

Etepali snorted. "They're suspicions, nothing more. I have no hard proof. Besides, I'm not a politician. All I could do was gather loyal soldiers. My army consists entirely of allied Household members—much as Field Marshal Tamas consolidated his most loyal troops in Adopest before his coup. Now I worry that I have brought all of Sedial's enemies together in a single spot to make them easier to deal with."

Vlora frowned, not entirely sure she understood the implication. It took a few moments for realization to dawn. "You think that the other two armies here are going to turn on you?"

"I believe they have orders to that effect, yes. Both generals are from Sedial's inner circle. They have positioned me between their armies instead of to one side, which I find odd. Further, we have no instructions to *actually* attack."

That healthy doubt returned to Vlora's breast. Hadn't Delia just told her that she expected an imminent attack? "Then what are you to do?"

"Keep you hemmed in until further orders. An odd thing to do when we outnumber you, isn't it?" Etepali pressed her lips into a firm line. "I suspect that, when the orders to attack *do* come, I will be pressed to attack first and take the worst casualties. After the battle, the other two armies will turn on me. At least, that's what *I* would do."

Vlora scoffed in disbelief, trying to wrap her head around all of this. She would have to try and confirm it, of course. But the possibility of inner turmoil among the Dynize could mean a change to everything! She could sit back and watch as the Dynize turned on one another, waiting to pounce at the opportune moment. Her feeling of elation grew and grew until another realization popped it like a lance through a boil.

"Does Sedial act in desperation?" she asked quietly.

"Why would he? He controls the entire southeast corner of Fatrasta. Lindet presses him fiercely, but there is no reason to believe she can win. He controls two of the godstones. His influence dictates the direction of both the Dynize government and her armies."

"And he's cunning?"

"Very. I don't use the world lightly."

If all of this was true, and Sedial was about to act against his enemies...it meant he was in position. He had two godstones, which meant that Styke had failed. Perhaps he only needed those two godstones for his plan to work? She shook off the uncertainty. That didn't matter, not right now. What mattered was that Sedial was confident enough in his position to act against his internal enemies. Time was running out.

"What will you do?" Vlora asked.

"The message I received from Yaret is four days old," Etepali replied carefully. "For all I know, Sedial has already finished the job. I will have to wait until I get further word. Not enough has happened for me to act directly."

"So you've come here to tell me what you can?"

"Yes. I'm in a precarious position. As I said, I have no proof of Sedial's intentions beyond Yaret's communiqué. Yet I may at any moment find myself at the end of an ally's sword." Etepali's face hardened, her fingers drawing into fists. "I am still a good Dynize citizen. But my loyalty to the Great Ka, such as it was, ends with the attempt on my cousin's life." Etepali stood suddenly, shaking her head as if coming out of a dream. "There is another thing."

Vlora watched Etepali carefully. "Yes?" she urged.

"Your politician, the Lady Snowbound."

"What about her?" Vlora felt her eyes narrow involuntarily.

"She has cut some kind of a deal. I don't know what it is, but she's been sneaking a stream of messengers in and out of the camps of my fellow generals. I've already been instructed that if fighting begins, I am to avoid her provosts."

Vlora grit her teeth, trying to decide if she could trust the old woman. There was a lot of information here—juicy, inflammatory bits that could change all of Vlora's plans.

"They are watching me, and I shouldn't be gone so long," Etepali said suddenly. She gave Vlora a piercing glance and, in a quick rush as if to get it all out before she could think better of it, she said, "The last I heard, Landfall was protected by seventy thousand soldiers. Roughly two-thirds of those are conscripts from Dynize and the Palo, and would fall beneath a stiff breeze. The rest are Sedial's best soldiers. The fortress is well protected by sorcery and gun emplacements." Her mouth snapped shut.

Vlora stood as well. Her breath was short now, her mind filled with possibilities and anxieties. "You know that I cannot trust you at your word."

Etepali gave a tired sigh. "I'm aware. We are still enemies, you and I, and our mutual trickery has marred the possibility of true cooperation. But I'm giving you this information in good faith. How you act upon it is up to you. I will give you one last assurance:

If I am ordered to attack, I will delay doing so for as long as possible."

"That is . . . generous."

Etepali put on her hat and gave Vlora a small bow before sweeping out of the tent without another word. The moment she was gone, Vlora began to pace, her mind on fire. After several minutes of consideration, she went to the flap of the tent and told Buden to summon a messenger.

Once the lad arrived, Vlora barked off a storm of orders. "Double—no, triple—the number of our scouts. The next few days I want to know everything about the Dynize. Their positioning, their maneuvers, the number of men on their front lines. If they so much as twitch in our direction or toward our flanks, I want to be informed immediately. Also, send an expedition up the river. There should be a tributary about seven miles to the north. I want them to find any keelboats up there and bring them down. Wake up Sabastenien. I want the expedition to come from his best troops, and I want them gone within the hour."

The messenger left at a sprint, and Vlora fell back into her chair to stew on all of this. Of everything she had been told, one piece of information kept floating to the forefront of her thoughts: Delia had betrayed her. If true, it would not come as a surprise. But how? What kind of a deal could she have cut with Ka-Sedial in such a short amount of time?

Her body wanted nothing more than to crawl back into bed and claim a few more hours of sleep, but her mind, she knew, wouldn't allow it. Grabbing a lantern and lighting it, she headed out and across to the general-staff tent to review her battle plans.

She had work to do.

CHAPTER 54

Styke sat in the Etzi compound canteen, breaking his fast with warm flatbread and snake-meat kabobs while Celine and Jerio played in the corner. It was a large, sprawling room with several dozen tables and two open doors into the kitchens. Most of the Household had already had their breakfast and begun their day, leaving Styke to eat in relative quiet as he shook the sleep from his head.

Celine and Jerio, he noted, had begun to allow other children into their little group. There were around half a dozen of them now, and as far as he could tell, they were playing at some kind of imaginary war. Celine was very obviously in charge, with Jerio as her second in command. The other children followed faux orders seriously, gathering into a line to "assault" a position on the other side of a table that they dutifully clambered over at Celine's shout.

Celine led the charge.

Styke finished his breakfast as the kids tended to their wounded and then regrouped for another attack. He checked his fingernails for blood, then leaned back in his chair to watch the door. He had expected an outburst by now—it wasn't all that far from noon, after all—but none had come.

As if in answer to his thoughts, the door to the canteen opened. Etzi strode in, pausing just long enough for his eyes to adjust to the lower light and then focusing on Styke. "Get dressed," he said stiffly. "We've been summoned to the Quorum Hall." He left without saying another word.

Styke took his time wiping crumbs from his chin and shirt and then climbed slowly to his feet. This summons was not unexpected. What *was* unexpected was that it came without any extra hullabaloo. No raised alarms. No rumors sweeping the city. No one in the compound acted cagey like they were keeping information from him, and he hadn't seen Etzi since yesterday.

He ambled over to the kids, getting Celine's attention with a wave. She broke off from her troops and joined him, breathless from another tumble over the enemy position. He touched her shoulder, frowning to himself. "I'm going with Etzi to the Quorum Hall."

"Again? I thought you were gonna try to finish the army today," she said, referring to the cavalry unit he'd been carving.

"Hopefully it won't be long. I'll work on it, promise." He turned away, letting Celine return to her friends, but waited a moment to catch Jerio's eye. The boy approached at a slight jerk of Styke's head.

"Keep an eye on her," Styke said in a low voice. "If something happens to me, you keep her safe. Understand?"

"Yes, sir!" Jerio snapped a very serious salute.

Styke watched them prepare for another charge, then headed to his room to don his dress uniform. He joined Etzi in the courtyard where the Household head had already climbed into a waiting carriage. Styke noted that the size of Etzi's honor guard seemed to increase with each subsequent visit—there had been just a handful the day they were ambushed with Zak's execution. Now there were thirty of them on foot and another four on horseback. Styke almost demanded his horse, but dismissed the notion when Etzi gestured through the door for him to climb inside.

They were soon rolling down the causeway that attached the compound to the city. Etzi sat in a glum silence for the first several minutes of the trip. Styke let him remain that way until he could no longer contain his own curiosity.

"Why have they summoned us?" he asked.

Etzi's gaze flicked to Styke's knife, lingered there, and then moved up to his face. "They found a head in the Quorum Hall this morning."

Styke pretended to be surprised. "Oh?"

"Yes."

"Is that why they're summoning us?"

Etzi paused for a beat. "Should it be?"

Styke returned his gaze silently, expressionless. Etzi had made it clear that he didn't want to know more than he needed to. Styke didn't see any reason to change that now.

Etzi cleared his throat and finally averted his gaze. "The head belongs to Ji-Patten. They haven't been able to find the body. The Quorum Hall is under guard at night, so no one has been able to explain how the head got there. I've been at an emergency session all morning." Etzi suddenly looked tired and worn. "A third of the Quorum thinks you did it. Another third refuses to believe that anyone, let alone a foreign soldier on his own, could possibly kill a dragonman."

"And the other third?"

"Divided. Foreign agents, not ruling out yourself, or infighting among Sedial's group, or even a mythical creature prowling the streets. We've kept information from leaking to the public so far, but it *will* happen sooner or later. There is nothing more terrifying than the fear of the mob. The head was found with a word written in blood on the floor—'traitor.' It was written in Dynize, which casts doubt on the possibility of its being a foreign agent."

Styke didn't respond, quietly feeling pleased with himself. He'd found a Dynize dictionary in Maetle's library the other day and checked to make sure he'd spelled and conjugated the word right. Nothing like casting a little doubt among one's enemies.

Etzi sighed. "To answer your question, I have no idea why you're being summoned. The messenger woke me up from a much-needed nap. The Quorum wasn't supposed to gather again until after dinner. There's either a mistake or..."

"Or they think I murdered one of their dragonmen."

Etzi scowled. "It must be a mistake. If you're being arrested, they would have shown up at my compound with several of his comrades."

They fell into an uncomfortable silence for the rest of the trip, arriving outside the Quorum Hall, where Etzi and Styke disembarked. Styke adjusted his overly warm jacket, tugging at the collar as he looked around the square. The crowd was thinner than usual, and he wondered if perhaps the rumors of Ji-Patten's discovered head had already begun to send the populace into a fear spiral—certainly not something he'd intended, but it could be a useful side effect.

He followed Etzi down the long hall, and they soon entered the Quorum Hall, only to find it practically empty. A handful of janitors cleaned the tiered seating, while small pockets of Household heads and representatives spoke in hushed tones. No one paid any mind to Etzi and Styke's entrance.

"I thought you said the Quorum summoned us?" Styke said.

"I did," Etzi replied, a look of confusion crossing his face. "Stay here." He hurried up the steps and out through another exit from the Quorum Hall, leaving Styke waiting on the speaker's dais. He pursed his lips, looking across to the few other occupants of the room, an uneasy feeling growing in his gut. His mind immediately leapt to suspicion. Had they been lured out of the compound for some reason? Were Sedial's people making some kind of play? Or was he just being paranoid?

Etzi returned a few moments later, shaking his head. "I just spoke with the Quorum clerk. He didn't send out a summons."

"Could this be a ruse?"

"To what end?"

"To get us out of the compound." Styke felt his shoulders tense. Celine. "We have to go back." He was already moving by the time he finished the words, half jogging out of the Hall. Etzi was close on his heels, and they reached the carriage and honor guard a moment later. "Back to the compound," Etzi barked. "And quickly!"

Styke settled in across from Etzi as the carriage began to jolt along the cobbles. He was a bundle of nerves now, his hand resting on his knife, the other clenched in a fist. A decent portion of Etzi's Household guard was with them right now, leaving the compound with just the men and women who worked there during the day. It was practically defenseless. He could feel a growing desperation and resisted the urge to shout out the window at the driver. He should have ridden Amrec, damn it.

The carriage turned a corner and suddenly lurched to a stop, nearly throwing Etzi on top of Styke. The lurch was accompanied by the swearing of the driver and several exclamations from the soldiers jogging alongside.

"Sir," a voice said, "we have a problem."

Etzi climbed out, and from Styke's viewpoint he could see the Household head pale visibly. He followed him into the street.

Their path had been blocked—the road cordoned off with carts, barrels, and any other large detritus that came readily to hand. This bit of road wasn't exactly an alley, but it wasn't an avenue, either—a rather narrow bend in the road with poor visibility and, more importantly, not nearly enough room to turn a carriage around. Crowded into the blockade was a mob of at least fifty men and women armed with clubs, torches, and machetes. They stared at Etzi's carriage in eerie silence.

"What is this?" Etzi demanded. "Move them aside!"

Several members of his guard blanched. The four on horseback rode forward hesitantly, and the captain of the guard demanded to speak with whoever was in charge of the barricade. Styke took several steps back through Etzi's guards and looked back around the corner, only to find that another, smaller mob had begun to assemble a barricade behind them. Styke swore and hurried back to Etzi.

"They're cutting us off," Styke said. "This is a damned trap. We've got to move now." He could see Etzi freeze in indecision, like a rabbit who'd just spotted a predator bearing down on him. Styke snatched him by the arm, giving him a shake.

"Sir," the captain of the guard called. "They want the foreigner."

Styke growled under his breath, turning back to the barricade. More people poured out of nearby buildings to join the mob, swelling the numbers. There were few guns among them, but he did see a handful of musket barrels poking out of windows above the street. His gut twisted. This was it, then. Styke's punishment for the murder of Ji-Patten. It had certainly been organized quickly enough.

Etzi seemed to shake himself from his panic. "Tell them that I am a Household head and to disperse immediately!" he called angrily. "This damned rabble can terrorize the citizenry, but I am a member of the Household Quorum!" He was shouting now, at the mob itself rather than at his guard captain.

Styke took a firm grip of Etzi's arm. "This isn't a mob," he warned. "Look at them. No shouting. No incoherence. I've faced mobs, and they're not this organized. They're cutting us off from behind. It's a trap set by Sedial's people." This wasn't law or politics. They were out of Etzi's realm now, and that moment of panic in the Household head had shown Styke what kind of mettle he was dealing with.

Etzi would have no choice but to hand him over, and Styke

struggled not to blame him for that. No time for blame. He mentally tracked his own path through the mob, finding where it was thinnest. He spotted a door that would take him into one of the nearby buildings. Once inside, he'd either hold out against the rabble or find a rear exit. After that, he'd have to make his way to Etzi's compound to fetch Amrec, Ka-poel, and Celine.

"Give us the foreigner, or face the consequences!" someone shouted. Etzi's guards looked to him for orders. Styke watched, tensed, for that look of defeat in Etzi's eyes and prepared to draw his knife and charge the rabble.

"Consequences?" Etzi suddenly roared, catching Styke off guard. "You speak of consequences! Your blood is on your own hands, you ingrates! To me, my soldiers, to me! Fix bayonets! Hurien, hold our withdrawal! Kepuli, abandon the carriage and lead us back the way we came. Cut down anyone who gets in our way!"

Styke suddenly found himself swept into the center of the guard, shoved shoulder-to-shoulder with Etzi. The group marched in lockstep back around the corner, fixing bayonets as they moved while a small portion of Etzi's guard leveled their weapons at the mob now behind them. Someone in the rabble gave a shout, and the muskets above them opened fire. One of Etzi's guards fell, and the rest shot blindly into the mob.

Styke lost sight of their rearguard as he and Etzi rounded the corner and approached the half-finished barricade going up to block their retreat. The guard lowered their bayonets as one and charged with a shout. They hit hard and fast, and it became clear that whoever had organized this rabble had underestimated Etzi's ability to think on his feet. The mob dissolved beneath the points of their bayonets, fleeing for the main avenue or nearby alleys. Less than half of them stood their ground.

Styke drew his knife, only for Etzi to snatch him by the forearm. "No!" Etzi snapped. "This blood is for us to spill—I don't want a single knife wound on any of Sedial's stooges."

Reluctantly, Styke returned his knife to its sheath.

The fight between Etzi's guard and roughly twice their number in armed commoners was short and bloody. Those who hadn't fled the initial charge were enthusiastic, but they had no chance against a wall of bayonets from a group of guardsmen who, Etzi had once told him, were mostly veterans of the civil war. Once the mob was dead, wounded, or scattered and the barricade claimed, Etzi began to bark orders.

"You, get the city guard! Kepuli, give Ben and me four men to get back to the compound. Use the rest to relieve our friends."

"Just four, sir?"

"I said four, didn't I? We'll take the main avenues, where they'll be loath to confront us. Now, go!"

Styke watched the guard captain gather his forces and head back around that corner. His adrenaline was up, his fury at the ambush just now following on the heels of unfulfilled bloodlust. He reluctantly followed Etzi and his four guards back to the main avenue, where they headed toward the compound using a long, very public route.

At one point he saw a column of city guards rushing toward the scene of the ambush. None of them seemed to even notice Etzi and Styke. The rest of the way back was uneventful, and they were soon inside the compound, where Etzi ordered the last of his guards to man the wall.

Styke found Celine still playing with Jerio and the others in the canteen. He looked in on her, resisting the urge to go give her a hug, and quietly backed out.

It did not take him long to pinpoint the fear he had felt during that ambush—the fear, not for his life, but that Celine would be left without his protection in a strange land. His heart was still hammering when Etzi's Household guard returned almost an hour later. They shouted for Maetle to attend the wounded, and they were carrying half a dozen covered litters between them—the dead from the ambush. Styke overheard Etzi's captain reporting that the city guard had driven off the rest of the mob, taking in a few for questioning.

Maetle appeared to tend to the wounded, and Etzi faded into one of the corridors, watching the triage pale-faced. Styke skirted the courtyard and came around from behind to join the Household head. Etzi blinked at Styke, then looked back at the dead and wounded. His expression was distant, shell-shocked. It seemed to take him a few moments to realize that Styke was even there. Then his expression hardened. "Did you kill Ji-Patten?"

"Do you really want to know?"

"Yes."

"Hold on," Styke said, returning to his room. He fetched one of Ji-Patten's knives and returned to Etzi in the corridor. "I was going to give it to Orz. A memento as to how your mother has been avenged."

Etzi took the knife in both hands, rotating it with his fingers, his gaze lingering on the bone-white blade. "How did he die?"

"Like a dog. Ka-poel ambushed him, and I finished him off."

"She broke a dragonman?"

"Yes."

Etzi took a few deep breaths, then put the bone knife in his pocket. "Good. He didn't deserve a better death."

"That's how I saw it."

Etzi looked up at Styke sharply. "This"—he thrust a hand toward the courtyard—"is an escalation. I cannot say whether it was planned before Ji-Patten's murder or in direct response to it, but that does not matter. Sedial's stooges have attacked a Household head. He has overplayed his hand, and I will make certain that he feels the consequences."

Styke felt, not for the first time, that things were spiraling well beyond his control. But this time he also felt that they might very quickly get beyond Etzi's, Sedial's, or anyone else's control as well.

Now, more than ever, he needed the Mad Lancers behind him. He silently urged Jackal to return with word of Ibana. "I appreciate you not handing me to the mob." He meant it. No need to puff up pleasantries to please his host. Etzi had likely saved his life, at the cost of many of his own guards.

"Do not thank me," Etzi answered angrily. "I am doing my duty toward my Household and my guest. That they thought I would hand you over without a fight isn't just folly on their part—it is an insult against me. I only have one regret."

"What's that?"

Etzi wiped a hand across his brow, gaze lingering on the wounded scattered across the courtyard. "That this feels like the first step toward more violence—and that we are at the center of it."

CHAPTER 55

Michel squatted in the offshoot of a tunnel in the Land-fall catacombs, watching the bobbing of lights pass just below him as hundreds of Yaret's Household members streamed by. Cupbearers walked up and down the column, giving instructions in low, calm voices, paying special attention to the inevitable handful of people who gave in to panic in the damp, cramped darkness of the tunnels. Michel checked his pocket watch by the light of his own lantern. It was almost four o'clock in the morning.

It had taken them four whole days to plan the exodus—two for Michel to verify Tenik's story and lay the groundwork for moving several hundred people into the tunnels, and another two days for Yaret to gather supplies, call in ranking Household members from the nearby army camps, and prepare his cupbearers for the job. As far as Michel knew, the whole thing had been airtight. Most of the Household didn't even know they were running for it until they were awakened from their beds and told to descend into the catacombs.

Still, he couldn't help the pervasive worry that something was going to go wrong. All it took was one spy to tip off Sedial to the flight. Michel scuffed the floor with the toe of his boot, trying to wrench his thoughts away from worry.

"I don't think anyone recognized you," he told Ichtracia.

She stood beside him, watching the political refugees with something between bemusement and irritation. "Nobody is even glancing this direction," she answered. "I'm not going to hang around long enough for them to start wondering. Besides, you said that one of Yaret's soldiers recognized me back at the park."

"He's been sworn to secrecy," Michel promised. "Only three people in the Household know you're in Landfall."

"Three too many," Ichtracia muttered, shaking her head. "Too late now, I suppose. How are you going to feed all these people?"

"I'm wondering the same thing." The words might as well have been Michel's, but they came from behind him. He stood up, nodding to Jiniel as she came up to stand between him and Ichtracia. "You're insane," she told him.

"I'm saving hundreds of people from the knife of a tyrant," he replied.

"With resources that could be used by Palo." The tone wasn't argumentative, but it did contain a light rebuke. Jiniel didn't agree with his decision, but they'd hashed out the plan over the last couple of days and decided that the benefits outweighed the costs. She seemed to realize whom she was standing beside and ducked her head at Ichtracia. "Sorry."

"Don't apologize to me. Yaret is no friend of mine."

Michel held up a hand to forestall further discussion as two figures pulled themselves away from the passing group and headed up the tunnel toward them. Michel picked up his lantern, holding it above his head until he could see that it was just Yaret and Tenik. They nodded to him solemnly, gave Ichtracia a wary glance, and looked curiously at Jiniel.

"This is a friend of mine," Michel said, gesturing to her. "The fewer names you know, the safer this whole process will be."

"For you," Tenik said. His expression was surly, his eyes red.

Michel gave him a worried glance. "Yes, for us."

Yaret waved away his cupbearer's concern. "What Tenik means to say," he said, bowing to Jiniel, "is thank you. You're saving a lot of people tonight."

"At least for now," Ichtracia reminded him. "Eventually, Sedial is going to figure out where you went and come looking for you."

"Yes, but this gives us a head start on him." Yaret sounded tired, but positive. "It gives us time to figure out how to get out of the city to unite with Etepali."

Michel squeezed Tenik's shoulder. "I'll do what I can on that front. Smuggling so many people out of Landfall is going to be a measure more difficult than having you all walk into a tunnel. But with this chaos, you might just be able to do so."

Tenik cast a dark look at his master. "They tried again tonight."

"Tried what?" There was a note of despair in Tenik's voice that worried Michel.

"Another assassin," Tenik said. "A lone dragonman. Killed two of our cupbearers. Seventeen of our soldiers. I..." He fell silent, squeezing his eyes shut.

Michel made a silent "ah" with his mouth. No wonder Tenik was in a dark mood.

"One of the men who died protecting me," Yaret said quietly, "was his cousin. They were very close." Michel thought he saw a trace of guilt cross Yaret's face, but he couldn't have been sure in the lantern light. Yaret cleared his throat. "I have some information that you might find useful. As a way of thanking you."

"Anything you can give us," Jiniel said.

Yaret produced a bundle from his jacket and handed it to her. "We intercepted a number of dispatches just a few hours ago. They *should* have come to us, but they were sent to another Household.

According to the dispatches, Lindet is giving Sedial's forces a pit of a time. She's pushed to within thirty miles of Landfall, but she's strung herself out. Our generals are still confident they can win, but have asked Sedial for more troops. Lindet is a more capable commander than anyone expected."

"That sounds about right," Michel said. Lindet's approach was a mixed blessing, depending on how he looked at it. She wasn't an ally, not by a long shot, but she *was* keeping Sedial very distracted right now.

"The problem is," Yaret went on, "most of the troops out fighting her belong to the Households on the purge list. Sedial is throwing them to the wolves and keeping his most loyal close to him. I've sent word to anyone affiliated with my Household to withdraw, and I know I'm not the only Household head to do so."

"Let's hope some of yours are able to get out of that quagmire," Jiniel said. To Michel's surprise, she sounded sincere. But then again, she'd always had a good grasp of nuance—knowing how to find allies among her enemies and when to forgive the latter. Michel wondered, if Lindet managed to win this thing, if Jiniel would be able to get any concessions out of her. Maybe. Lindet had always been good at making promises. Making her keep them was the difficult part.

"Any word on the violence in the city?" Michel asked, directing the question at both Jiniel and Yaret.

"Nothing on our end since nightfall," Jiniel said. "There was a riot in Proctor, but it burned itself out before it could get too dangerous."

Tenik spoke up. "Sedial is planning some kind of reprisal. We've been cut out of a lot of communication since that first assassination attempt, but we do know that he's sending some of his best soldiers into the city."

"That's not something I wanted to hear," Michel said, swearing softly.

"A show of force," Yaret said. "Constant patrols, tightened curfews." He rubbed his shoulders. "I'm worried what this means. Sedial doesn't usually escalate until he's ready to act."

"He's close," Ichtracia said, a sneer on her lips. "He's got the blood he needed to unlock the godstone. He has control of two of them. He might try to create a god with the power at his fingertips."

"Will that work?" Yaret asked with a shudder. "I thought he needed the third."

"Maybe." Ichtracia shifted from one leg to the other nervously. She looked angry and uncertain. "Maybe not."

A thought danced at the back of Michel's mind—something that had been floating around his head ever since he first met Sedial. "Are we still pretending that Sedial isn't just going to seize godhood for himself?" Tenik, Yaret, and Ichtracia all turned to Michel as if he'd just uttered the worst kind of blasphemy, staring at him with disbelief. He cautiously went on. "I don't know how it works, to be fair. But from what I understand, this new god doesn't just come out of nowhere. It's an ascension of sorts, for an actual person."

"It'll be the emperor," Yaret said confidently. "That was always the plan. Our emperor will become god, and have the power to hold us together..." He trailed off, looking at his two fellow Dynize. Tenik seemed even more glum than before. Ichtracia's disbelief slowly turned to horror.

"He's right," she breathed. "Pit, why did none of us see this before?"

"No," Yaret scoffed. "Not even Sedial would commit such a crime. He wants power, but to take the strength of the godstones for himself would be...I can't even think of a word for it!" He rounded on Ichtracia. "You really think he's capable of such a thing?"

She gave a reluctant nod. "He wants order. It's his greatest desire. What better way to do it than with the power of a god?" Her face screwed up, and for a moment Michel thought she might vomit. "I agree with Michel. It's something he would do."

Yaret swore softly. Michel could see his thoughts moving quickly, his expression hardening with resolve. "I see. Tenik, I want you to send runners to our closest allies. Tell them we think that Sedial is planning on seizing the god gift for himself."

"We don't have any proof," Tenik replied.

"It doesn't matter. Did you see my face? If it looked anything like yours, it shows how mindless we've become." He swore again. "None of us even considered the possibility, but once Michel spoke it aloud, it took very little to convince us of the truth of it. We *know* what kind of a man Sedial is. We've just denied it to ourselves. Go!"

Tenik gave Yaret a half bow and limped down the tunnel. Yaret slapped a fist against the wall and looked at Michel. The positive veneer that he'd worn a few minutes ago was gone and there was a deep sorrow in his eyes. "What ruin have I led my Household to?"

"No ruin yet," Michel said, hoping that he sounded reassuring.

"Even if we escape...we can't fight against a god."

"He has to *get* that godhood first," Ichtracia said, her lip curled.

"Who can stop him?" Yaret swayed slightly and waved off an offered hand. "I must see to my people. Thank you again, Michel. I would not have expected such a kindness from an ally, let alone..."

"A traitor?" Michel asked.

Yaret snorted. "That word will never be used to describe you again. Not in my Household. As far as I'm concerned, you are still Devin-Michel, a Yaret—if that title means anything when the week is through." He nodded again and headed down the tunnel.

Michel watched him go, worried. His suggestion that Sedial would seize the power of the godstones for himself had been halfway to a joke—he had assumed everyone thought the same thing. He hadn't expected it to have such a demoralizing effect on Yaret and Tenik. "Jiniel, can you set someone aside to make sure we help them as much as possible?"

Jiniel side-eyed Ichtracia. "We're stretched thin, Michel."

"Just one person. A liaison. Yaret may still be of use to us."

"What did you always tell me about being sentimental toward

your former targets?" That rebuke was back in her tone again. Ichtracia made an irritable grunt, and Michel put up a hand to forestall a fight.

"You're not wrong. But...I have to do this."

Jiniel seemed on the edge of objecting, but finally gave a nod.
"I'll provide a liaison."

"Thanks, I—"

Michel was cut off by someone shouting his name farther down
the tunnel. He turned to see a lantern rushing toward him, and the
figure holding it resolved into Tenik. The cupbearer held his leg,
limping quickly with a grimace of pain. "Michel!"

"I'm here! What is it?"

"One of my people just now reported in from the capital building. We sent him there to recover some of the Blackhat files, and he
overheard a meeting of a few of Sedial's lieutenants." Tenik looked
over his shoulder, then lowered his voice. "Sedial is moving on the
Depths."

"Moving on them?" Michel asked in confusion. "What do you
mean by that?"

"He has no patience for the riots. He's sent three Privileged to
put Greenfire Depths to the flame. He intends to destroy it completely, and everyone in it."

Michel felt like he'd been punched. "That's a hundred thousand people. More. He's just going to snuff them out? Damn it all!
When?"

"Just after dawn."

Michel spun to Jiniel. "Sound the alarm. Get a hold of everyone
you can. We need to evacuate the Depths!"

"Evacuate?" Jiniel hissed. "That would take days. Weeks!"

"You have just a few hours."

"We can at least get our people out. Come on!" Jiniel grabbed
Michel by the hand and began to pull him down the tunnel. He
escaped her grasp and turned to Ichtracia.

"You should stay here." The last word hadn't left his mouth when he finally caught sight of her face, shadows flickering in the lantern light. It was a mask of fury.

"No," she spat, striding past him.

"Wait!"

She didn't stop. "You are good at picking your fights, Michel. I'm picking mine. I won't let him do this. Not to all those people. They think the Palo don't have a Privileged. But you do. You have me."

Michel exchanged a glance with Tenik, then nodded to Jiniel. "Get our people out. Send runners to every Palo leader we know. Everyone who can't flee should be prepared to fight for their lives. We have to try to save who we can." He began to run.

"Where are you going?" she shouted after him.

"With Ichtracia. We're going to buy you as much time as we can!"

CHAPTER 56

It took Vlora's scouts an entire day to locate and retrieve the keel-boats that Etepali had told her would be hidden up the river. She watched as the group returned in the early hours of the morning, poling almost a hundred keelboats down the Hadshaw in silence while the din of a distant battle provided a backdrop. Bo stood to one side of her, Nila to the other, both of them still wearing their dressing gowns.

"Is there a reason you needed us up at this hour to watch some boats arrive?" Bo asked, stifling a yawn.

Vlora leaned on her sword, enjoying the way the soft mud of the riverbank felt spongy beneath her feet, alleviating some of her pain. "Yes."

"Are you going to tell us?" Nila asked.

"Prime claims that he knows what the pedestal actually is."

That seemed to wake them both up. "You're sure?" Bo asked. "We saw him just last night and he didn't mention anything. And wait . . . it's not a pedestal?"

"It seems he was working through the night and had some sort of epiphany. He's supposed to meet us here and give us a briefing, then the two of you are going to confirm his findings." Vlora checked her pocket watch. "In fifteen minutes."

"You could have let us sleep for fifteen more minutes," Nila protested.

"According to the man I had fetch you, none of the thirteen people in your tent were sleeping. Besides, I wanted you to get your heads right before he shows up."

Nila harrumphed. Bo looked down at his dressing gown. "I should have put on pants." He gestured at one of Vlora's messengers waiting just up the bank. "Hey, you. Yes, you. Go get me some pants!"

"And one of my dresses, dear," Nila said.

"And a dress!" Bo added. "Just ask for Javinia. She'll pick out the right ones." He sighed and produced his enormous pipe from the pocket of his dressing gown, puffing it to life. They were soon wreathed in a cloud of cherry-scented tobacco. Vlora waved a little away from her face and checked her pocket watch again, hoping that Prime would be early. She had a lot to do today.

"It's not enough," she muttered under her breath, counting the keelboats as they went by.

"What's not enough?" Bo asked.

She didn't answer, content to continue counting. She could feel him watching her and wondered if he'd already guessed her plan. As if to answer her question, he suddenly gave a soft "ah-ha!"

"Yes?" she asked.

"We're not going to fight them, are we?"

Vlora put a hand to her ear, feeling a momentary urge to play coy. "Isn't that fighting you hear?"

"No," Bo said slowly. "That is a cavalry screen." The report of artillery punctuated his statement. "And a bit of field gunnery to muddy the waters." He pointed to the empty river just to their south, where his sorcery had thrown up a simple, but effective, screen of mist that hid her mass of keelboats. "I *thought* that you were going to get all clever with the keelboats—use them to ferry men back and forth across the river so that we can use the river to our advantage while the Dynize cannot."

"That *was* my plan, yes," Vlora responded.

"But we're not going to do that anymore, are we? We're going right for the big prize: Landfall. What, exactly, did Etepali say to you when she visited the other day?"

"She said she's worried about getting stabbed in the back. They have no orders to attack us, and if they do get any, she's going to hold back as long as possible."

"Shouldn't we take advantage of her doubt in order to attack her two allies?"

"Fighting a foe with a two-to-one numerical advantage against us still isn't something I'd rush into," Vlora said. "But I'm also worried that they don't *need* to attack us. If Sedial is simply buying time so he can make his move…"

"Even without the third godstone?"

"Even without the third godstone," Vlora confirmed. "So…if we can get enough keelboats, we're going to make a run for it."

"And by *it*, you mean Landfall," Nila confirmed.

Vlora nodded.

"Right into the belly of the beast," Bo said. He thumbed a little more tobacco into his pipe and donned a nasty little smile. "That's going to be very dangerous."

"And there is no possible way Sedial will expect it. Have you been keeping a closer eye on Delia?"

"Of course. She's just going about her business, though. No evidence that she's betrayed us. Ah! Speaking of which…" Bo trailed off due to the sudden arrival of Delia Snowbound. The politician and her retinue crested a nearby hill and strode toward Vlora with purpose. "She doesn't look happy," Bo muttered under his breath.

Vlora tried a welcoming smile, but it felt like a grimace on her lips so she exchanged it for a neutral expression. "Good morning, Lady Snowbound. I trust you slept well?"

Delia thrust a finger at Vlora and began to talk even before she'd closed the distance between them. "What the pit are you up to?" she demanded. "I've just been informed that none of my messengers are allowed into or out of the camp."

"They're not," Vlora confirmed.

"Did we not have an understanding? Aren't I trying to end this war?"

"We do have an understanding," Vlora replied coolly. "That understanding is that I am still very much in charge of the army. We are at a critical moment, and I've suspended passes for nonvital personnel."

"You cannot!"

"I can, and I did." Vlora swallowed her annoyance and tried a different tactic. She still wasn't entirely certain that Delia had betrayed them. She needed to be careful. "This isn't personal, Delia. I'm undertaking a bit of very delicate maneuvering. That fighting you hear? Our entire cavalry force is out there providing a skirmisher's screen so that I can move my troops around with impunity. I don't want any of your messengers coming or going, because if they were to be questioned about my movements, it may ruin my entire strategy."

The reasonable tone seemed to have an effect on Delia. Her posture relaxed slightly and she sniffed at Bo and Nila's dressing gowns. "I thought you told me you weren't going to attack them."

"Not a real attack. Just a screening maneuver."

"And how long will this last?"

"Just the next thirty-six hours," Vlora said reassuringly.

"I see." Delia regarded Vlora with a cold look. "Are you going to tell me what those maneuvers are?"

"I'm not. As I said, they're very delicate. Very secret." Vlora spread her hands. "You're welcome to take it up with the general staff, but most of them are in the dark as well. They understand the need for keeping things quiet."

Delia sniffed again and, without another word, spun on her heel and marched back into camp. Vlora was glad to see her go, but she couldn't help but feel a little unsettled. She shouldn't have to distrust her political liaison so deeply. She should be able to discuss strategy openly. But here she was.

"That was bullshit, wasn't it?" Bo asked.

"Of course not."

"The general staff doesn't know we're making a run for Landfall?"

"Oh, *they* know. I told them about forty minutes ago. But they also know that it depends on us getting about fifty more keelboats. If we can't get the keelboats, then we're going to go to the second plan."

"Which is?"

"Break these two field armies right here and now, and then march to Landfall. Ah, here's Prime." She caught sight of the Predeii walking along the opposite bank, coming up from the keelboat where they'd secured the godstone. She headed toward the bridge and was followed by Bo and Nila. They met the old man halfway across, where he raised a hand in greeting and studiously avoided making eye contact with Nila.

"Good morning, Lady Flint. Borbador. Nila."

"Morning, Prime. So what is this damned thing that we captured? Was it worth the effort?"

Prime ran his fingers along the birthmark that crossed his face and scalp. "Yes, yes I do believe it was. And as I suspected, it is not a pedestal. Come with me."

The small group followed him back across the opposite bank and boarded the keelboat, where Prime brought their attention to a number of symbols chiseled into the stone. They were little more than gobbledygook to Vlora, but Nila and Bo just frowned. "I thought we agreed those are meaningless?" Bo said.

"We did!" Prime said excitedly. "But an old memory floated through my head last night, and I cross-referenced these symbols with a book I have outlining some of the very earliest known samples of Old Deliv. They match. At least, once you turn them upside down they do."

"And?" Vlora asked.

"And these symbols are a simple instruction. It translates very literally as 'Put the blood here.'" He pointed to the side of the stone, where there was a slight depression beneath the words. Or rather, Vlora realized, craning her head, just above the words. "Wait, are we looking at this thing sideways?"

"Sideways and upside down," Prime declared. He slapped the stone. "This is actually the top."

"'Put the blood here,'" Vlora mused. "I assume that's a sacrificial thing?"

"See this?" Prime said, hurrying around and climbing up a ladder until he was on the top of the stone. Vlora followed him. He pointed to a ridge, then produced a piece of paper. "This is a sketch I made of the godstone before we destroyed it. Once I realized that we were looking at the top rather than the side, and now we're standing on the side rather than the top, I surmised that this ridge fits against the base of the godstone. Like a puzzle piece."

Vlora looked down at Bo and Nila, who were still staring at the symbols. "Are you following any of this?"

Nila and Bo glanced at each other. Nila pointed to one of the symbols and said something in a low voice to Bo. He shook his head. She said something else, and he grimaced, then slowly nodded. Nila looked up at Prime. "You think it's an altar?"

"For blood sacrifices, yes," Prime replied matter-of-factly. "I believe that it is a sort of key to the godstone. The lines match up too well for it not to be. Slide it up against the base of the godstone, connect it via sorcery, then apply the required blood and…" He gestured expansively.

"You could have told me this before I climbed on the thing." Vlora had a sudden, powerful urge to bathe. She climbed down and headed to the riverbank, where she waited for her friends to join her. "So we know what it is. What do we do with it?"

"Destroy it, preferably," Prime said.

"What little blasting oil we have left we're saving for the godstone in Landfall."

Prime wrinkled his nose. "No doubt, they have uncovered a similar altar for the other godstone."

"We'll deal with that when we get to it." Vlora gazed at the thing, feeling deeply unsettled. An altar for blood sacrifices. She had no illusions about how the bone-eyes got their power, but an altar of this size seemed created for more than the occasional bit of blood. She could only imagine how many throats had been slit over this thing. "All right. We take it with us to Landfall. Once we rendezvous with the fleet, we put it on a ship and take it out to sea, where we dump it someplace deep."

"Isn't it dangerous to take it *toward* its original destination?" Prime asked.

"We're cut off from the coast by three field armies," Vlora replied flatly. "Do you have any better ideas?"

"I don't."

"The good news," Bo pointed out, "is that for Sedial to capture the damn thing he'll have to kill us all."

"That's not good news, dear," Nila said gently.

"It just means we won't have to deal with whatever god he creates."

Vlora rubbed her temples. "Yes, I suppose that's a silver lining." She looked up, taken aback by a sudden cheer around the bend of the river. The cheer carried on for several moments, then grew quiet. She could hear a ruckus in that direction and shook her head. "Any idea what's going on down there?" she asked.

"Beats me," Bo replied. "It's on the other side of our keelboat fleet."

Vlora walked back to the bridge and crossed to the riverbank and the edge of camp. Several more cheers had followed the first. She had half a mind to go find the source of it, but the sounds of gunshots from her cavalry screen seemed more worthy of her attention. She needed to check in with her officers and with the artillery— make sure everything was going smoothly. "Go put some pants on, and find out what everyone's cheering about," she tossed over her shoulder at Bo, heading up the side of the bank.

She hadn't reached the top of the hill when the gallop of hooves caught her attention. It was Davd, and his face was flushed. He sawed at the reins, calming his horse, and breathlessly saluted.

"What's going on?" Vlora asked.

Davd grinned down at her. "They're back!"

"Who's back?"

"The soldiers we left after Windy River. Vallencian and all the wounded."

Vlora waved at the news, pleased. That would be several hundred recovered veterans. She hadn't enjoyed leaving them behind, and rescuing them from the Fatrastans had been one of the things she'd worried about accomplishing before leaving the continent. "Good, good. Send the Ice Baron to see me when he gets the chance." She turned to go. "Wait, how did they find us?"

Davd's grin grew wider. "That's not all, ma'am. Colonel Olem is with them."

Vlora stood back, watching as dozens of keelboats poled up to the bank of the Hadshaw and began to disgorge the soldiers she had left in the care of the Ice Baron after the Battle of Windy River. The group included both wounded and recovered, and it appeared that they had brought with them far more supplies than they had when they had left. The mercenaries in their crimson uniforms embraced their regular-army brethren, the two groups intermingling happily. Spontaneous "huzzahs" broke out among reunited squads.

Vallencian stood out among the group, rushing back and forth, trying to keep everyone organized as they spilled off the keelboats. He was largely ignored. He finally threw his hands up in distress and looked around, his face lighting up when he spotted Vlora. She braced herself as he rushed up the hillside toward her.

"Lady Flint!" he bellowed.

"Vallencian," she replied, offering her hand. She tried not to be rude to the man who had cared for her wounded for the last few months, but she also looked around him, trying to pick Olem out of all the faces on the riverbank. It was so much harder without her sorcery. "Wait, don't..." Vallencian barely slowed as he barreled toward her, pulling her into a hug that lifted her clear off the ground. She bit her lip against the pain, forcing a grin onto her face, and gently patted him on the arm.

He set her down but kept his hands on her shoulders, holding her at arm's length like a parent seeing their child after a year away at school. "You are well?"

"Mending, yes."

"You've looked better, I'll admit."

"It was worse two months ago." For some reason, his concerned bluntness brought a smile to her lips.

"And it's behind you now. You're stronger, wiser." He slapped her on the shoulder, nearly knocking her off her feet. "I look forward to hearing the stories. Once we've kicked the Dynize out of Landfall, I insist that you stay at my home outside the city. We'll have food, drink, dancers. The finest of everything!" He gestured expansively, nearly smacking Vlora in the face. She leaned back.

"I'm not sure we'll be staying long enough for that. Besides, the last time I visited one of your houses, you didn't have any furniture."

Vallencian seemed to consider this. "I'll get some. For you."

"If I'm still in the city," Vlora promised.

"Good. Good! Now, I haven't had a drop of good whiskey in three days. Where can I find something to drink?"

Vlora opened her mouth to direct him toward the quartermaster with her blessings, only to find the words snatched from her tongue as her eyes fell on Olem. He'd appeared behind Vallencian as if by magic, and stood quietly with his hands clasped behind his back. Vlora stared at him, a rush of emotions tearing through her faster than she could understand them. Relief turned into guilt, which turned into anxiety, and then back again into relief. She studied his face. His hair was a little longer, his beard grown out. He wasn't wearing his uniform. His face was placid.

"Vallencian," she said quickly, "let me introduce you to Magus Borbador and Privileged Nila." Vlora spun toward Bo, who was approaching them as he buttoned up his jacket. "Borbador," she called, "this is my dear friend the Ice Baron. Make friends." She practically shoved Vallencian toward Bo and then spun back around to face Olem.

They watched each other from a half dozen paces apart. Vlora fought with the confusing jumble of emotions wrestling one another in her chest. Though he didn't look any older, she felt like she hadn't seen him in years.

"Ma'am," Olem said, breaking the silence. He removed his hat. "Colonel Olem reporting in. I've brought you thirty-seven keelboats and four hundred and eighty-nine fresh soldiers. I've also got extra supplies, courtesy of Lady Chancellor Lindet. Sorry I'm not in uniform. I seem to have left it back with the fleet."

Vlora took two steps closer to him. "I'm sorry," she whispered.

"Eh?" Olem leaned toward her, one finger behind his ear.

"I said I'm sorry."

"Ah, right. Just wanted to make sure I heard you."

"You're a prick."

Olem pursed his lips, the corners turned up. "Feeling better?"

"Slowly."

"Sorry I ran off. An uncle of mine used to say it's better to walk off anger than to vent it. I, uh, had to take a long walk."

Vlora closed the distance between them and slowly, timidly reached out to take Olem's hand. Without warning, Olem snatched her into a hug. Vlora wrapped her arms around his middle, squeezing with all her might, her face pressed against his chest. They remained that way for some time, until Vlora finally took a deep breath and released him. She took half a step back and wiped the corners of her eyes. "I've missed you."

"I've missed you, too. I've only heard a bit of what you've been up to, but it sounds like you've been a busy woman."

"That's one way of putting it."

Olem produced a cigarette from his breast pocket and a match from his cuff. Within seconds he was producing a fine cloud of white smoke. He gave a little cough, took the cigarette out of his mouth, and leaned forward and kissed her. It was the faintest of pecks, but it made Vlora's heart leap. Even the smell of his cigarette smoke was like the finest of colognes.

"Will you forgive me?" she asked.

"Already done." He took a drag on the cigarette. "You and I are too busy to hold grudges. I was either going to come back, or not."

"I'm glad you did."

"So am I. Now, I've got a message for you from Lindet."

Vlora's elation was slightly tempered. "What does *she* want?"

"She said for us to do what's necessary."

"She's not going to fight us for the godstone?" Vlora asked with a frown.

"That's what she claims. She's got a massive army, almost entirely conscripts, and they're giving the Dynize the pit not all that far from Landfall. But I don't think she can win a sustained war, and neither does she. The Dynize troops are too experienced and they're backed up by better sorcery."

"So we have her blessing to smash our way into Landfall and destroy the godstone?"

"That's the sum of it, yes."

"That's . . . a little disappointing."

"You'd rather we be spitting in her face throughout all of this?"

"Of course I would."

"Me, too." Olem smirked. "Unfortunately for us, she's a realist. She gave me these keelboats and the location of one of her military caches. To be honest, I'm glad you're here, because I really wasn't looking forward to carrying all of these supplies overland to meet up with you." He squeezed her hand and raised his chin to look toward the camp. "Do I hear gunshots?"

"Screening maneuver. Our cavalry are keeping the Dynize away from us so they don't see what I'm up to."

"How many Dynize?"

"Three field armies, but one of their generals is worried about being stabbed in the back and isn't going to attack us."

"Do you believe her?"

"Doesn't matter."

Olem cocked an eyebrow. "What do you mean, it doesn't matter?"

Vlora pointed upriver. "You see that fog?"

"I see a sorcerous mist. What do you have hidden under that?"

"Another four hundred keelboats, give or take. We're not going to fight these assholes. We're going to make a break for the city."

Olem gave a low whistle. "That sounds very dangerous."

"It will be. But with the keelboats you just brought, we should have enough to transport the entire army—minus the cavalry. They're going to screen for us and then ride hard downriver. I intend to hit Sedial before he even knows we're there." Vlora sucked in a quick breath, waiting for Olem to voice his objections. He was, after all, her sounding board and conscience. If he thought the gamble was too risky, he would say so.

Instead, he reached out and brushed some hair from her cheek. "I heard you weren't yourself."

"I wasn't. For a while."

"Well, this sounds a lot like my lady. I'm glad you're getting back to normal. Is there any chance you still have one of my spare uniforms in your trunk? I should probably get properly dressed if we're going to assault Landfall."

CHAPTER 57

Michel was swept along helplessly in the wake of Ichtracia's fury. They navigated the countless tunnels of the catacombs beneath the plateau, their path lit by flames flickering on the tips of Ichtracia's gloved fingers. Michel lost track of all sense of time during their journey, but the sun had already risen above the eastern horizon when they finally emerged into the streets of Landfall.

His first thought was that they were too late—but he didn't smell smoke and Ichtracia gave no indication that the Depths had already been assaulted with sorcery. His second thought was that something else was happening, and it didn't take him long to spot what.

Whole companies of soldiers had marched onto the plateau. Their helms and breastplates shone in the morning sun, blinding Michel as he and Ichtracia dashed from one alleyway to the next. As if in answer to the soldiers marching up the avenues, immense barricades had been thrown up to block their paths. Thousands of Palo, many of them likely still rioting and looting from the night before, had taken to the street with clubs, swords, blunderbusses, and any other weapon they could get a hold of. They screamed at the soldiers, who ordered them to stand down, hurling clay shingles from the roofs and tearing up paving stones for heavier ammunition.

Violence wasn't coming. Violence was *here*.

Michel emerged onto one of the streets behind a battalion of Dynize soldiers, all of them focused on Palo partisans shouting at them from second-story windows. He stared at the group in dismay as the commander very clearly vacillated between retreat and attack. Michel knew enough about uprisings to be confident that all these partisans would be dead by nightfall.

Ichtracia stumbled out of the alleyway behind him and turned her attention on the soldiers, raising her hands. Michel leapt back and grabbed her by the arm. "They'll be fine for now," he told her. "If we're still alive, we can come back and help after we stop the Privileged from destroying the Depths."

She hesitated only a moment before lowering her hands and giving him a determined nod. He tried to swallow his own terror at the realization that she'd been a hairsbreadth from attacking her own people—something she'd claimed she would avoid doing at all costs. He pulled her toward the next alley, where they cut across several more streets and then through a tenement, taking them behind the barricades.

As they neared the rim of Greenfire Depths, Ichtracia suddenly came to a halt, throwing her hand up. Michel froze while she stood stock-still, her chin lifted, sniffing the air like a hound at the hunt. After what felt like an eternity, she finally said, "They're here."

"The Privileged?"

"Yes. There are three of them, and they're not even bothering to hide." Her lip curled, and she pointed at the wall and then slightly to the left, and then farther to the left of that. "There, there, and there."

"Do you know them?"

"Doubtlessly. Our cabal is enormous, but not *that* enormous."

Michel watched the side of her face, wondering if she was about to get cold feet at the idea of attacking her companions. He could see a flurry of emotions playing out across her face, revealing that moment of weakness before her expression hardened once more. "It doesn't matter who they are," she continued. "They've come to slaughter innocent people."

She moved slowly, carefully, in a half crouch as they emerged from the alley. Michel followed her to their next hiding spot—an overturned cart off to one side of the street—and she raised her hand once more and turned to him. While her expression was cold and distant, he was surprised to see tears streaming down her cheeks. "Ichtracia?"

She suddenly reached out, touching his face with two gloved fingers. "I've liked you from the beginning, Michel. You made me laugh, but then you made me care about things. Thanks for that."

"I'm kind of sick of people thanking me for doing my job," Michel retorted with forced bravado. His own gut turned somersaults. "You don't need to thank me for anything. Just stay alive."

"I'm afraid that's not very likely. There's three of them and just one of me." She wiped her sleeve across her face. "You shouldn't make a Privileged cry, Michel."

"We can do this," Michel replied, biting his lip.

"No. *I* can do this. You're going to hide. You're not in charge this time, lover. I am. Now, go find Jiniel. Help her organize whatever needs to be done next." Without another word, Ichtracia broke from their hiding spot and began to sprint.

Michel tried to shout after her, but he choked on the words. She was soon gone, leaving him alone in what seemed like the only pocket of quiet in the entire city. He looked over his shoulder to the east, where he could now hear the reports of musket fire and the screams of men and women. The south echoed with the same language of the rioters—and the soldiers sent to put them down.

It was just a few blocks back to the catacombs. He *might* find relative safety down there—unless Ichtracia's fight with her countrymen collapsed the entire plateau. He grit his teeth and emerged from his hiding spot. Ichtracia did not deserve to die alone.

He ran along the street, perpendicular to the alley Ichtracia had disappeared into. The sound of an explosion nearly threw him off his feet, and he paused briefly to look toward the Depths, where a cloud of smoke now rose above the buildings nearest to him. No, not the Depths. That smoke was coming from the Rim. A thunderclap followed it, then a heart-wrenching sound like the world's largest pane of glass had just shattered. More smoke followed it.

He traveled three more blocks and took a hard right, dashing down an alleyway. The sorcerous cacophony continued, setting his teeth on edge and making his hands shake violently. Anyone with any brains would be sprinting in the opposite direction.

He emerged from the alley onto a narrow street that cut precariously along the Rim, and stopped to get his bearings.

A ways down, around the curve of the Rim, he caught sight of Ichtracia as a fireball appeared out of the sky and slammed into her. To Michel's shock, she seemed to absorb the sorcery with a flick of her wrist, emerging from it unscathed. A section of the Rim suddenly collapsed, dust exploding outward. Michel caught sight of the first Privileged—a woman who leapt from the falling ledge, barely making it to solid ground before more fireballs appeared in the air above her head and shot toward Ichtracia.

Michel searched for the second and third Privileged and found both of them standing between himself and the ongoing fight. The second Privileged watched the fight with clear confusion, gloved fingers pressed to his lips. The third Privileged was less than two dozen paces away, with his back toward Michel. He regarded the battle with disinterest before turning away and looking down at the Depths. A few moments passed before he raised his hands, and one of the tallest buildings in the Depths became enveloped in flames.

Michel crept toward the Privileged, trying to watch both Ichtracia's duel and the sorcerer at the same time. Another fire started down in the Depths, and then another. The Privileged smiled to himself. If he spotted Michel in his peripheral vision, he gave no indication. Michel removed the knuckledusters from his pocket.

A scream suddenly cut through the morning air, punctuated by another explosion. The Privileged looked toward Ichtracia's fight. Ichtracia made an emphatic gesture, bringing her whole arm around in a chopping motion. Her opponent reeled, screamed again, and then slumped.

The Privileged closest to Michel gave an irritated sigh and turned to Ichtracia, raising his hands.

"Hey," Michel said, sprinting the last few feet between them.

The Privileged whirled just as Michel's shoulder connected with his kidneys. The Privileged gave a gentle "Oof" and disappeared off the Rim. A series of crashes followed. Michel caught himself on a railing and peered over the edge, noting broken shingles and a torn storm drain. There was no sign of the body. Michel gripped the railing under him hard, trying to calm his nerves, then looked up to find the second Privileged had turned to stare at him.

His eyes were drawn past the Privileged to Ichtracia, and past her to a figure that had just emerged on the Rim over her shoulder, tugging on a pair of white, runed gloves.

A fourth Privileged.

"Look out!" Michel screamed.

"I told you to run!" she shouted back. She flipped one hand toward him, and he felt himself suddenly lifted and thrown, cartwheeling head over heels up and over three-story buildings. The last glimpse he caught of Ichtracia was one of surprise, as flame and rock crashed down over her in a spectacular explosion. Michel's flight was swift but steady, and he soared along in a clearly con-trolled bubble before it disappeared. He dropped the last dozen feet into a pile of rubble, catching himself with his three-fingered hand. The whole left side of him lit up with pain.

He lay that way for several seconds before the thought of Ichtra-cia being consumed by sorcery got him up and moving. He took one step, then another, forcing his body along until he was knocked backward by an unseen force. The air was smashed from his lungs, and he was thrown into the side of a building a split second before a rumbling sound reached him. Dust and flame coalesced, threaten-ing to suffocate him, until suddenly he could feel air reaching his lungs once more.

He lay unmoving, trying to peer through the dust. When it had cleared enough to see, he found himself looking at...nothing. Every building between him and the Rim was gone, leveled to scat-tered rubble. The corpses of unfortunate bystanders were barely recognizable in the mess, and it only took him a few moments of searching to see that Ichtracia was missing.

CHAPTER 58

Styke sat in the corridor outside his shared room, whittling horses by lamplight and listening to the distant sounds of a sleeping city. Talunlica was, in his experience, an extremely quiet city after dark, even with the riots that consumed the daylight. But that didn't mean it was silent—the rumble of delivery wagons, the march of patrolling city guards, the barking of dogs, the gentle lap of water against the compound's outer wall. He found those sounds, and the stillness of the compound, to be comforting in these hours of sleeplessness.

He finished one of the horses, holding it up to the lamplight to make small, final adjustments, before setting it aside and preparing a new piece of wood for whittling. He was almost finished with the entire set. All the whittling had given his hands something to do while he planned how, exactly, he was going to get Ka-poel near the godstone.

Etzi spoke of escalating conflict and his fears of violence. Styke longed for it. His knife hand twitched constantly, and last night he'd spent several hours in the stables seeing to all of the Lancers' horses, just to give himself something to do. He longed to throw himself back in the saddle, lower a lance, and charge an enemy.

But he had to keep himself in check. He was a guest here. Ka-poel and Celine were under his protection, and he was under Etzi's protection. He did not feel guilt over the mob attack yesterday, but he understood that it may have been in response to his murder of Ji-Patten and that he shouldn't be personally involved in further escalation. No need to push Etzi's hospitality.

Styke heard a throat clear and looked up from his whittling, expecting to find Etzi or Maetle out for a midnight stroll. Instead, he discovered a figure dressed in a loose Dynize traveling smock leaning on a wall at the end of the corridor as if he'd been watching Styke for several minutes.

"Jackal?" Styke asked cautiously.

The hood of the traveling cloak was thrown back to reveal the Palo warrior. Jackal approached, coming into the light of the lantern and lowering himself down beside Styke as if they were meeting casually in a park or on the street. Jackal had gotten significantly more weather-beaten in the last nine days: cheeks dark, hair looking redder. Perhaps it was the clothing, but he seemed oddly more Dynize, as if he'd been absorbing the energy of the people.

"Took you long enough," Styke snorted.

"Sorry. Took me longer than I expected to find Ibana—an alarm was put out after my escape and I had to take a longer route."

"But you *did* find her?" Styke set his whittling aside and stared at Jackal eagerly.

"Once I was away from the godstone, I just needed to avoid patrols and listen to the spirits." Jackal tapped the side of his head.

"And?"

"Roughly ninety percent of our fleet arrived safely. They put to shore at the rendezvous point almost a month ago. Just as Orz told us, the rendezvous was deep enough in the swamp that they haven't been discovered. The Dynize claim they tamed the Jagged Fens, but they've really only cleaned up a corridor along the main highway. Everywhere else . . ." Jackal shrugged. "Nobody goes that deep into the swamp, and Ibana has been being really damned careful. She even dismissed the fleet so they wouldn't be spotted from the sea."

Styke felt his eyes widen. "Dismiss the fleet? You're joking."

"Ibana seems confident that we'll be able to commandeer a fleet once we've accomplished our task."

"Does she have any idea how badly we messed up with the maps?" Styke gestured at the city around them.

"Some," Jackal answered hesitantly. "She's been using our Palo as scouts, hoping they blend in. They've hunted to conserve rations and stayed well away from the roads. They've lost some soldiers and horses to the ravages of the swamp, but were in higher spirits than I would have expected. So far, they haven't been discovered."

"You updated them?"

"I did. Ibana wasn't happy."

"I can imagine."

"But she's pleased that you're alive. She hid it well, but I could tell."

"What do you mean she 'hid it well'?"

"There was a lot of swearing and cursing your name. I got the feeling that she regretted dismissing the fleet and probably would have gone back to Fatrasta by now if she hadn't." Jackal hesitated again, long enough that Styke could tell he wanted to say something else.

"Spit it out," Styke said.

"Well," Jackal drew out the word. "They're running low on rations. Now that Ibana knows you're alive, and knows about Talunlica, she wants to move on the city."

Styke felt his stomach lurch. His wish for *something* to happen was about to come true. "How soon?"

"She was mobilizing everyone before I left."

"How long ago?"

"Two days."

"Shit." Styke spat the word and resisted the urge to throw his whittling knife across the corridor. "She needs to hold off. Sedial's goons are using the Lancers still imprisoned against me—the moment they find out we have an army here, they'll execute the lot."

"I told her about Zak. She said it was an acceptable loss."

Styke felt his hackles rise. "How could you possibly know about Zak? You were two days out of the city when it happened."

Jackal tapped the side of his head again. The damned spirits.

Styke swore. "She wants to get *me* killed, too?"

"She assumes you're safe enough."

"Like pit I am. Etzi has stood up for us so far, but I can't imagine me and Ka-poel will be welcome when they find out we have a foreign army on their shores."

Jackal spread his hands as a show of helplessness. "Ibana is champing at the bit."

"No stopping her. Damn it, she's supposed to be the cautious one." Styke rubbed furiously at his Lancer ring with one thumb. He should probably be happy to hear that the Mad Lancers were coming to get him. But the chaos in the city was too unpredictable. The appearance of a foreign army *might* make Talunlica fall to bits, allowing them to storm in and crush the city garrison. *Or* it might unite the Dynize against a common threat. Styke was willing to bet it would do the latter.

"All right," he breathed. "This is what we're going to do. I need you to return to Ibana as quickly as possible. If you can reach her before she leaves her hiding spot, you need to tell her to stay put—a direct order from me. If not...well, you need to keep her from riding into the city. It'll be a tempting target for her, but I want to have a couple of days to get me and the others out. Tell her to come within four miles and hold for my order. If she doesn't hear from me within a couple days, she can torch the city."

"Four miles, two days." Jackal nodded. "I'll ride as fast as I can."

"Good. Get moving."

Jackal disappeared as quickly as he'd appeared. Styke heard the scrape of someone shimmying over the compound wall but nothing else. He listened for several minutes and then, troubled, picked his whittling back up. No hope of sleep now, not unless he could calm himself down a little—and his mind was racing, his heart eager for a fight, but his thoughts cautious.

He was a fighter, not a strategist. A million variables could make things go wrong between now and Ibana's arrival. He resisted the urge to bolt right away—to saddle his horse, grab Ka-poel and Celine, and follow Jackal out of the city. Never mind the risk of such a flight; he refused to leave Markus, Sunin, and the rest to die in a Dynize prison.

He finally tossed aside his whittling and climbed to his feet.

It had been days since he'd spoken to Orz. The dragonman had been given a small recovery room just beside Maetle's infirmary, and according to the compound gossip, he was healing at an astonishing speed. He'd been seen walking on his own—albeit slowly—just yesterday. Unfortunately, Styke needed more than just "walking" right now. He approached Orz's quarters and knocked gently on the door before stepping inside. There wasn't much room to maneuver. Like every other building in the compound, it had been built to take up as little space as possible. Just stepping inside put Styke immediately beside the one small bed.

Styke felt something press against his inner thigh. The small hairs on the back of his neck stood on end. "It's Styke," he said.

"Should have known," Orz answered. "The emperor doesn't have any assassins that cast that big of a shadow." Orz's voice was weak, not much above a whisper. He pulled his knife away. "You have news?"

Styke lowered himself down beside Orz's head. The dragon-man hadn't attempted to sit up, eyeballing Styke from his supine position. Styke couldn't help but wonder if he didn't want to move, or couldn't. "Why does everyone seem to know things before me?"

"I heard someone slip over the wall, then bits of a whispered conversation, and then they went back over the wall. I can only assume it's the man you had break out of prison the day I woke up. Jackal, right?"

"That was halfway across the compound," Styke grumbled.

"I have very good hearing, and it's hard to sleep when Maetle won't give me more mala until tomorrow night."

Styke tapped the side of his ring. "You're right, I have news. Jackal found Ibana."

"Is she where she was supposed to be?"

"She is, and by some miracle she hasn't been discovered yet. But she's running low on rations and champing at the bit. As far as we know, she left the swamp the moment Jackal headed back to find me."

"So news might reach the city at any time." Orz sounded resigned.

"Correct."

"They'll come for us," Orz said. "It's just the excuse Sedial's people will need—perfectly justified."

"Agreed."

"And Etzi won't be able to protect us, whether or not he wants to. We should leave tonight."

Styke held up two fingers, unsure as to whether Orz could see them. "First, I'm not sure if you can ride. Second, I'm not leaving the rest of my Lancers in that prison to be tortured and executed."

"I can ride," Orz said. He sat up, as if to emphasize his health, but nearly toppled out of the bed. Styke caught him by his shoulder to steady him.

"I'm not leaving without them," Styke reiterated. "I don't mind throwing you over a saddle and putting your recovery back weeks—you'll survive. But the others..." Styke trailed off. He could practically *feel* Orz's disagreement. He probably agreed with

Ibana; the captured soldiers were acceptable casualties. If they were twenty random recruits, Styke might agree. But these were the oldest of his Lancers, men and women who'd been with him since the very beginning of the Fatrastan War for Independence, and some of them from even before that. "Do I tell Etzi about the army?"

Orz was silent for some time. Styke was beginning to think he'd nodded off, when he finally spoke again. "Etzi told me that you killed Ji-Patten."

"I did."

"You gave him one of Ji-Patten's knives. Who is the other for?"

"Markus. Zak's brother."

Another long pause. "I would have liked to have killed him myself."

"It wasn't a fair fight."

"Etzi told me that, too." Orz hesitated. "You should know something."

"What is that?"

"Etzi is making plans. Plans that he hasn't mentioned to you."

Styke took a sharp breath. "And?"

"He sees an opportunity in Ka-poel. He's been spending a lot of time with her as of late."

"No one told me this." Styke scowled.

"It has little to do with you, and everything to do with her."

"She is my ward." Styke felt himself growing angry and not a little bit confused. The fact that he hadn't noticed the two of them speaking even once indicated that they were going behind his back—and what purpose would there be in that unless it was about a betrayal?

"It doesn't involve you," Orz insisted, as if reading Styke's mind. "You have enough to think about that Ka-poel didn't want to bring it to your attention."

"What is 'it'?" Styke demanded.

"I don't know exactly."

"Then why bring it up?" Styke wanted to shake Orz by the throat.

"To warn you," Orz said flatly. "Etzi wants to use Ka-poel in his politics. He has confirmed her identity, and revealed her presence to several of his allies."

Styke felt like a cold bucket of water had been poured over him. "Did she agree to this?"

"It took some time for him to bring her around. She wants nothing more than to destroy the godstone and return to Fatrasta. But Etzi wants to use her as a counter for Sedial. She has the power, and she has the birthright. All she has to do is use them."

"And stick her neck into Dynize politics. The moment Sedial finds out for certain that Ka-poel is here, he will send dragonmen to fetch her."

"Etzi has been cautious," Orz said defensively.

"He better damn well have been." Styke swore. First Ibana, and now Ka-poel. He hadn't had control of things for a month, but what little agency he *did* have seemed to have disappeared in a puff of smoke. Nothing to do now but wait for the tidal wave to hit and hope he could ride it out. "What do I do with this?" he whispered to himself.

There was a beat of silence, and then Orz said, "If Ka-poel agrees to work with Etzi and his allies, you might be protected. She claims her birthright as an adviser of the emperor, denounces Ka-Sedial and the war with Fatrasta, and claims you and the Lancers as her bodyguard. It won't go down easily, but it might mean that the city doesn't immediately try to execute you and march an army out to meet Ibana."

"That sounds like a whole lot of being hopeful," Styke growled.

"I agree. But sometimes that's all we can do."

"You realize if this all goes south, you're going to die with me, right?" Styke said petulantly.

"I am very aware," Orz replied.

"Good. I just want to make sure." He felt a swirl of emotions, none of them positive. Beneath the eagerness to fight and the anger at this uncertainty, he felt fear—the world was about to explode around him, and Celine would no doubt be caught in the maelstrom. Etzi's Household, too, and though he didn't want to admit it, he did care. Etzi had shown his true colors yesterday, defending Styke at the cost of his own soldiers. He'd been a protective, loyal host, and the city was about to find out he'd been harboring an enemy officer. No matter how he spun it, he would lose out.

It did not leave a good feeling in the pit of Styke's stomach.

"You should try to get some sleep," Orz said gently.

"Small chance of that." Styke stood up, turning toward the door.

"Then what will you do?"

"The politics of all this are well beyond me, so I'm going to do the one thing I can to prepare: sharpen my knife and polish my armor."

CHAPTER 59

V lora awoke with a deep sense of unease, and it took her several moments of lying in the dark, listening to the creak of wood and the gentle sound of lapping water to remember where, exactly, she was: nestled among the barrels and crates of supplies in the shallow hold of a keelboat. She practiced deep, calming breaths as the befuddlement of sleep fled her mind. She was among friends, traveling quickly and with a plan. She was still Lady Vlora Flint, a former powder mage and current military commander.

Those simple realities made her feel only marginally better. Something was wrong, and she couldn't quite place it.

A small gasp escaped from her lips, and she rolled over to feel around in the bedroll beside hers. It was empty and cold—it hadn't been occupied for some time. But it *was* there. Olem *had* returned. She continued her breathing exercises and stumbled to her feet, wrapping a blanket around her shoulders. Bent almost double, she crept through the hold by feel alone, making her way out to the deck of the keelboat.

The deck was covered in the gently snoring forms of her body-guard and the resting polers, who, for sixteen hours each day, pro-pelled the boat down the Hadshaw. As her personal vessel, it was much less crowded than the rest of the flotilla, and she was able to pick her way among the sleeping bodies without the risk of actu-ally stepping on anyone. She approached the stern, where a lantern hung at head height illuminating a single figure sitting with his legs hanging off the deck. She would have been able to identify that sil-houette anywhere, but the whiff of cigarette smoke and the ember glowing in the dark removed all doubt.

She felt her mysterious anxiety drop slightly as she sat down beside Olem, her feet swinging just a couple of inches above the water.

"You should be sleeping," he said gently.

"I don't feel very well."

"Sick?"

"I don't think so." She searched for a way to describe it. "It's almost a gut feeling, like I know something is going to go wrong."

"That's natural. We're about to attack a superior force at their stronghold."

"But it's *not* that," Vlora continued.

"You're sure?" She could see him looking at her peculiarly by the lantern light.

"I don't know." She gave a frustrated sigh. It felt like her body was trying to tell her something, but she had absolutely no sense of *what*. It made her feel helpless and angry. She tried to shake it off. "Have we heard anything from Delia's people since we set off down the river?"

"No. The provosts managed to claim a handful of keelboats for themselves, so I know they're back there somewhere."

"Delia is probably furious that we're striking for the Dynize heart. We should have left them behind."

"Little chance of that."

"I suppose we can only hope we ruined whatever deal she struck with Ka-Sedial's generals. Oh well. What time is it?"

"I think it's around three."

"How far from Landfall are we?"

"Twenty miles, give or take."

"That close?" Vlora pictured a map in her mind. "We must have passed the Battle of Windy River site yesterday, then?"

"We did."

"I didn't even notice." She passed a hand across her face.

"You've been a bit preoccupied," Olem said reassuringly, reaching out to squeeze her hand.

They'd spent the last few days in the keelboat together, rarely more than a couple dozen paces apart, and somehow it felt like Olem had never left. Having him close again was like having a limb restored, and she wondered whether the sense of loss that had come with the loss of her sorcery had, in part, been a sense of loss of *him*. It seemed likely. There was still a thin barrier between them—hesitations, unshared thoughts—but it felt like something that would heal in time.

Then why did she feel so strangely right now?

"We should land tomorrow afternoon," Vlora told him. "Everyone has their orders?"

Olem lifted his gaze to look out over the river, where they could see the lights of dozens of their immense flotilla of keelboats. "They do," he confirmed. "We're moving too fast for scouts to be much good, but the riders we've sent out indicate that this region is almost abandoned. Lindet's forces are fifty miles or so to our west, so that's where all of the Dynize armies are focused. Aside from the little bit of traffic we've come across, this stretch is almost entirely undefended."

"Could it be a trap?"

Olem chuckled. "That nervous, huh?"

"I'm serious!"

"I don't think even Sedial could anticipate that you'd slip past three of his field armies and rush downriver in just a handful of days to confront him. If he's foreseen it, then we deserve to get our teeth kicked in."

"That's not reassuring." Vlora paused, considering all the plans and contingencies she'd made. During the day, looking upon her flotilla and excited by their swift travel, it was easy to feel as if she was on top of everything. But in the darkness of the night, when life felt so very fragile and the world so big, all the doubts began to creep in. What if her plans weren't good enough? What if her army wasn't up to the job? What if *she* wasn't? What if Sedial had more sorcery at his call, or men guarding his door, than she had expected?

"I've been putting on a confident face for the general staff to keep them on board with this plan," Vlora admitted, "but I'm terrified that I'm about to get us all killed."

"Hm," Olem grunted. "You have been downplaying the danger, but I don't think you're fooling anyone. We all know this is a mad dash to death or victory. Bo and Nila definitely do. The general staff are not a bunch of fools. Even the soldiers can sense it."

Vlora rubbed her eyes. "I should be taking it slower. I should have dismantled those three armies piece by piece and marched our way down the river destroying everything in our path slowly, cautiously. The Adran way."

"That's not the Adran way." Olem laughed.

She narrowed her eyes at him. "I don't think you're taking this seriously."

"Do you remember," he went on, "when Tamas tried to flank the Kez forces outside of Budwiel by transporting three brigades through a cave system?"

"Yes. And that didn't work out well for us."

"I could name several dozen maneuvers in Tamas's career that were equally as brash. Most of them *did* work out. The Adran way is to be the best at everything. Fewer troops, but better trained with better equipment and stronger lines. Quality over quantity. Driving ourselves like a spike right into Sedial's heart *is* the Adran way. The general staff knows that. And remember that most of them were present for Kresimir. They know the dangers we're facing unless we prevent Sedial from using that stone. They believe in the cause. They believe in *you*."

Vlora laid her head on Olem's shoulder. "Maybe you're right. I just need to stop worrying."

"Worrying is fine. But you shouldn't let it keep you from sleeping. You, of all people, need rest."

"I'm telling you, I don't think it's the worry. I...just feel strange." She rubbed her arms. "Jittery! That's the word. It must just be nerves."

At the word "jittery," Olem gave her a sharp glance. Vlora ignored it. There wasn't anything she could do but try to get some sleep. She'd already prepared all that she could, and her officers were taking care of all the smaller details. There was nothing to get excited about until her flotilla was spotted by the Dynize.

She looked over her shoulder, letting her gaze cross the sleeping forms on the deck and then turning it toward the river. Somewhere along the flotilla she could hear someone singing softly—no doubt a soldier who was having a hard time sleeping. It was a strange feeling, floating on a river the night before a battle with keelboat decks instead of tents, lanterns instead of cookfires, and the lapping of the water against the shores instead of the call of sentries. Somewhere in the distance she heard a horse whinny, and wondered how the cavalry were getting on. They'd ridden alongside the river, pushing themselves hard to keep up with the keelboats, and would be very tired by the time they reached Landfall. But their presence on the shore gave Vlora some comfort that her flotilla wouldn't be unexpectedly flanked.

Beside her, Olem suddenly rustled. "Stay here," he said. "I'll be right back." He climbed to his feet and disappeared into the cabin, leaving her alone in the darkness for a minute or two. When he returned, she felt a goblet pushed into her hand.

"What's this?"

"A bit of wine. Nothing fantastic, but..."

"Is there something to celebrate?" Vlora asked, giving it a sniff.

She could make out a cautious smile on Olem's face. "Just a hunch that you needed something to take the edge off."

Vlora snorted. "I *wish* it would take the edge off. Even being powder blind I can't get drunk." She took a hefty gulp of the wine anyway. She'd already swallowed when she tasted something peculiar, and then the full brunt of it hit her. "By Adom," she swore. "This is terrible." The sulfuric taste clung to her tongue no matter how much she sputtered. "What the pit is in..."

She trailed off as a little thrill spread throughout her mouth and into her blood and mind, lighting up her senses in a familiar, but decidedly subdued manner. Her hands began to tremble with excitement.

"Powder," Olem said. "Just a small spoonful."

"That's a good way to ruin a cup of wine," Vlora said, downing the rest of her glass. She tried not to let her excitement get the better of her as her senses sharpened. The sound of distant singing grew louder, the darkness of the night shifting before her eyes until she could pierce it without squinting. Even the terrible taste of the wine grew more pronounced. Her mind seemed to speed up to compensate for all this new information. She felt her hands tremble and her face flush. "How the pit..." she began, turning toward Olem.

He was watching her eagerly. "Is it working?"

"It is."

A grin cracked his face and he gave a little sigh of relief. "You would have been furious at me if it hadn't."

Vlora held her hand horizontally in front of her face. It only took a brief surge of willpower to still the trembling. The aches and pains and exhaustion were all still there, but they were in a distant place, locked in the corner of her mind, overpowered by the sudden arrival of her powder trance. "How did you know?"

"Your body was giving signs of withdrawal."

"I don't follow."

"That strange feeling you described," Olem said, waving one of his cigarettes under her nose. "It sounded a lot like how I feel when I haven't had one of these for a couple of days. It was the word 'jittery' that pulled it together for me. Cigarettes, mala, coffee. They don't affect powder mages the same way they do other people, but the fact that your body was suddenly having withdrawal effects, months after you lost your sorcery..." His grin grew wider. "Well? How is it?"

Vlora cautiously reached out with her senses. She could sense all the powder nearby, in the holds of the keelboats and in the horns and wrapped charges of the soldiers. She tried to temper her excitement and pulled away from it all mentally to try for a self-diagnosis. "Dulled."

"In what way?"

"Just...not as sharp as it used to be. I can't see as well in the dark, and the sounds aren't as pronounced. Maybe it's the wine you mixed it with, but I think I should be cautious."

"I agree. Your body is still healing."

She let out a shaky laugh and could hear her own relief in it. Her sorcery was back! Perhaps not as strong as it once was, but it was *there*. She could continue to heal. She could be a mage again. "It's going to be a pit of a time holding back once we get to Landfall."

"I expect you to do just that. Let Davd do the heavy lifting."

Vlora clenched her fists, unclenched them, and tried to stop grinning. For the first time in months the urge to blow something up was a joyous one rather than a furious reaction that ended in tears. She forced herself to pull back with her senses. More than enough chance to test them tomorrow. And Olem was right. She needed to be careful. Her sorcery might be back, but it could also be fragile. She would only use it in an emergency.

Leaning over, she kissed Olem gently. "Thank you."

"You would have figured it out eventually. But I know that jittery feeling." He tapped the side of his nose. "Now, have I woken you up or do you think you can get some more sleep?"

"I don't ever want to sleep again." Vlora looked out over the water once more. Her body had been her enemy these last couple of months. It was still a tangled mess of scars and still-healing wounds, but it was now tense with the desire for action. She could move her arms without hurting. Pit, she might actually be able to fight again. She got to her feet and looked down at Olem. "We might die tomorrow."

"Always a possibility," he conceded.

"Join me in the cabin?"

Olem took one last drag, flicked his cigarette into the water, and stood up. "Lead on, Lady Flint."

CHAPTER 60

Styke met with Etzi and Ka-poel on the small guard tower overlooking the causeway that connected Etzi's compound with the rest of the city. Beyond them, smoke rose from the northwest corner of the city and a mob of commoners swept down the closest main avenue just out of musket range, waving weapons and shouting angrily. Pavers, stones, and bricks were loosened and thrown through windows as the mob passed a nearby collection of shops, and citizens fled in all directions ahead of the chaos.

At this range, it was impossible to tell whether the mob was composed of Sedial's hired crew, an angry response to the former, or another group altogether that had formed spontaneously just to cause destruction. Whoever they were, they didn't seem interested in the causeway or the walled compound, a fact that visibly relieved the Household guard manning the walls.

Etzi himself watched the action with a stricken expression, alternating every few moments between grief and anger. "Sedial thought he could control the mob," he grumbled, "and instead he's done us all in." As if to punctuate his words, there was a sickening crash from a few streets over. A cloud of dust rose from a suddenly blank spot on the city vista, and Styke could only assume that one of the mobs had pulled down an entire city guard tower.

"Nobody can truly control a mob," Styke said, removing his ring and scratching beneath it.

"The Great Ka is a thousand miles away. He doesn't give a shit what's happening here." Etzi struck a fist against his palm. "Damned fool." He took a few deep breaths and turned to Styke and Ka-poel, looking them up and down for several moments before addressing Styke. "Orz says he told you about our dealings?" He gestured between himself and Ka-poel.

Styke tried not to be annoyed that he'd been left out. "He just said that you've been trying to get Ka-poel to enter the political arena."

"More or less."

Styke raised an eyebrow at Ka-poel.

I haven't decided yet, Ka-poel gestured.

"You *need* to decide," Etzi said urgently. "This is quickly growing beyond anyone's control. Mobs are crisscrossing the city, making it difficult for Households to communicate. Another couple of days and we may be cut off for weeks, left to hunker down behind the walls, where we try not to attract the attention of the rabble."

"Where's the city guard?" Styke asked.

"Half of them have joined the mobs." Etzi threw his hands up. "The rest have retired to their own Households to help keep order—I called back twenty of my own to man the walls." He fell silent, glaring at Ka-poel as if willing her to give him an answer, and then finally turning back to Styke. He set his jaw. "This is only going to get worse. Word has arrived of an army south of the city." His eyes narrowed. "*Your* army."

Styke leaned against the top of the compound wall, returning

Etzi's gaze coolly. So much for Jackal getting back to Ibana and keeping the Mad Lancers out of sight. "Oh," he replied.

"Oh? Is that it?" Etzi clenched his fists, unclenched them, and then tried to pace. He gave up when the space atop the tower proved too small. "You've taken my hospitality, and I've done you the courtesy of asking no questions, only to find out that you've somehow managed to land several thousand cavalry on my shores."

Styke drew his knife and used the tip to pick dirt from beneath his fingernails. "You said you didn't want to know."

"An enemy army is *need-to-know* amounts of urgency."

"How much *do* you know?" Styke asked.

"Orz has told me everything. I know about your separation from the fleet, your deal with him, and your uncertainty over the army. I also know that you've come here to attempt to destroy the godstone." His gaze flicked to Ka-poel, who returned the glance without expression.

Styke adjusted his stance casually, sweeping a quick look across the courtyard below them. Aside from the handful of guards manning the walls, no one had gathered in ambush or seemed prepared to rush him. Etzi hadn't summoned him to some sort of trap, which meant he wasn't about to turn on him.

Yet.

He returned his knife to its sheath and spread his hands. "So you know everything now. What are you going to do?"

"Under normal circumstances, there would already be a few dragonmen and dozens of city guard here to arrest you. The last message I got from my allies on the Quorum indicated that most everyone suspects that you have something to do with that army."

"But?" Styke voiced the unsaid word.

"But...no one is in any state to do anything about it. Factionalism is the word of the day. Most of our generals and fighting men are in Fatrasta. What few we have will remain with their

Households, and I have no doubt those Households will hunker behind their walls and hope that your cavalry will find it just as difficult to enter the city as the guard is finding it to restore order."

Styke snorted. "And if my soldiers decide to enter and put down the mob at the tip of a sword?"

"You may cow us by destroying an army or two, if it comes to that," Etzi said flatly, "but this is a city of a million people, and their blood is already up. Do you think even the best-trained cavalry in the world can tame that with a mere few thousand?"

Styke grunted a response. Etzi was probably right. He didn't want the Mad Lancers to have anything to do with dozens— maybe hundreds—of roaming mobs. Their one advantage was that they had a clear goal. Getting into the city, securing the godstone, and giving Ka-poel time to destroy it . . . well, that might be within reach.

Though when he ran the thought through his head a few times, it sounded more and more absurd. "You didn't answer my question," Styke said. "What are you going to do?"

Etzi stared at a new column of smoke just beginning to rise from the south. He scowled at it for a few moments. "I don't care about the godstone," he said quietly. "Other Households might risk lives to protect it, but not me. I'm going to get you and Orz out of the city, and my responsibility for you will be finished. Then I'm going to try to help rally the Household Quorum to fight you."

Styke knew it would go easier on both of them if they just tried to kill each other right now. But he could also see the defeated frustration in Etzi's eyes, and he knew for himself that he wasn't about to turn on his host in cold blood. Etzi had been too good to him. "I'm not leaving without my soldiers."

"Orz said you'd say that." Etzi's scowl deepened. "As soon as the rest of my Household comes in from the city guard, I'm sending them to the prison, where they will have orders to force their way

in, retrieve your soldiers, and bring them back here. After that"—
he made a "go away" gesture—"I'll turn you out."

"Won't that be dangerous?"

"Extremely. That short journey might take them the rest of
the day. But if it gets you out of the city without bloodshed..."
Etzi turned his attention back to Ka-poel, staring at her for several
moments. When no answer was forthcoming, he gave a frustrated
sigh and climbed down from the guard tower.

Styke watched a mob across the water to the north. They looked
like they were chasing someone, but they were too far away to tell.
"This dealing you've had with Etzi," he said. "What does he want?"
He turned back to Ka-poel and watched her hands.

She pursed her lips. *I wasn't trying to go behind your back*, she
gestured.

"That's not what I asked."

They want me to get involved.

"I picked up on that."

*Deeply involved. They want to present me to the emperor to take
Ka-Sedial's place as his highest adviser.*

Just as Orz had suggested. Styke wondered what Etzi's coalition
hoped to gain from this. Did they plan on using her as a puppet?
Because if so, they were about to bite off more than they could
chew. He glanced at the mobs and thought of Zak's execution.
Sedial projected enough fear from a thousand miles away to put a
whole city on edge and bend Households to his will. Perhaps Etzi
and his friends were just so desperate that they'd cling to anything.

"They know *exactly* who you are?"

She nodded.

"And they believe you?"

Another nod, this time less certain. *It may not matter to them.
I'm a powerful bone-eye, more than strong enough to challenge Sedial.
Perhaps that's all they care about.*

"But you haven't given them an answer."

Ka-poel hesitated.

"You're waiting for something," Styke realized aloud.

A nod.

"What?"

Taniel.

Styke frowned, then raised his eyebrows as he caught up mentally. She'd mentioned before that Taniel planned on catching up with him, but it had slipped his mind in the weeks since. "Taniel's coming *here*. To the city?"

He's currently on a fast ship heading toward us. I'm not going to throw myself into Dynize politics without consulting him.

Styke let out an uneasy breath. Taniel was a small army all on his own. Having him nearby would be an awfully huge relief. "Do you know how long until he arrives?"

She shook her head. *Days? A week at most.*

Too long for them to just sit on their thumbs for one man. Styke needed to move immediately. Once he had his soldiers back, he'd ride out of the city and join up with Ibana. They'd have to strategize from there, but he deeply suspected that they'd be riding back in within twenty-four hours, plowing through any mobs and guardsmen who got in their way. One objective. Accomplish, then pull out.

He wondered how hard it would be to kidnap or assassinate the emperor once they'd breached the palace complex. *That* might be their ransom back to Fatrasta.

He and Ka-poel watched the city for some time. A contingent of city guard soon approached down the causeway, were hailed by one of the watchmen, and let in. Less than an hour later, just as the afternoon began to wane, forty heavily armed and armored Household guardsmen were sent back down the causeway, heading toward the prison to retrieve Styke's soldiers.

He knew he should be with them, but Etzi had refused the offer. Styke's presence would just attract the attention of the mobs. And he was probably right. It didn't make Styke feel any better, letting another man's soldiers fight his battle for him.

Styke remained on the guard tower, watching the city, long after Ka-poel had headed back into the compound. Celine ran through the courtyard a handful of times, but he was otherwise left to his own devices.

He was about to head down to the canteen when a small group of horsemen appeared at the causeway, galloping at full speed out of the street and slowing only when they reached the gate. A flurry of words were exchanged between the couple of guards remaining in the compound and the new arrivals. Etzi was summoned and ordered the gate opened.

The group consisted of three women and two men. They were dusty, wild-eyed, and breathless from a hard ride. Four of them were dressed in Household livery and heavily armed, while the fifth carried herself with the unmistakable air of a politician. A Household head, probably. Styke noted cuts on all five of the horses, as if they'd ridden straight through the center of a mob to get here.

Styke climbed down from the guard tower to join Etzi and his guests in the courtyard.

A terse greeting was exchanged, and their leader eyeballed Styke. "We have to talk," she said to Etzi, her voice shaky.

"Ben," Etzi said by way of introduction, "this is Meln-Sika, one of my staunchest allies and head of the Sika Household. Would you mind giving us some privacy? Sika, we can speak in my office."

"No." The woman threw her hand up toward Styke. "Let the foreigner listen. We may need him."

Styke had already begun to head toward the canteen. He stopped himself and turned back, head cocked. There was real fear in Sika's voice. Something more than fear of the mobs. Etzi scowled between Styke and Sika, then gestured Styke to come in close.

Sika rummaged around inside her shirt for a moment and drew out a card.

"This is Ka-Sedial's seal," Etzi said, taking it in hand and opening it. His eyes scanned the single page. His face grew pale. He got to the bottom and then began to read it again, fingers trembling. He finally handed it back. "A purge order?" he whispered.

"From the Great Ka himself," Sika spat.

"I don't understand," Styke interjected. Even as the words left his mouth, something clicked in the back of his head; these might be the mysterious orders that Ji-Patten had alluded to the night he died.

Etzi and Sika exchanged a glance. "There's more," Sika told Etzi, then turned toward Styke to include him in the explanation. "Last night, a mob appeared outside of the Donnolian Household—one of our allies. From what I've been able to gather from the survivors, the mob was better armed than most and included a few city guardsmen. They claimed to have an arrest warrant for Donnolian himself. They even had legal paperwork. Once Donnolian opened the gates, the mob flooded in and massacred his entire Household."

"Donnolian is dead?" Etzi breathed.

"He is. The same thing has happened to two other Households, and maybe more that I haven't been able to get word to. A mob appeared outside my own gates a few hours ago, but I'd just been warned and my soldiers were able to scatter the rabble. We grabbed this"—she shook the purge order—"off one of their leaders."

It took Styke a few moments to catch up. "When you say that this is from Sedial..."

"Written in his own hand and sent from Fatrasta," Sika said. "He ordered it *weeks* ago. I've wondered why his allies haven't taken a stronger stance against Etzi's legal wrangling, and this is why—because they knew they'd get the order to kill us all anyway." Sika's voice dripped with fury. "The further chaos caused by these mobs is meant to screen their purge, to prevent us from uniting."

Styke took the purge order from Sika's hand. He'd only just begun attempting to learn how to read and write Dynize, so the few paragraphs were illegible to him. But the list of Household names that took up most of the page was unmistakable. Styke spotted both Sika and Etzi's names there, including a dozen other Households that he'd heard mentioned as in opposition of Sedial.

Etzi staggered over to a nearby wall and sagged against it. Styke turned to Sika. "Why the purge order?" he asked. "Why not just send it through one of his puppets?"

"It's the veneer of legality," Sika sneered.

"Why does that matter?" Styke asked. "He's murdering Dynize citizens."

"The Ka claims that he is purging enemies of the state. Anyone with a brain can see he's just consolidating his own power. But this list isn't everyone, of course. There are over a hundred neutral Households. An order written in his own hand is an official government act—those neutral Households are less likely to defend us if they believe that they won't be next."

"And your emperor is just going to let this happen?"

"That's the worst part." Etzi seemed to regain control of his senses, returning to the center of the courtyard and presenting the envelope to Styke. "The signature at the bottom belongs to the emperor. He *sanctioned* this."

Styke looked back and forth between the two Household heads. Sika wore a mask of anger, Etzi one of shock. But he could see the deep fear in the eyes of both of them. He realized that he was looking into the faces of two people who already considered themselves as good as dead.

That's why Sika wanted him to hear all of this. "You want my army," he said flatly.

"I haven't spoken to more than a few Household heads," Sika said quietly. "But the Great Ka has ordered our deaths. We can go quietly, or we can go fighting."

"And you want to invite a foreign army into the city?" Etzi asked in horror.

"Damn the city!" Sika spat. "Damn Sedial, and damn the emperor! This is not just about individual honor or loyalty to a higher cause!" She snatched the purge order from Styke's hand and thrust it into Etzi's face. "This orders the murder of our *entire* Households. Men, women, and children. If I thought my death would strengthen the empire, I would walk to it gladly. But I will not sacrifice the lives of thousands of people in my care just to give that old sack of shit the control he craves. Don't you dare tell me that you would, either."

A flurry of emotions crossed Etzi's face, and in the course of a few moments Styke saw him transform into the man who had ordered his soldiers to cut their way through an angry mob. His jaw tightened and he nodded at Sika. "You're right, I won't. But we don't stand a chance, divided as we are. Even if we ally ourselves with this cavalry force, we are still cut off from one another."

"I'm doing what I can," Sika said, throwing her arms up. "You're the third Household that I've managed to warn. The best we can do right now is spread information—the more of us who are able to recall our soldiers from the garrisons and close our gates, the more we may be able to weather these mobs. We get through the next few days and maybe we can rally our forces faster than Sedial."

She sounded confident, but Styke could tell she was clutching at straws. She was right that Sedial's allies were using the mobs to cover for their purge, but she couldn't possibly believe that Etzi and the rest would be able to gather more strength than Sedial, even if they managed to survive the initial bloodshed. Sedial had planned for this. His allies would have soldiers set aside to eventually put down the mobs and then crush any opposition that remained. And with the Households spread out across the city...

"We're undefended," Styke said.

"You're *what*?" Sika demanded.

Etzi took a deep breath. "I sent most of my soldiers to fetch Styke's men from the prison. They may not be back for hours."

"You damn well better hope that whoever is commanding the purge doesn't decide to get around to you until tomorrow," Sika said, throwing up her hands. "I can't spare anyone, I can't risk..." She trailed off helplessly.

"No need," Etzi said confidently. "We have good walls. My soldiers will be back within a few hours. We'll be fine."

"You're certain?"

"Certain. You're right. You can't spare anyone, and you can't stay here. You have to warn as many of our allies as you can. I'll send out a few runners of my own."

Styke side-eyed Etzi. Sending out messengers would deplete the few guards they had left. He swore inwardly, willing the guardsmen to return with his Lancers. Once they were back, he'd have options—defend Etzi, flee the city, or even escort Etzi's entire Household to a bigger compound. He tried to wrap his head around this new shift. He would use this civil strife to his advantage, of course, but he had to figure out exactly how to do it.

Did he go fetch Ibana and ride the army to the godstone, allowing the Dynize to slaughter one another? Or did he intervene on behalf of Etzi? The former was the smart thing to do. The latter was...the more honorable? The old Styke would have ridden away laughing. There was nothing better than an enemy at war with itself. But now?

Sika and her soldiers took some refreshment and ammunition, then disappeared back into the city. Once she was gone, Styke cornered Etzi. "If you can spare anyone—anyone—I need you to send them south with an update for my second-in-command. I'll write her a message myself."

"It'll be done."

"You also want to tell Ka-poel what's going on," he advised.

"We may already be a lost cause, unless your men can come quickly enough," Etzi responded.

"I can't promise that Ka-poel won't think otherwise, but once your soldiers bring mine back from the prison, I can get them armed and on horseback. We can at least escort your Household to somewhere more defensible."

Etzi passed a hand across his face. "I appreciate the offer, but there isn't anywhere more defensible. We have to make a stand here." He nodded to himself. "I will go make my case to Ka-poel."

He hadn't been gone more than ten minutes when Styke heard a warning shout from one of the guards. He climbed quickly to one of the towers and looked toward the city, where a mob had begun to gather at the end of the causeway. It was already fifty strong and growing quickly. He could see city guardsmen among them, and even while he watched, an officer detached from the mob and walked the length of the causeway. He stopped a few yards from the gate.

"I have an arrest warrant for Meln-Etzi!"

Etzi was summoned and climbed up beside Styke. He was ashen-faced, but steady. A single glance told Styke that Etzi knew exactly what this was. "I am Meln-Etzi," he told the officer.

"In the name of the emperor and the Great Ka, open this gate! You are under arrest for treason!"

"If I open this gate," Etzi whispered, "we will all die."

"Agreed," Styke said.

"But if I don't, they will storm the walls and destroy us anyway." He froze in place for several moments, then climbed down from the tower.

"Meln-Etzi!" the officer called. "Meln-Etzi, I demand you open this gate."

"Keep it closed," Etzi ordered. A small group had already begun to gather in the courtyard, and Etzi doled out tasks in a quick, efficient tone. "Maetle, get the youngest children and pregnant women into the smuggler hole. Send boats across the lake to our closest allies and tell them we need help. Open the armory for everyone else. We will try to stall for the return of our soldiers."

The group scattered without questioning the orders. Within

minutes people began flooding back in, wearing old, ill-fitting breastplates and morion helmets and carrying muskets from the Household armory. Styke watched them impassively, considering getting his own weapons, when he spotted Celine and Jerio.

Jerio was carrying a musket. The boy could barely lift it, but he was looking it over with the serious air of an experienced soldier. Styke could hear him arguing with Celine. "You are my guest," Jerio said, mimicking words that Styke had heard Etzi say on more than one occasion. "Join the children in the smuggler hole!"

"I'll man the walls," Celine insisted, grabbing for Jerio's musket. She put on a brave face, but Styke could see that the seriousness of the situation seemed to have struck her more deeply than it had Jerio. Her voice trembled. She was breathing hard. She was terrified.

Something inside Styke snapped. His face twisted, his gut clenching. He strode over to the arguing children and snatched the musket out of Jerio's hands. "You'll do no such thing," he ordered. The idleness and suppressed fury of the last couple of weeks finally overwhelmed him. He could barely see straight.

"Ben!" Celine turned on him, her eyes tearing. "They're going to kill my friends, Ben. We can't let them. I'll fight, I will!"

Styke grabbed them both by the shoulders and shoved them toward the stables. "No fighting. Take Jerio."

"I won't hide!" Celine yelled.

"Of course you won't, you little shit. Jerio, I want you to load my carbines. Celine."

Her tears were flowing freely now. "Ben?"

Styke reached out and wiped a tear away with his thumb. "Go get my armor ready."

CHAPTER 61

Styke ran a thumb along the base of his neck where enchanted steel pressed against his bare skin, adjusting the thick wool shirt he wore as a padding to protect him from such chafing. He wasn't just hot already—he was boiling—but the sensation of his armor once again resting on his shoulders made him forget every other ill, discomfort, and pain. The weight of it felt protective and reassuring, but it was the scent of sorcery that made his heart sing. That scent was just as potent as it was ten years ago. It swirled in his nostrils like the smell of a bitter beer.

One of the greatest dangers a soldier could face was the feeling of his own invincibility. It was a particular kind of stupidity that could get anyone killed. Styke had danced with such a feeling his whole life, but the armor? The armor removed that blind spot. It made him a walking fortress, with few weaknesses.

He stepped forward and finished adjusting Amrec's armor. The big warhorse shimmied and shook his head in protest at the weight of the draping chain mail, but Styke took him by the nose and whispered in his ear until he calmed. "You're fine, you big baby. We tried this on you back at Starlight. You can do this." He ran his hand along Amrec's flank, feeling for uncomfortable wrinkles in the chain. He could hear shouting just outside the stables. The mob was growing impatient, threatening to batter down the gate of the Etzi compound.

"How do I look?" Styke asked, presenting himself to his small audience.

Celine looked him up and down seriously. "Like a knight."

Jerio seemed more skeptical. He could hear the sounds outside and they were clearly getting to him. "You're sure it works?"

Styke breathed in that bitter draft of sorcery. "It works."

"My uncle is a captain. He says that armor, even enchanted armor, is no match for a good musket ball."

Styke reached up and grasped Amrec's saddle horn, put a foot in the stirrup, and pulled himself onto the warhorse. "Normally, I'd agree with him. But in this case…" He patted Amrec on the neck and nodded to the stable door. Celine ran to open it, but she was beaten by the door sliding open on its own.

"Ben, are you…" It was Etzi. The Household head froze at the sight of Styke, looking up with widening eyes. "What are you doing?"

"I'm going to disperse the mob."

Etzi scoffed in disbelief, then ran forward to take Amrec by the bridle. Amrec snorted and stomped at the gesture, and Etzi took a step back. "That's not just a mob. They have muskets and pikes. Real weapons. Whatever you think you can do with a set of enchanted armor, it's not enough. There are well over a hundred now. They'll pull you down and kill you." He took a deep breath and set his jaw. "I'm going to offer myself without opening the gate. I'm hoping that's enough to buy the rest of you some time."

Styke scratched at his neck. The wool shirt was slipping again. Even after months of freedom he still weighed two stone less than he had the last time he wore this armor. It wasn't dangerously loose, but it *was* uncomfortably so. "Move," he told Etzi.

Reluctantly, the Household head stepped aside. Styke gestured to Celine, who rushed to the corner of the stables and snatched up his helmet and lance. He took the helmet first, fitting it onto his head, enjoying the protective claustrophobia that still smelled of his decade-old sweat. He took his lance, ducked his head, and rode out of the stables.

A hodgepodge of Household members had gathered in the courtyard. They jumped out of the way as Styke entered their midst, staring. He wondered what was going through their heads and remembered the old days. Back in Landfall, the first few times the Lancers had worn their armor in public, everyone had thought them mad, imbeciles, fools clad in ancient vestments. It wasn't until they'd won battle after battle that they'd begun to chant when they entered a town.

"Open the gate," Styke ordered.

No one moved. A rock sailed over their heads and clattered against the wall of one of the buildings inside the compound. Another breached the compound gate, then another. A window shattered. Styke could see the fear on the faces of the Household members. Old women, young boys, invalids. All of them holding old muskets from the Household armory, all of them waiting for death to come streaming through that gate.

He wondered where his own fear lay. Etzi was right, of course. One man, even in enchanted armor, couldn't hold off an angry mob. The moment he slowed down, they would pull him from Amrec's back and find the chinks in his armor. Riding through that door might as well be a death sentence.

Fear, he decided, didn't factor into it. These people had hosted and protected him. They'd taken in Ka-poel and Celine. They'd treated him like one of their own. Now, with the mob banging at their door, they couldn't hope to protect themselves. But he *could* protect them. He could be their shield, buy them time until Etzi's guard returned with his Lancers. He was Ben Styke and, he decided, it was about time this goddamn continent learned what that meant.

He lowered his visor. "Open the gate!" he bellowed.

Celine and Jerio appeared, rushing through the courtyard and throwing themselves at the mighty bar that kept the door locked. They were too small, even together, to make it budge. Etzi arrived at their heels and put his back beneath the bar, snapping his Household members out of their fearful reverie. The bar was lifted, the heavy doors pulled back.

The first unlucky bastard to surge through the gate caught Amrec's front hooves to the chest, hurling his body into the bottlenecked crowd with enough force to dash a half dozen of them to the ground. The mob arrested its own forward momentum, causing several of them to fall off the sides of the causeway into the lake. Those closest to Styke scrambled backward, the heat of their fury dissipating at the point of Styke's lance and the spark of Amrec's hooves on the flagstones.

Styke advanced until Amrec was entirely on the causeway. He was surrounded now, though all those closest cowered in surprise at his advance. "Close the gates!" he called over his shoulder. He heard them creak closed behind him, then the boom of the bar being put back into place. He inhaled deeply, smelling the sorcery and sweat and fear and anger. He should be shivering in nervous anticipation, but instead he found a laugh rumbling up from his belly.

This was what he was made for.

"Who's in charge of this?" he demanded in Dynize.

The mob continued to claw a slow retreat, those in the front trying to move backward and those behind shoving forward. That retreat slowed to nothing when the weight of their more adventurous comrades kept them from being able to slip back farther.

"It's the foreign giant!" someone shouted.

"Give us Etzi," another whooped.

Styke swung his lance across the noses of the closest of the mob. "You don't want Etzi. You want me."

"He's a traitor!"

"Forget Etzi, this is the foreigner! Pull him from his horse!"

"You pull him from his horse," a young woman just out of reach of Styke's lance called over her shoulder. She turned and leapt into the water. A few others joined her. The rest of the mob held strong. Styke could *feel* them growing a backbone, realizing that this was just one man in some armor. He could hear whispered encouragement from the center of things, no doubt coming from Sedial's paid instigators. He tried to find anyone who looked like they held some sort of authority. He failed.

Amrec could feel it, too—that growing tension. Styke tightened his grip on his lance.

He saw a movement among the crowd. A young man lifted a musket, braced it on the shoulder of a comrade, and pulled the trigger. Styke saw the puff of smoke, heard the noise of the blast, and felt a ping against the visor of his helmet that jerked his head backward, all in a fraction of a second.

There was a shocked silence. Styke reached, left-handed, across his saddle and drew his carbine. He leveled it and pulled the trigger, dropping the shooter in a spray of blood.

All pit broke loose.

The mob surged forward with a howl. Styke holstered his carbine in one smooth motion, took the reins in one hand, and dug in his heels. Amrec leapt into the crowd without hesitation. Within moments they were speeding across the causeway, nearly three hundred stone of armored warhorse and rider plowing through bodies. Styke's lance tore the face off an old man throwing a rock, punched through shoulders and stomachs, quickly becoming too heavy to hold. He released the lance with a grunt, drawing his saber and laying about him. Bullets, pikes, rocks, and clubs all bounced off his armor. The cacophony of it was deafening, a bludgeoning that might have unhorsed a lesser man on a lesser horse.

He began to laugh, the mirth bubbling up from his stomach. It didn't take long for him to reach the end of the causeway and gain the main avenue. Amrec's momentum slowed as they rode into an even greater crowd. The avenue was packed, the mob here thick and angry. They swarmed like angry hornets, those with long weapons dashing forward to attempt to thrust them between Amrec's legs, others leaping out of the way.

Styke turned Amrec and drove him back to the causeway, clearing it completely in one swoop and then turning to ride back toward the city, plowing into the center of the mob. No one who could still stand remained in the causeway. The Household was safe. The entire fury of the mob was upon *him*.

Amrec danced through the furious crowd, hooves flashing tirelessly while Styke's saber rose and fell. He fought with one eye on the causeway, another on the mob, waiting for them to break.

But they didn't break. Organized city guard members, fighting as a unit, emerged from the mob. They gave up trying to shoot him and fixed their short plug bayonets. More pikes emerged, as if brought to them by auxiliaries hiding in the alleys. They began to rush Styke in determined waves, falling back from his mad flailing and then trying again.

Styke lost all concept of time. He felt himself begin to grow sluggish as he continued to fight, losing strength behind the swing of his saber. He could feel Amrec's exhaustion between his legs.

He heard Amrec's scream a moment before the horse lurched beneath him and fell. They both went down in a tumble, and only long-practiced instinct allowed Styke to throw himself free instead of being pinned beneath Amrec's weight. He rolled, losing his saber but drawing his knife, coming up unsteadily and turning his head toward his horse.

Amrec tried to regain his feet. Screamed again. The sound wrenched something inside of Styke, tearing out his guts as he watched Amrec fail, and try and fail again.

The distraction cost him. Styke felt a scrape against his armor and then a sting at his side. He whirled hard, only to find a Dynize face clinging close to him. It belonged to a middle-aged woman, who snarled through his visor. "From the Great Ka," she hissed. Styke gasped as her knife was pulled from his side, raised, bloody and dripping, and thrust toward his eyes. He barely registered the stark white bone of the knife, the black tattoos that spiraled up the woman's arm.

He only heard his horse screaming.

He slammed his head against her face, listening to the rasp of her blade sliding harmlessly along his visor. Blood sprayed from the impact, momentarily blinding him, but he had a hold of her with his left hand now and didn't need his sight. He felt the tip of his knife drag at her swamp-dragon-leather armor. Giving a roar, he punched it through with all his strength.

The dragonman sagged in his arms and he threw the disemboweled corpse into the crowd, then wrenched off his helmet so that he could clean the blood from his eyes. What he saw when his vision cleared was like something out of a nightmare.

Soldiers swarmed Amrec, trying to put down the screaming, flailing horse with their long pikes. More dashed toward Styke, while those closest to him stared at the body of their dragonman in shock. "Dogs!" he spat. "Cowards! Can't even put down a horse!" He steadied himself, his fury threatening to burst from his chest. Something caught the attention of several of the city guard, turning their heads. Styke took the opportunity to rock onto the balls of his feet and fling himself forward.

He crashed into them with reckless abandon. He thrust his knife with one hand and wielded his helmet like a club with the other. Within moments both gauntlets were soaked in blood. Guardsmen fell beneath him like bugs, their screaming and pleading falling on deaf ears.

He lost his helmet, turned, and snatched a man by the front of his shirt and drew his knife hand back.

"Ben!" the man wailed. "It's me!"

The blow almost fell. Styke yanked himself from his bloodlust, eyes focusing until he recognized Markus clutched in his out-stretched arm. He forced himself to let go, to lower his knife and look around. What he saw astounded him—armored figures riding down the Dynize mob, swarming around Styke at a charge. What remained of the city guard attempted to flee, only to run into the fixed bayonets of Etzi's Household guard marching up the avenue.

He stumbled back from Markus, taking deep breaths. One of the armored cavalry came to a stop in front of him, wrenching off her helmet. It was Ibana, and she barely paused to look at him before barking orders.

"Secure that alley! Don't let them get away! Leave a few alive for questioning! Gut the rest!" Her horse stamped and thundered beneath her, and Styke noticed distantly that the neck and forelegs of the beast were splattered in the blood of run-down enemies. He took a shaky breath.

"How did you find me?"

"Jackal's spirits warned us you'd gotten yourself into a situation," she said, her eyes still on the ensuing slaughter. "Looks like we arrived just in time."

Styke could no longer feel that joy of the battle. In its place was a hollow, distant grief. His gaze returned to Amrec, who now lay on his side, still but breathing. Styke could see now that one of Amrec's hooves was hanging by a sinew. The mad beast had tried to stand, even with a leg nearly cut off.

"No, you were too late," Styke told Ibana. "Give me your carbine."

CHAPTER 62

For the second time in his life, Michel watched as Landfall burned.

The first time had been during the revolution. Fatrastan partisans and Kez soldiers had fought back and forth across the plateau while Ben Styke's Mad Lancers barely kept the Kez fleet from landing reinforcements along the rocky shores. Lady Chancellor Lindet's armies had arrived in the nick of time, finally capturing Fort Nied and pushing the Kez into the ocean. This time, he saw no Mad Lancers in their gleaming armor. He saw no rescuing army.

Michel hid in a church bell tower and watched while frustrated Dynize soldiers raged back and forth across the plateau, continuing their slow and brutal suppression of the Palo rioters. Smoke rose from a dozen quarters, including Greenfire Depths. But the Depths *was* still there. It hadn't been destroyed by Privileged, and no new Privileged had been sent to finish the job.

It had been two days since he lost Ichtracia and his heart still hurt. He'd been unable to find so much as a body—hers, or the

Privileged she'd been fighting. He'd spent his time since dodging patrols, trying to find some kind of organization among the rioters, and looking for Jiniel. Mama Palo's headquarters was abandoned and refugees streamed out of the city by the thousands. If the Dynize cared about those that were fleeing, they made no move to stop them. The city had all their attention.

Despite the inevitable end to the uprising, hundreds of Palo fought on behind barricades or engaged the Dynize in long, running battles. Michel watched as they were snuffed out one at a time, and scoured the city for any sign of his allies. The church bell tower was one of his preordained meeting spots, and the ninth such spot that he'd checked. Yet there was still no sign of Jiniel or the others.

Michel saw a Dynize patrol gun down a lone stone-throwing Palo boy and averted his eyes. He'd expected violence at some point, but all of this? This was too much. This was not what he'd wanted. And yet he was responsible. He gathered up his pack of meager belongings scrounged from Mama Palo's headquarters and headed down from the bell tower, making his way across the empty church and standing by the door for a few minutes to listen for a break in the fighting outside.

"Michel!" The name was barked sharply, and it made him jump and spin. Across the room, back behind the altar, he spotted a familiar face, which brought a sigh of relief. It was Devin-Mezi, Jiniel's cousin. Michel put a hand over his heart and gave her a nod. She rushed across the room to him. "Pit and damnation, it *is* you. We thought we'd lost you."

"Not yet," Michel answered. "I've been looking for you as well. Where is Jiniel?"

"We retreated to the catacombs," Devin-Mezi said, looking Michel over with a scowl. "We're hiding with Yaret and his Household."

Michel nodded tiredly. "That makes sense. I lost my maps and I didn't really want to get lost down there looking for you."

"We have the maps," Devin-Mezi said reassuringly. "We got most of our people out of . . . well, never mind. I'll take you to Jiniel, she'll want to update you." Her scowl deepened. "Are you hurt?"

Michel instinctively hid his left hand. The wound had opened badly during the explosion that had ended Ichtracia's fight with the Privileged, and he hadn't been able to stop it from weeping blood since. A hasty, one-handed stitch job was all that was keeping it together. It hurt so badly that he could barely see, but he forced himself to think through it. He gave Devin-Mezi a tight grin. "Where's the closest entrance to the catacombs?"

They were able to make their way through the street fighting and descended into the plateau through the basement of a bakery. Devin-Mezi produced a hidden lantern and two pistols, one of which she handed to Michel. "Just in case," she told him. "Some of the soldiers have been venturing down here, but they rarely bother going very far for fear of getting lost."

Michel was too tired to harbor suspicions or fears. He followed Devin-Mezi through the maze of tunnels, descending deeper and deeper until they rounded a corner and suddenly spotted a pool of light. It was a sentry, a Palo who challenged them and stood aside when Devin-Mezi gave the password. Soon they were past, and descended still farther until they broke out into a number of large chambers well lit by oil lanterns and crowded with people, both Palo and Dynize.

Michel allowed himself to feel pain again at the sight of familiar faces, but forced himself to keep walking rather than collapse into a sobbing mess. Devin-Mezi continued to lead him through the group until they stopped outside of a chamber cordoned off by a cloak stretched across a string. She swept it aside. "I found him!"

Michel stumbled in after her and was mobbed by relieved faces, thumps on his back, whispered questions, and a jumble of news. He waved it all back, blinking through his pain, and collapsed into an offered chair before looking across the gathering. It consisted of

Jiniel and several of her lieutenants, Yaret, Tenik, and a handful of Yaret Household cupbearers.

"By Kresimir," Jiniel swore. "Michel, you are covered in blood."

"I need whiskey, a needle, thread, and someone with a steady hand," he answered.

Jiniel barked orders, and within minutes the supplies were brought. It was Tenik who knelt beside Michel with the needle and thread, taking a damp cloth to wash Michel's hand. Michel grimaced at every touch, but several swallows of whiskey took the edge off and allowed him to consider the faces before him with a little more clarity. He focused on Jiniel and pointed toward the rock above their heads.

"Have you been outside lately?"

She nodded. "We have word coming in from our people at a constant rate. All the coming and going is risky, but we're trying to stay on top of everything happening."

"Our people are getting slaughtered out there."

Jiniel cast her eyes downward. "I know."

And there was nothing she could do. There was nothing any of them could do. Michel stared at his hand, trying to make himself *think*. They needed a plan, no matter how simple or cowardly. Run away. Fight back. He could barely summon the energy to move, let alone make that decision. He took another swig of whiskey and thought about Ichtracia striding to her death to face down three Privileged. She would have won, too, if not for the fourth showing up. He winced as Tenik finished cleaning his hand and began to pick out the sloppy stitches he'd done himself.

"Do we have any plans?" Michel asked.

"We're working on it," Jiniel replied, exchanging a glance with Yaret. The Household head cleared his throat. "We've coordinated with some of the larger groups of fighters, and spread evacuation orders to as many communities as we can."

Yaret spoke up. "We just received word from Etepali. She's stuck up north between two of Sedial's armies and Lady Flint. She doesn't think she can slip away, but offers us succor if we can reach her."

Running away seemed like a *really* good idea right now. But how to get out of the city? "You should make a run for it," he told Yaret. "Right now, with all Sedial's focus on Lindet's armies and putting down the Palo."

"We're considering the idea," Yaret said seriously.

"Good." Michel turned his gaze on Jiniel, who grimaced at his hand until she noticed him watching her and tried to turn it into a smile.

"You and Ichtracia saved Greenfire Depths," she said. "I'm guessing the sorcerous fight on the Rim was the two of you."

"Just her," he said with a sad smile, shaking his head. Beside him, Tenik finally began to stitch his hand. He barely felt the in and out of the needle through his gloom.

"People are fleeing the Depths in droves," Jiniel continued. "No one is stopping them, and Sedial hasn't sent any more Privileged to start fires."

"I noticed that." Michel took a long look as Tenik continued the stitches on his ruined hand. "I couldn't even find a body."

Jiniel and Yaret looked at each other again. "Whose body?" Jiniel asked.

"Ichtracia's."

"But...she's still alive," Yaret said.

Michel rounded on him, nearly tearing out the new stitches. "No, she's not," he growled, the words tumbling out with more emotion than he'd meant. "I *saw* that sorcery. No one could have survived that."

Yaret did not shrink before his temper. "One of my cupbearers saw her after the battle. Sedial's people captured her. She was beaten up, but still alive." He leaned toward Michel. "The People-Eater doesn't die so easily."

Something flared in Michel's belly, stirring upward through his chest until it reached his mind. He could feel the gears there begin to grind. He sought to grasp onto that flicker of energy, to use it to pull himself from his sleep-deprived, painful lethargy. If Ichtracia *had* survived that fight, she would be in dire straits now. Sedial might punish her in some way. Pit, he might still have need of her blood. The very thought of her as a sacrifice made Michel retch. Something had to be done. But what? It would take the biggest army in the world to rescue her from Sedial—or the best spy. He wasn't the latter on the best of days, let alone in his current condition, and he didn't have the former.

"Where is Sedial?" Michel asked.

"We have contact with some sympathetic Households still near the capital building," Yaret said slowly. "They said that Sedial has retreated to the fortress down south."

"To use the stones?" Michel asked sharply.

"Or just to wait out the violence," Yaret said with a shrug.

There was the rustle of a soft voice outside the meeting chamber, and Tenik finished tying off Michel's stitches and climbed painfully to his feet to cross to the makeshift door. He spoke to someone on the other side, then turned to Yaret. "We have more information coming in from the plateau."

"Go on," Yaret urged.

"Sedial is gathering his troops, pulling them out of Upper Landfall."

"He's regrouping?" Michel guessed.

Tenik spoke to the messenger outside in a low voice before turning back to them. "We're not entirely sure. It seems he's massing troops on the southern bank of the Hadshaw. At least twenty thousand of them already."

"Twenty thousand," Michel breathed in disbelief.

"And rising. He's pulled *everyone* off the plateau. They just left in the middle of firefights and melees."

"He must be preparing for a new push into the city." Michel looked around at the faces of his friends, trying to make some sense of this.

"But why abandon good positions to do it?" Yaret asked.

No one seemed to know the answer. "Send out more people," Michel told Jiniel. "Even if our risk of being discovered goes up. We *have* to know what's going on." He was already considering courses of action, trying to come up with any idea, no matter how far-fetched, that would allow him to rescue Ichtracia. The fear that Ichtracia was about to be used as another blood sacrifice continued to grow. He kept it to himself. No need to spark a panic until they had a better plan. "How about your allies?" he asked Yaret. "Is there a staunch resistance against Sedial yet?"

"I've warned everyone on the purge list," Yaret replied, spreading his hands. "Seven of them are already dead. Several more have fled the city. A few have managed to withdraw all their troops and plan to make a stand, and the rest... well, the rest are hunkering down to wait out the violence, hoping that Sedial changes his mind. The damned fools. It would take an act of a god to get them to act, even on the eve of their own destruction."

"So no help from that quarter?"

"Maybe a small amount."

"The ones who plan on fighting back. Can you try to unite them?"

It was Tenik who answered. "We've been trying to do just that. It's going... all right. If we had two more weeks to work, we might be able to gather all of Sedial's enemies."

Michel sought a solution—*any* solution—and came up empty-handed. A commotion outside took Tenik back to the door, where he conferred with a new voice. There was an excited, quiet exchange and Tenik whirled on the room. "We know why Sedial is massing his troops!"

"Why?" Michel climbed to his feet, followed by everyone else in the room.

Tenik scoffed, double-checked with the messenger, then shook his head in disbelief. "We've spotted a flotilla. There are hundreds of keelboats coming down the Hadshaw. They're within miles of the city."

"Lindet?" Michel asked in confusion.

"No. It's Lady Flint and the Adrans."

A handful of gasps escaped the gathered lieutenants, and Yaret stared at Tenik. "How is that possible? We just heard from Etepali today and she said the Adrans were a five-day march north."

"It's the flotilla," Michel explained excitedly, already limping for the door. "With enough keelboats, Flint could bring everyone she has down the river in less than half the time it takes to march it. Try to organize the Palo on the plateau," he told Jiniel. "Put out fires and give us a semblance of order. Yaret, see if you can gather some of your allies during this respite."

"Where are you going?" Jiniel asked.

"If I'm going to get Ichtracia back, I'll need an army. And Lady Flint has the best one on the continent."

CHAPTER 63

Vlora stood on the prow of her keelboat, face to the wind, listening to the polers keep time as they worked their way up and down the sides of the vessel. The river was packed, hundreds of keelboats crammed together as close as they could manage without fouling their poles. All around her, soldiers double-checked their rifles and kit as their sergeants belted out encouragement, obscenities, and orders. She could *feel* the tension of the moment, her heart hammering at the prospect of the coming battle.

A light powder trance hummed in the back of her head, keeping her thoughts clear and her body limber. She didn't trust herself to take more than the smallest amount of powder, but this, she told herself, would be enough. As she scanned the horizon with her looking glass, she picked out the most important features in the landscape.

The largest was the Landfall Plateau, looming less than two miles from their current position and growing closer with every moment. Smoke rose from the city, telling a tale of internal strife, while people streamed out of the suburbs of Lower Landfall at an alarming rate. She put the refugees from her mind. They would not be a threat.

The threat, she found, was gathering on a bend in the river, just where the Hadshaw turned toward the ocean and the western bank became the southern bank. Thousands of soldiers—*tens of thousands*—mustered speedily on the plain. Their morion helmets and steel breastplates glittered in the afternoon sun as their officers tried to force them into formation. Thousands more streamed from the city, the suburbs, and from the mighty fortress half-constructed around the godstone south of the city.

"Looks like they knew we were coming," Bo said. He stood beside her, his own looking glass to his eye, gloves already donned. "Their scouts must be lightning fast."

"Or one of the armies we were facing up north sent their fastest messengers once we'd slipped away," Vlora replied. "They would have killed a horse to get here before us, but it *is* possible."

"Either way," Bo mused, "we're in for a fight."

"As expected. Do you see that bit of high ground at seven o'clock?"

"No...wait, yes. They're putting a couple of field guns into place."

"Looks like it." Vlora lowered her looking glass and turned to look back across the flotilla just in time to see another keelboat maneuver perilously close to hers. The polers on both vessels stopped their work as the two drifted together, and then Olem leapt onto hers. Once he was on board, the polers immediately began to move again. He brushed off the front of his uniform, gained his balance, and came to join her with a flushed face.

"I've leapt between horses before," he proclaimed, "but there's something about jumping keelboats that's even more terrifying. I've got news from the shore."

"Our cavalry?" Vlora asked.

"They're pretty exhausted from the ride down here," Olem reported. "Sabastenien says that he'd prefer not to use them unless absolutely necessary. He *has* been able to scout with spare horses."

"And?"

"We're looking at twenty-five thousand infantry, with the number rising quickly as they get reinforcements. They've got one heavy-gun emplacement up on the plateau, but it's not facing the river—it's facing west. It won't fire on our landing but it'll pound our flanks the moment we make a move toward the godstone. On the plain itself, they don't have a lot of good places to put field guns, but it looks like there are at least three different gun platforms for us to worry about."

As if to punctuate his point, a puff of smoke went up from the center of the massing defenders. Vlora thought she saw a splash some ways down the river. The report of a single artillery round hit them a moment later. "Getting their distance," she commented. "Anything else?"

"Yes. That fortress down south might not be finished, but it has some pretty nasty gun towers and sloped walls. If we do manage to take the field, that damned fortress is gonna be a whole different beast."

"We'll deal with that when we get to it," Vlora said. "Tell Sabastenien that I want his cavalry to harass the enemy's north flank. Tell him not to engage—just keep them nervous. I want Davd and Buden to keep those gun crews hopping until we can get close enough for Nila to take care of them. Norrine is on Privileged duty. Bo is going to do his best to keep us from getting hit too hard in the face when we land."

"Right away!" Olem signaled to a nearby keelboat and was soon leaping across, off to deliver Vlora's orders.

She took several deep breaths, willing herself steady, and glanced over at Bo. He was watching her with a note of concern. "What?"

"You ready for this?"

Vlora reached into her pocket for a powder charge, squeezing one end between two fingers until a few granules spilled out into her palm. With a thought, she ignited them, causing a small flash and wisp of smoke.

Bo raised both eyebrows. "I'll be damned."

"It's coming back," Vlora told him. "Not fast enough, and I'm not going to push myself, but it's there."

"Congratulations. Just promise me you won't do anything too stupid today."

"I'll try."

"I'm not reassured."

They continued down the river, the probing shots of shore artillery getting closer and closer as the flotilla approached. Small clusters of enemy troops began to appear on the bank, streaming in from some nearby camp. Vlora could tell at a glance that the troops were green, their officers struggling to keep them in order. She wondered if they would be the worst she faced, but immediately dismissed the thought. Sedial was too intelligent not to surround himself with at least a few brigades of veterans. He'd throw these greenhorns at her to tire her out, then unleash the veterans.

Olem returned. "Messages sent," he reported. "I'll be relieved when we get back on shore and I don't have to do that."

"Man up," Vlora told him playfully.

He scoffed, taking an offered rifle from one of Vlora's bodyguard and readjusting his bicorn hat. "I've never done a proper water landing before."

"It might get rough," Bo warned, raising his hands as a cannonball splashed down just a few hundred paces in front of them.

Vlora peered toward the shore, watching as the groups of soldiers grew thicker and more coherent. Their landing point was in the gentle shallows just at the bend of the river, and the enemy had clearly anticipated the spot. At least two brigades would oppose them there. She had more men, of course, but she was also leading them off several hundred keelboats. "Rough" might be an understatement.

"Oh," Bo suddenly said. "I brought you something." He fished into his pocket quickly and, before she could object, threw something over her neck. It was a red-and-blue-striped sash with a gold medallion stamped with the mountains of Adro over the teardrop of the Adsea. It took her a moment to recognize it, and when she did, she let out a gasp. The last time she'd seen this medallion was when it had been worn by Tamas to some state function. Though it had been his by right, he rarely wore it and never kept it displayed.

It was the decoration of a field marshal of Adro.

"This doesn't belong on me," she said in confusion, trying to take it off. Olem reached out and stopped her.

Bo said, "Remember when you accused me of bringing Taniel an army and then handing it to you when he didn't want it? Well, the army was never meant for Taniel. It was meant for *you*. Whether you like it or not, you're Field Marshal Flint now. The general staff voted on it yesterday. Unanimous. So keep the bloody thing on."

Vlora didn't know how to respond. She fingered the gold medallion, lost in memories for a brief moment until the report of cannon fire brought her back to the present. She drew her sword and turned around. To her surprise, hundreds of sets of eyes were already on her. The men crouched on their keelboats, bayonets fixed, rifles loaded. An eerie silence had fallen over the flotilla.

"My soldiers!" she called, loud and clear. "My friends! Today we do not fight for glory or riches. We do not fight for the immediate safety of our people or our borders. We fight a menace that we alone among modern men have faced before. Today we aim our weapons at a man who would be a god. Are you with me?" Thousands of men sprang to their feet, lifting rifles in the air, and let out a great cheer. "We will not allow this threat to rise!" she bellowed. "We will spit in the face of those who would rule the world!"

Vlora whirled, her sword thrust into the air. Ahead of her, the sandy riverbank loomed large as the keelboats turned toward it, rather than continuing on with the curve of the river. A cannonball suddenly whizzed past her head, tearing into a keelboat behind her and scattering dozens of soldiers. Their cheers did not die down— they only intensified.

Bo suddenly threw up his hands, fingers twitching. The air above them seemed to shatter and a cannonball careened off his sorcery, flying harmlessly toward the opposite bank. He grimaced, then his eyes widened. "Hold on!" he yelled, bracing himself against something only he could see.

Vlora *felt* the sorcery a half second before it collided with Bo's shield. Lightning webbed above them, crackling and hissing. A bolt of ice materialized over Bo's shoulder and lanced toward the bank. "Got him!" Bo crowed. "Norrine, you better hurry up if you want to kill those assholes before me! Nila, now!"

The moment Nila's name left Bo's lips, a column of blue fire sprouted from the keelboat to their right. The flames sizzled across the water, hitting the bank and turning as if they had a mind of their own. They cascaded across the bank, consuming infantrymen by the hundreds. Within seconds there was nothing but charred flesh and blackened grass on the riverbank, leaving Vlora with a beachhead several hundred yards deep and twice as wide. She braced herself as the polers suddenly dug in, slowing the boat until they slid almost gently onto the sandbar.

Vlora licked a few morsels of powder off her fingertips and drew her pistol, waving both pistol and sword in the air. "Charge!" she cried, leaping into the knee-deep water. Ten thousand voices answered her call, and the might of the Adran Army swarmed the shore.

Vlora's soldiers gained their beachhead and then some. Within thirty minutes the entire riverbank was theirs. Three Dynize gun emplacements lay in smoldering ruins thanks to Nila's sorcery. Marion-helmed Dynize casualties littered the field and filled it with the cries of the wounded. The rest of the Dynize had pulled back with startling alacrity—half fleeing, half retreating, but keeping the bulk of their army between Vlora and the godstone. The rest of the keelboats were unloaded, field guns rolled by plank onto the soft floodplains while Sabastenien's cavalry kept the Dynize nervous to the west.

During the landing, Vlora had twisted her ankle in the run toward shore. It was an undignified injury, and she paced to try and work out the pain. A bullet had grazed Olem's cheek, leaving him with a startling amount of blood across his chin and collar. Bo cleaned sand out of his prosthetic, while Nila had somehow managed to reach the shore without getting even the hem of her dress wet. Vlora ordered Burt's irregulars up to relieve the cavalry, and gazed toward the plateau, where she could just barely see the gun platform that would make her life miserable if she tried to march toward the godstone.

"I don't like it," she stated to no one in particular.

"Like what?" Olem asked, dabbing at his cheek with a handkerchief. He waved off a surgeon and walked over to join Vlora.

"They should have held us there," she replied. "They had enough men that even with a little bit of discipline, and backed up by their bone-eyes and Privileged, they should have contested that landing more fiercely."

Olem scowled and cast his gaze across the riverbank. "Now that you mention it..."

"I'm right, aren't I?"

"Only two Privileged and a single bone-eye," Olem said. "That seems like scant protection for all the soldiers he's sending out to meet us."

"Do they still have reinforcements coming in?"

"From everywhere, it seems. Our scouts estimate they now have thirty-five thousand soldiers on the field between us and the god-stone and still growing. So why are they holding off?"

Vlora brooded, staring toward the monolith she could see clearly just a couple miles to their south. It poked up from the center of that big, ugly fortress. She could once again sense that dark fore-boding from the godstone, putting her on edge, and she worried that it might affect her decision-making. "They might be stretched thin. The sorcerers, I mean. With Lindet to the west and a couple armies still up north and the losses we inflicted on their cabal dur-ing the siege of Landfall, they might just not be able to field very much sorcery against us, so they plan on a defensive battle."

"Possibly," Olem conceded.

There was a "but" in his tone. "What do you think it could be?"

"If he knew we were coming, what if he's just luring us toward the fortress? Does the godstone have any other powers that we're not aware of?"

The very suggestion made Vlora ill. "Ask Nila and Bo. Tell them to be ready for anything." She couldn't allow herself to hope that they'd *completely* caught Ka-Sedial with his pants down. But if she had, and there was a chance to avoid the coming bloodshed... "Get me a messenger to send to Ka-Sedial. He has thirty minutes to agree to surrender the godstone, or we're going to take it by force."

"Isn't that Delia's job?" Olem asked.

"Do you see Delia anywhere? Besides, we still don't know for sure whether she's betrayed us or not." The orders were relayed, and Vlora watched the messenger run off to find a political officer, then turned her attention back to the landing. Her soldiers were already falling into line, forming tight regiments with her best troops—some of them still wearing their Riflejack mercenary uniforms—composing the center. Auxiliaries commanded the right, while a staunch com-pany of grenadiers took her far left flank closest to the plateau, ready in case Sedial dispatched troops directly from the city.

Olem rushed back and forth, intercepting messengers, issuing commands, and keeping all of the minute details straight with an accuracy that Vlora couldn't hope to match. He soon returned to her side and, in a low voice, asked, "The afternoon is advancing. Are we going to attack tonight? Or should we dig in for camp?"

Vlora hesitated only a moment before answering. If they attacked and had a hard time making progress, they could be forced back into the keelboats overnight. But if they dug in and waited until dawn, it would give Sedial an immense amount of time to rearrange his defense.

And she still couldn't shake the feeling that he was simply buying time to use the godstones.

"Get our auxiliaries digging trenches on our flanks, but tell them to be ready to move at a moment's notice. We're attacking today unless Sedial surrenders."

The message was relayed, and Vlora was left to watch as the preparations continued. She dabbed a bit of powder on her tongue, relishing the sizzle that it sent through her body and wrestling with the urge to take more. Only a few minutes passed before a rider appeared, rushing toward Vlora and not bothering to dismount before belting out a warning.

"Lady Flint! Word from General Sabastenien. He says that the provosts have—"

"General Vlora Flint!" a voice boomed.

Vlora whirled from the rider, turning toward a column of provosts that had appeared between the lines of her own men. There were at least two hundred of them, pushing their way through the regular soldiery, and at their head was Provost Marshal Valeer. She fixed him with a cool look and crossed her arms.

"Valeer! I thought you'd wait in the wings until the real fighting was done. Are you here to lead the main charge?"

The provost marshal strode toward Vlora until he was mere paces away, his hand on his sword, his chin lifted and lip curled.

Olem subtly stepped out ahead of Vlora and ashed a cigarette toward Valeer. "It's 'Field Marshal' now," he said.

Valeer sniffed at the sash around Vlora's neck. "We'll see about that. Vlora Flint, you have orders to end this offensive immediately. Lady Snowbound has secured a cease-fire with the Great Ka of Dynize. Stand down, or face the consequences."

Vlora eyeballed Valeer's provosts as they fanned out to surround her and Olem, and noticed that both Bo and Nila were elsewhere—clearly something that Valeer had planned on. She maintained her cool demeanor. "Has she?"

"She has, and I'm here to insist that you give the order to stand down at this very moment."

"I won't give such an order until I hear the terms of the cease-fire."

"The terms are not your concern. The stability of Adran international relations is your concern, and you are on the very precipice of plunging us into an extended conflict that we cannot hope to win. Stand down!"

At a gesture from Olem, Vlora's bodyguard assembled from where they'd been resting nearby. Though heavily outnumbered, they shouldered their way through the provosts until they had joined Vlora's side. It was a show of solidarity that gave her a fresh breath of confidence. Beyond the cordon of provosts, officers and regular army soldiers began to take a great interest in the proceedings.

"Olem," Vlora said, not taking her eyes off Valeer, "send a runner to the general staff. Let them know they're to stand by for further orders."

"I said, '*Stand down*,'" Valeer snapped.

"I heard you the first several times," Vlora replied, "but like I said, I won't do any such thing until I know what deal the Lady Snowbound has made. Where is she?"

"With the Great Ka."

Vlora scoffed. Delia must have landed her provosts and practically sprinted off to meet with Sedial for her to have already made a deal. "And the terms of the cease-fire."

Valeer straightened his shoulders, drawing himself up. "While you played at soldier up north, we have been arranging for the end to hostilities. Lady Snowbound has handed over the capstone of the Yellow Creek godstone to the Dynize. In return, they have pledged—"

"You *what*?" Vlora snarled.

"We have handed over—"

She cut him off again, drawing her sword before she'd given the action conscious thought. "What insanity could have possibly compelled you to hand that madman the key to the power he seeks?"

"You *dare* to draw your sword at me?" Valeer replied, taking a step back and thrusting a finger toward her. "Your mad thirst for blood will see us all dead—Delia and I have taken steps to avoid that. We gave them the capstone the moment the army left the coast. Now, put up your sword if you ever want to see Adro again!"

"Take it from me," she snarled.

"We know your secret, Lady Flint," Valeer proclaimed haughtily. "You can't use your sorcery. Provosts! Arrest this woman in the name of the Republic of Adro!"

A moment of confusion hung in the air, and the provosts stared at their leader as if they couldn't imagine it would go this far. In that instant, Olem drew his sword and pistol and shouted, "The provosts have turned on Lady Flint. To arms!"

Vlora's bodyguard took two steps outward and lowered their bayoneted rifles, putting Vlora into the center of a steel hedgehog formation. The only opening faced Valeer, and the provost marshal drew his own sword and leapt toward her. He had barely made it half a step when a shot rang out in Vlora's ear. Valeer gave a gasp and stumbled back, staring at the smoke that rose from Olem's pistol. Clutching his chest, the provost marshal collapsed.

"If you set down your weapons right now, you will be allowed to return to your comrades alive," Olem said loudly.

The closest provosts looked down at their dying marshal, then at Olem. They were drawn from what little remained of the old nobility, and most of them had a good reason to personally dislike Vlora and Olem. But they also knew exactly where they were. She could see on their faces that they knew the improbability of their leaving this place alive if they tried to follow Valeer's last order.

Beginning with the few closest, they threw down their rifles.

"Get rid of this," Vlora said, gesturing to Valeer, "and escort these men to the rest of their comrades." The provosts were mobbed by the regular soldiery and swept away, while Vlora took advantage of the chaos to catch her breath. She could feel her heart hammering from the confrontation, and even another hit of powder couldn't keep her hands from shaking. She turned to Olem. "Do we know if our fleet has arrived to reinforce us from the coast?"

"They're supposed to be here tonight or tomorrow."

"Send a runner around the north side of the plateau to try and flag them down. We need to know if Delia really did secret away the capstone." She swore under her breath and realized that her adrenaline wasn't from the confrontation but from the implications of what Valeer had revealed. "All those meetings. Our own discussions. Delia played me for a fool the whole time. Damn it!" She turned toward Valeer, who lay on the ground nearby, supported by two of his men, blood leaking from his lips. He barely seemed to know where he was anymore, and would likely be dead within the hour. "Did Delia really think I'd just surrender?" she asked Olem. "Did she not understand that this is more important than anyone's career, including mine?" She caught herself just short of throwing her sword. "Recall the political officer," she belted at her cadre of waiting messengers. "Tell the general staff to prepare to advance."

"Ma'am!" a voice called. "I'm sorry to interrupt, but—"

"What is it?" Vlora demanded, whirling on a soldier standing just behind her.

The soldier had a Palo man by the collar. The Palo was of medium height with a short, wispy beard and a gaunt face. His left hand was wrapped in bloody bandages and looked like it was missing a couple of fingers. "Sorry, ma'am. He surrendered to our pickets. Claims he works for Taniel Two-shot and has urgent news. Thought you might want to talk to him."

The Palo removed his flatcap. "Michel Bravis, Son of the Red Hand, at your service."

CHAPTER 64

Michel's escort dragged him across the riverbank, follow-ing Lady Flint to where a handful of camp followers had hastily erected an open-sided tent. A handful of important-looking officers with gold epaulets on their Adran blues had already found the shade of the tent. A table was brought in and covered with maps and reports in the matter of a few moments. Lady Flint rounded the table, sorting the papers around with a critical eye, and then barked off a series of orders. Waiting messengers scattered like pigeons in every direction.

She finally turned toward Michel and frowned at his escort. "Dismissed," she said, and the man released Michel and took off after the messengers.

Michel stood just outside of the shade of the tent, looking around, hoping that he did not faint from loss of blood. His entire left arm throbbed from the pain in his hand, and while Tenik's stitches were tight, the new bandages were already soaked with blood. He wanted nothing more than to lie down on the ground and fall asleep. But he couldn't. Not while Ichtracia was still held by her grandfather.

"Taniel told me you were his best spy and to make contact when we reached Landfall," Vlora suddenly said, still looking at her maps. It took Michel a moment to realize she was talking to him, and he gratefully stepped under the tent.

"I'm flattered."

"And I would have completely forgotten if you hadn't shown up," Vlora said. Her tone was clipped—all business—and it seemed that every other breath was to give orders to another messenger or one of the officers gathered around. The command tent had, in just a few moments, become the nexus of the entire battle grinding into motion around them. "I'm a bit busy here, so you better make your report quickly." She looked up, over his head, squinting into the distance. "Start with what's going on in the city."

Michel took a moment to sort through everything in his head, ordering information from most to least important. "We discovered that Sedial used Palo blood to unlock the restrictions Ka-poel made to the Landfall godstone. The Palo have risen up, and there are riots, barricades, and fighting in the streets. At least, there were. He's ordered all of his soldiers out of Landfall to deal with you."

Vlora looked up at her second-in-command. Michel remembered Colonel Olem from his time as their Blackhat liaison, and the man hadn't changed a bit. He even had a cigarette still hanging out of the corner of his mouth. Olem gave Vlora a sharp nod. "That explains all the villages up north. They were probably using them for blood sacrifices as well."

"I don't follow," Michel said.

"Sedial's crimes extend far out of Landfall," Olem said, but did not explain further. "Go on."

"My people," Michel continued, "have made contact with Sedial's enemies among the Dynize. We're doing what we can to gather an internal resistance against Sedial, but I don't think there's real time to do anything. The godstones have been active for over a month now. We can only guess that he's waiting for the last godstone to make his move, but I suspect that if you win the day, he will attempt to use them regardless."

He now had Vlora's undivided attention. She peered at him thoughtfully, a serious look on her face. "He *does* have all three godstones."

"Oh."

"It's broken," Olem explained, "but he has the capstone. We have no idea if that's enough for him to act."

Michel took off his hat and ran his good hand through his hair, barking a laugh. It sounded desperate and manic to his ears. "If that's all there is to be had, then he's going to use them."

"You're sure?"

"I know what kind of man Sedial is. He will not risk losing this war." Michel gestured toward the godstone and the battle that had begun to join to their south. He could hear the shouts of officers, then the crack of muskets and rifles. A cloud of powder smoke rose into the air and great battle cries rose from the ranks. It all sounded so close that it made him want to run back to the relative protection of the catacombs. None of the assembled officers appeared to even notice the hubbub.

Vlora seemed to consider Michel's words. "Do you have any idea what kind of preparations he'll need to undertake to use the godstones?"

"No. Blood, probably."

"And do we have any idea what the godstones will do?" she asked Olem.

"Beyond making a god? Could be anything."

Vlora let out a soft laugh. "So we don't know when, and we don't know what, but we're sure that Sedial is about to do *something*. This is terrifying." She didn't look terrified. She looked annoyed, like someone who'd been given a bigger job than she'd expected and told to do it in half the time. "Fine. It's all the more important that we kick in his door and take away his toys. Olem, send word to the brigadiers that we're running out of time. Tell Silvia that she's to have the flares ready for when darkness falls. We're not stopping this offensive until we capture the fortress."

"The casualties—" Olem began.

Vlora took a sharp breath, cutting him off with a nod. "I accept the risk and the responsibility."

"Yes, ma'am." The orders were given, and Olem returned to her side. What he said next was in a low tone, just loud enough that Michel could hear. "We do have another option."

"Go on."

"We can try to kill him."

Vlora looked up from her maps once more. "If he shows his head, I've already given the mages permission to blow it off."

"He's not going to show his head," Olem replied, "but after dark we can send a couple of mages to scale the walls and seek him out."

Michel caught his breath, looking between the two Adrans. "There will be at least a handful of dragonmen and bone-eyes inside that fortress. And probably a garrison of thousands."

"It would be a suicide mission," Vlora agreed, rubbing her chin.

"But it might be worth it," Olem said.

Vlora began to pace, scowling at the ground at her feet. Michel could practically see her weighing her options. He couldn't imagine that even a powder mage could crack whatever guard Sedial had around him, but Vlora and Olem clearly thought otherwise.

He clenched his jaw, thinking of Ichtracia deep in the fortress. Alone, probably injured, awaiting whatever fate her grandfather had in store for her. Would she end up another sacrifice? Or just a casualty? And what happened if Vlora *did* kick in the door with artillery and sorcery and bayonets? Would Ichtracia survive the chaos that ensued? A plan began to form in Michel's head, and he

considered the idea of a couple of assassins not just for assassins'
sake, but as a distraction.

"It should be me," Vlora finally said.

The words were barely out of her mouth when Olem responded,
"Absolutely not."

"Tamas would have done it," Vlora responded, the corners of her
eyes hardening with stubbornness.

"*You're* not Tamas," Olem replied, and it became clear that this
was part of some wider argument that Michel could not fathom.
"And if the assassination fails, you need to be here to make sure the
army does not. Give me two of your mages and twenty grenadiers.
I can do it myself."

"No!" The word was almost desperate. "No," Vlora repeated.
"You're not going anywhere. If I'm vital, then you're vital."

Olem seemed about to argue his point, but shook his head.
"Then it's not happening."

"I'll do it." The voice cut through the tent, and a man shouldered his way through the small group to stand between Vlora and
Olem. He carried a rifle and wore one of the silver keg pins of a
powder mage.

Vlora cast him a hard look. "Davd. You're supposed to be on
artillery duty."

"Silvia has the enemy artillery contained," Davd reported. "At
least until we get within range of the fortress. I actually came to
suggest that we get someone close to deal with the artillery after
dark, but if you want to assassinate Ka-Sedial, I'm your man."

Vlora hesitated.

"All it takes is one bullet," Davd pointed out. "I can get in, find a
high spot, take a shot, and get out. If I can make it back to the base
of the wall, no dragonman will be able to catch up with me."

Olem and Vlora exchanged glances, and it became clear that
Olem was more in favor of the idea than his general. Michel could

feel his own hasty plans now falling into place. This could work. It *had* to work. He considered his discussions with Survivor and the route the old man had taken out of the fortress and across the marshes, painting it out in his head. "I can guide him there," he suddenly blurted.

Everyone looked in his direction, and he nodded with a confidence that he forced himself to feel. One distraction, even a failed attempt on Sedial's life, might be all he needed to get inside and retrieve Ichtracia. "I can do it," he insisted. "Give me the mage and I'll make sure he gets inside the fortress."

CHAPTER 65

Styke stood at the end of the causeway leading to Etzi's compound, facing the city and leaning on his broken lance. His side burned from the dragonman's knife, while the rest of his body ached from a pounding that would be a myriad of bruises in a couple of days.

If, that was, he could survive that long.

He couldn't take his eyes off Amrec's body. Someone from the Household had emerged an hour ago and covered it reverently with a blanket, but that just seemed to make the poor creature's corpse stand out more in the mess that remained of Sedial's hired mob. Maetle walked through it all, tending to the wounded on both sides but clearly out of her depth. No surgeon, no matter how skilled, was ready for their first time of seeing true carnage. Styke sympathized. In another time, he might have reveled at the destruction he had caused. But having to put a bullet in the head of his own horse had taken all the glory out of his deeds. He felt tired, hurting, and sick to his stomach.

Only a handful of his Lancers were to be seen. The rest rode through the borough, establishing order at the tips of their lances, forcing peace on the immediate area surrounding Etzi's compound. Occasionally a report came back to Styke. He barely listened. He'd put Ibana in charge of securing their location. He had no urge to deal with any more than he already had.

"Ben." The soft voice forced him to take his eyes off Amrec's covered corpse. Celine stood by his side. She looked across the mayhem with concern, then focused on his blood-covered face.

"I thought I told you to stay inside," Styke rebuked her gently.

"They sent me to get you."

"Who?"

"Etzi. Some of the Household heads have arrived. They're pressuring Ka-poel to take on the mantle of the Great Ka and ally the Mad Lancers with their faction. They think you'll help convince her."

"They didn't come out to get me themselves?" Styke scoffed.

"I think they're afraid of you."

Styke let his eyes play across what remained of the mob once more and tossed his broken lance aside. "Good." He let Celine take him by his gore-slick gauntlet and lead him back across the causeway. He walked with a bit of a limp, his side burning, wondering if he should get out of his armor and deal with this wound before he bled out. As they passed through the gates of the compound, Etzi's Household guard stared at Styke in silence. Only the boy, Jerio, approached him, holding up a mug of beer. Styke took it with grateful thanks, downing it in two long drafts, and then followed Celine into the Household amphitheater.

A table had been set up in the center of the space. Ka-poel sat at one end, Etzi at the other. Arrayed down either side were nine more figures. Styke had watched them all arrive, though he hadn't paid attention to their identities. He could only assume that these were the Household heads. The only one he recognized was Meln-Sika, the woman who'd warned Etzi about the covert purge.

"Please sit, Colonel Styke," Etzi said, pointing to the one empty chair at the table.

Styke looked down at his bloody armor, looked at the chair, then limped around to stand just behind Ka-poel. He gave each of the Household heads a long glance. A few of the Dynize shifted uncomfortably in their seats, while others regarded him warily, as if reassessing him.

It was Meln-Sika who finally cleared her throat. "This is a poor quorum, my friends, but I believe this is the best we can manage. The rest of our allies are either dead or trapped inside their compounds. Do I have unanimous agreement to continue?" The ten Household heads each raised a hand. Meln-Sika acknowledged the vote with a nod, then lifted her chin toward Ka-poel. "At this, our most desperate hour, will you put your lot in with us? Will you become the Great Ka and help us force the emperor to dismiss Ka-Sedial?"

To Styke's eyes, Ka-poel looked so small and fragile sitting there at his side. But her jaw was firm, her lips pursed. She began to gesture, and it was Celine who translated. *I am not a trained politician. If I take on the mantle of the Great Ka, I'm sure every one of you is already too aware at how much help I will need.*

"We'd be honored to stand by your side," Meln-Sika replied, bowing her head.

"That's not what she means," Styke grunted.

Ka-poel pointed at him, a small smile fluttering across her lips. *I will not be a puppet. You know my grandfather, so you already know my temperament. If you put me forward as Great Ka, you are accepting the risk of my rule. I will accept guidance. I will* not *be controlled.*

Silence descended at the table. Styke could see the Household heads considering her words. Etzi was the only one who seemed to take them as a matter of course and had already made his decision. "Understood," he told her. "Do you have further demands?"

Ka-poel's fingers flashed. *I am hesitant to make a decision without my husband, but I know that time is short and we cannot afford to wait for him.* She let out a soft sigh. *I have one further demand: that no one interfere when I destroy the godstone.*

Meln-Sika inhaled sharply. Several of the Household heads appeared visibly shocked. Once again, only Etzi was unsurprised, but Styke knew he had had several weeks to get to know Ka-poel. He knew what to expect. "It is our inheritance," Meln-Sika said, her shaky tone betraying her fear. "It is our hope as a people."

Hope? Ka-poel answered through Celine. Her lip curled as she gestured. *It is a rock imbued with the power of a million dead. There is no hope to be had from any of the godstones. They are nothing but an avenue toward power. The only hope the Dynize people need is that of unity.*

"We haven't had unity since our god was murdered," a man half-way down the table objected. "Not until Sedial gave us the hope of the godstones."

Sedial gave you the godstones because he knew that you all hated him so much, he could never unite you himself. I won't have that problem. Ka-poel tapped her fingers on the table thoughtfully before continuing. *I am here. I will destroy the godstone. Whether you choose to place me in a position of power once I have accomplished my task is up to you. Decide quickly.*

It was the second time speed had been mentioned, and Styke leaned down to whisper in her ear. "Are we in a rush?"

She nodded. *Yes.*

"Why?"

She did not answer the question. Etzi raised his hand and, once he had everyone's attention, said, "I've spoken with my brother. Based on the number of dragonman sightings throughout the city today, we estimate that the emperor is practically undefended. If we want to force him to renounce Ka-Sedial, this might be our only chance to do so." His expression hardened. "You," he said to Ka-poel, "may have to break Sedial's hold on the emperor before we can force his hand. I truly believe that Sedial would kill the emperor before relinquishing power."

Meln-Sika sniffed. "This assumes we agree to allow the destruction of the godstone."

"And if we don't?" Etzi rounded on his colleague, thrusting a hand toward Styke. "You expect us to fight Sedial's mobs *and* defend the godstone against the Mad Lancers? We have *no choice.* Ka-poel is right. The godstone was a symbol to unite us. If there is power to be got from it, do you think that Sedial will share? We do not need a god to make us whole again. We need a Great Ka who does not contrive to enslave us."

"We barely know her," Meln-Sika retorted. "How do we know that isn't exactly what she will do?"

Etzi threw up his hands. "We can have an enemy who will murder us all, or we can have an untested ally. There are no other choices—no one else has the birthright to unite us and the power to challenge Ka-Sedial. Choose your graves."

"I..." Meln-Sika began, only for Ka-poel to slam her fist on the table. The entire room jumped, including Styke, and he looked down to find Ka-poel leaning forward, eyes wild, a look of focus on her face. She gestured emphatically.

You must decide now! Celine translated.

"We've barely had time to discuss it," Meln-Sika objected.

Ka-poel lurched to her feet, and Styke reached out to catch her by the arm. She shook him off and glared at the group. *Ka-Sedial is preparing to move. Decide!*

Etzi blinked back at her for a moment, then gestured to the rest of the Household heads. "A vote, then, for our small quorum. Those willing to back Ka-poel as the Great Ka?" He raised his hand.

Two more hands shot up immediately. Three followed slowly.

Meln-Sika grimaced and hesitantly raised her own, and once she had acquiesced, the remaining four joined her. Another unanimous vote, though Styke could tell that many of them were unhappy with the speed at which the discussion had taken place. *Good,* Ka-poel gestured. *Styke, gather your Lancers. We go to the imperial palace immediately.*

Even Etzi was surprised by the declaration. "We should gather our forces," he said. "We can risk an hour or two to bring more Household heads and soldiers to our cause."

No, Ka-poel gestured. *We cannot. Sedial has begun the ritual to wake the godstones. If we do not go now, it will be too late.*

Styke heard a shout from Etzi's front gate and, within a few moments, the hammering of running feet. It was Maetle who burst into the meeting, shoving aside one of the Household head guards. "Meln-Etzi, Meln-Sika, Ka-poel! Something is happening to the godstone! The whole city glows red!"

While the others fell into confusion, Styke turned to Ka-poel. Her face grew determined, and she gestured to one side so that only he could see what she said.

Get me to the godstone. These fools have no idea what is about to happen. If I do not challenge Ka-Sedial now, there will be no challenge.

CHAPTER 66

Michel and Davd took a long, circuitous route through the coastal marshes and approached the fortress from the east. It took them more time than he would have liked, and it quickly became clear that the powder mage was impatient over how slowly Michel was moving. He couldn't shake the feeling that he should just give Davd some vague instructions and let him loose—but he knew this was his only chance of reaching Ichtracia. Artillery and sorcery crackled over a smoke-filled battlefield to their northwest as the Adran and Dynize war machines slammed into each other with a violence that Michel could feel in his bones even at a distance. The setting sun played through it all, turning the horizon a brilliant, black-tinged orange for the space of a few minutes.

Once they'd left the coastal marshes, they proceeded through a rubble field and ramshackle tent village full of frightened Palo laborers hunkering down to weather the distant battle and Landfall riots. Davd quickly captured a Dynize uniform jacket for himself, which he wore over his Adran blues. Michel expected martial law in the laborer village, but there appeared to be no one of consequence—whatever common soldiery still occupied the place kept their eyes glued to the battle. Michel and his companion passed unnoticed.

The fortress quickly loomed above them. It was a sprawling thing, far larger—and far less complete—than Michel had guessed. Much of the eastern wall was still covered in scaffolding, the lower stone blocks covered in a finishing mortar while many of the upper blocks had yet to be put in place. The area at the base of the wall was a mess of cranes, carts, tools, and stone.

Survivor had described his exit through the base of an incomplete well where a natural spring drained from the area. It took a moment's examination to find that the area had been walled in during the time since—a great culvert now drained into the old streambed. It was big enough to crawl through, but protected by thick iron bars.

"That's not going to work," Michel muttered to himself, squinting at the scaffolding along the wall. "That was our way in," he told Davd, "but it's been bricked up."

"I can climb that scaffolding."

"I was thinking the same thing."

The powder mage frowned at the top of the wall. "You don't need to come any farther. We're here. I'll find the son of a bitch."

"No," Michel said, almost too quickly. "I'm coming."

The words had barely left his mouth when Davd snatched him by the front of his shirt and threw him down behind a discarded stone block. Michel didn't even have the chance to voice an objection before a sudden crack split his ears. The very earth seemed to rumble. For a moment, Michel thought that it had started to rain heavily—only to realize that tiny pieces of stone were falling all around them in a fine hail. He put his hands over his head, listening to the disconcerting sound and staring at Davd.

"Flint's pushing hard!" Davd shouted, pointing above them.

Michel looked up to see that one of the gun towers less than fifty paces to their north had suddenly ceased to exist. A jagged stone remnant, wreathed in smoke and crackling with lightning, was all that remained. "If Nila is close enough to do that, the army is nearby!" Michel stared at Davd, trying to figure out why he was shouting, only to realize that the sound seemed distant and muddled. His ears rang.

"Are we still going in?" he shouted back.

"They might still stop her," Davd replied, regaining his footing and heading to the scaffolding. "You need to stay here. I can't wait for you."

Michel watched helplessly as Davd took a deep breath from something in his pocket, swung his rifle onto his back, and leapt onto the scaffolding. The leap seemed effortless but must have been six feet, and he scrambled up the scaffolding like a spider. He was at the top of the incomplete wall within moments, leaving Michel behind.

"Well, there goes my distraction." Michel swore under his breath and followed the powder mage. His ascent proved painfully slow, as his own lack of sorcery—and his ruined hand—kept him from making the leaps and quick judgment that Davd had displayed. Michel worked methodically, finding the ladders and safest routes, gaining each level with only a pause to listen to his ringing ears in an attempt to judge the distance of the armies clashing beyond the northern wall of the fortress.

Another explosion shook the scaffolding dangerously. Michel clung to the stone facade with all his might until the shaking had passed. He had no ability to judge whether the explosion had been sorcery or artillery.

He was just climbing through a gap left between two big stone blocks at the top when a sudden brilliance caught him off guard. The sun had almost completely set, leaving most of the fortress shrouded in darkness, and for a moment he thought that the

Dynize had begun firing flares. He squinted toward the sky, trying to find the source.

A thrill of fear went through him when he realized that the godstone had begun to *glow*. The triangular cap at the top bathed the battlefield in a yellow light as if a second sun had suddenly appeared. The fear almost sent Michel scrambling back to the dubious safety of the scaffolding, but he forced himself to roll off the wall and onto the unfinished battlements. He dropped into a crouch, squinting against the light of the godstone, and attempted to get his bearings.

The fortress was easily as big as the capital building up in Land-fall, sprawling and cavernous, but it became immediately clear that the builders had put all of their effort into the walls and gun towers. The inside was little more than a pit filled with the detri-tus of construction—scaffolding, cranes, stone. Michel could see everything from his hiding spot. The big fortress doors were kitty-corner from his position, flanked by high gun towers. The area swarmed with soldiers, running up and down wooden ramps car-rying ammunition up to the guns. While the fortress floor was a flurry of activity, everyone who wasn't focused on the defense was staring, dumbfounded, up at the godstone.

No one had noticed Michel. At least for the moment.

The godstone itself was protected by an inner keep that appeared to be finished. The high stone walls were clear of scaffolding; the mighty doors stood open and were heavily guarded. Even glancing in that direction gave Michel a dark sense of unease, though the glances he threw in that direction revealed that bodies were being carried out of the keep—an alarming number of them.

Something else caught his attention: a relatively small pyra-mid, a single piece of stone, sitting off to one side of the court-yard. Nobody appeared to pay it much mind, but it glowed with a less powerful crimson light, pulsing in time with the top of the godstone. This, he realized, must be the capstone that Flint had mentioned.

He hurried along the battlements parallel to the keep, toward the back of the fortress, his eyes on a ramp that would get him down to the main floor. There were a handful of buildings there—two long barracks, and a half-dozen smaller units, all made of wood. If Ichtracia was to be found, he had no doubt she was in one of those. He paused occasionally to watch for guards, taking advantage of the deep shadows thrown by the pulsating godstone to hide behind construction materials.

It was during one of these pauses that he spotted Davd. The powder mage had made it all the way around to the opposite side of the fortress, clearly heading toward an unfinished tower that would give him the best vantage point. Davd sprinted across the battlements, carving his way through a small group of Dynize soldiers, catching them unaware.

Michel watched his progress until one of the Dynize spotted him. An alarm was raised quickly despite the overwhelming thunder of the artillery, and a great deal of attention shifted to Davd. The attention, he realized, was both a boon and a bane. It would allow Michel to sneak through more easily, but it may just have ruined their shot at killing Sedial before this could get any worse.

"Good luck," he wished the powder mage, and descended from the wall toward the barracks below.

He was about halfway down when his head began to hurt. It was a stabbing pain, like the worst kind of hangover, and it made him stumble and nearly plummet from the ramps. He caught himself on the building, rubbing furiously at his temples. For the briefest moment, he couldn't remember where he was. The confusion passed and he forced himself back to his feet, taking the descent with more caution.

The ramp turned at an alcove that led into a hallway in the outer wall. Michel paused, watching for guards, and then turned down the ramp. Or, at least, that's what he'd intended to do.

Instead, he continued forward, walking down the hallway at a leisurely pace. The rest of his body still seemed to obey him—his head still turned, his arms worked—everything but his legs. Confusion grew to irritation, and then to concern, and then to panic all in the space of a dozen steps. His adrenaline kicked into overdrive as he fought with his own body, trying to get himself to turn around.

It was in vain. He continued down the hall guided by the light of the godstone until the hallway turned with the angle of the wall. He was presented with a door on his right, flanked by a pair of Dynize dragonmen. The two glanced at Michel curiously, and he tried to scramble backward, only to find that even his arms wouldn't obey him anymore.

"He's here to see me," a voice called from within. Michel felt himself seized with fear as he finally realized what was happening. His body began to sweat and shake uncontrollably, and he strolled right between the two dragonmen and through the door.

It was a small room—meant to be a guard post, perhaps, or maybe an officer's bedroom. It was occupied by a writing desk and a single stool, the latter of which was positioned beside a slit of a window that overlooked the inner fortress. Ka-Sedial sat on the stool, smiling pleasantly, head craned as he watched something that only he could see. Ichtracia sat on the floor behind him. She was still wearing the same vest and pants she'd had on four days ago. She was covered in bruises, her face a bloody mess, the left cheek marred by a burn scar that extended from her temple down the side of her neck. She wore a strange yoke—a wooden beam that ran behind her neck and held both of her arms up where her hands could be seen clearly. Each individual finger was locked separately in a tiny vise.

"Hello, Michel," Sedial said pleasantly, turning away from the window. "You may have noticed that Ka-poel is no longer protecting you." Michel's eyes darted to the writing desk, where a vial of blood sat beside a purple, withered finger. His blood. His finger. His terror escalated beyond the ability for rational thought.

At his name, Ichtracia's head rolled and her eyes flickered. A bit of drool trickled out of the corner of her mouth.

"She's quite drugged," Sedial said. "Helpless as a babe." He brushed his fingertips across Ichtracia's forehead, then briefly touched the yoke behind her shoulders. "The brace is just an extra precaution. What's wrong, Michel? I've left you your ability to speak. No witty reply? No desperate plea to release Ichtracia?" Sedial grimaced, as if realizing how petty he sounded, and glanced back out the window. "I have to admit, when you popped back into the periphery of my senses, I was more than a little surprised that you were coming *here*. Well, maybe it shouldn't have been a surprise. You're an arrogant little spy. The powder mage *was* a surprise... but my dragonmen will deal with him soon."

Sedial slapped his knees happily and stood up, knuckling his back like an old man preparing for a walk in the park. "It's almost time, my boy! You're going to have a great honor, you know." He grasped a leather cord, tugging it gently until Ichtracia shifted onto her knees and then climbed, awkwardly, to her feet. Her eyes were red and unfocused, and Michel felt his chest tightening with fear and anger at the sight of someone so strong brought so low. He suddenly turned without giving his body instructions to do so, and followed as Sedial led Ichtracia out into the hall.

"You seem to be in a very good mood for someone who's about to be crushed by the Adran Army," Michel said as they walked down the hall. It was the best jab he could muster, but it had no strength to it. His voice was dull. Defeated.

Sedial didn't respond, heading out onto the ramp and descending to the inner fortress, Ichtracia following in a stupor, and Michel unable to do anything but tag along behind. He could sense the dragonmen take up position behind him, but when he tried to turn his head, he found that he could not. He prayed for the crack of Davd's rifle and a magical bullet splitting Sedial's skull. It didn't come.

"We've caught up so much over the last few days, she and I," Sedial said over his shoulder, giving a little tug to Ichtracia's leash. "She says you're in love with her. Is that true?"

Michel bit down on his tongue until a pressure deep inside his belly forced him to speak. "I don't know." A well of emotion followed the words and, if he'd been allowed, he might have begun to sob.

Sedial looked a little disappointed. "She's fairly confident. You must at least care if you've come to try and fetch her. Ah, well. 'Care' is good enough for my purposes." They rounded the inner keep that housed the godstone and paused beside the big doors while soldiers carried out another corpse, then proceeded inside. Unlike the rest of the fortress, the keep was pristine and orderly. There was no rubble or equipment. The floors and walls were polished white marble. There was nothing inside except the godstone and twenty or so attendants. A wide, bloody altar lay at the base of the obelisk.

Michel fought Sedial's hold harder, calling out for Ka-poel in his mind. There was no answer.

Sedial stopped in front of the altar, a little frown on his face, blood pooling around his sandals. A blast shattered the air, and one of the gun towers fell silent. "They . . . you," he said to Michel, "all think me a monster. It's so strange to me. All I'm trying to do is impose order, and yet my enemies swarm like locusts." He gave a little sigh. "It won't matter in a few minutes. Up you go!" He prodded Ichtracia, forcing her up a little stepladder onto the blood-soaked altar. Michel thought he saw a flicker in her eyes and a twitch in her shoulders. He silently willed her to fight.

Instead, she lowered herself to her knees. One of the dragonmen climbed up beside her and carefully removed the yoke holding her arms and hands, then pushed her gently onto her back.

"She thought," Sedial said as he watched the proceeding, "that I needed her blood to unlock Ka-poel's hold on the godstone. I *did* need blood, quite a lot of it, but what I needed *her* for? Well, my granddaughter is no ordinary sacrifice. To open the godstone to me, the blood needs *power*. She has it in spades. She, Michel, is going to help me change the world. It's a good death. Unlike yours." He patted Michel affectionately on the shoulder and handed him a knife. "Up you go."

Michel's terror reached a crescendo as he ascended the step-ladder. Darkness touched the corners of his vision as he fought the compulsion with every ounce of his being. He screamed at himself to stop—to turn and plunge the knife into Sedial's chest. Instead, he turned on his heel and knelt down beside Ichtracia. He raised the knife.

"Wait," Sedial said. "It must be coordinated with a sacrifice at the main godstone in Talunlica." He paused, lips moving silently as if speaking to a voice in his head. Another moment passed. "Ah, yes. We are in position. Go ahead, Michel."

Tears streamed down Michel's face as his arms plunged downward. The knife rammed between Ichtracia's ribs. She let out a muted gasp, body twitching, and he jerked the knife out of her, sagging back onto his knees. He could do nothing but watch her chest as the blood bubbled out of it.

Sedial tsked. "You missed her heart, my boy. I suppose this *is* your first time. Shall we try again?"

"Please don't," Michel whispered as his hands jerked back up, holding the knife above Ichtracia's chest. He felt a brief breeze on the side of his neck and heard something like a sigh.

"Ah. No need. That was enough blood," Sedial said happily. "Look."

Michel was allowed to turn his head toward the godstone. A

rectangle had appeared on the stone surface, about the size of a door. It glowed with the same light as the top of the godstone, though greatly muted. Michel suddenly felt hot breath on his ear and could sense that Sedial had stepped onto the altar with him.

"I don't know what attention I'll be able to turn toward mortal pleasures once I am a god. But I promise that I'll make a special point of attending to you. The anguish you have felt these last few moments is nothing." Another affectionate pat on Michel's shoulder. "I go into the Else!" Sedial announced to his assistants, straightening his back and squaring his shoulders to the godstone. "Hold this room against any attack until I have returned."

Without a backward glance, Sedial strode through the glowing door into the godstone.

CHAPTER 67

Styke had to admit that the procession making its way down the main avenue to the emperor's palace was an impressive one. At its head were the Mad Lancers—nearly four hundred heavy cavalry garbed in ancient armor, the skull-and-lance flag fluttering over their heads. Behind them came the Household heads and their guards. Taking up the rear were the Adran cavalry Styke had borrowed from Flint what felt like years ago, still commanded by Major Gustar. Everyone rode at attention, eyes keen, knowing that they were putting on a show for the palace.

The rest of the Mad Lancers, mostly recruits from their trek across Fatrasta, kept the Dynize mob and their loyalist backers from bothering the procession. Styke could hear the sounds of screaming and carbine shots coming from all around them, and could see fighting across the lake. He tried to ignore it. He had a more important job to do.

Even focusing on that was proving to be a challenge. Styke swayed in his saddle, feeling light-headed from loss of blood. He hadn't bothered to tell anyone about the wound in his side, and he wondered if that had been a mistake. The whole area screamed with each bounce of the saddle of his borrowed horse, and blood dripped down the side of his armor. He caught a few concerned glances from the Lancers, but no one asked him about the wound.

The group reached the great gates of the palace complex, and Styke raised one gauntlet to halt the column, giving the palace a once-over with a critical eye. It had been built for show rather than to withstand a siege. The walls couldn't have been more than twenty feet high, the arch above the gate made out of wood instead of stone. Both arch and gate were brightly painted. Styke got the feeling that people weren't supposed to actually attack the emperor. Something about sacrilege. He didn't much care.

Above the wall, just a few blocks to his left, rose the godstone. The top of the pillar shone like the sun, causing walls and buildings to cast long shadows and forcing Styke to shade his eyes as he looked up to the silent row of morion-helmed soldiers arrayed on the top of the wall. The soldiers were dressed and armed just like any Dynize infantry or Household guard, but they also wore full face masks painted in the same bright turquoise, yellows, greens, and blues as the palace gate.

"I'm glad you're here," Styke said quietly to the Lancer beside him.

Ibana snorted. "Saved your life. Again."

"That you did."

She must have heard something in Styke's voice, because Ibana's expression softened and she reached over to touch her gauntlet to his. "I'm glad you're still alive."

They shared a companionable silence until Etzi joined them at the front of the column, riding out a few paces ahead with his Household standard flying above his horse. He called up to the imperial guard. "The Household Quorum demands an audience with the emperor. Open the gates!"

One of the guards removed his mask and leaned over the wall.

"I see only foreigners and traitors. The gates will remain closed. Disperse at once."

Etzi cast Styke an uncertain glance. Styke said quietly to Ibana, "If they let us in, I want you to figure out exactly how many soldiers are inside and put yourselves between them and Ka-poel."

"I get the feeling they're not going to do that," Ibana replied.

"Then we're going to gain the palace by force."

"Still want to know how many guard they have?"

"We can count the corpses later."

Ibana gave him a toothy grin. Another day, Styke might have returned it. He touched his side and grimaced up at the imperial guard, who was still staring arrogantly back down at Etzi. The Household head hesitated a few moments and cleared his throat.

"You see before you members of the Household Quorum and our allies. We seek a peaceful resolution to what has occurred today. Open the gates so that we may speak to the emperor. No one else has to die."

The guard captain gestured dismissively. "You've had your warning."

Styke urged his horse up beside Etzi's. "They're not going to negotiate."

"Perhaps if we—"

Ka-poel rode up from the column and flashed a handful of signals at Styke.

They're just buying time, Styke translated to Etzi. "She says we don't have hours to spare. We might not have minutes."

Even now, after all that had occurred, it was clear Etzi was loath to order an attack on the imperial palace. Styke didn't have the same reservations. He nodded to Ibana, and she lifted her voice. "Open the gates or we will open them for you!"

A musket shot rang out, ricocheting off the cobbles just in front of Etzi's horse. A warning shot. They shouldn't have bothered.

"Go!" Styke snapped to Etzi, lowering his visor and putting himself between the wall and Ka-poel.

"No?" Ibana boomed. "You heard 'em, boys! Tear down the gates!"

A number of things happened at once. At Ibana's order, the Lancers fanned out in front of the gate, each soldier producing a rope and grapple. The imperial guard produced their muskets and opened fire, their bullets whizzing around Styke's head, pinging off his armor. Ka-poel produced her satchel, flipping it open with one hand and raising the other into the air above it. Tiny wax dolls appeared, floating around her head like wasps. One of the imperial guard suddenly turned on his companion with a bayonet. Another produced a knife and disappeared. The shouting of the officers became desperate screams, and their hail of bullets was reduced to a sprinkle as they attempted to put down their own companions.

Dozens of Lancers threw their grapples over the gateway arch. The ropes were secured to saddles and the horses began to strain. Ibana shouted orders. More grapples were added. Styke watched the process silently, listening to the fighting among the guards. He could *smell* the coppery bite of sorcery now, though he wasn't sure whether it was coming from Ka-poel or the godstone. He took a few deep breaths, patting the neck of his borrowed horse.

With a final shout from Ibana, horses working in concert, the Lancers ripped down the arch. One of the doors was torn clear off its hinges, while the other screeched and bent at an angle, still holding on. Styke drew his sword. "Lancers, with me!"

They thundered into the palace, emerging into a wide parade ground and fanning out. There were at least two companies of imperial guard waiting for them, and even with Ka-poel's interference, the resistance was brutal. Styke felt the crunch of bodies beneath his horse's chest armor and swung his sword in a fury as bayonets surrounded him. For a moment he felt he would be overwhelmed, but the sheer weight of the column riding in through the gate pushed back the Dynize and soon he was surrounded by his own men. Horses fell to bayonets, men and animals screaming, as the Mad Lancers took the gate.

He was suddenly free of the mob, his sword slick, gripping the saddle horn to keep from falling to the ground. The chaos of the battle raged around him. He turned to find Ka-poel at his side. She slapped his armor and gestured emphatically. *We have no time! This way!* She suddenly charged through the melee, bent over her horse, machete in hand, galloping at speed with seemingly no thought for the danger. Styke had no choice but to follow.

Instead of heading deeper into the palace, Ka-poel turned and rode parallel to the wall. They ducked beneath an arch, thundered down a long, narrow corridor, and emerged into an enormous garden.

Ka-poel reined in and dismounted expertly. Styke did the same, holding his side, sword in one hand. The garden was several acres— a pristine little slice of heaven with ponds, streams, decorative trees, flowers, and more. The sound of the fighting, though Styke knew it was close, seemed miles away. His nose twitched at the fragrant smell of sorceries that he could not identify but that presented a subtle undercurrent to the powerful reek of blood.

The godstone stood in the center of the garden. Vines grew around its base like it was some old ruin, and the place might have been a perfect picture of peace were it not for the dozens of bodies stacked on the far side of the garden. An altar sat before the godstone, covered in blood, one final corpse wearing the gloves of a Privileged sprawled across its center. A light had appeared in the shape of a doorway just above the altar. Ka-poel strode toward that light with purpose.

"You cannot go that way," a voice called.

What Styke had initially taken for a corpse along the far wall suddenly stood up. It was a man in his forties, face and head shaved clean but with the skin and features of a Palo. To Styke's surprise, the man was at least as tall as him, if not taller. Black tattoos swirled around his wrists, bare chest, and neck, and his torso was covered in blood spatter. Even at this distance, even in the shadow of the godstone, the man smelled of sorcery. He watched Ka-poel and Styke through bored, half-lidded eyes.

"Why do you not obey me?" His voice was a deep rumble. "I am Emperor Janen. I am obeyed."

Ka-poel's hands flashed. *Deal with him. Be careful. He is like Taniel.*

"What do you mean he's like Taniel?" Styke asked.

Without answering, Ka-poel suddenly broke into a sprint, heading straight for the godstone. Styke swore and did the same. Though they should have beaten the emperor there by twenty paces, he crossed the space in the blink of an eye, one hand outstretched to snatch at Ka-poel. Styke flung his sword overhand and the emperor spun, batting it out of the air as if it were a lazily thrown ball.

The distraction allowed Styke several more strides, and when the emperor turned to grab Ka-poel, Styke slammed into him from the side. He put every ounce of strength into the tackle, and all the weight of his body and armor behind it. Janen fell beneath him, and they hadn't even hit the ground before Styke was drawing his knife.

He barely pulled it halfway from its sheath when he felt a palm connect with his chest. His breath was snatched from him, several of his ribs giving a sickening crack that he felt from his fingertips to his toes. The blow sent him reeling. Janen was on him in an instant, the emperor's face marred by a mildly annoyed frown. Styke threw a punch with his left hand. Janen grabbed his fist and almost casually gave a squeeze.

Ensorceled steel bent under the strength. Styke felt a scream wrench itself from his mouth as his hand was crushed inside his gauntlet, pain lancing up his arm and making his knees weak. He fought through it and jabbed with his now-drawn knife, catching the emperor under the ribs. The tip of Styke's blade had barely pierced the skin when a backhand caught him on the chin. He spun bodily, helpless to catch himself, and landed on his back a dozen feet away, disoriented and in pain.

Janen strode toward him, wearing that same irritated frown.

Styke felt three of his teeth loose in his mouth. Blood poured from his lips. In all his life, he had never been manhandled by strength even a tenth of what the emperor had. He knew, in that instant, that he was going to die. Behind Janen, Ka-poel reached the altar and dove headfirst into the glowing light. She disappeared in a wink.

The emperor inhaled sharply and spun toward the altar. Styke tried to lift himself up, unsure whether Janen could follow Ka-poel through that door. He had to keep the bastard distracted. But how?

The crack of a gun jolted Styke out of his painful half stupor. Janen jerked, swatting at the back of his head as if stung by a bee. Styke craned his head to look for the source of the shot, hoping to find Ibana or Jackal or, preferably, all of the Mad Lancers together. Instead he saw a man drop from the outer wall and land on his feet as if the fall was nothing.

"Is she inside?" Taniel demanded, discarding his smoking pistol.

"She is," Styke croaked. He spat out one of his teeth.

"Then you've done your part. I'll deal with Sedial's creature." Taniel drew his sword and darted forward.

CHAPTER 68

Michel couldn't remember the last time he really, truly cried. He'd cried in pain before, certainly. He'd wept over the deaths of his friends. But the sobs that wracked his body came out in horrid, anguished yowls, tearing his throat raw. He clutched at Ichtracia, trying to regain control of himself, only half aware of the chaos around him.

Dragonmen and Privileged ran out of the keep. The doors were closed and barred. Blasts shook the ground beneath them and plaster fell from the keep walls. Hundreds of people shouted in Dynize.

Michel could not have said how long it had been since Sedial stepped through the portal, but there came a moment when he realized that he was no longer controlled. He held Ichtracia to his chest. He'd shifted onto his knees. The realization of sudden freedom broke through to him like a lightning strike and he wrestled down the sobs and wiped a grimy sleeve across his eyes. He lowered Ichtracia back to the ground, tearing away her vest, pressing his palm to her chest wound to try to stem the flow of blood.

He'd missed her heart.

Blood bubbled up through his fingers. He pressed harder, and Ichtracia suddenly gurgled. Her eyes opened wide, the whites turned red from the mala used to drug her. A single bubble of blood appeared on her lips. It popped. Another formed, and he realized she was trying to speak.

"I'm sorry," he said. "I'm sorry. I'm sorry. I'm sorry." His palm slipped off the wound. He tried to put it back, barely able to see through the hazy mist in his eyes.

To his shock, Ichtracia shifted in his arms. It was slow, gradual, and he might not have felt it if he didn't see her hand suddenly fall out of her pocket. She was wearing one of her hidden gloves, still attached to her vest by several strings. The glove was black with blood. She tugged weakly, trying to free the glove, then seemed to give up. Her body sagged. Michel tore the strings and clutched at her hand, pressing the gloved fingers against her own wound. "Come on! You can stop the bleeding!"

Michel felt a firm hand suddenly grasp him by the shoulder. He was torn away from Ichtracia and turned toward a dragon-man, who, staring down at Michel, seemed about to toss him aside. Michel tried to struggle, looking back toward Ichtracia. The other hand fell from her pocket, wearing a glove.

The tips of Ichtracia's fingers twitched.

A roar filled Michel's ears. Heat pricked at his face like the embers of a fire, and he suddenly found himself unhanded. He wrapped his arms around himself to try to stop his trembling as he was buffeted by unseen forces.

Within moments, nothing remained of Sedial's guards. Soldiers, dragonmen, Privileged. At least two dozen people had been turned to ash in an instant. He let out a gasp and dropped back to his knees beside Ichtracia. He patted her cheek, then checked her pulse. He could feel nothing.

No conscious thought propelled him forward. With a surge of

strength, Michel scooped his arms beneath Ichtracia and lifted her to his chest. Slowly, one leg at a time, he got his feet beneath him. He hesitated, only for a moment, staring at the unknown glow of oblivion. In two strides, he stepped through the portal and into the godstone.

Michel stepped into a deafening silence. He was in a room of gray brick whose dimensions seemed to shift between blinks—the ceiling high, then low; the walls near, then far. Three glowing doors hovered in the air at a constant distance from one another, providing something for Michel's mind to grasp onto. Equidistant between them was a spot of the blackest black Michel had ever seen. It tugged at his eye, at once revolting and pleasing, hanging suspended above the ground. It couldn't have been much bigger than an apple.

Michel took a step forward, trying to think through his disorientation. There was something wrong with this place—something that pressed on the edges of his mind and flickered across his vision, yet he could not place it. It took him several moments to realize that no color existed here, that he could only see black, white, and gray. But that wasn't what was driving him mad.

He took another step, trying to remember his purpose. Beneath his feet, the brick felt spongy and loose. He smiled at the sensation, bouncing himself up and down on the balls of his feet. He looked down at Ichtracia's blood-soaked body. It seemed to weigh nothing. He couldn't recall why he had brought her here, or why he cared.

It took several more moments before he realized that they were not alone. Two figures stood on either side of the blackest black. They faced each other, their bodies frozen, their eyes locked. Michel could hear words, slow and muted, as if through a thick wall. He strained to hear them and in the effort of that focus saw their lips moving.

"You can't waste it," Ka-Sedial said.

A faint flicker of surprise registered in the back of Michel's head as Ka-poel answered him aloud, "And yet I won't let you take it."

"You have no choice. It *cannot* be wasted," Sedial replied. "We are here. The power must be seized. Neither of us can imagine the consequences of leaving without it." His frozen body seemed to lean forward ever so slightly. "You don't have to oppose me, child. This rite of power is older than Kresimir. Blood is meant to be spilled. It is meant to be *used*. We can share it." He moved closer to the blackest black.

A bead of sweat rolled down Ka-poel's brow and dripped from her chin. "I don't need more power. I have no use for it."

"Everyone has a use for power." Sedial moved backward a fraction of an inch. "You and I. We split it between us, as Kresimir split the power with his siblings. We can do great things." He trembled slightly, moving back even more.

Ka-poel's eyes suddenly flicked toward Michel. In the flash of an instant his warping reality seemed to stabilize, and he remembered the reason for the tears on his cheeks. "You can't be here!" Ka-poel told him. "It will kill you!"

"Your sister," Michel gasped. "She…" He couldn't finish, lifting Ichtracia's body with all his might, offering it toward Ka-poel. There was a flicker of hesitation in her eyes. Ka-Sedial suddenly surged forward, his frozen body stopping within inches of the blackest black. A snarl crept onto his lips, determination straining in his eyes. Something seemed to peel off the tips of Ka-poel's fingers—a shadow, floating, back and forth like a feather, toward Michel. It landed softly on Ichtracia's brow.

"It's all I can spare," Ka-poel said, her voice trembling. "You have to go. You will die."

"I'll die with her, then," Michel said. He could feel his mind slipping again, that momentary control beginning to wane.

"Let him die," Sedial rasped. "Let them all die. Break free of your worldly cares. You can be a god, Ka-poel!" The old man's fingers reached slowly toward the blackest black, as if moving through molasses.

Michel's reality began to unravel. Ichtracia slipped from his fingers, forgotten. His eyes locked on the blackest black. He wanted to walk toward it, but found that he could not. Something seemed to touch his collar. Ichtracia lay in a pool of blood at his feet. She began to recede farther from him, and he reached out to grasp her, but didn't have the strength to do it. Something—someone—was pulling him backward. He craned in confusion.

Lady Flint stood just inside the door through which Michel had entered. She didn't seem bothered by the room, her jaw set and her eyes steady. "You heard the woman," she told him. "Out."

Michel felt himself flung toward the portal and watched helplessly as the room with the blackest black disappeared. He stumbled onto the bloodstained altar in the fortress near Landfall. The room was filled with Adran soldiers, most of them badly wounded. Olem stood between a pair of Privileged as one of them treated a gash in his forehead. Understanding returned, and Michel threw himself back toward the portal, only to slam against rock. He pawed at the warm stone and let out a howl of grief.

The portal was gone.

Vlora tossed the spy back into the real world and turned to face the two figures squared off over the blackest black. She walked toward them, finding that the closer she drew, the harder it was to proceed. Halting her advance, she walked around to one side where she could see both faces. Though they looked frozen, like fish on ice, her sorcerous senses screamed, alerting her to the unseen conflict raging between them. Her nostrils burned from powder, her body weak from all those injuries at the Crease.

"You came," Ka-poel suddenly said.

"Chasing him." Vlora nodded. "I didn't expect to find you here."

She tried to take a step forward. It felt like stepping into a tub full of honey. "Lost half my army and a bunch of good friends to do it, but I'm here. Wherever *here* is. The Else?"

"Yes."

Vlora looked around at the strange brick room. There was no source for the light that illuminated them, though the world was swirling with pastels of sorcery. The colors coalesced around Ka-poel and her grandfather until they seemed to *become* that blackest black. Vlora pointed at it in question.

"The souls of a million damned," Ka-poel told her. "Or the sorcerous essence of their blood. Whatever you want to call it—the heart of the godstones. How man becomes god."

"Did Kresimir build this?"

"I don't know."

"Why isn't he talking?" Vlora gestured at Ka-Sedial.

"Because he's not letting himself be distracted." Ka-poel fell silent, the frozen expression on her face slowly becoming a scowl. Both she and her grandfather were sweating profusely. Sedial was closer to the blackest black, his fingertips drifting toward it.

Vlora watched them struggle for a few more moments and stepped back, drew her pistol, and fired.

"Wait!" Ka-poel's warning came too slow. The shot echoed through the room. Vlora could *see* the bullet race toward Ka-Sedial's head. But as it grew closer, it too slowed, and the bullet came to a stop not an inch from his temple. Ka-poel gave an angry grunt. "Attacking him won't do any good. We can manipulate this place to a point. That's why you can't come closer."

Vlora glared at the offending bullet and drew her sword. "You're certain about that?"

Ka-poel didn't answer, but Vlora saw Sedial's eyes flicker toward her as she began to wade through the honey-like air, her blade extended. She thought she heard a distant rumble, disturbing the silence of the room.

"You shouldn't be here," Sedial suddenly spoke up.

"Neither should you," Vlora retorted. She took a hit of powder—too much, more than she should dare in her fragile state—and pushed forward.

"This is my birthright!" Sedial snapped. "This is *my* power to take. You have no place here, powder mage. You can look into the Else, but you cannot enter."

Vlora felt herself buffeted by...something. Ka-poel moved slightly toward the blackest black, Sedial twitched away from it. Vlora continued to push her weakened body, summoning from the well deep within her—all her anger, her frustration, her determination. She extended her arm, plunging her sword toward Sedial's throat, like trying to push the blade through the center of a tree. The metal began to bend, and Sedial's fingers regained their lost ground in his reach for the blackest black.

"Nobody wants you as their god," Vlora hissed.

"No one gets to choose their god," Sedial said. He suddenly lurched to one side, shaking his head in confusion. His fingers slipped past the blackest black, and the bullet suspended in air continued along its path, whizzing past his ear and smacking into the far wall in a puff of plaster. Vlora's own body was released, the force of her own momentum carrying her past Sedial. Ka-poel let out a gasp, stumbled, and would have fallen if not caught by an arm. The woman—the corpse—that Michel left on the floor clutched at Ka-poel, holding her up, and waved a blood-soaked gloved hand at Sedial.

"Ichtracia! You must not manipulate the elements in this place!" Sedial barked.

Ichtracia raised both her hands. That distant rumble occurred once more, and the Privileged laughed. "That wasn't me, Grandfather."

"It's the damned powder mage! This place was not built for her kind!" Sedial spun toward Vlora as she picked herself up off the floor. He extended one hand toward her, and she felt herself propelled toward one of the glowing portals. "Help me get her out, and we can share this power! Ichtracia...my Mara. Give me your strength."

The Privileged stared back at Sedial for a few moments. "No," she said softly.

The rumbling grew louder. A crack formed along one wall, spidering out into many. Sedial looked around desperately, panic in his eyes. "Damn you. It'll kill us all!" There was a flicker at the edges of Vlora's awareness, a shadow cast across the far wall in the shape of a tall, fat man with a ladle in one hand and an apron around his belly.

"Adom?" Vlora asked in the stillness of the moment.

The figure winked and was gone. The rumblings stopped, and the thick air released Vlora, allowing her to move again.

Sedial leapt for the blackest of black. Ka-poel was quicker. One hand darted forward, plunging into the sorcerous maelstrom. All around them, the Else began to crumble.

Michel sat on the edge of the altar, soaked in the blood of Ichtracia and who knew how many other sacrifices, cradling his ruined hand. Adran soldiers rushed around him, officers barking orders, messengers giving reports, while the distant sound of musket fire was occasionally punctuated by the roar of cannons. From what Michel had gathered just listening to the chatter around him, they'd captured the fortress at great cost. The Dynize still outnumbered them, menacing from every direction.

Olem strode through the middle of it all, a pillar of calm in the chaos, listening to a string of bad news without so much as a blink.

"Sir, confirmation from the Ninth. General Sabastenien has succumbed to his wounds!"

"Send a field promotion to his second-in-command," Olem responded.

"The Third is buckling on our western flank, they're requesting reinforcements."

"Give them two companies from the Seventh and have them pull back three hundred yards."

"Sir, word from Privileged Nila. She's taken care of that regiment of cavalry trying to cut us off from the north, but she's burned out bad."

"Tell her to retreat, and make sure Magus Borbador knows not to take any offensives. We *need* him to neutralize any Privileged they have left."

"Sir, report from Captain Norrine. Captain Buden is down. Another one of those damned dragonmen."

"Is he still alive?"

"She didn't say."

"Send a medic and a stretcher. Get him out of there. How's Davd?"

A medic appeared through the doors of the keep, hands covered in blood, and answered the question with the shake of his head.

Olem swore. "Listen up, everyone! We're down to one powder mage and one Privileged. Our field guns are knackered and the Dynize seem pretty pissed off that we've captured their damned obelisk. I'm not sure if we can hold this position, but we're damn well going to try. The good news is our fleet has arrived and shelled the living piss out of everything the Dynize had holding the harbor, which gives us a corridor of retreat and relief. I want all wounded evacuated in that direction. Get to it!"

The orders were followed within moments, wounded being loaded into stretchers while reinforcements took to the fortress walls with their rifles. Michel watched it all with a dense numbness, wondering if he should follow them toward Landfall. Even getting down from the altar seemed like an impossible task. Maybe it was fitting that he should stay here and die when the Dynize recaptured the fort.

"Michel!"

He jumped, realizing that Olem stood directly in front of him. "Huh? Sir?"

"You've lost a lot of blood, soldier. You should get out of here."

Michel shook his head and pulled his mangled hand closer to his chest. "I'm not leaving without Ichtracia."

"That's a bold thing to say, but you're only going to get in the way."

"I'm not leaving."

"Pit. Well, I'm giving Vlora five more minutes and then requesting volunteers to hold the keep and sending everyone else to fight their way toward the coast. If you want to die with those of us that stay, you're more than welcome to do so." Olem abruptly turned and shouted at a messenger, striding away to a flurry of reports.

Michel lifted his eyes to the godstone, *willing* that portal to reappear. Only blank stone stared back at him. He felt himself tilting, his head foggy. The practical spy within him formulated a plan to retreat with the Adrans, make use of their medics, then get himself to a hideaway within the catacombs where he could recover through whatever was to follow this battle. He squeezed his eyes shut and scooted off the edge of the altar, gaining his feet. There was no point in remaining. He'd done all he could do.

A popping sound, like a rifle going off behind his ear, made him jump. He spun back toward the godstone only to see that a great crack had formed, running lengthwise all the way up and down the monument. The whole thing shifted, and half of it looked like it was about to fall but, at the last moment, settled in on its own weight. Michel was so transfixed by the break that he almost missed the two figures who'd appeared on the altar.

Vlora and Ichtracia leaned against each other, their clothes steaming. Michel felt himself brushed aside as Olem rushed to the altar and helped Vlora down. The two leapt into a conference, and within moments Vlora was ordering a fighting retreat from the godstone. The Adrans began to pick up their things, ready to leave now that their general had returned.

Michel wanted to rush to Ichtracia, but it was all he could do to stay standing as she came to join him. She was covered in blood, still wearing her gloves, her vest hanging loose to reveal that the great wound he'd given her under Sedial's influence was healed without a scar. He could tell from the slump of her shoulders that she was in pain, and her eyes still held the redness of a deep mala binge.

"You look as bad as I feel," she said.

"That good?" Michel swayed, seeing darkness at the corners of his vision. "I'm glad you're back."

"Michel?"

Her voice sounded distant. Michel's head felt heavy, and he abruptly dropped to his knees, casting about for a soft spot to sit. "I'm just going to lie down for a while," he told her. "Sorry I stabbed you."

CHAPTER 69

Styke leaned against a tree in the godstone garden and worked to remove his ruined gauntlet. From his teeth to his toes, *everything* hurt. It was as if he'd been hit by a runaway mule cart, and he still couldn't quite grasp just how easily the emperor had manhandled him. The supernatural strength was beyond anything he'd ever witnessed.

Across the garden, at the base of the godstone, Taniel and the emperor tore into each other like two fighting cockerels. The emperor had snatched up his own sword. Both men were obviously trained duelists. Their movements were a blur, their hands darting like humming-birds, their footwork raising a cloud of dust around them. Even for someone like Styke, who had watched and participated in fights his entire life, it was difficult to tell what, exactly, was happening.

It was clear, however, that Taniel was not winning. Blood soaked his face and shirt, rivulets of dirty sweat trickling down his neck. The emperor fought with a look of focus, and not a single sword stroke marred his bare chest.

Styke gasped as the gauntlet finally came off. He dropped it to the ground and examined his hand. His left and ring fingers were likely broken. The other three seemed to work, and the hand itself was undamaged. He discarded the ruined gauntlet, trying to catch his breath, wondering how many ribs were cracked and how much blood he'd lost.

A shout tore his eyes off the duel and made him peer around the tree against which he'd been resting. A door leading into the palace complex had opened not far from where he'd entered, and a group of soldiers in their imperial garb and lacquered masks emerged from within. There were seven in total, and they froze in wonder at their emperor battling the Kressian stranger.

Their pause only lasted a few moments. One barked to the others, and they began to jog toward the godstone, loosening swords and checking their pistols. Styke felt his head sag in painful exhaustion.

Summoning what reserves he could find deep within himself, he limped along behind a screen of bushes, coming up on the line of guardsmen at an angle, reaching them just a few moments before they reached his borrowed horse. He lurched out from behind the bushes and slammed his right gauntlet in between the eyes of their leader, dropping him like a stone, then drew his knife.

The guardsmen were not dragonmen, but that was where Styke's fortunes ended. The fall of their leader seemed to barely faze them, and five of them fanned out while the closest to Styke leapt toward him with sword drawn.

Styke caught the swing on his left vambrace and jabbed with his knife. Even as his counterstroke skidded off the guard's ceremonial armor and sank into the flesh just below his arm, Styke knew he was moving too slowly. A pistol shot went off to his side, and he felt the rattle of a bullet hitting one of his pauldrons. A quick, shouted exchange took place between the remaining guards as he attempted to pull his blade out of their companion. Someone stepped up to

Styke's side, and before he could react, the butt of a pistol cracked him on the temple.

The blow would have dropped a lesser man. As it was, Styke stumbled back, stunned, stars floating across his vision. He might have fallen if his back had not come in contact with a tree. He let it take his weight, grateful for the moment of rest, and blinked hard to try to clear his swimming vision.

A scream issued from somewhere nearby, attracting the attention of his assailants. Styke took the opportunity to spit blood into the face of the closest guard and fall forward among them, knife swinging. It was sloppy work, but he managed to drop two before the other three withdrew. He stumbled after them, knife cutting a graceless arc in the air, grumbling curses at their backs.

He found another tree to take his weight and turned to look after his retreating opponents, only to discover that he'd gotten mixed up in the melee. He was no longer between them and their emperor, and they'd chosen to leave him to go help their ward.

The scream, it seemed, had come from the emperor. His face was torn open from brow to chin, a neat, bloody gash cut through his nose and lips. Despite the wound, he seemed to have doubled his efforts, backing a vindicated-looking Taniel toward the corner of the garden.

Styke's opponents didn't reach their emperor. The crack of firearms tore through the air behind Styke, and all three men collapsed in a hail of bullets. Styke whirled, nearly losing his balance, to find a line of dismounted Lancers and Household guards just inside the grotto, their weapons smoking. Ibana emerged into the garden behind them, followed closely by Etzi.

Ibana's measured pace was doubled when she laid eyes on Styke. She jogged over to him, her armor rattling, and ducked beneath his shoulder. "By Adom, Ben, you look like death!"

"I'm fine." He tried to wave her off.

"What the pit happened to your hand?"

He gestured toward the emperor. "Him."

Etzi and his Household guards watched the duel with eyes wide. No one moved to interfere. "The emperor," Etzi said in an awed whisper, "has been given strength by the bone-eyes. We found one of them just in the main hall, face withered, barely able to stand. The emperor must be drawing power off of them in incredible amounts. Who is that man, and how is he able to fight the might of the imperial cabal?"

"That," Styke said, "is Ka-poel's husband."

"Incredible," Etzi breathed, "but still, he cannot win, not against—"

Whatever he was about to say was cut off by a crack that cut the air in two. It was as if a cannon had gone off in the garden, and everyone around Styke flinched away from the sound. All eyes were drawn to the godstone. A new crack ran, jagged and splintering, from base to capstone. On the altar, clothes smoking, were two figures.

Ka-poel stood like an avenging angel, head held high, ignoring the old man on his knees in front of her. She grasped him by the nape of the neck and threw him forward, off the altar, where he gave a pitiful cry and curled up into a ball.

In that moment Taniel suddenly surged forward, batting aside the emperor's sword and plunging his own blade two-handed into the emperor's sternum. The emperor gasped loudly and back-pedaled toward the godstone. Somehow, despite two feet of steel through his chest, he remained standing. It wasn't until he finally turned toward the godstone and his eyes fell upon Ka-poel—and then the old man at his feet—that he finally teetered. Blood dripping from his lips, the emperor of Dynize collapsed.

"Leave him!" Ka-poel snapped. The sound brought a halt to Etzi and the Household guards, who had begun to rush toward their fallen emperor. It also elicited a look of surprise from Taniel. "Finish destroying the imperial guard," Ka-poel ordered. She gestured at the old man at her feet. "Then bring him and any survivors to the throne room. We have much to discuss."

Styke felt light-headed and dizzy. He began to chuckle.

"What's so funny?" Ibana demanded.

Styke continued to laugh until it hurt. He clutched his side, nearly sticking himself with his own knife. "She went in there looking for a god and came back out with a voice."

It took over an hour for the Lancers and the Household guards working together to clear the imperial complex. Messengers were sent in every direction with the intent of halting further violence, but even after that hour Styke could still hear the crack of carbines or the occasional clash of swords somewhere off within the complex grounds.

Beyond the walls, Talunlica continued to burn as mobs and soldiers raged back and forth across the city.

The imperial throne room was a long, high-ceilinged chamber made of brightly painted wood, lit by gas lanterns along both sides and gas chandeliers hanging at intervals. The flags of several hundred Households flew from the rafters, marching their way up to the very throne itself, which was a single piece of red stone carved into the likeness of twin swamp dragons.

The room was filled with spectators: wounded Lancers and Household guards, captured imperial soldiers and bureaucrats. The Household heads who had accompanied them stood in close conference with Ka-poel and Taniel near the throne. Styke rested his head against the wall off to one side, just trying to keep from falling over. Maetle had given him a splint for his fingers and bandages for his side, but he could tell from Ibana's worried glances that he looked like he was knocking on death's door. He was weak with blood loss, his armor covered in blood.

Someone called for attention. Styke opened his eyes, realizing he'd been dozing on his feet, and lifted his head toward the throne. The Household heads, Etzi among them, left the dais to take up positions at the front of the crowd. Styke watched their faces, curious at the various reactions: hope, joy, confusion. Fear.

Only Ka-poel and Taniel remained on the dais. They waited until the Household heads were in their places and then Ka-poel took up a position just in front of the throne. Taniel joined her.

Everyone's attention was on Ka-poel. No one spoke. No one even seemed to breathe.

"Where is my grandfather?" she suddenly asked.

A few moments passed before a pair of Lancers dragged in the old man whom she'd brought with her through the godstone. The resemblance was uncanny, but Styke had somehow expected more from the Great Ka. Sedial seemed unharmed, but everything about him was broken: His face was pale, his eyes empty, his mouth hanging slack. He was left to sit on the top step of the dais, staring blankly at the floor. A line of drool dripped from his chin.

Ka-poel looked down at him for some time, leaving the entire hall in breath-bated silence. Her lip curled. Her eyes narrowed. She finally sniffed and took a deep breath.

"The emperor is dead," she said. Her voice carried clearly, echoing off every corner of the room. "The Great Ka has been driven mad by what he saw in the godstone. The imperial cabal will take a century to recover from the losses they've incurred from this war, and the mighty armies of Dynize have been reduced by hundreds of thousands.

"You have nothing," she continued. "You are a divided country with broken ideals and a shattered reputation that will not survive the modern world. Many of your greatest Households have been destroyed this very day by the machinations of Ka-Sedial. You have nothing...except me.

"I don't want to be your god. But it was either me or him." She nudged Sedial with one toe. "I will not answer prayers. I will not perform miracles. But I will be your goddess—your empress—and I will help you put back together the pieces of this shattered land.

You've got what the Great Ka promised you. You've got a new god. Will you accept me?"

The final question was almost timid in its asking, entirely different from the tone of the rest of her speech. Styke was certain that if the assembled Households said no, she would leave them all without a second thought.

The question left an ominous silence, which continued for over a minute, and then two. Slowly, one by one, the Household heads began to kneel. They were followed by a wave of every Dynize in the room, from the Household guards to their prisoners. Only the present Lancers, still wearing their armor, most of them wounded and slick with gore, remained on their feet. They looked toward Styke. As did Ka-poel and Taniel.

"Colonel Ben Styke," Ka-poel intoned, "I would like the Mad Lancers to form an imperial guard for my new government. Will you carry our standard below your own?"

Below. The word punched a laugh out of Styke's belly, one so hard that he almost fell over from the pain. He wiped tears from the corners of his eyes. "You're already very good at this, my little blood-witch friend."

Several of the Household heads inhaled sharply. Ka-poel smirked.

"Even being a god, I imagine there will be a lot of cleaning up to do," Styke continued. "There will be a lot of violence."

"There will," she agreed.

Styke glanced at Ibana. She just shrugged. He said, "I'll think about it. I'll have to consult the men."

"Can I heal your wounds?" Ka-poel asked. Her tone was gentle.

"You're a Privileged now?"

"No. I'm something different."

"Ah. Good for you. Will I die from these wounds?"

"I don't believe so."

Styke considered the offer. He was no stranger to sorcerous

healing, but he could feel his own stubbornness taking hold in his gut. He was no man to feel beholden to a god. "A little pain is good for a man," he finally said, pulling himself away from the wall. He limped to the center of the throne room and turned his back on Ka-poel, walking slowly toward the exit. He heard Etzi's voice hiss behind him.

"Where are you going?" Etzi demanded. "You're witnessing the birth of a god!"

"Gods," Styke replied, waving him off. "Emperors. Countries. Bah. I'm giving the order for the Mad Lancers to regroup and await new commands, then I'm going to find my daughter."

Michel had done a lot of insane things in his life—he'd manipulated strong men, lied to friends, defied dictators, and even cut off his own finger for the sake of disguise. Despite all of this, he had never before been as nervous as he was as the riverboat delivered him and Ichtracia directly to a small launch off the side of the imperial palace in Talunlica.

He'd tried to marvel at the city to keep himself distracted. It really was an incredible place, one that he knew he'd enjoy touring at length, but even his arrival in a country that had been closed off to outsiders for a hundred years did nothing to pull his mind away from the coming meeting. He tried rehearsing what he'd say. He played games in his head. He read books. Nothing seemed to work.

The dock was not a large one, mostly taken up by large, brightly colored vessels in the purple and turquoise of the imperial household. Their riverboat slid into the one open spot, porters jumping out to secure the boat and then unload the luggage in a flurry of activity. Despite all the strangeness of this place, the pair waiting to meet them were a familiar sight, one that took the edge off Michel's nerves.

Taniel Two-shot stood with his hands clasped behind his back. He wore the flowing-cut jacket and pants of a Dynize uniform, but with the Adran blue and silver-and-crimson trim in contrast to all the turquoise around them. At his side was a tall figure in ancient-looking armor. The visor was open to reveal a scarred, hard-faced Kressian woman. He didn't recognize her, but he did recognize the skull-and-lance insignia attached to her left pauldron.

One of the porters gestured for them to come ashore, and Michel looked at Ichtracia. Her expression was cool, unreadable, and arrogant, but when she squeezed the tips of his fingers gently, he could feel that she was trembling. Taniel stepped forward to offer her his hand, which she accepted. Michel followed.

"Ichtracia, Michel. It's good to see you again. This is Ibana je Fles, the captain of the imperial guard. Sorry that Ka-poel isn't here to meet you. One of her audiences has run long, but she'll end it the moment she knows you're in the palace."

Pleasantries were exchanged, and they followed Taniel along the dock and into the palace. Michel lagged behind, considering their surroundings, trying to work through his nerves. They were getting worse with every step.

Taniel didn't seem to notice, talking while they walked. "I'm glad you were able to make it so quickly. I'm sure everything between here and in Fatrasta is still in absolute chaos."

"You have no idea," Ichtracia replied. "Peace is still holding, but everyone who doesn't have orders to remain in Landfall is trying to get back here. They're terrified of what will happen to them if things break down, now that the armies are leaving."

It had only been two months since the end of hostilities, and if anything, Ichtracia was playing down the uncertainty and panic of everyone who'd been involved in the war. When she and Michel left, Landfall had felt like a powder keg, with the Palo, Kressians, and Dynize all sitting on the knife's edge, wondering what would happen now that Dynize had a new empress. Michel wondered if he should speak up, but rejected the thought. Taniel would no doubt corner him later for a full debriefing. Besides, this was no longer his place. He wasn't a Privileged or a relative or a politician or anyone important. He was just another spy without orders.

They walked through the long, high-ceilinged palace corridors. Servants seemed to flutter everywhere, always on Michel's periphery but never crossing their paths. They reached a junction at which Ibana was called away by a soldier. Michel watched her go, and finally spoke up.

"Wasn't she Ben Styke's second-in-command?"

Taniel nodded.

"So the Mad Lancers really did invade Dynize all on their own?"

"Accompanying Ka-poel, yes." Taniel chuckled. He looked older than he'd been, but significantly less tired. "Once Ka-poel seized the throne, we offered the Mad Lancers a place at Ka-poel's side." He paused thoughtfully. "Styke turned us down. Ibana did not."

"He turned her down?" Ichtracia asked, dumbfounded. "You don't turn down honors from the empress of Dynize!"

"I think," Taniel said, "that Ka-poel is going to be a different kind of ruler than your people are used to, for both good and ill. Besides, it wouldn't have mattered who made the offer. Styke wasn't interested. He . . . got something else for our gratitude, though."

They rounded another corner, and Ichtracia suddenly came to a stop. There, at the other end of the hall, surrounded by a small entourage, was Ka-poel. Ka-poel wore a uniform much like Taniel's, but colored with the purple and turquoise with accents that matched his Adran colors. She raised a hand to cut off someone who'd been speaking with her, then made a sharp gesture. The entourage scattered.

A few seconds of silence followed, and the two sisters ran toward each other, falling into a long embrace. To Michel's surprise, they began talking almost immediately. He stared, dumbfounded. "She can talk?" he asked Taniel.

Taniel watched the reunion with a small smile. "Something she gained when she went into the godstone to oppose Sedial. We have no idea how or why."

"Is she..." Michel swallowed. "Is she really a god?"

Taniel glanced at him sidelong. "What have you heard?"

"Only a few rumors since we arrived. The Dynize here are whispering about it, but we didn't find out anything about it in Fatrasta."

"It's...complicated."

"That's not a no."

"There was a lot of power in those godstones, enough to make many gods. Ka-poel took some of it. The rest, well...she used the rest to destroy the godstones themselves. We're hoping that's enough to seal the Else away forever."

"I see." Michel regarded Ichtracia and Ka-poel warily, his stomach tying itself in knots.

"Is something wrong?" Taniel asked with a frown.

"I'm out of my element," Michel demurred. "In more ways than one." He tried to ignore the concerned glance that Taniel cast him. "So, if Pole is the new empress, then what are you?"

"I'm her consort," Taniel answered.

"Not the emperor?"

He sniffed and shook his head. "That would be neither politically expedient nor something I desire. I don't need power or responsibilities. I'd far rather stand behind her than beside her. It frees me up to protect her from everyone in this damned country who is angry she seized power."

"Isn't she immortal now?"

"Maybe? Maybe not. We're not going to test it. For now, we're going to stitch the country back together—to unite them, open the borders, and bring them into the modern age. Once that's done"—he shrugged—"we hope to reach a point at which Dynize doesn't need a monarch and we can just disappear."

"That sounds ideal."

"There's a lot of work to do between now and then. You'll be pleased to know we've already opened up conversations with the Palo in Landfall. We have a lot of leverage over Lindet, and we're going to use it to make sure she changes the way the Palo are treated."

"I'm very glad to hear that," Michel replied. When he and Ichtracia left Landfall, Jiniel had already sent messengers directly to Ka-poel. He had high hopes.

"Speaking of which..." Taniel trailed off as the two sisters finally came to join them. Ka-poel beamed openly. Ichtracia was more guarded, her expression fit for the People-Eater that the palace servants had expected to return, but she clutched her older sister's hand so tightly that both their fingers turned white. Taniel nodded to Ka-poel. "Should we get this over with?"

Ka-poel greeted Michel with a small smile, and his nerves almost set him shaking. He interjected before she could say anything. "Look, I'm not sure if I belong here. If you can point me somewhere out of the way, I'll let you two..." He trailed off. "Get what over with?"

"It's good to see you, Michel," Ka-poel said. She sounded so much like Ichtracia that it was uncanny.

Michel looked between her and Taniel, wondering what they were up to. He gave a half bow. "Empress."

"Oh, stop that. You can be formal in public because it's expected, but not within the palace grounds." Ka-poel took a deep breath and exchanged a smirk with her husband. "Michel and Ichtracia, we have tasks for you, if you're willing. Ichtracia, I'd like you to become the magus of my new imperial cabal. Michel, I want you to be the imperial spymaster. I can think of no two people I'd rather have at my back."

For her part, Ichtracia seemed to absorb the news as if she expected it. Michel felt his mouth fall open. "You're joking?"

"Of course not," Ka-poel said, looking vaguely annoyed. "Why would I joke about that?"

"I..." Michel sucked on his teeth and took a deep breath. He finally got a grasp on his nerves, pulling them all tight until he could talk without a tremble in his voice. He made eye contact with Ichtracia. Only a moment ago she had exclaimed that one does not turn down honors from the ruler of Dynize. "Does this change that thing we'd discussed?"

"Not for me it doesn't. Does it for you?"

"No."

It seemed to be Taniel and Ka-poel's turn to be confused. They both watched Michel with a sudden trepidation. Michel kept his eyes on Ichtracia for a few more moments before turning to her sister. God, empress, or simply his former employer—he could do this. "Ichtracia and I are getting married. We want to spend a few months here, but then we've been invited to visit the Palo Nation in northern Fatrasta and we figure that would be a good place for both of us, where no one knows nor cares who we are."

"Oh." The response came from Taniel and Ka-poel at the same time. Michel bit his tongue. He was going to marry the sister of the new Dynize empress. He should be asking for permission, not *telling* them. But Ichtracia had made it clear that she was no one's property anymore. If he hadn't told them, she would have. He braced himself, waiting for the rebuke to come.

The silence was just beginning to get awkward when Ka-poel suddenly grinned. "Congratulations! That's...not what I expected."

Still as stone-faced as ever, Ichtracia slipped away from her sister and took Michel's hand. "We've spent a lot of time together this last year. We'd like to spend more, and without responsibilities."

"I think we can understand that," Taniel said. "It doesn't mean we won't try to talk you into something. An ambassadorship, maybe?" He pressed on, before either of them felt the need to answer. "It doesn't matter. We have plenty of time to discuss it. I made sure the palace chancellor cleared out Pole's schedule for the day. Shall we go find lunch?"

Michel felt all the nerves that had turned his body into a twisted bundle these last couple of weeks finally relax. His legs felt spongy, but his chest felt light. "That sounds great. You can help me convince Ichtracia to agree to meet my mother when we go back through Fatrasta."

V lora stood on the ramparts of Fort Nied, staring at the Landfall Plateau, which rose sharply above her, wondering if she would ever see the city again. It was a strange thought, at once somber and relieving. What had begun with her landing not far from this spot for some light mercenary work to get her out of Adro for a few years had ended with her fighting two major battles at the city, clashing with a dictator and a wannabe god, and getting thousands of her soldiers killed.

She'd made her mark on Fatrasta, and Fatrasta, for good or ill, had damned well made its mark on her.

"Lady Flint!" a voice called up at her from within the fort. "We'll need a decision in thirty minutes, ma'am!"

Vlora acknowledged the warning with a raised hand, her gaze still lifted to the Landfall. Six months after the end of what people had taken to calling the Godstone War, the city was a shadow of its former self. Piles of rubble still remained of buildings destroyed in the initial Dynize shelling, alongside the burned-out husks of those torched during the Palo uprising that accompanied the climax of the war. Despite all the destruction still evident, there was new growth to be seen if one knew where to look: the skeletons of new construction, fresh-faced buildings only just finished, and the thick traffic of a population finally trickling back to their homes.

Vlora pulled her thoughts away from Landfall and turned her eyes toward the harbor, where two ships lay at anchor. One of them was a big, powerful, clumsy ship with black sails—closer to a floating palace than to a true ship of the line. It had brought with it a number of Dynize diplomats and fresh correspondents from the new Dynize empress less than a week ago. The other ship was small and fast, a Rosvelean-built vessel flying Adran colors.

Both ships had orders to sail to their countries of origin with the next outgoing tide.

"Vlora?"

Vlora lifted her head from her contemplations and turned toward the stairs, where Olem had appeared. He paused briefly, cigarette smoke streaming from his nostrils, then ashed his cigarette and joined her.

"Still haven't decided?" he asked.

Vlora shook her head. "Are the last of the coffins on board the Adran ship?"

"They are," he answered.

"Davd and Sabastenien?"

"It'll be a good trip for them. The captain assures me that none of the coffins will slide around."

"Good. I . . . I still wonder if I did the right thing."

"We all wonder that," Olem responded.

"That I did the right thing?"

"Each of us wonder about ourselves," he amended.

"I was joking."

Olem snorted and leaned over to give her a peck on the cheek before lighting a new cigarette. "You're going to have to decide. You have twenty-five minutes before our luggage has to be loaded into one of those ships."

Vlora pulled a pair of letters from her jacket, opened them both, then spread them on the ramparts, using one hand to smooth the folds. On the left was a letter from Taniel, inviting her and Olem to visit the court of the new Dynize empress. On the right was a letter from the government of Adro, demanding that Vlora return to Adro to answer for getting Adran soldiers involved in a foreign war.

She considered that second letter. Most of her soldiers had gone home months ago, accompanying Bo, Nila, and the fleet. This was, after all, no longer an Adran matter. Their army was dissolved, the matter put to rest. They had won. Vlora had stopped a would-be god.

She hadn't told anyone but Olem about that moment in the Else, when Ka-poel seized that blackest of black. None of the new "empress's" correspondents had referred to her godhood. She wondered how long until the news got out—how long until her compatriots back home found out that she had, in fact, failed in her mission.

She wondered if Ka-poel was equipped for godhood, or if a new nightmare had been born.

"If we go home," she told Olem, "there is a distinct possibility that we will both be arrested and court-martialed. Delia has been there for four months, putting her own spin on what happened here, no doubt telling everyone that you murdered Provost Marshal Valeer in cold blood."

If the prospect of facing a trial bothered Olem, it didn't show on his face. "Bo and Nila have both been back for a couple of months, as well as most of the general staff. After Delia's betrayal, they won't let her lies stand."

"And yet our arrest is still a possibility."

Olem tapped his finger on the letter from Adro. "It is," he conceded. "We could go to Dynize. Taniel has as much promised you a letter of recommendation, an ambassadorship, and the full protection of the Dynize throne."

"And it would give us a chance to see what Ka-poel has really become," Vlora mused.

"Last I heard, Major Gustar is still hanging around there to make sure Adro has *some* representation in the Dynize court until a proper ambassador arrives. It would be good to see him."

Vlora looked from one letter to the other, then back again. A war raged in her chest as she considered the possibilities of both, the benefits and the dangers. There were too many to name. The idea of returning to Adro and facing a country that had made it clear it didn't want its war heroes around anymore was terrifying. The possibility of conflict—of putting her talents to use in Dynize—had a certain allure.

"You support whichever decision I make?" she asked Olem, though she'd asked him the same a dozen times in the last few days.

"I do."

She picked up the letter from Dynize, folded it, and placed it back in her pocket. "No more running from home," she told him, taking the other letter and handing it to him. "I have a story to tell in Adro, and I'm going to tell it, no matter what Delia and her friends try to do to us."

"It'll be good to see the mountains again," Olem said, a small smile spreading across his face. "What about Ka-poel?"

"I'm tired, Olem. God or not, it's going to take her years to repair Dynize. I think I've earned time to deal with more personal

matters. Besides." She frowned, thinking back to those few minutes in the Else. "Adom was *there*, and he did not stop her. I have
the feeling things are going to work out."

"Right. I suppose we can ask him in person in a couple of
months." Olem offered her his arm. "Well, my Lady Flint. Will
you accompany me to our ship?"

She hooked her arm into his. "Gladly."

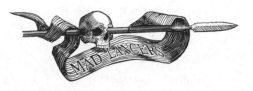

Styke watched a tree fall, listening to the satisfying snap of limbs as it gained speed in its descent and finally crunched to the ground with a sound that echoed throughout the forest. He took a deep breath, wiping sweat from his brow, and shouldered his ax. His left hand hurt terribly, the fingers that Emperor Janen broke still aching on cool days, and his side decidedly tender after so much hard labor.

But both pains were good ones. They reminded him that he was alive, but mortal.

Styke proceeded to strip the tree of all its branches—a job that took him several hours. By the time he was finished, it was getting near noon and Celine had joined him, setting up two armies of carved cavalry on the nearby stump of a tree he'd felled last week. Styke watched her play with the two warring forces for a few moments, then fetched a reinforced leather strap. Wrapping the strap around the trunk of the tree, then around his shoulders, Styke dragged the trunk across the soft ground until he'd removed it from the area that would be, one of these days, his new house and yard.

"You know we have horses, right, Ben?" Celine called from her play.

Styke reached his destination and dropped it, letting it roll down a slight incline toward a pile of other trunks. "No need to use a horse for what a man can do on his own."

A sudden neigh caught Styke's attention, turning his gaze away from his own horse pen and toward the forest. About thirty yards away, watching him from their mounts, was a small procession. His sister sat at the front—straight-backed and proper in her saddle, face expressionless. A number of bodyguards and servants were arrayed around her, most of them looking far more impressed than their master.

Once she knew she'd been spotted, Lindet flipped the reins and approached. Styke wiped his face with his shirt.

"After all you've been through," Lindet said as she approached, "you're still an ox. I can't believe it."

Styke stretched his hand and ignored a twinge in his side. "You expect me to fall to sloth in my retirement?"

"I didn't expect you to retire," she snorted. At a gesture, her companions came to a stop, while Lindet herself brought her horse right up next to Styke and dismounted. She draped the reins over a nearby branch. "Let me get something straight: This new Dynize empress pries the entire Hammer out of my hands as a concession for removing her armies peaceably from Fatrasta, and then turns around and gives it to you? What the pit did you do in Dynize to earn that kind of gratitude?"

"It's just a bit of land."

"It's thousands of square miles of land, largely unpopulated, with several abandoned frontier forts and a proper fortress on the coast. And I'm to understand you own it all, now?" Lindet's tone seemed to waver between impressed and annoyed.

Styke scratched the back of his head, stifling a smile. "I've given a lot of it to my old Lancers, and I let the towns keep their land, but yeah. I own the Hammer."

"What are you going to do with it?"

"Damned if I know. I've never actually owned land before. For now, I'm going to build a cabin, then get working on a stable. I figure in a few years I can have a proper horse farm up and running. I've also been promised three hundred Dynize horses. I'm gonna start breeding them with some of ours and see what comes out the other side."

Lindet sighed. "You. A horse farmer. There's been a lot of madness in my life the last couple of years, but this might be the most insane." She waved away a fly, but managed to turn it into a dismissive gesture. "Fine. Show me the grave."

Styke glanced at Lindet's retinue. They were still mounted, and keeping their distance. He let his grin drop and jerked his head. "This way." He led Lindet away from his new clearing and about fifty yards through the woods, then across a river and past an arrow-shaped boulder. At the base of a big beech tree sat a rectangle of white marble, marked with the name "Marguerie je Lind." Styke had only done basic maintenance on the small memorial since that night crossing the Hammer last year. It was a shaded, pleasant spot, but he half expected Lindet to demand why he hadn't erected something more grand.

Instead, his sister pursed her lips and gazed down at the marble marker, hands clasped, regarding it in silence for several minutes. "I always wondered where you buried her."

"I thought you didn't want to know," Styke replied. Out of the corner of his eye he spotted Celine hanging around, close enough to eavesdrop but far enough to remain respectful.

"I didn't," Lindet replied. "At least, I thought I didn't. I believed her weak for being unable to protect herself from *him*. But I've reassessed those beliefs."

Styke was tempted to reignite an argument long forgotten. He bit his tongue. "That's good."

A smile touched the corners of Lindet's mouth, as if she knew what he was thinking. "I'm on a tour of the country," she suddenly said, looking up to meet his eye.

"Oh?"

"It's been almost a year since the war ended. Relations with the Nine are normalizing. The Dynize empress, beyond the initial concessions she wrung out of me, has been nothing but warm. The Palo are icy but coming around. It's time to rebuild in earnest, and I need to know every corner of the country that requires help so that I can distribute it."

"I see." Styke eyeballed his sister. There was something different about her—a very faint hesitation that had never been there before. "I was in Bellport a few weeks ago. The newspapers are claiming that you're going to remain Lady Chancellor for six more years and then hold a general election. Is that true?"

"It is."

"I wouldn't have pegged you for giving up power."

"I wouldn't have pegged you for becoming a horse farmer," she shot back.

"That's fair." Styke looked around until he found one of his spare lances that he'd left against a nearby tree. He leaned on it, still watching his sister. "Will the election be real?"

Lindet seemed to consider this question for several moments. Speaking in a quiet voice, she said, "I've spent the last ten years preparing for a Dynize invasion that I was certain would come sooner rather than later. It arrived as I suspected, and yet even with all my sacrifices and preparations and control, I still wasn't ready. It...it taught me a valuable lesson.

"Next week I'm announcing the dissolution of the Blackhats. No more secret police. No more systematic oppression. It didn't work before and now that I see that, well..." She shrugged. "I can either spend the rest of my life trying to hold on to power for fear of what will happen when I lose it, or I can put into place a system in which I can retire in peace without everyone on the continent hating me. So, yes. The elections will be real."

"Will you run in them?"

"It depends on whether I've managed to get everyone to forget how much they hate me by then."

"That's awfully ambitious for six years," Styke said glibly.

"Have you ever known me *not* to be ambitious?"

"Point taken." Styke tapped his ring against his lance. "Will you stay a couple days? We haven't spoken at length in... quite some time."

"No, we haven't."

"I've got a proper house in a nearby town, until I've finished building my new one here."

For the first time since she was a little girl, Styke saw his sister smile—a real smile, without cruelty or hidden intention. "I'd like that, thank you." She reached into her pocket and pulled out an envelope. "I heard you legally adopted the girl?"

Styke gave those papers a wary glance. "I did."

"Good. This is a list of schools in Fatrasta, and the best universities in the world. I know you're a fan of learning in the saddle, but my niece *will* be educated. We can discuss those options over dinner tonight." Glancing once more down at their mother's grave, Lindet turned to walk back toward her waiting retinue.

Celine waited until she'd gone before joining Styke at the graveside. He looked down at her and snorted. "Lindet wants to send you to school."

"I heard," she replied thoughtfully. "I'm not sure that I'll like school."

"It would be good for you."

"Did you go to school?"

"I did. Boarding, then university, then the continental military academy. Hated every minute of it, but I did learn a few things. Would you rather go off to school now, or help me get the horse farm set up first?"

Celine's forehead creased. She stared at nothing in deep thought, then looked up at him. "Why didn't you tell Auntie Lindet about your deal with Ka-poel?"

"Telling her to her face that a foreign empress has made me her prison warden won't go over well. She might be learning, but Lindet is still a proud woman. Either she'll get thirsty for power again and find out that I'm here to check her power, or it'll never come up. I'm hoping it's the latter."

Celine nodded along with the explanation. "When will Lindet want me to go to school?"

"Immediately, I'm guessing."

"And when will Ibana be back from Dynize?"

"She's going to oversee the new imperial guard for another year, then join us. She wants to rebuild her father's smithy over there." Styke pointed off into the woods.

Celine considered for several more moments. "I'd like to be here to watch your new town grow. I can go to school when I'm older, right?"

"Absolutely." Styke took his lance and walked over to his mother's grave. He leaned on the shaft, sinking it butt-down into the soft earth until the point was at chest level. Removing his big Lancer ring, he placed it on the tip of the lance and stepped back to view his handiwork. Nodding to himself, he offered his hand to Celine. "Agreed. Now, let's go pretend to be interested in Lindet's schools."

ACKNOWLEDGMENTS

Thank you to my wonderful editor, Brit Hvide, for helping me finish out this series with a bang. Thanks to my fantastic agent, Caitlin Blasdell, and all her colleagues at Liza Dawson Associates, without whom the Powder Mage universe wouldn't be what it is today. Also thank you to the awesome staff at Orbit who work hard to make sure that my books are edited, marketed, printed, given cover art, and so much more.

Thanks to my wife, Michele, for all the work she's spent editing this and all the previous books—for giving me great ideas and pointing out where I go wrong and cheering me on when I get it right.

And of course, thanks to my beta readers, Mark Lindberg and Peter Keep, for taking a look at an early manuscript and giving me valuable feedback. Their help has saved me countless headaches.

Finally, thanks again to my old editor Devi Pillai. Her job change may have prevented her from finishing out the series, but she's the one who gave me my first big break and bought both the Powder Mage Trilogy and Gods of Blood and Powder. Without her support I probably wouldn't have gotten this far.